EPIC

TITANS & GIANTS MYTHS & TALES

ANTHOLOGY OF CLASSIC TALES

Foreword by Debbie Felton

FLAME TREE PUBLISHING

TALES

This is a FLAME TREE Book

Publisher & Creative Director: Nick Wells
Editorial Director: Catherine Taylor
Project Editor: Jocelyn Pontes
Special thanks to Michael Kerrigan

FLAME TREE PUBLISHING
6 Melbray Mews, Fulham,
London SW6 3NS, United Kingdom
www.flametreepublishing.com

First published 2024

24 26 28 27 25
1 3 5 7 9 10 8 6 4 2

ISBN: 978-1-80417-800-3
Special ISBN: 978-1-80417-945-1

The cover image is created by Flame Tree Studio based on artwork by Slava Gerj, Gabor Ruszkai and Adwo. Internal decorations are courtesy Shutterstock.com and the following artists: Kozyreva Elena, Vector Tradition, Alpha Factory Std and Karlionau (story headers).

A copy of the CIP data for this book is available from the British Library.

Printed and bound in China

EPIC

TITANS & GIANTS MYTHS & TALES

ANTHOLOGY OF CLASSIC TALES

Foreword by Debbie Felton

FLAME TREE PUBLISHING

TALES

Contents

Foreword

'THERE WERE GIANTS in the earth in those days', as one translation of Genesis 6:4 says, hearkening back to a time before recorded history when strange and powerful creatures were believed to walk the earth. Contemporary with the biblical tradition, ancient Greek myths tell not only of giants but also of Titans, godlike beings who existed even before the cosmos as we know it was formed. The Titans may be unique to Greek myth, but cultures around the world have preserved myths, folktales, and legends about giants and Titan-like entities. Such stories convey both awe and fear: how amazing was it that in our world there existed mighty beings who towered over us, who could be aggressive and dangerous, but who just might, on occasion, be benevolent? Perhaps more importantly, why do we tell stories about such entities?

Some of these stories are etiological, providing explanations for how the world came to be as it is, sometimes down to wonderfully specific details such as the origin of the edelweiss flower or of the Belgian flag. In this and other respects, the stories often reflect the cultures they come from. Frost Giants routinely appear in stories from colder countries such as Scandinavia and the Swiss Alps, while Sun and River Giants populate tales from Brazil, a country with a warm climate and many large rivers. Giants in tales from Japan, a nation surrounded by water, inhabit their own dreadful islands.

In addition to culturally specific aspects, many stories of giants from around the world demonstrate similar themes. The giants often, unfortunately, represent native, less 'civilized' peoples who were rightly (from the stories' perspective) conquered by their seemingly more sophisticated colonizers, as when Gogmagog is vanquished by Corineus. These giants are characterized as hateful, arrogant, and, most significantly, as sub-human and therefore as unworthy of compassion; indeed, the human characters often demonstrate more compassion towards animals than towards the giants. Notably, in many of the tales originating in Europe, the giants are clearly pagans who smell 'Christian blood' and want to kill the humans (who are assumed to be Christians) and cook them in a stew – anthropophagy being an undeniable sign of barbarism as far as these stories are concerned.

Related to the theme of giants as primitive natives to be conquered is the way giants are often used in the stories to highlight the importance of intelligence, wit, and courage – traits many giants sorely lack. Giants may function as subsidiary elements in these stories, where they are used to characterize the human protagonists as exceptionally clever or brave despite their disadvantageously small size; whether a noble prince on a quest to save a princess or a kingdom, a lowly tailor out to seek his fortune, or a humble fisherman hoping for a good catch, humans who have their wits about them can trick the crass, cruel, and foolish giants, whose lumbering size is frequently associated with diminished brainpower. But at times, a modern audience may even feel sorry for these giants, who are often cheated out of an agreement, have their magical items stolen and used against them, or are otherwise treated poorly for no reason other than being a giant and therefore by their mere nature undeserving of fair dealings.

At the same time, we find stories where giants who, despite initially seeming threatening, prove themselves surprisingly kind, friendly, and understanding even when humans behave badly, or giants who unexpectedly respond well when treated kindly. Some of these benevolent giants even join forces with humans to defeat the hateful giants who threaten them. Overall, the stories about Titans and giants in this collection ask us to consider what we, as humans, value in ourselves and others. Is it courage, compassion, intelligence, loyalty, kindness, or – we might hope – a combination of all these and other positive traits? And, finally, these stories may help us understand how we should treat each other, no matter our differences.

Debbie Felton
Professor of Classics, University of Massachusetts Amherst

Publisher's Note

TALES OF GIANTS have an immensely powerful hold on our imagination. The idea of these beings towering over us, of their every step making the ground shudder, is awe-inspiring. Add to that the primeval origins of the god-like Titans of Greek mythology, and heroes' triumph over such omnipotence, and truly we have the ingredients for gripping storytelling. In this anthology we have endeavoured to collect a thoughtfully curated cross-section of varied stories from worldwide folklore and fairy tale, featuring giants of all kinds.

As always, we must remind the reader that, as tales from mythology and folklore are principally derived from an oral storytelling tradition, their written representation depends on the transcription, translation and interpretation by those who heard them and first put them to paper, and also on whether they are recently re-told versions or more directly sourced from original first-hand accounts. The stories in this book are a mixture, and you can learn more about the sources and authors at the back of the book. Due to the historical nature of such texts, we're aware that there may be some language used which has the potential to cause offence to the modern reader. However, wishing to overall preserve the integrity of the writing, rather than imposing contemporary sensibilities, we have left it largely unaltered.

For this reason too, please note that spellings may differ between stories depending on their origins – for example if the source is Greek (like Hesiod's *Theogony*) you will find 'Heracles', while stories that used later Roman sources will spell this character as 'Hercules'.

We also ask the reader to remember that while the myths and tales are timeless, much of the factual information, opinions regarding the nature of countries and their peoples, as well as the style of writing in this anthology, are of the era during which they were written.

EPIC TALES

TITANS & GIANTS MYTHS & TALES

ANTHOLOGY OF CLASSIC TALES

Foreword by Debbie Felton

FLAME TREE PUBLISHING

Titans & Giants in Myth & Folklore

Introduction

'THE HEBREW CHRONICLERS tell us', the story-collector Gertrude Landa tells us in her turn,

> *that the giants of their land were the children of the fallen angels who took to themselves wives from the beautiful daughters of men. When these huge beings had consumed the possessions of their neighbours, they began to devour even the human beings themselves; and from this horrible example men came to kill and eat birds, animals and fishes.*

This tradition takes giants to be not just big and frightening but essentially malign – and exemplary in their evil. The Book of Genesis, it might be thought, provides – in the story of Adam and Eve and their first disobedience – an adequate explanation for the origins of what Christians would call 'original sin'. But mythology is constantly coming up with alternatives here, refinements there in what seems to be a never-ending effort, not just to entertain with a ceaseless stream of stories, but to apprehend and illustrate the infinite variety of human life. Here, then, we have another take on the 'Fall of Man'.

A Greek Gallimaufry

Classical Greek civilization has for centuries been taken as in some sense paradigmatic, at least in a 'Western' tradition which, in modern times, by no means restricted to the 'West', has wielded disproportionate influence on the world at large. Order, logic, coherence and consistency… These are the sort of values it exemplifies. Not, however, in its mythology. A look at Greek myth, with a specific focus on the Titans and Giants which we see centred in this collection, reveals a bewildering anarchy of ideas and imagery. Far from finding a Parthenon of elegant regularity and symmetry in the stories of the Greeks, we get a Gordian Knot of tangled narratives and jumbled themes.

Titanic

The Titans, we are told in Hesiod's *Theogony*, *c.* 700 BCE, were not just giant in stature: they were, to all intents and purposes, the world's first gods. The children of Gaia (the Earth) and Uranus (Heaven, and Gaia's son and husband), they were twelve in all: six brothers and six sisters. They included Oceanus – as his name suggests, the ocean, encompassing both the Mediterranean and the Atlantic, as well as the great river seen as encircling the earth. Hyperion, whose name means 'He who walks on high', was associated with the heavens. He was father in his turn to Helios (the Sun), Selene (the Moon) and Eos (Dawn).

Theia (also known as Aethra) shared some of her brother's brilliance: by tradition she gave gold and silver their distinctive shine. Mnemosyne, their sister, was a personification of memory. She would be mother to the Muses – nine divine maidens who inspired the different sciences and arts. Iapetus is only vaguely defined, though his relationship with Oceanus' daughter Clymene produced a second generation of Titans – including Atlas (who carried the heavens on his shoulders) and Prometheus (who would one day give men the gift of fire). Iapetus was seen as having been the ultimate ancestor of humankind. Thus far, the antique order seems essentially benign: these Titans are not monsters but personifications or emblems of things in what would seem their natural and normal order. It also, moreover, appears to represent a sort of matriarchy, all life and power springing from the common earth-mother Gaia.

Castrating Kronos

But events would take a decidedly different turn in the developing Greek tradition. Gaia was angered by Uranus' insistence that their youngest children, also immense of stature – the monstrous, hundred-handed Hecatoncheires and the one-eyed Cyclopes – should spend their lives imprisoned in the bowels of the earth, in Tartarus. The Earth Mother made a sickle which she gave to Kronos, her youngest son, so he could castrate his father and usurp his throne.

A cruel father had his punishment, but Kronos' coup would merely replace one patriarchy with another. Marrying his sister Rhea, he conducted himself as the original and ultimate 'alpha male', shoring up his dominance by swallowing all their children as they were born. One alone escaped: the infant Zeus was smuggled to safety in Crete, where he grew to manhood plotting revenge against his unnatural sire. The god of open sky and mountaintop, he was armed with flashing thunderbolts, and established his seat on the heights of Greece's highest peak, Mount Olympus, from where he led his own family in war against the Titans (now regurgitated so as to be able to help in their father's defence). The Cyclopes came to Zeus' assistance – skilled smiths, they forged the thunderbolts he fought with and fought alongside him in this *Titanomachy* ('War with the Titans'). As did Prometheus, at this stage at least a loyal supporter of Zeus and his new order. The final victory of Zeus' Olympians marked not only the end of the region's pre-Greek period but the inauguration of a new, and more recognizably 'modern' male-supremacist theology.

Born in Blood

In parallel with this tradition, though, the Greek mythological record also gives us a *Gigantomachy*. Another battle between Zeus and his company and a race of mighty giants; another defence of the Olympian order against earth-born barbarism and chaos. Beyond their participation in this war, little is known about the *Gigantes* or 'Giants'. Except that they sprang to life out of the blood that splashed forth from Uranus' genitals, severed by Kronos' sickle; they were conventionally seen as being loyal to Gaia as Mother Earth. (Another drop of blood landed in the sea off the coast of Kythera, a tiny island south of Greece, giving rise to Aphrodite, goddess of love.)

Symbolically, then, the Giants stood for the primeval matriarchal order, whilst simultaneously embodying masculine stature and brute strength – and standing in a strange sibling-relation with the idea of feminine allure. The Greek mythic record as a whole, indeed, is so complex, so sometimes-contradictory so just-about-invariably-confusing as to make us wonder just how reliable a 'mythic record' can ever be; whether it can really be a 'record' in any meaningful sense at all. Oceanus is at once a personage and a place, an element, an aspect of the world; Mnemosyne is simultaneously a goddess and an idea. Kronos contrives to be both an instrument of matriarchal vengeance and an emblem of patriarchal tyranny.

Drama and Dream

We have, accordingly, to be careful when we try to identify a straightforward symbolic meaning in any giant or titan in any story. The theories Sigmund Freud proposed a century ago have suggested exhilaratingly illuminating insights but even so, taken uncritically, may still mislead. His psychoanalytic exploration of the realm of dream – and his appreciation that myths might be seen (and so 'read' and interpreted) as a culture's collective dreamlife – allowed a new understanding of just what myths might mean; of the important cultural assumptions they might encode. And yet, in making the comparison with dream – notoriously weird in its narratives and unstable in its structuring logics – he reminds us that we can't expect the kind of coherence we would look to find in a more conventionally authored text. Add in the innumerable layers of detail accrued by each story over generations of transmission through the oral tradition and, conversely, the 'refinements' made by modern collectors and editors, and we have good reason to exercise a certain caution.

That said, it isn't difficult to see the story of Kronos and Uranus as just the sort of lurid psychodrama Freud found surging beneath the surface of the well-ordered Viennese bourgeois family. Since his time, indeed, a loose consensus has been reached amongst researchers that the giant in the myth or fairy story often serves to symbolize the powerfully intimidating presence of the father. In Freud's view, notoriously, the son saw his sexual desire for his mother as being thwarted by his father, his rival – and, potentially, a crushing, castrating threat. To the little boy, the towering figure of his father is a phallic symbol in itself; an object of conscious love, no doubt, but also of a deep subconscious fear.

Freud and the Father

How far real-life families actually work this way is questionable, to put it mildly – twenty-first-century psychotherapy has been extremely selective in the use it's made of Freud. But his intuitive understanding of how art and literature appeal to us still seems extraordinary: we often find his theories strike a chord. Certainly in myths, which do indeed appear to tap into the subconscious of the culture that produced them just as dreams do into the individual subject's secret self.

And Freud did seem to sum up the narrative arc of a great many giant-killing stories (the English tale 'Nix Nought Nothing', in this collection, for example) when he observed: 'A hero is a man who stands up manfully against his father and in the end ... victoriously overcomes him' (*Moses and Monotheism*, 1938). That the father could be metaphorical, more an oppressive psychological situation than a literal parent is evident from a story like the Brazilian 'The Forest Lad and the Wicked Giant' whose hero has a kind and caring father.)

On Trial

Might it not be fair to say that, in Freud's aphorism, the 'father' is whatever we're most in awe of? That the hero's triumph lies in overcoming his greatest fear? Whatever else we think of him, the giant is a daunting enemy. In facing him, we set ourselves the utmost test. The idea that it's a trial – of strength, of courage, of resolve – is laid out most clearly in Arthurian romance: the knight's 'quest' is explicitly a test of just this kind. The knight's journey is one of adventure but also, very obviously, of growth. In braving its dangers, he no doubt demonstrates his dedication to his hero's calling but he also obviously tempers the steel of his resolve. In defying the giant, defeating the dragon, and rescuing the damsel in distress, he shows himself a valiant defender of the weak.

But nobility isn't just for the nobility. Born of a peach stone and brought up by a poor old peasant couple, Momotaro, the 'Peach's Son' in the Japanese story, will grow up to do battle with a great many ogres and free the maidens held prisoner by the wicked Demon King. If his victories prove his worth as a warrior, his narrative arc overall may be seen to underline the true value of the obscure couple who took him in and brought him up from infancy.

It has often been glossed over in its innumerable shorter retellings, but the English classic 'Jack and the Beanstalk' is likewise the story of a test. Feckless and naïve, Jack is the despair of his old mother (who admittedly has spoiled him). Finally, she snaps: '"O you wicked child! by your ungrateful course of life you have at last brought me to beggary and ruin!"' His thoughtlessness is 'cruel', she points out, and has brought her to absolute penury. Forced to sell the cow, and sending Jack off to market with it, she's again reduced to tears of helpless rage when he comes home having sold it for a handful of brightly coloured beans. The story as it unfolds sees Jack's true character subjected to exacting tests, in which he's at last able to show that he's more than a selfish, stupid boy. He's also subjected to a form of Freud's test of heroism, for (as his fairy guardian will reveal to him) his clash with the giant is to be all about the vindication – and avenging – of his father.

People of the Past

Whatever else our father might be, he has to be older than us, to belong to a different generation. Giants in legend typically hark back to a time before our own. One way, then, in which the 'father' they represent might be stood up to and mythically 'overcome' is in the progress we see ourselves – as a civilization – having made. This was of course in part the function of the Titans in ancient Greece – even in antiquity, they seemed to represent a different age. So it has remained into our own day. 'Long ages ago,' begins the Swiss story 'The Mountain Giants',

> *when the round earth was being shaped, and the ice was melting, to give way to the green fields and flowers, huge monsters, bears, wolves and other wild animals were the only living creatures in Switzerland. Then the giants arrived in the world.*
>
> *When, by and by, human beings came into the land, they told their children that the mountains were what were left of the earth's crust, after it had shrunk into peaks and ridges, bumps and hollows, like an apple, when baked in the oven, making crusts, points and wrinkles. The valleys had been sunk, by the giants walking about on the earth, while it was yet soft.*

The giants' impact was not just geomorphological: to Switzerland's storytellers they also served as an important moral warning. The Alpine rivers, they reported,

were formed by the weeping of the giants' wives and daughters, when they were badly treated; for these rough fellows, husbands and brothers, did not know how to be kind to their female kin.

The only way the giants were able to make their women obey them, when they were bad tempered, or naughty, or scolded too much, was to use shovels, pokers, clubs, and straps on them. This clumsy and cruel way of keeping the family in order, was because the giants had not yet learned to love, but were like brutes and knew only about force.

They were, in short, like humans who hadn't learned to be humane. Nor acquired the knowledge or skills now associated with civilization. They were, the narrative continues, witheringly, 'very stupid, as compared with men'.

Their brains were more like those of babies, and they were not half as smart as boys and girls are today. They did not know enough even to plough the ground, and raise wheat, and rye, and oats, and to make porridge, to say nothing of bread and cakes, and pies and doughnuts. They could not melt lead, or work iron, or make tools, but depended on their muscles, because these were huge and tough, so that they bulged out; for the giants had terrific strength, like bulls and elephants. Though their brains were so small, their limbs were like pillars, much thicker than piano legs, and their arms were like iron. They could only make hammers, or chisels, knives and scrapers of stone, and clubs of wood, for they knew no better, and never went to school or college.

Guileless Galumphers

There's wit and artifice in this modern version – William Elliot Griffis was no rustic storyteller – but the mocking tone is to be found in earlier tales. Giants were always as much ridiculed as feared. This mild disdain reflects the pride that people took in the progress they felt their societies had made. Giants, when they weren't actually monstrous like the ancient Cyclopes (or monstrously vain, like the beautiful Vukub in the Mayan story), were just like men and women in everything but size. It made sense, then, for popular tales to highlight the superior sophistication of ordinary mortals; it allowed them to feel good about themselves.

About their mental quickness in particular. The giant was by definition a great deal bigger than a man or woman and vastly superior in strength, but these weren't the things by which people really set most store in modern times. Big and boorish, clumsy and credulous, rendered vulnerable by his bulk and brutish mind, the giant was a *reductio ad absurdum* of the way they saw their own more primitive forebears. They measured their society's progress by the distance they felt they'd come since their earliest ancestors chased around after prehistoric game or scratched a living from the soil with sticks. Homer's account of Odysseus' clash with Polyphemus is just the earliest example we have of a long and illustrious line of stories in which quick-thinking humans get one over on an ostensibly terrifying giant, as Conall Cra-Bhuidhe does in the Hebridean story of that name and we see the tailor do in the Swiss story of 'The Tailor and the Giant'. Jack the Giant Killer, in the famous Cornish story, combines courage and cleverness in equal measure, much as Mirza does in the Punjabi tale of that name.

Enchantments and Charms

Sometimes, as in the Serbian story 'The Biter Bit', the hero has magical assistance. In the Norse tale, 'When Thor went to Jotunheim', the god of thunder, strong as he already is, still needs the help of a magic belt of strength. Another belt is given to the young Romanian hero of 'The Giants and the Herd-Boy'. This one gives its wearer the power of invisibility. Magic is a subject all its own. The North African Berber tale 'The Three Treasures of the Giants' is first and foremost a story of enchantment. The giants only feature as the owners of the 'treasures': a magic table which on command can furnish 'the dinner of an emperor', a cornet which can call up an army of any size, and a bag which contains an unlimited supply of castles. With their help, poor put-upon Jack is able to outdo his elder brothers and redress the injustice he's always faced as youngest in the family.

Other things can also help to tip the balance the hero's way. In the Irish story 'The Son of the King of Erin and the Giant of Loch Léin', the power of love prevails. The king's son is hopelessly ill-equipped to carry out any of the impossible tasks the giant sets him but the giant's daughter falls for him so she helps him through. Either way, the narrative makes plain that humans may have other attributes which more than compensate for their physical shortcomings and make it possible for them to contend with any giant. It's a sister's love that, in the Native American story, endows the infant Dais Imid ('He of the Little Shell') with the magic shell which will prove a powerful protector his whole life long.

Back-Door Benevolence?

It may seem meretricious to suggest that, if a giant's monstrous evil provides the test that establishes a hero's valour, that evil has ultimately shown itself a force for good. Yet, within the structure of the story, it may well be so. In any case, human nature being what it is, it was always inevitable that the folkloric record would throw up at least a sprinkling of more benevolent giants. First, of course, because we go to folktales above all for their infinite variety; then because we can't help feeling for the underdog. And, as eccentric as it may sound to see the giant that way in his immediate context in the story, there's no doubt that he's something of a whipping-boy in folklore's wider moral scheme.

Modern literary writers have certainly felt a certain sympathy. Oscar Wilde's 'The Selfish Giant' (1888) is, as his story's title suggests, as curmudgeonly and cruel as any in the folklore, but is given the chance of redemption – which in the end he gladly takes. More recently, Michael Morpurgo's Gentle Giant (2003) saves a girl from drowning in the lake beside his island home – and by doing so saves himself from his loneliness and despair. Morpurgo's moral take is modern: his giant is undoubtedly big and intimidating – so much so that the local people won't go near him. What in an earlier age would have seemed his 'wickedness' and 'cruelty' are, for the twenty-first century reader, more readily understood as an abrasiveness born of isolation and sadness. The giant isn't 'bad' – he's just misunderstood.

Friendly giants are to be found in more traditional folktales too. In the Hungarian story, 'The Strong Prince', for example, an orphaned prince and his mother, the widowed queen, leave their palace, stunned by their bereavement, and wander off into the forest. There they are beset by robbers who take all they own. The attackers don't just disarm the prince – stripping him of his sword: they blind him, gouging out his eyes; altogether as comprehensive a Freudian castration as we could find. In this instance, however, the giant–father comes to the rescue. The giant who lives in the nearby castle gives them sanctuary and support. He washes the boy's eyes and replaces them in his head. Sending out his magical emissaries, a monkey, a fox and a squirrel, he recovers the prince's sword – symbolically, of course, restoring him to manhood. He would restore him to his kingdom too, but the prince has fallen head-over-heels in love with the giant's daughter and decides to stay in the woods with his mother and with this new family.

'Greater than Any...'

Then there's Stoom, in the Dutch story 'The Ice King and his Wonderful Grandchild', for example. So important is the Ice King, Uller, that he takes care of the Norse god Odin's throne throughout the winter months, setting up amidst the snows of the North Pole or high up on some Alpine peak. Uller is irascible. When the mischievous fire fairy, Vuur, courts his six daughters and is slow to make his mind up which he fancies most, the Ice King makes him marry them all at once.

Regen, this collective bride is called, and they give birth to a gender-non-specific child to whom they give the Dutch name Stoom. (This name of course means 'steam', of whose power and technological applications the rest of the story is pretty much an allegory.) Stoom takes after its father in its light-heartedness and love of pranks. 'In the kitchen,' we are told,

> *it would make the iron kettle lid flop up and down with a lively noise. If it were confined in a vessel, whether of iron or earthenware, when set over the fire, it would blow the pot or kettle all to pieces, in order to get out. Thinking itself a great singer, it would make rather a pleasant sound, when its mother let it come out of a spout. Yet it never obeyed either of its parents. When they tried to shut up Stoom inside of anything, it always escaped with a terrible sound. In fact, nothing could long hold it in, without an explosion.*

Stoom ventures down into the bowels of the earth, to places where streams of water meet the deep fires that are always burning there. Awful earthquakes result as Stoom tries to escape. No one knows how to handle Stoom – yet people do learn quickly enough that, treated properly, Stoom will be a strong and loyal servant, driving locomotives, ships and submarines, and, generally speaking, 'greater than any giant or fairy ever was'.

A Matter of Time

Even by the surrealistic standards of mythology, Stoom's birth to half a dozen different mothers is unusual. So too is the gender-neutral way in which it is introduced. This doesn't last too long, in truth. Within a few paragraphs (and without acknowledgement) the narrator slips into default-masculinizing mode, bestowing he/him pronouns on our hero. 'His' story is striking too, however, in its evident modernity – at least in the form in which it's been collected and retold here. Since when did folktales deal in trains and submarines? Simultaneously, and as important, though: what we're reading seems antiquated. Since when were such forms of transport powered by steam?

Most of the stories collected here are several centuries old. Some date back millennia, indeed. The poems of 'Homer' (no single poet of that name is actually known to have existed) are believed to have been composed some time in the eighth century BCE. That said, the translations offered here were, inevitably, made much more recently – in the late-nineteenth and early twentieth centuries. And, in a sense, it can be said that no poem is older than its translation, which will inevitably be shaped by the biases, preoccupations and tastes of the translator's age. The gap in time may be much less extreme, but this is true for the other tales assembled here.

In truth, though, as we saw with Stoom's steam engines, the more modern a retelling, the more quickly it may date. As with technology, so with social attitudes: the last century has seen a transformation in many of our deepest assumptions about everything from sexual politics to disability, from race to class. The folk tradition is 'traditional' by definition – and we don't now necessarily find the assumptions of a Victorian lady or Edwardian gentleman much more sympathetic than we do those of Homer's warriors. As Freud would have been first to see, though, any excavation of the folkloric past is bound to bring up material which may make us shudder now, along with modes of expression that we don't now find acceptable. In the end, though, in the interests of intellectual integrity, we have to take these stories as we find them, with all they offer us in colour, energy and human truth.

Gods, Warriors & Heroes of Old

Introduction

"'OH, GIANT,' QUOTH JACK, 'where are you now?'" No exploit establishes the status of a hero so irrefutably as his triumph over an enemy many times his size. Jack the Giant Killer's opponent, in the English story, is so big he makes the Mount of Cornwall quake. Appropriately enough, Jack attacks the landscape itself, digging an enormous pit for the giant to fall into.

This section considers the role of giants in cosmogony and creation myths and other stories in which the world, and our environment, was shaped. Giants in the earliest legends often literally built the world, carving out oceans or throwing up mountain ranges. Myths do not necessarily heed the normal rules of reason, but it still makes intuitive sense for the being who held the heavens up, or the father of the sun, to have a certain stature. It's a rough and ready guide, admittedly, but great size is an easy way of representing more general significance, so gods, like the early Greek Titans or those of the West African Yoruba, were often imagined as giants. Or, of course, as in the case of Jack, giants could be the measure of the greatness of those who fought and defeated them, from Odysseus's legendary victory over Polyphemus to Cornish Corineus's over Gogmagog. Divine supremacy itself may have to be established in conflict with outsized enemies: in both the Greek and Norse traditions the gods fight bitter wars with giants.

The Theogony of Hesiod

FROM THE HELICONIAN MUSES let us begin to sing, who hold the great and holy mount of Helicon, and dance on soft feet about the deep-blue spring and the altar of the almighty son of Cronos, and, when they have washed their tender bodies in Permessus or in the Horse's Spring or Olmeius, make their fair, lovely dances upon highest Helicon and move with vigorous feet. Thence they arise and go abroad by night, veiled in thick mist, and utter their song with lovely voice, praising Zeus the aegis-holder and queenly Hera of Argos who walks on golden sandals, and the daughter of Zeus the aegis-holder bright-eyed Athene, and Phoebus Apollo, and Artemis who delights in arrows, and Poseidon the earth-holder who shakes the earth, and reverend Themis and quick-glancing Aphrodite, and Hebe with the crown of gold, and fair Dione, Leto, Iapetus and Cronos the crafty counsellor, Eos and great Helius and bright Selene, Earth too, and great Oceanus, and dark Night, and the holy race of all the other deathless ones that are for ever. And one day they taught Hesiod glorious song while he was shepherding his lambs under holy Helicon, and this word first the goddesses said to me – the Muses of Olympus, daughters of Zeus who holds the aegis:

"Shepherds of the wilderness, wretched things of shame, mere bellies, we know how to speak many false things as though they were true; but we know, when we will, to utter true things."

So said the ready-voiced daughters of great Zeus, and they plucked and gave me a rod, a shoot of sturdy laurel, a marvellous thing, and breathed into me a divine voice to celebrate things that shall be and things there were aforetime; and they bade me sing of the race of the blessed gods that are eternally, but ever to sing of themselves both first and last. But why all this about oak or stone?

Come thou, let us begin with the Muses who gladden the great spirit of their father Zeus in Olympus with their songs, telling of things that are and that shall be and that were aforetime with consenting voice. Unwearying flows the sweet sound from their lips, and the house of their father Zeus the loud-thunderer is glad at the lily-like voice of the goddesses as it spread abroad, and the peaks of snowy Olympus resound, and the homes of the immortals. And they, uttering their immortal voice, celebrate in song first of all the reverend race of the gods from the beginning, those whom Earth and wide Heaven begot, and the gods sprung of these, givers of good things. Then, next, the goddesses sing of Zeus, the father of gods and men, as they begin and end their strain, how much he is the most excellent among the gods and supreme in power. And again, they chant the race of men and strong giants, and gladden the heart of Zeus within Olympus – the Olympian Muses, daughters of Zeus the aegis-holder.

Them in Pieria did Mnemosyne (Memory), who reigns over the hills of Eleuther, bear of union with the father, the son of Cronos, a forgetting of ills and a rest from sorrow. For nine nights did wise Zeus lie with her, entering her holy bed remote from the immortals. And when a year was passed and the seasons came round as the months waned, and many days were accomplished, she bare nine daughters, all of one mind, whose hearts are set upon song and their spirit free from care, a little way from the topmost peak of snowy Olympus. There are their bright dancing-places and beautiful homes, and beside them the Graces and Himerus (Desire) live in delight. And they, uttering through their lips a lovely voice, sing the laws of all and the goodly ways of the immortals, uttering their lovely voice. Then went they to Olympus, delighting in their sweet voice, with heavenly song, and the dark Earth resounded about them as they chanted, and a lovely sound rose up beneath their feet as they went to their father. And he was reigning in Heaven, himself holding the lightning and glowing thunderbolt, when he had overcome by might his father Cronos; and he distributed fairly to the immortals their portions and declared their privileges.

These things, then, the Muses sang who dwell on Olympus, nine daughters begotten by great Zeus, Cleio and Euterpe, Thaleia, Melpomene and Terpsichore, and Erato and Polyhymnia and Urania and Calliope, who is the chiefest of them all, for she attends on worshipful princes: whomsoever of Heaven-nourished princes the daughters of great Zeus honour, and behold him at his birth, they pour sweet dew upon his tongue, and from his lips flow gracious words. All the people look towards him while he settles causes with true judgments: and he, speaking surely, would soon make wise end even of a great quarrel; for therefore are there princes wise in heart, because when the people are being misguided in their assembly, they set right the matter again with ease, persuading them with gentle words. And when he passes through a gathering, they greet him as a god with gentle reverence, and he is conspicuous amongst the assembled: such is the holy gift of the Muses to men. For it is through the Muses and far-shooting Apollo that there are singers and harpers upon the Earth; but princes are of Zeus, and happy is he whom the Muses love: sweet flows speech from his mouth. For though a man have sorrow and grief in his newly troubled soul and live in dread because his heart is distressed, yet, when a singer, the servant of the Muses, chants the glorious deeds of men of old and the blessed gods who inhabit Olympus, at once he forgets his heaviness and remembers not his sorrows at all; but the gifts of the goddesses soon turn him away from these.

Hail, children of Zeus! Grant lovely song and celebrate the holy race of the deathless gods who are for ever, those that were born of Earth and starry Heaven and gloomy Night and them that briny sea did rear. Tell how at the first gods and Earth came to be, and rivers, and the boundless sea with its raging swell, and the gleaming stars, and the wide Heaven above, and the gods who were born of them, givers of good things, and how they divided their wealth, and how they shared their honours amongst them, and also how at the first they took many-folded Olympus. These things declare to me from the beginning, ye Muses who dwell in the house of Olympus, and tell me which of them first came to be.

Verily at the first Chaos came to be, but next wide-bosomed Earth, the ever-sure foundations of all the deathless ones who hold the peaks of snowy Olympus, and dim Tartarus in the depth of the wide-pathed Earth, and Eros (Love), fairest among the deathless gods, who unnerves the limbs and overcomes the mind and wise counsels of all gods and all men within them. From Chaos came forth Erebus and black Night; but of Night were born Aether and Day, whom she conceived and bore from union in love with Erebus. And Earth first bore starry Heaven, equal to herself, to cover her on every side, and to be an ever-sure abiding-place for the blessed gods. And she brought forth long hills, graceful haunts of the goddess-Nymphs who dwell amongst the glens of the hills. She bore also the fruitless deep with his raging swell, Pontus, without sweet union of love. But afterwards she lay with Heaven and bore deep-swirling Oceanus, Coeus and Crius and Hyperion and

Iapetus, Theia and Rhea, Themis and Mnemosyne and gold-crowned Phoebe and lovely Tethys. After them was born Cronos the wily, youngest and most terrible of her children, and he hated his lusty sire.

And again, she bore the Cyclopes, overbearing in spirit, Brontes, and Steropes and stubborn-hearted Arges, who gave Zeus the thunder and made the thunderbolt: in all else they were like the gods, but one eye only was set in the midst of their foreheads. And they were surnamed Cyclops (Orb-eyed) because one orbed eye was set in their foreheads. Strength and might and craft were in their works.

And again, three other sons were born of Earth and Heaven, great and doughty beyond telling, Cottus and Briareos and Gyes, presumptuous children. From their shoulders sprang an hundred arms, not to be approached, and each had fifty heads upon his shoulders on their strong limbs, and irresistible was the stubborn strength that was in their great forms. For of all the children that were born of Earth and Heaven, these were the most terrible, and they were hated by their own father from the first.

And he used to hide them all away in a secret place of Earth so soon as each was born, and would not suffer them to come up into the light: and Heaven rejoiced in his evil doing. But vast Earth groaned within, being straitened, and she made the element of grey flint and shaped a great sickle, and told her plan to her dear sons. And she spoke, cheering them, while she was vexed in her dear heart:

"My children, gotten of a sinful father, if you will obey me, we should punish the vile outrage of your father; for he first thought of doing shameful things."

So she said, but fear seized them all, and none of them uttered a word. But great Cronos the wily took courage and answered his dear mother:

"Mother, I will undertake to do this deed, for I reverence not our father of evil name, for he first thought of doing shameful things."

So he said: and vast Earth rejoiced greatly in spirit, and set and hid him in an ambush, and put in his hands a jagged sickle, and revealed to him the whole plot.

And Heaven came, bringing on night and longing for love, and he lay about Earth spreading himself full upon her.

Then the son from his ambush stretched forth his left hand and in his right took the great long sickle with jagged teeth, and swiftly lopped off his own father's members and cast them away to fall behind him. And not vainly did they fall from his hand; for all the bloody drops that gushed forth Earth received, and as the seasons moved round she bore the strong Erinyes and the great Giants with gleaming armour, holding long spears in their hands and the Nymphs whom they call Meliae all over the boundless Earth. And so soon as he had cut off the members with flint and cast them from the land into the surging sea, they were swept away over the main a long time: and a white foam spread around them from the immortal flesh, and in it there grew a maiden. First she drew near holy Cythera, and from there, afterwards, she came to sea-girt Cyprus, and came forth an awful and lovely goddess, and grass grew up about her beneath her shapely feet. Her gods and men call Aphrodite, and the foam-born goddess and rich-crowned Cytherea, because she grew amid the foam, and Cytherea because she reached Cythera, and Cyprogenes because she was born in billowy Cyprus, and Philommedes because she sprang from the members. And with her went Eros, and comely Desire followed her at her birth at the first and as she went into the assembly of the gods. This honour she has from the beginning, and this is the portion allotted to her amongst men and undying gods – the whisperings of maidens and smiles and deceits with sweet delight and love and graciousness.

But these sons whom be begot himself great Heaven used to call Titans (Strainers) in reproach, for he said that they strained and did presumptuously a fearful deed, and that vengeance for it would come afterwards.

And Night bore hateful Doom and black Fate and Death, and she bore Sleep and the tribe of Dreams. And again the goddess murky Night, though she lay with none, bore Blame and painful Woe, and the Hesperides who guard the rich, golden apples and the trees bearing fruit beyond glorious Ocean. Also she bore the Destinies and ruthless avenging Fates, Clotho and Lachesis and Atropos, who give men at their birth both evil and good to have, and they pursue the transgressions of men and of gods: and these goddesses never cease from their dread anger until they punish the sinner with a sore penalty. Also deadly Night bore Nemesis (Indignation) to afflict mortal men, and after her, Deceit and Friendship and hateful Age and hard-hearted Strife.

But abhorred Strife bore painful Toil and Forgetfulness and Famine and tearful Sorrows, Fightings also, Battles, Murders, Manslaughters, Quarrels, Lying Words, Disputes, Lawlessness and Ruin, all of one nature, and Oath who most troubles men upon Earth when anyone wilfully swears a false oath.

And Sea begat Nereus, the eldest of his children, who is true and lies not: and men call him the Old Man because he is trusty and gentle and does not forget the laws of righteousness, but thinks just and kindly thoughts. And yet again he got great Thaumas and proud Phoreys, being mated with Earth, and fair-cheeked Ceto, and Eurybia who has a heart of flint within her.

And of Nereus and rich-haired Doris, daughter of Ocean the perfect river, were born children, passing lovely amongst goddesses, Ploto, Eucrante, Sao, and Amphitrite, and Eudora, and Thetis, Galene and Glauce, Cymothoe, Speo, Thoe and lovely Halie, and Pasithea, and Erato, and rosy-armed Eunice, and gracious Melite, and Eulimene, and Agaue, Doto, Proto, Pherusa, and Dynamene, and Nisaea, and Actaea, and Protomedea, Doris, Panopea, and comely Galatea, and lovely Hippothoe, and rosy-armed Hipponoe, and Cymodoce who with Cymatolege and Amphitrite easily calms the waves upon the misty sea and the blasts of raging winds, and Cymo, and Eione, and rich-crowned Alimede, and Glauconome, fond of laughter, and Pontoporea, Leagore, Euagore, and Laomedea, and Polynoe, and Autonoe, and Lysianassa, and Euarne, lovely of shape and without blemish of form, and Psamathe of charming figure and divine Menippe, Neso, Eupompe, Themisto, Pronoe, and Nemertes who has the nature of her deathless father. These fifty daughters sprang from blameless Nereus, skilled in excellent crafts.

And Thaumas wedded Electra the daughter of deep-flowing Ocean, and she bore him swift Iris and the long-haired Harpies, Aello (Storm-swift) and Ocypetes (Swift-flier) who on their swift wings keep pace with the blasts of the winds and the birds; for quick as time they dart along.

And again, Ceto bore to Phoreys the fair-cheeked Graiae, sisters grey from their birth: and both deathless gods and men who walk on Earth call them Graiae, Pemphredo well-clad, and saffron-robed Enyo, and the Gorgons who dwell beyond glorious Ocean in the frontier land towards Night where are the clear-voiced Hesperides, Sthenno, and Euryale, and Medusa who suffered a woeful fate: she was mortal, but the two were undying and grew not old. With her lay the Dark-Haired One in a soft meadow amid spring flowers. And when Perseus cut off her head, there sprang forth great Chrysaor and the horse Pegasus who is so called because he was born near the springs (pegae) of Ocean; and that other, because he held a golden blade (aor) in his hands. Now Pegasus flew away and left the Earth, the mother of flocks, and came to the deathless gods: and he dwells in the house of Zeus and brings to wise Zeus the thunder and lightning. But Chrysaor was joined in love to Callirrhoe, the daughter of glorious Ocean, and begot three-headed Geryones. Him mighty Heracles slew in sea-girt Erythea by his shambling oxen on that day when he drove the wide-browed oxen to holy Tiryns, and had crossed the ford of Ocean and killed Orthus and Eurytion the herdsman in the dim stead out beyond glorious Ocean.

And in a hollow cave she bore another monster, irresistible, in no wise like either to mortal men or to the undying gods, even the fierce Echidna who is half a nymph with glancing eyes and fair cheeks, and half again a huge snake, great and awful, with speckled skin, eating raw flesh beneath the secret parts of the holy Earth. And there she has a cave deep down under a hollow rock far from the deathless gods and mortal men. There, then, did the gods appoint her a glorious house to dwell in: and she keeps guard in Arima beneath the earth, grim Echidna, a nymph who dies not nor grows old all her days.

Men say that Typhaon the terrible, outrageous and lawless, was joined in love to her, the maid with glancing eyes. So she conceived and brought forth fierce offspring; first she bore Orthus the hound of Geryones, and then again she bore a second, a monster not to be overcome and that may not be described, Cerberus who eats raw flesh, the brazen-voiced hound of Hades, fifty-headed, relentless and strong. And again she bore a third, the evil-minded Hydra of Lerna, whom the goddess, white-armed Hera nourished, being angry beyond measure with the mighty Heracles. And her Heracles, the son of Zeus, of the house of Amphitryon, together with warlike Iolaus, destroyed with the unpitying sword through the plans of Athene the spoil-driver. She was the mother of Chimaera who breathed raging fire, a creature fearful, great, swift-footed and strong, who had three heads, one of a grim-eyed lion; in her hinderpart, a dragon; and in her middle, a goat, breathing forth a fearful blast of blazing fire. Her did Pegasus and noble Bellerophon slay; but Echidna was subject in love to Orthus and brought forth the deadly Sphinx which destroyed the Cadmeans, and the Nemean lion, which Hera, the good wife of Zeus, brought up and made to haunt the hills of Nemea, a plague to men. There he preyed upon the tribes of her own people and had power over Tretus of Nemea and Apesas: yet the strength of stout Heracles overcame him.

And Ceto was joined in love to Phorcys and bore her youngest, the awful snake who guards the apples all of gold in the secret places of the dark Earth at its great bounds. This is the offspring of Ceto and Phorcys.

And Tethys bore to Ocean eddying rivers, Nilus, and Alpheus, and deep-swirling Eridanus, Strymon, and Meander, and the fair stream of Ister, and Phasis, and Rhesus, and the silver eddies of Achelous, Nessus, and Rhodius, Haliacmon, and Heptaporus, Granicus, and Aesepus, and holy Simois, and Peneus, and Hermus, and Caicus fair stream, and great Sangarius, Ladon, Parthenius, Euenus, Ardescus, and divine Scamander.

Also she brought forth a holy company of daughters who with the lord Apollo and the Rivers have youths in their keeping – to this charge Zeus appointed them – Peitho, and Admete, and Ianthe, and Electra, and Doris, and Prymno, and Urania divine in form, Hippo, Clymene, Rhodea, and Callirrhoe, Zeuxo and Clytie, and Idyia, and Pasithoe, Plexaura, and Galaxaura, and lovely Dione, Melobosis and Thoe and handsome Polydora, Cerceis lovely of form, and soft-eyed Pluto, Perseis, Ianeira, Acaste, Xanthe, Petraea the fair, Menestho, and Europa, Metis, and Eurynome, and Telesto saffron-clad, Chryseis and Asia and charming Calypso, Eudora, and Tyche, Amphirho, and Ocyrrhoe, and Styx who is the chiefest of them all. These are the eldest daughters that sprang from Ocean and Tethys; but there are many besides. For there are three thousand neat-ankled daughters of Ocean who are dispersed far and wide, and in every place alike serve the earth and the deep waters, children who are glorious among goddesses. And as many other rivers are there, babbling as they flow, sons of Ocean, whom queenly Tethys bore, but their names it is hard for a mortal man to tell, but people know those by which they severally dwell.

And Theia was subject in love to Hyperion and bore great Helius (Sun) and clear Selene (Moon) and Eos (Dawn) who shines upon all that are on Earth and upon the deathless Gods who live in the wide Heaven.

And Eurybia, bright goddess, was joined in love to Crius and bore great Astraeus, and Pallas, and Perses who also was eminent among all men in wisdom.

And Eos bore to Astraeus the strong-hearted winds, brightening Zephyrus, and Boreas, headlong in his course, and Notus – a goddess mating in love with a god. And after these Erigenia bore the star Eosphorus (Dawn-bringer), and the gleaming stars with which Heaven is crowned.

And Styx the daughter of Ocean was joined to Pallas and bore Zelus (Emulation) and trim-ankled Nike (Victory) in the house. Also she brought forth Cratos (Strength) and Bia (Force), wonderful children. These have no house apart from Zeus, nor any dwelling nor path except that wherein God leads them, but they dwell always with Zeus the loud-thunderer. For so did Styx the deathless daughter of Ocean plan on that day when the Olympian Lightener called all the deathless gods to great Olympus, and said that whosoever of the gods would fight with him against the Titans, he would not cast him out from his rights, but each should have the office which he had before amongst the deathless gods. And he declared that he who was without office and rights as is just. So deathless Styx came first to Olympus with her children through the wit of her dear father. And Zeus honoured her, and gave her very great gifts, for her he appointed to be the great oath of the gods, and her children to live with him always. And as he promised, so he performed fully unto them all.

But he himself mightily reigns and rules.

Again, Phoebe came to the desired embrace of Coeus.

Then the goddess through the love of the god conceived and brought forth dark-gowned Leto, always mild, kind to men and to the deathless gods, mild from the beginning, gentlest in all Olympus. Also she bore Asteria of happy name, whom Perses once led to his great house to be called his dear wife. And she conceived and bore Hecate whom Zeus the son of Cronos honoured above all. He gave her splendid gifts, to have a share of the earth and the unfruitful sea. She received honour also in starry Heaven, and is honoured exceedingly by the deathless gods. For to this day, whenever any one of men on Earth offers rich sacrifices and prays for favour according to custom, he calls upon Hecate. Great honour comes full easily to him whose prayers the goddess receives favourably, and she bestows wealth upon him; for the power surely is with her. For as many as were born of Earth and Ocean amongst all these she has her due portion. The son of Cronos did her no wrong nor took anything away of all that was her portion among the former Titan gods: but she holds, as the division was at the first from the beginning, privilege both on Earth, and in Heaven, and in sea. Also, because she is an only child, the goddess receives not less honour, but much more still, for Zeus honours her. Whom she will she greatly aids and advances: she sits by worshipful kings in judgment, and in the assembly whom she will is distinguished among the people. And when men arm themselves for the battle that destroys men, then the goddess is at hand to give victory and grant glory readily to whom she will. Good is she also when men contend at the games, for there too the goddess is with them and profits them: and he who by might and strength gets the victory wins the rich prize easily with joy, and brings glory to his parents. And she is good to stand by horsemen, whom she will: and to those whose business is in the grey discomfortable sea, and who pray to Hecate and the loud-crashing Earth-Shaker, easily the glorious goddess gives great catch, and easily she takes it away as soon as seen, if so she will. She is good in the byre with Hermes to increase the stock. The droves of kine and wide herds of goats and flocks of fleecy sheep, if she will, she increases from a few, or makes many to be less. So then, albeit her mother's only child, she is honoured amongst all the deathless gods. And the son of Cronos made her a nurse of the young who after that day saw with their eyes the light of all-seeing Dawn. So from the beginning she is a nurse of the young, and these are her honours.

But Rhea was subject in love to Cronos and bore splendid children, Hestia, Demeter, and gold-shod Hera and strong Hades, pitiless in heart, who dwells under the earth, and the loud-crashing Earth-Shaker, and wise Zeus, father of gods and men, by whose thunder the wide Earth is shaken. These great Cronos swallowed as each came forth from the womb to his mother's knees with this intent, that no other of the proud sons of Heaven should hold the kingly office amongst the deathless gods. For he learned from Earth and starry Heaven that he was destined to be overcome by his own son, strong though he was, through the contriving of great Zeus. Therefore he kept no blind outlook, but watched and swallowed down his children: and unceasing grief seized Rhea. But when she was about to bear Zeus, the father of gods and men, then she besought her own dear parents, Earth and starry Heaven, to devise some plan with her that the birth of her dear child might be concealed, and that retribution might overtake great, crafty Cronos for his own father and also for the children whom he had swallowed down. And they readily heard and obeyed their dear daughter, and told her all that was destined to happen touching Cronos the king and his stout-hearted son. So they sent her to Lyetus, to the rich land of Crete, when she was ready to bear great Zeus, the youngest of her children. Him did vast Earth receive from Rhea in wide Crete to nourish and to bring up. Thither came Earth carrying him swiftly through the black night to Lyctus first, and took him in her arms and hid him in a remote cave beneath the secret places of the holy Earth on thick-wooded Mount Aegeum; but to the mightily ruling son of Heaven, the earlier king of the gods, she gave a great stone wrapped in swaddling clothes. Then he took it in his hands and thrust it down into his belly: wretch! he knew not in his heart that in place of the stone his son was left behind, unconquered and untroubled, and that he was soon to overcome him by force and might and drive him from his honours, himself to reign over the deathless gods.

After that, the strength and glorious limbs of the prince increased quickly, and as the years rolled on, great Cronos the wily was beguiled by the deep suggestions of Earth, and brought up again his offspring, vanquished by the arts and might of his own son, and he vomited up first the stone which he had swallowed last. And Zeus set it fast in the wide-pathed Earth at goodly Pytho under the glens of Parnassus, to be a sign thenceforth and a marvel to mortal men. And he set free from their deadly bonds the brothers of his father, sons of Heaven whom his father in his foolishness had bound. And they remembered to be grateful to him for his kindness, and gave him thunder and the glowing thunderbolt and lightening: for before that, huge Earth had hidden these. In them he trusts and rules over mortals and immortals.

Now Iapetus took to wife the neat-ankled mad Clymene, daughter of Ocean, and went up with her into one bed. And she bore him a stout-hearted son, Atlas: also she bore very glorious Menoetius and clever Prometheus, full of various wiles, and scatter-brained

Epimetheus who from the first was a mischief to men who eat bread; for it was he who first took of Zeus the woman, the maiden whom he had formed. But Menoetius was outrageous, and far-seeing Zeus struck him with a lurid thunderbolt and sent him down to Erebus because of his mad presumption and exceeding pride. And Atlas through hard constraint upholds the wide Heaven with unwearying head and arms, standing at the borders of the Earth before the clear-voiced Hesperides; for this lot wise Zeus assigned to him. And ready-witted Prometheus he bound with inextricable bonds, cruel chains, and drove a shaft through his middle, and set on him a long-winged eagle, which used to eat his immortal liver; but by night the liver grew as much again everyway as the long-winged bird devoured in the whole day. That bird Heracles, the valiant son of shapely ankled Alcmene, slew; and delivered the son of Iapetus from the cruel plague, and released him from his affliction – not without the will of Olympian Zeus who reigns on high, that the glory of Heracles the Theban-born might be yet greater than it was before over the plenteous Earth. This, then, he regarded, and honoured his famous son; though he was angry, he ceased from the wrath which he had before because Prometheus matched himself in wit with the almighty son of Cronos. For when the gods and mortal men had a dispute at Mecone, even then Prometheus was forward to cut up a great ox and set portions before them, trying to befool the mind of Zeus. Before the rest he set flesh and inner parts thick with fat upon the hide, covering them with an ox paunch; but for Zeus he put the white bones dressed up with cunning art and covered with shining fat. Then the father of men and of gods said to him:

"Son of Iapetus, most glorious of all lords, good sir, how unfairly you have divided the portions!"

So said Zeus whose wisdom is everlasting, rebuking him. But wily Prometheus answered him, smiling softly and not forgetting his cunning trick:

"Zeus, most glorious and greatest of the eternal gods, take which ever of these portions your heart within you bids." So he said, thinking trickery. But Zeus, whose wisdom is everlasting, saw and failed not to perceive the trick, and in his heart he thought mischief against mortal men which also was to be fulfilled. With both hands he took up the white fat and was angry at heart, and wrath came to his spirit when he saw the white ox-bones craftily tricked out: and because of this the tribes of men upon Earth burn white bones to the deathless gods upon fragrant altars. But Zeus who drives the clouds was greatly vexed and said to him:

"Son of Iapetus, clever above all! So, sir, you have not yet forgotten your cunning arts!"

So spake Zeus in anger, whose wisdom is everlasting; and from that time he was always mindful of the trick, and would not give the power of unwearying fire to the Melian race of mortal men who live on the Earth. But the noble son of Iapetus outwitted him and stole the far-seen gleam of unwearying fire in a hollow fennel stalk. And Zeus who thunders on high was stung in spirit, and his dear heart was angered when he saw amongst men the far-seen ray of fire. Forthwith he made an evil thing for men as the price of fire; for the very famous Limping God formed of Earth the likeness of a shy maiden as the son of Cronos willed. And the goddess bright-eyed Athene girded and clothed her with silvery raiment, and down from her head she spread with her hands a broidered veil, a wonder to see; and she, Pallas Athene, put about her head lovely garlands, flowers of new-grown herbs. Also she put upon her head a crown of gold which the very famous Limping God made himself and worked with his own hands as a favour to Zeus his father. On it was much curious work, wonderful to see; for of the many creatures which the land

and sea rear up, he put most upon it, wonderful things, like living beings with voices: and great beauty shone out from it.

But when he had made the beautiful evil to be the price for the blessing, he brought her out, delighting in the finery which the bright-eyed daughter of a mighty father had given her, to the place where the other gods and men were. And wonder took hold of the deathless gods and mortal men when they saw that which was sheer guile, not to be withstood by men.

For from her is the race of women and female kind: of her is the deadly race and tribe of women who live amongst mortal men to their great trouble, no helpmeets in hateful poverty, but only in wealth. And as in thatched hives bees feed the drones whose nature is to do mischief – by day and throughout the day until the sun goes down the bees are busy and lay the white combs, while the drones stay at home in the covered skeps and reap the toil of others into their own bellies – even so Zeus who thunders on high made women to be an evil to mortal men, with a nature to do evil. And he gave them a second evil to be the price for the good they had: whoever avoids marriage and the sorrows that women cause, and will not wed, reaches deadly old age without anyone to tend his years, and though he at least has no lack of livelihood while he lives, yet, when he is dead, his kinsfolk divide his possessions amongst them. And as for the man who chooses the lot of marriage and takes a good wife suited to his mind, evil continually contends with good; for whoever happens to have mischievous children lives always with unceasing grief in his spirit and heart within him; and this evil cannot be healed.

So it is not possible to deceive or go beyond the will of Zeus; for not even the son of Iapetus, kindly Prometheus, escaped his heavy anger, but of necessity strong bands confined him, although he knew many a wile.

But when first their father was vexed in his heart with Obriareus and Cottus and Gyes, he bound them in cruel bonds, because he was jealous of their exceeding manhood and comeliness and great size: and he made them live beneath the wide-pathed Earth, where they were afflicted, being set to dwell under the ground, at the end of the Earth, at its great borders, in bitter anguish for a long time and with great grief at heart. But the son of Cronos and the other deathless gods whom rich-haired Rhea bore from union with Cronos, brought them up again to the light at Earth's advising. For she herself recounted all things to the gods fully, how that with these they would gain victory and a glorious cause to vaunt themselves. For the Titan gods and as many as sprang from Cronos had long been fighting together in stubborn war with heart-grieving toil, the lordly Titans from high Othyrs, but the gods, givers of good, whom rich-haired Rhea bore in union with Cronos, from Olympus. So they, with bitter wrath, were fighting continually with one another at that time for ten full years, and the hard strife had no close or end for either side, and the issue of the war hung evenly balanced. But when he had provided those three with all things fitting, nectar and ambrosia which the gods themselves eat, and when their proud spirit revived within them all after they had fed on nectar and delicious ambrosia, then it was that the father of men and gods spoke amongst them:

"Hear me, bright children of Earth and Heaven, that I may say what my heart within me bids. A long while now have we, who are sprung from Cronos and the Titan gods, fought with each other every day to get victory and to prevail. But do you show your great might and unconquerable strength, and face the Titans in bitter strife; for remember our friendly kindness, and from what sufferings you are come back to the light from your cruel bondage under misty gloom through our counsels."

So he said. And blameless Cottus answered him again: "Divine one, you speak that which we know well: nay, even of ourselves we know that your wisdom and understanding is exceeding, and that you became a defender of the deathless ones from chill doom. And through your devising we are come back again from the murky gloom and from our merciless bonds, enjoying what we looked not for, O Lord, son of Cronos. And so now with fixed purpose and deliberate counsel we will aid your power in dreadful strife and will fight against the Titans in hard battle."

So he said: and the gods, givers of good things, applauded when they heard his word, and their spirit longed for war even more than before, and they all, both male and female, stirred up hated battle that day, the Titan gods, and all that were born of Cronos together with those dread, mighty ones of overwhelming strength whom Zeus brought up to the light from Erebus beneath the earth. An hundred arms sprang from the shoulders of all alike, and each had fifty heads growing upon his shoulders upon stout limbs. These, then, stood against the Titans in grim strife, holding huge rocks in their strong hands. And on the other part the Titans eagerly strengthened their ranks, and both sides at one time showed the work of their hands and their might. The boundless sea rang terribly around, and the Earth crashed loudly: wide Heaven was shaken and groaned, and high Olympus reeled from its foundation under the charge of the undying gods, and a heavy quaking reached dim Tartarus and the deep sound of their feet in the fearful onset and of their hard missiles. So, then, they launched their grievous shafts upon one another, and the cry of both armies as they shouted reached to starry Heaven; and they met together with a great battle-cry.

Then Zeus no longer held back his might; but straight his heart was filled with fury and he showed forth all his strength. From Heaven and from Olympus he came forthwith, hurling his lightning: the bold flew thick and fast from his strong hand together with thunder and lightning, whirling an awesome flame. The life-giving Earth crashed around in burning, and the vast wood crackled loud with fire all about. All the land seethed, and Ocean's streams and the unfruitful sea. The hot vapour lapped round the Earth-born Titans: flame unspeakable rose to the bright upper air: the flashing glare of the thunder-stone and lightning blinded their eyes for all that there were strong. Astounding heat seized Chaos: and to see with eyes and to hear the sound with ears it seemed even as if Earth and wide Heaven above came together; for such a mighty crash would have arisen if Earth were being hurled to ruin, and Heaven from on high were hurling her down; so great a crash was there while the gods were meeting together in strife. Also the winds brought rumbling earthquake and duststorm, thunder and lightning and the lurid thunderbolt, which are the shafts of great Zeus, and carried the clangour and the war cry into the midst of the two hosts. An horrible uproar of terrible strife arose: mighty deeds were shown and the battle inclined. But until then, they kept at one another and fought continually in cruel war.

And amongst the foremost Cottus and Briareos and Gyes insatiate for war raised fierce fighting: three hundred rocks, one upon another, they launched from their strong hands and overshadowed the Titans with their missiles, and buried them beneath the wide-pathed Earth, and bound them in bitter chains when they had conquered them by their strength for all their great spirit, as far beneath the earth to Tartarus. For a brazen anvil falling down from Heaven nine nights and days would reach the Earth upon the tenth: and again, a brazen anvil falling from Earth nine nights and days would reach Tartarus upon the tenth. Round it runs a fence of bronze, and night spreads in triple line all about it like a neck-circlet, while above grow the roots of the earth and unfruitful sea. There by the counsel of

Zeus who drives the clouds the Titan gods are hidden under misty gloom, in a dank place where are the ends of the huge Earth. And they may not go out; for Poseidon fixed gates of bronze upon it, and a wall runs all round it on every side. There Gyes and Cottus and great-souled Obriareus live, trusty warders of Zeus who holds the aegis.

And there, all in their order, are the sources and ends of gloomy Earth and misty Tartarus and the unfruitful sea and starry Heaven, loathsome and dank, which even the gods abhor.

It is a great gulf, and if once a man were within the gates, he would not reach the floor until a whole year had reached its end, but cruel blast upon blast would carry him this way and that. And this marvel is awful even to the deathless gods.

There stands the awful home of murky Night wrapped in dark clouds. In front of it the son of Iapetus stands immovably upholding the wide Heaven upon his head and unwearying hands, where Night and Day draw near and greet one another as they pass the great threshold of bronze: and while the one is about to go down into the house, the other comes out at the door.

And the house never holds them both within; but always one is without the house passing over the Earth, while the other stays at home and waits until the time for her journeying come; and the one holds all-seeing light for them on Earth, but the other holds in her arms Sleep the brother of Death, even evil Night, wrapped in a vaporous cloud.

And there the children of dark Night have their dwellings, Sleep and Death, awful gods. The glowing Sun never looks upon them with his beams, neither as he goes up into Heaven, nor as he comes down from Heaven. And the former of them roams peacefully over the Earth and the sea's broad back and is kindly to men; but the other has a heart of iron, and his spirit within him is pitiless as bronze: whomsoever of men he has once seized he holds fast: and he is hateful even to the deathless gods.

There, in front, stand the echoing halls of the god of the lower-world, strong Hades, and of awful Persephone. A fearful hound guards the house in front, pitiless, and he has a cruel trick. On those who go in he fawns with his tail and both his ears, but suffers them not to go out back again, but keeps watch and devours whomsoever he catches going out of the gates of strong Hades and awful Persephone.

And there dwells the goddess loathed by the deathless gods, terrible Styx, eldest daughter of back-flowing Ocean. She lives apart from the gods in her glorious house vaulted over with great rocks and propped up to Heaven all round with silver pillars. Rarely does the daughter of Thaumas, swift-footed Iris, come to her with a message over the sea's wide back.

But when strife and quarrel arise among the deathless gods, and when any of them who live in the house of Olympus lies, then Zeus sends Iris to bring in a golden jug the great oath of the gods from far away, the famous cold water which trickles down from a high and beetling rock. Far under the wide-pathed Earth a branch of Oceanus flows through the dark night out of the holy stream, and a tenth part of his water is allotted to her. With nine silver-swirling streams he winds about the Earth and the sea's wide back, and then falls into the main; but the tenth flows out from a rock, a sore trouble to the gods. For whoever of the deathless gods that hold the peaks of snowy Olympus pours a libation of her water is forsworn, lies breathless until a full year is completed, and never comes near to taste ambrosia and nectar, but lies spiritless and voiceless on a strewn bed: and a heavy trance overshadows him. But when he has spent a long year in his sickness, another penance and an harder follows after the first. For nine years he is cut off from the eternal gods and never joins their councils of their feasts, nine full years. But in the tenth year he comes again to join the assemblies of the deathless gods who live in the house of Olympus. Such an oath, then, did the gods appoint the eternal and primaeval water of Styx to be: and it spouts through a rugged place.

And there, all in their order, are the sources and ends of the dark Earth and misty Tartarus and the unfruitful sea and starry Heaven, loathsome and dank, which even the gods abhor.

And there are shining gates and an immoveable threshold of bronze having unending roots and it is grown of itself. And beyond, away from all the gods, live the Titans, beyond gloomy Chaos. But the glorious allies of loud-crashing Zeus have their dwelling upon Ocean's foundations, even Cottus and Gyes; but Briareos, being goodly, the deep-roaring Earth-Shaker made his son-in-law, giving him Cymopolea his daughter to wed.

But when Zeus had driven the Titans from Heaven, huge Earth bore her youngest child Typhoeus of the love of Tartarus, by the aid of golden Aphrodite. Strength was with his hands in all that he did and the feet of the strong god were untiring. From his shoulders grew an hundred heads of a snake, a fearful dragon, with dark, flickering tongues, and from under the brows of his eyes in his marvellous heads flashed fire, and fire burned from his heads as he glared. And there were voices in all his dreadful heads which uttered every kind of sound unspeakable; for at one time they made sounds such that the gods understood, but at another, the noise of a bull bellowing aloud in proud ungovernable fury; and at another, the sound of a lion, relentless of heart; and at anothers, sounds like whelps, wonderful to hear; and again, at another, he would hiss, so that the high mountains re-echoed. And truly a thing past help would have happened on that day, and he would have come to reign over mortals and immortals, had not the father of men and gods been quick to perceive it. But he thundered hard and mightily: and the Earth around resounded terribly and the wide Heaven above, and the sea and Ocean's streams and the nether parts of the Earth. Great Olympus reeled beneath the divine feet of the king as he arose and Earth groaned thereat. And through the two of them heat took hold on the dark-blue sea, through the thunder and lightning, and through the fire from the monster, and the scorching winds and blazing thunderbolt. The whole Earth seethed, and sky and sea: and the long waves raged along the beaches round and about, at the rush of the deathless gods: and there arose an endless shaking. Hades trembled where he rules over the dead below, and the Titans under Tartarus who live with Cronos, because of the unending clamour and the fearful strife. So when Zeus had raised up his might and seized his arms, thunder and lightning and lurid thunderbolt, he leaped from Olympus and struck him, and burned all the marvellous heads of the monster about him. But when Zeus had conquered him and lashed him with strokes, Typhoeus was hurled down, a maimed wreck, so that the huge Earth groaned. And flame shot forth from the thunder-stricken lord in the dim rugged glens of the mount, when he was smitten. A great part of huge Earth was scorched by the terrible vapour and melted as tin melts when heated by men's art in channelled crucibles; or as iron, which is hardest of all things, is softened by glowing fire in mountain glens and melts in the divine Earth through the strength of Hephaestus. Even so, then, the Earth melted in the glow of the blazing fire. And in the bitterness of his anger Zeus cast him into wide Tartarus.

And from Typhoeus come boisterous winds which blow damply, except Notus and Boreas and clear Zephyr. These are a god-sent kind, and a great blessing to men; but the others blow fitfully upon the seas. Some rush upon the misty sea and work great havoc among men with their evil, raging blasts; for varying with the season they blow, scattering ships and destroying sailors. And men who meet these upon the sea have no help against the mischief. Others again over the boundless, flowering Earth spoil the fair fields of men who dwell below, filling them with dust and cruel uproar.

But when the blessed gods had finished their toil, and settled by force their struggle for honours with the Titans, they pressed far-seeing Olympian Zeus to reign and to rule over them, by Earth's prompting. So he divided their dignities amongst them.

Now Zeus, king of the gods, made Metis his wife first, and she was wisest among gods and mortal men. But when she was about to bring forth the goddess bright-eyed Athene, Zeus craftily deceived her with cunning words and put her in his own belly, as Earth and starry Heaven advised. For they advised him so, to the end that no other should hold royal sway over the eternal gods in place of Zeus; for very wise children were destined to be born of her, first the maiden bright-eyed Tritogeneia, equal to her father in strength and in wise understanding; but afterwards she was to bear a son of overbearing spirit, king of gods and men. But Zeus put her into his own belly first, that the goddess might devise for him both good and evil.

Next he married bright Themis who bore the Horae (Hours), and Eunomia (Order), Dike (Justice), and blooming Eirene (Peace), who mind the works of mortal men, and the Moerae (Fates) to whom wise Zeus gave the greatest honour, Clotho, and Lachesis, and Atropos who give mortal men evil and good to have.

And Eurynome, the daughter of Ocean, beautiful in form, bore him three fair-cheeked Charites (Graces), Aglaea, and Euphrosyne, and lovely Thaleia, from whose eyes as they glanced flowed love that unnerves the limbs: and beautiful is their glance beneath their brows.

Also he came to the bed of all-nourishing Demeter, and she bore white-armed Persephone whom Aidoneus carried off from her mother; but wise Zeus gave her to him.

And again, he loved Mnemosyne with the beautiful hair: and of her the nine gold-crowned Muses were born who delight in feasts and the pleasures of song.

And Leto was joined in love with Zeus who holds the aegis, and bore Apollo and Artemis delighting in arrows, children lovely above all the sons of Heaven.

Lastly, he made Hera his blooming wife: and she was joined in love with the king of gods and men, and brought forth Hebe and Ares and Eileithyia.

But Zeus himself gave birth from his own head to bright-eyed Tritogeneia, the awful, the strife-stirring, the host-leader, the unwearying, the queen, who delights in tumults and wars and battles. But Hera without union with Zeus – for she was very angry and quarrelled with her mate – bore famous Hephaestus, who is skilled in crafts more than all the sons of Heaven.

But Hera was very angry and quarrelled with her mate. And because of this strife she bore without union with Zeus who holds the aegis a glorious son, Hephaestus, who excelled all the sons of Heaven in crafts. But Zeus lay with the fair-cheeked daughter of Ocean and Tethys apart from Hera...deceiving Metis (Thought) although she was full wise. But he seized her with his hands and put her in his belly, for fear that she might bring forth something stronger than his thunderbolt: therefore did Zeus, who sits on high and dwells in the aether, swallow her down suddenly. But she straightway conceived Pallas Athene: and the father of men and gods gave her birth by way of his head on the banks of the River Trito. And she remained hidden beneath the inward parts of Zeus, even Metis, Athena's mother, worker of righteousness, who was wiser than gods and mortal men. There the goddess (Athena) received that whereby she excelled in strength all the deathless ones who dwell in Olympus, she who made the host-scaring weapon of Athena. And with it (Zeus) gave her birth, arrayed in arms of war.

And of Amphitrite and the loud-roaring Earth-Shaker was born great, wide-ruling Triton, and he owns the depths of the sea, living with his dear mother and the lord his father in their golden house, an awful god.

Also Cytherea bore to Ares the shield-piercer Panic and Fear, terrible gods who drive in disorder the close ranks of men in numbing war, with the help of Ares, sacker of towns: and Harmonia whom high-spirited Cadmus made his wife.

And Maia, the daughter of Atlas, bore to Zeus glorious Hermes, the herald of the deathless gods, for she went up into his holy bed.

And Semele, daughter of Cadmus was joined with him in love and bore him a splendid son, joyous Dionysus – a mortal woman an immortal son. And now they both are gods.

And Alemena was joined in love with Zeus who drives the clouds and bore mighty Heracles.

And Hephaestus, the famous Lame One, made Aglaea, youngest of the Graces, his buxom wife.

And golden-haired Dionysus made brown-haired Ariadne, the daughter of Minos, his buxom wife: and the son of Cronos made her deathless and unageing for him.

And mighty Heracles, the valiant son of neat-ankled Alemena, when he had finished his grievous toils, made Hebe the child of great Zeus and gold-shod Hera his shy wife in snowy Olympus. Happy he! For he has finished his great works and lives amongst the dying gods, untroubled and unaging all his days.

And Perseis, the daughter of Ocean, bore to unwearying Helios Circe and Aeetes the king. And Aeetes, the son of Helios who shows light to men, took to wife fair-cheeked Idyia, daughter of Ocean the perfect stream, by the will of the gods: and she was subject to him in love through golden Aphrodite and bore him neat-ankled Medea.

And now farewell, you dwellers on Olympus and you islands and continents and thou briny sea within. Now sing the company of goddesses, sweet-voiced Muses of Olympus, daughter of Zeus who holds the aegis – even those deathless one who lay with mortal men and bore children like unto gods.

Demeter, bright goddess, was joined in sweet love with the hero Iasion in a thrice-ploughed fallow in the rich land of Crete, and bore Plutus, a kindly god who goes everywhere over land and the sea's wide back, and him who finds him and into whose hands he comes he makes rich, bestowing great wealth upon him.

And Harmonia, the daughter of golden Aphrodite, bore to Cadmus Ino and Semele and fair-cheeked Agave and Autonoe whom long haired Aristaeus wedded, and Polydorus also in rich-crowned Thebe.

And the daughter of Ocean, Callirrhoe was joined in the love of rich Aphrodite with stout-hearted Chrysaor and bore a son who was the strongest of all men, Geryones, whom mighty Heracles killed in sea-girt Erythea for the sake of his shambling oxen.

And Eos bore to Tithonus brazen-crested Memnon, king of the Ethiopians, and the Lord Emathion. And to Cephalus she bore a splendid son, strong Phaethon, a man like the gods, whom, when he was a young boy in the tender flower of glorious youth with childish thoughts, laughter-loving Aphrodite seized and caught up and made a keeper of her shrine by night, a divine spirit.

And the son of Aeson by the will of the gods led away from Aeetes the daughter of Aeetes the Heaven-nurtured king, when he had finished the many grievous labours which the great king, over bearing Pelias, that outrageous and presumptuous doer of violence, put upon him. But when the son of Aeson had finished them, he came to Iolcus after long toil bringing the coy-eyed girl with him on his swift ship, and made her his buxom wife. And she was subject to Iason, shepherd of the people, and bore a son Medeus whom Cheiron the son of Philyra brought up in the mountains. And the will of great Zeus was fulfilled.

But of the daughters of Nereus, the Old Man of the Sea, Psamathe the fair goddess, was loved by Aeacus through golden Aphrodite and bore Phocus. And the silver-shod goddess Thetis was subject to Peleus and brought forth lion-hearted Achilles, the destroyer of men.

And Cytherea with the beautiful crown was joined in sweet love with the hero Anchises and bore Aeneas on the peaks of Ida with its many wooded glens.

And Circe the daughter of Helius, Hyperion's son, loved steadfast Odysseus and bore Agrius, and Latinus who was faultless and strong: also she brought forth Telegonus by the will of golden Aphrodite. And they ruled over the famous Tyrenians, very far off in a recess of the holy islands.

And the bright goddess Calypso was joined to Odysseus in sweet love, and bore him Nausithous and Nausinous.

These are the immortal goddesses who lay with mortal men and bore them children like unto gods.

But now, sweet-voiced Muses of Olympus, daughters of Zeus who holds the aegis, sing of the company of women.

The Titans

CHAOS, EREBUS AND NYX were deprived of their power by Aether and Hemera, who did not long enjoy the possession of the sceptre; for Uranus and Gaea, more powerful than their progenitors, soon forced them to depart, and began to reign in their stead. They had not dwelt long on the summit of Mount Olympus, before they found themselves the parents of twelve gigantic children, the Titans, whose strength was such that their father, Uranus, greatly feared them. To prevent their ever making use of it against him, he seized them immediately after their birth, hurled them down into a dark abyss called Tartarus, and there chained them fast.

This chasm was situated far under the earth; and Uranus knew that his six sons (Oceanus, Coeus, Crius, Hyperion, Iapetus, and Cronus), as well as his six daughters, the Titanides (Ilia, Rhea, Themis, Thetis, Mnemosyne, and Phoebe), could not easily escape from its cavernous depths. The Titans did not long remain sole occupants of Tartarus, for one day the brazen doors were again thrown wide open to admit the Cyclopes – Brontes (Thunder), Steropes (Lightning), and Arges (Sheet-lightning) – three later-born children of Uranus and Gaea, who helped the Titans to make the darkness hideous with their incessant clamor for freedom. In due time their number was increased by the three terrible Centimani (Hundred-handed), Cottus, Briareus, and Gyes, who were sent thither by Uranus to share their fate.

Greatly dissatisfied with the treatment her children had received at their father's hands, Gaea remonstrated, but all in vain. Uranus would not grant her request to set the giants free, and, whenever their muffled cries reached his ear, he trembled for his own safety. Angry beyond all expression, Gaea swore revenge, and descended into Tartarus, where she urged the Titans to conspire against their father, and attempt to wrest the sceptre from his grasp.

All listened attentively to the words of sedition; but none were courageous enough to carry out her plans, except Cronus, the youngest of the Titans, more familiarly known as Saturn, who found confinement and chains peculiarly galling, and who hated his father for his cruelty. Gaea finally induced him to lay violent hands upon his sire, and, after releasing him from his bonds, gave him a scythe, and bade him be of good cheer and return victorious.

Thus armed and admonished, Cronus set forth, came upon his father unawares, defeated him, thanks to his extraordinary weapon, and, after binding him fast, took possession of the vacant throne, intending to rule the universe for ever. Enraged at this insult, Uranus cursed his son, and prophesied that a day would come when he, too, would be supplanted by his children, and would suffer just punishment for his rebellion.

Cronus paid no heed to his father's imprecations, but calmly proceeded to release the Titans, his brothers and sisters, who, in their joy and gratitude to escape the dismal realm of Tartarus, expressed their willingness to be ruled by him. Their satisfaction was complete, however, when he chose his own sister Rhea (Cybele, Ops) for his consort, and assigned to each of the others some portion of the world to govern at will. To Oceanus and Thetis, for example, he gave charge over the ocean and all the rivers upon earth; while to Hyperion and Phoebe he entrusted the direction of the sun and moon, which the ancients supposed were daily driven across the sky in brilliant golden chariots.

The Giant Who Shines in the Sky

IN THE DAYS WHEN THE OLYMPIANS still walked at times among men, Zeus and Poseidon and Hermes once found themselves benighted in a lonely region of the rough Bœotian country.

As darkness fell, they passed a little hut by the roadside. The farmer stood in the doorway, enjoying the cool of the evening after his day's toil; and seeing the wayfarers plodding along, he invited them in to pass the night.

"My house is poor enough," said he, "but such as it is, it is yours."

The three gods entered. The farmer, Hyrieus by name, set food and drink before them, waited upon them, gave up his own pallet to make them comfortable and entertained these nameless wanderers like distinguished guests, all with the utmost simplicity and good feeling.

The Olympians were touched by this rough herdsman's fine hospitality. They consulted together in whispers when they had finished their meal.

Then: "Is there anything you wish for, host?" enquired Hermes as spokesman.

Hyrieus started. "Well," said he, "of course there is, but that's past mending."

"What is it?" persisted Hermes.

"I had a wife," said the herdsman, "whom I loved so that when she died I vowed never to marry again. So all these years I have lived alone, and alone I shall live till the end. Yet a man cannot help wishing for a son to drive away the loneliness of the winter evenings and to be a prop to him in his old age. Probably you will laugh at me for a foolish person: for I mean to keep my vow, and yet I wish for a son."

"Those who know do not laugh at honesty," replied Hermes. "And I say to you that he who gives all freely never fails to receive. I noticed that you killed your only ox to provide meat for our meal: bring me his hide."

Hyrieus stared at him, doubtful. He feared he was being made the butt of some jest. But the stranger's open smile promised something quite different. Much wondering, he went out into the darkness and after a while returned with the hide of the ox which he had sacrificed to hospitality. He did not regret the act, but he could not help thinking of the morrow as he handled the still warm skin of this faithful companion and servant. What would he do without its aid? And what did this mysterious person mean by his odd request? He spoke as a man having authority, however, and there was nothing for it save to obey and see what might befall.

Hermes took the hide, and bade him fetch a spade. The three mysterious visitors went out into the night. Hyrieus, peering out after them, saw them bury the ox skin in front of his house, with strange and secret ceremonies. Without knowing why, he trembled. He trembled still more when they returned, for the strangers seemed to have become suddenly majestic, awe-inspiring.

The bearded one, who had not spoken hitherto, looked solemnly upon the herdsman. Instinctively the Bœotian fell into an attitude of worship.

"You shall have your wish," announced this one, in tones that filled the low-raftered room like a mighty wind. "Next spring you shall have a son – and such a son as mortal never yet had."

The three retired for the night. When Hyrieus woke, as usual, with the dawn, they had disappeared. He went about his labours, sorely increased by the loss of his ox, pondering deeply on what had occurred. Many a time he looked at the little patch of freshly turned earth, but something forbade him to investigate. And then the autumn rains came and obliterated the spot; and the winter snows covered all; and everything was as it had been, save for the insistent recollection in the farmer's heart. Many times he laughed at his folly; yet in the still evenings as he sat before his fire, he knew that he expected – something.

Winter passed at length. Spring painted the hills with yellow and white and pink blossoms. And its soft unfolding promises seemed to reinforce that secret hope, which defied reason, and which persisted in the heart of Hyrieus. As he sat outdoors in the long twilight evenings, instead of crouching close to his scanty fire, every sound of the reawakening earth had a new meaning. Even the still white calm of snow-capped Parnassus, far to the west, seemed to presage some great happening. For the first time since his youth he really heard the shrill voices of the frogs in the neighbouring marsh: it was as if even these tiny creatures were repeating the promise made him by his mysterious visitors. And then he would smile sadly at his senile credulity and, remembering the reality of the morrow's hard work, would plod stiffly into his solitary hut and seek on his pallet bed that dream land where all things are possible.

One morning he rose with even more than his usual reluctance to exchange for the hard grubbing reality the vague but delightful fancies which had filled the night. Force of habit made him swallow a few mouthfuls of his coarse breakfast. Mechanically he stepped outside towards the day's work that awaited him.

The sun was just rising over the low ridge that thrust itself into the bend of the Asopus River. Instinctively his gaze went towards the spot where the strange trio had performed their mysterious rites, past which gurgled a little stream.

He stopped short, startled out of his dreamy reverie. His eyes rounded in astonishment.

That spot of earth had remained bare, though all around it the lush grass and many-coloured flowers had woven an intricate tapestry. It was this strange fact which had continually reinforced his wonder and his superstitious belief.

But overnight a sudden transformation had taken place. The whole space was one mass of asphodels in full bloom. The sun's level rays fell upon their white blossoms, amid which the meandering threads of crimson looked like blazing hieroglyphs.

Hyrieus looked in bewilderment, mixed with a kind of awe. Slowly he advanced towards this bed of blossoms which had appeared so suddenly. Then he cried out.

For there, cradled in the asphodels, lay a babe – such a child as his eyes had never yet beheld. Shapely and beautiful, and of such size as made one think of the Heroes of legend, he slept peacefully.

Overcoming his timidity at last, Hyrieus gently picked up the sleeping infant. When the big blue eyes opened and a sleepy smile came over the child's face, the honest farmer's heart overflowed with joy at this realization of his wildest dreams. Marvelling again at the weight of his burden, he took this earth-born son into his cottage, laid him on his own bed, and sat watching his slumber in a sort of ecstasy. From that time he was father and mother both to the child, carrying it with him when he went about his necessary labour afield, and watching over it with an anxious care into which his whole existence seemed concentrated.

The boy was well worth these pains and pride. He never cried; and he seemed perfectly happy and contented when couched in a nest of soft grass and dry leaves under the open sky, where his foster-father, as he toiled, could keep an eye on him. Moreover, the youngster grew like some sturdy young bull. He had no teething troubles; presently he was eating the same food that served Hyrieus himself – with all the choicest portions for his share; and he found his legs almost as quickly as a young partridge.

In fact, by the time when ordinary children are beginning to toddle uncertainly, this boy, whom Hyrieus had named Orion, was as tall as his foster-father. Nor did he cease his prodigious growth when he reached the ordinary limits of mankind: not even Otus and Ephialtes, who rebelled against the gods and strove to set Mt. Ossa upon Pelion that they might scale Olympus itself – not even these gigantic youths could compare with Orion. And we have the word of Odysseus who beheld them among the shades in Hades that those portentous twins were at nine years of age fifty-four feet in height and some thirteen across the shoulders.

He was as handsome as one of the immortals, too, this Orion. Well proportioned and graceful in spite of his size, he roamed the woods and fields with the agility and tirelessness of one of the wild creatures whose ways seemed to have an endless fascination for him.

Hyrieus began to fare better than ever before, for the boy would return from these expeditions with rabbits and hares, with quails, wood pigeons, partridges and ducks, which he had snared or caught with his hands by some sudden pounce after a long stalk.

Presently his foster-father showed him how to make a bow and arrows; and one day the youngster proudly appeared before the hut with a roebuck upon his shoulders. It was not long before he had learned to outwit the great red stags of the hills, to chase successfully the long-horned wild goats, and even to bring back chamois from the precipitous fastnesses of rocky, fir-clad Mt. Cithæron, or the crags of two-peaked Helicon. By the time he had reached his early teens he was already a mighty hunter, who had met and vanquished the lynx, the wolf and the brown bear, who could stand up to the charge of an infuriated wild boar, and whose chief desire was to take in fair fight the lion skin he wished for a cloak.

Fierce as he was, however, in attacking some snarling wild beast with his great club, he was always gentle and thoughtful to his foster-father; and Hyrieus many a time blessed the day when his hospitality had fallen upon such fruitful soil. To be sure, as the good farmer grew old, his unbounded pride in the feats of this stripling cast at times a reflected glory upon himself: there were moments when he looked upon Orion's great muscles and the trophies of his strength and fleetness almost as if these were to be credited to his very own flesh and blood. Yet in the bottom of his heart there was ever a slight feeling of awe at this prodigy who had come to comfort his old age; and this was deepened when he learned of one strange power which the youth possessed.

Exulting in his own swiftness of foot, Orion was one day chasing a roebuck, endeavouring to run down the bounding little creature on equal terms. The deer made for the river, and finding itself hard pressed, sprang in and swam the wide stream. Orion, close behind, excitedly plunged in after his quarry; and though the water was far above his head, he actually gained upon the deer in crossing, caught it on the opposite shore, and bore the carcass home in triumph. It seemed perfectly natural to him to be able to walk through the water, without touching bottom, almost as easily as on dry land; but Hyrieus was filled with astonishment at his story and could scarcely credit it until he saw the youth a few days later perform the same miraculous feat in the neighbouring lake, advancing with great strides through fifty feet of water, only his head showing above the surface. Unknown to either of them, this was the natal gift of Poseidon, god of the sea and waters. Orion troubled himself little enough about whence it came or its singularity; but from that hour rivers and lakes were no obstacle to him, and when he roamed further and reached the great sea itself, he found himself master of even this, and able to travel through the salt surge and the heaving waves of Poseidon's own domain. Thereafter, the farthest confines of Greece, nay even Thrace, Macedon and remote Illyria, could not satisfy this passion for wandering. He learned to know the aspect of inaccessible Olympus from the north and west as well as the familiar one from the south. The unknown, with its new animals and fresh landscapes, ever called him on to wider and wider swings from his Bœotian home.

When he reached young manhood, all who beheld him agreed that he was handsomest among the sons of men – if indeed he were of human origin. The maidens of Tanagra, Thebes and Platæa did not say so much, but their eyes spoke for them when the swift-footed young hunter sped past. As for him, he seemed to see none of them save Side, whose tall beauty and dignity marked her out among all the graceful girls of that land; and he only knew that when he looked upon her he was filled with a vague unrest.

The time came for the festival of the Great Dædala, when, once in sixty years, all the folk celebrated the reconciliation of Zeus and Hera.

From every corner of Bœotia the people gathered. In solemn procession, headed by the priests, they fared forth into an ancient forest, where giant oaks stood shoulder to shoulder so that their mighty boles were in sunless gloom.

The priest set some boiled meat on the ground. Breathlessly the great assemblage watched in silence as the birds dropped through the air to their feast.

Presently a raven appeared. A long sigh of expectant excitement went up from the crowd. The glossy black bird lit near the meat, and walked awkwardly towards it, cocking an impudent eye towards the motionless creatures who watched him so intently. Assured of their harmlessness, he seized a piece of this Heaven-sent dinner and flapped away with his prize. Every gaze was focused upon him.

As he lit on the lower branch of a huge oak some distance off, a tremendous shout from hundreds of throats rang through the gloomy forest. Everyone rushed to the tree thus selected. Amid songs and clamour, men with axes cut down this giant growth. And when it crashed to earth, another shout alarmed the birds and beasts for miles about.

Swiftly the skilled axemen hewed out an image from a section of the trunk. With deft fingers the women dressed this image in snowy bridal garments.

When all was ready, it was lifted into a clumsy wain, with solid hewed-out wheels, drawn by a white bullock. Beside it was seated the most beautiful virgin as bridesmaid; and Orion's heart throbbed violently as he saw the stately Side take her place in this seat of honour.

The wain started back out of the wood, followed by a piping and dancing throng of worshippers. At the edge of the forest they were met by another procession, escorting the thirteen other images which commemorated all the Little Dædala festivals since the last great celebration.

Chanting and dancing, the whole multitude moved down to the Asopus River; after a ceremony of purification, they set out for Mt. Cithæron.

Here the fourteen wains were dragged to the very summit of the mountain. The images were placed on the altar of square blocks of wood, and brushwood was heaped over all. After sacrifices had been performed – a he-goat to Zeus, and a cow to Hera – a torch was set to this sacred pile, and in a moment the whole was a vast pillar of fire, leaping a hundred feet into the air and visible for miles and miles in every direction.

It was a prodigious and awe-inspiring spectacle. But Orion saw only Side in her calm and lofty beauty. For the first time he realized that there were other things necessary to his happiness besides chasing the red deer and the snarling wolf.

He sought her parents and demanded her. And when they found that Side, so sure of herself and so scornful of all suitors, had lost her heart to this tall, impetuous youth, they gave their consent.

The wedding was the occasion of another celebration almost as joyous as one of the lesser Dædala, for all the countryside was proud of the unmatched beauty of Side, and Orion's renown had spread far and wide.

Each guest seemed to vie with all the others in complimenting Side, who had never looked more lovely or more unapproachable than in her bridal array. So loud and extravagant was this chorus of praise that it aroused the jealousy of some of her comrades.

"After all," broke out a black-eyed maiden spitefully, "she is the daughter of crooked-legged Alpheus. One might think, to hear them go on, that it was Hera herself who was being married to this wild man."

Orion, beside his bride, heard the taunt, and turned upon the speaker.

"I have never seen Hera," said he. "But I have seen Side – and she is beyond compare with any mortal I know. Until I behold the Goddess face to face and find I am mistaken, I shall believe that even on Olympus there is none that can challenge my bride."

The guests gasped and drew back a space at this audacious sacrilege. Side, however, smiled, well pleased. For in her secret heart she thought her ardent lover spoke but the truth, and that had she been in Hera's place there would have been no need of the reconciliation with Zeus, for which the Dædala was held.

The large-eyed Queen of Heaven heard the rash speech and saw the presumption of this earth-born maiden. Her majestic brows knitted in anger – and it was as if a cloud passed across the face of the sun. Sternly she refused the wedding sacrifice to herself, the Perfecter and Fulfiller, and all the folk were aghast at this portent.

But Side still smiled, serene in her blind conceit.

"Am I not perfect enough for you to worship?" said she softly to Orion.

His ardent answer was interrupted by a crash of thunder from the clear sky. Swiftly a great darkness fell upon the smiling plain. The merrymakers were blanched with fear as this blackness engulfed everything. They spoke in strained whispers. Darker and darker it grew, till one could not see his terrified neighbour's face. Even the murmurings ceased. All waited for some dread happening, they knew not what.

The silence was pierced by a sudden scream.

"Side!" cried Orion. "Side! Where are you?" He rushed wildly about, upsetting all in his path.

There was the sound of a rushing wind, nothing more. Then the gloom lifted as mysteriously as it had come.

But the bride was nowhere to be found. The wedding party crept to their homes. No earthly eye ever again beheld the presumptuous Side. The wise ones whispered that the enraged Hera had cast her into Hades for her sacrilege. Once more Orion roamed the forests, more fiercely than ever.

It chanced one day, as he crashed through the thick bushes beside a river in hot chase of a noble stag, that he came suddenly upon a group of seven nymphs who, garlanded with flowers, were dancing upon the carpet of green moss.

They ceased their song at the sight of him and huddled together behind the tallest in affright. This one, however, looked at him in bold defiance. She was Maia, eldest of these seven daughters of Atlas, and such was her beauty that it had already touched the heart of the Father of the gods himself. Straight and slender she stood, gazing under level brows at the intruder as if challenging him to approach one under the protection of Zeus.

There was something about her proud carriage and the perfect oval of her face that made Orion think of his lost Side. The stag was forgotten. Impulsively he stepped forward to speak to her.

As this giant youth, with his torn and shaggy skin garment, and all flushed with the excitement of his chase, came closer, even Maia's bravery forsook her. She gave a cry of alarm, and all the seven turned and fled through the forest. Orion pursued them, as instinctively as he would have dashed after a startled roe. But to his surprise and chagrin they proved almost as fleet-footed as himself. He would hear them ahead, or catch a glimpse of them between the tree trunks, and plunge towards the spot – only to be baffled time and again. At length, after hours of pursuit, he was compelled to own himself beaten and give up for the time.

The next day found him casting about like any deerhound for this elusive quarry. Yet they were as wary as he, and while he sighted them across a valley and renewed his efforts to the utmost, he never succeeded in drawing even as close as the first time, since the frightened nymphs had a trick of twisting and turning when hard pressed that always succeeded in carrying them out of sight and hearing.

This went on day after day till it became his main occupation, and while hunting game the thought of the fair Maia ever kept him on the alert. More than once he almost outwitted her and her sisters, and his determination became only hotter as time passed.

At last his opportunity came – five years after that first memorable meeting. From a hilltop he spied the group in the lush meadow by the river, pelting each other with anemones. Cautiously he crept along back of the ridge till he reached a point where he felt sure he could cut them off from the protecting forest. Then he leaped to his feet and started down the steep hillside as he had never run before.

Watchful from many alarms, they saw him almost immediately. With shrieks of terror they fled up the gentle slope. As he had foreseen, it became a race to see which should first reach the nearest tongue of forest that thrust towards the river.

Breathless but triumphant, Orion found himself at the edge of the tangled thicket. The group of maidens halted fifty feet away, all except Maia weeping and crouching to the ground. In the open they were absolutely at his mercy.

Slowly he advanced towards them, wondering more than ever at the grace and charm of the leader, who faced him this time with less defiance, yet without any of the despair shown by her sisters. She called aloud upon Zeus for aid.

Closer and closer Orion approached, with never a word. Then with the same swift motion in which he was wont to pounce upon a trembling hare, he caught at his prize – and remained in this position, staring stupidly at seven white pigeons that fluttered away just out of his grasp and soared upward till they disappeared into the blue of the sky.

Zeus had listened to the prayer of Maia, and in his sovereign power he caught up all the seven into the firmament and translated them into stars, the shining Pleiades.

For the second time in his life Orion realized with dull resentment that there were unseen powers beyond his own. Like some wounded wolf he sought a couch in a cave, beneath a great overhanging rock in the nearby ravine, and lay there nursing his grievance.

When he finally came forth, the fair land of Hellas had become distasteful to him. He set forth to find some country beyond the seas where he might still be mightiest of all, and where naught could remind him of these rebuffs.

Wide were his wanderings across the mighty sea. Even to Scylla and Charybdis he came, and there left perpetual memorials of his might. For on the Sicilian coast, where fell Charybdis threatened every mariner, he built a sickle-shaped strip of protecting rock that formed the safe harbour of Zancle, where, thanks to this shelter, the great city of Messina was to rise. Also, across the strait from hideous, six-headed Scylla he hurled into the open sea a rocky mass that now juts from the shore as the promontory of Pelorus – whereon he reared a temple to his protector Poseidon, in which the inhabitants religiously adored the sea-god for thousands of years thereafter. For a time he dwelt in the mountains of Hera, whence fiery Ætna could be seen to the north, rumbling and spouting forth flame as the colossal Enceladus still struggled beneath its weight.

But he could not long be content in any one place; so when he had mastered all the difficulties of rugged Sicily, he set forth once more.

This time he fared eastward again till he came into the smiling waters of the Ægean, and reached the craggy isle of Chios, where fig tree, palm and vine grew under the soft Ionian sky.

King Œnopion ruled this land of ease and plenty, and his daughter Merope was famed through all Ionia for her beauty.

Hardly had Orion beheld this princess when he found his heart burn within him at the sight or thought of her. Boldly he demanded her in marriage.

But King Œnopion, proud of his lineage as son of Dionysus and Ariadne, thought it far from fitting that his daughter should wed this wandering woodsman, superhuman as his strength might be. Not venturing to express his feeling openly to his formidable, self-invited guest, he still managed to delay giving a decisive answer.

After the fashion of lovers of all times, Orion made offering of his special capacities. The wild creatures of Chios had a hard time, for not only must skins and furs and venison be laid at the feet of the beautiful Merope, but he caught at the suggestion of the King that he should free the island from the lions and other dangerous beasts which then ravaged it and held all the inhabitants in terror.

To Œnopion's disappointment he proved fiercer than the bears and lions, even than the dreaded sharks of the sea. Instead of being devoured as the King had hoped, he brought back one trophy after another, always demanding, with outdoor directness, the thing he had set his heart on.

His scanty patience was exhausted long before the wily monarch's stock of pretexts. His nature and habit had ever been to seize what he wanted: in his usual headlong fashion he attempted openly to carry off Merope by force; and failing in his first effort, made no secret of his intention to try again.

The wily Œnopion concealed his resentment and bade the headstrong suitor to a banquet. In friendly fashion he plied him with heady wine from the luscious grapes of Ariusia.

Then, when even his giant strength was relaxed, the royal slaves set upon him, blinded him, and cast him out upon the seashore to perish.

As the salt spray dashing over his face brought him to full consciousness, he roared aloud in pain and wrath. The people in the city miles away trembled at that sound; and Œnopion regretted to the bottom of his cowardly heart that he had not slain this giant when he was in his power.

Orion bathed his face in the lapping waves and got slowly on his feet. His first instinct was to grope his way back to the palace and take swift revenge upon the King for his treachery. But a few faltering steps convinced him of the folly of attempting this in his helpless state.

He turned again towards the sea, in which he now felt almost as much at home as on land. Keeping the fresh breeze full in his face, and calling aloud upon Poseidon, he waded into the waves. With no clear idea of where he was going, he set forth.

Northward he fared, finding relief in his mighty strides through the cool waters, and in the wind that blew full upon his fevered eyes. Hour after hour he sped on tirelessly, his thoughts still in such a ferment of rage that he could make no calm or reasoned plan.

Without knowing it, he arrived off the western point of Lesbos. Suddenly there broke upon his fantastic plans for revenge a mighty pulsing beat, which came muffled, from far away, through water and air. Instinctively he proceeded towards the sound; and as he advanced it grew ever louder, till he fancied it seemed like the clangour of a vast anvil under the strokes of some super-smith.

In fact he was approaching the isle of Lemnos, where dwelt and laboured the cunningest of all smiths, the lame god Hephæstos. Here, in a cavern stretching down beneath the ocean floor, he had had his workshop ever since Zeus had hurled him from Olympus, and here he wrought such marvels as the arms of Achilles, the sceptre of Agamemnon, and the fatal necklace of Harmonia.

Guided by the ringing hammer strokes, Orion at length reached this subterranean forge and told his story. The immortal craftsman was moved to see such bodily perfection marred and helpless through loss of sight.

He called one of his workmen. "Take Cedalion with you," he said. "He will guide you to the spot where the Sun rises. I know Helios well: did I not make the golden boat which carries him back each night, along the border of the earth, to the east once more? Before his gleaming eyes every darkness must retreat; for the All-seer pierces through any blackness. It is from him alone that you may recover your eyesight."

Overjoyed at any definite hope, Orion placed Cedalion on his shoulders, hastened up from the cavern, and once more plunged into the rolling breakers.

Directed by him he carried, he journeyed eastward, eastward ever. Past many a strange land he sped, holding to the mark as a homing-pigeon holds towards his distant remembered cote.

Long and weary was the way; but nothing mattered save to press on towards the god of light. And at last he reached that lovely bay in the ultimate East where Helios mounts the sky each morn behind his snow-white steeds.

Here he placed Cedalion on his feet again. The latter prostrated himself face to earth, lest he be smitten by the terrible brilliance of the Sun god. But Orion stood erect, awaiting the coming of the Day.

The brooding night trembled and drew back. Through the morning mist appeared Eos, goddess of the dawn and herald of her brilliant brother. New-risen from her ocean-couch, with ruddy hair streaming above her saffron-coloured mantle, she advanced in her golden chariot, while her rosy fingers sprinkled dew upon the earth from the vase she carried. The dawn breeze struck mysterious notes of music from her tresses like those of an Æolian harp.

Orion could not see this gracious vision as he stood there stark and expectant. Yet some influence of the colourful morning freshness which faced him softened his countenance into a smile of pleasure.

And as Eos looked upon the perfectness of his strong, beautiful youth, she loved him. Bending down, she pressed a kiss upon his forehead, whispering: "Be of good heart. Helios comes."

She passed on. The heavens blazed with purple and crimson and gold streamers, shooting up to the zenith from the corona of the rising Sun god.

Out of the rippling blue waters of the bay lifted his majestic visage. The intolerable gleam of his eyes fell full upon the sightless orbs of Orion.

Instantly the blinded giant saw once more. But seeing, he was constrained for the first time in his life to bow his head before that fiery glance. When the god had whirled on upward, he picked up the trembling Cedalion, set him on his shoulders again, and turned back towards Lemnos, for his wrath still burned hotly against Œnopion. Yet amid his grim thoughts of vengeance, ever and again there sounded those faint music-breaths that had come to him when Eos passed by; and ever and again he would feel her soft lips against his brow.

Like some dripping sea monster, he stepped upon the beach of Chios. Overbearing all who would stay him, he drove on towards the palace. Œnopion, however, had been warned of his coming and had hastily hid himself in a labyrinthine cavern beneath the ground.

Search as he might, Orion could not discover his enemy, and was reluctantly forced to forego the retribution he had planned.

He thought then to leave this ill-omened isle. But the next morning Eos, who had not forgotten him, carried him off to Delos. Since her Titan husband had been slain by the lightning of Zeus, she claimed the right to marry this handsome hunter. But the council of the gods rejected her plea. She dared not resist this supreme decree, so sorrowfully she left him.

Now this tiny isle of Delos had been the birthplace of Apollo and Artemis. Formerly called Ortygia, it had floated hither and thither before the winds; but when Leto came to give birth to these twin children of Zeus, and found no refuge elsewhere in all the world, the mighty ruler of Olympus fixed it firmly in its place by four chains of adamant; and for ever after it was sacred to the three divinities, though more particularly to Apollo.

Little reverence or awe was there in Orion's mind, however, when he found himself alone upon this rocky islet. He realized that for a third time invisible powers had come between him and the woman he thought his; worst of all, there was no one against whom he could direct the hot resentment that flexed every mighty muscle of his body.

His consuming wrath made some action a necessity. He started up the craggy slope of Mt. Cynthos, bursting through the tangled thicket, leaping from one boulder to another, striding across deep clefts in the rock – with a vague idea that from the commanding summit of the hill he might spy one of these hidden enemies who thus thwarted him.

As he squeezed through a narrow pass at the foot of a riven face of rock, his hunter's eye caught the black spot marking a cave entrance; and the grizzly hairs at the opening told him it was a wolf's den. He paused instinctively and peered into the gloom of the cavern. A chorus of high yapping barks proclaimed the presence of a family of cubs.

He hesitated a moment, wondering if he could force his broad shoulders through the opening. Then he sprang to his feet and faced about, as he heard behind him a snarl that threatened instant danger.

A few feet away, the head of a huge she-wolf protruded from the glossy green leaves of the dense laurel. The creature had just dropped a fawn it had been bringing home, and the bleeding carcass lay unheeded at the edge of the thicket. Its green eyes blazed with deadly intention; the long hair on its neck bristled up straight around the blood-spotted jaws into a Medusa's head of terror.

Orion had barely time to throw up one guarding arm, when the fierce brute sprang at his throat. Even the wild boar at bay has no fury comparable with that of the hunting wolf-mother, protecting her young. But for the giant's instinctive defensive movement, it might have gone badly even with him. As it was, the dripping teeth caught hold of a fold of his skin garment, and he staggered against the rock wall at the impact of the animal landing on his shoulder.

This death-grapple quite suited the hunter's own savage mood. His eyes blazed as balefully as those of the wolf. With a motion as swift as that of a panther he gripped the animal's upper jaw with his right hand. Heaving it free from his shoulder, his left hand caught the lower jaw before those wicked fangs had time to close upon his fingers.

Then, putting forth his full might, he fairly tore the struggling beast's jaws asunder, and dashed it lifeless against a boulder.

He was a superb figure as he stood there in the full vigour of his aroused powers. It might have been one of the Titan brood defying any force of earth or heavens. Yet instead of being monstrous, he was beautiful – manhood in its perfection though enlarged far beyond common humanity.

"Well done!" said a clear voice behind him. "A fitting end for the fawn-killer."

Orion turned – and to his surprise, his limbs trembled as they had not done at the sight of the attacking brute.

A tall maidenly figure stood beside a cypress tree whose twisted roots disappeared into a rock crevice. She held a bow, and her right hand still gripped the long arrow which she had clearly been holding sighted against the wolf, ready to discharge the instant the man seemed to be getting the worst of the struggle.

Her embroidered chiton was girt to the knees; her long hair, intricately woven about her head, was bound by a fillet on which shone a silver crescent; upon her feet were Cretan sandals, whose crossing thongs were held by embossed silver clasps. Slender, youthful, alive with vitality, with great sparkling eyes and smiling lips, she seemed, as she replaced the arrow in her quiver, to breathe forth that very spirit of the forest which had ever drawn Orion into the most intimate depths of nature's wildnesses. Indeed, as he gazed stupidly at this radiant creature, she appeared like the very embodiment of all his deepest longings, unexpressed and even unrealized by himself.

"Ai!" she exclaimed. "Never have I seen such a one among the sons of men. I am Artemis. Henceforth we shall hunt together, you and I."

For the first time in his life Orion felt humble. It was not that she named herself daughter of Zeus: but to have the companionship of this Shining One in the life he loved was a boon which no strength of his could win; and his heartbeat with lowly gratitude.

Then the self-sufficient man reasserted himself. "Let us go," said he. "There is no creature of the woods that can escape or defy me."

The goddess smiled, as if pleased with his boastfulness. "This isle will hardly contain such hunters as we. Let us go to Crete. There are mountains that dwarf Ossa and Pelion. There we may range from the perpetual snow of Ida to the olive-filled vales of Iardanos."

Joyfully Orion strode beside her down the rugged side of Cynthos. He hoped they might encounter some monster, that he might at once protect his companion and show his power. And Artemis, perceiving his thought, smiled again in pleasure.

Southward, across the sea they journeyed to the land of Minos. And here they spent long golden days in roaming over the length and breadth of this isle of mountains and caves and upland pasture plateaus and fertile sea-level valleys. They waged relentless war against the killers that preyed upon the wild herds whom Artemis held under her protection: till to this day it is recorded that not a wolf can be found in Crete, plentiful as they still are in neighbouring lands.

Orion was well content. Life had become an infinitely richer thing than he had ever imagined, even when he had thought it at the full. For once he was willing to wait patiently for that which he most desired.

For this Comrade was the true woman he had ever sought. Daughter of Zeus though she was, terrible as was her wrath, proud as she might be of her title of Parthenos, he felt sure she belonged to him, and that each new day's varied experience bound them together the more indissolubly.

And it is written that the Goddess herself felt the bond. She recognized her mate according to the decrees of nature. And she made no secret of her intention to wed this earth-born one.

Then bright Apollo, twin brother of the huntress, waxed wroth and determined to avert this disgrace. And because even he hesitated to thwart her openly, he had recourse to guile.

It chanced towards dusk one summer's eve that Artemis stood by the seashore. Contrary to his wont, Orion had gone off alone on an expedition to a neighbouring island.

He was now returning, progressing through the water with mighty strides, but so distant that his head seemed but a tiny speck upon the horizon.

Suddenly Apollo descended to his sister's side. Playfully he began to rally her upon her vaunted skill with the bow, at which he himself was unexcelled.

When her pride was aroused, he declared that she could not hit that black spot which seemed to move towards them – probably a porpoise.

Quickly the piqued Goddess seized an arrow from the quiver on her shoulder. Steadily she drew her bow till the arrowhead touched her finger. Firmly she loosed it. The string gave a mighty twang. The shaft sped seaward, true to the mark.

Artemis turned in triumph, but Apollo had vanished. A vague uneasiness filled her breast. The surf seemed to beat against the sands in lamentation, growing louder and yet louder.

Then urged on by Poseidon, the waves passed from one to another, and presently laid at her feet – the dead body of her Comrade, whom she had thus unwittingly slain.

At that the Huntress knew what it was to weep, even as the daughters of men. Bitterly she reproached Apollo, wildly she reproached herself.

Hope sprang up again within her as she thought of Asclepius. Well she knew the skill of this child of Apollo, who had added to his inheritance all the wisdom of Chiron the centaur. His feats of healing had approached miracles, and it was whispered that he had even essayed with success the final miracle of restoring the dead to life. He could not refuse his aid to her.

Swiftly she bore away the body across the sea to Argolis, where the temple of Asclepius stood near Epidaurus.

Unwillingly the sage of healing hearkened to her plea, for he feared to exercise his art upon one who had presumed to alliance with divinity. Yet to his father's twin he could refuse nothing.

He set about his work. Skilfully he compounded elixirs; solemnly he performed the mystic rites of his craft.

But at the moment of consummation, his forebodings proved but too well founded. All-seeing Zeus perceived the confusion that must result on earth if such resurrection were permitted; so he hearkened to the protests of Hades, and suddenly slew the too-wise physician with one of his thunderbolts.

So far the Thunderer did listen to the prayers of Artemis: he placed the beautiful giant on high as a constellation in the sky.

There you may see him still if you are of the hunting craft and sally forth after wildfowl before Eos flushes the eastern sky. The three stars in a straight line in his jewelled belt gleam as the most conspicuous ornament of the spangled sky; below an even larger white star, Rigel, marks the giant's left foot; while topaz Betelgeuse blazes on his shoulder at an equal distance above. At his heels follows his faithful dog, where Sirius now gleams white, but looked redly down some thousands of years ago. Before him, with fair Maia chief among them, still fly the Pleiades, though he heeds them not.

Thus, "gliding through the silent sphere … and girt with gold," the giant hunter seeks his lost Artemis still.

How Zeus Fought with Titans and Giants

WE THINK OF ZEUS as the mightiest god of Greece, accompanied by his servants Force, Might and Victory – the Cloud-Gatherer, the Rain-Giver, the Thunderer, the Lightning-Hurler, the Sender of Prodigies, the Guider of Stars, the Ruler of other gods and men, whom even Poseidon the Earth-Shaker must obey. The very name reverberates with majesty, power, dominion.

But the beginnings of this vast deity were in darkness and danger.

True, the reign of his father Kronos was that Golden Age when, in the fresh morning of the world, Heat and Cold were not yet at strife, the Seasons had not begun their mystic dance, and one mild and equable climate stretched from pole to pole; when the trees bore fruit and the vine her purple clusters all the year, and honeydew dripped from the laurel and juniper which are now so bitter; when flowers of every hue filled the air with perpetual fragrance, the lion gambolled with the kid, and the unfanged serpent was as harmless as the dove; when over-curious Pandora not yet having released her boxful of ills, men had neither care nor sickness nor old age, but after centuries of blissful calm, faded like flowers and became kindly spirit-guardians of their successors.

Yet amid this charming serenity Kronos could never forget the curse of his father Uranus whom he had overthrown, and the prophecy that he himself should in his turn be cast down by his own children.

Wherefore being resolved to defeat that prophecy, he swallowed each child his wife Rhea brought forth, as soon as it was born. When Rhea had thus lost five babes – Hestia, Demeter, Hera, Hades and Poseidon – and knew herself about to bear yet another, she made her prayer to Uranus her ancient sire, imploring counsel and aid.

But only a faint, vast murmur thrilled through the sky:

"My voice is but the voice of winds and tides, no more than winds and tides can I avail. Pray thou to thy puissant Mother: in me, dispossessed of godhead, is no succour more."

So the Titaness betook her to Earth, and the mighty Mother gave her counsel how to outwit grim Kronos. And Rhea fled through the swift, dark night to a secret thicket upon a hill of Arcadia. There was born a mighty babe, whom she called Zeus. At her prayer Mother Earth smote the mountain, and there gushed forth a bounding stream, in which she laved the infant. Then she gave him to the nymph Neda who bore him swiftly across the sea to Crete, hiding him in a cave upon a dense and wooded mountain named Ida.

She entrusted the child to Adrastea and Ida, nymphs of the mountain, to be reared in secret. But Rhea took a huge stone and wrapped it in swathes, and brought it to Kronos, then sovereign of the gods, saying: "Behold, I have borne my lord another son."

Naught said he, but snatched the stone and greedily swallowed it, nothing doubting that it was the newborn child. Thus his wife deceived him, for all his cunning.

Rhea might not so much as see her babe, lest Kronos should spy her from his throne on high; but the child thrived, laid in a golden winnowing-fan for a good omen, tended by the gentle nymphs, and nourished on the wild honey they gathered for him and on the milk of a mountain goat. Around him danced the fierce Curetes, Earth-born warriors, who performed their war-dances, rattling and clashing their weapons whenever the infant cried, lest Kronos should hear him.

So the child Zeus increased daily in beauty and stature, nor was it long before he gave proof of his godhead in wondrous wise. Two years his goat foster-mother suckled him: snow-white she was, with jet black horns and hooves, the most beauteous of her kind, and her name was Amalthea. Then, on a day while the young god played with her after his wont, he grasped one of her curved horns as she made pretence of butting, and broke it clean off.

Tears stood in the creature's eyes, and she looked reproachfully on her fosterling. But the little god ran to her and threw his arms about her shaggy neck, bidding her be comforted, for he would make amends; with that he laid his right hand on the goat's head, and immediately a new horn sprouted full-grown. And he took up the horn he had broken, and gave it to the nymphs, saying, "Kindly nurses, in recompense of your care, Zeus gives you Amalthea's Horn, which shall be to you a horn of plenty. As for her, when I come into my kingdom, I will be mindful of my foster-mother; she shall not die but be changed into one of the bright signs of Heaven." Thus Zeus promised, and fulfilled his word in the aftertime, for faithful and true are the promises of the Immortals. But when the nymphs had taken the Horn of Amalthea, behold – they found it brimful of all manner of luscious fruits, of the finest wheat flour, and sweet butter, and golden honeycomb. They shook all out, laughing in delight, and one cried: "Here were a feast for the gods, had we but wine thereto!" No sooner said she this than the Horn bubbled over with ruby wine; for this was the magic in it, that it never grew empty, and yielded its possessors whatsoever food or drink they desired.

Now when Earth saw that Zeus was come to the prime of his mighty youth, she sent to him one of the daughters of Oceanus named Metis, which is, being interpreted, 'Counsel'. And Metis came and stood before him in the Idaean Mount and said: "I have an errand unto thee, O king that shalt be hereafter."

And Zeus said: "Is it a foe's errand, or a friend's? Who sent thee hither, and who art thou?"

And she said: "Metis is my name, a daughter of Oceanus the old, and my errand is from Earth, the All-Mother. She bids thee take this herb I bring and go straight to Kronos in his golden house on high; tell him not who or whence thou art, but cause him to swallow the herb unweeting, and it shall work mischief to him and good to thee. Delay not, for the hour is at hand when Kronos must pay full measure for the outrage he did his sire, as it is ordained."

"Tell me," said Zeus, "how knows Earth that such an hour is at hand, and by whom is the vengeance ordained?"

Metis answered: "There are Three Sisters, daughters of Primeval Night, Grey Virgins, older than Time, who sit for ever in the shades of underground, spinning threads of divers colours from their golden distaffs; and the threads are the lives of gods and men. As the sisters twine them, sad-hued or bright, so is the lot of each living soul, mortal or immortal; there is none among the gods, nor shall be, that may escape the lot spun for him, nor avail to turn those spinners from their task. Hasting not, resting not, without knowledge, without pity, the Three Fates work on. But as they twirl the spindles, they sing the Song of the Morrow; and Earth, she only, understands that song; hence it is she knows what is coming upon Kronos."

Then Zeus arose and went up to the heavenly palace halls; there he found Kronos feasting, and quaffing honey-coloured nectar, wine of the gods. Kronos asked him who he was, and Zeus answered: "I am Prometheus, son of Iapetus thy brother, who greets thee well by me." Then Kronos bade him welcome, and they drank and caroused together. But when they had well drunk, Zeus put the herb of Earth into his father's cup, unmarked of him.

And Kronos no sooner swallowed it than a marvel past thought befell; for he disgorged from his giant maw first the stone Rhea gave him (which stone was ever afterwards preserved as a pious memorial at Delphi) and then her two sons and daughters three, no longer babes but full-grown.

Forthwith Zeus made himself known to his brethren, and the young gods seized their father and bound him in chains. But ancient Kronos cried for aid to his Titan kindred, with a voice like the tempest's roar; and they came swiftly in their might; and the young gods could not stand before them, but fled out of Heaven to the cloudy top of Mount Olympus, that great peak robed in eternal snows.

There they abode as in a citadel, and thence it is that Zeus and the family of Zeus are called 'the Olympians' to this day.

The Titans occupied Mt. Othrys to the south, and the broad plains of Thessaly in between show even yet the shattered rocks and rent surface from the struggle which ensued.

For now there was war in Heaven; ten years the Elder Gods fought against the Olympians and neither side could win the mastery. But one amongst the Titans would not fight against Zeus; for being endued with wisdom and foresight about all gods, he perceived that the day of Kronos must shortly have an end and his sceptre pass to another. This was Prometheus, whom Asia, daughter of Oceanus, bore to Iapetus, son of Earth. Fain would he have dissuaded his father and brother from taking arms in a lost cause, and for the sake of one who, himself a usurper, must now reap as he had sown; but they would not heed, trusting in their own giant strength.

At last Zeus sought counsel of Mother Earth and she spake this oracle unto him out of the cave that is in rocky Pytho – *"He that will conquer in this strife, let him set free the captives in Tartarus."* For Earth had long borne Kronos a grudge, because he would not release the Hundred-handed and the Cyclopes from that abyss of darkness; therefore she willingly revealed to Zeus the secret of victory. But naught knew he of those giants or their fate, nor so much as the name of Tartarus, which none among the Heaven-dwelling gods will utter for very loathing; so the saying of Earth was dark to him, and he was much disheartened. Then Prometheus, knowing what had befallen, came to Zeus on Olympus and said: "Son of Kronos, though I fight, I may not do so against my kin; fight against thee I will not, for that were idle folly, seeing the Fates will have thee Lord of all. Let there be peace between me and thee, and I will interpret the oracle Earth has given thee."

And Zeus heard him gladly, and said: "For this good turn, count me thy debtor and fast friend evermore."

Then straightway they two fared through the Underworld to the gates of unplumbed Tartarus, where by the Titan's aid Zeus slew the snake Campé, their grisly warder, and delivered the captives.

And amazed was the leader of the younger gods at the sight of these monstrous first children of Earth. For each of the three Hundred-handed, Briareus, Cottus and Gyges, had moving ever from his shoulders a hundred arms, not brooking approach, while above this threatening display rose fifty heads. As for the Cyclopes, Brontes, Steropes and Arges, they resembled the Titans, save that each had a single round eye in the centre of his forehead. They had shown from birth such overbearing spirit and terrific strength, tossing whole hills with their forests about like balls, that even Uranus had feared them and thrust them into Tartarus ere they were grown.

Zeus rejoiced at these mighty allies. But fell fighters as they were, their greatest aid was not in their strength but their skill. For the Cyclopes made themselves a smithy in the glowing heart of Mt. Ætna, and there they wrought such gifts for their deliverers as only they could fashion. To Poseidon they gave his trident with prongs of adamant; and to Hades a cap of darkness whose wearer was invisible to gods and men; while for Zeus himself they forged the kingliest weapons of all: the thunderbolts and the blasting, zig-zagged lightning.

Then Zeus set before them all the nectar and ambrosia of the gods, and addressed them: "Hear me, illustrious children of Earth and Heaven, that I may speak what my spirit within my breast prompts me to speak. For a very long time have we been fighting for the mastery, the Titan gods and we who are sprung from Kronos. Now show your invincible might against the Titans, in gratitude for your deliverance to the light from bondage in murky gloom."

The blameless Cottus answered: "Excellent Lord, we are aware that thy wisdom is most high, and thy mind, and that thou hast been to the immortals an averter of destruction. Wherefore we will now protect thy dominion in fell conflict, fighting stoutly against the Titans."

And all the gods applauded, female as well as male, and they rushed to combat. The Titans on their side were no less eager, and as the battle joined, the boundless sea re-echoed terribly, and Earth resounded, and broad heavens groaned as it shook, and vast Olympus swayed on its base, and even to murky Tartarus came the hollow sound of feet and battle-strokes. And as the two sides came together, their great war cry reached to the starry Heaven above.

Now Zeus loosed his fury, and the bolts with thunder and lightning shot so fast and fiercely from his mighty hand that Earth crashed in conflagration, and the forests crackled with fire; the ocean's streams began to boil, while the vapour encircled the Titans, and the incessant, dazzling flashes bereft their eyes of sight, gods as they were.

Fearful heat spread everywhere, and it seemed as if Earth and Heaven were clashing together and falling into ruins. At the same time the winds spread abroad smoke and battle-cry and crash of missiles, as the Hundred-handed, insatiable in war, advanced, hurling three hundred vast rocks at a time against the enemy.

Before this combination of terrors even the Titans could not stand. They were dashed from their battlements and fell like shooting stars nine days and nights to earth, then on down for nine days and nights more to Tartarus. Here were they bound and cast into that dismal abyss, behind a triple brazen wall built by Poseidon, around which Night is poured in three rows. And the Hundred-handed were set to guard them.

Kronos and a few others escaped to the north, and there made head for a time, sheltered against Zeus's thunderbolts in caverns of the hills. But there came to the Olympians two mighty twin shapes, Force and Might, followed by their sister, beauteous-ankled Victory (from whose shoulders waved great eagles' wings) – all children of Styx; and those two illustrious ones announced to Zeus that henceforth they were his servants, and that their sister, Victory, would ever follow them.

So with these ministers, Zeus went forth once more; and the remainder of the Titans fled westward beyond the utmost limits of Earth. But huge Atlas, brother of Prometheus, was overtaken, and him Zeus stationed on the very verge of the Earth, before the clear-voiced Hesperides, sentencing him to bear for ever on his shoulders the weight of the vast sky.

Having thus achieved the victory, Zeus gave to Hades dominion over the Underworld, to Poseidon the Sea, and took himself the realm of the Æther and the Earth, rewarding all those who had assisted him, and especially honouring Styx, mother of Force, Might and Victory, so that thenceforth the most sacred and inviolable oath for an immortal was to swear by Styx.

Mother Earth was far from pleased at this outcome. Her imprisoned first-born children had been released only to have her other beautiful Titan sons and daughters take their places in Tartarus. In revenge she brought forth a brood of Giants to war with the young gods. These were huge and invincible creatures with ghastly faces and long, thick, matted hair hanging from their heads and chins; instead of feet they had scaly dragons' tails. Their birthplace was in Phlegra or Pallene. The most redoubtable among them were Porphyrion and Alcyoneus. The latter was immortal so long as he fought on the same part of the Earth on which he was born, and he soon distinguished himself by carrying off the cattle of the Sun and Moon.

With these and their brethren – Enceladus, Pallas, Clytius, Polybotes, Hippolytus and others – were joined Otus and Ephialtes, children of Poseidon, who, says Homer, grew nine inches every month, and who when they were only nine years old had captured war-god Mars himself and held him prisoner more than a year.

Now the oracle revealed to the gods that the giants could be destroyed only in combat with a mortal. Gæa (Earth) had learned this, and sought by means of magic herbs to make her offspring invulnerable also to mortals.

But Zeus anticipated her: he forbade the Dawn, the Moon and the Sun to shine, cut off the medicinal herbs with which Earth had plastered her offspring, and sent Athena to summon Heracles to take part in the combat.

This savage group of Giants then attacked the Olympians, hurling great masses of rock, tree-trunks lashed together, and blazing brands against the sky. But the distance was too great for them to do much damage, so they tried to scale Heaven itself. When their trees fastened together proved too short, Otus and Ephialtes set about another attempt: upsetting Mt. Ossa they began to roll it towards Mt. Olympus, intending to pile the lofty peak of Pelion on that, and thus reach their enemies.

Then Zeus rose in his majesty. With a thunderbolt he hurled the mountain back to its former place, the Olympians all dashed down, riding on the winds, and a mighty battle followed which lasted a whole day.

Heracles drew his great death-dealing bow and slew Alcyoneus with an arrow. But as soon as he touched the earth he rose with renewed life and strength. Whereupon wise Athena counselled the hero to grasp the monster by the foot and drag him out of Pallene, his birthplace. He did so, and Alcyoneus died.

At this Porphyrion in hot rage hurled the island of Delos at Zeus and rushed upon Heracles and Hera. As the giant laid hold of the goddess's swathing veils, she cried out for help, and the thunderbolt of Zeus and Heracles' arrow smote Porphyrion simultaneously.

As for the rest, Apollo shot out the left eye of Ephialtes, and Heracles the right. Dionysus killed Eurytus with his sacred wand, while Clytius was thrust through by Hecate or Hephæstus with glowing ironstone. Enceladus fled across the sea, but Athena seized a great triangle of rock and cast it upon him – and when trees and soil formed on this, it was called the island of Sicily.

As Virgil's wandering hero, Æneas, sings:

Here, while from Aetna's furnaces the flame
Bursts forth, Enceladus, 'tis said, doth lie,

Scorched by the lightning. As his wearied frame
He shifts, Trinacria, trembling at the cry
Moans through her shores, and smoke involves the sky.

Athena, terrible in her battle-wrath, next killed and flayed Pallas and put his skin over her own body while the combat lasted – whence comes her name of Pallas Athene. Polybotes, chased by Poseidon over the sea, came to Cos; here the sea-god tore off a piece of the island and buried him under it, where now is Nisyron.

Hermes, concealed by the helmet of Hades, killed Hippolytus, while Artemis slew Gration. So the Fates ended Agrius and Thoon with brazen clubs. The rest Zeus crushed with thunderbolts, and Heracles finished with his deadly arrows.

Then in hot wrath Earth brought forth the most terrific monster yet seen. Typhon was he called, the greatest of Earth's children, half man and half animal: he was human to the loins and was so huge that he towered over the mountains while his head knocked against the stars. His outstretched arms reached from sunrise to sunset, and a hundred dragon heads shot from his shoulders. Instead of legs he moved on vast, rustling snaky coils; his whole body was feathered; bristly hair floated in the wind from his head and chin, and fire streamed from his eyes.

Such a monster was Typhon.

Hurling clusters of rocks up at Heaven, he ran with hisses and screams, while a red mass of flame bubbled from his mouth.

When the gods saw him charge on Heaven, they fled to Egypt, where they wandered about in the shapes of animals, pursued by him.

Zeus hurled thunderbolts as long as he was afar off. When he came nearer, the god's iron sickle made him flee, and Zeus pursued him to the Caucasus that towers over Syria. There he came up with him, covered with wounds, and joined in a hand-to-hand grapple.

But Typhon held him off, wrapping his snaky limbs around him, snatched away the sickle, and cutting out the sinews of the god's hands and feet, put him on his shoulders and carried him across the sea to Cilicia.

Here in a cavern he threw him down, put away the sinews wrapped in a bearskin, and set as a guard over the helpless god Delphyne, a young she-dragon, half human, half animal.

But cunning Hermes stole away the sinews and secretly replaced them in Zeus's wrists and ankles. Then Zeus gathered himself together, and his former powers came upon him, and he rose to his seat in Heaven in a car drawn by winged horses.

Again he hurled his thunderbolts upon Typhon and pursued the monstrous giant to Mt. Nysa, where the Fates outwitted the fugitive: for, persuaded by them that he would thereby get greater powers, he ate of the ephemeral poison fruits.

Then the chase became more furious. They came to Thrace where Typhon fought with whole peaks of the Hamus Mountains; and when these were hurled back on him by the Thunderer, his blood gushed out over them so that these are called the 'bloody mountains' to this day.

And at last, as Typhon was compelled to flee across the Sicilian sea, Zeus threw the towering mountain of Ætna on top of him and buried him there for ever. Here he lies still, turning and groaning at times, while fires blaze up from the hurled lightning.

After that there was nobody in Heaven, earth or the underworld who dared dispute the supreme dominion of Zeus.

The Eleventh Labour of Hercules

ONE OF THE MOST DIFFICULT of Hercules' labours was to procure the golden apples that the Hesperides, daughters of Hesperus, god of the west, guarded very jealously. At the foot of the tree coiled a fierce dragon whose nostrils poured out fire, and whose deadly breath would have slain any venturesome robber, even if he had escaped the dragon's claws. As Hercules did not know in what part of the great glowing west the Garden of the Hesperides lay, he wandered many miles before he met with anyone who could direct him where to go. The first help he received was from the nymphs of the Eridanus River, who were sporting on the riverbank and called to Hercules to come and join in their games. Much as he would have liked to rest, the hero dared not tarry; but he begged the friendly nymphs to tell him the way to the Garden of the Hesperides. They could not help him, but they advised him to go to old Proteus, "the Ancient of the Deep," who could tell him whatever he wished to know better than anyone else. So Hercules went down to the seashore, and found the hoary god asleep in his cool green cave. Knowing the old man's wiles, the hero grasped him firmly and held him fast through all the bewildering changes by which he sought to frighten away the stranger. At last, finding himself securely caught, the Wizard assumed his own form, and asked Hercules what it was that he wished to know. The hero stated his errand, and Proteus told him, "in words that ne'er deceive," that he must find the giant Titan Atlas who alone knew where the Garden of the Hesperides lay.

Hercules then started again on his search, and in the course of his journey came to the Caucasus Mountains, where he found Prometheus, the stealer of the sacred fire, bound with adamantine chains to the rock, while a vulture daily feasted on his liver. Hercules killed the foul bird, broke the chains, and set Prometheus free; and in return for his deliverance the grateful Titan directed his rescuer where to find the giant Atlas. Following Prometheus's advice, Hercules travelled straightway to Africa; and on the way he passed through the land of the Pygmies, a tiny race of warriors who waged continual warfare with neighbouring tribes, and especially with their deadly enemies, the cranes. Hercules was not aware that he had reached the country of the Pygmies; but one day, when he had fallen asleep from weariness, he was wakened by sharp prickings over his body; and looking around he saw a host of diminutive men, attacking him with their tiny weapons. The hero laughed at these brave efforts, caught up a few of the doughty little warriors, and, wrapping them in his lion skin, carried them back with him to the court of Eurystheus.

As he journeyed through Africa in search of Atlas, Hercules came to the country of Anteus – a mighty giant and wrestler, and the son of Terra, the Earth. All strangers who came into the land were obliged to wrestle with him, and if they were defeated, they were immediately killed. As no one had ever overcome Anteus, he had brought an untimely death on many a brave hero; so Hercules was eager to defeat him and avenge the unknown dead. As soon as they had grappled for the first struggle, the slayer of the Hydra knew that he had met more than his equal in strength. For a long time they wrestled, Anteus growing stronger after each fall, and Hercules growing fainter from every additional blow of the giant's hand. Again and again the undaunted hero threw his adversary to the ground, but Anteus rose with redoubled vigour and continued the unequal contest. Then, all at once, Hercules remembered the tale he had once heard told of a giant who drew strength from his mother Earth; and believing that this was the case with Anteus, he made a mighty effort and lifted the giant from the ground. Anteus struggled to get his feet again on the earth; but Hercules kept him in the air, and held him there until he felt the powerful body beginning to weaken. Little by little the miraculous strength oozed away, and soon Anteus grew so weak that Hercules easily crushed the limp form with his hands.

The hero then travelled on in search of Atlas, whom he finally found standing on the coast of Africa, with the great weight of the heavens resting on his broad shoulders. As Hercules looked up at the enormous figure, which reached so far into the clouds that nothing could be seen above his waist, he noticed that the forests had grown up so thick and tall all around that only a glimpse of the giant's huge legs could be seen through the heavy foliage. As the hero stood watching this figure that for centuries had stood here in obedience to the divine command of Jupiter, he saw dark clouds beginning to gather about the giant's head, and soon a storm broke over the sea and land. Amid the beating of the rain and the crash of the thunder, Hercules thought he heard the voice of Atlas speaking to him; but it might have been only a peal of thunder. When the storm was over and the mists rolled away from the earth, Hercules saw the head of Atlas through rifts in the scurrying clouds. The snow-white hair gave the giant's face a benign look as it fell thick and white over the stooping shoulders that bore so terrible a weight. In a voice that he strove hard to make gentle, Atlas asked the hero what he was seeking, and Hercules told him that he had come to get some of the golden apples from the Garden of the Hesperides. Atlas laughed at these words, and his great shoulders shook so with merriment that a few of the stars fell out of their places. Then he told Hercules that such a feat was impossible even to so great a hero; but that if someone would take the heavens from his shoulders for a few hours, he himself would get the apples.

Hercules was delighted with this offer of assistance, and agreed to take the giant's burden while the latter went on his friendly errand. Very carefully Atlas transferred the heavens to the shoulders of Hercules, and then sped westward to the Garden of the Hesperides. The hero was a bit troubled when he saw Atlas shake his huge shoulders and stretch himself in delight at his freedom, for it would be strange, indeed, if the giant were ready to resume his burden after having tasted the joy of liberty. With some anxiety Hercules watched him step into the sea that came only to his knees though he had waded out a mile from the shore. As Atlas went deeper and deeper into the waves, at first his huge bulk loomed like a cliff against the horizon; but soon it dwindled into a mere speck, and was presently lost to view. How long he stood holding the heavens Hercules never knew; but he found himself growing very weary of his burden, and anxious over Atlas's long absence. Suddenly he saw a dark spot on the horizon, and he knew that it was the giant returning.

It had not been a difficult task for Atlas to reach the Garden, or to pluck the golden apples from the carefully guarded tree; and Hercules, delighted with the giant's success, thanked him for his trouble and asked him politely to take the sky again on his shoulders, for the journey back to the court of Eurystheus was a long one. Now Atlas had no desire to stand for another dozen centuries with his old burden; and seeing a good opportunity of getting rid of it for ever, he told Hercules that he would carry the apples to Eurystheus himself; and meanwhile the hero could keep the heavens supported until Atlas returned. Pretending that he was quite satisfied with this arrangement, Hercules bade the giant goodbye; then hastily asked him to wait a moment while he made a pad for his shoulders to ease the weight of the unaccustomed burden. The unsuspicious giant good-naturedly agreed to this, and took the heavens from Hercules; but instead of making a cushion, the hero picked up the golden apples, which Atlas had dropped on resuming his burden, and started back to his own country, leaving the giant to stand on the seashore for ever, or until the pitying gods should release him.

The Odyssey: Book X (Extract)

Aeolus, The Laestrygones, Circe

"THENCE WE WENT ON TO THE AEOLIAN ISLAND where lives Aeolus son of Hippotas, dear to the immortal gods. It is an island that floats (as it were) upon the sea, iron bound with a wall that girds it. Now, Aeolus has six daughters and six lusty sons, so he made the sons marry the daughters, and they all live with their dear father and mother, feasting and enjoying every conceivable kind of luxury. All day long the atmosphere of the house is loaded with the savour of roasting meats till it groans again, yard and all; but by night they sleep on their well made bedsteads, each with his own wife between the blankets. These were the people among whom we had now come.

"Aeolus entertained me for a whole month asking me questions all the time about Troy, the Argive fleet, and the return of the Achaeans. I told him exactly how everything had happened, and when I said I must go, and asked him to further me on my way, he made no sort of difficulty, but set about doing so at once. Moreover, he flayed me a prime ox-hide to hold the ways of the roaring winds, which he shut up in the hide as in a sack – for Jove had made him captain over the winds, and he could stir or still each one of them according to his own pleasure. He put the sack in the ship and bound the mouth so tightly with a silver thread that not even a breath of a side-wind could blow from any quarter. The West Wind which was fair for us did he alone let blow as it chose; but it all came to nothing, for we were lost through our own folly.

"Nine days and nine nights did we sail, and on the tenth day our native land showed on the horizon. We got so close in that we could see the stubble fires burning, and I, being then dead beat, fell into a light sleep, for I had never let the rudder out of my own hands, that we might get home the faster. On this the men fell to talking among themselves, and said I was bringing back gold and silver in the sack that Aeolus had given me. 'Bless my heart,' would one turn to his neighbour, saying, 'how this man gets honoured and makes friends to whatever city or country he may go. See what fine prizes he is taking home from Troy, while we, who have travelled just as far as he has, come back with hands as empty as we set out with – and now Aeolus has given him ever so much more. Quick – let us see what it all is, and how much gold and silver there is in the sack he gave him.'

"Thus they talked and evil counsels prevailed. They loosed the sack, whereupon the wind flew howling forth and raised a storm that carried us weeping out to sea and away from our own country. Then I awoke, and knew not whether to throw myself into the sea or to live on and make the best of it; but I bore it, covered myself up, and lay down in the ship, while the men lamented bitterly as the fierce winds bore our fleet back to the Aeolian island.

"When we reached it we went ashore to take in water, and dined hard by the ships. Immediately after dinner I took a herald and one of my men and went straight to the house of Aeolus, where I found him feasting with his wife and family; so we sat down as suppliants on the threshold. They were astounded when they saw us and said, 'Ulysses, what brings you here? What god has been ill-treating you? We took great pains to further you on your way home to Ithaca, or wherever it was that you wanted to go to.'

"Thus did they speak, but I answered sorrowfully, 'My men have undone me; they, and cruel sleep, have ruined me. My friends, mend me this mischief, for you can if you will.'

"I spoke as movingly as I could, but they said nothing, till their father answered, 'Vilest of mankind, get you gone at once off the island; him whom heaven hates will I in no wise help. Be off, for you come here as one abhorred of heaven.' And with these words he sent me sorrowing from his door.

"Thence we sailed sadly on till the men were worn out with long and fruitless rowing, for there was no longer any wind to help them. Six days, night and day did we toil, and on the seventh day we reached the rocky stronghold of Lamus – Telepylus, the city of the Laestrygonians, where the shepherd who is driving in his sheep and goats (to be milked) salutes him who is driving out his flock (to feed) and this last answers the salute. In that country a man who could do without sleep might earn double wages, one as a herdsman of cattle, and another as a shepherd, for they work much the same by night as they do by day.

"When we reached the harbour we found it land-locked under steep cliffs, with a narrow entrance between two headlands. My captains took all their ships inside, and made them fast close to one another, for there was never so much as a breath of wind inside, but it was always dead calm. I kept my own ship outside, and moored it to a rock at the very end of the point; then I climbed a high rock to reconnoitre, but could see no sign neither of man nor cattle, only some smoke rising from the ground. So I sent two of my company with an attendant to find out what sort of people the inhabitants were.

"The men when they got on shore followed a level road by which the people draw their firewood from the mountains into the town, till presently they met a young woman who had come outside to fetch water, and who was daughter to a Laestrygonian named Antiphates. She was going to the fountain Artacia from which the people bring in their water, and when my men had come close up to her, they asked her who the king of that country might be, and over what kind of people he ruled; so she directed them to her father's house, but when they got there they found his wife to be a giantess as huge as a mountain, and they were horrified at the sight of her.

"She at once called her husband Antiphates from the place of assembly, and forthwith he set about killing my men. He snatched up one of them, and began to make his dinner off him then and there, whereon the other two ran back to the ships as fast as ever they could. But Antiphates raised a hue-and-cry after them, and thousands of sturdy Laestrygonians sprang up from every quarter – ogres, not men. They threw vast rocks at us from the cliffs as though they had been mere stones, and I heard the horrid sound of the ships crunching up against one another, and the death cries of my men, as the Laestrygonians speared them like fishes and took them home to eat them. While they were thus killing my men within the harbour I drew my sword, cut the cable of my own ship, and told my men to row with all their might if they too would not fare like the rest; so they laid out for their lives, and we were thankful enough when we got into open water out of reach of the rocks they hurled at us. As for the others there was not one of them left.

The Outwitting of Polyphemus

TROY HAD FALLEN. After ten years' siege by a hundred thousand of Greece's mightiest warriors, the ramparts built by Poseidon had still proved impregnable to assault; the fell arrows of Heracles added to this host had failed to accomplish what Heracles himself had done single-handed. But finally, at the appointed time, stratagem had succeeded where force had proved of no avail: the monstrous wooden horse, within which crouched wily Odysseus and his chosen band, had wrought Ilium's downfall – leaving the world even till this day a pregnant proverb: to beware the enemy bearing gifts.

Among the Greeks summoned by King Menelaus to recapture Helen the incomparable, there was none to equal Odysseus as a combined warrior, leader and counsellor. To him had been awarded the celestial arms of Achilles; it was he who secretly stole away the Palladium, the guardian image whose presence made Troy invulnerable; through his counsel and under his leadership, the fateful wooden horse had brought the final victory.

He had done his utmost to evade the call to Troy in the first place, for the oracle had foretold that if he went, it would be twenty years before he should again see his beloved isle of Ithaca.

It had already taken half of this daunting term to complete the object of the expedition. But now the Trojan stronghold was a fiery memory. Helen was restored to her rightful husband. There remained merely the voyage of a few hundred miles back, through the island-studded Ægean and around the Peloponnesus, to bring him once more to his own kingdom, to that patient Penelope who awaited his return, and the baby son (now a baby no longer but the "discreet" Telemachus), to whom his sire was but a name. Surely the soothsayer must have erred: it could not take years for his galleys to cover the distance over which his heart and thoughts sped so swiftly.

Yet it was with a solemn countenance that the hero made offerings to the gods, and bade his followers loose the sails of his twelve stout ships before the southwest breeze. For none knew better than he how little might the utmost human skill and wisdom avail against the decrees of Olympus.

No such forebodings clouded the minds of his islanders. The thought of home, after these years of toil and peril, ran through their veins like an elixir. With shouts of joy, as dawn broke fresh and clear, each crew raced its long-keeled, high-prowed galley down the sloping beach. Dripping, they scrambled aboard, every man to his thwart. In unison the oars hit the water with powerful strokes, to the measure of an exultant chant. The yards were hoisted, sails unclewed, lowered and made fast. Under the following wind and the rowers' vigour, the vermillion-cheeked galleys leaped like live things across the quiet waters that curled about their prows.

It was not so quiet as they passed out of the protected harbour, for the stiff breeze was beginning to make the leaping waves blossom into white; but with yards braced and oars bending, they stood away stoutly into the northwest. Between Lemnos and Imbros they passed, forced ever more to northward by the growing wind, till they could see the wooded heights of Samothrace to leeward; and while most of the unthinking rejoiced to feel the plunging vessels speed so fast through the waves, Odysseus was far from satisfied, realizing that they were now headed almost directly away from their proper course.

He was glad enough as darkness began to fall, to see ahead the mountainous shore of Thrace, and to beach his vessels beneath the stars on the sandy strip, near the mouth of a cove, which his careful eye had noted.

Morning showed them hard by the chief town of the Ciconians, who inhabited those shores. They were barbarians, these Thracians, and proper spoil for warlike Greeks. Launching his galleys and leaving guards aboard, Odysseus led his Ithacans against this city of Ismaurus, sure of an easy victory as had been theirs so often before.

In one swift assault they overwhelmed the place, sacked it, and divided the booty. Then the prudent leader ordered an instant retreat to the waiting vessels.

But his inflamed soldiers, who had drunk deep of Thracian wine, could no longer be controlled. They began to slaughter the crook-horned oxen and the sheep, preparing by the shore for a triumphant carouse. All night the wild feast lasted.

Then, when discipline was relaxed, what had been foreseen by their leader came to pass. The Ciconians who had escaped had called upon their neighbours for aid. At dawn these began to gather, on horseback, in war chariots, on foot, thick as leaves and flowers in spring.

The Greeks now listened to their leader. It was too late to take to the swift ships, but they set themselves in battle array as the enemy burst upon them. Stoutly they fought, while the brass-tipped spears carried death to both sides. For nearly the whole day they managed to hold their ground against the pressing multitude; but towards sunset the numbers of the foe began to tell. The Grecian line was turned; man after man went down; and when they finally fled aboard the galleys in rout, seventy-two of their company were missing.

Glad to have escaped alive, the survivors did not leave till they had performed the last sacred rites, calling aloud three times to each of their slain comrades by name that their spirits might be guided back to Hellas. Then, with aching hearts, they sped from that ill-omened shore, while Odysseus prayed to Zeus for a favouring north wind.

The Cloud-gatherer heard, but answered in anger. The sky to northward grew black and lowering. So suddenly did the storm-clouds overspread the heavens that it seemed as if night had tumbled headlong upon the quaking fleet. Suddenly the wind leaped upon them, hurling the galleys apart as by a giant hand. The sails were torn to tatters by the tempest; the fury of the gale and the overwhelming rain forced the crews below, while the ships pitched and wallowed as they drove before the wind. Seeing that their only chance for life was to get under the lee of some protecting shore, the crews came up once more, each rower staggered to his seat, and they set to work to force their labouring craft towards land.

Two days and nights they toiled, till even their tough hands were blistered and raw, and their exhausted muscles could scarcely grip the oars. They reached the shelter of a promontory at length and rested there, amazed to find themselves still afloat.

By the next morning the gale seemed to have blown itself out, so they hoisted their yards, set sail, and stood south before a following wind and sea.

Again the hopes of all ran high, as they coasted along the mountainous shores of Eubœa, and turned southwest towards the long point of the Peloponnesus.

Still the favouring breeze swept them on. They doubled the dreaded cape of Maleia, and held west, now doubting not at all that in two days at the most their straining eyes would behold the rock cliffs of Ithaca. Only the face of Odysseus was stern and set, as he pondered in his mind the doleful prediction which had clouded his thoughts so many years.

Indeed, he was hardly surprised when, as they swept around the next jutting point, they were suddenly thrown aback by a squall from the north, accompanied by such a head sea that they were forced to put about and run before it, as far back as Cythera.

Even here they could make no harbour but drifted on helplessly before the furious gale. Nine days and nights they were tossed about, not knowing where they were or whither they were being carried.

On the tenth the fury of the wind abated, and they sighted an unknown shore. Odysseus stood in close to land, anchored, and sent a party ashore for fresh water. They prepared food on the beach, and ate and drank greedily after their exhausting vigil.

The leader then despatched two sailors inland, with a third as a herald, to see what manner of folk inhabited these shores.

They did not return, so he set out after them himself. He soon came upon them amid a company of the natives, and perceived that the trouble arose from the friendliness of these, not from any desire to harm the visitors. For this was the famed land of the Lotus-eaters, and after their custom they had given the sailors their own flowery food: straightway the wanderers had lost all remembrance of their errand, of ships, comrades, leader and home; they desired naught save to eat of the lotus for ever in this place of pleasant dreams.

Finding that they hearkened neither to his commands nor entreaties, Odysseus dragged them weeping back to the ships by very force, bound them fast, and stowed them under the rowers' benches. In haste he bade his crews embark, lest they too eat of this insidious food; and the moment they were safely aboard, the oars beat the water into foam, as they swept ahead to whatever might next await them.

On they cruised, across strange seas, with no knowledge of how to steer, but impelled ever forward on a chance course. It did not seem to matter particularly when they ran into a fog so thick that they could scarcely see far enough about to keep together.

Murky night settled down upon them. The blore of wind and sea seemed to increase and fill all space; yet there was no sign of rocks or breakers ahead, nor could straining eyes make out anything to steer by. They could but hold on their course, in dread of what any moment might bring, while the all-pervading roar grew ever more threatening.

Then, as if by magic, the tossing galleys suddenly rode peacefully on calm water. The thunderous roar was stilled, so that one might hear the ripple of the curling wavelets about the bows. And presently the staunch galleys slid gently up on a sloping beach.

Still they could see naught about them. But it was enough for those hardened wanderers that they were once more safe for the moment. Lowering all the sails, they stumbled ashore, lay down on the sand, and fell into the heavy sleep of passed fatigue and danger.

Rosy-fingered dawn opened their eyes upon a scene of beauty. They lay at the head of a landlocked basin, through whose narrow entrance, between tall cliffs, they had unwittingly steered safely in the blackness of the night. Close beside them a silvery stream rippled its way to the bay, from a cleft in the rock set about with dark poplars. Lush meadows, suitable for plough land and vineyards, stretched from the shore back to the wooded hills that hemmed in their refuge. Everything that nature unaided could provide was there, awaiting only the labour of men to turn it all into fruitfulness and homes; and the hearts of these storm-tossed mariners relaxed in pleasure as they gazed upon the charming prospect.

On making a circuit of the island, they found its forest-covered rocks even more immediately interesting than the meadows about the harbour, for innumerable wild goats made it their home, and the sight of these bounding figures turned their thoughts to hunting and food.

Bows and hunting spears were quickly brought from the ships; and separating into three bands, they entered ardently upon the chase. Nor was it long before they returned to the beach heavily laden with toothsome game. Nine goats there were for each of the twelve galleys, and to the leader were allotted ten more. Then, until the setting of the sun, they sat and feasted on this welcome meat, with ruddy wine from the ample store which they had brought away in jars as part of the spoil from the citadel of the Ciconians.

There was no sign of human beings on their island. But from the ridge they had marked a much larger one just behind it, with a wide harbour, across the mouth of which their resting-place lay. These rugged shores rose cliff-like from the water, carrying the eye back to higher and higher mountains, till it rested in wonder upon a gigantic peak that seemed to pierce the very sky. From the snows about its crest rose a threatening column of smoke – for this was that veritable Ætna with which all-powerful Zeus had at last overwhelmed the fleeing Typhon who had once driven the gods from Olympus.

In the calm of the evening the Greeks could hear across the narrow channel the bleat of sheep and goats, and sounds like those from the dwellings of men, but tremendous and awe-inspiring. Wondering what manner of folk these might be, they laid them down upon the beach and slept.

At dawn Odysseus held a council.

"You, my friends," said he, "stay here, while I with my own crew explore this neighbouring isle. I must first discover whether its people be churlish and savage, or if they observe the sacred rites of hospitality to strangers."

Quickly the cables were loosed, the rowers took their places at the pins, and the galley leaped forward out of the bay and around the point of the island. In a short time they were entering the harbour on the opposite shore.

Hardly had they passed the outer point when they stopped rowing in wonder. High up above them was a great cave in the face of the mountain. Dense masses of laurel grew all about its entrance. In front was an enclosure, walled in by huge boulders and by massive trunks of tall pine and oak trees. Clearly this was the abode of some creature who kept flocks and herds: but what sort of being must it be who could build such a colossal wall or need such quarters?

Odysseus bade his crew stay on the galley and guard it with their lives. Twelve men, upon whom he could rely, he picked to accompany him. In a goatskin bottle he carried his choicest offering – some of the dark sweet wine given him by the priest of Apollo at Ismaurus, in gratitude for his protection when they had despoiled the Ciconians; it had been reserved for the priest himself and two others only of his household, and so potent was it that, when a cupful was mixed with twenty times as much water, its aroma still filled the nostrils.

Cautiously the adventurer climbed up the ascent, followed by his twelve companions. No human being was in sight as they passed through the enclosure; but when they entered the cave, there were plentiful signs of recent habitation. On one side were pens filled with lambs and kids, the newborn in one, each older group to itself. Milking pails, huge bowls of milk set for cream, others of curd and of whey, and crates filled with cheeses stood all about, in vast size and profusion like everything else.

All they saw was so suggestive of an owner far outside the limits of ordinary men, that his followers at once besought him to make off with as many cheeses, lambs and kids as they could carry aboard, and to hasten quickly from that terrifying abode. But Odysseus refused. Confident in the powers of his tongue and sword, he resolved to await the return of this mighty cave-dweller, both to satisfy his own curiosity and in the hope of receiving the customary gifts. Bitterly was he to regret his decision before many hours had passed.

Meanwhile, under his bidding, the Greeks kindled a fire, made burnt offering to the gods, and satisfied their hunger with some of the cheese. Then they sat about in the gloomy cave, awaiting its master's homecoming.

Everything combined to make them apprehensive, and the nerves of all save Odysseus soon became taut enough. Hardened as they had become to danger and the unknown, they started in spite of themselves at every sound from the forest and thicket outside. And each time they would cast sidelong glances at one another and at their unmoved leader, striving to appear as unconcerned as he.

The sun in the west had begun to throw a long slanting tongue of light through the rock portal when unmistakable evidence came to their ears. Amid the bleating of returning flocks, there sounded the regular beat of what could only be mighty footsteps – footsteps which made even the solid rock quiver, and for which only the sights about them could have prepared their minds. Nearer and nearer they came, and even those bronzed faces grew pale.

Suddenly the sunlight streaming into the cave was darkened by a vast shape. It did not enter, but tossed in the whole bole of a blasted pine, whose dry limbs crashed and splintered as it fell. The tumbling Greeks sprang back to a dark corner: even their awed imaginations had not conceived of such gigantic strength.

Presently a mass of ewes began to jostle in through the doorway; clearly the rams and he-goats were to be left outside, and these were the milkers of the herd.

Behind them came the monstrous creature, and to the crouching watchers it appeared as if some mountain peak from the range they had seen were walking in upon them. Yet this prodigy, which seemed to fill the whole cave, was built like a man in all respects save one: one great eye only he bore, in the centre of his forehead. Savage and uncouth he was, with matted hair, and yellow tusks at the corner of his mouth like some ancient wild boar. And wise Odysseus knew that this was one of the famed Cyclopes who acknowledged not even the sovereignty of Olympus.

That baleful eye apparently did not perceive the terrified group huddled into the shadow. The monster turned as he entered, and laid hold of a huge stone which stood beside the portal. Such was its size that a score of ox-teams could not have started it from its place; but the intruders saw him wrap his great arms about the mass: the muscles stood out like cables as, lifting the boulder clear from the floor, he placed it in front of the entrance for a door stone, completely blocking the exit.

Dark as it now was within, he at once set to work at milking, placing half the milk in vessels for curdling, and filling with the rest a bowl in which two ordinary men could have stood upright and which would have held ten amphoræ of wine of ten gallons each. This done, he put the lambs and kids beneath their mothers.

Breaking off great limbs of the tree he had brought in as if they were twigs, he kindled a roaring fire. The leaping flames lit up the gloomy cavern. As the giant turned, the baleful glance of his single eye fell upon the cowering Ithacans.

"Ha!" he roared, in a voice that beat upon them like a gale of wind. "Who are you? Where have you come from across the seas? You look to me like some of those sea-rovers who bring no good to those they visit."

Though his companions, stout men all, seemed utterly overwhelmed by the savage's voice and aspect, Odysseus made answer boldly:

"We are Achæans, homeward bound from Troy, but driven by adverse winds across the sea. Through many wanderings Zeus has brought us hither. Subjects of Agamemnon are we, most famous of men, so great a city he took. Here by chance, we ask of you food and shelter, and the gift which is the stranger's due. Even you, O mighty one, must respect the gods. And Zeus is the protector of the stranger and suppliant."

Rough was the monster's reply:

"Stupid or ignorant you must be to threaten me with the gods. The Cyclopes care not for Zeus or his ægis: we are mightier than he, and in this world the strong is the master. Not for the wrath of Zeus would I spare you. But where is your ship? On this shore or the far one? Answer."

Odysseus was not to be beguiled so simply. "Poseidon, the Earth-shaker, wrecked my ship," he declared, "and cast her on the rocky point at the island's end. Only I, with these men, escaped."

Without a word, the Cyclops leaped forward. His hairy arms shot forth. In each huge hand he seized one of the startled seamen. Before the luckless ones had time so much as to call aloud, he had dashed out their brains upon the rocky floor. Then, like some lion of the mountains, he tore them limb from limb and devoured them, washing down his horrible meal with draughts of milk.

Paying no heed to the sighs and tears and calls upon Zeus of the survivors, he stretched his gorged bulk at full length among his flock and slept, filling the cave with the sound of his noisome breathing.

Shaken with wrath at the outrage and the contempt, Odysseus was about to creep upon the sleeping horror and thrust his sharp sword into his vitals. He had marked the very spot, resolving to make sure first by feeling for the heartbeat with his hand.But he reflected that this meant certain destruction for all, since they could by no possibility move the enormous door-stone. As best they might then, he and his crushed followers waited for the dawn.

They were not long left in doubt as to the monster's intentions towards the rest of them. At daybreak he stretched himself, rose yawning, and kindled the fire. Again he milked his herd and cared for them. Again he seized two struggling victims and slaughtered and devoured them for his morning meal.

Moving aside the boulder, he drove out goats and sheep, and replaced the door-stone as one might put the lid on a quiver. They heard his vast footfalls dying away, and his hoarse calls to his flock, as he drove them over the hills to pasturage. Penned up inexorably, they must await his return and its fresh horrors.

Sick at heart as he was, Odysseus thought only of revenge. Earnestly he besought Athene for wisdom.

Studying every object in the place, his eye returned again and again to the bole of a green olive tree which lay beside the pen. In size it was fit for the mast of a merchant ship of twenty oars, breasting the open sea; yet clearly the Cyclops was drying it out to use for a club-like staff.

Long did the hero ponder. And at last his jaw set and a grim smile played upon his face. His plan was made.

While his followers bemoaned their fate, he stepped across the cavern, drew his short sword and hacked off a six-foot section of this tree-trunk. Rolling it across to his men, he bade them shape it down. When it was smooth, he pointed the tip and charred it in the blazing fire till the point was hard. This weapon he hid carefully beneath the dry dung with which the cave was littered.

He explained to his wondering comrades that his idea was to thrust this great stake into the giant's eye while he slept; and he suggested that they choose by lot four of their number who should help him in this daring attack.They did so, and Odysseus noted with satisfaction that chance had given him the very resolute helpers he would have selected. Heartening them as best he could, through the long trying hours of inaction, the leader awaited their jailer's return.

Towards evening they heard those same portentous sounds of the monster's coming. The door-stone was lifted aside. In poured the jostling flocks. To the delight of Odysseus not a sheep was left outside: that fitted in exactly with his crafty scheme. He contained himself while the giant performed his evening tasks; even when two more of the Greeks were slain and devoured, he made no sign.

When this ghastly meal was despatched, however, he stepped forward, holding in his hands a bowl filled with the dark Ciconian wine.

"Here, Cyclops," said he. "Drink after your meal and see what we had aboard our ship. I brought it as an offering, thinking it might move you to send me home. But you defy the laws. How shall a stranger ever come to you again from any people after such a wicked deed?"

The giant drained the bowl at one draught, and a look of pleasure spread over the horrible features.

"Give me more, friend," he said. "And tell me your name that I may please you with a stranger's gift. The Cyclops' fruitful fields bear grapes with delicious wine in their heavy clusters; but this is truly nectar and ambrosia."

Odysseus refilled the bowl with the sparkling wine, and again the giant gulped it down. A third time it was replenished, and quickly emptied. Noticing that the potent drink was beginning to affect even that huge body, Ulysses answered his question:

"You ask my name: I will tell it, and do you fulfil your promise of a stranger's gift. My name is Noman. Noman am I called by mother, father and all my comrades."

With a drunken chuckle the Cyclops answered:

"Noman I will eat last, after all his comrades: that is the stranger's gift."

With that, he sank back, overcome by the wine. In a few moments he was sleeping, gorged and intoxicated, horrible to see and hear.

The moment had come. Odysseus seized the clumsy stake, and thrust the point into the embers of the fire, urging his men to be of stout heart and take their one chance.

When the point of the green olive trunk was aglow and ready to burst into flame, he snatched it from the fire. His four helpers took it like a battering-ram. Odysseus himself, standing on a projecting point of rock, grasped the butt firmly.

At the word of command, as if they were boring a ship-beam with a drill, the four plunged the smouldering point into the giant's eye with all their strength, while their leader twisted the weapon violently.

The effect was startling. Blood bubbled around the point. The great eyeball hissed like water into which a smith has plunged hot iron to temper it. With a roar that almost deafened them, the giant came to life, and his mighty upheaval hurled the men hither and thither. He wrenched the stake from his eye and hurled it from him in a frenzy. But the breathless and terrified sailors perceived with relief that the work had been well done: the monster was blind.

Beside himself with pain and anger he shouted at the top of his voice to his fellow Cyclopes who lived in the other caves along the windy heights. The hearts of the Greeks stood still with fear as they felt the earth quiver beneath running feet, and heard the cries of the gathering giants.

Presently a mighty voice from without demanded:

"What has happened to you, Polyphemus, that you rend the night with your screams and keep us all from sleep? Is someone carrying off your flocks? Are you being murdered by craft or force?"

"Friends," fairly blubbered the giant. "Noman is murdering me by craft. Force there is none."

"If no man harms you," came the reply, "the ill must come from Zeus and that you cannot fly. Pray to your father Poseidon."

Despite the calls and curses of the wounded one, the terrific company strode off, never suspecting the truth; and Odysseus laughed in his heart at the success of his simple stratagem.

Groaning in agony, Polyphemus groped about with his hands till he found the door-stone, moved it aside and seated himself with hands outstretched, to lay hold of his enemies in case they tried to escape with the sheep.

But Odysseus had foreseen this contingency, and now set quickly about the final move of his careful plan. He had observed that some of the rams were of a specially fine breed, very large, and covered with a long, heavy, blue fleece. Separating these from the rest, he quietly bound them together in groups of three with willow withes from the Cyclops' bed. The middle one of each of these three carried a man beneath him, guarded on each side by an unridden animal. The largest of the flock he selected to carry himself, hanging beneath his shaggy belly and gripping his back from each side with arms and hands completely buried in the enormous fleece. Having made their preparations in absolute silence, they anxiously awaited the coming of the day.

As the first ruddy streaks of dawn became visible through the cave mouth, the rams hastened out, eager for pasture, while the unmilked ewes bleated in distress about the enclosure.

Polyphemus, moaning and muttering threats, ran his hands over the back of every sheep before he would permit it to go out. Stupidly, he never thought of feeling beneath, where the trembling seamen hung in dread of being detected.

One after another passed safely out of that gloomy cavern into the fresh freedom of the morning. Last of all came the great leader ram with its human freight.

"What, my pet!" exclaimed the Cyclops as he felt the creature's back. "Why are you the hindmost of the flock? You were never a laggard, but always first to crop the tender grass, first to drink at the stream, first to turn homeward at night. Ah, you miss your master's eye, which that villain and his vile crew have put out. Noman it was – but I will have him yet. If only you could speak and tell me where he is skulking, how quickly would I dash out his brains. That would help some in the misery that scoundrel has brought upon me."

He freed the ram and it trotted quickly out. The moment they were safely away from the enclosure, Odysseus dropped to earth and helped his comrades to free themselves. Then they hastily drove off the fat rams towards the shore, casting many an anxious glance behind them, for they feared that at any moment the Cyclops might discover the trick and come down upon them.

They reached the ship where their staunch comrades welcomed them as men returned from the dead. Checking their laments for the luckless ones who had perished, Odysseus ordered them to toss the rams aboard as quickly as they might. The rowers leaped to their places; the oars hit the water in unison; the galley sped away from that accursed shore.

When they had reached the limit of hailing distance, Odysseus stood up on the poop and shouted to the cave above:

"Cyclops, those were not a weakling's comrades upon whom you wrought your brutality. It was destined that your crime should find you out, wretch who dared to devour a guest within your house. For this has Zeus chastised you, Zeus and all the gods of Olympus."

The giant heard, and knew himself outwitted. Frantic with rage, he sprang forth from the cabin, tore up a boulder that looked like a whole hilltop, and hurled it towards the sound of the taunting voice.

The mass of rock fell in front of the galley; and it sent such a wave surging backward that the vessel was washed clean back to shore.

It would have fared badly then with the adventurers had the giant been able to see their plight, for they were easily within his grasp. But Odysseus seized a setting pole and shoved off again, making signs with his head to the rowers to pull their hardest.

They put twice as wide a space as before between them and the enemy. Then Odysseus rose again to speak to him. Beneath their breath his men implored him to desist:

"O foolhardy one, why rouse this savage who even now drove us back to shore with his missile? We thought all was over then. Had he heard but a whisper he would have crushed us beneath some jagged mass of granite."

Their leader was not to be moved.

"Cyclops," he cried proudly, "if ever man asks you of your blinded eye, say it was the deed of Odysseus, spoiler of cities, Laertes' son, whose home is Ithaca."

At that Polyphemus groaned dolefully.

"Surely the ancient oracles are come upon me! A soothsayer once dwelt here, Telemus the renowned. He told me I should lose my sight through one Odysseus; but I watched for some mighty one – and now this miserable pigmy has blinded me after overcoming me with wine. Nevertheless, come hither, Odysseus, that I may bestow on you the stranger's gift and beg the Land-shaker to speed you on your journey. His son am I; he can heal me if he will."

Odysseus laughed in scorn. "Would I might as surely strip you of life and send you to Hades as it is sure the Earth-shaker will never heal your eye."

Then for the first time in his life the monster prayed, stretching forth his hands to the sky:

"Hear me, thou girder of the land, dark-haired Poseidon. If I am truly thine, and thou art called my father, vouchsafe no coming home to this Odysseus, spoiler of cities, Laertes' son, whose home is Ithaca. Yet if it be his lot to see his friends once more, and reach his stately home and native land, late let him come, in evil plight, with loss of all his crew, on the vessel of a stranger, and may he at his home find trouble."

He finished. His anger burst forth fiercely once more. Heaving up another rock far larger than the first, he swung it back and forth, put forth his utmost strength and hurled the mountainous mass out to sea. It struck behind the galley, which shot up as if lifted by a tidal wave.

Odysseus called his order; the oars struck the water; the tough shafts bent with the strain; but in a few moments the galley was riding safe beyond the whirlpool and speeding towards the outer island.

But through all the rejoicings with which they met their comrades in the other ships, through the feast, and through the propitiatory sacrifice, the heart of Odysseus was heavy within him.

It was with a solemn brow that he loosed sail at dawn next day and set forth to accomplish what remained of his amazing destiny.

The Third Voyage of Sinbad the Sailor

AFTER A VERY SHORT TIME the pleasant easy life I led made me quite forget the perils of my two voyages. Moreover, as I was still in the prime of life, it pleased me better to be up and doing. So once more providing myself with the rarest and choicest merchandise of Bagdad, I conveyed it to Balsora, and set sail with other merchants of my acquaintance for distant lands. We had touched at many ports and made much profit, when one day upon the open sea we were caught by a terrible wind which blew us completely out of our reckoning, and lasting for several days finally drove us into harbour on a strange island.

"I would rather have come to anchor anywhere than here," quoth our captain. "This island and all adjoining it are inhabited by hairy savages, who are certain to attack us, and whatever these dwarfs may do we dare not resist, since they swarm like locusts, and if one of them is killed the rest will fall upon us, and speedily make an end of us."

These words caused great consternation among all the ship's company, and only too soon we were to find out that the captain spoke truly. There appeared a vast multitude of hideous savages, not more than two feet high and covered with reddish fur. Throwing themselves into the waves they surrounded our vessel. Chattering meanwhile in a language we could not understand, and clutching at ropes and gangways, they swarmed up the ship's side with such speed and agility that they almost seemed to fly.

You may imagine the rage and terror that seized us as we watched them, neither daring to hinder them nor able to speak a word to deter them from their purpose, whatever it might be. Of this we were not left long in doubt. Hoisting the sails, and cutting the cable of the anchor, they sailed our vessel to an island which lay a little further off, where they drove us ashore; then taking possession of her, they made off to the place from which they had come, leaving us helpless upon a shore avoided with horror by all mariners for a reason which you will soon learn.

Turning away from the sea we wandered miserably inland, finding as we went various herbs and fruits which we ate, feeling that we might as well live as long as possible though we had no hope of escape. Presently we saw in the far distance what seemed to us to be a splendid palace, towards which we turned our weary steps, but when we reached it we saw that it was a castle, lofty, and strongly built. Pushing back the heavy ebony doors we entered the courtyard, but upon the threshold of the great hall beyond it we paused, frozen with horror, at the sight which greeted us. On one side lay a huge pile of bones – human bones, and on the other numberless spits for roasting! Overcome with despair we sank trembling to the ground, and lay there without speech or motion. The sun was setting when a loud noise aroused us, the door of the hall was violently burst open and a horrible giant entered. He was as tall as a palm tree, and perfectly black, and had one eye, which flamed like a burning coal in the middle of his forehead. His teeth were long and sharp and grinned horribly, while his lower lip hung down upon his chest, and he had ears like elephant's ears, which covered his shoulders, and nails like the claws of some fierce bird.

At this terrible sight our senses left us and we lay like dead men. When at last we came to ourselves the giant sat examining us attentively with his fearful eye. Presently when he had looked at us enough he came towards us, and stretching out his hand took me by the back of the neck, turning me this way and that, but feeling that I was mere skin and bone he set me down again and went on to the next, whom he treated in the same fashion; at last he came to the captain, and finding him the fattest of us all, he took him up in one hand and stuck him upon a spit and proceeded to kindle a huge fire at which he presently roasted him. After the giant had supped he lay down to sleep, snoring like the loudest thunder, while we lay shivering with horror the whole night through, and when day broke he awoke and went out, leaving us in the castle.

When we believed him to be really gone we started up bemoaning our horrible fate, until the hall echoed with our despairing cries. Though we were many and our enemy was alone it did not occur to us to kill him, and indeed we should have found that a hard task, even if we had thought of it, and no plan could we devise to deliver ourselves. So at last, submitting to our sad fate, we spent the day in wandering up and down the island eating such fruits as we could find, and when night came we returned to the castle, having sought in vain for any other place of shelter. At sunset the giant returned, supped upon one of our unhappy comrades, slept and snored till dawn, and then left us as before. Our condition seemed to us so frightful that several of my companions thought it would be better to leap from the cliffs and perish in the waves at once, rather than await so miserable an end; but I had a plan of escape which I now unfolded to them, and which they at once agreed to attempt.

"Listen, my brothers," I added. "You know that plenty of driftwood lies along the shore. Let us make several rafts, and carry them to a suitable place. If our plot succeeds, we can wait patiently for the chance of some passing ship which would rescue us from this fatal island. If it fails, we must quickly take to our rafts; frail as they are, we have more chance of saving our lives with them than we have if we remain here."

All agreed with me, and we spent the day in building rafts, each capable of carrying three persons. At nightfall we returned to the castle, and very soon in came the giant, and one more of our number was sacrificed. But the time of our vengeance was at hand! As soon as he had finished his horrible repast he lay down to sleep as before, and when we heard him begin to snore I, and nine of the boldest of my comrades, rose softly, and took each a spit, which we made red-hot in the fire, and then at a given signal we plunged it with one accord into the giant's eye, completely blinding him. Uttering a terrible cry, he sprang to his feet clutching in all directions to try to seize one of us, but we had all fled different ways as soon as the deed was done, and thrown ourselves flat upon the ground in corners where he was not likely to touch us with his feet.

After a vain search he fumbled about till he found the door, and fled out of it howling frightfully. As for us, when he was gone we made haste to leave the fatal castle, and, stationing ourselves beside our rafts, we waited to see what would happen. Our idea was that if, when the sun rose, we saw nothing of the giant, and no longer heard his howls, which still came faintly through the darkness, growing more and more distant, we should conclude that he was dead, and that we might safely stay upon the island and need not risk our lives upon the frail rafts. But alas! morning light showed us our enemy approaching us, supported on either hand by two giants nearly as large and fearful as himself, while a crowd of others followed close upon their heels. Hesitating no longer we clambered upon our rafts and rowed with all our might out to sea. The giants, seeing their prey escaping them, seized up huge pieces of rock, and wading into the water hurled them after us with such good aim that all the rafts except the one I was upon were swamped, and their luckless crews drowned, without our being able to do anything to help them. Indeed I and my two companions had all we could do to keep our own raft beyond the reach of the giants, but by dint of hard rowing we at last gained the open sea. Here we were at the mercy of the winds and waves, which tossed us to and fro all that day and night, but the next morning we found ourselves near an island, upon which we gladly landed.

There we found delicious fruits, and having satisfied our hunger we presently lay down to rest upon the shore. Suddenly we were aroused by a loud rustling noise, and starting up, saw that it was caused by an immense snake which was gliding towards us over the sand. So swiftly it came that it had seized one of my comrades before he had time to fly, and in spite of his cries and struggles speedily crushed the life out of him in its mighty coils and proceeded to swallow him. By this time my other companion and I were running for our lives to some place where we might hope to be safe from this new horror, and seeing a tall tree we climbed up into it, having first provided ourselves with a store of fruit off the surrounding bushes. When night came I fell asleep, but only to be awakened once more by the terrible snake, which after hissing horribly round the tree at last reared itself up against it, and finding my sleeping comrade who was perched just below me, it swallowed him also, and crawled away leaving me half dead with terror.

When the sun rose I crept down from the tree with hardly a hope of escaping the dreadful fate which had over-taken my comrades; but life is sweet, and I determined to do all I could to save myself. All day long I toiled with frantic haste and collected quantities of dry brushwood, reeds and thorns, which I bound with fagots, and making a circle of them under my tree I piled them firmly one upon another until I had a kind of tent in which I crouched like a mouse in a hole when she sees the cat coming. You may imagine what a fearful night I passed, for the snake returned eager to devour me, and glided round and round my frail shelter seeking an entrance. Every moment I feared that it would succeed in pushing aside some of the fagots, but happily for me they held together, and when it grew light my enemy retired, baffled and hungry, to his den. As for me I was more dead than alive! Shaking with fright and half suffocated by the poisonous breath of the monster, I came out of my tent and crawled down to the sea, feeling that it would be better to plunge from the cliffs and end my life at once than pass such another night of horror. But to my joy and relief I saw a ship sailing by, and by shouting wildly and waving my turban I managed to attract the attention of her crew.

A boat was sent to rescue me, and very soon I found myself on board surrounded by a wondering crowd of sailors and merchants eager to know by what chance I found myself in that desolate island. After I had told my story they regaled me with the choicest food the ship afforded, and the captain, seeing that I was in rags, generously bestowed upon me one of his own coats. After sailing about for some time and touching at many ports we came at last to the island of Salahat, where sandal wood grows in great abundance. Here we anchored, and as I stood watching the merchants disembarking their goods and preparing to sell or exchange them, the captain came up to me and said,

"I have here, brother, some merchandise belonging to a passenger of mine who is dead. Will you do me the favour to trade with it, and when I meet with his heirs I shall be able to give them the money, though it will be only just that you shall have a portion for your trouble."

I consented gladly, for I did not like standing by idle. Whereupon he pointed the bales out to me, and sent for the person whose duty it was to keep a list of the goods that were upon the ship. When this man came he asked in what name the merchandise was to be registered.

"In the name of Sinbad the Sailor," replied the captain.

At this I was greatly surprised, but looking carefully at him I recognized him to be the captain of the ship upon which I had made my second voyage, though he had altered much since that time. As for him, believing me to be dead it was no wonder that he had not recognized me.

"So, captain," said I, "the merchant who owned those bales was called Sinbad?"

"Yes," he replied. "He was so named. He belonged to Bagdad, and joined my ship at Balsora, but by mischance he was left behind upon a desert island where we had landed to fill up our water-casks, and it was not until four hours later that he was missed. By that time the wind had freshened, and it was impossible to put back for him."

"You suppose him to have perished then?" said I.

"Alas! yes," he answered.

"Why, captain!" I cried, "look well at me. I am that Sinbad who fell asleep upon the island and awoke to find himself abandoned!"

The captain stared at me in amazement, but was presently convinced that I was indeed speaking the truth, and rejoiced greatly at my escape.

"I am glad to have that piece of carelessness off my conscience at any rate," said he. "Now take your goods, and the profit I have made for you upon them, and may you prosper in future."

I took them gratefully, and as we went from one island to another I laid in stores of cloves, cinnamon, and other spices. In one place I saw a tortoise which was twenty cubits long and as many broad, also a fish that was like a cow and had skin so thick that it was used to make shields. Another I saw that was like a camel in shape and colour. So by degrees we came back to Balsora, and I returned to Bagdad with so much money that I could not myself count it, besides treasures without end. I gave largely to the poor, and bought much land to add to what I already possessed, and thus ended my third voyage.

When Sinbad had finished his story he gave another hundred sequins to Hindbad, who then departed with the other guests, but next day when they had all reassembled, and the banquet was ended, their host continued his adventures.

The Creation of the Universe

BEFORE THE UNIVERSE WAS CREATED, there existed only a vast expanse of sky above and an endless stretch of water and uninhabited marshland below. Olorun, the wisest of the gods, was supreme ruler of the sky, while Olokun, the most powerful goddess, ruled the seas and marshes. Both kingdoms were quite separate at that time and there was never any conflict between the two deities. Olorun was more than satisfied with his domain in the sky and hardly noticed what took place below him. Olokun was content with the kingdom she occupied, even though it contained neither living creatures nor vegetation of any kind.

But the young god Obatala was not entirely satisfied with this state of affairs, and one day, as he looked down from the sky upon the dull, grey terrain ruled by Olokun, he thought to himself:

"The kingdom below is a pitiful, barren place. Something must be done to improve its murky appearance. Now if only there were mountains and forests to brighten it up, it would make a perfect home for all sorts of living creatures."

Obatala decided that he must visit Olorun, who was always prepared to listen to him.

"It is a good scheme, but also a very ambitious one," Olorun said to Obatala. "I have no doubt that the hills and valleys you describe would be far better than grey ocean, but who will create this new world, and how will they go about it?"

"If you will give me your blessing," Obatala replied, "I myself will undertake to do this work."

"Then it is settled," said Olorun. "I cannot help you myself, but I will arrange for you to visit my son Orunmila. He will be able to guide you."

Next day, Obatala called upon Orunmila, the eldest son of Olorun, who had been given the power to read the future and to understand the secret of existence. Orunmila produced his divining tray, and when he had placed sixteen palm nuts on it, he shook the tray and cast its contents high into the air. As the nuts dropped to the ground, he read their meaning aloud:

"First, Obatala," he announced, "you must find a chain of gold long enough for you to climb down from the sky to the watery wastes below. Then, as you descend, take with you a snail shell filled with sand, a white hen, a black cat and a palm nut. This is how you should begin your quest."

Obatala listened attentively to his friend's advice and immediately set off to find a goldsmith who would make him the chain he needed to descend from the sky to the surface of the water below.

"I would be happy to make you the chain you ask for," said the goldsmith, "provided you can give me all the gold I need. But I doubt that you will find enough here for me to complete my task."

Obatala would not be dissuaded, however, and having instructed the goldsmith to go ahead with his work, he approached the other sky gods and one by one explained to them his purpose, requesting that they contribute whatever gold they possessed. The response was generous. Some of the gods gave gold dust, others gave rings, bracelets or pendants, and before long a huge, glittering mound had been collected. The goldsmith examined all the gold that was brought before him, but still he complained that there was not enough.

"It is the best I can do," Obatala told him. "I have asked all of the other gods to help out and there is no more gold left in the sky. Make the chain as long as you possibly can and fix a hook to one end. Even if it fails to reach the water below, I am determined to climb down on it."

The goldsmith worked hard to complete the chain and when it was finished, the hook was fastened to the edge of the sky and the chain lowered far below. Orunmila appeared and handed Obatala a bag containing the sand-filled snail's shell, the white hen, the black cat and the palm nut, and as soon as he had slung it over his shoulder, the young god began climbing down the golden chain, lower and lower until he saw that he was leaving the world of light and entering a world of twilight.

Before long, Obatala could feel the damp mists rising up off the surface of the water, but at the same time, he realized that he had just about reached the end of his golden chain.

"I cannot jump from here," he thought. "If I let go of the chain I will fall into the sea and almost certainly drown."

And while he looked around him rather helplessly, he suddenly heard a familiar voice calling to him from up above.

"Make use of the sand I gave you," Orunmila instructed him, "toss it into the water below."

Obatala obeyed, and after he had poured out the sand, he heard Orunmila calling to him a second time:

"Release the white hen," Orunmila cried.

Obatala reached into his bag and pulled out the white hen, dropping her on to the waters beneath where he had sprinkled the sand. As soon as she had landed, the hen began to scratch in the sand, scattering it in all directions. Wherever the grains fell, dry land instantly appeared. The larger heaps of sand became hills, while the smaller heaps became valleys.

Obatala let go of his chain and jumped on to the solid earth. As he walked he smiled with pleasure, for the land now extended a great many miles in all directions. But he was proudest of the spot where his feet had first landed, and decided to name this place Ife. Stooping to the ground, he began digging a hole, and buried his palm nut in the soil. Immediately, a palm tree sprang up from the earth, shedding its seeds as it stretched to its full height so that other trees soon shot up around it. Obatala felled some of these trees and built for himself a sturdy house thatched with palm leaves. And here, in this place, he settled down, separated from the other sky gods, with only his black cat for company.

The Story of the Hero Makóma

ONCE UPON A TIME, at the town of Senna on the banks of the Zambesi, was born a child. He was not like other children, for he was very tall and strong; over his shoulder he carried a big sack, and in his hand an iron hammer. He could also speak like a grown man, but usually he was very silent.

One day his mother said to him: "My child, by what name shall we know you?"

And he answered: "Call all the head men of Senna here to the river's bank." And his mother called the head men of the town, and when they had come he led them down to a deep black pool in the river where all the fierce crocodiles lived.

"O great men!" he said, while they all listened, "which of you will leap into the pool and overcome the crocodiles?" But no one would come forward. So he turned and sprang into the water and disappeared.

The people held their breath, for they thought: "Surely the boy is bewitched and throws away his life, for the crocodiles will eat him!" Then suddenly the ground trembled, and the pool, heaving and swirling, became red with blood, and presently the boy rising to the surface swam on shore.

But he was no longer just a boy! He was stronger than any man and very tall and handsome, so that the people shouted with gladness when they saw him.

"Now, O my people!" he cried waving his hand, "you know my name – I am Makóma, 'the Greater'; for have I not slain the crocodiles in the pool where none would venture?"

Then he said to his mother: "Rest gently, my mother, for I go to make a home for myself and become a hero." Then, entering his hut, he took Nu-éndo, his iron hammer, and throwing the sack over his shoulder, he went away.

Makóma crossed the Zambesi, and for many moons he wandered towards the north and west until he came to a very hilly country where, one day, he met a huge giant making mountains.

"Greeting," shouted Makóma, "who are you?"

"I am Chi-éswa-mapíri, who makes the mountains," answered the giant, "and who are you?"

"I am Makóma, which signifies 'greater,'" answered he.

"Greater than who?" asked the giant.

"Greater than you!" answered Makóma.

The giant gave a roar and rushed upon him. Makóma said nothing, but swinging his great hammer, Nu-éndo, he struck the giant upon the head.

He struck him so hard a blow that the giant shrank into quite a little man, who fell upon his knees saying: "You are indeed greater than I, O Makóma; take me with you to be your slave!" So Makóma picked him up and dropped him into the sack that he carried upon his back.

He was greater than ever now, for all the giant's strength had gone into him; and he resumed his journey, carrying his burden with as little difficulty as an eagle might carry a hare.

Before long he came to a country broken up with huge stones and immense clods of earth. Looking over one of the heaps he saw a giant wrapped in dust dragging out the very earth and hurling it in handfuls on either side of him.

"Who are you," cried Makóma, "that pulls up the earth in this way?"

"I am Chi-dúbula-táka," said he, "and I am making the riverbeds."

"Do you know who I am?" said Makóma. "I am he that is called 'greater'!"

"Greater than who?" thundered the giant.

"Greater than you!" answered Makóma.

With a shout, Chi-dúbula-táka seized a great clod of earth and launched it at Makóma. But the hero had his sack held over his left arm and the stones and earth fell harmlessly upon it, and, tightly gripping his iron hammer, he rushed in and struck the giant to the ground. Chi-dúbula-táka grovelled before him, all the while growing smaller and smaller; and when he had become a convenient size Makóma picked him up and put him into the sack beside Chi-éswa-mapíri.

He went on his way even greater than before, as all the river-maker's power had become his; and at last he came to a forest of bao-babs and thorn trees. He was astonished at their size, for everyone was full grown and larger than any trees he had ever seen, and close by he saw Chi-gwísa-míti, the giant who was planting the forest.

Chi-gwísa-míti was taller than either of his brothers, but Makóma was not afraid and called out to him: "Who are you, O Big One?"

"I," said the giant, "am Chi-gwísa-míti, and I am planting these bao-babs and thorns as food for my children the elephants."

"Leave off!" shouted the hero, "for I am Makóma, and would like to exchange a blow with thee!"

The giant, plucking up a monster bao-bab by the roots, struck heavily at Makóma; but the hero sprang aside, and as the weapon sank deep into the soft earth, whirled Nu-éndo the hammer round his head and felled the giant with one blow.

So terrible was the stroke that Chi-gwísa-míti shrivelled up as the other giants had done; and when he had got back his breath he begged Makóma to take him as his servant. "For," said he, "it is honourable to serve a man so great as thou."

Makóma, after placing him in his sack, proceeded upon his journey, and travelling for many days he at last reached a country so barren and rocky that not a single living thing grew upon it – everywhere reigned grim desolation. And in the midst of this dead region he found a man eating fire.

"What are you doing?" demanded Makóma.

"I am eating fire," answered the man, laughing; "and my name is Chi-ídea-móto, for I am the flame-spirit, and can waste and destroy what I like."

"You are wrong," said Makóma; "for I am Makóma, who is 'greater' than you – and you cannot destroy me!"

The fire-eater laughed again, and blew a flame at Makóma. But the hero sprang behind a rock – just in time, for the ground upon which he had been standing was turned to molten glass, like an overbaked pot, by the heat of the flame-spirit's breath.

Then the hero flung his iron hammer at Chi-ídea-móto, and, striking him, it knocked him helpless; so Makóma placed him in the sack, Woro-nówu, with the other great men that he had overcome.

And now, truly, Makóma was a very great hero; for he had the strength to make hills, the industry to lead rivers over dry wastes, foresight and wisdom in planting trees, and the power of producing fire when he wished.

Wandering on he arrived one day at a great plain, well watered and full of game; and in the very middle of it, close to a large river, was a grassy spot, very pleasant to make a home upon.

Makóma was so delighted with the little meadow that he sat down under a large tree, and removing the sack from his shoulder, took out all the giants and set them before him. "My friends," said he, "I have travelled far and am weary. Is not this such a place as would suit a hero for his home? Let us then go, tomorrow, to bring in timber to make a kraal."

So the next day Makóma and the giants set out to get poles to build the kraal, leaving only Chi-éswa-mapíri to look after the place and cook some venison which they had killed. In the evening, when they returned, they found the giant helpless and tied to a tree by one enormous hair!

"How is it," said Makóma, astonished, "that we find you thus bound and helpless?"

"O Chief," answered Chi-éswa-mapíri, "at midday a man came out of the river; he was of immense stature, and his grey moustaches were of such length that I could not see where they ended! He demanded of me 'Who is thy master?' And I answered: 'Makóma, the greatest of heroes.' Then the man seized me, and pulling a hair from his moustache, tied me to this tree – even as you see me."

Makóma was very wroth, but he said nothing, and drawing his fingernail across the hair (which was as thick and strong as palm rope) cut it, and set free the mountain-maker.

The three following days exactly the same thing happened, only each time with a different one of the party; and on the fourth day Makóma stayed in camp when the others went to cut poles, saying that he would see for himself what sort of man this was that lived in the river and whose moustaches were so long that they extended beyond men's sight.

So when the giants had gone he swept and tidied the camp and put some venison on the fire to roast. At midday, when the sun was right overhead, he heard a rumbling noise from the river, and looking up he saw the head and shoulders of an enormous man emerging from it. And behold! right down the riverbed and up the riverbed, till they faded into the blue distance, stretched the giant's grey moustaches!

"Who are you?" bellowed the giant, as soon as he was out of the water.

"I am he that is called Makóma," answered the hero; "and, before I slay thee, tell me also what is thy name and what thou doest in the river?"

"My name is Chin-débou Máu-giri," said the giant. "My home is in the river, for my moustache is the grey fever-mist that hangs above the water, and with which I bind all those that come unto me so that they die."

"You cannot bind me!" shouted Makóma, rushing upon him and striking with his hammer. But the river giant was so slimy that the blow slid harmlessly off his green chest, and as Makóma stumbled and tried to regain his balance, the giant swung one of his long hairs around him and tripped him up.

For a moment Makóma was helpless, but remembering the power of the flame-spirit which had entered into him, he breathed a fiery breath upon the giant's hair and cut himself free.

As Chin-débou Máu-giri leaned forward to seize him the hero flung his sack Woro-nówu over the giant's slippery head, and gripping his iron hammer, struck him again; this time the blow alighted upon the dry sack and Chin-débou Máu-giri fell dead.

When the four giants returned at sunset with the poles they rejoiced to find that Makóma had overcome the fever-spirit, and they feasted on the roast venison till far into the night; but in the morning, when they awoke, Makóma was already warming his hands at the fire, and his face was gloomy.

"In the darkness of the night, O my friends," he said presently, "the white spirits of my fathers came unto me and spoke, saying: 'Get thee hence, Makóma, for thou shalt have no rest until thou hast found and fought with Sákatirína, who has five heads, and is very great and strong; so take leave of thy friends, for thou must go alone.'"

Then the giants were very sad, and bewailed the loss of their hero; but Makóma comforted them, and gave back to each the gifts he had taken from them. Then bidding them "Farewell," he went on his way.

Makóma travelled far towards the west; over rough mountains and water-logged morasses, fording deep rivers, and tramping for days across dry deserts where most men would have died, until at length he arrived at a hut standing near some large peaks, and inside the hut were two beautiful women.

"Greeting!" said the hero. "Is this the country of Sákatirína of five heads, whom I am seeking?"

"We greet you, O Great One!" answered the women. "We are the wives of Sákatirína; your search is at an end, for there stands he whom you seek!" And they pointed to what Makóma had thought were two tall mountain peaks. "Those are his legs," they said, "his body you cannot see, for it is hidden in the clouds."

Makóma was astonished when he beheld how tall was the giant; but, nothing daunted, he went forward until he reached one of Sákatirína's legs, which he struck heavily with Nu-éndo. Nothing happened, so he hit again and then again until, presently, he heard a tired, far-away voice saying: "Who is it that scratches my feet?"

And Makóma shouted as loud as he could, answering: "It is I, Makóma, who is called 'Greater'!" And he listened, but there was no answer.

Then Makóma collected all the dead brushwood and trees that he could find, and making an enormous pile round the giant's legs, set a light to it.

This time the giant spoke; his voice was very terrible, for it was the rumble of thunder in the clouds. "Who is it," he said, "making that fire smoulder around my feet?"

"It is I, Makóma!" shouted the hero. "And I have come from far away to see thee, O Sákatirína, for the spirits of my fathers bade me go seek and fight with thee, lest I should grow fat, and weary of myself."

There was silence for a while, and then the giant spoke softly: "It is good, O Makóma!" he said. "For I too have grown weary. There is no man so great as I, therefore I am all alone. Guard thyself!" And bending suddenly he seized the hero in his hands and dashed him upon the ground. And lo! instead of death, Makóma had found life, for he sprang to his feet mightier in strength and stature than before, and rushing in he gripped the giant by the waist and wrestled with him.

Hour by hour they fought, and mountains rolled beneath their feet like pebbles in a flood; now Makóma would break away, and summoning up his strength, strike the giant with Nu-éndo his iron hammer, and Sákatirína would pluck up the mountains and hurl them upon the hero, but neither one could slay the other. At last, upon the second day, they grappled so strongly that they could not break away; but their strength was failing, and, just as the sun was sinking, they fell together to the ground, insensible.

In the morning when they awoke, Mulímo the Great Spirit was standing by them; and he said: "O Makóma and Sákatirína! Ye are heroes so great that no man may come against you. Therefore ye will leave the world and take up your home with me in the clouds." And as he spake the heroes became invisible to the people of the Earth, and were no more seen among them.

How Odin Lost His Eye

IN THE BEGINNING OF THINGS, before there was any world or sun, moon and stars, there were the giants; for these were the oldest creatures that ever breathed. They lived in Jotunheim, the land of frost and darkness, and their hearts were evil. Next came the gods, the good Æsir, who made earth and sky and sea, and who dwelt in Asgard, above the heavens. Then were created the odd little dwarfs, who lived underground in the caverns of the mountains, working at their mines of metal and precious stones. Last of all, the gods made men to dwell in Midgard, the good world that we know, between which and the glorious home of the Æsir stretched Bifröst, the bridge of rainbows.

In those days, folk say, there was a mighty ash-tree named Yggdrasil, so vast that its branches shaded the whole earth and stretched up into heaven where the Æsir dwelt, while its roots sank far down below the lowest depth. In the branches of the big ash-tree lived an odd family of creatures. First, there was a great eagle, who was wiser than any bird that ever lived – except the two ravens, Thought and Memory, who sat upon Father Odin's shoulders and told him the secrets which they learned in their flight over the wide world. Near the great eagle perched a hawk, and four antlered deer browsed among the buds of Yggdrasil. At the foot of the tree coiled a huge serpent, who was always gnawing hungrily at its roots, with a whole colony of little snakes to keep him company – so many that they could never be counted. The eagle at the top of the tree and the serpent at its foot were enemies, always saying hard things of each other. Between the two skipped up and down a little squirrel, a tale-bearer and a gossip, who repeated each unkind remark and, like the malicious neighbour that he was, kept their quarrel ever fresh and green.

In one place at the roots of Yggdrasil was a fair fountain called the Urdar-well, where the three Norn-maidens, who knew the past, present and future, dwelt with their pets, the two white swans. This was magic water in the fountain, which the Norns sprinkled every day upon the giant tree to keep it green – water so sacred that everything which entered it became white as the film of an eggshell. Close beside this sacred well the Æsir had their council hall, to which they galloped every morning over the rainbow bridge.

But Father Odin, the king of all the Æsir, knew of another fountain more wonderful still; the two ravens whom he sent forth to bring him news had told him. This also was below the roots of Yggdrasil, in the spot where the sky and ocean met. Here for centuries and centuries the giant Mimer had sat keeping guard over his hidden well, in the bottom of which lay such a treasure of wisdom as was to be found nowhere else in the world. Every morning Mimer dipped his glittering horn Giöll into the fountain and drew out a draught of the wondrous water, which he drank to make him wise. Every day he grew wiser and wiser; and as this had been going on ever since the beginning of things, you can scarcely imagine how wise Mimer was.

Now it did not seem right to Father Odin that a giant should have all this wisdom to himself; for the giants were the enemies of the Æsir, and the wisdom which they had been hoarding for ages before the gods were made was generally used for evil purposes. Moreover, Odin longed and longed to become the wisest being in the world. So he resolved to win a draught from Mimer's well, if in any way that could be done.

One night, when the sun had set behind the mountains of Midgard, Odin put on his broad-brimmed hat and his striped cloak, and taking his famous staff in his hand, trudged down the long bridge to where it ended by Mimer's secret grotto.

"Good day, Mimer," said Odin, entering; "I have come for a drink from your well."

The giant was sitting with his knees drawn up to his chin, his long white beard falling over his folded arms, and his head nodding; for Mimer was very old, and he often fell asleep while watching over his precious spring. He woke with a frown at Odin's words. "You want a drink from my well, do you?" he growled. "Hey! I let no one drink from my well."

"Nevertheless, you must let me have a draught from your glittering horn," insisted Odin, "and I will pay you for it."

"Oho, you will pay me for it, will you?" echoed Mimer, eyeing his visitor keenly. For now that he was wide awake, his wisdom taught him that this was no ordinary stranger. "What will you pay for a drink from my well, and why do you wish it so much?"

"I can see with my eyes all that goes on in heaven and upon earth," said Odin, "but I cannot see into the depths of ocean. I lack the hidden wisdom of the deep – the wit that lies at the bottom of your fountain. My ravens tell me many secrets; but I would know all. And as for payment, ask what you will, and I will pledge anything in return for the draught of wisdom."

Then Mimer's keen glance grew keener. "You are Odin, of the race of gods," he cried. "We giants are centuries older than you, and our wisdom which we have treasured during these ages, when we were the only creatures in all space, is a precious thing. If I grant you a draught from my well, you will become as one of us, a wise and dangerous enemy. It is a goodly price, Odin, which I shall demand for a boon so great."

Now Odin was growing impatient for the sparkling water. "Ask your price," he frowned. "I have promised that I will pay."

"What say you, then, to leaving one of those far-seeing eyes of yours at the bottom of my well?" asked Mimer, hoping that he would refuse the bargain. "This is the only payment I will take."

Odin hesitated. It was indeed a heavy price, and one that he could ill afford, for he was proud of his noble beauty. But he glanced at the magic fountain bubbling mysteriously in the shadow, and he knew that he must have the draught.

"Give me the glittering horn," he answered. "I pledge you my eye for a draught to the brim."

Very unwillingly Mimer filled the horn from the fountain of wisdom and handed it to Odin. "Drink, then," he said, "drink and grow wise. This hour is the beginning of trouble between your race and mine." And wise Mimer foretold the truth.

Odin thought merely of the wisdom which was to be his. He seized the horn eagerly, and emptied it without delay. From that moment he became wiser than anyone else in the world except Mimer himself.

Now he had the price to pay, which was not so pleasant. When he went away from the grotto, he left at the bottom of the dark pool one of his fiery eyes, which twinkled and winked up through the magic depths like the reflection of a star. This is how Odin lost his eye, and why from that day he was careful to pull his grey hat low over his face when he wanted to pass unnoticed. For by this oddity folk could easily recognize the wise lord of Asgard.

In the bright morning, when the sun rose over the mountains of Midgard, old Mimer drank from his bubbly well a draught of the wise water that flowed over Odin's pledge. Doing so, from his underground grotto he saw all that befell in heaven and on earth. So that he also was wiser by the bargain. Mimer seemed to have secured rather the best of it; for he lost nothing that he could not spare, while Odin lost what no man can well part with – one of the good windows wherethrough his heart looks out upon the world. But there was a sequel to these doings which made the balance swing down in Odin's favour.

Not long after this, the Æsir quarrelled with the Vanir, wild enemies of theirs, and there was a terrible battle. But in the end the two sides made peace; and to prove that they meant never to quarrel again, they exchanged hostages. The Vanir gave to the Æsir old Niörd the rich, the lord of the sea and the ocean wind, with his two children, Frey and Freia. This was indeed a gracious gift; for Freia was the most beautiful maid in the world, and her twin brother was almost as fair. To the Vanir in return Father Odin gave his own brother Hœnir. And with Hœnir he sent Mimer the wise, whom he took from his lonely well.

Now the Vanir made Hœnir their chief, thinking that he must be very wise because he was the brother of great Odin, who had lately become famous for his wisdom. They did not know the secret of Mimer's well, how the hoary old giant was far more wise than anyone who had not quaffed of the magic water. It is true that in the assemblies of the Vanir Hœnir gave excellent counsel. But this was because Mimer whispered in Hœnir's ear all the wisdom that he uttered. Witless Hœnir was quite helpless without his aid, and did not know what to do or say. Whenever Mimer was absent he would look nervous and frightened, and if folk questioned him he always answered: –

"Yes, ah yes! Now go and consult someone else."

Of course the Vanir soon grew very angry at such silly answers from their chief, and presently they began to suspect the truth. "Odin has deceived us," they said. "He has sent us his foolish brother with a witch to tell him what to say. Ha! We will show him that we understand the trick." So they cut off poor old Mimer's head and sent it to Odin as a present.

The tales do not say what Odin thought of the gift. Perhaps he was glad that now there was no one in the whole world who could be called so wise as himself. Perhaps he was sorry for the danger into which he had thrust a poor old giant who had never done him any wrong, except to be a giant of the race which the Æsir hated. Perhaps he was a little ashamed of the trick which he had played the Vanir. Odin's new wisdom showed him how to prepare Mimer's head with herbs and charms, so that it stood up by itself quite naturally and seemed not dead. Thenceforth Odin kept it near him, and learned from it many useful secrets which it had not forgotten.

So in the end Odin fared better than the unhappy Mimer, whose worst fault was that he knew more than most folk. That is a dangerous fault, as others have found; though it is not one for which many of us need fear being punished.

The Theft of the Hammer

IT WAS TO THE SWEET AND LOVING GOD BALDUR that the earth owed its warmth and beauty, its rich fruit and its rare harvests. How the Frost Giants hated Baldur, and how they struggled year after year to wrest the earth from him!

They hated the warmth Baldur brought with him, for it destroyed their power. They hated the sweet flowers and the soft grass and the tiny leaves that everywhere peeped out when the winds whispered, "Baldur is coming, Baldur is coming."

But no sooner had Baldur turned away and said, "Goodbye, dear Earth, for a little time, remember Baldur loves you and will come back again to you," than the Frost Giants would creep out from their mountain gorges and burst forth upon the fields and forests.

The tiny bubbling brooks they would seal with their cruel chains of ice; even the great rivers could not hold their freedom against the giant power.

Like angry fiends they would seize upon the leaves and tear them from the trees. The tiny flowers hung their heads and shrivelled with fear when they approached; nor were the Frost Giants content until the whole earth lay brown and cold and barren beneath their hand. Then, all beauty swept away, they covered over all, their silent sheet of snow, and stood, grim sentinels, cold and hard, guarding their work of destruction and desolation.

There was deep silence when the Frost Giants reigned; no sound was heard save the sad moaning among the branches of the forest, as the firs and pine trees bent towards each other and whispered of the days when Baldur shone upon them.

But the Frost Giants never yet had conquered; never yet had Baldur failed to return to the trees and flowers and rivers and streams that he loved so well.

At his first step upon the ice, a crackling sound was heard – a sound which awoke the sleeping earth and warned the Frost Giants to flee to their mountains.

"Baldur has come! Baldur has come!" the birds and every living thing would cry; and a rustle and sound of music would thrill the waiting earth.

Then came always a mighty battle. The Frost Giants lashed the waters and rocked the trees. The winds shrieked, the sky grew cold and black. The snows fell and the driving rain beat against the earth. But Baldur, the quiet, firm, loving Baldur always conquered. How, he himself could hardly tell. He did not fight; he did not storm. He only bent his shining face over the struggling earth and waited.

Little by little, when their fury was spent, the Frost Giants, defiant but conquered, retreated. The great sheets of ice broke up, and the rivers rushed forth singing their mad songs of joy and freedom. The snows faded away, and one by one the little flowers peeped forth again.

All now was happiness and warmth and fragrance; the flowers bloomed; the fruits turned mellow; the sky grew warm; and the pines and fir trees breathed deep sighs of rest and contentment that once again sweet Baldur was among them.

And not only did the Frost Giants hate Baldur, but they hated Frey, who often robbed them of the fruits and flowers they loved to breathe their bitter breath upon and kill. Thor, too, they hated; for with his magic hammer, he now, more than ever, loved to bring forth the lightning and the thunder, and to send down upon the earth refreshing showers of soft, warm rain.

As the Frost Giants scowled down from their icy castles, and saw the little flowers turn up their happy faces to drink in the sparkling drops, and heard the birds trill their happy songs, and smelled the rich fragrance of the damp firs and pines, they roared with anger and vexation.

"Let us revenge ourselves upon this insolent Thor who robs us of our rights," they bellowed to each other across the great valleys that separated their giant peaks.

"We can do nothing so long as he holds the magic hammer," growled one.

"We must steal the hammer from him," shouted another.

"Steal the hammer! Steal the hammer!" shouted all the giants until the very skies echoed with the words.

"And I will be the one to steal it," bellowed Thrym, the strongest and greatest giant of them all.

"And, moreover, I will go at once to the city of Asgard. The gods are asleep. With my great eye, I can see even now the hammer lying beside the sleeping Thor. Guard my castle. I am gone."

And putting on the guise of a great bird, Thrym spread his wings and flew across the black night to Asgard. The gods shivered in their sleep as he entered and breathed his breath upon the summer air of heaven, but knew not what had chilled them.

In the morning there was a heavy frost upon the gateways. There was a chill in the air. For Thrym, the Frost Giant, had crept in upon them. He had crept even to the hall in which the mighty Thor was sleeping. He had crept close beside the mighty god – and the magic hammer was gone.

The Finding of the Hammer

"MY HAMMER! MY HAMMER!" thundered Thor, awaking and finding it gone.

The gods in all Asgard awoke with a start.

"What a crash of thunder! So quick, so sharp!" cried the earth-people; for they did not know it was a cry of rage from Thor.

"Loki," thundered Thor again. "Put you on wings. Go you to the home of the Frost Giants and bring back my hammer. Someone of them has stolen it. Go! Go! I say."

And Loki, who had been a very obedient servant to Thor since his theft of the golden hair of Sif, put on the magic wings and fled away.

"What brings you here in the land of the Frost Giants?" growled Thrym, as Loki alighted before him.

"I have come for the hammer you have stolen from Thor," answered Loki boldly, seeing at once, from the jeering look in Thrym's eye, that he was the thief.

"You will never find it," sneered Thrym. "It is well hidden; but I will send it back to you if Odin will send me Freyja for my wife."

Loki begged and coaxed and threatened; but it was all of no avail. "Never," bellowed Thrym, "until you send Freyja to me."

"She shall go," thundered Thor, when Loki came back to Asgard. "Whatever the price, the hammer must be brought back. Asgard is not safe without it."

But Freyja was as fierce as had been Thrym himself. "I will not go," she insisted. "Never! Never! Never will I go!"

"I say you must," thundered Thor. But although Thor's thunders were terrible and his frown was deep and inky black, Freyja was not to be moved either by pleading or threatening.

"Go yourself," said she. "Dress yourself as a goddess and go." Nor would she listen even to another word. Thor thundered and rumbled and rolled. It was all of no avail. Freyja was a goddess and would not be driven.

"I will go," said Thor at last. "Bring me a bridal dress. Hang a necklace around my neck. Bind a bridal veil about my head. The giants are as stupid as they are large; and I will set forth in the name of Freyja to meet the giant Thrym."

Thor was quickly dressed, and the bridal party set forth across the sky in the chariot of the Sungod. How the thunder rolled! How the lightning flashed from the angry eyes of Thor! How he grumbled and rumbled!

Jotunheim was reached. The Sungod lowered his chariot behind the hills; and a soft, red light spread over the earth and sky as the bridal party entered the castle of the giant Thrym.

"Freyja has come! Freyja has come!" bellowed Thrym. "Come, come, everyone to the bridal feast! Come, come to the feast of Thrym and Freyja!"

The giants in all the mountains round about answered to the call of Thrym. An hour, and the huge castle was filled with the huge guests. A great feast was held. But through it all Thor sat silent and motionless. Indeed, he dared not move; he dared not speak lest the thunder burst forth from his lips, or the lightning shoot forth from his eyes.

"Now lift the veil from Freyja's face," bellowed Thrym, when all save the bride herself had eaten and drank their fill. "Let me see the eyes of my bride. Let us all look upon the face of my goddess bride."

"Not yet," whispered Loki coming forward; "it was the command of Thor that the veil should not be lifted, nor should you claim Freyja for your own, until the hammer was placed in her hand, to be returned to the gods."

"Bring in the hammer! Bring in the hammer!" roared Thrym, full of loud, good humour.

The hammer was brought. Hardly could Thor wait to have it placed in his hand.

His thunder began to rumble. There was a dangerous light in his eyes; but Thrym and the guests saw none of this. But hardly was the hammer within his reach when forth Thor sprang, seized it in his clutched fingers, tore aside the bridal veil, and with a rumble and a roar that shook the mountains of Jotunheim and razed the great stone castles to the ground, he poured out his lightning upon the giants, one and all. Right and left he swung the mighty weapon; the giants quaked and trembled with terror; Thrym ran and hid himself behind a mountain; the air was white with lightning; the hills rang with the crashings of the thunder; the seas lashed and foamed and answered back the echoes; the walls of Jotunheim shook and trembled.

And now the chariot of the Sungod was near at hand. Into it Thor and Loki leaped, and were borne back to the city of the gods. The hammer was restored. Again Thor held it in his mighty grasp. He held it, and Asgard once more was safe.

When Thor Went to Jotunheim

ODIN, HE OF THE NINE-AND-FORTY NAMES, dwelt in bright Asgard with his fellow Æsir and Asynjar. Father of gods and men though he was, born though he was of a giant mother, there was bitter strife between him and the vast Frost and Mountain Giants, the seed of Ymir's feet. They alone ventured openly to dispute his sovereignty.

Mightiest of the other twelve Æsir was the All-father's eldest Earth-born son, Thor. Two goats of magical powers drew his chariot; iron gauntlets he had with which to grasp Miolnir, the hammer that none might withstand; when he girded about his loins the belt of strength, even his god-like might was doubled. He alone of all the gods must wade the mist-rivers and ascend into Asgard on foot, lest his flaming, thundering chariot destroy Bifrost, the trembling rainbow bridge over which all the rest of the celestial company rode daily to and from the judgment-seat below.

Many a Frost Giant had been dashed down into the gloom of Nifelhel by this Miolnir-hammer, which the dwarf artist Sindre had forged for the Asa god; but this monster race held the secrets of black sorcery, and in this way they were at times a match for the powers of Asgard.

So Thor discovered on a certain expedition.

One day he left his vast mansion Bilskirnir, with its five hundred and forty halls, and accompanied by Loki, set out towards Jotunheim. Northward they journeyed a whole day, in the goat-drawn car, till they came to Alfheim, where the sons of Ivalde guarded the southern shores of the great sea against the giants who dwelt beyond it, lest these attempt to attack Asgard from his side.

As was his custom, Thor stopped for the night at the house of Egil, the master archer, able to travel on his skis over both snow and water: brother, too, he was to Volund, craftiest of smiths, who was later to forge the sword of victory, fatal even to the gods. There dwelt with Egil his foster-son Thialfi, who had been found as an infant on a tide-washed sandbar of the sea: he was swiftest of foot of all who lived in Midgard, the home of men; for in truth he was that same Frey who afterwards sat in Asgard. He and his sister Roska were very dear to Egil.

Right welcome was Thor to Egil. Yet when mealtime came there was a scarcity of food for the company.

"Little shall that trouble us," cried Thor, with his rumbling laugh that shook the hall. "The meat I like best is that which carries me when I do not carry it."

Followed by Loki and the wondering Thialfi, he strode out into the darkness to where his strong-horned goats were stalled.

Smiling at the boy's amazement, he killed the beautiful creatures, skinned them, cut up the carcasses with great care, and put the flesh into the kettles to stew. When the meal was ready, he invited all to join, and while Thialfi found it hard to forget the trim and graceful animals, so full of life and spirit, he had to admit that he had never before tasted such delicious fare.

"Eat your fill, everybody," said Thor. "None need go hungry when Tanngniast and Tanngrisnir are on the board. But one caution I must give: not a bone must be broken. When we are through, let the boy gather every bone, sort out the two sets, and put one pile in each of the skins by the hearth yonder."

When all were satisfied, Thor and Egil fell to talk, recounting their expeditions against the foes of the gods in Jotunheim, while Thialfi obediently gathered together the bones, and arranged them in the hides.

An evil smile flitted over the thin face of crafty Loki as he perceived that the two warriors had become completely absorbed in their tales of past exploits. Thor was now reminding Egil of that famous adventure when he himself, wounded in the forehead, had borne his companion with a frozen foot across the foggy Elivagar water and its magic terrors. He was lost to everything that went on around him, laughing aloud and smiting his great thigh as he lived over those moments of tense excitement.

As Thialfi knelt at the other end of the wide hearth, painstakingly striving to complete his task, he started at a low whisper from the shadow beyond.

"Did you like the meat?"

"Yes," answered the boy in surprise, looking up. He could hardly see the features of his questioner, but the eyes gleamed, almost like the blaze from the burning logs in the fireplace.

"You have not tasted the best yet," said the smooth voice. "The real strength and sweetness is in the marrow."

Thialfi stared at him.

"Yes, that is like honey, and he who eats of it can go for days without any other nourishment. Nor can I imagine why he was so stingy as to withhold the best."

Still the youth did not know what to say.

"Better try it," continued Loki. "That long leg bone there is just full of sweetness."

"Oh no," said Thialfi, involuntarily lowering his voice to the same pitch. "He forbade us to break any of them."

"What nonsense. Why should you be so careful of that rubbish? You saw yourself what he did to the living animals: how could he really mind after that if just one picked bone were a little chipped? You'll never have another chance to taste such fare as only those in Asgard know."

"I don't like to," whispered the boy. "He might be angry."

"Angry! He'll never know. Why should he poke about and find a piece at the bottom of the pile? And if he should notice it, it would simply be an accident that might have happened a dozen times already."

Thialfi hesitated.

"It makes no difference to me, of course," went on the tempter. "But I don't see why you should be deprived of the best part when it can't possibly hurt anybody to take it. Besides, I've heard you were a wonderful runner, and I have an idea that the one who tastes of that marrow will find his powers marvellously increased."

The youth's eyes shone: he was proud of his ability to outstrip all with whom he had raced, and he could not resist this idea.

Glancing over his shoulder, he saw the pair still deep in their reminiscences. With a sudden impulse he thrust the leg bone beneath his skin coat, and went quietly out into the darkness. Gently he chipped off a piece of the bone and sucked out the marrow. It was delicious, as Loki had said, and his excited imagination made him fancy he could already feel a waxing of vigour in his muscles. Yet it was with a guilty feeling that he stole back and hid the fractured piece at the bottom of one of the piles. Well pleased was Loki, for he believed he had without danger to himself sown enmity between these two defenders of Asgard.

Presently all went to bed. Silence fell upon the great hall and the sleeping-rooms; but Thialfi trembled and started and tossed, a prey to terrifying dreams.

It was still dark within the hall when Thor rose, though outside the dawn light began to show in the east. He kindled the fire on the spreading hearth, and the leaping flames soon brightened the place. Thialfi awoke. From his couch he could see past the drawn skin curtain into the large apartment. A feeling of panic crept over him as he saw the huge distorted shadow which the fire threw against the wall, now shrinking, now shooting up to monstrousness. For the shadow was busy with something that lay beside the hearth – and the youth remembered only too well that all was not right with the contents of those skins.

Thor placed the two goats' pelts before him. He took out his great hammer, Miolnir, and waved it solemnly over the piles, muttering potent words. Thialfi stretched forward breathlessly to see.

What was his amazement when the bundles of dead bones began to stir. The hides moved and stretched and rounded. Before his unbelieving eyes the two trim goats stood up alive, vigorous and handsome as ever.

But no! One was not as he had been. The poor creature was lame; it limped, dragging one hind leg, as it moved.

Thialfi crouched down again, trembling, as he saw the big man bend swiftly to examine the injured leg.

Then there was a roar of anger which shook the beams. Everybody was running in. Miolnir was out once more, not to restore life this time – far from it: Thor was vowing vengeance and threatening to destroy his friend Egil and the whole household for the injury done to this cherished possession; his red hair stood out like flames about his massive head; he gripped the terrible hammer so hard that the joints of his fingers showed white in the firelight.

At that Thialfi dragged himself forward. Half dead with fear, he confessed what he had done, saying not a word of Loki's tempting.

Egil, as much disturbed as his guest, protested his desire to make amends.

"Payment is due," said he. "It is for you to state the price."

The sight of the frightened youth had somewhat calmed Thor's anger. This graceful, slender body was no fit object for Miolnir's weight. Slowly his vast muscles relaxed.

"It is the law," said he. "Let him pay who committed the fault: he and his sister shall be my bond-servants from this day forth."

This punishment seemed mild enough to Thialfi; for he was secretly drawn to this open-faced mighty one whose blue eyes harboured no meanness, and who was clearly good-natured despite his sudden bursts of fierceness. Moreover, the prospect of roaming abroad with him was far from displeasing. As for the beautiful Roska – she had nothing to say about it. Anyhow, where Thialfi went was the place she would choose to be.

So peace was restored, and all sat down to the morning meal content, save crafty Loki.

Leaving the goats with Egil, Thor and his companions set forth on foot. The chill mists and unfathomed depths of the Elivagar sea had no terrors for him; but when they had passed over its expanse, they came to a strange and gloomy country surrounding the stronghold of the giants.

Endlessly the forest stretched away; and all day they wandered through its pathless mazes without sight of any human being. There was no sign of even beast or bird, and while swift-footed Thialfi, who carried Thor's wallet, scoured the thickets on either side, all his wood-craft failed to discover anything in the way of food.

Darkness settled down upon them almost as soon as the sun disappeared. The question of a place to spend the night became urgent. Searching on all sides in the gathering dusk, they finally came upon a large structure with an entrance that took up the whole width of one end.

No one appeared or answered to their shouts; so they entered and lay down in the main hall, glad of any place to lay their heads after their exhausting day.

Towards midnight, when they were all slumbering soundly, they were rudely awakened by an earthquake which shook the whole building. Leaping to their feet, they staggered to and fro over the heaving floor, expecting each moment to feel the roof fall upon their heads. But the swaying stopped presently and Thor bade them seek some place of safety.

To the right they found a smaller chamber, without any door or curtain; and the three crept into the farthest corner of this and dropped down, trembling with fear. Thor, however, remained at the entrance. Holding Miolnir ready, he stayed on guard the rest of the night, listening to an extraordinary noise like a rushing wind which he could hear outside from time to time.

As soon as it was light, he stepped out of the building to investigate this roaring sound.

There, stretched out on the ground, was a monstrous creature, so huge that he looked like the fallen trunk of some primeval fir tree. He was fast asleep, and it was his snoring which had sounded like a howling winter gale.

Many a giant as Thor had seen and encountered, the bulk of this man-mountain made him pause in astonishment. Then he quietly girded about him the belt of strength, for if ever he needed to double his powers it was now.

Just then the giant opened his eyes, which looked like muddy lakes. He yawned, stretched himself and stood up – and his head was almost lost in the tops of the trees.

For the only time in his history Thor hesitated to join in open battle.

"Who are you?" he asked.

"My name is Skrymir," said the other. His voice was like the bellow of the thunder, and Loki, Thialfi and Roska ran to the entrance and looked out at the reverberating sound.

"As for you," continued the giant, "I know you well: you are Asa-Thor. But what have you done with my glove?"

With that he stretched down his big hand towards the awed group of three, which scattered before him; and they realized that the building in which they had lodged was the creature's glove, the smaller room to which they had fled being the thumb.

"Shall we travel together?" asked Skrymir, smiling in a way that made Thor's cheeks burn.

"As you will," replied the latter.

Thereupon the giant sat down, opened a prodigious wallet, and fell to his breakfast; but Thor and his comrades drew apart by themselves and shared their scanty stock of provisions.

When they had finished –

"Here," said Skrymir, "let me carry your food. It will not weigh me down."

So saying, he thrust Thor's wallet into his own and started off through the forest with such tremendous strides that they could hardly keep in sight of him.

All day long he led them at this pace amid the endless woods; and Roska for one was more than glad, despite her brother's aid, when dusk brought him to a halt beside an ancient oak.

"We have loitered along slowly enough," he said, "yet I suppose it is time to sleep. I am not hungry; you can take the wallet and get your own meal. If you need a roof over your heads, my glove is there."

He stretched himself out and presently was snoring so that one could have heard him a mile away.

Dark and silent, Thor finally took the leather bag, to get out their food. His feelings were not smoothed when he found he could not untie the knots. In growing anger he worked away at the stubborn thongs, but he could make no impression on the hard knots. Then, his patience exhausted, he tried to break the fastenings. Still they defied his efforts.

Enraged at being thus trifled with, he grasped Miolnir, stepped forward, and dashed it at the giant's head.

Skrymir stirred himself slightly.

"What was that – a leaf?" he asked sleepily. "Have you little ones supped yet? Have you gone to sleep?"

"We are just lying down," muttered Thor. Puzzled and upset, he strode off and lay down under another oak.

But he could not sleep. The stertorous snores of the giant seemed to mock him.

Finally he sprang up again and walked cautiously back. The moonlight shone full on the giant's bulky form. Heaving his hammer aloft, he launched it with such violence that the head buried itself in Skrymir's skull.

"What's happening?" called out the giant, rolling over. "An acorn dropped right on my head. How do you fare, Thor?"

"All right," called back the other, stealing away behind the tree trunks. "I woke when you called out. There is plenty of time to sleep yet."

Again all was quiet, except in Thor's breast, where rage and humiliation contended in a turmoil. He forced himself to lie still, calming his burning wrath with the assurance that when the moment came for a third blow, he would take ample revenge for this disgrace. The creature did not exist who could treat Asa-Thor in this manner.

A long time he waited both to recover his poise and to be sure the other was really asleep again. At length, a little before daybreak, he rose softly, and again approached the slumbering giant.

His hands ran over the magic belt as if to draw from it the last bit of aid. Gripping Miolnir with both hands, he summoned up every power of his heaving muscles. The remembrance of his failures burned in his veins and seemed to double his strength and determination.

He whirled Miolnir about his head, and brought it down with his utmost force upon the sleeper. To his grim satisfaction, he saw it smash into the giant's cheek up to the very handle.

To his consternation, Skrymir sat up and appeared to brush something from his face.

"There must be birds roosting in this tree," said he disgustedly. "How can one sleep when they are scratching moss and bark loose so that it falls over one's head?"

He looked about.

"What! Are you awake, too, Thor? I suppose it is time to get up anyhow; for you say you want to get to Utgard. The city is not far now. I must warn you, though, of one thing. I have heard you whispering together as if you thought my size was something remarkable; but if you go to Utgard, you will see many far taller than I. So I counsel you against making much of yourselves, for Utgard-Loki's men will have little patience with the boasting of such mannikins. Indeed, if you are wise, you will turn back at once. However, if you persist in your folly, your road lies east. I go northward, to those cliffs in the distance yonder."

He threw his wallet over his shoulder and went off, unheeding Thor's resentful glare.

Following his directions, the party presently passed out of the forest, and travelled over a wide plain.

Towards noon they came upon the city of Utgard. So lofty were its walls and buildings that their heads bent back on their necks as they gazed up to the pinnacles of the towers.

When they came close, they saw nobody; but a vast gate of ponderous bars closed the way. It was locked and bolted. After trying for some time to call a keeper, and then to unfasten the gate, Thor and his comrades squeezed between the bars and entered the silent city.

They went through one deserted street after another, till they saw before them a magnificent palace, whose door stood wide. Walking boldly in, they found themselves in a hall that dwarfed anything they had ever beheld. Sitting on benches were ranged two lines of men, the first glance at whom convinced the travellers that Skrymir had spoken truly.

Advancing to the raised seat, they saluted the ruler, Utgard-Loki. But the king gazed at them with a smile. Thor was by no means accustomed to such scornful treatment, and his companions could perceive his heat growing as this contemptuous silence continued.

At length the king spoke:

"It is tedious to ask for tidings of a long journey; yet if I mistake not, that little one there must be Asa-Thor."

"Possibly," he went on, addressing Thor directly, "you may be more than you appear. What can you do, you and these with you? No one stays in Utgard unless he can in some feat of skill or strength excel all others."

"I have a feat," spoke up Loki. "I can eat quicker than any here. I am ready to prove it against all."

"That will be worth seeing, if you can make your boast good," said the giant king. "It shall be put to the test."

He called to one named Logi, sitting on a further bench. A trough filled with fresh meat was brought in, and placed between the two. At the signal, both began to eat, one from each end.

Loki strove his utmost, and yet when he reached the middle of the trough he met his antagonist there. Moreover, it was seen that while he had devoured all the flesh on his side, Logi had consumed flesh, bone and the trough to boot. There could be no gainsaying that the visitor was vanquished.

"And what can you do?" asked Utgard-Loki, looking at Thialfi.

"I can run," said the youth.

"We shall soon see about that. Let us go outside to the course."

The whole company went forth to a level stretch of plain. A slim youth whom they called Hugi took his place beside Thialfi. The latter, who had never been beaten in swiftness, smiled confidently.

The word was given. The two runners were off like arrows from the bow. But Thialfi could hardly credit his eyes when, before he had covered half the distance to the turning-point, he met Hugi coming back already.

"You will have to ply your legs better than that," said Utgard-Loki, "if you expect to win in this company."

A second course was run. Thialfi strained every nerve and muscle to the utmost. His heartbeat as if it would burst through his ribs. Yet Hugi reached the goal when he was still a bowshot off.

"You run bravely," remarked the king. "Still, it seems to me this match will not be yours. The third trial must decide."

Once more they toed the mark and sped away. Thialfi did his best, but he was wearied with his last effort; his swift adversary crossed the finish line ere he had quite gone halfway.

The whole assemblage declared there was no need of further trial. Utgard-Loki turned to Thor.

"We have heard much of your prowess, Asa. What is your choice to prove to us that rumour's tales are true?"

"I will drink a draught with any of you," growled Thor between his teeth.

"Excellent," returned the king. He led the way back into the hall, and bade his cup-bearer bring the drinking-horn. It was borne forth.

"A good drinker," remarked Utgard-Loki, "empties this at a single draught. Some men make two of it. The puniest of all can take it off in three."

Thor looked at the horn critically. It did not appear of extra size, though the end stretched away behind the bearer. Moreover, he was very thirsty. So little doubt had he of emptying it at a draught, that he did not pause to take breath, but set it to his lips and pulled long and deeply.

He set it down with a clatter, thinking to ask for more. To his chagrin, he could hardly perceive any lowering of the liquor.

"Well!" exclaimed the king. "Surely that is not much for Asa-Thor to boast of. I would not have believed it if it had been told me. Perhaps, though, you were saving yourself for a second draught."

Without answering, Thor seized the horn once more and quaffed a mighty draught. Yet on looking in, it seemed as if he had made less impression than before. Still the vessel could now be carried without spilling.

The king shook his head. "A man must use his own sort of skill. Certainly, though, you have left most of the task for your last attempt. I fear your reputation here will hardly match what you have in Asgard if this is a sample of your prowess."

Too angry to speak now, Thor grasped the horn again. Tilting it back, he drank and drank till he thought he would burst with the effort. But when he could do nothing more, he found he had emptied only the top inch or two.

He handed the horn back to the cup-bearer.

"I see plainly," said Utgard-Loki, "that what we have heard of you was a traveller's tale. Still, do you wish to try something else? I confess it does not seem likely that you will bear away many prizes here."

"I know," Thor replied doggedly, "that such draughts would not be accounted small among the Æsir – but I will attempt another feat. What have you to propose?"

"We have a game here, a sort of childish exercise. Before witnessing this last performance, I would scarce have dared mention it to Asa-Thor. It is merely lifting my cat from the floor."

A large grey cat walked out, its tail held high.

Thor looked at it, uncertain.

"He is large – for a cat," said the king.

Stung to the quick, Thor stepped forward, put a hand under the beast's belly and lifted hard.

The cat arched his back, not resisting at all. Heave and strain as he might, Thor could only get one paw off the floor.

"I imagined as much," said Utgard-Loki. "Even my cat is too large for such a little one."

"Little I may be," cried Thor. "Yet let me see the man here who will wrestle with me at this moment."

Utgard-Loki looked at the massive figures ranged along the benches.

"I see no one small enough for that. If you must wrestle, however – call old Elli, the nurse. She has thrown many a better man than you have yet proved yourself."

In came a bent, withered, toothless old crone. At the king's bidding, she grappled with the aroused Thor.

Violently he strove, till the muscles on his arms and legs stood out like ropes. Locking his mighty arms, he strained this way and that. The more he put forth his power, the firmer did the frail old woman seem to stand.

Then Thor began to feel an inexorable grip tightening upon himself. He struggled as if his very life hung on the issue. Yet his legs began to bend. Presently he was forced down upon one knee.

Old Elli released him and hobbled off. With heaving breast, dripping sweat, and vastly ashamed, Thor stood up before them.

"We need hardly further trial," said Utgard-Loki. "Besides, it grows late. Show them to the guest seats."

They were made welcome, and feasted that night with good cheer.

Next morning they prepared to depart. Utgard-Loki saw that they were bountifully provided with food and drink. He himself conducted them to the gate of the city.

"Well, Asa-Thor," said he, as they were about to separate, "are you satisfied with your visit to Utgard? Have you seen more powerful rulers elsewhere on your journeys?"

"Truly," replied honest Thor, "I have brought great shame upon the Æsir. Justly will ye say that I am one of little worth."

"Hardly that," said the giant king. "Now that you are outside of my city – which with my consent you will never enter again – I must tell you the truth. Had I imagined your powers and how near they would have brought me to disaster, you would by no means have seen the inside of it this time.

"Know, then, that I have deceived you all along with illusions.

"The wallet you could not open in the forest was bound with invisible iron wire. The least of the three strokes of your hammer would have ended my days: I brought before me a rocky mountain which you could not see; in this you will find three deep ravines, made by those blows.

"The contests here were illusions likewise.

"Though Loki ate like hunger, Logi who outmatched him was ardent fire itself.

"Of Hugi it was thought: how could even swift Thialfi keep pace with him?

"The horn you tried to empty reached to the sea; when you come to the shore you will see your draughts have caused the ocean itself to ebb. When we saw you lift one of the cat's paws from the floor, we were all terror-stricken: for the cat was in reality the great Midgard serpent which encompasses the whole earth. Nurse Elli was in fact old age – and never yet has man wrestled with her as have you.

"Therefore, let us never meet again. For in spite of all the marvels of your strength, you can never prevail against me because of my illusions."

Wild with anger, Thor laid hold of Miolnir. But Utgard-Loki had vanished. He would have destroyed the city, but even that had disappeared, leaving only a smooth and verdant plain.

There was no help for it save to return to their own land; and in truth as the Asa reflected upon what had happened, he was not so ill pleased as before.

Especially did he recall his feat of lifting the Midgard serpent; and the remembrance of his incredible exploit fired him with a resolution to match himself once more against this monstrous world-encircling progeny of Loki.

It was not long thereafter when he determined to wait no more for this. So hastily did he set out that he took neither car, nor goats, nor followers.

In the semblance of a young man he travelled forth, and at dusk came to the dwelling of a giant named Hymir, who lived by the Elivagar water.

Here he passed the night. At the evening meal he alone ate two of the oxen Hymir had prepared.

"I shall have to go fishing tomorrow to feed you," grumbled the host.

In the morning Hymir made his boat ready to go fishing. Thor offered to accompany him.

"Much use a midget like you would be," returned the giant. "You can eat, of a certainty; but rowing is quite another matter. Worse than that, you would get cold and terrified if I go out to my fishing-grounds and stay as I am accustomed to."

Sorely tempted to try Miolnir on the giant's skull, Thor dissembled:

"I will row as far as you say. We shall see which wishes to turn back first. What bait do we use?"

"Get a bait for yourself," returned the surly fellow.

Thor walked off to where the herd of oxen grazed. The leader was a huge coal-black bull. Seizing the beast by its horns, the Asa wrung off its head, carried it back to the boat and threw it in.

"Better if you had sat still," grumbled Hymir.

They pushed the boat through the breakers and put out to sea, each rowing with a pair of oars. Thor was aft, and Hymir was amazed to see how the boat shot through the waves, even against the strong wind.

Before long the giant pulled in his oars.

"Here is where I catch flat fish," said he.

"No, no; further out," said Thor, pulling harder than ever.

"Stop!" cried Hymir after a while. "We are getting near the dwelling of the Midgard serpent."

"Further out is better fishing," declared Thor; and he rowed on in spite of his companion's protests.

He stopped at last. Muttering, Hymir threw out his line. Presently he drew up a whale. Then another took hold.

Meanwhile Thor had taken out a line and hook, the size of which caused the giant to stare. Fastening the gory bull's head on the hook, he dropped it far down into the depths, till it actually reached the bottom.

He did not have to wait long. Something far down there seized the bait. The line tautened. Thor jerked violently. When the monster felt the hook, it pulled so hard that Thor was forced to hold on to the rowing pins to avoid being dragged overboard.

Then the Asa's spirit waxed high. He hauled at the line so that his feet went through the bottom of the boat and down to the ocean floor. Yet ever he pulled, so stoutly that presently the hideous head of the Midgard snake appeared above the surface.

Nothing daunted by the floods of venom which the beast spouted out at him, Thor darted fiery glances at his enemy, still striving to lift the head into the boat.

Hymir, however, terrified beyond measure and feeling the craft sink beneath him, took his knife out of the sheath and cut the line just as Thor launched his hammer.

The monster fell back and sank again to his immemorial abode.

We know not whether those speak truly who declare that Miolnir struck off its head at the bottom of the sea, or whether it still lies encircling the earth. But it is related among the exploits of Alexander the Great that being lowered in a glass cage to the depths of the ocean he beheld a prodigious monster going past, and sat for two days, watching its body ooze along all the time, before its 'tail and hinder parts' appeared. Which sounds as if Thor had not made a thorough job of it.

Certain it is, however, that Hymir said no word till they were again at the shore. Then he muttered:

"Do your share: carry the whales in or make the boat fast."

Whereupon Thor picked up boat, oars, whales and all, and bore the whole thing up the wooded hillside to the Jotun's dwelling.

The Stolen Wine

Part One

THERE HAD LAIN FOR AGES UPON AGES, hidden away in the great rocky cellar of one of the giant's castles, a cask of wine, which had been stolen from the gods.

Never before had the gods been able to learn what had become of it; what giant had stolen it, nor in what castle it was hidden.

But now that Odin had become All-wise, nothing could be concealed from him.

"I know at last where the wine lies hidden," said Odin one day to his son, Thor; "and I shall set forth to find it."

Thor brought down his hammer with a thud. "Let me go with you," cried he, springing up. "And let me fell to the earth with one blow of my magic hammer the giant who has stolen, and has kept hidden all these ages, our precious wine."

"No;" answered Odin, "this time I must go alone. The wine is guarded day and night, and it will not be easy to bring it away, even when I have found it. But watch for me, dear son. One day there will come, beating its wings against the shining gates of our city, a great white eagle. Do not harm the eagle. Open the gates to him; for that eagle will be Odin, returning with the stolen wine to our city of Asgard."

Then Odin put aside his sparkling crown and laid down his sceptre. His wonderful blue mantle, studded with stars and fastened always with a pale crescent moon, he also threw aside, and stepped forth in the garb of a common labourer. "It is in this guise that I shall win my way to the giant's castle," said Odin; and in a second he had passed out from the hall and was gone.

It was the giant, Suttung, that had stolen the wine, and it was in his castle that it had lain hidden all these years.

Now, of all the strong castles of all the giants, Suttung's castle was the strongest. The cellar was cut into the solid rock. Moreover, three sides of the castle rose in solid walls of granite; while the fourth, no less firm and strong, was built of massive blocks bound with hoops and bars and bolts of strongest iron and steel.

Now, Suttung had a brother, Bauge, who was a giant farmer. He kept nine strong slaves, half giants themselves, to do his work for him.

As Odin approached the fields of Bauge's farm, he saw the nine men hard at work.

"Your scythes are dull," said he, as he drew near.

"Yes, but we have no whetstone to sharpen them upon," answered the workmen, the great drops standing out upon their foreheads.

"I will sharpen them on mine," said Odin, drawing one from his pocket.

"It is a magic whetstone!" cried the men as they saw it work. "Give it to us. We need it more than you. Give it to us. Give it to us."

"Take it, then," answered Odin, throwing it high in the air and walking off.

"It is mine! It is mine! Let me have it! Give it to me! I will have it! Out of the way! It shall be mine!" screamed and quarrelled the nine men as they pushed and crowded, each one determined to catch the whetstone as it came down to earth.

At last it fell. Then a fiercer battle followed. The angry men fell upon each other. They dragged and pulled and threw each other to the ground. They pounded each other; they struck at each other with their scythes. On and on they fought. Hour after hour the battle waged; till at last the Sun god, in sheer dismay at so unloving a sight, hid his face behind the hills, and the nine men lay dead upon the fields.

It was an hour later when Odin reached the castle of Bauge.

"Can you give me shelter for the night?" he asked, as the giant appeared at the door of his castle.

"Yes, I can give you shelter; but you must look elsewhere for your breakfast. A strange thing has happened. My nine slaves, while at work in the field, have fallen in battle upon each other, and have killed each other. Not one of them is left alive to serve me."

"They must have been idle, quarrelsome fellows," answered Odin.

"They were, indeed," answered Bauge; "but how shall I get my work done without them?"

"I will do the work for you," answered Odin.

"You! There is but one of you, even if you were willing to try," answered Bauge with but little interest.

"But I can do the work of any nine workmen that ever served you."

The giant laughed. "A remarkable workman. Pray, do you ask the wages of nine men as well?"

"I ask no wages," answered Odin. "I only ask that, as my pay when the work is done, you shall give me a draught of wine from the cask hidden in your brother's cellar."

Bauge stared. "How did you know there is a cask in my brother's cellar?" he gasped.

"It is enough that I know it," answered Odin coldly.

Bauge looked at Odin. "He is better than no man," he thought to himself. "I may as well get what work from him I can, before he finds that no being on earth can enter that cellar or force my brother to give away one drop of that wine."

"Very well, you may go to work," he said aloud. "I cannot promise you that we can make our way into my brother's cellar; but I will do what I can to help you."

"That is all I ask," answered Odin. "Now let me sleep, for I am tired; and if I am to do nine men's work, I must have nine men's sleep."

"And must you have nine men's food?" cried Bauge.

"I think it very likely," answered Odin with an odd smile. "Now let me sleep."

Part Two

"What is your name?" asked Bauge of his new workman when they set forth the next morning to the fields.

"You may call me Bolverk," answered Odin.

"Will one name be enough for all nine of you?" said Bauge with a disagreeable curling of his upper lip.

"I will not burden your giant mind with more than one," Odin answered, a funny little twinkle in his eye.

The giant gave a furious grunt. He did not quite know whether his new workman was stupid, or, whether under all his seeming meekness, it might not be that he was making fun of him.

Well, Bauge set Bolverk to work, and then, lazy fellow that he was, stretched himself out on a mountainside to watch.

"That new workman of mine," he bellowed, calling the attention of a neighbour giant to Odin at work in the field; "do you see him down there among the corn? He says he can do nine men's work."

"A workman usually thinks himself equal to any nine other workingmen," roared back the neighbour. "Of course you have agreed to give him nine men's wages?"

Then the two giants roared with laughter. They thought they had said a very bright thing, and very likely they had. It is only because you and I are mere earth-children that we do not think so too.

As the days went on, Bauge began to laugh less and to wonder more at his strange workman. He worked on quietly from sunrise till sunset. He did not seem to hurry in his work; he did not work over hours. But, strange to say, the work went on, as the workman had promised. No nine men could have done more or could have done it better.

It was harvest time when Odin came; the time when Frey, the god of the fields and of all that grows, glides around among his children and covers them over, or gathers in their wealth and beauty. Like the kind, loving father he is, he whispers to them now of Njord who so soon will come, sweeping across the earth, breathing his cold freezing breath upon all the world, and covering it over with the cold white sheet that kills the flowers and the fruits. He teaches his children to curl themselves up beneath the earth until the cruel Njord is gone. For Njord seeks to kill the tiny leaves and buds, and shrivel the radiant flowers, that, through all the long, warm summer days, have lifted their faces so brightly to their good friend, the Sun god.

Perhaps it was because Frey and Odin worked together that there were such rare crops, and that the harvesting went on so smoothly. Certain it was that all the fields were cleared, the cellars were filled, and all was ready for the long, cold months to come, when cruel Njord was king.

Even Bauge was in good humour. "You are indeed a wonderful workman," he said to Odin, as the last cellar was fastened and he sat down to rest.

"You are kind," answered Odin, the funny little twinkle coming again into his eyes. "Perhaps you would be willing to come with me now to your brother, that I may drink from the cask of wine that he keeps so closely guarded in his cellar."

Bauge began to feel uncomfortable. "He will not allow either you or me to so much as look upon that wine. You cannot have it."

"Bauge," said Odin, growing very tall and godlike, his wonderful eyes flashing with a light like fire, "you promised to do all you could to help me. Come and do as I bid you."

Bauge stared. His first thought was to kill the workman on the spot: but there was something about him, he hardly knew what, that made him, instead, rise and follow Odin to the brother's castle.

"Tell me which cellar holds the wine," said Odin when they had reached the brother's mountain.

"This one," answered Bauge.

"Now take this auger. Make a hole with it through the solid wall."

Bauge obeyed like one in a dream. It was a magic auger. How it worked! How the powdered stone flew in a cloud about his face!

"This is a very—" Bauge stopped. What had become of his workman? Not a soul was in sight. Odin had disappeared. And to this day the giant never knew what became of him, nor does his brother know who stole his wine from the cellar.

The stupid Bauge stood staring, now at the auger, now at the hole in the wall. He saw a little worm climb up the wall and disappear through the hole. That is all he ever saw or ever knew.

The little worm laughed to itself as it crept in out of sight. "You are very stupid, Bauge, not to know me."

Reaching the inner side of the wall, the little worm stopped to look about. There stood the cask; and beside it sat the daughter of the giant. "Poor girl," said Odin – I mean, said the worm – to himself. "It is a bitter fate to be doomed to sit for ever in this wretched dungeon watching your father's stolen treasure. But be happy. Soon you will be free. There will be no wine to watch."

The young giantess must have heard his words, for she looked up. There, just in front of the hole, the ray of light falling full upon his golden hair, stood a most beautiful youth. He looked so kindly upon her, and his eyes were so full of pity!

Her heart went out to him at once.

"I am very tired," said he gently. "So very tired. I have come a long, long distance. My home is far from here. I cannot tell you how far – but very, very far. If you would give me just one draught from the cask of wine."

The poor girl, grateful for the sound of a friendly voice, and for the sight of a human face, arose and lifted the lid for him.

Odin leaned over the cask. He put his lips to the wine and drank.

"You are very thirsty," said the giantess.

"Very," answered Odin, drinking on and on.

"You are very thirsty," said the giantess again.

"Very," answered Odin, still drinking on and on and on.

"You are very thirsty," said the giantess again; this time louder, her voice filled with fear.

"Very," answered Odin, still drinking on and on and on and on. Nor did he stop till every drop was gone and the cask stood dry and empty.

The young giantess, realizing all too late that the wine was stolen, ran to the cellar gateway, shouting as only a giant can shout for help.

The gateway flew open. In rushed the giants, Bauge and his brother.

"The wine! The wine!" they cried.

"Stolen, stolen!" sobbed the giantess, her sobs shaking even the solid cellar walls.

"The thief! The thief!" cried the giants. "Where is the thief?"

But there was no thief to be found. There stood the empty cask. But the thief? There was no living creature to be seen.

No living creature? I should not have said quite that. For there arose from a darkened corner of the cellar a beautiful, great white bird. Its wings brushed against the sides of the gateway as it passed. Then higher and higher, up, up, far, far away beyond the sea, above the clouds it soared, nor rested till its great wings beat against the golden bars of the shining gates of Asgard.

The Apples of Life

Part One

AMONG THE GODS IN ASGARD dwelt the beautiful Idun, the goddess whose care it was to guard the apples of life.

"Idun," Odin had said as he gave into her hands the rosy apples, "to guard these apples and keep them for ever from all harm, is to do a greater service for Asgard than even Thor, with his mighty thunders, or Baldur, with his warm light, can do; for these are the apples of everlasting youth. Without them, what would Asgard be more than the cities of Midgard or of Jotunheim? What would the gods be more than the mortals of Midgard or the giants of Jotunheim? So guard them well, beautiful Idun, for to them you owe your beauty, even as we owe to them our never-fading youth."

One day, when all was quiet and peaceful and happy in the city of Asgard, Loki, feeling within him the stirring of his own evil heart, betook himself to Midgard in search of mischief. The peace and quiet of Asgard he could no longer endure. Then, too, it was to him a cruel delight to shoot his arrows into the lives of the helpless children of Midgard and make them sad.

O, Loki was a cruel god! "Surely," Odin would sometimes say, as he looked upon him and thought of the wretchedness that yet would fall on Asgard through Loki's wicked deeds, "surely, Loki has the spirit of a Frost Giant; and the Frost Giants are bitter, bitter foes to Asgard."

This day Loki longed for mischief. "I will go down to Midgard and find some happy heart to sadden," said he, his eyes shining with their wicked light.

Down the rainbow bridge he hastened, and, with a light bound, sprang upon a bright tree in the beautiful land of Midgard.

"Who are you?" cried he, seeing in the tree beside him a great, white bird.

But the bird made no reply; he only winked, and blinked, and stared at Loki, and crooned, and pruned his feathers.

"Do you not know a god speaks to you?" stormed Loki, growing angry even with a bird.

Still no answer.

"Was ever there such a stupid bird? Indeed, like the people of Midgard, you seem to have no wisdom," sneered Loki. And determined to vent his evil mood, he seized a branch and began to beat the bird.

Then a strange thing happened. The bird, who all this time had seemed so stupid – too stupid even to fly away – now seized upon the bough and held it fast. Loki pulled and pulled with all his godlike strength. He could not move it; it was as if held in the grasp of a giant.

"Stupid bird!" sneered Loki, when he found he could do the bird no harm. "I will not stay in the tree with such a stupid creature."

A strange sound – almost like a laugh of triumph – squeezed itself out from the beak of the big bird.

"Go, Loki, go at once. Go back to Asgard; or perhaps you would like to go with me to Jotunheim," spoke the bird at last. And as he spoke, he spread his wings and arose high in the air. Alas, alas for Loki, as the bird rose, he rose too; nor could he free himself. He screamed, he fought, he begged, he strove with all his godlike arts to free himself, but all in vain.

On, on they flew, the bird and Loki, across the sky, over and under and between the clouds, across the great wide sea, at last across the snow-white peaks, down, down to a castle in Jotunheim, in the land of the mighty Frost Giants, the terrible, the dreaded enemies of the gods.

"Let me free! Let me free!" foamed Loki, struggling against the bird, whose magic held him fast.

"I will never let you free," answered the bird, throwing off his disguise and standing forth a giant foe; "I will never let you free except on one condition."

"I grant it! I grant it! Whatever it is, I grant it," cried the coward, caring for nothing but to free himself.

"The condition is this," continued the giant coolly: "I will let you free if you will bring me, without delay, the apples of everlasting youth – the apples that Idun guards and watches over, locked so closely in the golden casket in the city of Asgard."

Loki stared. He caught his breath. To give up the apples of life – the fruit by which the gods were kept for ever young and strong and beautiful – that was too great a thing to ask even of Loki, evil as he was.

"There are no such apples," answered he, trying, as cowards always do, to hide himself behind a lie. "There are no such apples."

"Very well," answered the giant, opening a great dungeon door, and thrusting Loki in. "When you are ready to do what I say, you may come out; never until then." The great dungeon door creaked upon its terrible hinges and Loki was alone, a prisoner, at the mercy of the Frost Giant.

Loki howled and beat against the walls of the dungeon.

"Are you ready to do what I asked of you?" asked the Frost Giant, opening the great door the next morning.

"There are no such apples," cried Loki. "On my honour as a god, I swear it!"

The giant made no reply. The heavy door creaked again, and Loki was alone.

"Are you ready to do what I asked of you?" asked the Frost Giant, opening the great door the second morning.

"Anything in all Asgard, O Giant, I promise you – anything but the apples," cried Loki.

The giant made no reply. The heavy door creaked again, and Loki was alone.

"Are you willing to do what I asked of you?" asked the Frost Giant, opening the great door the third morning.

"One of the apples, O Giant, I might steal from Idun and escape with before the fruit was missed," Loki began.

The giant made no reply. The heavy door creaked again and Loki was alone.

"Are you ready to do what I asked of you?" asked the Frost Giant, opening the great door the fourth morning.

"Yes, two of the three apples will I promise to bring you. With even one left, the gods might be content; for even then their lives would be far longer than the life of mortals."

The giant made no reply. The heavy door creaked again and Loki was alone.

"Are you ready to do what I asked of you?" asked the Frost Giant, opening the great door the fifth morning.

"Yes," answered Loki, meekly.

"You are willing to bring the apples of life?"

"Yes."

"And you will bring all three of them?"

"Yes."

"And you will bring them at once?"

"Yes."

"Go, then. I will go with you. Outside the walls of the shining city I will wait for you to bring the apples to me."

Then putting on the guise of birds, the two set forth, reaching the gateway of the city just as the Sungod was pouring down his flood of red and golden light upon the shining spires. The whole city lay bathed in the sunset splendour.

"Idun," said Loki, going directly to her, "it is well you guard so closely these golden apples of life. Without them we should grow old and die, even as wretched mortals grow old and die."

"Indeed, it would fare ill with us if harm came to these precious apples," answered Idun. "See the rich bloom upon them. If that were lost, then would our bloom be lost as well, and we should grow old and wrinkled."

"Yes," answered Loki; "and still – it seems very strange – but outside the gate of our city, just on the outer walls, are growing apples, looking so like these I cannot tell them one from the other. Bring your apples with you and let us see if they are alike. If they should prove to be, then I will gather them for you, and we will put them all together in the golden casket."

"How strange!" thought Idun innocently.

The Frost Giant, in his great bird guise, wheeled round and round, impatiently awaiting the coming of Idun and the apples. Hardly had the gates closed upon her, when down he swooped, seized her in his great strong beak, and flew with her across the sea to his home among the mountains.

The days rolled on and on. The Sungod rose, and drove his chariot across the sky, and sank behind the distant purple hills a thousand times.

There was a gloom, a shadow over Asgard; for the gods were growing old. The life had gone out of their eyes; their smooth round faces had grown thin and peaked; their step was halting, and the feebleness of age was falling upon them.

"It is Loki who has done this," thundered Thor one day, when, from old age and weakness, he had been defeated in a battle with the now ever-youthful giants. "It is Loki who has done this, and we will bear it no longer. Look at Odin; even he grows weak and bent and trembling. He is like the old men in Midgard. He, Odin, the All-father."

Thor's indignation waxed stronger and stronger. He set forth in search of Loki. "I will not even wait for him to come," he thundered, seizing his hammer and setting forth. "I shall find him, the evil-hearted, somewhere making mischief among the innocent people of Midgard," said he.

Part Two

"Henceforth, O evil-hearted, cruel Loki," burst forth the angry Thor, "henceforth Thor guards the walls of Asgard. Midgard, the skies, he shall forsake; no more will he brew storms; never shall the thunder roll nor the lightning flash; for Thor will watch for ever upon the battlements of Asgard the approach of the evil god who has brought such grief upon us. Never shall he enter the gates of the city again. Let him dare approach even to the golden gates, and Thor will smite him with his mighty hammer."

Loki quailed before the fury of the great god Thor. To be an outcast from Asgard, even he could not bear. "Spare me, spare me!" whined the cowardly Loki. "Spare me once more, and I will go again to Jotunheim. I will bring back Idun and the three apples of life."

Thor stood looking at the cowardly Loki. He longed to strike him with the hammer; to kill him with his thunderbolt; to scorch him with his lightning arrows. But, evil as he was, Loki was immortal; he was the son of Odin.

"Go, then, you mischief-making, evil-hearted son of unhappy Odin! Go; and whether success is yours or not, remember Thor guards the walls of Asgard and watches with his thunders for your return. Never, never, as long as Thor wields the mighty hammer, and holds the powers of thunder and lightning, shall Loki enter the golden city without the golden apples of immortal life."

Without another word, Loki put on his guise of a great white bird and sped across the sea and sky, again to the land of Jotunheim.

Straight down he swooped upon the castle of the giant who, all this time, had kept Idun imprisoned in a strong walled tower of solid rock.

The giant was out upon the sea. "And it is well for me," thought Loki, "that he is. No power in Midgard or in Asgard could wrest these precious apples from the giant's grasp."

One quick look out over the mountains and down upon the sea, and Loki seized Idun in his talons, changed her at once into a nut, the apples safe within the shell, and swept away towards Asgard.

But alas for Loki! The giant had heard the whirr of the great white wings. Leaping to his feet in his boat, he scanned the sky with his sharp giant eye. "It is Loki! It is Loki!" bellowed he, catching sight of the great white bird among the clouds. "It is Loki! It is Loki! No bird of Midgard flies so high nor sweeps the air with such mighty wings."

With one great giant pull, he shot his boat upon the shore; with one great giant bound he struck the mountain top.

"The apples of life! The apples of life!" he thundered. "Gone! Gone! The apples of life are gone!"

One second, and putting on the guise of a great grey eagle he shot up into the sky in swift pursuit of Loki. The Sungod hid his chariot behind a cloud that the shadows might protect and cover Loki. Thor sent forth his thunder. The skies blackened; the wind beat back the great grey eagle; the lightning staggered and blinded him. Still on and on he flew, gaining in spite of all upon the track of Loki.

Every eye in Asgard was strained; every giant in Jotunheim stood breathless upon his mountain. The great round faces of the giants grew tense; the wrinkled aged faces of the gods grew pale. It was a terrible race. It was a race for life and health and everlasting youth.

"Build fires upon the walls! Heap up the brush! Stand ready with the tapers!" cried Odin, who foresaw the end.

The brush is heaped. Each god stands ready, his haggard face growing whiter and thinner with fright and dread and eagerness.

Already the rush of Loki's wings are heard. The eagle follows close. Nearer and nearer they come, closer and closer is the race. One moment more! – One second! – The frightened eyes of Loki can be seen, so near he is. Thor sends his blinding fire once more across the eagle's track. It reels, for an instant it falls back. In that one second, with one last mighty stroke, Loki clears the walls and falls, exhausted, breathless, almost dead upon the golden pavement of the city.

"The fires! The fires! The fires!" cried Odin. An instant, and there rises from the walls great sheets of blaze. The brush crackles and snaps and sends up great tongues of fire. The eagle, angry, desperate, and blinded by the lightning sweeps on, straight towards them. Like a foolish moth, he bears down upon the city, into the very heart of the blaze. A sudden crackling, a cry of pain, a cloud of black, black smoke, and the great grey eagle falls a helpless mass upon the pavement beside the breathless Loki.

The haggard faces flush with hope and joy. The apples are safe. Idun has come back, the apples again are theirs, and life and joy and eternal youth once more are with them.

Now the goddess of music bursts forth again in song; the god of poetry pours forth his melody; a feast is spread, and the gods and goddesses once more eat of the wonderful apples of life. The colour comes back into their faded cheeks; light again flashes from their eyes. Youth and health and strength are theirs again. Peace reigns once more in Asgard.

The Giant Behind the Waterfall

THE GIANTS LINGERED LONGER in the Far North than elsewhere. About two hundred years after the death of Charlemagne there was living in Iceland a saga hero named Grettir the Strong. He was the most powerful man ever known in the north country. More than once he had overcome dreaded berserkers in their battle fury; on a narrow path on a cliff face he conquered a huge bear with his naked hands, holding off the infuriated beast by the ears till he could topple it over the precipice; but his strength and high spirit brought him great reverses and caused him to be an outlaw for much of his troubled life.

During his wanderings through the wild unknown regions as a forest man, he spent one winter under the Geitland glacier where the hot springs made a fair grassy valley; and here he was intimate with a giant named Thorir, whose daughters were glad to see him because not many people came there.

Finding it dull, he resumed his travels, and came into Bardadal. Here at Sandhaugar dwelt then Steinvor, a widow with young children. The place had an evil name from a strange happening.

Two winters before Steinvor had gone as usual to celebrate Yule at the neighbouring town of Eyjardalsa, while her husband, Thorsteinn the White, stayed at home. Men lay down to sleep in the evening, and in the night they heard a great noise in the room near the bondi's (farmer's) bed. No one dared to get up to see what was the matter, because there were so few of them. The mistress of the house returned home the next morning, but her husband had disappeared and no one knew what had become of him. So the next season passed. The following winter the mistress wanted to go to mass, and told her servant to stay at home; he was very unwilling but said she should be obeyed. It happened just as before; this time the servant disappeared. People thought it very strange and found some drops of blood upon the outer door, so they supposed that some evil spirit or troll must have carried off both the men.

This story had spread all through the district. It came to the ears of Grettir, who being well accustomed to deal with ghosts and spectres turned his steps thither and arrived on Yule-eve at Sandhaugar. He was disguised as was now his custom, because his enemy Thorir had set a price on his head, and called himself Gest.

The lady of the house saw that he was enormously tall, and the servants were terribly afraid of him. He asked for hospitality; the mistress told him that food was ready for him but that he must see after himself. He said he would, and added:

"I will stay in the house while you go to mass if you would like it."

She said: "You must be a brave man to venture to stay in this house."

"I do not care for a dull life," he said.

Then she said: "I do not want to remain at home, but I cannot get across the river."

"I will come with you," said the pretended Gest. So she made ready to go to mass with her little daughter. It was thawing outside; the river was flooded and was covered with ice.

"It is impossible for man or horse to cross," said Steinvor.

"There must be fords," said Gest. "Do not be afraid."

"First carry the maiden over; she is lighter."

"I don't want to make two journeys of it," said he; "I will carry you in my arms."

She crossed herself and said: "That is impossible; what will you do with the girl?"

"I will find a way," said Gest.

Taking them both up, he set the girl on her mother's knee, while he bore them both on his left arm, keeping his right arm free.

So he carried them across. They were too frightened to cry out. The river came up to his breast, and a great piece of ice came against him, which he pushed off with the hand that was free. Then the stream became so deep that it broke over his shoulder, but he waded on vigorously till he reached the other bank and put them on shore.

The mistress reached Eyjardalsa for mass and everyone wondered how she had crossed the river. She said she did not know whether it was a man or a troll who had carried her over. The priest said it was certainly a man, though unlike other men. "Let us keep silent over it; may be that he means to help you in your difficulties."

She stayed there that night.

Meanwhile Grettir had waded back. It was nearly dark by the time he got home to Sandhaugar and called for some food. When he had eaten something he told the servants to go to the other end of the hall. Then he got some boards and loose logs and laid them across the hall to make a great barricade so that none of the servants could get across. No one dared to oppose him or to object to anything. The entrance was in the side wall of the hall under the back gable, and near it was a cross bench upon which Grettir laid himself, keeping on his clothes, with a light burning in the room. So he lay till into the night.

Towards midnight he heard a loud noise outside, and very soon there walked a huge troll-wife into the room. She carried a trough in one hand and a rather large cutlass in the other. She looked around the room as she entered, and on seeing Grettir lying there she rushed at him; he started up and attacked her furiously.

They fought long together; she was the stronger but he evaded her skilfully. Everything near them and the panelling of the back wall were broken to pieces. She dragged him through the hall door out to the porch, where he resisted vigorously. The troll-wife wanted to drag him out of the house, but before that was done they had broken up all the fittings of the outer door and borne them away on their shoulders. Then she strove to get to the river and among the rocks. Grettir was terribly fatigued, but there was no choice but either to brace himself or be dragged down to the rocks.

All night long they struggled together, and he thought he had never met with such a monster for strength. She gripped him so tightly to herself that he could do nothing with either hand but cling to her waist.

When at last they reached a rock by the river he swung the monster around and got his right hand loose. Then he quickly seized the short sword he was wearing, drew it, and struck at the troll's right shoulder, cutting off her right arm and releasing himself. She sprang among the rocks and disappeared in the waterfall. Grettir, very stiff and tired, lay long by the rock.

At daylight he went back to the hall and lay down on his bed, blue and swollen all over.

When Steinvor came home she found the place all in disorder. She went to the stranger and asked him what had happened, and why everything was broken to pieces. He told her the whole adventure, just as it had happened. She thought it a matter of great moment and asked him who he was. He told her the truth, said that he wished to see a priest, and asked her to send for one. She did so; Steinn the priest came to Sandhaugar and soon learnt that it was Grettir, the son of Asmund, who had come there under the name of Gest.

The priest asked him what he thought had become of Steinvor's husband and servant who had disappeared; Grettir said they must have been taken among the rocks. The priest said he could not believe that unless he gave some evidence of it. Grettir declared that later it would become known, and the priest went home. Grettir lay many days in his bed, and the lady did all she could for him.

He himself always declared that the troll woman sprang among the rocks in the waterfall when she was wounded, but the men of Bardadal have a tale that day dawned upon her while they were wrestling, so that when he cut off her arm she lost her powers and is still standing there on the mountain in the likeness of a hideous woman. However that may be, the dwellers in the valley kept Grettir's secret so that he was safe from his enemies and the blood-feud while he lay helpless.

One day that winter, after Yule, Grettir went to Eyjardalsa and met Steinn, to whom he said: "I see, priest, that you have little belief in what I say. Now I wish you to come with me to the river and see for yourself what probability there is in it."

The priest did so. When they reached the falls they saw a cave up under the rocks. The cliff was there so steep that no one could climb it, and it was nearly ten fathoms down to the water. They had a rope with them.

"It is quite impossible for anyone to get down there," said the priest.

Grettir answered: "It is certainly possible; and men of high mettle are those who would feel themselves happiest there. I want to see what there is back of the fall. Do you mind the rope."

The priest said he could do so if he chose. He drove a stake into the ground and laid stones against it.

Grettir now fastened a stone in a loop at the end of the rope, and lowered it from above into the water.

"How do you mean to go?" asked Steinn.

"I don't mean to be bound when I come into the fall," Grettir said. "So my mind tells me."

Then he prepared to go; he had few clothes on, and only a short sword; no other arms. He jumped from a rock and got down to the fall. The priest saw the soles of his feet, but after that did not know what had become of him.

Grettir dived beneath the fall. It was very difficult swimming because of the currents, and he had to dive to the bottom to get behind the pouring wall of water. There was a rock where he came up, and a great cave behind the fall in front of which the water streamed down.

He went into the cave, where there was a large fire burning, and a horrible great giant, most fearful to behold, sitting before it.

As Grettir entered the giant sprang up, seized a halberd and struck at him, for he could both strike and thrust with it. It had a wooden shaft and was of the kind called 'heptisax.' Grettir struck back with his sword and cut through the shaft.

Then the giant tried to reach up backward to a sword which was hanging in the cave, and at that moment Grettir struck at him and cut open his lower breast and stomach so that all his entrails fell out into the river and floated down the stream.

The priest, who was sitting by the rope, saw the water all thickened and bloody and lost his head, making sure that Grettir was killed. He left the rope and ran off home, where he arrived in the evening and told them for certain Grettir was dead, and said it was a great misfortune to have lost such a man.

Grettir struck few more blows at the giant before he was dead. He then entered the cave, kindled a light and explored. It is not told how much treasure he found there, but there is said to have been some. He stayed there till late into the night, and found the bones of two men which he carried away in a skin.

Then he came out of the cave, swam to the rope and shook it, thinking the priest was there; finding him gone he had to climb up the rope hand over hand, and so reached the top.

He returned to Eyjardalsa and carried the skin with the bones in it into the vestibule of the church, together with a rune-staff, upon which were most beautifully carved the following lines:

Into the fall of the torrent I went;
Dank its maw towards me gaped.
The floods before the ogress' den
Mighty against my shoulder played.

And then:

Hideous the friend of Mella came,
Hard were the blows I dealt upon her.
The shaft of Heptisax was severed,
My sword has pierced the monster's breast.

There too it was told how Grettir had brought the bones from the cave.

When the priest came to the church the next morning, he found the staff and all that was with it and read the runes. Grettir had returned to Sandhaugar.

When Steinn met Grettir again he asked him exactly what had happened, and Grettir told him. He declared the priest had held the rope very faithlessly, and Steinn admitted that it was true.

Men felt no doubt that these monsters were responsible for the disappearance of Thorsteinn and his servant, nor was there any haunting or ghost-walking there afterwards; Grettir had evidently cleared the land of them.

The bones were buried by the priest in the churchyard. Grettir stayed that winter in Bardadal, though unknown to those who sought his blood.

The Turke and Gawain

A TERRIBLE BROOD OF GIANTS once lived on the Isle of Man – as anyone in western England could have told you a hundred years ago, or five hundred for that matter. Today this island of Mona in the Irish Sea produces nothing stranger than Manx tail-less cats and a hard-headed race of people who cling most obstinately to their old Norse and Celtic customs, with 'deemsters' to judge them and a Legislature and Lieutenant-governor of their own for their 20,000 inhabitants.

But away back in the days of great King Arthur it was common knowledge that a horde of giants had driven out the first fairy population of the island, and, after ruling many generations in the usual discourteous fashion of giants, had been themselves overpowered by the mighty enchanter Merlin, and lay spellbound for ever in vast subterranean chambers beneath their ancient palace.

And if you have any doubts about this, and find it difficult to verify the tale by consulting a Manxman (or better still an aged Manxwoman) – why you need only turn to *The History and Description of the Isle of Man*, wherein Mr Waldron only seventy years ago related all the facts as to 'Curious and Authentick Relations of Apparitions of Giants that have lived under the castle from time immemorial. Likewise many comical and entertaining stories of the pranks played by fairies, &c.'

He himself saw beneath Douglas Fort the "very strong and secret apartment underground, having no passage to it but a hole, which is covered with a large stone, and is called to this day 'The great man's chamber.'" Also many wise ones told him how several venturesome spirits who ventured down to the subterranean chambers at Castleton, and not one of them ever returned to give an account of what he had undoubtedly seen – except one foolhardy individual, full of 'Dutch courage,' who risked the attempt in spite of the grisly fate of his predecessors. This lucky person related upon his return that, after traversing interminable black passages, he at last reached a light and a magnificent dwelling, in which lay a monster fourteen feet long and ten or eleven feet around – whereat, like a wise and prudent man, he retraced his steps without further investigation.

And there is more vivid testimony than this. Probably five or six centuries back, an unknown minstrel made a ballad telling all about this giant brood and what befell the valiant Sir Gawain upon his adventure into that dread island.

A few portions of this ballad are lost (they were used to light the fires by the maids in Humphrey Pitt's house in Shropshire, where Bishop Percy, about 1760, found the old seventeenth century manuscript book containing it!) But the course of the tale is plain, and the romance stands here essentially as it was written down about 1650, having been passed on orally for hundreds of years before that.

* * *

Listen, lords great and small, what adventures did befall in England, where hath been the knights that held the Round Table, doughty warriors and keen.

All England both east and west, lords and ladies of the best, they busked them and made them bowne, and as King Arthur sate in his seat – lords served him at his meat – there came a man into the hall. He was not tall, but he was broad, made like a turke (a dwarf) in his legs and thighs. Said he:

"Is there any will, as a brother, give me a buffet and take another – if any be so hardy?"

Then spoke that crabbed knight, Sir Kay:

"Man, thou seemest not so strong in wit if thou be not adread, for there are knights within this hall will fell thee to the ground with one buffet. Be thou never so stalwart of hand, I dare safely sweare I shall bring thee to the ground."

Then spake that worthy knight Sir Gawain:

"Cousin Kay, thou speakest unworthily, and rude is thy answer. If this man wants wit, small honour to thee if thou shouldst kill him."

The dwarf answered threateningly: "Come on, the better of you two, though ye be fierce as any wild boar."

With that Gawain rose and smote him, but not with his full strength, lest he slay him outright. But to his surprise the dwarf did not go down before his blow but withstood it. Then the dwarf looked upon him menacingly and said:

"Be sure that when the time comes this buffet thou hast given me shall be well quitted. But before that thou must go with me on an adventure – and I shall make thee thrice as afraid as ever man was on this middle earth ere thou see this court again."

"I plight my troth," said Gawain. "I dare go with thee and never fly. Never will I flee from an adventure, be it jousting or any other tournament."

The dwarf took leave of the crowned King, and Sir Gawain made ready his armour and steed. They rode northwards two days and more. By then Sir Gawain was sore hungered and had great need of meat and drink. The dwarf knew he needed food and spoke rough words to him, holding his head high:

"Gawain, where is all thy plenty? The other day thou wast served with dainties and gave no part to me, but bruised me with a buffet: therefore thou shalt have mickle care and shalt see adventures. I only would I had here King Arthur and many of thy fellows in brotherhood that are wont to strive for mastery."

He led Sir Gawain to a high hill. Suddenly the earth opened and closed again, and Gawain began to dread; the murk came down and the light disappeared; and a storm of snow and rain, with thunder and lightning, broke upon them.

Sir Gawain sighed heavily. "Such weather," said he, "saw I never before, in no place that I have ever been."

The dwarf paid no attention and led him on for a long journey, till at last they came in sight of a noble castle standing close beside the sea. "We shall go in," said the guide, "but take heed that if thou seest anyone within, thou speak not to man nor woman. Yea, even if they address thee, on thy peril see thou makest them no answer but only unto me."

So they rode up to the castle and Sir Gawain lighted off his horse. The dwarf, being on foot already, led him through the gates. Here they found chamber, bower and hall, with rich railings and most seemly to look upon. In the hall a board was spread with all manner of meat and drink for any grooms who might win thither. Sir Gawain would have fallen to that fare, but the dwarf bade him leave it alone on his peril so that he waxed anxious.

Said Gawain: "Man, I marvel that thou mayst spare none of these victuals when there is such great plenty here. Yet do I marvel more, by my fay, that I see neither man nor man, woman nor child. I had liever now be free to eat my fill of this fair meat than to have all the gold in Christendom."

At that the dwarf went forth and immediately returned, bringing meat and drink of the finest.

"Eat, Gawain," said he, "and refresh thy spirit. In faith thou shalt labour and sweat ere thou get more food."

When the knight had drunk ale and wine, he said: "I will, without boast or threat, be ready at thy bidding. Yet I would pray thee rather to give me my buffet and let me go my way for I would not longer be in this place."

The dwarf reminded him of his plighted word presently, and led him without again. There lay a boat by the shore; and, obeying his guide, Sir Gawain turned loose his charger. Indeed there was naught else he could do.

"I plight my troth to thee," said the dwarf, "he shall be here when thou comest again."

They sailed across the water for the space of an hour, when there appeared before them an island whereon stood a fair castle whose like the knight had ne'er beheld.

Said the dwarf: "Gawain, we have come thus far without scathe; but now cometh the performance of thine oath. In yonder castle dwells the King of Man. He is a soldan of heathenesse, and he hath with him such a hideous rout of giants as one might not match did he seek far and near as wide as the world. Many adventures are before you; and doubt not that we shall be assailed before we win hence again. But an ye take good heed to me I shall help ye in need; and I trow there is none so strong in stoure that he shall gainsay us."

They landed and came into the great hall, where sat the King of Man, grim and terrible.

"Ah, Sir Gawain, stiff and stoure," said he, "how fareth thine uncle King Arthur? And that bishop, Sir Bodwine, that will not let my goods alone but spiteth them every day? He preaches much of a crown of thorns; but an ever I catch him he shall think such a crown but play. Sit down at my board, Sir Knight."

"Nay, that may not be," said Sir Gawain. "I trow a venturous knight shall sit down in no king's hall ere he have assayed adventures."

"Fair may it fall ye then, Gawain," said the King. "Go, fetch me forth my tennis ball," quoth he to those who stood near, "for I will see this knight play."

So they brought in a huge ball, all of brass; and behind it came a hideous company of giants. They were seventeen in number, and the least of them was half as tall again as the knight.

Gawain looked on these monstrous creatures who laughed and showed their foul teeth in pleasure at the prospect of dashing out his brains in the course of this strange game. Then he looked at the ball of brass, and knew there was no man in all England able to so much as carry it, much less play at hand-ball with it as was proposed. And in his heart he began to feel great fear that he was here presently to be shamed and slain. Just then the dwarf spoke privily in his ear.

To the grim King the knight said: "This is too easy a play for a proven knight. This boy of mine will play for you."

Then one of the giants struck the great heavy ball; and the dwarf struck it back so mightily that it flew clean out of the hall door and out of sight.

"Of a truth, that is a strong boy you have," said the King. "Now let us try at casting the axletree."

So they brought forth a monstrous axletree such as only one of the giants could so much as lift. The tallest of the giants made a cast from the other end of the hall, so that the tremendous mass crashed down before the feet of the knight and his companion. Gawain made a sign; whereat the dwarf picked up the huge axletree and hurled it so shrewdly that it thrust through one of the giants, and he fell down with grisly groaning.

"Take away the axletree," said the King. "Such a boy saw I never before; yet, as I may thrive, he shall be better assayed ere he go. This third adventure is the last before me at this time."

All turned towards a monstrous brazier which stood in the hall, within whose great iron bars there blazed coals and wood.

"Gawain," said a giant, "do you begin the play. A great giant lifted up this brazier and set it down fairly with one hand. When you have essayed it, one of us shall answer you."

Sir Gawain was never so disturbed since he was a man on middle earth. Then he bethought him and turned to the dwarf.

"Lift this brazier, boy," said he, "that is so worthily wrought."

At that the dwarf sprang forward, and seized the huge knobs of the iron brazier which rose far above his head. Then he lifted it clear and swung it thrice about his head, that the coals and red brands flew out over the hall floor, and they had much ado to put out the fire.

The King waxed wroth and he bade them lay hands on the knight; and before he could draw his sword they had disarmed him and bound him fast. The King had him taken aside and spoke to him privily.

"Ah, Gawain," said the King, "evil was the day for thee that thou camest hither. Full many a knight, mickle of might and strong in battle, hath come before thee, and all of them I have slain through my mastery. Never went there away one to tell the tale. Nor shalt thou go, fell though thou beest, nor none that belongeth to King Arthur."

The dwarf had drawn on a cloak of invisible grey and followed them, himself unseen in this weed. He heard all this, and followed still when the King led Gawain into a fast dungeon where stood a great cauldron of boiling lead. The molten lead bubbled and spattered; and before it stood a loathly giant with an iron pronged fork in his hand. The giant looked eagerly upon the captive knight.

The King said to his monster: "Here are none but we two: do what is best."

But at that instant the dwarf discovered himself in his weed of invisible grey; and at the sight the giant cried out in fear.

The dwarf leaped upon him, gripped him mightily about the waist, and cast him all as he was into the cauldron of molten lead, holding him down with the prongs till he was scalded to death.

Sir Gawain turned to the King: "But thou agreest to be baptized, thine hour is come."

The King in anger spat upon him; and the dwarf seized him and hurled him into the fire to perish. Then he said to Sir Gawain:

"Master, the peril is past. Yet let us not tarry to complete this adventure."

So they went through the castle and slew all that foul company except such as were willing to become Christian men. And they found there vast treasure of gold and silver. Then the dwarf brought a golden basin, fit for an emperor, and a well-tempered sword, and fell on his knees before Gawain, and said:

"If ever I did aught for thee, take this keen sword and strike off my head."

"Now God forfend!" exclaimed Gawain. "Not for all the red gold would I have thee slain."

"Have done, my master. I have no dread. In this basin let me bleed and thou shalt see a new play."

Sorrowfully, Gawain took the brand, and with one blow he smote off his head. And when the blood fell into the golden basin, the dwarf stood up in his own guise of a stalwart knight. Sir Gromer he was hight.

"Blessed be thou, Sir Gawain. Well hast thou quitted me for my aid."

Then they went throughout the castle and released many a captive knight and lady who had been held there in dolour. And after they had feasted they crossed the ocean water and returned to King Arthur's court, where there was great joy of the seventeen bright ladies thus restored.

Sir Gromer, the former dwarf, went down upon his knee before Arthur:

"Sir King, an it please you, crown Gawain King of Man."

But Gawain kneeled beside him and said: "Nay, Lord, not I; give it to him, for he won it."

Then said Arthur: "Take thou the kingdom, Sir Gromer; for I see that Gawain will never consent."

And it was so.

Jack the Giant-Killer

WHEN GOOD KING ARTHUR REIGNED, there lived near the Land's End of England, in the county of Cornwall, a farmer who had one only son called Jack. He was brisk and of a ready lively wit, so that nobody or nothing could worst him.

In those days the Mount of Cornwall was kept by a huge giant named Cormoran. He was eighteen feet in height, and about three yards round the waist, of a fierce and grim countenance, the terror of all the neighbouring towns and villages. He lived in a cave in the midst of the Mount, and whenever he wanted food he would wade over to the mainland, where he would furnish himself with whatever came in his way. Everybody at his approach ran out of their houses, while he seized on their cattle, making nothing of carrying half a dozen oxen on his back at a time; and as for their sheep and hogs, he would tie them round his waist like a bunch of tallow-dips. He had done this for many years, so that all Cornwall was in despair.

One day Jack happened to be at the town hall when the magistrates were sitting in council about the Giant. He asked: "What reward will be given to the man who kills Cormoran?" "The giant's treasure," they said, "will be the reward." Quoth Jack: "Then let me undertake it."

So he got a horn, shovel, and pickaxe, and went over to the Mount in the beginning of a dark winter's evening, when he fell to work, and before morning had dug a pit twenty-two feet deep, and nearly as broad, covering it over with long sticks and straw. Then he strewed a little mould over it, so that it appeared like plain ground. Jack then placed himself on the opposite side of the pit, farthest from the giant's lodging, and, just at the break of day, he put the horn to his mouth, and blew, Tantivy, Tantivy. This noise roused the giant, who rushed from his cave, crying: "You incorrigible villain, are you come here to disturb my rest? You shall pay dearly for this. Satisfaction I will have, and this it shall be, I will take you whole and broil you for breakfast." He had no sooner uttered this, than he tumbled into the pit, and made the very foundations of the Mount to shake. "Oh, Giant," quoth Jack, "where are you now? Oh, faith, you are gotten now into Lob's Pound, where I will surely plague you for your threatening words: what do you think now of broiling me for your breakfast? Will no other diet serve you but poor Jack?" Then having tantalized the giant for a while, he gave him a most weighty knock with his pickaxe on the very crown of his head, and killed him on the spot.

Jack then filled up the pit with earth, and went to search the cave, which he found contained much treasure. When the magistrates heard of this they made a declaration he should henceforth be termed

JACK THE GIANT-KILLER

and presented him with a sword and a belt, on which were written these words embroidered in letters of gold:

"Here's the right valiant Cornish man,
Who slew the giant Cormoran."

The news of Jack's victory soon spread over all the West of England, so that another giant, named Blunderbore, hearing of it, vowed to be revenged on Jack, if ever he should light on him. This giant was the lord of an enchanted castle situated in the midst of a lonesome wood. Now Jack, about four months afterwards, walking near this wood in his journey to Wales, being weary, seated himself near a pleasant fountain and fell fast asleep. While he was sleeping, the giant, coming there for water, discovered him, and knew him to be the far-famed Jack the Giant-Killer by the lines written on the belt. Without ado, he took Jack on his shoulders and carried him towards his castle. Now, as they passed through a thicket, the rustling of the boughs awakened Jack, who was strangely surprised to find himself in the clutches of the giant. His terror was only begun, for, on entering the castle, he saw the ground strewed with human bones, and the giant told him his own would ere long be among them. After this the giant locked poor Jack in an immense chamber, leaving him there while he went to fetch another giant, his brother, living in the same wood, who might share in the meal on Jack.

After waiting some time Jack, on going to the window, beheld afar off the two giants coming towards the castle. "Now," quoth Jack to himself, "my death or my deliverance is at hand." Now, there were strong cords in a corner of the room in which Jack was, and two of these he took, and made a strong noose at the end of each; and while the giants were unlocking the iron gate of the castle he threw the ropes over each of their heads. Then he drew the other ends across a beam, and pulled with all his might, so that he throttled them. Then, when he saw they were black in the face, he slid down the rope, and drawing his sword, slew them both. Then, taking the giant's keys, and unlocking the rooms, he found three fair ladies tied by the hair of their heads, almost starved to death. "Sweet ladies," quoth Jack, "I have destroyed this monster and his brutish brother, and obtained your liberties." This said he presented them with the keys, and so proceeded on his journey to Wales.

Jack made the best of his way by travelling as fast as he could, but lost his road, and was benighted, and could not find any habitation until, coming into a narrow valley, he found a large house, and in order to get shelter took courage to knock at the gate. But what was his surprise when there came forth a monstrous giant with two heads; yet he did not appear so fiery as the others were, for he was a Welsh giant, and what he did was by private and secret malice under the false show of friendship. Jack, having told his condition to the giant, was shown into a bedroom, where, in the dead of night, he heard his host in another apartment muttering these words:

"Though here you lodge with me this night,
You shall not see the morning light
My club shall dash your brains outright!"

"Say'st thou so," quoth Jack; "that is like one of your Welsh tricks, yet I hope to be cunning enough for you." Then, getting out of bed, he laid a billet in the bed in his stead, and hid himself in a corner of the room. At the dead time of the night in came the Welsh giant, who struck several heavy blows on the bed with his club, thinking he had broken every bone in Jack's skin. The next morning Jack, laughing in his sleeve, gave him hearty thanks for his night's lodging. "How have you rested?" quoth the giant; "did you not feel anything in the night?" "No," quoth Jack, "nothing but a rat, which gave me two or three slaps with her tail." With that, greatly wondering, the giant led Jack to breakfast, bringing him a bowl containing four gallons of hasty pudding. Being loath to let the giant think it too much for him, Jack put a large leather bag under his loose coat, in such a way that he could convey the pudding into it without its being perceived. Then, telling the giant he would show him a trick, taking a knife, Jack ripped open the bag, and out came all the hasty pudding. Whereupon, saying, "Odds splutters hur nails, hur can do that trick hurself," the monster took the knife, and ripping open his belly, fell down dead.

Now, it happened in these days that King Arthur's only son asked his father to give him a large sum of money, in order that he might go and seek his fortune in the principality of Wales, where lived a beautiful lady possessed with seven evil spirits. The king did his best to persuade his son from it, but in vain; so at last gave way and the prince set out with two horses, one loaded with money, the other for himself to ride upon. Now, after several days' travel, he came to a market-town in Wales, where he beheld a vast crowd of people gathered together. The prince asked the reason of it, and was told that they had arrested a corpse for several large sums of money which the deceased owed when he died. The prince replied that it was a pity creditors should be so cruel, and said: "Go bury the dead, and let his creditors come to my lodging, and there their debts shall be paid." They came, in such great numbers that before night he had only tuppence left for himself.

Now Jack the Giant-Killer, coming that way, was so taken with the generosity of the prince that he desired to be his servant. This being agreed upon, the next morning they set forward on their journey together, when, as they were riding out of the town, an old woman called after the prince, saying, "He has owed me tuppence these seven years; pray pay me as well as the rest." Putting his hand to his pocket, the prince gave the woman all he had left, so that after their day's food, which cost what small spell Jack had by him, they were without a penny between them.

When the sun got low, the king's son said: "Jack, since we have no money, where can we lodge this night?"

But Jack replied: "Master, we'll do well enough, for I have an uncle lives within two miles of this place; he is a huge and monstrous giant with three heads; he'll fight five hundred men in armour, and make them to fly before him." "Alas!" quoth the prince, "what shall we do there? He'll certainly chop us up at a mouthful. Nay, we are scarce enough to fill one of his hollow teeth!"

"It is no matter for that," quoth Jack; "I myself will go before and prepare the way for you; therefore stop here and wait till I return." Jack then rode away at full speed, and coming to the gate of the castle, he knocked so loud that he made the neighbouring hills resound. The giant roared out at this like thunder: "Who's there?"

Jack answered: "None but your poor cousin Jack."

Quoth he: "What news with my poor cousin Jack?"

He replied: "Dear uncle, heavy news, God wot!"

"Prithee," quoth the giant, "what heavy news can come to me? I am a giant with three heads, and besides thou knowest I can fight five hundred men in armour, and make them fly like chaff before the wind."

"Oh, but," quoth Jack, "here's the king's son a-coming with a thousand men in armour to kill you and destroy all that you have!"

"Oh, cousin Jack," said the giant, "this is heavy news indeed! I will immediately run and hide myself, and thou shalt lock, bolt, and bar me in, and keep the keys until the prince is gone." Having secured the giant, Jack fetched his master, when they made themselves heartily merry whilst the poor giant lay trembling in a vault under the ground.

Early in the morning Jack furnished his master with a fresh supply of gold and silver, and then sent him three miles forward on his journey, at which time the prince was pretty well out of the smell of the giant. Jack then returned, and let the giant out of the vault, who asked what he should give him for keeping the castle from destruction. "Why," quoth Jack, "I want nothing but the old coat and cap, together with the old rusty sword and slippers which are at your bed's head." Quoth the giant: "You know not what you ask; they are the most precious things I have. The coat will keep you invisible, the cap will tell you all you want to know, the sword cuts asunder whatever you strike, and the shoes are of extraordinary swiftness. But you have been very serviceable to me, therefore take them with all my heart." Jack thanked his uncle, and then went off with them. He soon overtook his master and they quickly arrived at the house of the lady the prince sought, who, finding the prince to be a suitor, prepared a splendid banquet for him. After the repast was concluded, she told him she had a task for him. She wiped his mouth with a handkerchief, saying: "You must show me that handkerchief tomorrow morning, or else you will lose your head." With that she put it in her bosom. The prince went to bed in great sorrow, but Jack's cap of knowledge informed him how it was to be obtained. In the middle of the night she called upon her familiar spirit to carry her to Lucifer. But Jack put on his coat of darkness and his shoes of swiftness, and was there as soon as she was. When she entered the place of the Old One, she gave the handkerchief to old Lucifer, who laid it upon a shelf, whence Jack took it and brought it to his master, who showed it to the lady next day, and so saved his life. On that day, she gave the prince a kiss and told him he must show her the lips tomorrow morning that she kissed last night, or lose his head.

"Ah!" he replied, "if you kiss none but mine, I will."

"That is neither here nor there," said she; "if you do not, death's your portion!"

At midnight she went as before, and was angry with old Lucifer for letting the handkerchief go. "But now," quoth she, "I will be too hard for the king's son, for I will kiss thee, and he is to show me thy lips." Which she did, and Jack, when she was not standing by, cut off Lucifer's head and brought it under his invisible coat to his master, who the next morning pulled it out by the horns before the lady. This broke the enchantment and the evil spirit left her, and she appeared in all her beauty. They were married the next morning, and soon after went to the court of King Arthur, where Jack for his many great exploits, was made one of the Knights of the Round Table.

Jack soon went searching for giants again, but he had not ridden far when he saw a cave, near the entrance of which he beheld a giant sitting upon a block of timber, with a knotted iron club by his side. His goggle eyes were like flames of fire, his countenance grim and ugly, and his cheeks like a couple of large flitches of bacon, while the bristles of his beard resembled rods of iron wire, and the locks that hung down upon his brawny shoulders were like curled snakes or hissing adders. Jack alighted from his horse, and, putting on the coat of darkness, went up close to the giant, and said softly: "Oh! are you there? It will not be long before I take you fast by the beard." The giant all this while could not see him, on account of his invisible coat, so that Jack, coming up close to the monster, struck a blow with his sword at his head, but, missing his aim, he cut off the nose instead. At this, the giant roared like claps of thunder, and began to lay about him with his iron club like one stark mad. But Jack, running behind, drove his sword up to the hilt in the giant's back, so that he fell down dead. This done, Jack cut off the giant's head, and sent it, with his brother's also, to King Arthur, by a waggoner he hired for that purpose.

Jack now resolved to enter the giant's cave in search of his treasure, and, passing along through a great many windings and turnings, he came at length to a large room paved with freestone, at the upper end of which was a boiling cauldron, and on the right hand a large table, at which the giant used to dine. Then he came to a window, barred with iron, through which he looked and beheld a vast number of miserable captives, who, seeing him, cried out: "Alas! young man, art thou come to be one amongst us in this miserable den?"

"Ay," quoth Jack, "but pray tell me what is the meaning of your captivity?"

"We are kept here," said one, "till such time as the giants have a wish to feast, and then the fattest among us is slaughtered! And many are the times they have dined upon murdered men!"

"Say you so," quoth Jack, and straightway unlocked the gate and let them free, who all rejoiced like condemned men at the sight of a pardon. Then searching the giant's coffers, he shared the gold and silver equally amongst them and took them to a neighbouring castle, where they all feasted and made merry over their deliverance.

But in the midst of all this mirth a messenger brought news that one Thunderdell, a giant with two heads, having heard of the death of his kinsmen, had come from the northern dales to be revenged on Jack, and was within a mile of the castle, the country people flying before him like chaff. But Jack was not a bit daunted, and said: "Let him come! I have a tool to pick his teeth; and you, ladies and gentlemen, walk out into the garden, and you shall witness this giant Thunderdell's death and destruction."

The castle was situated in the midst of a small island surrounded by a moat thirty feet deep and twenty feet wide, over which lay a drawbridge. So Jack employed men to cut through this bridge on both sides, nearly to the middle; and then, dressing himself in his invisible coat, he marched against the giant with his sword of sharpness. Although the giant could not see Jack, he smelt his approach, and cried out in these words:

"Fee, fi, fo, fum!
I smell the blood of an Englishman!
Be he alive or be he dead,
I'll grind his bones to make me bread!"

"Say'st thou so," said Jack; "then thou art a monstrous miller indeed."

The giant cried out again: "Art thou that villain who killed my kinsmen? Then I will tear thee with my teeth, suck thy blood, and grind thy bones to powder."

"You'll have to catch me first," quoth Jack, and throwing off his invisible coat, so that the giant might see him, and putting on his shoes of swiftness, he ran from the giant, who followed like a walking castle, so that the very foundations of the earth seemed to shake at every step. Jack led him a long dance, in order that the gentlemen and ladies might see; and at last to end the matter, ran lightly over the drawbridge, the giant, at full speed, pursuing him with his club. Then, coming to the middle of the bridge, the giant's great weight broke it down, and he tumbled headlong into the water, where he rolled and wallowed like a whale. Jack, standing by the moat, laughed at him all the while; but though the giant foamed to hear him scoff, and plunged from place to place in the moat, yet he could not get out to be revenged. Jack at length got a cart-rope and cast it over the two heads of the giant, and drew him ashore by a team of horses, and then cut off both his heads with his sword of sharpness, and sent them to King Arthur.

After some time spent in mirth and pastime, Jack, taking leave of the knights and ladies, set out for new adventures. Through many woods he passed, and came at length to the foot of a high mountain. Here, late at night, he found a lonesome house, and knocked at the door, which was opened by an aged man with a head as white as snow. "Father," said Jack, "can you lodge a benighted traveller who has lost his way?" "Yes," said the old man; "you are right welcome to my poor cottage." Whereupon Jack entered, and down they sat together, and the old man began to speak as follows: "Son, I see by your belt you are the great conqueror of giants, and behold, my son, on the top of this mountain is an enchanted castle, this is kept by a giant named Galligantua, and he by the help of an old conjurer betrays many knights and ladies into his castle, where by magic art they are transformed into sundry shapes and forms. But above all, I grieve for a duke's daughter, whom they fetched from her father's garden, carrying her through the air in a burning chariot drawn by fiery dragons, when they secured her within the castle, and transformed her into a white hind. And though many knights have tried to break the enchantment, and work her deliverance, yet no one could accomplish it, on account of two dreadful griffins which are placed at the castle gate and which destroy everyone who comes near. But you, my son, may pass by them undiscovered, where on the gates of the castle you will find engraved in large letters how the spell may be broken." Jack gave the old man his hand, and promised that in the morning he would venture his life to free the lady.

In the morning Jack arose and put on his invisible coat and magic cap and shoes, and prepared himself for the fray. Now, when he had reached the top of the mountain he soon discovered the two fiery griffins, but passed them without fear, because of his invisible coat. When he had got beyond them, he found upon the gates of the castle a golden trumpet hung by a silver chain, under which these lines were engraved:

"Whoever shall this trumpet blow,
Shall soon the giant overthrow,
And break the black enchantment straight;
So all shall be in happy state."

Jack had no sooner read this but he blew the trumpet, at which the castle trembled to its vast foundations, and the giant and conjurer were in horrid confusion, biting their thumbs and tearing their hair, knowing their wicked reign was at an end. Then the giant stooping to take up his club, Jack at one blow cut off his head; whereupon the conjurer, mounting up into the air, was carried away in a whirlwind. Then the enchantment was broken, and all the lords and ladies who had so long been transformed into birds and beasts returned to their proper shapes, and the castle vanished away in a cloud of smoke. This being done, the head of Galligantua was likewise, in the usual manner, conveyed to the Court of King Arthur, where, the very next day, Jack followed, with the knights and ladies who had been delivered. Whereupon, as a reward for his good services, the king prevailed upon the duke to bestow his daughter in marriage on honest Jack. So married they were, and the whole kingdom was filled with joy at the wedding. Furthermore, the king bestowed on Jack a noble castle, with a very beautiful estate thereto belonging, where he and his lady lived in great joy and happiness all the rest of their days.

Gogmagog

AFTER THE TROJAN WAR, Æneas, fleeing from the desolation of the city, came with Ascanius by ship unto Italy. There, for that Æneas was worshipfully received by King Latinus, Turnus, King of the Rutulians, did wax envious and made war against him. When they met in battle, Æneas had the upper hand, and after that Turnus was slain, obtained the kingdom of Italy and Lavinia the daughter of Latinus. Later, when his own last day had come, Ascanius, now king in his stead, founded Alba on Tiber, and begat a son whose name was Silvius. Silvius, unknown to his father, had fallen in love with and privily taken to wife a certain niece of Lavinia, who was about to become a mother. When this came to the knowledge of his father Ascanius, he commanded his wizards to discover whether the damsel should be brought to bed of a boy or a girl. When they had made sure of the matter by art magic, they told him that the child would be a boy that should slay his father and his mother, and after much travel in many lands, should, albeit an exile, be exalted unto the highest honours. Nor were the wizards out in their forecast, for when the day came that she should be delivered of a child, the mother bore a son, but herself died in his birth.

Howbeit, the child was given in charge unto a nurse, and was named Brute.

At last, after thrice five years had gone by, the lad, bearing his father company out a-hunting, slew him by striking him unwittingly with an arrow. For when the verderers drave the deer in front of them, Brute thinking to take aim at them, smote his own father under the breast. Upon the death of his father he was driven out of Italy, his kinsfolk being wroth with him for having wrought a deed so dreadful. He went therefore as an exile into Greece, and there he met with the descendants of Helenus, son of Priam, then held in bondage by the Greeks. Freeing these countrymen by a sudden attack on the Greek stronghold, and capturing Pandrasus himself, the valiant adventurer presently sailed away with the king's daughter for a wife, and a ransom of over three hundred ships laden with treasure and provisions.

They ran on together for two days and a night with a fair current of wind, and drew to land at a certain island called Leogecia, which had been uninhabited ever since it was laid waste by pirates in the days of old. Howbeit, Brute sent three hundred men inland to discover by whom it might be inhabited. Who, finding not a soul, slew such venison of divers kinds as they found in the glades and the forests.

They came, moreover, to a certain deserted city, wherein they found a temple of Diana. Now in this temple was an image of the goddess, that gave responses, if haply it were asked of any votary that there did worship.

At last they returned to their ships, laden with the venison they had found, and report to their comrades the lie of the land and the situation of the city, bearing the Duke on land that he make repair unto the temple, and after making offerings of propitiation, enquire of the deity of the place what land she would grant them as a fixed abiding place. By the common consent of all, therefore, Brute took with him Gerion the augur, and twelve of the elders, and sought out the temple, bringing with them everything necessary for making sacrifice. When they arrived, they surrounded their brows with garlands, and set up three altars according to immemorial wont, before the holy place, to the three Gods, Jove, to wit, and Mercury, as well as to Diana, and made unto each his own special libation. Brute himself, holding in his right hand a vessel full of sacrificial wine and the blood of a white hind before the altar of the goddess, with face upturned towards her image, broke silence in these words: –

Goddess and forest Queen, the wild boar's terror,
Thou who the maze of heaven or nether mansions
Walkest at will, vouchsafe they rede to earthward!
Tell me what lands thy will it is we dwell in?
What sure abode? Lo, there to Thee for ever
Temples I vow, and chant of holy maidens!

After he had nine times repeated this, he walked four times round the altar, poured forth the wine he held upon the hearth of offering, laid him down upon the fell of a hind that he had stretched in front of the altar, and after invoking slumber fell on sleep. For as at that time it was the third hour of the night, wherein are mortals visited by the sweetest sleep. Then it seemed him the goddess stood there before him, and spake unto him on this wise: –

Brute – past the realms of Gaul, beneath the sunset
Lieth, an island, girt about by ocean,
Guarded by ocean – erst the haunt of giants,
Desert of late, and meet for this thy people.
Seek it! For there is thine abode for ever.
There by thy sons again shall Troy be builded;
There of thy blood shall Kings be born, hereafter
Sovran in every land the wide world over.

On awakening from such a vision, the Duke remained in doubt whether it were a dream that he had seen, or whether it were the living goddess herself who had thus foretold the land whereunto he should go. At last he called his companions and related unto them from first to last all that had befallen him in his sleep. They thereupon were filled with exceeding great joy, and advise that they should at once turn back to their ships, and while the wind was still blowing fair, should get under way as quickly as possible full sail for the west in search of that land which the goddess had promised.

Nor did they tarry. They rejoined their comrades and launched out into the deep, and after ploughing the waves for a run of thirty days, made the coast of Africa, still not knowing in which direction to steer their ships. Then came they to the Altars of the Phileni, and the place of the Salt-pans, steering from thence betwixt Ruscicada and the mountains Azarae, where they encountered sore peril from an attack by pirates. Natheless, they won the victory, and went on their way enriched by the spoil and plunder they had taken.

From thence, passing the mouth of the River Malva, they arrived in Mauritania, where lack of food and drink compelled them to disembark, and dividing themselves into companies, they harried the whole region from end to end. When they had revictualled their ships, they made sail for the Columns of Hercules, where they saw many of the monsters of the deep called Sirens, which surrounded the ships and well-nigh overwhelmed them. Howbeit, they made shift to escape, and came to the Tyrrhene Sea, where they found nigh the shore four generations born of the exiles from Troy, who had borne Antenor company in his flight. Their Duke was called Corineus, a sober-minded man and excellent in counsel, mighty in body, valiance and hardiness, insomuch as that if it were he had to deal with a giant in single combat he would straightway overthrow him as though he were wrestling with a lad. Accordingly, when they knew the ancient stock whereof he was born, they took him into their company, as well as the people whereof he was chieftain, that in after-days were called Cornishmen after the name of their Duke. He it was that in all encounters was more help to Brute than were any of the others.

Then came they to Aquitaine, and entering into the mouth of the Loire, cast anchor there. Here they abode seven days and explored the lie of the land. Goffarius Pictus then ruled in Aquitaine, and was King of the country, who, hearing the rumour of a foreign folk that had come with a great fleet and had landed within the frontier of his dominions, sent envoys to make enquiry whether they demanded peace or war?

While the legates were on their way to the fleet, they met Corineus who had just landed with two hundred men to hunt for venison in the forest. Thereupon they accosted him, and asked him by whose leave he hath thus trespassed into the King's forest to slay his deer? And when Corineus made them answer, that in such a matter no leave nor licence whatever could be held as needful, one of their number, Imbert by name, rushed forward, and drawing his bow, aimed an arrow at him. Corineus avoided the arrow, and ran in upon Imbert as fast as he might, and with the bow that he carried all-to-brake his head in pieces. Thereupon the rest fled, just making shift to escape his hands, and reported the death of their fellow to Goffarius.

The Duke of the Poitevins, taking the matter sorely to heart, forthwith assembled a mighty host to take vengeance upon them for the death of his messenger. Brute, hearing tidings of his coming, set guards over his ships, bidding the women and children remain on board while he himself along with the whole flower of his army marcheth forth to meet the enemy.

When the engagement at last began, the fighting was fierce on both sides, and after they had spent a great part of the day in battling, Corineus thought it a shame that the

Aquitanians should hold their ground so stoutly, and the Trojans not be able to press forward to the victory. So taking heart afresh, he called his own men apart to the right of the battle, and forming them in rank made a rapid charge upon the enemy; and when, with his men in close order, he had broken the front ranks, he never stinted striking down the enemy till he had cut his way right through the battalion, and forced them all to flee. Good luck had supplied the place of a sword he lost with a battle-axe, wherewith he cleft in twain any that came next him from the crown of the head right down to the girdle-stead.

Brute marvels; his comrades and even the enemy marvel at the hardihood and valour of the man, who, brandishing his battle-axe among the flying host, added not a little terror by shouting, "Whither fly ye, cowards? Whither fly ye, cravens? Turn back, I tell ye, turn, and do battle with Corineus! Shame upon ye! So many thousands as are ye, do ye flee before my single arm? Flee then! And take with ye at least this comfort in your flight, that it is I who am after ye, I who ere now have so oft been wont to drive the Tyrrhene giants in flight before me, and to hurl them to hell by threes and fours at a time!"

At these words of his a certain earl named Subardus with three hundred men turned back and charged down upon him. But Corineus, in raising his shield to ward the blow, forgot not the battle-axe he held in his hand. Lifting it overhead, he smote him a buffet upon the top of his helmet that cleft him right through into two halves. After this, he straightway rusheth in amongst the rest, whirling his axe, and a passing furious slaughter he maketh. Hurrying hither and thither, he avoideth receiving a single stroke, but never resteth a moment from smiting down his enemies. Of one he loppeth off hand and arm, of another he cleaveth the shoulders from the body, of another he striketh off the head at a single blow, of another he severeth the legs from the thigh. All dash headlong upon him only; he dasheth headlong in upon them all.

Brute, who beholdeth all this, glowing with love of the man, hurrieth forward with a company to succour him. Then ariseth a mighty shouting betwixt the two peoples – the strokes were redoubled, and passing bloody was the slaughter on the one side and the other.

But it endureth not long. The Trojans won the day, and drove King Goffarius and his Poitevins in flight before them. Goffarius, escaping by the skin of his teeth, betook him into the parts of Gaul to have succour of his kinsfolk and acquaintance. At that time twelve kings there were in Gaul, each of equal rank, under whose dominion the whole country was ruled. They all received him kindly, and with one accord did pledge them to drive out from the frontiers of Aquitaine this foreign folk that had arrived there.

Brute, overjoyed at the said victory, enricheth his comrades with the spoils of the slain, and after again forming the ranks in companies, he leadeth his host inland with the intention of sacking the whole country and loading his ships with the countless treasure. Accordingly, he burneth the cities in all directions, fire after fire, and ransacketh their hidden hoards; even the fields were laid waste, and citizen and countryman alike and subjected to a piteous slaughter, his aim being to exterminate the unhappy race to the last man. But after that he had thus visited with bloodshed well-nigh the whole of Aquitaine, he came into the place where now standeth the city of Tours, which, as Homer beareth witness, he afterwards himself builded. Finding, after diligent survey that the place was convenient as a refuge, he there decided to pitch his camp, so that if need were he could betake him thereinto. For sore misgiving had he by reason of the arrival of Goffarius, who had marched into the neighbourhood along with the Kings and

Princes of Gaul and a mighty host of armed warriors to do battle against him. When his camp was fully finished, he awaited Goffarius for two days therein, confident alike in his own prudence and in the hardihood of the young men whereof he was the chieftain.

Now, when Goffarius heard of the Trojans being there, he advanced by forced marches day and night until he came well within sight of Brute's camp. Gazing grimly thereon, yet somewhat smiling withal, he burst forth into these words:

"Alas! what grievous destiny is here? Have these ignoble exiles pitched their camp within dominions of mine? To arms, ye warriors, to arms! And charge through their serried ranks! Right soon may we take captive this herd of half-men like sheep and hold them in bondage throughout our realm."

Forthwith, all they that he had brought with him leapt to arms, and marched upon their enemies ranked in twelve battalions. But not after any woman wise did Brute range his men and march to meet them. Prudently instructing his troops as to what they were to do, how to advance and in what order to hold their ground, he gave the word to charge.

At the first onset, the Trojans for a time had the upper hand, and fearful was the slaughter they made of the enemy, for nigh two thousand of them fell, and the rest were so daunted at the sight that they all but turned to flee. But where the numbers of men are the greater, there the more often doth victory abide. In this case, therefore, the Gauls, albeit that at first they were beaten back, yet being thrice so many as their enemies, made shift to form themselves again in rank and charged in again on every side against the Trojans, whom they compelled after much bloodshed to take refuge in the camp.

Having thus obtained the victory, they beleaguered them within the camp, never thinking but that before they departed thence the besieged would either offer their necks to the fetters, or suffer a cruel and lingering death from the pangs of hunger.

In the meanwhile, on the night following, Corineus entered into counsel with Brute, and agreed with him that he would issue forth of the camp that same night by certain byways, and would lie hidden in the neighbouring forest until daybreak. And when Brute, issuing forth just before dawn, should be engaged in battle with the enemy, he himself with his company should attack them in the rear, and charging in upon them put them to the sword. Brute applauded this device of Corineus, who, cautiously issuing forth as he had proposed with three thousand men, betook him to the depths of the forest.

Accordingly, when the morrow morning began to break, Brute ordained his men in companies, and opening the gates of the camp, marched forth to battle. The Gauls straightway set themselves to oppose him, and disposing their troops in battle array came to close quarters with him. Many thousands of men were at once cut down on both sides, and many were the wounds given and received, for not a man spareth his adversary.

It chanced that a certain Trojan was there present named Turonus, a nephew of Brute's, than whom there was none more valiant and hardy save only Corineus himself. He with his single sword slew no less than six hundred men. Unhappily he was slain before his time by a sudden onslaught of the Gauls; and the foresaid city of Tours acquired the name thereof by reason of his being there buried.

And while the troops on both sides were in the very thickest of the battle, Corineus came upon them of a sudden and charged the enemy at the double in the rear. Straightway the others, pressing forward from the front, renew the attack more hotly and strain them to the utmost to complete the slaughter. The Gauls were aghast with dismay even at the very shout of the Cornishmen as they charged in on the rear, and thinking that they were more in number than they were, fled, hot foot, from the field. The Trojans were on their heels hewing them down in pursuit, nor ceased they to follow them up until the victory was their own.

Brute, nevertheless, albeit he were right glad at heart to have achieved so signal a triumph, was sore grieved by anxiety on one account, for he saw that, whilst his own numbers were minished daily, those of the Gauls were daily multiplied. Wherefore, seeing it was doubtful whether he could any longer hold out against them, he chose rather to retire to his ships while the greater part of his army was still whole and the glory of the victory still fresh, and to set sail in quest of the island which the divine monition had prophesied should be his own. Nor was there any tarriance. With the assent of his men, he returned to his fleet, and after loading his ships with all the treasures and luxuries he had acquired, he re-embarked, and with a prosperous wind sought out the promised island, where he landed at last in safety at Totnes.

At that time the name of the island was Albion, and of none was it inhabited save only by a few giants. Natheless the pleasant aspect of the land, with the abundance of fish in the rivers and deer in the choice forests thereof did fill Brute and his companions with no small desire that they should dwell therein. Wherefore, after exploring certain districts of the land, they drove the giants they found to take refuge in the caverns of the mountains, and divided the country among them according as the Duke made grant thereof.

They began to till the fields, and to build them houses in such sort that after a brief space ye might have thought it had been inhabited from time immemorial. Then, at last, Brute calleth the island Britain, and his companions Britons, after his own name, for he was minded that his memory should be perpetuated in the derivation of the name. Whence afterward the country speech, which was aforetime called Trojan or crooked Greek, was called British.

But Corineus called that share of the kingdom which had fallen unto him by lot Cornwall, after the manner of his own name, and the people Cornishmen, therein following the Duke's example. For albeit that he might have had the choice of a province before all the others that had come thither, yet was he minded rather to have that share of the land which is now called Cornwall, whether from being, as it is, the *cornu* or horn of Britain, or from a corruption of the said name Corineus.

For naught gave him greater pleasure than to wrestle with the giants, of whom was greater plenty there than in any of the provinces that had been shared amongst his comrades. Among others was a certain hateful one by name Gogmagog, twelve cubits in height, who was of such lustihood that when he had once uprooted it, he would wield an oak tree as lightly as it were a wand of hazel.

Brute, having thus got footing in Britain, was preparing to improve the same, when Albion, who had named this island after his own name – by which it is sometimes called at this day – having intelligence thereof, raised his whole power, being men of gigantic stature, and vast strength, and bearing for their arms huge clubs of knotty oak, battle-axes, whirlbats of iron and globes full of spikes, fastened to a long pole by a chain; and with these, he fell upon the invaders on a certain day when Brute was holding high festival to the gods.

A bloody battle was fought, wherein the Trojans were worsted and many of them slain, and their whole army was forced to retire.

Brute, hereupon considering the disadvantage between his men and the giants, devised a stratagem to overthrow them, by digging in the night a very long and deep trench, at the bottom impaling it with sharp stakes, and covering it with boughs and rotten hurdles, on which he caused to be laid dried leaves and earth, only leaving some passages, well known to his men by particular marks.

This being done, he dared the giants to a second battle, which Albion readily accepted; and the fight being begun, after some dispute, Brute seemed to retire; whereupon the giants pressed on him with great fury; and the Trojans retiring nimbly beyond their trench made a stand, and ply'd them with a shower of darts and arrows, which manner of fight they were unacquainted with, whereby many of them were slain. However, Albion encouraging his men to come to handy strokes with their enemies, they rushed forward, and the vanguard immediately perished in the trenches; and the Trojans continuing to shoot their arrows very thick, the giants were put to flight, and pursued into Cornwall; where, in another bloody fight, Albion was slain by Brute, fighting hand to hand.

But his huge brother, Gogmagog, Brute had commanded to be taken alive as he was minded to see a wrestling bout betwixt him and Corineus, who was beyond measure keen to match himself against such monsters.

So Corineus, overjoyed at the prospect, girt himself for the encounter, and flinging away his arms, challenged him to a bout at wrestling.

At the start, on the one side stands Corineus, on the other the giant, each hugging the other tight in the shackles of their arms, both making the very air quake with their breathless gasping. It was not long before Gogmagog, grasping Corineus with all his force, brake him three of his ribs, two on the right side and one on the left.

Roused thereby to fury, Corineus gathered up all his strength, heaved him up on his shoulders and ran with his burden as fast as he could for the weight to the seashore nighest at hand. Mounting up to the top of a high cliff, and disengaging himself, he hurled the deadly monster he had carried on his shoulder into the sea, where, falling on the sharp rocks, he was mangled all to pieces and dyed the waves with his blood, so that ever thereafter that place from the flinging down of the giant hath been known as Lamgoemagot, to wit, 'Gogmagog's Leap,' and is called by that name unto this present day.

Corineus tells of his own exploit in the old tragedy of 'Locrine':

When first I followed thee and thine brave King,
I hazarded my life and dearest blood,
To purchase favour at your princely hands,
And for the same in dangerous attempts,
In sundry conflicts, and in divers broils,
I shew'd the courage of my manly mind:
For this I combatted with Gathelus,
The brother to Goffarius of Gaul;
For this I fought with furious Gogmagog,
A savage captain of a savage crew;
And for these deeds brave, Cornwall I received,
A grateful gift given by a grateful King;
And for this gift, this life and dearest blood
Will Corineus spend for Brutus' sake.

He does not, however, relate the most wonderful part of the affair, which comes to us through Fulke Fitz-Warine, an outlawed baron of the thirteenth century. Fulke tells how after Gogmagog was slain, a spirit of the devil entered into his body, and came into these parts, and long held possession of the country that never Briton dared to inhabit it. And how afterwards, King Bran, the son of Doneval, caused the ancient city of the giants to be rebuilt, repaired the walls, and strengthened the great fosses, and he became Burgh and Great March. And the devil came by night and took away everything that was therein, since which time nobody has ever inhabited there.

But Payn Peverel, a proud and courageous knight, heard this story, and determined to brave the demon. The latter appeared, in a fearful tempest, under the semblance of Gogmagog; he carried in his hand a great club, and from his mouth cast fire and smoke, with which the whole town was illuminated. However, devoutly making the sign of the Cross, the knight attacked him so fiercely with his trusty sword that ere long the demon cried for mercy – and disclosed the secret treasures of the town, promising Payn that he should be lord of all that soil.

Another account says that there were two brothers, Gog and Magog, who were taken prisoners by Brute and led in triumph to the place where London now stands; and when a palace was erected by the side of the River Thames, on the present site of Guildhall, these two giants were chained to the palace gates as porters. In memory of which their effigies, after their deaths, were set up as they now appear in Guildhall.

Certain it is that these two colossal figures, the older carrying a 'morning star' (the spiked globe fastened to a long pole by a chain with which horsemen used to demolish their enemies in a *mêlée*) have kept 'watch and ward' over London gates for centuries – and were believed by thousands of children to descend from their pedestals and go to dinner when St. Paul's clock struck twelve.

In 1415 victorious Henry V was welcomed into London by a male and female giant standing at the entrance to the Bridge, the man holding an axe and a bunch of keys; a few years later Henry VI was similarly greeted; in 1554, upon the public entry of Phillip and Mary, two great images of giants stood at the bridge, one named Gogmagog the Albion, one Corineus; and all through the sixteenth and seventeenth centuries these mighty reminders of the old tale figured in public pageants.

These figures were made only of wicker-work and pasteboard, put together with great art and ingenuity; and these two terrible original giants had the honour yearly to grace my Lord Mayor's show, being carried in great triumph in the time of the pageants; and when that eminent service was over, remounted their old stations in Guildhall, till by reason of their very great age, old time, with the help of a number of city rats and mice, had eaten up all their entrails. The dissolution of the two old, weak and feeble giants gave birth to the two present substantial and majestic giants; who, by order, and at the City charge, were formed and fashioned. Captain Richard Saunders, an eminent carver in King Street, Cheapside, was their father; who, after he had completely finished, clothed and armed these, his two sons, they were immediately advanced to their lofty stations in Guildhall, which they have peacefully enjoyed ever since the year 1708.

For over two hundred years now these fourteen-foot hollow wooden figures have stood in the Guildhall, one holding his spiked ball, the other a halberd. Many a parade have they figured in; many a child has been frightened by them; many a visitor has wondered at them; but few enough have ever read the tale of Corineus's encounter with the terrible original.

Battle with the Fomorians

from 'The Quest of the Children of Tuirenn'

NUADA OF THE SILVER HAND rose to become King of the Tuatha Dé Danann during the most savage days of the early invasions. The Fomorians, a repulsive band of giant sea-pirates, were the fiercest of opponents who swept through the country destroying cattle and property and imposing tribute on the people of the land. Every man of the Tuatha Dé Danann, no matter how rich or poor, was required to pay one ounce of gold to the Fomorians, and those who neglected to pay this tax at the annual assembly on the Hill of Uisneach were maimed or murdered without compassion. Balor of the Evil Eye was leader of these brutal invaders, and it was well known that when he turned his one glaring eyeball on his foes they immediately fell dead as if struck by a thunderbolt. Everyone lived in mortal fear of Balor, for no weapon had yet been discovered that could slay or even injure him. Times were bleak for the Tuatha Dé Danann, and the people had little faith in King Nuada, who appeared powerless to resist Balor's tyranny and oppression. As the days passed by, they yearned for a courageous leader who would rescue them from their life of wretched servitude.

The appalling misery of the Tuatha Dé Danann became known far and wide and, after a time, it reached the ears of Lugh of the Long Arm of the fairymounds, whose father was Cian, son of Cainte. As soon as he had grown to manhood, Lugh had proven his reputation as one of the most fearless warriors and was so revered by the elders of Fairyland that they had placed in his charge the wondrous magical gifts of Manannan the sea-god, who had protected their people for countless generations. Lugh rode the magnificent white steed of Manannan, known as Aenbarr, a horse as fleet of foot as the wailing gusts of winter, whose charm was such that no rider was ever wounded while seated astride her. He had the boat of Manannan, which could read a man's thoughts and travel in whatever direction its keeper demanded. He also wore Manannan's breastplate and body armour, which no weapon could ever pierce, and he carried the mighty sword known as 'The Retaliator', which could cut through any battle shield.

The day approached once more for the People of Dana to pay their annual taxes to the Fomorians, and they gathered together, as was customary, on the Hill of Uisneach to await the arrival of Balor's men. As they stood fearful and terrified in the chill morning air, several among them noticed a strange cavalry coming over the plain from the east towards them. At the head of this impressive group, seated high in command above the rest, was Lugh of the Long Arm, whose proud and noble countenance mirrored the splendour of the rising sun. The King was summoned to witness the spectacle, and he rode forth to salute the leader of the strange army. The two had just begun to converse amiably when they were interrupted by the approach of a grimy-looking band of men, instantly known to all as Fomorian tax-collectors. King Nuada bowed respectfully towards them and instructed his subjects to deliver their tributes without delay. Such a sad sight angered and humiliated Lugh of the Long Arm, and he drew the King aside and began to reproach him:

"Why do your subjects bow before such an evil-eyed brood," he demanded, "when they do not show you any mark of respect in return?"

"We are obliged to do this," replied Nuada. "If we refuse we would be killed instantly and our land has witnessed more than enough bloodshed at the hands of the Fomorians."

"Then it is time for the Tuatha Dé Danann to avenge this great injustice," replied Lugh, and with that, he began slaughtering Balor's emissaries single-handedly until all but one lay dead at his feet. Dragging the surviving creature before him, Lugh ordered him to deliver a stern warning to Balor:

"Return to your leader," he thundered, "and inform him that he no longer has any power over the People of Dana. Lugh of the Long Arm, the greatest of warriors, is more than eager to enter into combat with him if he possesses enough courage to meet the challenge."

Knowing that these words would not fail to enrage Balor, Lugh lost little time preparing himself for battle. He enlisted the King's help in assembling the strongest men in the kingdom to add to his own powerful army. Shining new weapons of steel were provided, and three thousand of the swiftest white horses were made ready for his men. A magnificent fleet of ships, designed to withstand the most venomous ocean waves, remained moored at port, awaiting the moment when Balor and his malicious crew would appear on the horizon.

The time finally arrived when the King received word that Balor's fierce army had landed at Eas Dara on the northwest coast of Connacht. Within hours, the Fomorians had pillaged the lands of Bodb the Red and plundered the homes of noblemen throughout the province. Hearing of this wanton destruction, Lugh of the Long Arm was more determined than ever to secure victory for the Tuatha Dé Danann. He rode across the plains of Erin back to his home to enlist the help of Cian, his father, who controlled all the armies of the fairymounds. His two uncles, Cu and Cethen, also offered their support, and the three brothers set off in different directions to round up the remaining warriors of Fairyland.

Cian journeyed northwards, and he did not rest until he reached Mag Muirthemne on the outskirts of Dundalk. As he crossed the plain, he observed three men, armed and mailed, riding towards him. At first he did not recognize them, but as they drew closer, he knew them to be the sons of Tuirenn, whose names were Brian, Iucharba and Iuchar. A long-standing feud had existed for years between the sons of Cainte and the sons of Tuirenn, and the hatred and enmity they felt towards each other was certain to provoke a deadly contest. Wishing to avoid an unequal clash of arms, Cian glanced around him for a place to hide and noticed a large herd of swine grazing nearby. He struck himself with a druidic wand and changed himself into a pig. Then he trotted off to join the herd and began to root up the ground like the rest of them.

The sons of Tuirenn were not slow to notice that the warrior who had been riding towards them had suddenly vanished into thin air. At first, they all appeared puzzled by his disappearance, but then Brian, the eldest of the three, began to question his younger brothers knowingly:

"Surely, brothers, you also saw the warrior on horseback," he said to them. "Have you no idea what became of him?"

"We do not know," they replied.

"Then you are not fit to call yourselves warriors," chided Brian, "for that horseman can be no friend of ours if he is cowardly enough to change himself into one of these swine. The instruction you received in the City of Learning has been wasted on you if you cannot even tell an enchanted beast from a natural one."

And as he was saying this, he struck Iucharba and Iuchar with his own druidic wand, transforming them into two sprightly hounds that howled and yelped impatiently to follow the trail of the enchanted pig.

Before long, the pig had been hunted down and driven into a small wood, where Brian cast his spear at it, driving it clean through the animal's chest. Screaming in pain, the injured pig began to speak in a human voice and begged his captors for mercy:

"Allow me a dignified death," the animal pleaded. "I am originally a human being, so grant me permission to pass into my own shape before I die."

"I will allow this," answered Brian, "since I am often less reluctant to kill a man than a pig."

Then Cian, son of Cainte, stood before them with blood trickling down his cloak from the gaping wound in his chest.

"I have outwitted you," he cried, "for if you had killed me as a pig, you would only be sentenced for killing an animal, but now you must kill me in my own human shape. And I must warn you that the penalty you will pay for this crime is far greater than any ever paid before on the death of a nobleman, for the weapons you shall use will cry out in anguish, proclaiming your wicked deed to my son, Lugh of the Long Arm".

"We will not slay you with any weapons in that case," replied Brian triumphantly, "but with the stones that lie on the ground around us." And the three brothers began to pelt Cian with jagged rocks and stones until his body was a mass of wounds, and he fell to the earth battered and lifeless. The sons of Tuirenn then buried him where he had fallen in an unmarked grave and hurried off to join the war against the Fomorians.

With the great armies of Fairyland and the noble cavalcade of King Nuada at his side, Lugh of the Long Arm won battle after battle against Balor and his men. Spears shot savagely through the air and scabbards clashed furiously until, at last, the Fomorians could hold out no longer. Retreating to the coast, the terrified survivors and their leader boarded their vessels and sailed as fast as the winds could carry them, back through the northern mists towards their own depraved land. Lugh of the Long Arm became the hero of his people, and they presented him with the finest trophies of valour the kingdom had to offer, including a golden war chariot studded with precious jewels, which was driven by four of the brawniest milk-white steeds.

Conall Cra Bhuidhe

CONALL CRA BHUIDHE was a sturdy tenant in Eirinn: he had four sons. There was at that time a king over every fifth of Eirinn. It fell out for the children of the king that was near Conall, that they themselves and the children of Conall came to blows. The children of Conall got the upper hand, and they killed the king's big son. The king sent a message for Conall, and he said to him – "Oh, Conall! what made thy sons go to spring on my sons till my big son was killed by thy children? but I see that though I follow thee revengefully, I shall not be much the better for it, and I will now set a thing before thee, and if thou wilt do it, I will not follow thee with revenge. If thou thyself, and thy sons, will get for me the brown horse of the king of Lochlann, thou shalt get the souls of thy sons."

"Why," said Conall, "should not I do the pleasure of the king, though there should be no souls of my sons in dread at all. Hard is the matter thou requirest of me, but I will lose my own life, and the life of my sons, or else I will do the pleasure of the king."

After these words Conall left the king, and he went home: when he got home he was under much trouble and perplexity. When he went to lie down he told his wife the thing the king had set before him. His wife took much sorrow that he was obliged to part from herself, while she knew not if she should see him more. "Oh, Conall," said. she, "why didst not thou let the king do his own pleasure to thy sons, rather than be going now, while I know not if ever I shall see thee more?" When he rose on the morrow, he set himself and his four sons in order, and they took their journey towards Lochlann, and they made no stop but (were) tearing ocean till they reached it. When they reached Lochlann they did not know what they should do. Said the old man to his sons – "stop ye, and we will seek out the house of the king's miller."

When they went into the house of the king's miller, the man asked them to stop there for the night. Conall told the miller that his own children and the children of the king had fallen out, and that his children had killed the king's son, and there was nothing that would please the king but that he should get the brown horse of the king of Lochlann. "If thou wilt do me a kindness, and wilt put me in a way to get him, for certain I will pay thee for it."

"The thing is silly that thou art come to seek," said the miller; "for the king has laid his mind on him so greatly that thou wilt not get him in any way unless thou steal him; but if thou thyself canst make out a way, I will hide thy secret."

"This, I am thinking," said Conall, "since thou art working every day for the king, that thou and thy gillies should put myself and my sons into five sacks of bran."

"The plan that came into thy head is not bad," said the miller. The miller spoke to his gillies, and he said to them to do this, and they put them in five sacks. The king's gillies came to seek the bran, and they took the five sacks with them, and they emptied them before the horses. The servants locked the door, and they went away.

When they rose to lay hand on the brown horse, said Conall, "You shall not do that. It is hard to get out of this; let us make for ourselves five hiding holes, so that if they perceive us we may go in hiding." They made the holes, then they laid hands on the horse. The horse was pretty well unbroken, and he set to making a terrible noise through the stable. The king perceived him. He heard the noise. "It must be that that was my brown horse," said he to his gillies; "try what is wrong with him."

The servants went out, and when Conall and his sons perceived them coming they went into the hiding holes. The servants looked amongst the horses, and they did not find anything wrong; and they returned and they told this to the king, and the king said to them that if nothing was wrong that they should go to their places of rest. When the gillies had time to be gone, Conall and his sons laid the next hand on the horse. If the noise was great that he made before, the noise he made now was seven times greater. The king sent a message for his gillies again, and said for certain there was something troubling the brown horse. "Go and look well about him." The servants went out, and they went to their hiding holes. The servants rummaged well, and did not find a thing. They returned and they told this. "That is marvellous for me," said the king: "go you to lie down again, and if I perceive it again I will go out myself." When Conall and his sons perceived that the gillies were gone, they laid hands again on the horse, and one of them caught him, and if the noise that the horse made on the two former times was great, he made more this time.

"Be this from me," said the king; "it must be that someone is troubling my brown horse." He sounded the bell hastily, and when his waiting man came to him, he said to him to set the stable gillies on foot that something was wrong with the horse. The gillies came, and the king went with them. When Conall and his sons perceived the following coming they went to the hiding holes. The king was a wary man, and he saw where the horses were making a noise. "Be clever," said the king, "there are men within the stable, and let us get them somehow." The king followed the tracks of the men, and he found them. Every man was acquainted with Conall, for he was a valued tenant by the king of Eirinn, and when the king brought them up out of the holes he said, "Oh, Conall art thou here?" "I am, O king, without question, and necessity made me come. I am under thy pardon, and under thine honour, and under thy grace." He told how it happened to him, and that he had to get the brown horse for the king of Eirinn, or that his son was to be put to death.

"I knew that I should not get him by asking, and I was going to steal him."

"Yes, Conall, it is well enough, but come in," said the king. He desired his look-out men to set a watch on the sons of Conall, and to give them meat. And a double watch was set that night on the sons of Conall. "Now, O Conall," said the king, "wert thou ever in a harder place than to be seeing thy lot of sons hanged tomorrow? But thou didst set it to my goodness and to my grace, and that it was necessity brought it on thee, and I must not hang thee. Tell me any case in which thou wert as hard as this, and if thou tellest that, thou shalt get the soul of thy youngest son with thee." "I will tell a case as hard in which I was," said Conall.

"I was a young lad, and my father had much land, and he had parks of year-old cows, and one of them had just calved, and my father told me to bring her home. I took with me a laddie, and we found the cow, and we took her with us. There fell a shower of snow. We went into the herd's bothy, and we took the cow and the calf in with us, and we were letting the shower (pass) from us. What came in but one cat and ten, and one great one-eyed fox-coloured cat as head bard over them. When they came in, in very deed I myself had no liking for their company. 'Strike up with you,' said the head bard, I why should we be still? and sing a cronan to Conall Cra-Bhui.' I was amazed that my name was known to the cats themselves. When they had sung the cronan, said the head bard, 'Now, O Conall, pay the reward of the cronan that the cats have sung to thee.' 'Well then,' said I myself, 'I have no reward whatsoever for you, unless you should go down and take that calf.' No sooner said I the word than the two cats and ten went down to attack the calf, and, in very deed, he did not last them long. 'Play up with you, why should you be silent? Make a cronan to Conall Cra-Bhui,' said the head bard. Certainly I had no liking at all for the cronan, but up came the one cat and ten, and if they did not sing me a cronan then and there! 'Pay them now their reward,' said the great fox-coloured cat. 'I am tired myself of yourselves and your rewards,' said I. 'I have no reward for you unless you take that cow down there.' They betook themselves to the cow, and indeed she did not stand them out for long.

"'Why will you be silent? Go up and sing a cronan to Conall Cra-Bhui,' said the head bard. And surely, oh, king, I had no care for them or for their cronan, for I began to see that they were not good comrades. When they had sung me the cronan. they betook themselves down where the head bard was. 'Pay now their reward,' said the head bard; and for sure, oh, king, I had no reward for them; and I said to them, 'I have no reward for you, unless you will take that, laddie with you and make use of him.' When the boy heard this he took himself out, and the cats after him. And surely, oh, king, there was 'striongan' and catterwauling between them. When they took themselves out, I took out at a turf window that was at the back of the house. I took myself off as hard as I might into the wood. I was swift enough and strong at that time; and when I felt the rustling 'toirm' of the cats after me I climbed into as high a tree as I saw in the place, and (one) that was close in the top; and I hid myself as well as I might. The cats began to search for me through the wood, and they were not finding me; and when they were tired, each one said to the other that they would turn back. 'But,' said the one-eyed fox-coloured cat that was commander-in-chief over them, 'you saw him not with your two eyes, and though I have but one eye, there's the rascal up in the top of the tree.' When he had said that, one of them went up in the tree, and as he was coming where I was, I drew a weapon that I had and I killed him. 'Be this from me!' said the one-eyed one – 'I must not be losing my company thus; gather round the root of the tree and dig about it, and let down that extortioner to earth.' On this they gathered about her (the tree), and they dug about her root, and the first branching root that they cut, she gave a shiver to fall, and I myself gave a shout, and it was not to be wondered at. There was in the neighbourhood of the wood a priest, and he had ten men with him delving, and he said, 'There is a shout of extremity and I must not be without replying to it.' And the wisest of the men said, 'Let it alone till we hear it again.' The cats began, and they began wildly, and they broke the next root; and I myself gave the next shout, and in very deed it was not weak. 'Certainly,' said the priest, 'it is a man in extremity – let us move.' They were setting themselves in order for moving. And the cats arose on the tree, and they broke the third root, and the tree fell on her elbow. I gave the third shout. The stalwart men hasted, and when they saw how the cats served the tree, they began at them with the spades; and they themselves and the cats began at each other, till they were killed altogether – the men and the cats. And surely, oh king, I did not move till I saw the last one of them falling. I came home. And there's for thee the hardest case in which I ever was; and it seems to me that tearing by the cats were harder than hanging tomorrow by the king of Lochlann.

"Oh! Conall," said the king, "thou art full of words. Thou hast freed the soul of thy son with thy tale; and if thou tellest me a harder case than thy three sons to be hanged tomorrow, thou wilt get thy second youngest son with thee, and then thou wilt have two sons."

"Well then," said Conall, "on condition that thou dost that, I was in a harder case than to be in thy power in prison tonight." Let's hear," said the king. – "I was there," said Conall, "as a young lad, and I went out hunting, and my father's land was beside the sea, and it was rough with rocks, caves, and geos. When I was going on the top of the shore, I saw as if there were a smoke coming up between two rocks, and I began to look what might be the meaning of the smoke coming up there. When I was looking, what should I do but fall; and the place was so full of manure, that neither bone nor skin was broken. I knew not how I should get out of this. I was not looking before me, but I was looking over head the way I came – and the day will never come that I could get up there. It was terrible for me to be there till I should die. I heard a great clattering 'tuarneileis' coming, and what was there but a great giant and two dozen of goats with him, and a buck at their head. And when the giant had tied the goats, he came up and he said to me, 'Hao O! Conall, it's long since my knife is rusting in my pouch waiting for thy tender flesh.' 'Och!' said I, 'it's not much thou wilt be bettered by me, though thou should'st tear me asunder; I will make but one meal for thee. But I see that thou art one-eyed. I am a good leech, and I will give thee the sight of the other eye.' The giant went and he drew the great cauldron on the site of the fire. I myself was telling him how he should heat the water, so that I should give its sight to the other eye. I got heather and I made a rubber of it, and I set him upright in the cauldron. I began at the eye that was well, pretending to him that I would give its sight to the other one, till I left them as bad as each other; and surely it was easier to spoil the one that was well than to give sight to the other.

"When he 'saw' that he could not see a glimpse, and when I myself said to him that I would get out in spite of him, he gave that spring out of the water, and he stood in the mouth of the cave, and he said that he would have revenge for the sight of his eye. I had but to stay there crouched the length of the night, holding in my breath in such a way that he might not feel where I was.

"When he felt the birds calling in the morning, and knew that the day was, he said – "Art thou sleeping? Awake and let out my lot of goats." I killed the buck. He cried, 'I will not believe that thou art not killing my buck.' 'I am not,' said I, 'but the ropes are so tight that I take long to loose them.' I let out one of the goats, and he was caressing her, and he said to her, 'There thou art thou shaggy, hairy white goat, and thou seest me, but I see thee not.' I was letting them out by the way of one and one, as I flayed the buck, and before the last one was out I had him flayed *bag wise*. Then I went and I put my legs in place of his legs, and my hands in place of his fore legs, and my head in place of his head, and the horns on top of my head, so that the brute might think that it was the buck. I went out. When I was going out the giant laid his hand on me, and he said, 'There thou art thou pretty buck; thou seest me, but I see thee not.' When I myself got out, and I saw the world about me, surely, oh, king! joy was on me. When I was out and had shaken the skin off me, I said to the brute, 'I am out now in spite of thee.' 'Aha!' said he, 'hast thou done this to me. Since thou were so stalwart that thou hast got out, I will give thee a ring that I have here, and keep the ring, and it will do thee good.' 'I will not take the ring from thee,' said I, 'but throw it, and I will take it with me.' He threw the ring on the flat ground, I went myself and I lifted the ring, and I put it on my finger. When he said me then. 'Is the ring fitting thee?' I said to him, 'It is.' He said, 'Where art thou ring?' And the ring said, 'I am here.' The brute went and he betook himself towards where the ring was speaking, and now I saw that I was in a harder case than ever I was. I drew a dirk. I cut the finger off from me, and I threw it from me as far as I could out on the loch, and there was a great depth in the place. He shouted, 'Where art thou, ring?' And the ring said, 'I am here,' though it was on the ground of ocean. He gave a spring after the ring, and out he went in the sea. And I was as pleased here when I saw him drowning, as though thou shouldst let my own life and the life of my two sons with me, and not lay any more trouble on me.

"When the giant was drowned I went in, and I took with me all he had of gold and silver, and I went home, and surely great joy was on my people when I arrived. And as a sign for thee, look thou, the finger is off me."

"Yes, indeed, Conall, thou art wordy and wise," said the king. "I see thy finger is off. Thou hast freed thy two sons, but tell me a case in which thou ever wert that is harder than to be looking on thy two sons being hanged tomorrow, and thou wilt get the soul of thy second eldest son with thee."

"Then went my father," said Conall, "and he got me a wife, and I was married. I went to hunt. I was going beside the sea, and I saw an island over in the midst of the loch, and I came there where a boat was with a rope before her and a rope behind her, and many precious things within her. I looked myself on the boat to see how I might get part of them. I put in the one foot, and the other foot was on the ground, and when I raised my head what was it but the boat over in the middle of the loch, and she never stopped till she reached the island. When I went out of the boat the boat returned where she was before. I did not know now what I should do. The place was without meat or clothing, without the appearance of a house on it.

I raised out on the top of a hill. I came to a glen; I saw in it, at the bottom of a chasm, a woman who had got a child, and the child was naked on her knee, and a knife in her hand. She would attempt to put the knife in the throat of the babe, and the babe would begin to laugh in her face, and she would begin to cry, and she would throw the knife behind her. I thought to myself that I was near my foe and far from my friends, and I called to the woman, 'What art thou doing here?' And she said to me, 'What brought thee here?' I told her myself word upon word how I came. 'Well then,' said she, 'it was so I came also.' She showed me to the place where I should come in where she was. I went in, and I said to her, 'What was in fault that thou wert putting the knife on the neck of the child.' 'It is that he must be cooked for the giant who is here, or else no more of my world will be before me.' I went up steps of stairs, and I saw a chamber full of stripped corpses. I took a lump out of the corpse that was whitest, and I tied a string to the child's foot, and a string to the lump, and I put the lump in his mouth, and when it went in his throat he would give a stretch to his leg, and he would take it out of his throat, but with the length of the thread he could not take it out of his mouth. I cast the child into a basket of down, and I asked her to cook the corpse for the giant in place of the child. 'How can I do that?' said she, 'when he has count of the corpses.' 'Do thou as I ask thee, and I will strip myself, and I will go amongst the corpses, and then he will have the same count,' said I. She did as I asked her. We put the corpse in the great cauldron, but we could not put on the lid. When he was coming home I stripped myself, and I went amongst the corpses. He came home, and she served up the corpse on a great platter, and when he ate it he was complaining that he found it too tough for a child.

"'I did as thou asked me,' said she. 'Thou hadst count of the corpses thyself, and go up now and count them.' He counted them and he had them. 'I see one of a white body there,' said he. 'I will lie down a while and I will have him when I wake.'

When he rose he went up and gripped me, and I never was in such a case as when he was hauling me down the stair with my head after me. He threw me into the cauldron, and he lifted the lid and he put the lid into the cauldron. And now I was sure I would scald before I could get out of that. As fortune favoured me, the brute slept beside the cauldron. There I was scalded by the bottom of the cauldron. When she perceived that he was asleep, she set her mouth quietly to the hole that was in the lid, and she said to me 'was I alive.' I said I was. I put up my head, and the brute's forefinger was so large, that my head went through easily. Everything was coming easily with me till I began to bring up my hips. I left the skin of my hips about the mouth of the hole, and I came out. When I got out of the cauldron I knew not what to do; and she said to me that there was no weapon that would kill him but his own weapon. I began to draw his spear, and every breath that he would draw I would think I would be down his throat, and when his breath came out I was back again just as far. But with every ill that befell me I got the spear loosed from him. Then I was as one under a bundle of straw in a great wind, for I could not manage the spear. And it was fearful to look on the brute, who had but one eye in the midst of his face; and it was not agreeable for the like of me to attack him. I drew the dart as best I could, and I set it in his eye. When he felt this he gave his head a lift, and he struck the other end of the dart on the top of the cave, and it went through to the back of his head. And he fell cold dead where he was; and thou mayest be sure, oh king, that joy was on me. I myself and the woman went out on clear ground, and we passed the night there. I went and got the boat with which I came, and she was no way lightened, and took the woman and the child over on dry land; and I returned home."

The king's mother was putting on a fire at this time, and listening to Conall telling the tale about the child. "Is it thou," said she, "that were there?"

"Well then," said he, "'twas I."

"Och! och!" said she, "'twas I that was there, and the king is the child whose life thou didst save; and it is to thee that life thanks might be given." Then they took great joy.

The king said, "Oh Conall, thou camest through great hardships. And now the brown horse is thine, and his sack full of the most precious things that are in my treasury."

They lay down that night, and if it was early that Conall rose, it was earlier than that that the queen was on foot making ready. He got the brown horse and his sack full of gold and silver and stones of great price, and then Conall and his four sons went away, and they returned home to the Erin realm of gladness. He left the gold and silver in his house, and he went with the horse to the king. They were good friends evermore. He returned home to his wife, and they set in order a feast; and that was the feast, oh son and brother!

Amadis Among the Giants

KING LISUARTE OF GREAT BRITAIN WAS AT TABLE; the cloths were removed, and Galaor, Florestan and Agrayes were about him. These were among his foremost knights, but they grieved for the absence of their brother and kinsman, the incomparable Amadis of Gaul; he, for love and worship of the peerless Oriana, the king's daughter, had long wandered about in disguise, performing such exploits as made the whole world ring with his renown. Sometime he was known as the Child of the Sea, later as the Knight of the Green Sword, and at this time he went by the name of Beltenebros, or the Fair Mystery. And among his deeds had been the slaying of King Abies of Ireland, whose limbs were as those of a giant, and who numbered among his allies many astonishing fierce giants.

Then there came a strange knight into the palace, all armed except his head and his hands, and with him two squires, and he carried in his hand a letter sealed with five seals, which on his knees he presented to the king, saying:

"Let this be read, and then I will say for what I am come."

Lisuarte perceived that it was a letter of credence and bade him speak his errand.

Then said the knight: "King, I defy thee on the part of Famongomadan, the Giant of the Boiling Lake; Cartadaque, his nephew, giant of the Defended Mountain; Madanfabul, his marriage-brother, the giant of the Vermillion Tower; and for Quadragante, brother of King Abies of Ireland, and Arcalaus the Enchanter:

"They tell thee that thy death, and the death of all who call themselves thine is in their hands, for they are coming against thee on King Cildadan's side. Howbeit, if thou wilt give thy daughter Oriana to Madasima, the fair daughter of Famongomadan, to be her damsel and servant, they will not injure thee, nor be thine enemies, but will give her in marriage when it is time, to Basogante, Madasima's brother, who doth well deserve to be lord of her and thy land.

"Therefore, King, look to thy choice! Such peace or such war."

Lisuarte smiled when he began to reply, as one who set at naught the defiance. "Knight," said he, "better is a dangerous war than a dishonourable peace: a bad account should I render to him who hath placed me in this high rank, if for lack of heart I should so shamefully debase it. Tell them I would rather choose war with them all the days of my life, and death in that war at last, than consent to the peace they offer. Tell me where I may send a knight to carry them this answer."

"They may be found," replied the ambassador, "in the Boiling Lake, which is in the Isle of Mongaza."

So it was done, and a knight of King Lisuarte's carried them his reply defying them to the utmost.

Now Amadis was at a nunnery, being but barely recovered of severe wounds. He sent Enil, his squire for the time, to the next town to get arms made for him, a green shield with as many golden lions as it could hold, and to buy him a horse, and a sword and breastplate, the best he could find. For he purposed to ride to Millaflores to see Oriana, the lady of all his thoughts.

In twenty days all was ready, as he had ordered it; and at the end of that time arrived Durin, who brought word from her who was called the one without a peer. Then he walked apart with Durin, and heard the message of Oriana, and also how his brethren were to be in the battle against Cildadan and the giants, and of the defiance that Famongomadan had sent, and how he demanded Oriana to be serving-damsel to his daughter till he should give her in marriage to his son. When he heard this, his flesh shook with exceeding anger, and he resolved in himself, so soon as he had seen his lady, to undertake no adventure till he had found Famongomadan, and fought with him a combat for the utterance of what he had dared propose.

That night Amadis, still going by the name of Beltenebros even to his companion, took leave of the nuns, and early the next day, armed in his green armour, he set forth, and Enil with him carrying his shield and helmet and lance. The day was clear, and he feeling himself in his strength and once more in arms, began to manage his horse so skilfully that Enil said to him:

"I know not, sir, what the strength of your heart may be, but I never saw a knight appear so well in arms."

"The worth," quoth Amadis, "lies in a good heart, not in a good appearance. Happy dole hath he whom God has gifted with both. You have judged the one, judge the other as you shall see it deserves when put to proof."

Seven days they travelled without adventure, and Amadis, as he drew nearer, wore his helmet that he might not be known. On the eighth, as they were passing the foot of a mountain, they met a knight upon a large bay horse, so huge in stature that he appeared to be a giant, and two squires carrying his arms.

He cried out with a loud voice to Amadis: "Stop, Sir Knight, till you have told me what I want to know."

Amadis looked at the stranger's shield, and seeing there golden flowers in a field azure, he knew it was Don Quadragante, brother to King Abies of Ireland and his own deadly foe. Yet, remembering Famongomadan, he would willingly now have avoided battle; as also, because he was on his way to Oriana, and feared lest the great prowess of this knight should cause him some delay. Howbeit he stopt, and bade Enil give him his arms, if they were wanted.

"God protect you!" quoth Enil. "He looks to me more like a devil than a knight."

"He is no devil," said Amadis, "but a right good knight, of whom I have heard heretofore."

By this time Quadragante was come up, and said to him: "Knight, you must tell me if you belong to the household of King Lisuarte."

"Why ask you?"

"Because I have defied him and all his household, and kill all of them whom I meet."

Amadis felt his anger rising, and replied: "You are one of those who hath challenged him?"

"I am; and I am he who will do to him and his all the evil in my power."

"And who are you?"

"My name is Don Quadragante; and I am brother to that King Abies who was foully slain by an unknown knight of Lisuarte's."

"Certes, Don Quadragante, notwithstanding your high lineage and your great prowess in arms, this is great folly in you to defy the best king in the world. They who undertake more than they can effect are rather rash than hardy. I am not this king's vassal, nor am I of his land, but for his goodness my heart is disposed to serve him, so that I may count myself among those whom you have defied; if you choose battle with me, you may have it; if not, go your way."

"I believe, knight," said Quadragante, "you speak thus boldly because you know me so little; pray you, tell me your name."

"They call me Beltenebros: you will know me by it no better than before, for it is a name of no renown; but, though I am of a far land, I have heard that you are seeking Amadis of Gaul, and, by what I hear of him, it is no loss to you that you cannot find him."

"What!" quoth Quadragante. "Do you prize him, whom I hate so much, above me? Know that your death-hour is arrived. Take thy arms and defend thyself if thou canst."

"I might do it with some doubt against others, but can have none in opposing thee, who art so full of pride and threats."

Then they ran their course; both felt the shock: the horse of Amadis reeled, and he himself was wounded at the nipple of the breast. Quadragante was unhorsed and hurt in the ribs. He rose and ran at Amadis, who did not see him, for he was adjusting his helmet, and mortally stabbed his horse. Amadis leaped off and went against him sword in hand in great anger.

"There was no courage in this," he cried. "Your own horse was strong enough to have finished the battle without this villainy."

The blows fell as thick and loud as though ten knights had been in combat, for both put forth all their strength and skill, and the fight lasted from the hour of terce till vespers; but then Quadragante, overcome with fatigue and with a blow that Amadis gave him on the helmet, fell down senseless.

Amadis took off his helmet to see if he were dead; the air revived him; he placed the sword-point at his face, saying:

"Remember thy soul, for thou art a dead man."

"Ah, Beltenebros," cried he, "for God's sake let me live, for my soul's sake."

"Yield thyself vanquished then, and promise to fulfill what I command."

"I will fulfill your will to save my life," said Quadragante, "but there is no reason wherefore I should confess myself vanquished: he is not vanquished who in his defence hath shown no fear, doing his utmost till strength and breath fail him and he falls; but he who does not do what he could have done, for lack of heart."

"You say well," said Amadis, "and I like much what I have heard from you; give me your hand and your promise then." And he called the squire to witness it:

"You shall go forthwith to the court of King Lisuarte, and remain there till Amadis arrives, and then you shall pardon him for the death of your brother, King Abies; for they by their own will fought in lists together, and such revenge, even among those of meaner degree, ought not to be pursued. However, you shall make null the defiance against King Lisuarte, and not take arms against those in his service."

All this did Quadragante promise against his will and in the fear of death. He then ordered his squires to make a litter and remove him; and Amadis, mounting the bay horse of his antagonist, gave his arms to Enil and departed.

Four damsels, who were hawking with a merlin, had seen the battle, and they now came up and requested the unknown would go to their castle, where he should be honourably welcomed, for the good will which he had manifested to King Lisuarte. He thankfully accepted their hospitality, being sore wearied with the struggle, and accompanied them. They found no other wound than that upon his breast, which bled much; howbeit in three days he departed.

On the second day at noon, from a hill top he beheld the city of London, and, to the right thereof, the castle of Miraflores, where his lady Oriana then abode. Here he stood a while, gazing and devising how he might despatch Enil.

Presently he was taunted by a company of knights to joust with them, and at last he rode against them and overthrew all ten, one after another.

Then came he, being athirst, to the Fountain of the Three Channels, and tarried there a while, discoursing with some damsels who were on their way to the court, and determining to fix upon this as a meeting place with Enil after he had been to his lady.

While they were talking, there came along the road a waggon drawn by twelve palfreys, and on it were two dwarfs who drove. There were many knights in chains in the waggon, and their shields were hanging at the side, and many damsels and girls among them weeping and lamenting loudly.

Before it went a giant, so great that he was fearful to behold; he rode a huge black horse, and he was armed with plates of steel, and his helmet shone bright, and in his hand he had a boar spear, whose point was a full arm's-length long. Behind the waggon was another giant, who appeared more huge and terrible than the first.

The damsels with Amadis seeing them were greatly terrified, and hid themselves among the trees. Presently the giant who rode foremost turned to the dwarfs and cried:

"I will cut you into a thousand pieces if you suffer these girls to shed their own blood, for I mean to do sacrifice with it to my God, whom I adore."

When Amadis heard this he knew it was Famongomadan, for he had a custom to sacrifice damsels to an idol in the Boiling Lake, by whose advice and words he was guided in everything. At this time Amadis did not wish to encounter him, because he hoped shortly to be with Oriana, and also because his joust with the ten knights had wearied him; but he knew the knights in the waggon, and saw that Princess Leonoreta and her damsels were there, for Famongomadan, who always took his waggon with him to carry away all he could find, had seized them in their tents.

Immediately he mounted, and called to Enil for his arms. But Enil said:

"Let those devils pass by first."

"Give me!" quoth Amadis. "I shall try God's mercy before they pass, to see if I can redress this villainy."

"O, sir," cried the squire, "why have you so little compassion on your youth? If the best twenty knights of King Lisuarte's court were here, they would not venture to attack them."

"Care thou not for that," replied his master. "If I let them pass without doing my best I should be unworthy to appear among gallant men: you shall behold my fortune."

Enil gave him his arms, weeping, and Amadis then descended the sloping ground to meet them. He looked towards Miraflores as he went, and said:

"O Oriana, my lady, never did I attempt adventure confiding in my own courage, but in you: my gentle lady, assist me now, in this great need."

He felt his full strength now, and all fear was gone, and he cried out to the dwarfs to stop.

When the foremost giant, Famongomadan, heard him, he came towards him with such rage that smoke came through the vizor of his helmet, and he shook his boar spear so forcefully that its ends almost met.

"Unhappy wretch!" cried he. "Who gave thee boldness enough to dare appear before me?"

"That Lord," quoth Amadis, "whom thou hast offended, who will give me strength today to break thy pride."

"Come on! Come on!" cried the giant. "And see if his power can protect thee from mine."

Amadis fitted the lance under his arm and ran against him full speed: he smote him below the waist with such exceeding force that the spear burst through the plates of steel, and ran through him, even so as to strike the saddle behind, that the girths broke and he fell with the saddle, the broken lance remaining in him. His boar spear had taken effect upon the horse of Amadis and mortally wounded him. The knight leaped off and drew his sword.

Famongomadan rose up so enraged that fire came from him, and he plucked the lance from his wound, and threw it at Amadis so violently that if the shield had not protected his helmet, it would have driven him to the ground; but his own bowels came out with the weapon, and he fell, crying:

"Help, Basagante! I am slain."

At this the other giant came up as fast as his horse could carry him: he had a steel axe in his hand, and with this he thought to have cut his enemy in two; but Amadis avoided the blow, and at the same time struck the giant's horse; the stroke fell short, but the tip of his sword cut through the stirrup-leather, and cut the leg also half through.

The giant in his fury did not feel the wound, though he missed the stirrup: he turned and raised his axe again. Amadis had taken the shield from his neck, and was holding it by the throngs: the axe fell on it and sank in and drove it from his hands to the ground. He had made another stroke; the sword wounded Basagante's arm, and, glancing below upon the plates of fine steel, broke, so that only the handle remained in his hand.

Not for this was he a whit dismayed; he saw the giant could not pluck his axe from the shield, and he ran and caught it by the handle also. Both struggled for the weapon; it was on that side where the stirrup had been cut away, so that Basagante lost his balance: the horse started and he fell; and Amadis got the battle-axe.

The giant drew his sword in vast fury, and would have run at the knight, but the nerves of his leg were cut through; he fell upon one knee, and Amadis smote him on the helmet, that the laces burst and it fell off. He, seeing his enemy so near, thought with his sword, which was very long, to smite off his head; the blow was aimed too high, it cut off the whole crown of the helmet, and cut away the hair with it. Amadis drew back; the helmet fell over his head upon his shoulders, and Leonoreta and the damsels, who were on their knees in the waggon praying to God to deliver them, tore their hair and began to shriek and call upon the Virgin, thinking he was surely slain. He himself put up his hand to feel if he were wounded to death, but feeling no harm made again at the giant, whose sword falling upon a stone in the last blow had broken.

Basagante's heart failed him now; he made one stroke more and cut the knight slightly in the leg with the broken sword; but Amadis let drive the battle-axe at his head: it cut away the ear and the cheek and the jaw, and Basagante fell, writhing in the agony of death.

At this time Famongomadan had taken off his helmet, and was holding his hands upon his wound to check the blood. When he saw his son slain he began to blaspheme God and His Mother Holy Mary, saying that he did not so much grieve to die as that he could not now destroy their monasteries and churches, because they had suffered him and his son to be conquered by one knight.

Amadis was then upon his knees returning thanks to God when he heard the blasphemer, and he exclaimed:

"Accursed of God and of His Blessed Mother! Now shalt thou suffer for thy cruelties. Pray to thine idol that, as thou hast shed so much blood before him, he may stop this blood of thine from flowing out with thy life."

The giant continued to curse God and his saints. Then Amadis plucked the boar spear from the horse's body, and thrust it into the mouth of Famongomadan, and nailed him backward to the earth.

He then put on Basagante's helmet that he might not be known, and mounting the other's horse rode up to the waggon and broke the chains of all who were prisoners therein. And he besought them to take the bodies of the giants to King Lisuarte, and say they were sent him by a strange knight called Beltenebros; and he begged the princess to permit him to take the black horse of Famongomadan, because it was a strong and handsome horse, and he would ride him in the battle against King Cildadan.

The bodies of the giants were so huge that they were obliged to bend their knees to lay them in the waggon.

Leonoreta and her damsels made garlands for their heads, and being right joyful for their deliverance, entered London singing in triumph. Much was King Lisuarte astonished at their adventure, and the more for Quadragante had already presented himself on the part of Beltenebros, of whom nothing else was known.

"I would he were among us," said the King. "I would not lose him for anything that he could ask and I could grant."

As for the further exploits of Amadis; and how, by the side of his brethren and the king, he conquered all those island giants in pitched battle; and how he slew the unspeakable monstrous offspring of the giant of Devil's Island that was called the Endriago; and how he and the peerless Oriana, in whom all beauty was centred, proved in the Firm Island those final adventures of the Arch of True Lovers and of the Forbidden Chamber; – are not these and many things beside written in the Portuguese chronicler's tale of *Amadis of Gaul*? And was this not one of the only three romances spared by the good Curate when he purged Don Quixote's library with fire – for that forsooth it was the best of all the romances?

Pan Gu and the Creation of the Universe

AT THE VERY BEGINNING OF TIME, when only darkness and chaos existed and the heavens and the earth had not yet been properly divided up, the universe resembled the shape of a large egg. And at the centre of this egg, the first living creature one day came into being. After many thousands of years, when he had gathered sufficient strength and energy and had grown to the size of a giant, the creature, who gave himself the name of Pan Gu, awoke fully refreshed from his long rest and stood upright within his shell. He began to yawn very loudly and to stretch his enormous limbs, and as he did so, the walls of the egg were cracked open and separated into two even portions. The lighter, more fragile, part of the egg floated delicately upwards to form the white silken sheet of the sky, while the heavier, more substantial part, dropped downwards to form the earth's crusty surface.

Now when Pan Gu observed this, he was happy and proud to have created some light in place of the darkness and chaos out of which he had emerged. But at the same time, he began to fear that the skies and the earth might fuse once more, and he stood and scratched his huge head, pondering a solution to the problem. And after he had thought things through for quite a while, he decided that the only way to keep the two elements at a safe distance from each other was to place his own great bulk between them. So he took up his position, heaving and pushing upwards against the sky with his hands and pressing downwards into the earth with all the weight of his massive feet until a reasonable gap had been formed.

For the next eighteen thousand years, Pan Gu continued to push the earth and the sky apart, growing taller and taller every day until the gap measured some thirty thousand miles. And when this distance between them had been established, the sky grew firm and solid and the earth became securely fixed far beneath it. Pan Gu then looked around him and seeing that there was no longer any danger of darkness returning to the universe, he felt at last that he could lay down and rest, for his bones ached and he had grown old and frail over the years. Breathing a heavy sigh, he fell into an exhausted sleep from which he never awoke. But as he lay dying, the various parts of his vast body were miraculously transformed to create the world as we mortals know it today.

Pan Gu's head became the mountain ranges; his blood became the rivers and streams; the hairs on his head were changed into colourful and fragrant blossoms and his flesh was restored to become the trees and soil. His left eye was transformed into the sun and his right eye became the moon; his breath was revived in the winds and the clouds and his voice resounded anew as thunder and lightning. Even his sweat and tears were put to good use and were transformed into delicate droplets of rain and sweet-smelling morning dew.

And when people later came to inhabit the earth, they worshipped Pan Gu as a great creator and displayed the utmost respect for all the natural elements, believing them to be his sacred body spread out like a carpet before them beneath the blue arch of the heavens.

The Great Stone Fire Eater

AGES AGO, THERE LIVED A GREAT FIRE SPIRIT inside of a mountain to the southwest of Seoul, the capital of Korea. He was always hungry and his food was anything that would burn. He devoured trees, forests, dry grass, wood, and whatever he could get hold of. When those were not within his reach, he ate stones and rocks. He enjoyed the flames, but threw the hard stuff out of his mouth in the form of lava.

This Fire Monster spent most of his time in a huge volcano some distance away, but in sight of the capital. The city people used to watch the smoke coming out of the crater by day and issuing in red fire, between sunset and sunrise, until all the heavens seemed in flames. Then, they said, the Fire Spirit was lighting up his palace. On cloudy nights the inside of the volcano glowed like a furnace. The moulten mass inside the crater was reflected on the clouds, so that one could almost see into the monster's belly.

But nothing tasted so good to the Fire Eater as things which men built, such as houses, stables, fences, and general property. An especial titbit, that he longed to swallow, was the royal palace.

Looking out of its crater one day, he saw the king's palace all silver bright and brand new, rising in the City of Seoul. Thereupon he chuckled, and said to himself, for he was very happy:

"There's a feast for me! I'll just walk out of my mountain home and eat up that dainty morsel. I wonder how the king will like it."

But the Fire Spirit was in no hurry. He felt sure of his meal. So he waited until his friend, the South Wind, was prepared to join him.

"Let me know when you're ready," said the Fire Spirit to the South Wind, "and we'll have a splendid blaze. We'll go up at night and enjoy a lively dance before they can get a drop of water on us. Don't let the rain-clouds know anything about our picnic."

The South Wind promised easily, for she was always glad to have a frolic.

So when the sun went down and it was dark, the Fire Spirit climbed out of his rocky home in the volcano and strode towards Seoul. The South Wind pranced and capered with him until the streets of the capital were so gusty that no one with a wide-brimmed hat dared go outdoors, lest, in a lively puff, he might lose his head-gear. As for the men in mourning, who wear straw hats a yardstick wide and as big and deep as wash-tubs, they locked themselves up at home and played checkers. By the time all the palace guards were asleep the Fire Spirit was ready. He said to the South Wind:

"Blow, blow, your biggest blast, as I begin to touch the roofs of the smaller houses. This will whet my appetite for the palace, and then together we'll eat them all up."

Not till they heard a mighty roar and crackling did the people in Seoul push back their paper windows to find out what was the matter. Oh, what a blaze! It seemed to mount to heaven with red tongues that licked the stars. Those who could see in the direction of the palace supposed the sun had risen, but soon the crash of falling roofs and mighty columns of smoke and flame, with clouds of sparks, told the terrible story. By the time the sun did rise, there was nothing but a level waste of ashes, where the large buildings had been. Even the smoke had been driven away by the wind.

When the king and his people in the palace enclosure, who had saved their lives by running fast, thought over their loss, they began to plan how to stop the Fire Monster, when he should take it into his head to saunter forth on another walk and gobble up the king's dwelling.

A council of wise men was called to decide upon the question. Many long heads were bowed in hard thought over the matter. All the firemen, stone-cutters, fortune-tellers, dragon tamers, geomancers and people skilled in preventing conflagrations were invited to give their advice about the best way to fight the hungry Fire Demon.

After weeks spent in pondering the problem they all agreed that a dragon from China should be brought over to Korea. If kept in a swamp and fed well, he would surely prevent the Fire Imp from rambling too near Seoul. Besides, the dragon knew how to amuse and persuade the South Wind not to join in the mischief.

So, at tremendous cost and trouble, one of China's biggest dragons, capable of making rain and of spouting tons of water on its enemies, was shipped over and kept in a swamp. It was honoured with a royal decoration, allowed to wear a string of amber beads over its ear, given a horsehair hat, a nobleman's girdle and fed all the turnips it desired to eat. In every way it was treated as the king's favourite.

But it was all in vain. Money and favour were alike wasted. The petted dragon made it rain too often, so that the land was soaked. Then when told not to do this, it grew sulky and neglected its duty. Finally it became fat and lazy and one night fell asleep when it ought to have been on guard, for the winds were out on a dance.

Seeing his jailer thus caught napping, the Fire Imp leaped out of its volcano prison, rode quickly on the South Wind to Seoul and in a few hours had again swallowed the royal palace. There was nothing seen next day except ashes, which the Fire Monster cared no more for than we for nutshells when the kernels are eaten up.

With big tears in their eyes, the king and his wise men met together again to decide on a new scheme to keep off the Fire Imp. They were ready to drown him, or to see him get eaten up, because he had twice swallowed up the palace. They sent the Chinese dragon home and this time, besides the fortune-tellers and the stone-cutters, the well-diggers were invited also. For many days the wise men studied maps, talked of geography, looked at mountains, valleys, and the volcano, and studied air currents. Finally one man, famous for his deep learning about wood and water, forests and rivers, spoke thus:

"It is evident that the fire has always come from the southwest and up this valley," pointing to a map.

"True, true," shouted all the wise men.

"Well, right in his path let us dig a big pond, a regular artificial lake and very deep, into which the Fire Monster will tumble. This will put him out and he can get no further."

"Agreed, agreed," shouted the wise men in chorus. "Why did we not think of this before?"

All the skilful diggers of wells and ditches were summoned to the capital. With shovel and spade they worked for weeks. Then they let in water from the river until the pond was full.

So everybody in Seoul went to bed thinking that the king's palace was now safe surely.

But the Fire Imp, seeing the dragon gone and his opportunity come, climbed out of his volcano and moved out for another meal. This time, the South Wind was busy elsewhere and could not go with him. So he went alone, but coming to the pond, tumbled and wet himself so badly that he was chilled and nearly put out when he got to the palace, which was only half burned. So he went home growling and hungry.

Again the wise men were called and the first thing they did was to thank the boss well-digger, who had made the pond. The king summoned him into his presence to confer rank upon him and his children. He was presented with four rolls of silk, forty pounds of white ginseng, a tiger-skin robe, sixty dried chestnuts and forty-four strings of copper cash. Loaded with such Korean wealth and honours, the man fell on his hands and knees and thanked His Majesty profusely.

Then they called the master stone-cutter or chief of the guild and asked him if he could chisel out the figure of a beast that could eat flames and be ugly enough to scare away the Fire Imp.

The master had long hoped that he would be invited to rear this bit of sculpture, but hitherto the king and Court had feared it might cost too much.

So the order was given, and out of the heart of the mountains, a mighty block of white granite was loosed and brought to Seoul on rollers, pushed, pulled, and hoisted by thousands of labourers. Then, hidden behind canvas, to keep the matter secret, lest the Fire Imp should find it out, the workmen toiled. Hammers and chisels clinked, until on a certain day the Great Stone Flame Eater was ready to take his permanent seat in front of the palace gate, as guardian of the royal buildings and treasures.

The Fire Imp laughed when the South Wind told him of what the Koreans in the capital were doing, even though she warned him of the danger of his being eaten up.

"I shall walk out and see for myself anyhow," said the Fire Imp.

One night he crept out quietly and moved towards the city. He was nearly drowned in the pond, but plucking up courage, he went on until he was near the king's dwelling. Hearing the Fire Imp coming, the Great Flame Eater turned his head and licked his chops in anticipation of swallowing the Fire Imp whole, as a toad does a fly.

But one sight of the hideous stony monster was enough for the Fire Imp. There, before him, on a high pedestal was something never before seen in heaven or on Earth. It had enormous fire-proof scales like a salamander, with curly hair like asbestos and its mouth was full of big fangs. It was altogether hideous enough to give even a Volcano Spirit a chill.

"Just think of those jaws snapping on me," said the Fire Imp to himself, as he looked at them and the fangs. "I do believe that creature is half alligator and half water-tortoise. I had better go home. No dinner this time!"

So by his freezing glance alone, the Great Flame Eater frightened away the Fire Imp, so that he never came again and the royal palace was not once burned. Today the ugly brute still keeps watch. You have only to look at him to enjoy this story.

A Giant's Rock-Throwing

A POINT OF LAND on the northwestern coast of the island Oahu is called Ka-lae-o-Kaena which means "The Cape of Kaena."

Out in the ocean a short distance from this cape lies a large rock which bears the name Pohaku-o-Kauai, or rock of Kauai, a large island northwest of Oahu. This rock is as large as a small house.

There is an interesting legend told on the island of Oahu which explains why these names have for generations been fastened to the cape and to the rock. A long, long time ago there lived on the island Kauai a man of wonderful power, by the name of Hau-pu. When he was born, the signs of a demi-god were over and around the house of his birth. Lightning flashed through the skies, and thunder reverberated, rolling along the mountainsides.

Thunder and lightning were very rare in the Hawaiian Islands, and were supposed to be connected with the birth or death or some very unusual occurrence in the life of a chief.

Mighty floods of rain fell and poured in torrents down the mountainsides, carrying the red iron soil into the valleys in such quantities that the rapids and the waterfalls became the colour of blood, and the natives called this a blood-rain.

During the storm, and even after sunshine filled the valley, a beautiful rainbow rested over the house in which the young chief was born. This rainbow was thought to come from the miraculous powers of the newborn child shining out from him instead of from the sunlight around him. Many chiefs throughout the centuries of Hawaiian legends were said to have had this rainbow around them all their lives.

Hau-pu while a child was very powerful, and after he grew up was widely known as a great warrior. He would attack and defeat armies of his enemies without aid from any person. His spear was like a mighty weapon, sometimes piercing a host of enemies, and sometimes putting aside all opposition when he thrust it into the ranks of his opponents.

If he had thrown his spear and if fighting with his bare hands did not vanquish his foes, he would leap to the hillside, tear up a great tree, and with it sweep away all before him as if he were wielding a huge broom. He was known and feared throughout all the Hawaiian Islands. He became angry quickly and used his great powers very rashly.

One night he lay sleeping in his royal rest-house on the side of a mountain which faced the neighboring island of Oahu. Between the two islands lay a broad channel about thirty miles wide. When clouds were on the face of the sea, these islands were hidden from each other; but when they lifted, the rugged valleys of the mountains on one island could be clearly seen from the other. Even by moonlight the shadowy lines would appear.

This night the strong man stirred in his sleep. Indistinct noises seemed to surround his house. He turned over and dropped off into slumber again.

Soon he was aroused a second time, and he was awake enough to hear shouts of men far, far away. Louder rose the noise mixed with the roar of the great surf waves, so he realized that it came from the sea, and he then forced himself to rise and stumble to the door.

He looked out towards Oahu. A multitude of lights were flashing on the sea before his sleepy eyes. A low murmur of many voices came from the place where the dancing lights seemed to be. His confused thoughts made it appear to him that a great fleet of warriors was coming from Oahu to attack his people.

He blindly rushed out to the edge of a high precipice which overlooked the channel. Evidently many boats and many people were out in the sea below.

He laughed, and stooped down and tore a huge rock from its place. This he swung back and forth, back and forth, back and forth, until he gave it great impetus which added to his own miraculous power sent it far out over the sea. Like a great cloud it rose in the heavens and, as if blown by swift winds, sped on its way.

Over on the shores of Oahu a chief whose name was Kaena had called his people out for a night's fishing. Canoes large and small came from all along the coast. Torches without number had been made and placed in the canoes. The largest fish-nets had been brought.

There was no need of silence. Nets had been set in the best places. Fish of all kinds were to be aroused and frightened into the nets. Flashing lights, splashing paddles, and clamor from hundreds of voices resounded all around the nets.

Gradually the canoes came nearer and nearer the centre. The shouting increased. Great joy ruled the noise which drowned the roar of the waves.

Across the channel and up the mountainsides of Kauai swept the shouts of the fishing-party. Into the ears of drowsy Hau-pu the noise forced itself. Little dreamed the excited fishermen of the effect of this on far-away Kauai.

Suddenly something like a bird as large as a mountain seemed to be above, and then with a mighty sound like the roar of winds it descended upon them.

Smashed and submerged were the canoes when the huge boulder thrown by Hau-pu hurled itself upon them.

The chief Kaena and his canoe were in the centre of this terrible mass of wreckage, and he and many of his people lost their lives.

The waves swept sand upon the shore until in time a long point of land was formed. The remaining followers of the dead chief named this cape "Kaena."

The rock thrown by Hau-pu embedded itself deeply in the bed of the ocean, but its head rose far above the water, even when raging storms dashed turbulent waves against it. To this death-dealing rock the natives gave the name "Rock of Kauai."

Thus for generations has the deed of the man of giant force been remembered on Oahu, and so have a cape and a rock received their names.

Quests & Trials of Strength & Wit

Introduction

TOLD HERE IN THE STORY of 'A Son of Anak', the biblical confrontation between David and Goliath is pretty much paradigmatic of the giant's role in a certain kind of myth. Goliath, the Anakite in question, is not just huge but cruel and arrogant – and, of course, an implacable enemy of the Jews. In facing him, David is armed not only with his trusty sling and his heroic courage, but with the support of his people and of his God. "Thou comest to me with a sword and with a spear, and with a shield: but I come to thee in the name of the Lord," he cries.

We've already seen that the giant's size, strength and malevolence can provide a handy yardstick for the military prowess and moral stature of the hero who defeats him. We see this borne out in a fair few thrilling stories here. But we also see the many different ways heroes can overcome what appear impossible odds when they have the cunning and resourcefulness required. The protagonist in the German story 'The Brave Little Tailor' could hardly be less convincing as a warrior-hero, and yet he cuts the giant down to size.

A Son of Anak: David and Goliath

THERE WAS WAR MANY YEARS between the children of Israel and the Philistines.

And it came to pass while Saul was King that the Philistines gathered together a great army, and marched into the land of Judah against the Israelites, and encamped in a plain near Shochoh. So Saul also drew out his army and hurried forward, and occupied a hill overlooking this plain; whereupon the Philistines were forced to leave their position and to establish themselves on another hill across the valley of Elah from Saul's camp.

While the armies thus faced each other, there came one day out of the ranks of the Philistines a champion named Goliath. Very terrible he was to behold, for he was of the race of those sons of Anak for fear of whom the Israelites under Moses had murmured and had been therefore condemned to wander forty years in the wilderness. And while Joshua had finally led them across the Jordan after the death of Moses, and had smitten the Anakim and overcome them, there had remained three cities where their seed still dwelt – Gaza, and Gath and Ashdod; and it was from Gath that this Goliath had come with the invading army.

He was half as tall again as an ordinary man, something over nine feet. His brazen breastplate alone weighed as much as a man; on his head was a helmet of brass; and he carried over his shoulder a mighty spear which looked like a weaver's beam and the head of which alone weighed twenty-five pounds. Brazen greaves were upon his legs, and he bore a shield of gleaming brass.

This daunting figure advanced boldly into the plain, between the two armies drawn up in battle array, and in a great voice cried out:

"Why are ye come out to set your battle in array? Am not I a Philistine and ye servants of Saul? Choose you a man for you and let him come down to me.

"If he be able to fight with me, and to kill me, then will we be your servants: but if I prevail against him and kill him, then shall ye be our servants, and serve us.

"I defy the armies of Israel this day; give me a man, that we may fight together."

Now this was quite customary in the olden times: many a great issue had been decided by the combat of two champions. Moreover, there were brave men enough in the army of the Israelites, for Saul had had war all his days, against the children of Moab and the Amalekites, against Ammon, Edom and Zoab; and when he had seen any strong or valiant fighter among his people, he had straightway taken him unto him. But at the sight of this huge, brazen warrior, his hardiest veterans turned pale and trembled – for was it not a saying passed on from father to son for many generations: "Who shall stand before the sons of Anak?"

So, among all those thousands there was not found one so much as to answer to the giant's challenge. Which, when he perceived, he reviled them and returned to his own people.

The next day he came forth again, morning and evening, and the day after that, and each day following, always repeating his challenge in the face of all the force, and taunting them bitterly. Wherefore Saul was greatly troubled, for he knew well that this open fear of the giant would fight more overwhelmingly against his soldiers, when battle was joined, than the mighty Philistine himself and all his host. He offered, therefore, great riches to any man who would go forth against the challenger; whosoever should slay him should have the king's daughter to wife, and his father's house should be free in Israel. Yet even this could not prevail upon any to stand before the Philistine, so that for forty days he braved and insulted the whole army without response.

Now there were three brothers among those who followed Saul, Eliab, Abinadab and Shammah. They were sons of Jesse, who dwelt but ten or twelve miles from the battlefield in the hills near Bethlehem. This Jesse had a fourth son, David, who was but a stripling and tended his father's sheep.

He was a ruddy youth, of fair gaze, and beautiful to look upon. So cunning a musician was he that when an evil spirit of melancholy had descended upon the king, one of his servants had brought the boy to harp to his master; and the youth's skill in charming away this evil spirit had given him favour in Saul's sight, so that he had kept him before him and made him his armour-bearer. But when the three older sons of Jesse had joined the army gathered against the Philistines, David had returned to his duties with his father's flocks.

It chanced at this time that Jesse called David to him:

"Take now," said he, "this bushel of parched corn and these ten loaves and carry them swiftly to the camp to thy brethren.

"And carry these ten cheeses to the captain of their thousand, and see how thy brethren fare and bring me word again."

So David arose very early in the morning and left the sheep with a keeper and went as his father had commanded to the camp by the valley of Elah.

It was an easy journey for one who spent his days abroad with the sheep, and the sun was but lately up when he reached the encampment.

All was noise and confusion as he arrived, for both hosts were setting themselves in battle array, army against army. So the youth left his burdens with the keeper of the supplies, and ran in among the ranks until he found his brethren and said unto them: "Peace be with you."

As he talked with them, the Philistine champion appeared on the opposite slope. According to his wont, he challenged the whole army and reviled them, while the men of Israel drew back, sore afraid as before.

David heard his insults, and heard also the talk of those who stood by: what great things King Saul had promised to any who might overthrow him, and how long his boast and defiance had gone unquestioned.

"What shall be done," he enquired of his neighbours, "to the man that killeth this Philistine and taketh away the reproach from Israel? For who is this uncircumcised Philistine that he should defy the armies of the living God?"

They answered and told him what the king had promised: "So shall it be done to the man that killeth him."

His eldest brother Eliab heard these questionings, and his anger was kindled against David. He turned upon him, saying:

"Why comest thou down hither? And with whom hast thou left those few sheep in the wilderness? I know thy pride and forwardness: thou art come down that thou mightest see the battle."

"What have I now done?" replied the youth. "Was there not a cause for my coming?"

He turned away and again asked the nearest soldier of the affair, receiving the same answer. And someone came to Saul, relating the words the stripling had spoken. Saul sent for him.

As soon as he stood in the king's presence, David broke out, pointing to the distant figure of the giant:

"Let no man's heart fail because of him; thy servant will go and fight with this Philistine."

"Thou art not able to go against this Philistine to fight with him," answered Saul; "for thou art but a youth, and he is a man of war from his childhood up."

"Thy servant kept his father's sheep," urged the young man, "and there came a lion and a bear and took a lamb out of the flock.

"And I went out after the lion and smote him and delivered the lamb out of his mouth: and when he arose against me, I caught him by the hair and smote him, and slew him.

"Thy servant slew both the lion and the bear: and this uncircumcised Philistine shall be as one of them, seeing he hath defied the armies of the living God."

When Saul saw the eagerness and confidence of this handsome young shepherd, he was reminded of the deed of his son Jonathan when, accompanied only by his armour-bearer, he had climbed up into the enemy's garrison at Michmash, and slain twenty men within the space of half an acre, and started the rout of the whole army of the Philistines which had been about to overrun the land.

"Go," said he, "and the Lord be with thee."

So he armed David with his own armour and put a helmet on his head. And David girded on the king's sword and tried to walk; but he found himself so unaccustomed to the armour that he said to the king:

"I cannot go with these; for I have not proved them."

So he removed the armour, and set out in his shepherd's clothes, with his staff in his hand and his sling hanging from his girdle. This latter was the weapon he knew, and it was by no means to be despised. The plain piece of leather with thongs attached to each end, by means of which a stone could be hurled, was perhaps the very earliest means of fighting at a distance; and it was the traditional arm of more than one nation of the Syrian region. Among the Benjaminites, when they fought with Israel, there were seven hundred chosen men, left-handed, every one of whom could sling stones at a hair's-breadth and not miss; and an expert slinger had the advantage, against a warrior armed with sword and spear, of being able to deliver an attack long before he himself was threatened.

The youth walked to the brook and carefully selected five rounded stones of the right size, which he put into the wallet slung over his shoulder. Then, in the full sight of both armies, he advanced against the giant warrior in his gleaming harness, who stood brandishing his great spear and shouting his scorn.

Seeing David approach, he came forward, preceded by his shield-bearer. But perceiving only this fresh-faced stripling in his skin garment, he was filled with contempt at such an antagonist.

"Am I a dog," he cried, "that thou comest to me with staves?"

Cursing the youth by his heathen gods, he shouted: "Come to me, and I will give thy flesh to the fowls of the air, and to the beasts of the field."

Calmly David answered:

"Thou comest to me with a sword and with a spear, and with a shield: but I come to thee in the name of the Lord of hosts, the God of the armies of Israel, whom thou hast defied.

"This day will the Lord deliver thee into my hand; and I will smite thee, and take thy head from thee; and I will give the carcasses of the host of the Philistines this day unto the fowls of the air, and to the wild beasts of the earth; that all the assembly may know there is a god in Israel."

Enraged at this insolence, the Philistine champion hastened forward to smite down this boaster with one blow.

But David ran towards him. And as he ran he took one of the stones and placed it in his sling. Whirling it about, he hurled it so shrewdly that the stone struck Goliath full in the forehead, burying itself in the skull.

Down crashed that giant bulk to earth. The shield-bearer fled aghast back to his own lines. Running up to his prostrate adversary, the youth drew the giant's sword from its sheath, and, while the multitude looked on in awed silence, he hewed the Philistine's head from his body.

At that the Israelites set up a shout which echoed from hill to hill. The Philistine host turned and fled in utter panic, while Saul's men slaughtered them all the way to the gates of Gath, making great spoil of their belongings.

But David took the giant's sword and placed it in the sanctuary of Nob, where it was to serve him in dire need, at a later day.

And Saul set him over all his men of war.

The Giant Builder

AGES AND AGES AGO, when the world was first made, the gods decided to build a beautiful city high above the heavens, the most glorious and wonderful city that ever was known. Asgard was to be its name, and it was to stand on Ida Plain under the shade of Yggdrasil, the great tree whose roots were underneath the earth.

First of all they built a house with a silver roof, where there were seats for all the twelve chiefs. In the midst, and high above the rest, was the wonder-throne of Odin the All-Father, whence he could see everything that happened in the sky or on the earth or in the sea. Next they made a fair house for Queen Frigg and her lovely daughters. Then they built a smithy, with its great hammers, tongs, anvils and bellows, where the gods could work at their favourite trade, the making of beautiful things out of gold; which they did so well that folk name that time the Golden Age. Afterwards, as they had more leisure, they built separate houses for all the Æsir, each more beautiful than the preceding, for of course they were continually growing more skilful. They saved Father Odin's palace until the last, for they meant this to be the largest and the most splendid of all.

Gladsheim, the home of joy, was the name of Odin's house, and it was built all of gold, set in the midst of a wood whereof the trees had leaves of ruddy gold – like an autumn-gilded forest. For the safety of All-Father it was surrounded by a roaring river and by a high picket fence; and there was a great courtyard within.

The glory of Gladsheim was its wondrous hall, radiant with gold, the most lovely room that time has ever seen. Valhalla, the Hall of Heroes, was the name of it, and it was roofed with the mighty shields of warriors. The ceiling was made of interlacing spears, and there was a portal at the west end before which hung a great grey wolf, while over him a fierce eagle hovered. The hall was so huge that it had 540 gates, through each of which 800 men could march abreast. Indeed, there needed to be room, for this was the hall where every morning Odin received all the brave warriors who had died in battle on the earth below; and there were many heroes in those days.

This was the reward which the gods gave to courage. When a hero had gloriously lost his life, the Valkyries, the nine warrior daughters of Odin, brought his body up to Valhalla on their white horses that gallop the clouds. There they lived for ever after in happiness, enjoying the things that they had most loved upon earth. Every morning they armed themselves and went out to fight with one another in the great courtyard. It was a wondrous game, wondrously played. No matter how often a hero was killed, he became alive again in time to return perfectly well to Valhalla, where he ate a delicious breakfast with the Æsir; while the beautiful Valkyries who had first brought him thither waited at table and poured the blessed mead, which only the immortal taste. A happy life it was for the heroes, and a happy life for all who dwelt in Asgard; for this was before trouble had come among the gods, following the mischief of Loki.

This is how the trouble began. From the beginning of time, the giants had been unfriendly to the Æsir, because the giants were older and huger and more wicked; besides, they were jealous because the good Æsir were fast gaining more wisdom and power than the giants had ever known. It was the Æsir who set the fair brother and sister, Sun and Moon, in the sky to give light to men; and it was they also who made the jewelled stars out of sparks from the place of fire. The giants hated the Æsir, and tried all in their power to injure them and the men of the earth below, whom the Æsir loved and cared for. The gods had already built a wall around Midgard, the world of men, to keep the giants out; built it of the bushy eyebrows of Ymir, the oldest and hugest of giants. Between Asgard and the giants flowed Ifing, the great river on which ice never formed, and which the gods crossed on the rainbow bridge. But this was not protection enough. Their beautiful new city needed a fortress.

So the word went forth in Asgard – "We must build us a fortress against the giants; the hugest, strongest, finest fortress that ever was built."

Now one day, soon after they had announced this decision, there came a mighty man stalking up the rainbow bridge that led to Asgard city.

"Who goes there!" cried Heimdal the watchman, whose eyes were so keen that he could see for a hundred miles around, and whose ears were so sharp that he could hear the grass growing in the meadow and the wool on the backs of the sheep. "Who goes there! No one can enter Asgard if I say no."

"I am a builder," said the stranger, who was a huge fellow with sleeves rolled up to show the iron muscles of his arms. "I am a builder of strong towers, and I have heard that the folk of Asgard need one to help them raise a fair fortress in their city."

Heimdal looked at the stranger narrowly, for there was that about him which his sharp eyes did not like. But he made no answer, only blew on his golden horn, which was so loud that it sounded through all the world. At this signal all the Æsir came running to the rainbow bridge, from wherever they happened to be, to find out who was coming to Asgard. For it was Heimdal's duty ever to warn them of the approach of the unknown.

"This fellow says he is a builder," quoth Heimdal. "And he would fain build us a fortress in the city."

"Ay, that I would," nodded the stranger. "Look at my iron arm; look at my broad back; look at my shoulders. Am I not the workman you need?"

"Truly, he is a mighty figure," vowed Odin, looking at him approvingly. "How long will it take you alone to build our fortress? We can allow but one stranger at a time within our city, for safety's sake."

"In three half-years," replied the stranger, "I will undertake to build for you a castle so strong that not even the giants, should they swarm hither over Midgard – not even they could enter without your leave."

"Aha!" cried Father Odin, well pleased at this offer. "And what reward do you ask, friend, for help so timely?"

The stranger hummed and hawed and pulled his long beard while he thought. Then he spoke suddenly, as if the idea had just come into his mind. "I will name my price, friends," he said, "a small price for so great a deed. I ask you to give me Freia for my wife, and those two sparkling jewels, the Sun and Moon."

At this demand the gods looked grave; for Freia was their dearest treasure. She was the most beautiful maid who ever lived, the light and life of heaven, and if she should leave Asgard, joy would go with her; while the Sun and Moon were the light and life of the Æsir's children, men, who lived in the little world below. But Loki the sly whispered that they would be safe enough if they made another condition on their part, so hard that the builder could not fulfill it. After thinking cautiously, he spoke for them all.

"Mighty man," quoth he, "we are willing to agree to your price – upon one condition. It is too long a time that you ask; we cannot wait three half-years for our castle; that is equal to three centuries when one is in a hurry. See that you finish the fort without help in one winter, one short winter, and you shall have fair Freia with the Sun and Moon. But if, on the first day of summer, one stone is wanting to the walls, or if anyone has given you aid in the building, then your reward is lost, and you shall depart without payment." So spoke Loki, in the name of all the gods; but the plan was his own.

At first the stranger shook his head and frowned, saying that in so short a time no one unaided could complete the undertaking. At last he made another offer. "Let me have but my good horse to help me, and I will try," he urged. "Let me bring the useful Svadilföri with me to the task, and I will finish the work in one winter of short days, or lose my reward. Surely, you will not deny me this little help, from one four-footed friend."

Then again the Æsir consulted, and the wiser of them were doubtful whether it were best to accept the stranger's offer so strangely made. But again Loki urged them to accept. "Surely, there is no harm," he said. "Even with his old horse to help him, he cannot build the castle in the promised time. We shall gain a fortress without trouble and with never a price to pay."

Loki was so eager that, although the other Æsir did not like this crafty way of making bargains, they finally consented. Then in the presence of the heroes, with the Valkyries and Mimer's head for witnesses, the stranger and the Æsir gave solemn promise that the bargain should be kept.

On the first day of winter the strange builder began his work, and wondrous was the way he set about it. His strength seemed as the strength of a hundred men. As for his horse Svadilföri, he did more work by half than even the mighty builder. In the night he dragged the enormous rocks that were to be used in building the castle, rocks as big as mountains of the earth; while in the daytime the stranger piled them into place with his iron arms. The Æsir watched him with amazement; never was seen such strength in Asgard. Neither Tŷr the stout nor Thor the strong could match the power of the stranger. The gods began to look at one another uneasily. Who was this mighty one who had come among them, and what if after all he should win his reward? Freia trembled in her palace, and the Sun and Moon grew dim with fear.

Still the work went on, and the fort was piling higher and higher, by day and by night. There were but three days left before the end of winter, and already the building was so tall and so strong that it was safe from the attacks of any giant. The Æsir were delighted with their fine new castle; but their pride was dimmed by the fear that it must be paid for at all too costly a price. For only the gateway remained to be completed, and unless the stranger should fail to finish that in the next three days, they must give him Freia with the Sun and Moon.

The Æsir held a meeting upon Ida Plain, a meeting full of fear and anger. At last they realized what they had done; they had made a bargain with one of the giants, their enemies; and if he won the prize, it would mean sorrow and darkness in heaven and upon earth. "How did we happen to agree to so mad a bargain?" they asked one another. "Who suggested the wicked plan which bids fair to cost us all that we most cherish?" Then they remembered that it was Loki who had made the plan; it was he who had insisted that it be carried out and they blamed him for all the trouble.

"It is your counsels, Loki, that have brought this danger upon us," quoth Father Odin, frowning. "You chose the way of guile, which is not our way. It now remains for you to help us by guile, if you can. But if you cannot save for us Freia and the Sun and Moon, you shall die. This is my word." All the other Æsir agreed that this was just. Thor alone was away hunting evil demons at the other end of the world, so he did not know what was going on, and what dangers were threatening Asgard.

Loki was much frightened at the word of All-Father. "It was my fault," he cried, "but how was I to know that he was a giant? He had disguised himself so that he seemed but a strong man. And as for his horse – it looks much like that of other folk. If it were not for the horse, he could not finish the work. Ha! I have a thought! The builder shall not finish the gate; the giant shall not receive his payment. I will cheat the fellow."

Now it was the last night of winter, and there remained but a few stones to put in place on the top of the wondrous gateway. The giant was sure of his prize, and chuckled to himself as he went out with his horse to drag the remaining stones; for he did not know that the Æsir had guessed at last who he was, and that Loki was plotting to outwit him. Hardly had he gone to work when out of the wood came running a pretty little mare, who neighed to Svadilföri as if inviting the tired horse to leave his work and come to the green fields for a holiday.

Svadilföri, you must remember, had been working hard all winter, with never a sight of four-footed creature of his kind, and he was very lonesome and tired of dragging stones. Giving a snort of disobedience, off he ran after this new friend towards the grassy meadows. Off went the giant after him, howling with rage, and running for dear life, as he saw not only his horse but his chance of success slipping out of reach. It was a mad chase, and all Asgard thundered with the noise of galloping hoofs and the giant's mighty tread. The mare who raced ahead was Loki in disguise, and he led Svadilföri far out of reach, to a hidden meadow that he knew; so that the giant howled and panted up and down all night long, without catching even a sight of his horse.

Now when the morning came the gateway was still unfinished, and night and winter had ended at the same hour. The giant's time was over, and he had forfeited his reward. The Æsir came flocking to the gateway, and how they laughed and triumphed when they found three stones wanting to complete the gate!

"You have failed, fellow," judged Father Odin sternly, "and no price shall we pay for work that is still undone. You have failed. Leave Asgard quickly; we have seen all we want of you and of your race."

Then the giant knew that he was discovered, and he was mad with rage. "It was a trick!" he bellowed, assuming his own proper form, which was huge as a mountain, and towered high beside the fortress that he had built. "It was a wicked trick. You shall pay for this in one way or another. I cannot tear down the castle which, ungrateful ones, I have built you, stronger than the strength of any giant. But I will demolish the rest of your shining city!" Indeed, he would have done so in his mighty rage; but at this moment Thor, whom Heimdal had called from the end of the earth by one blast of the golden horn, came rushing to the rescue, drawn in his chariot of goats. Thor jumped to the ground close beside the giant, and before that huge fellow knew what had happened, his head was rolling upon the ground at Father Odin's feet; for with one blow Thor had put an end to the giant's wickedness and had saved Asgard.

"This is the reward you deserve!" Thor cried. "Not Freia nor the Sun and Moon, but the death that I have in store for all the enemies of the Æsir."

In this extraordinary way the noble city of Asgard was made safe and complete by the addition of a fortress which no one, not even the giant who built it, could injure, it was so wonder-strong. But always at the top of the gate were lacking three great stones that no one was mighty enough to lift. This was a reminder to the Æsir that now they had the race of giants for their everlasting enemies. And though Loki's trick had saved them Freia, and for the world the Sun and Moon, it was the beginning of trouble in Asgard which lasted as long as Loki lived to make mischief with his guile.

The Five Brothers

ONCE UPON A TIME, long years ago, when giants still lived upon the earth, there dwelt an old man and his wife in a small wooden hut, sheltered from the rough winter winds by the tall mountains and rocks that surrounded it. The world would have said they were very poor; but they thought themselves rich, for they had five handsome, healthy boys, who were the delight of their eyes. There was only a year's difference in age between the lads, and they were always together.

One day, the old couple went to cut grass on a slope some distance off, leaving the boys alone at home. It was a bright, warm morning, and, tired of playing indoors, the children went out into the little garden, and soon their merry shouts were heard echoing from the hills. Presently, up the path towards them came an old woman, feeble and lame.

"May an old woman beg for a draught of water?" she said, in a weak voice.

Stopping their games at once, the eldest boy ran to the well, while the others made her sit down by the door and rest. In a moment he was back with a pitcher of cool, sparkling water.

"There, grannie," he said, "that will refresh you. I let the bucket run down ever so far, to make the water nice and cold."

The old dame thanked him heartily, and, having quenched her thirst, asked what their names were. The boys laughed merrily.

"We have no names," they said. "We are all so near in age that we do everything together; and when father or mother want anything they just call out 'Boys!' and there we are, always at hand."

"You have kind hearts," the old woman said, "you are good to the aged and feeble. I was nearly dying of thirst, and could not have gone further without your help. Would that I could reward you as I should like! Alas! I have not the power. But one thing I can do for you. You shall no longer be nameless. I am going to bestow a name on each. You, my young cup-bearer," turning to the eldest boy, "shall be called 'Watchwell'; your brothers, 'Holdwell,' 'Hitwell,' 'Spywell,' and 'Climbwell.' May these names in the future bring you good fortune, as a reward for your kindness to a poor old woman."

Then she bade them goodbye, reminded them once more of their names, told them to act up to them, and turned away down the path.

In the evening, when their parents returned, the boys related what had occurred, and repeated the strange names they had been given. The old people were much astonished, and asked where the stranger had come from, and all particulars about her. But the boys could only tell what had happened, and the whole thing would soon have been forgotten, had it not been for the names. These they did not forget, and, strange to say, the more they were used the more the owner of each name seemed to develop the special quality that his name denoted, Watchwell, in addition, constituting himself the general guardian of the five. Was there a burden to carry, Holdwell's strong arms were ready. Did the parents require fagots for the winter, Hitwell would cut a pile, up in the dark pine woods on the mountains, that gladdened their hearts. Not a rabbit or bird could escape the keen eyes of Spywell, and by constant practice little Climbwell could scale the steepest cliffs along the fiord.

Years rolled on; the bright boys had grown up into tall, handsome young men, and all this time they had never crossed the high rocky hills that walled in their valley, never seen the great world that lay outside. But now that they were men, a great wish was rising in their hearts to go forth from the old home and play their part among other men. The old people gave them their blessing, and bade them continue to stand by one another as they had ever done, for, if they only did that, there was nothing they could not achieve.

And so the young men departed, following the steep track over the high mountains at first, and then gradually leaving the hill country behind them as they went ever onwards. Sometimes they rested at a farmhouse, sometimes in a village, but nowhere did they find any permanent work. Many a farmer would gladly have engaged Watchwell and Spywell to guard his flocks, but he had no employment for Holdwell and Climbwell, and when the two last could have joined the village lads in fishing or seabird hunting, there was, again, no post for the other three. Still, they would not be discouraged. They had stout hearts and strong limbs, and the good fortune they sought must be found elsewhere. So on they went, climbing high mountains and fording swift rivers, till at last they entered an interminable dark pine wood with a tangled undergrowth of brambles and tall ferns. Hitwell cleared a path before them, and at length they emerged on a vast plain.

The sun was setting, and pouring a flood of crimson, gold, and purple over the scene before them. The rays lit up the tall spires and high grey walls of a large city, and turned the broad, flowing river that encircled it into molten gold.

The brothers stood still entranced.

"It must be the city of the king," cried Watchwell, at length.

"Yes," said Spywell; "look, there is the royal flag flying on the tower of the palace."

They soon traversed the plain, and as darkness began to fall, they arrived at the great drawbridge over the river, and were directed to the palace by the warder. The king received them, and listened to their request for employment in his service. The brothers were such fine, handsome fellows that he was much taken with them as they stood before him. They were very tall, and had bright blue eyes and fair curling hair. He told them that he could give employment to all five if they would remain throughout the winter at his court, and watch and guard his daughters at the coming Christmas Eve.

"Do not, however, pledge yourselves to stay, until you learn the nature of the task that lies before you," he said. "For I have made a vow that the life of the next man who fails in this duty shall be forfeited. Perhaps you five brothers acting together can be more careful than strangers. Now listen. Two years ago," he went on, "I had five fair daughters, but, alas! the Christmas before last my golden-haired Elma disappeared mysteriously in the dead of night. Search was made in all directions; no trace of her could be found. Last Christmas Eve the princesses' apartments were carefully watched and guarded; no strangers were admitted, only old and faithful servants were near them. But when morning came, Irene, my second daughter, was nowhere to be found, nor was there any sign of her captors' footsteps near the window of the room where she slept. I have now made a vow, and I shall keep it; but I also offer a reward. He who defends them faithfully this year shall wed the next eldest princess who would without his care have disappeared, and he shall be to me as a son. It will be death or honour. Choose, young men, now, while you are still quite free."

"We will stay and guard the princesses," they cried with one voice. "It is a task that will call all our qualities into full play. No robber can escape the eyes of Spywell, Holdwell will act up to his name, till Climbwell and Hitwell reach him, and I," and Watchwell drew himself up proudly, "I will be the one to forfeit my life if we fail."

So they remained at the court, and became great favourites with the king, who began to feel almost sorry that he had imposed sentence of death on the man who should fail to defend his daughters. He, therefore, determined to do what he could to make them safe, and caused a great tower to be built on to the palace with thick walls and windows very high up, and here the princesses were to sleep on Christmas Eve.

And now the time drew near. As usual great festivities were held for several days. On the last night, when the dancing and merry-making were all over, the three princesses – Frida, Ida and Meya – were led to the tower by the king, attended by their ladies. As they lay down on the big couch, covered with silken embroideries, he bade them a last good night, and charged the five brothers to guard them with their lives. Then he left the tower, double locking the great iron door that led into the rest of the castle. All was still. The brothers lay down on a rough bench in the ante-chamber, but the door of the princesses' room was wide open, and a lamp was kept burning there.

It had been a long and tiring day, and the younger brothers were soon fast asleep. But Watchwell never closed an eye. Wrapped in his long cloak, he leant against the wall and watched.

The night drew on. But what was that? He thought he saw a dark shadow slowly approach the window of the princesses' room. As he looked, a monstrous hand opened the lattice, and stretched out gropingly towards the couch on which the king's daughters lay asleep.

Watchwell touched his brothers. In an instant Holdwell had grasped the mysterious hand so tightly that the owner could not move it; and Hitwell, with one blow of his sword, severed it from the wrist. A terrible wild cry of pain and baffled anger filled the air, and, looking forth, the brothers saw a fearful giant striding rapidly away from the palace, and shaking his remaining hand threateningly towards the tower. The noise had aroused the king, who was quickly on the spot, while Watchwell and his brothers hurried after the monster. Faster and faster he went, seeing he was pursued, but, though he was speedily out of sight, Spywell's keen eye traced his footsteps all the way.

On, on, on they went, till at last they came to the foot of a high mountain. Steep and precipitous before them the sides rose up – no foothold to be seen anywhere. Climbwell, however, never hesitated. He showed his brothers a strong silken cord that he always carried with him, then, making a bold spring to a tiny ledge he had noticed, he commenced to climb, never taking a false step, till he reached the summit in safety. Then, lowering the silken rope, he drew up his brothers one after the other.

When they reached the top they found an enormous cavern, and just inside the entrance sat a huge giantess, on a low stool, crying bitterly. The brothers asked what ailed her.

"What matters it to you?" she said, and cried more than ever. But at last she told them that the previous night her husband had lost one of his hands, and she feared he would die, he was in such terrible pain. Then they told her that they could heal her husband if she would let them in, but "no one," they said, "must be there but ourselves; we must bind all others lest they should find out the secret of our healing power."

The giantess, who was quite as wicked as her husband, and had hoped to entice these young men, by her pretended grief, into the cavern, so as to provide a dinner for herself and her husband, did not at all like the suggestion of being bound. But she thought, perhaps, they might be able to heal her husband first, so she submitted for the moment, comforting herself with the hope that she could easily break the rope and set herself free when the young men had cured her husband.

Holdwell bound her with Climbwell's strong silken rope, and then they passed into the inner cavern. The giant was lying on his couch, and gave a howl of rage when he saw them. But, crippled by the loss of his hand, he was no match for the young men, who speedily put an end to him. Then they also killed the wicked giantess, who had quite a heap of human bones beside her, and proceeded to explore the inner cavern. They thought it might, perhaps, contain some hidden treasure. But nothing was to be found, and they were on the point of leaving, when Spywell descried a small door cunningly let into the rock. Speedily breaking it open, a subterranean passage was seen, leading to another cavern, and there they discovered the two lost princesses – Elma, very pale and emaciated; whilst Irene, who had not been imprisoned so long, was more rosy and not so thin. The giant had evidently intended securing all five princesses before eating them.

The king's daughters were greatly overjoyed when they saw their noble deliverers, and heard that they were prisoners no longer. They quickly departed, Spywell and Climbwell having discovered an easier road for them to return by.

They arrived at the palace as night was falling, and the joy of the king at having his five daughters united once more can well be imagined.

A great banquet was hastily prepared, and before the assembled nobles and guests he related the brave deeds of Watchwell and his brothers, and announced that he had decided to wed his five daughters to the five heroes. "It is but right and fitting that men such as these, brave, noble and true, should reign over this land when I am gone," he said, "and to whom could I more worthily entrust my dear daughters than to those who have saved their lives?"

Never was there so magnificent a wedding-feast. It lasted a whole month, and the dresses of the five princesses were perfect marvels of gold and silver embroidery and precious stones. Then to each brother was appointed a position in the State which would call his special quality into play. They lived long and happily with their respective wives, greatly beloved and honoured by all, and when at length the old king died, Watchwell succeeded to the throne, and his wise and good reign, together with his beautiful and beloved Queen Elma, is still spoken of to this day.

The Horse Gullfaxi and the Sword Gunnfoder

MANY, MANY YEARS AGO there lived a king and queen who had one only son, called Sigurd. When the little boy was only ten years old the queen, his mother, fell ill and died, and the king, who loved her dearly, built a splendid monument to his wife's memory, and day after day he sat by it and bewailed his sad loss.

One morning, as he sat by the grave, he noticed a richly dressed lady close to him. He asked her name and she answered that it was Ingiborg, and seemed surprised to see the king there all alone. Then he told her how he had lost his queen, and how he came daily to weep at her grave. In return, the lady informed him that she had lately lost her husband, and suggested that they might both find it a comfort if they made friends.

This pleased the king so much that he invited her to his palace, where they saw each other often; and after a time he married her.

After the wedding was over he soon regained his good spirits, and used to ride out hunting as in old days; but Sigurd, who was very fond of his stepmother, always stayed at home with her.

One evening Ingiborg said to Sigurd: "Tomorrow your father is going out hunting, and you must go with him." But Sigurd said he would much rather stay at home, and the next day when the king rode off Sigurd refused to accompany him. The stepmother was very angry, but he would not listen, and at last she assured him that he would be sorry for his disobedience, and that in future he had better do as he was told.

After the hunting party had started she hid Sigurd under her bed, and bade him be sure to lie there till she called him.

Sigurd lay very still for a long while, and was just thinking it was no good staying there any more, when he felt the floor shake under him as if there were an earthquake, and peeping out he saw a great giantess wading along ankle deep through the ground and ploughing it up as she walked.

"Good morning, Sister Ingiborg," cried she as she entered the room, "is Prince Sigurd at home?"

"No," said Ingiborg; "he rode off to the forest with his father this morning." And she laid the table for her sister and set food before her. After they had both done eating the giantess said: "Thank you, sister, for your good dinner – the best lamb, the best can of beer and the best drink I have ever had; but – is not Prince Sigurd at home?"

Ingiborg again said, "No"; and the giantess took leave of her and went away. When she was quite out of sight Ingiborg told Sigurd to come out of his hiding-place.

The king returned home at night, but his wife told him nothing of what had happened, and the next morning she again begged the prince to go out hunting with his father. Sigurd, however, replied as before, that he would much rather stay at home.

So once more the king rode off alone. This time Ingiborg hid Sigurd under the table, and scolded him well for not doing as she bade him. For some time he lay quite still, and then suddenly the floor began to shake, and a giantess came along wading halfway to her knees through the ground.

As she entered the house she asked, as the first one had done: "Well, Sister Ingiborg, is Prince Sigurd at home?"

"No," answered Ingiborg, "he rode off hunting with his father this morning"; and going to the cupboard she laid the table for her sister. When they had finished their meal the giantess rose and said: "Thank you for all these nice dishes, and for the best lamb, the best can of beer and the nicest drink I have ever had; but – is Prince Sigurd really not at home?"

"No, certainly not!" replied Ingiborg; and with that they took leave of each other.

When she was well out of sight Sigurd crept from under the table, and his stepmother declared that it was most important that he should not stay at home next day; but he said he did not see what harm could come of it, and he did not mean to go out hunting, and the next morning, when the king prepared to start, Ingiborg implored Sigurd to accompany his father. But it was all no use, he was quite obstinate and would not listen to a word she said. "You will have to hide me again," said he, so no sooner had the king gone than Ingiborg hid Sigurd between the wall and the panelling, and by-and-by there was heard once more a sound like an earthquake, as a great giantess, wading knee deep through the ground, came in at the door.

"Good day, Sister Ingiborg!" she cried, in a voice like thunder. "Is Prince Sigurd at home?"

"Oh, no," answered Ingiborg, "he is enjoying himself out there in the forest. I expect it will be quite dark before he comes back again."

"That's a lie!" shouted the giantess. And they squabbled about it till they were tired, after which Ingiborg laid the table; and when the giantess had done eating she said: "Well, I must thank you for all these good things, and for the best lamb, the best can of beer and the best drink I have had for a long time; but – are you quite sure Prince Sigurd is not at home?"

"Quite," said Ingiborg. "I've told you already that he rode off with his father this morning to hunt in the forest."

At this the giantess roared out with a terrible voice: "If he is near enough to hear my words, I lay this spell on him: Let him be half scorched and half withered; and may he have neither rest nor peace till he finds me." And with these words she stalked off.

For a moment Ingiborg stood as if turned to stone, then she fetched Sigurd from his hiding-place, and, to her horror, there he was, half scorched and half withered.

"Now you see what has happened through your own obstinacy," said she; "but we must lose no time, for your father will soon be coming home."

Going quickly into the next room she opened a chest and took out a ball of string and three gold rings, and gave them to Sigurd, saying: "If you throw this ball on the ground it will roll along till it reaches some high cliffs. There you will see a giantess looking out over the rocks. She will call down to you and say: 'Ah, this is just what I wanted! Here is Prince Sigurd. He shall go into the pot tonight'; but don't be frightened by her. She will draw you up with a long boat hook, and you must greet her from me, and give her the smallest ring as a present. This will please her, and she will ask you to wrestle with her. When you are exhausted, she will offer you a horn to drink out of, and though she does not know it, the wine will make you so strong that you will easily be able to conquer her. After that she will let you stay there all night. The same thing will happen with my two other sisters. But, above all, remember this: should my little dog come to you and lay his paws on you, with tears running down his face, then hurry home, for my life will be in danger. Now, goodbye, and don't forget your stepmother."

Then Ingiborg dropped the ball on the ground, and Sigurd bade her farewell.

That same evening the ball stopped rolling at the foot of some high rocks, and on glancing up, Sigurd saw the giantess looking out at the top.

"Ah, just what I wanted!" she cried out when she saw him; "here is Prince Sigurd. He shall go into the pot tonight. Come up, my friend, and wrestle with me."

With these words she reached out a long boat hook and hauled him up the cliff. At first Sigurd was rather frightened, but he remembered what Ingiborg had said, and gave the giantess her sister's message and the ring.

The giantess was delighted, and challenged him to wrestle with her. Sigurd was fond of all games, and began to wrestle with joy; but he was no match for the giantess, and as she noticed that he was getting faint she gave him a horn to drink out of, which was very foolish on her part, as it made Sigurd so strong that he soon overthrew her.

"You may stay here tonight," said she; and he was glad of the rest.

Next morning Sigurd threw down the ball again and away it rolled for some time, till it stopped at the foot of another high rock. Then he looked up and saw another giantess, even bigger and uglier than the first one, who called out to him: "Ah, this is just what I wanted! Here is Prince Sigurd. He shall go into the pot tonight. Come up quickly and wrestle with me." And she lost no time in hauling him up.

The prince gave her his stepmother's message and the second largest ring. The giantess was greatly pleased when she saw the ring, and at once challenged Sigurd to wrestle with her.

They struggled for a long time, till at last Sigurd grew faint; so she handed him a horn to drink from, and when he had drunk he became so strong that he threw her down with one hand.

On the third morning Sigurd once more laid down his ball, and it rolled far away, till at last it stopped under a very high rock indeed, over the top of which the most hideous giantess that ever was seen looked down.

When she saw who was there she cried out: "Ah, this is just what I wanted! Here comes Prince Sigurd. Into the pot he goes this very night. Come up here, my friend, and wrestle with me." And she hauled him up just as her sisters had done.

Sigurd then gave her his stepmother's message and the last and largest ring. The sight of the red gold delighted the giantess, and she challenged Sigurd to a wrestling match. This time the fight was fierce and long, but when at length Sigurd's strength was failing the giantess gave him something to drink, and after he had drunk it he soon brought her to her knees. "You have beaten me," she gasped, so now, listen to me. "Not far from here is a lake. Go there; you will find a little girl playing with a boat. Try to make friends with her, and give her this little gold ring. You are stronger than ever you were, and I wish you good luck."

With these words they took leave of each other, and Sigurd wandered on till he reached the lake, where he found the little girl playing with a boat, just as he had been told. He went up to her and asked what her name was.

She was called Helga, she answered, and she lived nearby.

So Sigurd gave her the little gold ring, and proposed that they should have a game. The little girl was delighted, for she had no brothers or sisters, and they played together all the rest of the day.

When evening came Sigurd asked leave to go home with her, but Helga at first forbade him, as no stranger had ever managed to enter their house without being found out by her father, who was a very fierce giant.

However, Sigurd persisted, and at length she gave way; but when they came near the door she held her glove over him and Sigurd was at once transformed into a bundle of wool. Helga tucked the bundle under her arm and threw it on the bed in her room.

Almost at the same moment her father rushed in and hunted round in every corner, crying out: "This place smells of men. What's that you threw on the bed, Helga?"

"A bundle of wool," said she.

"Oh, well, perhaps it was that I smelt," said the old man, and troubled himself no more.

The following day Helga went out to play and took the bundle of wool with her under her arm. When she reached the lake she held her glove over it again and Sigurd resumed his own shape.

They played the whole day, and Sigurd taught Helga all sorts of games she had never even heard of. As they walked home in the evening she said: "We shall be able to play better still tomorrow, for my father will have to go to the town, so we can stay at home."

When they were near the house Helga again held her glove over Sigurd, and once more he was turned into a bundle of wool, and she carried him in without his being seen.

Very early next morning Helga's father went to the town, and as soon as he was well out of the way the girl held up her glove and Sigurd was himself again. Then she took him all over the house to amuse him, and opened every room, for her father had given her the keys before he left; but when they came to the last room Sigurd noticed one key on the bunch which had not been used and asked which room it belonged to.

Helga grew red and did not answer.

"I suppose you don't mind my seeing the room which it opens?" asked Sigurd, and as he spoke he saw a heavy iron door and begged Helga to unlock it for him. But she told him she dared not do so, at least if she did open the door it must only be a very tiny chink; and Sigurd declared that would do quite well.

The door was so heavy that it took Helga some time to open it, and Sigurd grew so impatient that he pushed it wide open and walked in. There he saw a splendid horse, all ready saddled, and just above it hung a richly ornamented sword on the handle of which was engraved these words: "He who rides this horse and wears this sword will find happiness."

At the sight of the horse Sigurd was so filled with wonder that he was not able to speak, but at last he gasped out: "Oh, do let me mount him and ride him round the house! Just once; I promise not to ask any more."

"Ride him round the house!" cried Helga, growing pale at the mere idea. "Ride Gullfaxi! Why, Father would never, never forgive me if I let you do that."

"But it can't do him any harm," argued Sigurd; "you don't know how careful I will be. I have ridden all sorts of horses at home, and have never fallen off, not once. Oh, Helga, do!"

"Well, perhaps, if you come back directly," replied Helga, doubtfully; "but you must be very quick, or Father will find out!"

But, instead of mounting Gullfaxi, as she expected, Sigurd stood still.

"And the sword," he said, looking fondly up to the place where it hung. "My father is a king, but he has not got any sword so beautiful as that. Why, the jewels in the scabbard are more splendid than the big ruby in his crown! Has it got a name? Some swords have, you know."

"It is called 'Gunnfjoder,' the 'Battle Plume,'" answered Helga, "and 'Gullfaxi' means 'Golden Mane.' I don't suppose, if you are to get on the horse at all, it would matter your taking the sword too. And if you take the sword you will have to carry the stick and the stone and the twig as well."

"They are easily carried," said Sigurd, gazing at them with scorn; "what wretched dried-up things! Why in the world do you keep them?"

"Father says that he would rather lose Gullfaxi than lose them," replied Helga, "for if the man who rides the horse is pursued he has only to throw the twig behind him and it will turn into a forest, so thick that even a bird could hardly fly through. But if his enemy happens to know magic, and can throw down the forest, the man has only to strike the stone with the stick, and hailstones as large as pigeons' eggs will rain down from the sky and will kill everyone for twenty miles round."

Having said all this she allowed Sigurd to ride "just once" round the house, taking the sword and other things with him. But when he had ridden round, instead of dismounting, he suddenly turned the horse's head and galloped away.

Soon after this Helga's father came home and found his daughter in tears. He asked what was the matter, and when he heard all that had happened, he rushed off as fast as he could to pursue Sigurd.

Now, as Sigurd happened to look behind him he saw the giant coming after him with great strides, and in all haste he threw the twig behind him. Immediately such a thick wood sprang up at once between him and his enemy that the giant was obliged to run home for an axe with which to cut his way through.

The next time Sigurd glanced round, the giant was so near that he almost touched Gullfaxi's tail. In an agony of fear Sigurd turned quickly in his saddle and hit the stone with the stick. No sooner had he done this than a terrible hailstorm burst behind, and the giant was killed on the spot.

But had Sigurd struck the stone without turning round, the hail would have driven right into his face and killed him instead.

After the giant was dead Sigurd rode on towards his own home, and on the way he suddenly met his stepmother's little dog, running to meet him, with tears pouring down its face. He galloped on as hard as he could, and on arriving found nine men-servants in the act of tying Queen Ingiborg to a post in the courtyard of the palace, where they intended to burn her.

Wild with anger Prince Sigurd sprang from his horse and, sword in hand, fell on the men and killed them all. Then he released his stepmother, and went in with her to see his father.

The king lay in bed sick with sorrow, and neither eating nor drinking, for he thought that his son had been killed by the queen. He could hardly believe his own eyes for joy when he saw the prince, and Sigurd told him all his adventures.

After that Prince Sigurd rode back to fetch Helga, and a great feast was made which lasted three days; and everyone said no bride was ever seen so beautiful as Helga, and they lived happily for many, many years, and everybody loved them.

Anent the Giant Who Did Not Have His Heart About Him

ONCE UPON A TIME there was a king who had seven sons, and he was so fond of them that he never could bear to have them all away from him at once, and one of them always had to stay with him. When they had grown up, six of them were to go forth and look for wives; but the youngest the king wanted to keep at home, and the others were to bring along a bride for him. The king gave the six the handsomest clothes that had ever been seen, clothes that glittered from afar, and each received a horse that had cost many hundred dollars, and so they set forth. And after they had been at the courts of many kings, and had seen many princesses, they at last came to a king who had six daughters. Such beautiful princesses they had not as yet met with, and so each of them paid court to one of them, and when each had won his sweetheart, they rode back home again. But they were so deeply in love with their brides that they altogether forgot they were also to bring back a princess for their young brother who had stayed at home.

Now when they had already covered a good bit of the homeward road, they passed close to a steep cliff-side where the giants dwelt. And a giant came out, looked at them, and turned them all to stone, princes and princesses. The king waited and waited for his six sons; but though he waited and yearned, they did not come. Then he grew very sad, and said that he would never really be happy again. "If I did not have you," he told his youngest, "I would not keep on living, so sad am I at having lost your brothers."

"But I had already been thinking of asking your permission to set out and find my brothers again," said the youngest.

"No, that I will not allow under any circumstances," answered the father, "otherwise you will be lost to me into the bargain." But the youth's mind was set on going, and he pleaded so long that finally the king had to let him have his way. Now the king had only a wretched old nag for him, since the six other princes and their suite had been given all the good horses; but that did not worry the youngest. He mounted the shabby old nag, and "Farewell, Father!" he said to the king. "I will surely return, and perhaps I will bring my six brothers back with me." And with that he rode off.

Now when he had ridden a while he met a raven, who was lying in the road beating his wings, and unable to move from the spot because he was so starved. "O, dear friend, if you will give me a bite to eat, then I'll help you in your hour of direst need!" cried the raven. "I have not much food, nor are you likely to be able to help me much," said the king's son, "but still I can give you a little, for it is easy to see you need it." And with that he gave the raven some of the provisions he had with him. And when he had ridden a while longer, he came to a brook, and there lay a great salmon who had gotten on dry land, and was threshing about, and could not get back into the water. "O, dear friend, help me back into the water," said the salmon to the king's son, "and I will help you, too, in your hour of greatest need!"

"The help you will be able to give me will probably not amount to much," said the prince, "but it would be a pity if you had to lie there and pine away." And with that he pushed the fish back into the water. Then he rode on a long, long way, and met a wolf; and the wolf was so starved that he lay in the middle of the road, and writhed with hunger. "Dear friend, let me eat your horse," said the wolf. "My hunger is so great that my very inwards rattle, because I have had nothing to eat for the past two years!"

"No," said the prince, "I cannot do that: first I met a raven, and had to give him my provisions; then I met a salmon and had to help him back into the water; and now you want my horse. That will not do, for what shall I ride on then?"

"Well, my dear friend, you must help me," was the wolf's reply. "You can ride on me. I will help you in turn in your hour of greatest need."

"The help you might give me would probably not amount to much; but I will let you eat the horse, since you are in such sorry case," returned the prince. And when the wolf had eaten the horse, the prince took the bit and put it in the wolf's mouth, and fastened the saddle on his back, and his meal had made the wolf so strong that he trotted off with the king's son as fast as he could. He had never ridden so swiftly before. "When we have gone a little further I will show you the place where the giants live," said the wolf; and in a short time they were there. "Well, this is where the giants live," said the wolf. "There you see your six brothers, whom the giant turned into stone, and yonder are their six brides; and up there is the door through which you must pass."

"No, I would not dare do that," said the king's son. "He would murder me."

"O no," was the wolf's reply, "when you go in you will find a princess, and she will tell you how to set about getting rid of the giant. You need only do as she says." And the prince went in, though he was afraid. When he entered the house the giant was not there; but in one of the rooms sat a princess, just as the wolf had said, and such a beautiful maiden the youth had never seen. "Now may God help you, how did you get in here?" cried the princess, when she saw him. "It is certain death for you. No one can kill the giant who lives here, for he hasn't his heart about him."

"Well, since I do happen to be here, I will at least make the attempt," said the prince. "And I want to try to deliver my brothers, who stand outside, turned to stone, and I would like to save you as well."

"Well, if you insist upon it, we must see what we can do," replied the princess. "Now you must crawl under the bed here, and must listen carefully when I talk to the giant. But you must not make a sound." The prince slipped under the bed, and no sooner was he there than the giant came home.

"Hu, it smells like the flesh of a Christian here!" he cried. "Yes," said the princess, "a jackdaw flew by with a human bone, and let it fall down the chimney. I threw it out again at once, but the odour does not disappear so quickly." Then the giant said no more about it. Towards evening he went to bed, but after he had lain there a while, the princess, who sat looking out of the window, said: "There is something I would have asked you about long ago, if only I had dared."

"And what may that be?" enquired the giant. "I would like to know where you keep your heart, since you do not have it about you?" said the princess. "O, that is something you need not ask about; at any rate, it lies under the threshold of the door," was the giant's reply. "Aha," thought the prince under the bed, "that is where we will find it!"

The next morning the giant got up very early, and went into the forest, and no sooner had he gone than the prince and the king's daughter set about looking for the heart under the threshold of the door. Yet no matter how much they dug and searched, they found nothing. "This time he has fooled us," said the princess. "We'll have to try again." And she picked the loveliest flowers she could find and strewed them over the threshold – which they had put to rights again – and when the time drew near for the giant's return, the king's son crept under the bed once more. When he was beneath it, the giant came.

"Hu hu, I smell human flesh!" he cried. "Yes," said the princess. "A jackdaw flew by with a human bone in her beak, and she let it fall down the chimney. I threw it out at once, but I suppose one can still smell it." Then the giant held his tongue, and said no more about it. After a time he asked who had strewn the flowers over the threshold. "O, I did that," said the princess. "What does it mean?" the giant then asked. "O, I am so fond of you that I had to do it, because I know that is where your heart lies."

"Yes, of course," said the giant, "but it does not happen to lie there at all."

When he had gone to bed, the princess sat looking out of the window, and again asked the giant where he kept his heart, for she was so fond of him, said she, that she wanted to know above all things. "O, it is in the wardrobe there by the wall," said the giant. "Aha," thought the king's son under the bed, "that is where we will find it!"

The next morning the giant got up early, and went into the forest, and no sooner had he gone than the prince and the king's daughter set about looking for his heart in the wardrobe. Yet no matter how much they looked, they did not find it. "Well, well," said the princess, "we will have to try once more." Then she adorned the wardrobe with flowers and wreaths, and towards evening the king's youngest son again crawled under the bed. Then the giant came:

"Hu hu, it smells of human flesh here!" he cried.

"Yes,"' said the princess. "A jackdaw just this moment flew by with a human bone in her beak, and she let it fall down the chimney. I threw it out again at once, but it may be that you can still smell it." When the giant heard this, he had nothing further to say about it. But not long afterward he noticed that the wardrobe was adorned with flowers and wreaths, and asked who had done it.

"I," said the princess.

"What do you mean by such tomfoolery?" asked the giant.

"O, I am so fond of you that I had to do it, since I know that is where your heart lies," was the reply of the princess.

"Are you really so stupid as to believe that?" cried the giant.

"Yes, surely, I must believe it," said the princess, "when you tell me so."

"How silly you are," said the giant, "you could never reach the place where I keep my heart."

"But still I would like to know where it is," answered the princess. Then the giant could no longer resist, and at last had to tell her the truth.

"Far, far away, in a lake there lies an island," said he, "and on the island stands a church, and in the church there is a well, and in the well floats a duck, and in the duck there is an egg, and in the egg – is my heart!"

The next morning, before dawn, the giant went to the forest again. "Well, now I must get under way," said the prince, "and it is a way I wish I could find." So he said farewell to the princess for the time being, and when he stepped out of the door, the wolf was standing there waiting for him. He told him what had happened at the giant's, and said that now he would go to the well in the church, if only he knew the way. The wolf told him to climb on his back. He would manage to find the way, said he. And then they were off as though they had wings, over rock and wood, over hill and dale. After they had been underway for many, many days, they at last reached the lake. Then the king's son did not know how they were to get across. But the wolf told him not to worry, and swam across with the prince to the island. Then they came to the church. But the church-key hung high up in the tower, and at first the king's son did not at all know how they were to get it down. "You must call the raven," said the wolf, and that is what the king's son did. And the raven came at once, and flew right down with the key, and now the prince could enter the church. Then, when he came to the well, there was the duck, sure enough, swimming about as the giant had said. He stood by the well and called the duck, and at last he lured her near him, and seized her. But at the moment he grasped her and lifted her out of the water, she let the egg fall into the well, and now the prince again did not know how he was to get hold of it. "Well, you must call the salmon," said the wolf. That is what the king's son did, and the salmon came at once, and brought up the egg from the bottom of the well. Then the wolf told him to squeeze the egg a little. And when the prince squeezed, the giant cried out. "Squeeze it again!" said the wolf, and when the prince did so, the giant cried out far more dolefully, and fearfully and tearfully begged for his life. He would do all the king's son asked him to, said he, if only he would not squeeze his heart in two.

"Tell him to give back their original form to your six brothers, whom he turned to stone, and to their brides, as well; and that then you will spare his life," said the wolf, and the prince did so. The giant at once agreed, and changed the six brothers into princes, and their brides into kings' daughters. "Now squash the egg!" cried the wolf. Then the prince squeezed the egg in two, and the giant burst into pieces.

When the king's youngest son had put an end to the giant in this way, he rode back on his wolf to the giant's home; and there stood his six brothers as much alive as ever they had been, together with their brides. Then the prince went into the hill to get his own bride, and they all rode home together. And great was the joy of the old king when his seven sons all returned, each with his bride. "But the bride of my youngest is the most beautiful, after all, and he shall sit with her at the head of the table!" said the king. And then they had a feast that lasted for weeks, and if they have not stopped, they are feasting to this very day.

The Three Dogs

ONCE UPON A TIME there was a king who went forth into the world and fetched back a beautiful queen. And after they had been married a while God gave them a little daughter. Then there was great rejoicing in the city and throughout the country, for the people wished their king all that was good, since he was kind and just. While the child lay in its cradle, a strange-looking old woman entered the room, and no one knew who she was nor whence she came. The old woman spoke a verse over the child, and said that she must not be allowed out under the open sky until she were full fifteen years of age, since otherwise the mountain troll would fetch her. When the king heard this he took her words to heart, and posted guards to watch over the little princess so that she would not get out under the open sky.

Some time afterward, God gave the royal pair another little daughter, and again the whole kingdom rejoiced. But the wise old woman once more put in an appearance, and warned the king not to let the princess out under the open sky until she were full fifteen years of age. And then, after a time, God gave the royal pair a third daughter. This time, too, the old woman appeared, and repeated what she had already twice said. Then the king was much grieved; for he loved his children above everything in the world. Therefore he gave strict orders that the three princesses were always to be kept beneath the roof of the castle, and that none were to dare transgress against this command.

Now a long time passed, and the king's daughters grew up and became the most beautiful maidens of whom one has ever heard tell. Then war broke out and the king, their father, had to leave them. One day, while he was away at war, the three princesses were sitting in the window and looking out, watching the sunshine on the little flowers in the garden. And they felt a great desire to play with the lovely flowers, and begged their guards to let them go into the garden for a little while. But this their guards would not allow, for they feared the king's anger. Yet the king's daughters pleaded so very sweetly that they could not deny their pleas and they let them have their way. But the princesses did not have long to walk about, for no sooner were they beneath the open sky, than a cloud came suddenly down, and bore them off, and all attempts to regain possession of them were fruitless; though search was made in every direction.

Then the whole kingdom mourned and grieved, and one may imagine that the king was anything but happy when he returned home and learned all that had happened. Yet what is done cannot be undone, and in the end they had to resign themselves to it. And since the king knew of no other way to help himself, he had proclaimed throughout the kingdom that whoever would deliver his three daughters out of the power of the mountain troll should have one of them for his bride, and with her half of the kingdom. When this became known in foreign lands, many youths set forth with horses and followers to seek the princesses. At the king's court were two princes who also went forth to see whether fortune would be kind to them. They armed themselves in the best possible way with coats of mail and costly weapons, and bragged and boasted that they would not return without having done what they set out to do.

And now we will let the king's sons ride out over the world on their quest, while we turn to other people. Far, far out in the wild wood there lived a poor widow who had an only son who drove his mother's pigs to pasture every day. And as he crossed the fields, he whittled himself a flute, and amused himself playing it. And he played so sweetly that he warmed the cockles of the hearts of all those who heard him.

Now it chanced that the young swine-herd once sat in the wood blowing his flute, while his three pigs were digging under the pine-roots. And an old, old man came along, with a beard so long and so broad that it hung far below his girdle. The old man had a large, powerful dog with him. When the youth saw the great dog, he thought to himself: "If a fellow had a dog like that to keep him company here in the wilderness, he might consider himself lucky." And when the old man noticed this, he began: "That is why I have come, for I want to exchange my dog for one of your pigs." The youth was at once willing, and closed the bargain. He received the great dog, and gave up the grey pig in place of it. Then the old man went his way. But as he left he said: "You have reason to be satisfied with our exchange, for that dog is not like other dogs. His name is 'Take Hold!' and whatever you tell him to take hold of he will seize, even though it were the grimmest of trolls." Thereupon they parted, and the youth thought that fortune had indeed favoured him.

In the evening he called his dog and drove his pigs home. But when his old mother heard that he had given away the grey pig for a dog, she was angry beyond measure, and gave her son a good drubbing. The youth told her to calm herself; but all in vain, the longer it lasted the more furious she became. Then, since he did not know what else to do, he called out to his dog: "Take hold!" At once the dog ran up, seized the old mother and held her so tightly that she could not move. But otherwise he did her no harm. And now she had to promise her son to make the best of the matter, and then they were friends once more.

The following day the youth went to the wood again, with his dog and the two pigs. After a time he sat down and played his flute as usual, and the dog danced to his playing with such skill that it was nothing short of a miracle. And as he was sitting there, the old man with the grey beard came out of the wood again, and with him another dog, no smaller than the first. When the youth saw the handsome beast he thought to himself: "If a fellow had that dog to keep him company here where it is so lonely, he need have no fear." When the old man noticed this, he began: "That is why I have come, for I want to exchange my dog for one of your pigs." The youth did not lose any time, but agreed to close the bargain. He received the great dog, and gave up one of his pigs in place of it. Then the old man went his way. Yet before he left he added: "You have reason to be well satisfied with your purchase, for this dog is not like the other dogs. His name is 'Tear!' and if you give him something to tear, he will tear it to pieces, even though it were the grimmest of trolls." Then they parted. But the youth was happy in the idea that he had made a capital exchange; although he knew that his old mother would not be content with it. And when evening came, and the youth went home, his old mother was no less angry than she had been before. But this time she did not venture to beat her son, because she was afraid of the great dogs. Yet, as is usual, when women have scolded long enough, they stop of their own accord – and that is what happened in this case. The youth and his mother made peace with each other; though the mother thought to herself that the damage done could not well be repaired.

On the third day the youth went into the wood again with his pig and two dogs. He felt very happy, seated himself on a tree-stump and played his flute as usual. And the dogs danced to his playing with such skill that it was a pleasure to watch them. As the youth was sitting there in peace and quiet, the old grey-beard once more came out of the wood. This time he had a third dog with him, who was as large as both the others together. When the youth saw the handsome animal he could not help but think: "If a fellow had this dog to keep him company in the wilderness, he would have no cause for complaint." The old man at once began: "That is why I have come, in order to sell my dog, for I can see you would like to have him." The youth was at once willing and agreed to close the bargain. So he received the great dog and gave up his last pig in place of it. Then the old man went his way. Yet before he went he said: "You will be satisfied with your exchange, for this dog is not like other dogs. His name is 'Hark!' and his hearing is so keen that he hears everything that happens, though it be happening many miles away. He even hears the grass and the trees grow." Then they parted in the friendliest spirit. But the youth was happy in the thought that now he need fear nothing in the world. And then, when evening came on, and the swine-herd went home, his mother was very sad to think that her son had sold all they possessed. But the youth told her to be of good courage, since he would see to it that they did not suffer want. And when he spoke to her in such a cheerful manner, she grew content again, and decided that he had spoken in wise and manly fashion. Then when day dawned the youth went hunting with his dogs, and came back at evening with as much game as he could possibly carry. And he continued to go hunting in this way for a time until his old mother's storeroom was well provided with meat and all sorts of good things. Then he bade his mother a fond farewell, called his dogs, and said he was going to wander out into the world and try his fortune.

And he fared forth over mountains and tangled ways, and came into the heart of a sombre forest. There he met the grey-beard of whom I have already told you. And when he met him the youth was much pleased, and said: "Good day, grandfather, and thanks for the last time!" And the old man replied: "Good day to you, and whither away?" The youth answered: "I am wandering out into the world to see what fortune has in store for me." Then the old man said: "Keep right on going till you come to the royal castle, and there your fortune will take a turn." And with that they parted. The youth followed the old man's advice and for a time wandered on straight ahead. When he came to a tavern he played his flute and let his dogs dance, and was never at a lack for bed and board, and whatever else he might want.

After he had wandered long and far, he at length came to a great city, whose streets were filled with people. The youth wondered what it all meant, and at last reached the spot where, to the sound of bell, the king's proclamation was being cried – that whoever should deliver the three princesses out of the power of the troll, would receive one of them, and half the kingdom as well. Now he understood what the old man had meant. He called his dogs, and went to the king's castle. But there all had been grief and mourning since the day the king's daughters had disappeared. And of them all the king and queen were the most sorrowful. Then the youth went to the keeper of the door, and asked him whether he might play and show his dogs before the king. The courtiers were willing, for they hoped it might make him feel more cheerful. So he was admitted and allowed to show his tricks. And when the king had heard him play, and had seen the skilful dancing of his dogs, he grew quite merry, and none had seen him as happy during all the seven long years that had passed since he had lost his daughters.

When the dance was over, the king asked the youth what he asked as a reward for having given him such a pleasure. The youth answered: "My Lord King, I did not come to you to win gold and gear. But I have another request to make: that you allow me to set out and search for your three daughters, carried away by a mountain troll." When the king heard this his thoughts once more grew gloomy, and he replied: "You need not even think of delivering my daughters. It is no child's play, and your betters have already attempted it in vain. Yet should it really come to pass that you deliver one of the princesses, you may be sure that I will not break my word." So he took leave of the king and set forth. And he decided to take no rest until he had found what he sought.

Now he passed through many broad kingdoms without meeting with any special adventures. And wherever he went his dogs followed him. 'Hark!' ran along and listened for anything worth hearing to be heard around them; 'Take Hold!' carried his master's knapsack and 'Tear!' who was the strongest, carried his master when the latter was weary. One day 'Hark!' came running up hastily, and told his master that he had gone to a high mountain, and had heard the king's daughter, who sat within it and span, and that the troll was not at home. This greatly pleased the youth, and he hurried towards the mountain together with his three dogs. When they got there 'Hark!' said: "There is no time to lose. The troll is only ten miles away, and I can already hear the golden horseshoes of his steed ringing on the stones." The youth now ordered his dogs to break down the door into the mountain, and they did. And as he stepped into the mountain he saw a lovely maiden, sitting in the mountain-hall, winding a golden thread on a golden spindle. The youth went up and greeted the lovely girl. Then the king's daughter was much surprised and said: "Who are you that dare to venture into the giant's hall? During all the seven long years I have been sitting here in the mountain I have never yet seen a human being." And she added: "For heaven's sake hasten away before the troll returns home, or else your life will be forfeit!" But the youth was unafraid, and said that he would await the giant's return without fear.

While they were talking together, the giant came riding along on his colt shod with gold. When he saw the gate standing open he grew furiously angry and shouted till the whole mountain shook: "Who has broken my mountain door?" The youth boldly answered: "I did, and now I shall break you as well! 'Take Hold!' seize him! 'Tear!' and 'Hark!' tear him into a thousand pieces." No sooner had he spoken than the dogs rushed up, fell upon the giant and tore him into countless pieces. Then the princess was happy beyond measure and said: "God be praised, now I am freed!" And she fell upon the youth's neck and gave him a kiss. But he did not wish to stay there any longer, saddled the giant's colt, loaded it with all the gold and gear he found in the mountain, and hastily went away with the king's beautiful daughter.

They passed on together a long distance. Then, one day, 'Hark!' who always ran ahead scouting, came quickly back to his master, and told him he had been near a high mountain, and had heard the king's second daughter sitting within it winding golden yarn, and that the troll himself was not at home. This was very welcome news for the youth, and he hurried towards the mountain with his faithful dogs. Now when they drew near 'Hark!' said: "There is no time to lose. The giant is only eight miles away, and I can already hear the golden horseshoes of his steed ringing on the stones." The youth at once ordered his dogs to break down the door into the mountain, no matter which way. And when he stepped into the interior of the mountain he saw a lovely maiden sitting in the mountain hall, winding golden yarn on a golden windle. The youth went up and greeted the lovely girl. The king's daughter was much surprised and said: "Who are you that dare to venture into the giant's hall? During all the seven years I have been sitting here in the mountain I have never yet seen a human being." And she added: "For heaven's sake, hasten away, for if the troll comes your life will be forfeit!" But the youth told her why he had come, and said that he would await the troll's return quite undisturbed.

While they were still talking together, the giant came riding on his steed shod with gold, and drew up outside the mountain. When he noticed that the great door was open, he grew furiously angry, and shouted till the mountain trembled to its very roots. He said: "Who has broken my mountain door?" The youth boldly answered: "I have, and now I shall break you as well! 'Take Hold,' seize him! 'Tear!' and 'Hark!' tear him into a thousand pieces!" The dogs at once rushed up, threw themselves upon the giant, and tore him into as many pieces as leaves fall in the autumn. Then the king's daughter was happy beyond measure and cried: "God be praised, now I am freed!" And she fell upon the youth's neck and gave him a kiss. He led the princess to her sister, and one can imagine how glad they were to see each other again. Then the youth packed up all the treasures he found in the mountain hall, loaded them on the giant's steed, and went his way with the king's two daughters. And they wandered along for a long time. Then, one day, 'Hark!' who always ran ahead scouting, came hastily to his master and told him that he had been near a high mountain, and had heard the king's third daughter sitting within and weaving a web of gold, and that the troll was not at home. This was very welcome news for the youth, and he hastened towards the mountain, followed by his three dogs. When he drew near 'Hark!' said: "There is no time to lose, for the giant is only five miles away. I can already hear the golden horseshoes of his steed ringing on the stones." Then the youth at once ordered his dogs to break down the door into the mountain, by hook or by crook. And when he stepped into the mountain, he saw a girl sitting in the mountain hall, weaving a web of gold. But this maiden was lovely beyond all measure, with a loveliness exceeding all the youth had ever thought to find on earth. He now went up and greeted the lovely maiden. Then the king's daughter was much surprised and said: "Who are you that dare to venture into the giant's hall? During all the seven long years I have been sitting here in the mountain I have never yet seen a human being." And she added: "For heaven's sake, hasten away before the troll comes, or else your life will be forfeit!" But the youth was full of confidence, and said he would gladly venture his life for the king's lovely daughter.

While they were still talking the giant came riding along on his colt shod with gold, and drew up at the foot of the mountain. When he went in he saw that uninvited guests had arrived, and was much frightened; for well he knew of the fate that had befallen his brothers. He therefore thought it advisable to fall back upon cunning and treachery, for he had not dared to venture on open battle. For that reason he made many fine speeches, and was very friendly and smooth with the youth. Then he told the king's daughter to prepare a meal in order to show his guest all hospitality.

And since the troll knew so well how to talk, the youth allowed himself to be beguiled by his smooth words, and forgot to be on his guard. He sat down to the table with the giant; but the king's daughter wept secretly, and the dogs were very restless; though no one paid them any attention.

When the giant and his guest had finished their meal, the youth said: "Now that I have satisfied my hunger, give me something to quench my thirst!" The giant replied: "On the mountain-top is a spring in which bubbles the clearest wine; but I have no one to fetch it." The youth answered: "If that be all that is lacking, one of my dogs can go up." Then the giant laughed in his false heart, for nothing suited him better than to have the youth send away his dogs. The youth ordered 'Take Hold!' to go to the spring, and the giant handed him a great tankard. The dog went; yet it was easy to see that he did not go willingly; and the time passed and passed and he did not return.

After a while the giant said: "I wonder why your dog stays away so long? Perhaps you would let another of your dogs go and help him; for the way is long and the tankard is heavy." The youth did not suspect any trickery and agreed. He told 'Tear!' to go and see why 'Take Hold!' had not yet come. The dog wagged his tail, and did not want to leave his master. But the youth did not notice it and drove him off himself. Then the giant laughed heartily, and the king's daughter wept, yet the youth paid no attention; but was merry and at his ease, played with his sword, and dreamed of no danger.

Thus a long time passed; but nothing was heard of the wine nor of the dogs. Then the giant said: "I can see that your dogs do not do as you bid them, otherwise we should not have to sit here and thirst. I think it would be well if you let 'Hark!' go up and see why they do not come back." The youth agreed, and told his third dog to hurry to the spring. But 'Hark!' did not want to, and instead crept whining to his master's feet. Then the youth grew angry and drove him off by force. And when he reached the top of the mountain he shared the fate of the others, a high wall rose round about him, and he was made a prisoner by the giant's magic power.

Now that all three dogs were gone, the giant rose, and suddenly looked altogether different. He took down a long sword from the wall, and said: "Now I will do what my brothers did not do, and you must die at once, for you are in my power!" Then the youth was frightened, and he regretted he had allowed his dogs to leave him. He said: "I do not ask for my life, since in any event the time will come when I must die. But I would like to repeat the Lord's Prayer, and play a psalm on my flute, for such is the custom in my country." The giant granted his prayer, but said that he would not wait long. So the youth kneeled and began to blow his flute till it sounded over hill and dale. And that very moment the magic wall was broken and the dogs were freed. They came rushing on like the storm-wind, and fell upon the mountain troll. The youth at once rose and said: "'Take Hold!', seize him! 'Tear!' and 'Hark!' tear him into a thousand pieces!" Then the dogs flung themselves on the giant and tore him into countless pieces. Then the youth took all the treasures that lay in the mountain, hitched the giant's horses to a gilded wagon, and drove off as fast as he could.

Now when the king's daughters met again there was great joy, as may well be imagined, and all thanked the youth for delivering them out of the power of the mountain trolls. But the youth fell deeply in love with the youngest princess, and they promised to be true to each other. So the king's daughters passed on their way with music and merriment of every kind, and the youth served them with all the honour and courtesy due maidens of gentle birth. And while they were underway the princesses toyed with the youth's hair, and each tied her golden ring in his locks for remembrance.

One day while they were still underway, they met two wanderers, who were travelling the same road. The clothes of the two strangers were torn and their feet were sore, and their whole appearance showed that they had a long journey behind them. The youth stopped his wagon, and asked them who they were and whence they came. The strangers answered that they were two princes, and had gone forth to search for the three maidens in the mountain. But fortune had not favoured them; and now they had to return home more like journeymen than kings' sons. When the youth heard this he felt sorry for the two wanderers, and asked whether they would like to ride with him in his handsome wagon. The princes thanked him profusely for his offer. They drove on together, and came to the kingdom over which the father of the princesses reigned.

Now when the princes learned that the youth had delivered the king's three daughters, a great jealousy took possession of them, and they thought of how badly they had fared in their own venture. And they took counsel together as to how they might get the better of the youth, and win power and glory for themselves. But they hid their evil plot till a favourable opportunity arose for carrying it out. Then they suddenly threw themselves on their comrade, seized him by the throat and strangled him. And then they threatened to kill the princesses if they did not swear to keep silence. And since the king's daughters were in the power of the princes, they did not dare say no. But they felt very sorry for the youth who had given up his life for them, and the youngest princess mourned with all her heart, and all her happiness was at an end.

After this great wrong the princes drove to the royal castle, and one may well imagine how happy the king was to get back his three daughters. In the meantime the poor youth lay like dead off in a gorge in the forest. Yet he was not quite dead, and his faithful dogs lay about him, kept him warm, and licked his wounds. And they did not stop until their master came back to life again. When he was once more well and strong he set out, and after many difficulties came to the royal castle in which the princesses dwelt.

When he came in the whole court was full of joy and merriment, and from the king's hall came the sound of dancing and string music. That surprised him greatly, and he asked what it all meant. The serving-man answered: "You must come from far away, since you do not know that the king has regained his daughters who were in the power of the mountain troll. This is the oldest princess's wedding-day."

The youth then asked after the youngest princess, and when she was to marry. But the serving-man said that she did not want a husband, and wept the live-long day, though no one knew why. Then the youth felt happy once more; for now he knew that she loved him, and had kept faith with him.

The youth now went to the keeper of the door, and bade him tell the king that a guest had arrived who would add to the merriment of the wedding festivities by showing his dogs. This was to the king's liking, and he ordered that the stranger receive the best possible treatment. And when the youth stepped into the hall, the whole wedding company were astounded by his skill and his manly bearing, and all agreed that so handsome a youth was rarely seen. But no sooner had the king's three daughters recognized him, than they jumped up from the table, and flung themselves on his neck. And then the princes thought it best to make themselves scarce. But the king's daughters told how the youth had freed them, and the rest of their adventures; and to make quite certain they looked for their rings among his locks.

Now when the king heard of the trickery and treachery the two strange princes had used, he grew very angry and had them driven ignominously forth from the castle. But he received the brave youth with great honour, as he had deserved, and he was married to the king's youngest daughter that selfsame day. After the king's death the youth was chosen king of all the land, and a gallant king he was. And there he lives with his beautiful queen, and is reigning there happily to this very day. And that is all I have to do with it.

The Golden Ball

THERE WERE TWO LASSES, daughters of one mother, and as they came from the fair, they saw a right bonny young man stand at the house-door before them. They never saw such a bonny man before. He had gold on his cap, gold on his finger, gold on his neck, a red gold watch-chain – eh! but he had brass. He had a golden ball in each hand. He gave a ball to each lass, and she was to keep it, and if she lost it, she was to be hanged. One of the lasses, 'twas the youngest, lost her ball. I'll tell thee how. She was by a park-paling, and she was tossing her ball, and it went up, and up, and up, till it went fair over the paling; and when she climbed up to look, the ball ran along the green grass, and it went right forward to the door of the house, and the ball went in and she saw it no more.

So she was taken away to be hanged by the neck till she was dead because she'd lost her ball.

But she had a sweetheart, and he said he would go and get the ball. So he went to the park-gate, but 'twas shut; so he climbed the hedge, and when he got to the top of the hedge, an old woman rose up out of the dyke before him, and said, if he wanted to get the ball, he must sleep three nights in the house. He said he would.

Then he went into the house, and looked for the ball, but could not find it. Night came on and he heard bogles move in the courtyard; so he looked out o' the window, and the yard was full of them.

Presently he heard steps coming upstairs. He hid behind the door, and was as still as a mouse. Then in came a big giant five times as tall as he, and the giant looked round but did not see the lad, so he went to the window and bowed to look out; and as he bowed on his elbows to see the bogles in the yard, the lad stepped behind him, and with one blow of his sword he cut him in twain, so that the top part of him fell in the yard, and the bottom part stood looking out of the window.

There was a great cry from the bogles when they saw half the giant come tumbling down to them, and they called out, "There comes half our master, give us the other half."

So the lad said, "It's no use of thee, thou pair of legs, standing alone at the window, as thou hast no eye to see with, so go join thy brother"; and he cast the lower part of the giant after the top part. Now when the bogles had gotten all the giant they were quiet.

Next night the lad was at the house again, and now a second giant came in at the door, and as he came in the lad cut him in twain, but the legs walked on to the chimney and went up them. "Go, get thee after thy legs," said the lad to the head, and he cast the head up the chimney too.

The third night the lad got into bed, and he heard the bogles striving under the bed, and they had the ball there, and they were casting it to and fro.

Now one of them has his leg thrust out from under the bed, so the lad brings his sword down and cuts it off. Then another thrusts his arm out at other side of the bed, and the lad cuts that off. So at last he had maimed them all, and they all went crying and wailing off, and forgot the ball, but he took it from under the bed, and went to seek his true love.

Now the lass was taken to York to be hanged; she was brought out on the scaffold, and the hangman said, "Now, lass, thou must hang by the neck till thou be'st dead." But she cried out:

"Stop, stop, I think I see my mother coming!
O mother, hast brought my golden ball
And come to set me free?"

"I've neither brought thy golden ball
Nor come to set thee free,
But I have come to see thee hung
Upon this gallows-tree."

Then the hangman said, "Now, lass, say thy prayers for thou must die." But she said:

"Stop, stop, I think I see my father coming!
O father, hast brought my golden ball
And come to set me free?"

"I've neither brought thy golden ball
Nor come to set thee free,
But I have come to see thee hung
Upon this gallows-tree."

Then the hangman said, "Hast thee done thy prayers? Now, lass, put thy head into the noose."

But she answered, "Stop, stop, I think I see my brother coming!" And again she sang, and then she thought she saw her sister coming, then her uncle, then her aunt, then her cousin; but after this the hangman said, "I will stop no longer, thou'rt making game of me. Thou must be hung at once."

But now she saw her sweetheart coming through the crowd, and he held over his head in the air her own golden ball; so she said:

"Stop, stop, I see my sweetheart coming!
Sweetheart, hast brought my golden ball
And come to set me free?"

"Aye, I have brought thy golden ball
And come to set thee free,
I have not come to see thee hung
Upon this gallows-tree."

And he took her home, and they lived happy ever after.

The Giant of St. Michael's Mount

MANY ARE THE TALES of King Arthur's valiant Round Table of knights – whose deeds have been sung almost more than those of the King himself. But from the day when as a "damoiseau of some fifteen years" (men say in the sixth century after Christ), Arthur was crowned as successor to Uther Pendragon, he was an example of chivalry to his whole court.

"He was a very virtuous knight, right worthy of praise, whose fame was much in the mouths of men. To the haughty he was proud; but tender and pitiful to the simple. He was a stout knight and a bold: a passing crafty captain, as indeed was but just, for skill and courage were his servants at need: and large of his giving. He was one of Love's lovers; a lover also of glory; and his famous deeds are right fit to be kept in remembrance. He ordained the courtesies of courts, and observed high state in very splendid fashion. So long as he lived and reigned he stood head and shoulders above all princes of the earth, both for courtesy and prowess, as for valour and liberality."

Having settled his own realm in peace and restored the kingdom to its ancient borders, he conquered Ireland, Norway, Denmark and Flanders; and, after a nine-years' war, added France to his dominions.

To him, thus flushed with victory, came ambassadors from the Emperor of Rome, bidding him to appear at that city and make restitution for his wrongful attacks on the empire's provinces, or to expect to be haled thither in bonds for judgment by the senate.

The king's answer was to summon a vast army, commit the realm to the care of his nephew Mordred (who afterward wrought such bale to that noble company), and set out over sea for Rome – "not to carry tribute, but to seek it."

* * *

A puissant and well-armed host it was that set forth; and the warrior-monarch who led them was arrayed in harness that surpassed all his followers. His thigh-pieces were of steel, wrought strong and fairly by some cunning smith. His hauberk was stout and richly chased, even such a vesture as became so puissant a king. Upon him was girt his sword, Excalibur. Mighty was the glaive, and long in the blade. It was forged in the Isle of Avalon, and he who brandished it naked in his hand deemed himself a happy man.

His helmet gleamed upon his head. The nasal was of gold; circlets of gold adorned the head-piece, with many a clear stone; and a dragon was fashioned for its crest. This helm had once been worn by Uther his sire. The king was mounted upon a destrier (charger), passing fair, strong, and speedy, loving well the battle. About his neck was set his shield, all clean of elephant's bone (ivory), on which was painted in several colours the image of Our Lady of St. Mary. The lance he carried was named Ron: it was a strong shaft, tough and great, sharp at the head, and very welcome at need in the press of battle. It had been made in Caermarthen by a smith that hight Griffin, and King Uther had carried it before time.

Setting out from Southampton with his great host, the king sailed for France; and though the mariners, steering by the stars, "were very fearful of the dark," the ships came safely to haven very early in the morning at Barfleur in Normandy.

They had been but a little while in the land when tidings were brought to the king that a marvellously strong giant, newly come to that land, had carried off Helen, the niece of his kinsman, Hoel.

This doleful lady the giant, named Dinabuc, had taken to a high place known as St. Michael's Mount, though in that day there was neither church nor monastery on the cliff, but all was shut close by the waves of the sea.

The adventure which followed was told many times in the old days, by Wace, Layamon and others. Let us listen to the unknown romancer of the fourteenth century who left us *Le Morte Arthure*.

* * *

When they had reached the shore and raised their tents, a templar came and informed the king: "Here, too, is a tyrant who torments thy people, a great giant of Genoa engendered by fiends; he hath devoured more than five hundred people and also many infants and free-born children. This hath been his sustenance now for seven winters and yet is the glutton not sated so well it pleaseth him. In the country of Cotentin no people has he left outside the strong castle enclosed within walls – for he has completely destroyed all the children of the commons and carried them to his crag and devoured them there. The Duchess of Brittany he has taken today near Reynes as she rode with her fair knights, and led her to the mountain where he abideth. We followed afar off, more than five hundred barons and citizens and noble bachelors, but he reached the crag: she shrieked so loud: the horror of that creature I shall never forget. She was the flower of France or of five realms, and one of the fairest that was ever formed, the gentlest jewel accounted by lords from Genoa to Geron, by Jesus of Heaven! She was thy wife's cousin, as thou mayest know, and sprung from the noblest race that reign in this earth. As thou art a righteous king, take pity on the people and endeavour to avenge them that are thus affronted."

"Alas," said the king, "so long as I have lived had I known of this it had been well: it has not happened fairly but fallen foul that this fiend hath destroyed the fair lady. I had leifer than all France this fifteen winters that I had been before that fellow a furlong away when he laid hold of that lady and led her to the mountains; I had left behind my life ere she had suffered harm. But can you tell me the crag where lives that man? I will go to that place and speak with him, to deal with that tyrant for treason to his lord, and make a truce for a time till it may happen better."

"Sire, see ye yon foreland with yonder two fires? There lurks that fiend – ask when thou mayest, upon the crest of the crag by a cold well that encloses the cliff within its clear stream: there wilt thou find dead folk without number, more florins i' faith than in all the rest of France, and more treasure hath that traitor unlawfully got than there was in Troy, I trow, what time it was conquered."

Then the noble king sighed for pity of those people, went right to a tent and rested no longer, he weltereth and wrestleth with himself and wringeth his hands – there was no wight in the world that knew what he wanted. He called Sir Cayous who served with the cup and Sir Bedivere the bold that bore his great brand.

"Look to it that after evensong ye be armed full well and mounted on horses by yonder thicket – by yon blithe stream, for I will pass privately in pilgrimage that way at supper-time when the lords are served to seek a saint by yon salt streams on St. Michael's Mount where miracles are seen."

After evensong King Arthur himself went to his wardrobe and took out his clothes – he armed him in a jerkin with a rich golden fringe, and above that laid a jeryn of Acre right over, and above that a coat of gentle mail – a tunic of Jerodyn with edges frayed. He drew on a bacenett of burnished silver – the best that was in Basill with rich borders: the crest and the crown enclosed so fair with clasps of bright gold adorned with stones – the visor and the aventail equipped so fair without a flaw, with eyelets of silver; his gauntlets gaily gilded and engraved at the borders with grains and balls of most glorious hue; he bore a broad shield and calls for his sword, he jumped on a brown steed and waits on the heath. He rises in his stirrups and stands aloft, he strains himself stoutly and looks forth, then he spurs the bay steed and rides to the thicket and there his knights await him gallantly arrayed.

They rode by that river that runneth so swift where the trees overstretch with fair boughs, the roe and the reindeer run recklessly there in thickets and rose-gardens to feast themselves. The thickets were in blossom with may-flowers, with falcons and pheasants of fair hues – all the birds lived there which fly with wings, for there sang the cuckoo full loud on the bushes, with all birds of merriment they gladden themselves: the voice of the nightingale's notes was sweet, they strove with the throstles three hundred at once, that this murmur of water and singing of birds might cure him of ill who never was whole.

Then move these folk quickly and alighted on foot and fastened their fair steeds afar off; then the king sternly told his knights to abide with their horses and come no further, "For I will seek this saint by myself and speak with this master man who guards this mountain, and then shall ye partake of the Sacrament one after the other honourably at St. Michael's full mighty with Christ!"

The king climbs the crag with cliffs full high, to the top of the crag he climbs aloft; lifts up his umbrer and looks about him keenly, receiving the cold wind on his face to comfort him; two fires he finds flaming full high – for a quarter of a furlong he thus walks between them: along the way by the well he wanders on to get to know of the warlock and where he abides.

He moves to the port fire and even there he finds a very woeful widow wringing her hands and weeping with painful tears on a grave newly marked in the soil since midday it seemed. He saluted her sorrowfully with becoming words and straightway asked after the fiend. Then this woeful widow joylessly greeted him, rose up on her knees and clasped her hands, saying: "Unhappy man, thou speakest too loudly; if yon warlock heareth he will devour us both. Cursed be the wight that directed thee hither, that made thee to travel here in these wild parts. I warn thee for thy honour thou seekest sorrow. Whither hastenest thou, man? Thou seem'st unhappy, goest thou to slay him with thy bright sword? Wert thou wightier than Wade or Gawayn thou shouldest win no honour. I warn thee beforehand: thou crossedst thyself unsafely to seek these mountains; six such as thou were not sufficient to cope with him alone. For an thou seest him alone, thy heart will fail thee to cross thyself safely, so huge he seemeth.

"Thou art noble and fair and in the flower of thy manhood, but thou art doomed already, by my fay, and that I foretell thee. Were there fifty such as thee in the field or on the fair earth – the monster with his fist would fell you all. Lo! here the dear duchess – today was she taken – deep buried in the ground – he murdered this mild lady ere midday was rung – without any mercy I wot not why, he slew her churlishly, and here have I embalmed her and buried her afterwards. For the grief of this incurable woe I shall never be happy again. Of all the friends she had, none followed after her but I, her foster-mother of fifteen winters: to move from this foreland I shall never attempt, but shall be found in this field till I am left dead."

Then answered Sir Arthur to that old wife: "I am come from the conqueror courteous and noble, as one of the most noble of Arthur's knights, a messenger to this vile wretch for the benefit of the people, to speak with this master man who guards this mountain: to treat with this tyrant for the treasure of lands and to make truce foretime till it may turn out better."

"Fie, thy words are but wasted," quoth that wife then, "for he sets but little by both lands and people. Nor of rents of red gold he troubles, but he will break the law when he chooses himself, without the permission of any, as lord of his own.

"But he hath a mantle which he keeps for himself that was spun in Spain by special women and afterwards adorned in Greece full fairly: it is covered all over with hair and embroidered with the beards of valiant kings, woven and combed that knights may know each king by his colour, in his home there he abides. Here he seizes the revenues of fifteen kingdoms each Easter evening, however it so happens that they send it themselves for the safety of the people – at that season with certain knights, and he has asked Arthur all these seven winters. Therefore he herds here to outrage his people until the King of Britain has fed his lips and sent his beard to that bold monster with his best knights; unless thou hast brought that beard go thou no further, for it is bootless that thou shouldst stay for aught else: for he has more treasure to take when he likes than ever had Arthur or any of his forefathers. If thou hast brought the beard, he will be more pleased than if thou gavest him Burgundy or Britain: but take care for love's sake that thou keep thy lips silent so that no word escape from them whatever betides; see that thy present be ready and trouble him but little, for he is at his supper and will be easily angered. And now take my advice and remove thy clothes and kneel in thy mantle and call him thy lord. He sups all this season on seven children of the commons, chopped up on a charger of pure white silver with pickles and finely ground spices and wines of Portugal mixed with honey. Three luckless damsels turn his spits."

"Ha! I have brought the beard," quoth he, "for thus it pleaseth me, forth then will I go and bear it myself. But, pray, if thou wilt tell me where this monster abideth, I shall commend thee an I live, so help me our Lord!"

"Go straight to the fire," quoth she, "that flames so high: there lurks that fiend as thou wilt discover: but thou must go somewhat to the south, sidling a little, for his power of smelling extends over six miles."

The source of the smoke he sought speedily, crossed himself safely with certain words, and going to the side he caught sight of the fiend as she said, unseemly supping alone. He lay at full length reposing foully, the thigh of a man's limb he lifted up by the haunch, his back and the lower parts and his broad loins he baked at the dreadful fire, and he was breechless: there were roasting full rudely dreadful meats of men and cattle bound together, a large pot crammed with anointed children, some spitted like birds, and women turned them.

And then this comely king's heart was sorely grieved because of his people at the place where he stood. Then he girded on his shield and hesitated no longer, he brandished his bright sword by its bright hilt, went forth to the fiend with a rough determination, and loudly hailed that giant with fierce words:

"Now may Almighty God that ruleth us all give thee sorrow and trouble, thou glutton, that liest there for the foulest monster that was ever formed – foully thou feedest thyself – the devil take thy soul! Here is unclean quarry, fellow, by my troth – refuse of all creatures – thou cursed wretch, because thou hast killed anointed children thou hast made martyrs and taken away the lives of those who are broached here on spits in this place and slaughtered by thy hand. I shall work thee thy punishment as thou greatly deservest, by the might of St. Michael who guardeth this mountain: and for this fair lady that thou hast left dead; gird thyself, thou son of a dog, the devil take thy soul, for thou shalt die today through the force of my arm."

Then was the glutton dismayed and glared unseemly; he grinned like a greyhound with grisly teeth; he gaped and groaned aloud with grievous gestures for wrath with the good king who spake to him in anger. His hair and his forelock were matted together and hung before his face for about half a foot. His brow and forehead were all like the skin of a frog and seemed freckled, hook-nosed like a hawk and a fierce bird, and hairy round his hollow eyes with overhanging brows: rough as a dog-fish – hardly could he be seen, so was he hid in that mass of hair: ears he had full huge and ugly to see, with horrible eyes and burning withal: flat-mouthed like a flounder with grinning lips, and the flesh in his front teeth as foul as a bear. His beard was rough and black and reached to his breast, fat like a porpoise with a huge carcass, and flesh still hung in shreds from his foul lips. Bull necked was that giant and broad of shoulders, with a streaked breast like a boar with long bristles. Rough arms like oak-branches with gnarled sides – limbs and loins right hateful to see, believe ye in truth; shovel-footed was that man and he seemed to straddle, with unshapely shanks shuffling together: thick thighs like a giant and thicker in the haunch – fat as a hog, full terrible he looked. Whoever might reckon faithfully the full length of this man, from the face to the foot, he was five fathoms long.

Then he started up sturdily on two stiff shanks and soon caught up a club of bright iron. He would have killed the king with his keen weapon, but through the wisdom of Christ, the carle failed. The crest and the corona and the silver clasps cleanly with his club he crashed down to the earth.

The king raises his shield and covers himself completely, and with his fierce weapon reaches him a blow, right full in the face he struck him so that the burnished blade reached to his brains – he wiped his face with his foul hands and strikes fast at Arthur's face fiercely thereafter. The king changes his foot and withdraws a little; had he not escaped that blow he had fared evil; he follows up fiercely and strikes a blow high up on the haunch with his hard weapon, that half a foot of the weapon is hidden in the flesh: the monster's hot blood runs down the hilt; even to the entrails he strikes the giant.

Then he groaned and he roared and roughly strikes full eagerly at Arthur, and on the earth strikes a sword's length within the sward, he smites at once so that the king nearly swooned from the force of his blow. But yet the king nimbly and swiftly strives, he smites with the sword so that it gashed the giant's loins; and the blood gushes out so that it makes all the ground slimy on which he stands.

Then he cast down his club and seized the king – on the top of the crag he caught him in his arms and enfolded him securely to crush his ribs: so tightly held he him that his heart was near to bursting. Then the doleful damsels fell down on the earth, kneeling and crying and wringing their hands. "Christ deliver yonder knight and keep him from grief, and never let that fiend take his life."

Yet the warlock was so mighty that he crushed him under; fiercely they wrung and wrestled together, they weltered and wallowed on those rushes, they tumbled and turned about and tore their clothes – roughly from the top they tumbled down together, Arthur sometimes on top and sometimes beneath – from the crest of the hill right down to the hard rock – they ceased not until they reached the brink of the sea. But Arthur with his dagger smote the giant until it sank right up to the hilt in him. The thief in his death-struggle grasped him so fiercely that three ribs in the king's side were thrust asunder.

Then Sir Cayous the Keen, moved in sorrow for the king, said, "Alas, we are undone, my lord is overthrown – fallen down with a fiend – it is all over! We must be forfeit and banished for ever." They lifted up his hauberk and felt beneath – his stern and his haunches, too, right up to his shoulders, his flanks and his loins and his fair sides, both his back and his breast and his bright arms. They were glad when they found no flesh wounds, and for that they were joyed, these gentle knights.

"Now certes," said Sir Bedivere, "it seemeth by my Lord! He seeketh saints but seldom, wherefore he grips the tighter that thus seizes this saint's body out of these high cliffs, to carry forth such a man to clothe him in silver. By Michael, of such a fellow I have great wonder than ever our Sovereign Lord should suffer him in Heaven: if all saints be such who serve our Lord, I shall no saint be ever, by my father's soul!"

Then laughed the bold king at Bedivere's words – "This saint have I sought, so help me our Lord! Wherefore draw out thy sword and pierce him to the heart; make certain of this fellow, he hath angered me sorely. I have not fought with such a wight these fifteen winters, but in the mountains in Wales I met such another. He was the strongest by far that I ever met, and had not my fortune been favourable, dead would I be now."

* * *

The other whom the king had in mind was Ryence (or Riton), a Welsh giant who in his day made war on divers kings. Of these some were slain in battle, and others remained captive in his hand. Alive or dead, Ryence used them despitefully; for it was his wont to shave the beards of these kings, and purfle therewith a cloak of furs that he wore, very rich. Vainglorious beyond measure was Ryence of his embroidered cloak. Now by reason of folly and lightness, Ryence sent messages to Arthur, bidding him shave his beard, and send it forthwith to the giant, in all good will. Since Arthur was a mightier lord and a more virtuous prince than his fellows, Ryence made covenant to prefer his beard before theirs, and hold it in honour as the most silken fringe of his mantle. Should Arthur refuse to grant Ryence the trophy, then nought was there to do but that body to body they must fight out their quarrel, in single combat, alone. He who might slay his adversary, or force him to own himself vanquished, should have the beard for his guerdon, together with the mantle of furs, fringes and garniture and all. An old ballad describes the scene at Camelot when this impudent message arrived:

As it fell out on a Pentecost day,
King Arthur at Camelot kept his court royall,
With his faire queene Dame Guenever the gay;
And many bold barons sitting in hall;
With ladies attired in purple and pall;
And heraults in hewkes, hooting on high,
Cryed, Largesse, Largesse, Chevaliers tres-hardie.

A doughty dwarfe to the uppermost deas
Right pertlye gan pricke, kneeling on knee;
With Steven fulle stoute amids all the preas,
Sayd, Nowe sir King Arthur, God save thee and see!
Sir Ryence of North-Gales greeteth well thee,
And bids thee thy beard anon to him send,
Or else from thy jaws he will it off rend.

For his robe of state is a rich scarlet mantle,
With eleven kings beards bordered about,
And there is room lefte yet in a kantle,
For thine to stande, to make the twelfth out:
This must be done, be thou never so stout;
This must be done, I tell thee no fable,
Maugre the teethe of all thy round table.

When this mortal message from his mouthe past,
Great was the noyse bothe in hall and in bower:
The king fum'd; the queene screecht; ladies were aghast;
Princes puffd; barons blustred; lords began lower;
Knights stormed: squires startled, like steed in a stower;
Pages and yeomen yell'd out in the hall,
Then in came Sir Kay, the king's seneschal.

Silence, my soveraignes, quoth this courteous knight,
And in that stound the stowre began still:
Then the dwarfe's dinner full deerely was dight;
Of wine and wassel he had his wille:
And, when he had eaten and drunken his fill,
An hundred pieces of fine coyned gold
Were given this dwarf for his message bold.

But say to Sir Ryence, thou dwarf, quoth the king,
That for his bold message I do him defye;
And shortlye with basins and pans will him ring
Out of North-Gales; where he and I
With swords, and not razors, quickly shall trye,
Whether he, or King Arthur will prove the best barbor;
And therewith he shook his good sword Escalabor.

King Arthur met this upstart in battle on a high mountain, and there the king slew Ryence with the sword, spoiling him of that rich garment of furs, with its border of dead men's beards.

And now as he looked down at the loathly Dinabuc he realized that he had this time conquered a monster more loathly and misshapen, a giant more horrible, bigger and mightier than was Ryence, even in the prime of his youth and strength.

When he had thought upon these things the king said to his comrades:

"Anon strike off his head and put it on a stake, give it to thy squire, for he is well mounted: bear it to Sir Howel, who is in sore straits, and bid him take heart, for his enemy is destroyed: then bear it to Barfleur and fasten it on iron and set it on the barbican for men to see: my sword and my broad shield lie upon the moor on the crest of the crag where first we fought, and the club thereby all of bright iron, that hath killed many a Christian in the land of Cotentin: go to the foreland and fetch me that weapon, and let us go back to our fleet where it lies in the water. If thou wilt have any treasure take whatever thou likest: I will have the mantle and the club, I covet naught else."

Now they go to the crag, these comely knights, and brought him the broad shield and his bright weapon, the club and the cloak too. Sir Cayous himself goes with the conqueror to show the kings whom the king had with him in secret, while bright day climbed up above through the clouds.

By that time a great noise was there at the court, and in front of the comely king they kneeled all together, "Welcome, our liege lord, too long hast thou fought, our governor under God, ablest and most noble, to whom grace is granted and given at his will. Now thy happy arrival hath comforted us all, thou hast in thy royalty revenged they people. Through help of thy hand thine enemy is destroyed that overcame thy people and reft them of their children: never was there kingdom so readily relieved of its troubles."

Then the conqueror speaks Christianlike to his people, "Thank ye God," quoth he, "for his grace and no man, for man's deed it never was but His own might, or a miracle of His Mother's, who is so mild to all." He called then the boatmen sharply at once to hasten with the shoremen to shift the goods.

"All that great treasure which the traitor won, see it be given to the commons, clergy, and others of the country; see it be dealt out to my dear people so that none may complain, under penalty of your lives." He ordered his cousin with knightly words to build a church on the rock where the body lay, and a convent therein for service to Christ, in memory of that martyr who rests in the mountain.

And that beautiful pinnacled church, thrusting up from the island's rocky cliffs towards the sky, you may see at this very day.

The Giant's Cliff

THERE WAS ONCE A GIANT IN IRELAND, and his name was Mahon McMahon and he lived inside the cliffs that rose up straight from the sea. No one had ever seen door or window in the cliffs, and no one knew how the giant got in or out, but still it was said that he lived there, and there were those who told of how they had heard a strange sound of beating and the ringing of metal sounding from within, and had seen smoke rising up from the crevices.

Back from the sea, but yet not so very far from the cliffs, there was a fine big house, and a man by the name of Thomas Renardy lived in it. He was a married man, and he and his wife had one son, a pretty little boy named Philip, and he was the joy of their life and the light of their eyes.

With every year the boy grew handsomer and finer, till he was the admiration of all who saw him. All day he played about in the sun and the wind, and when his mother called him in to meals he came, and as soon as he had finished he was out again.

So he grew till he was seven years old, and then one day his mother called him, but he did not come. She hunted him high, and she hunted him low, but nowhere could she find him. Then the neighbours joined in the search. They were out hallooing over the hills and through the forest, and over by the cliffs where the sea beats high, but there was no answer to their calling, nor did they see aught of him, and his mother was left sorrowing.

A sad and smileless woman was she after that, and months rolled up into years, until the years were seven; and at the end of that time her grief for him was as green as at the beginning.

Now there was a blacksmith in that country who was a great reader of dreams. People came from far and near to tell him their dreams and to ask the meaning of them. The name of the blacksmith was Robert Kelly, and he was a great hand at the forge. One night the blacksmith had a dream of his own, and a curious dream it was.

He dreamed a little lad came riding up on a great white horse. He was a handsome little fellow, with yellow hair and blue eyes, and Robert took him, from his size and looks, to be about seven years old, but at the same time there was something curious about him that made the blacksmith think he might be older.

"Robert Kelly, do you remember me?" asked the lad.

"I can't say that I do," answered the blacksmith, "and yet there's something about you that makes me feel I may have seen you before."

"Then have you forgotten Phil Renardy who was lost away seven long years ago?"

Now the blacksmith knew of whom the boy had reminded him. It was of that little lost lad of the Renardys.

"But that was seven long years ago, as you said," replied the blacksmith, "and by this time Phil would be about fourteen years old. You will never be him."

"Nevertheless I am," said the boy. "It was the giant Mahon McMahon that stole me away seven years ago when I was playing near the cliffs, and I have been living with him and serving him ever since, and in the halls of the giant we who serve him never grow old, but stay as we were when he first brought us there."

Now all the while the blacksmith knew he was asleep, and he thought this dream of his was the strangest dream he had ever heard of.

"Now I will tell you why I have come here," the boy went on; and he told Kelly how the very next night the seven years of his service were up. "Every seven years," said he, "the giant's door stands open from the stroke of midnight till cock's crow the next morning. There is only one way to get to his door, and that is by way of the sea."

The lad then begged and implored the blacksmith to get a boat and row out to the cliff the next night, and to wait there until midnight, when the house opened. The blacksmith was then to seek through it until he found the lad and then he was to bring him away with him.

"And tomorrow, when my first seven years of service is up, is the only time you can do it," said he. "If you will not, then I can never escape, but must stay there in service to the giant for always."

Then Kelly, who still knew he was asleep, said, "But after all, this is all in a dream, and when I waken I'll think there's no meaning to it."

"Then I'll give you a token to prove to you that this is no common dreaming," said Philip. With that he turned his horse about, and the horse lashed out at the blacksmith with his hind leg, and the hoof struck him on the forehead with such force that it seemed as though his head would be crushed in.

The blacksmith cried out with the blow and woke to find the blood streaming down his face, and when he had wiped it away and was able to examine his forehead, there was the mark of a horseshoe on it.

Robert said nothing to anyone about his dream, not even when they saw the mark on his forehead and wondered about it, so they thought that in some way when he was shoeing a horse it must have managed to kick him. But that night he went secretly to a friend of his who had a boat and asked him whether he would row him out in front of the cliffs just before midnight.

The friend was loath to do it, for he had small liking for going out at night on the sea and to a place that was but ill thought of; for there were all these tales about sounds that had been heard from inside the cliff and that they might be made by Mahon McMahon.

However, in the end Robert persuaded him, and a little before midnight they set out. There was enough moonlight for them to see the way to go, and as they rowed towards the cliffs, Robert told his friend, for the first time, why he was coming there and what he hoped to do.

"And whether it was a dream or no I can't tell you," said he, "for I was sleeping, and yet here, all the same, is the mark of the horse's hoof on my forehead."

Well, the friend thought it a strange tale. "And it's hard to believe there's any truth in it," said he; "but here we are in front of the cliffs, and this night will prove the worth of your dreaming."

He held the boat there in front of the rocks with his oars, and the minutes slipped by, and neither of the men spoke, and everything was silent. Then from far away, and faintly, they heard the village clock strike twelve.

Again they waited, and then suddenly and without a sound the front of the cliff opened, and they saw a portico down almost on a level with the water, and a great door opening out upon it. Inside the door were steps cut in the rock and leading up and out of sight. A light shone out through the door and across the water, but it was not very bright.

"Here is where I chance it," said the blacksmith. "Row me up close so that I may step out on the portico, for according to my dream, it's in there I must go if I am to find little Philip Renardy."

The whole matter was so strange that his friend tried to dissuade him from going, but the blacksmith would not listen to him.

"I've a sign from him on my forehead," he said, "and go I must and will. Do you wait here for me till cock's crow, and if I haven't come by then, there's no use in your waiting longer."

His friend rowed him up close to the edge of the portico, and the blacksmith climbed out on it, and watchfully he crept over to the door and peered in. Everything was still, and he saw nothing but the steps leading upward, and they were so high, each one of them, that it was as much as he could do to climb them.

He carried a ploughshare that he had brought with him from his smithy, for somehow he thought a ploughshare might be a good weapon if he needed one. And anyhow, it gave him some sort of a feeling of courage to have hold of it.

He climbed the steps, one after another, and that took him some time, and then he came into a great hall, and in the centre of it was a table hewn out of rock.

Around this table sat seven giants. They sat there bending forward as though they were consulting with each other, but none of them moved or spoke, or even so much as winked an eyelid. They might have been carven figures, for all the signs of life they gave.

At the head of the table sat a giant with a long beard, and he had been sitting there so long that his beard had grown into the slab of rock that was the top of the table.

Robert Kelly stood there looking at them for a while, and then, as none of them took any notice of him, he called in a loud voice, "Is anyone among you named Mahon McMahon?"

At that the giant at the head of the table started up so suddenly that the pulling out of his beard split the rock of the table into pieces, but none of the others stirred nor looked at him.

"I am Mahon McMahon," cried the giant. "And what do you come seeking me for?"

"I have come here in search of little Phil Renardy," cried the blacksmith boldly, "and I have been told that you are the one who can tell me where to find him."

The giant looked at him in silence for a bit, and then he said, "Yes, I can tell you where to find him, and better than that, I can even show you where he is."

He then led the way into a great stone chamber on beyond the hall, and it was glowing with fires, and there in it were a great number of young lads. It seemed to the blacksmith that there were hundreds of them, and they were all busy at some kind or other of metal work.

When Mahon McMahon came in, they stopped their work and stood back against the wall, and the blacksmith saw that not one among them looked to be more than seven years old, and they were all so much alike that they might have been brothers.

"If you are a friend of Phil Renardy, no doubt you can choose him from all others," said the giant. "And now look about you, and if you can tell me at the first telling which is he, then you may take him away with you, and no harm to anyone. But if you cannot tell me, then it was an ill hour for you when you entered my house, for you'll never go out again."

This frightened the blacksmith, but still he kept his wits about him and looked carefully from one lad to the other, but for the life of him he could not tell of a surety which was Phil Renardy, for he had no clear remembrance of him.

In order to gain time he said to the giant, "And are all these fine lads servants of yours?"

"They are," replied Mahon McMahon, "and it has taken me a long time to gather them together."

"You must be a good master," went on Robert Kelly, "for they all look rosy and in good condition, and I'm sure you treat them well, and they must be fond of you." He thought by talking in this way he might flatter the giant and put him in a good humour.

"That is a true word you have spoken," said the giant, "and I'm sure you must be an honest man, so let us shake hands upon it."

He held out his hand to the blacksmith, but when Bob Kelly looked at it, it was so thick and broad and cruel looking that he was afraid to trust his own hand to it. "For if he were to take the fancy," thought Bob, "he could crush it as easily as I could crush a rotten potato." So, instead of putting his hand into the giant's, he put the ploughshare in it, and the giant shut his fingers tight on it, so that it crumpled up as though the iron had no more strength in it than a piece of paper.

"Praises be it was not my hand he was squeezing," thought Robert Kelly.

"You have a strong hand," said the giant, "but you need a stronger than that if you're to shake hands with Mahon McMahon."

Then all the little lads burst into laughter, but through their laughter he thought he heard someone sighing, "Robert Kelly! Robert Kelly! I am here behind you."

He turned about quickly, and there behind him was one lad among them who was not laughing. And like a flash the blacksmith seized hold of him and cried out, "This is Phil Renardy, and the one I would take with me."

"Bad cess to you!" cried the giant, "but you've chosen rightly."

Then all grew dark, but Robert Kelly kept tight hold of the boy he had chosen, and he could hear many voices about him, crying, "Happy Philip Renardy! Happy Philip Renardy!"

The next he knew the sun was shining, and he was lying on the grass at the top of the cliff, and the little lad was watching beside him.

"And are you of a truth the little Philip Renardy who's been lost for so long?" asked Kelly.

"I am that one," replied the lad, "and it is you who have saved me; and now let us be up and off, for my heart is aching within me for a sight of my mother."

So the blacksmith rose up, and took the little lad's hand and led him to the big house of the Renardys, and the lad seemed to know the way better than he did. And no sooner did Mrs. Renardy see him than she knew the lad as her son and was like to have gone distracted with the joy of it. That was a comfort to Bob Kelly, too, for all the time he had kept wondering whether by chance he might not have brought back the wrong boy with him.

When he at last left them and went back to his smithy, he found quite a crowd gathered there, talking about him, for when he hadn't come back to the boat his friend had made sure the cliff had closed on him, and that mortal eye would never again behold him.

But when the people who had gathered heard his tale, there was great rejoicing, and all the bells of the village were rung, and a great crowd hurried away to the Renardy's house to get a glimpse of the boy who had been stolen by the giant.

Soon after his return, the boy began to grow again, but he never became very big, and there was always something a bit strange about him, though after a while he married and had children of his own who were fine stout fellows, and all of them were wonderful workers in metals.

As for Robert Kelly, his adventures were the making of him, for people came from everywhere to have him do their work for them, so as to have a chance to hear him tell his story. Moreover, Philip taught him some of the secrets of working with metal that he had learned in the giant's house, so that he became quite famous.

But the giant was never heard of again, and no more sounds came from within the cliff house, so it was supposed that he had left that part of the country and chosen some other place as his dwelling.

The Son of the King of Erin and the Giant of Loch Léin

ON A TIME, THERE LIVED A KING AND A QUEEN IN ERIN, and they had an only son. They were very careful and fond of this son; whatever he asked for was granted, and what he wanted he had.

When grown to be almost a young man the son went away one day to the hills to hunt. He could find no game – saw nothing all day. Towards evening he sat down on a hillside to rest, but soon stood up again and started to go home empty-handed. Then he heard a whistle behind him, and turning, saw a giant hurrying down the hill.

The giant came to him, took his hand, and said: "Can you play cards?"

"I can indeed," said the king's son.

"Well, if you can," said the giant, "we'll have a game here on this hillside."

So the two sat down, and the giant had out a pack of cards in a twinkling. "What shall we play for?" asked the giant.

"For two estates," answered the king's son.

They played: the young man won, and went home the better for two estates. He was very glad, and hurried to tell his father the luck he had.

Next day he went to the same place, and didn't wait long till the giant came again.

"Welcome, king's son," said the giant. "What shall we play for today?"

"I'll leave that to yourself," answered the young man.

"Well," said the giant, "I have five hundred bullocks with golden horns and silver hoofs, and I'll play them against as many cattle belonging to you."

"Agreed," said the king's son.

They played. The giant lost again. He had the cattle brought to the place; and the king's son went home with the five hundred bullocks. The king his father was outside watching, and was more delighted than the day before when he saw the drove of beautiful cattle with horns of gold and hoofs of silver.

When the bullocks were driven in, the king sent for the old blind sage (Sean dall Glic), to know what he would say of the young man's luck.

"My advice," said the old blind sage, "is not to let your son go the way of the giant again, for if he plays with him a third time he'll rue it."

But nothing could keep the king's son from playing the third time. Away he went, in spite of every advice and warning, and sat on the same hillside.

He waited long, but no one came. At last he rose to go home. That moment he heard a whistle behind him, and turning, saw the giant coming.

"Well, will you play with me today?" asked the giant.

"I would," said the king's son, "but I have nothing to bet."

"You have indeed."

"I have not," said the king's son.

"Haven't you your head?" asked the giant of Loch Léin, for it was he that was in it.

"I have," answered the king's son.

"So have I my head," said the giant; "and we'll play for each other's heads."

This third time the giant won the game; and the king's son was to give himself up in a year and a day to the giant in his castle.

The young man went home sad and weary. The king and queen were outside watching, and when they saw him approaching, they knew great trouble was on him. When he came to where they were, he wouldn't speak, but went straight into the castle and wouldn't eat or drink.

He was sad and lamenting for a good while, till at last he disappeared one day, the king and queen knew not whither. After that they didn't hear of him – didn't know was he dead or alive.

The young man after he left home was walking along over the kingdom for a long time. One day he saw no house, big or little, till after dark he came in front of a hill, and at the foot of the hill saw a small light. He went to the light, found a small house, and inside an old woman sitting at a warm fire, and every tooth in her head as long as a staff.

She stood up when he entered, took him by the hand, and said, "You are welcome to my house, son of the king of Erin." Then she brought warm water, washed his feet and legs from the knees down, gave him supper, and put him to bed.

When he rose next morning he found breakfast ready before him. The old woman said: "You were with me last night; you'll be with my sister tonight, and what she tells you to do, do, or your head'll be in danger. Now take the gift I give you. Here is a ball of thread: do you throw it in front of you before you start, and all day the ball will be rolling ahead of you, and you'll be following behind winding the thread into another ball."

He obeyed the old woman, threw the ball down and followed. All the day he was going up hill and down, across valleys and open places, keeping the ball in sight and winding the thread as he went, till evening, when he saw a hill in front, and a small light at the foot of it.

He went to the light and found a house, which he entered. There was no one inside but an old woman with teeth as long as a crutch.

"Oh! then you are welcome to my house, king's son of Erin," said she. "You were with my sister last night; you are with me tonight; and it's glad I am to see you."

She gave him meat and drink and a good bed to lie on.

When he rose next morning breakfast was there before him, and when he had eaten and was ready for the journey, the old woman gave him a ball of thread, saying: "You were with my younger sister the night before last; you were with me last night; and you'll be with my elder sister tonight. You must do what she tells you, or you'll lose your head. You must throw this ball before you, and follow the clew till evening."

He threw down the ball: it rolled on, showing the way up and down mountains and hills, across valleys and braes. All day he wound the ball; unceasingly it went till nightfall, when he came to a light, found a little house, and went in. Inside was an old woman, the eldest sister, who said: "You are welcome, and glad am I to see you, king's son."

She treated him as well as the other two had done. After he had eaten breakfast next morning, she said: –

"I know well the journey you are on. You have lost your head to the Giant of Loch Léin, and you are going to give yourself up. This giant has a great castle. Around the castle are seven hundred iron spikes, and on every spike of them but one is the head of a king, a queen, or a king's son. The seven hundredth spike is empty, and nothing can save your head from that spike if you don't take my advice.

"Here is a ball for you: walk behind it till you come to a lake near the giant's castle. When you come to that lake at midday the ball will be unwound.

"The giant has three young daughters, and they come at noon every day of the year to bathe in the lake. You must watch them well, for each will have a lily on her breast – one a blue, another a white, and the third a yellow lily. You mustn't let your eyes off the one with the yellow lily. Watch her well: when she undresses to go into the water, see where she puts her clothes; when the three are out in the lake swimming, do you slip away with the clothes of Yellow Lily.

"When the sisters come out from bathing, and find that the one with the yellow lily has lost her clothes, the other two will laugh and make game of her, and she will crouch down crying on the shore, with nothing to cover her, and say, 'How can I go home now, and everybody making sport of me? Whoever took my clothes, if he'll give them back to me, I'll save him from the danger he is in, if I have the power.'"

The king's son followed the ball till nearly noon, when it stopped at a lake not far from the giant's castle. Then he hid behind a rock at the water's edge, and waited.

At midday the three sisters came to the lake and, leaving their clothes on the strand, went into the water. When all three were in the lake swimming and playing with great pleasure and sport, the king's son slipped out and took the clothes of the sister with the yellow lily.

After they had bathed in the lake to their hearts' content, the three sisters came out. When the two with the blue and the white lilies saw their sister on the shore and her clothes gone, they began to laugh and make sport of her. Then, cowering and crouching down, she began to cry and lament, saying: "How can I go home now, with my own sisters laughing at me? If I stir from this, everybody will see me and make sport of me."

The sisters went home and left her there. When they were gone, and she was alone at the water crying and sobbing, all at once she came to herself and called out: "Whoever took my clothes, I'll forgive him if he brings them to me now, and I'll save him from the danger he is in if I can."

When he heard this, the king's son put the clothes out to her, and stayed behind himself till she told him to come forth.

Then she said: "I know well where you are going. My father, the Giant of Loch Léin, has a soft bed waiting for you – a deep tank of water for your death. But don't be uneasy; go into the water, and wait till I come to save you. Be at that castle above before my father. When he comes home tonight and asks for you, take no meat from him, but go to rest in the tank when he tells you."

The giant's daughter left the king's son, who went his way to the castle alone at a fair and easy gait, for he had time enough on his hands and to spare.

When the Giant of Loch Léin came home that night, the first question he asked was, "Is the son of the king of Erin here?"

"I am," said the king's son.

"Come," said the giant, "and get your evening's meat."

"I'll take no meat now, for I don't need it," said the king's son.

"Well, come with me then, and I'll show you your bed."

He went, and the giant put the king's son into the deep tank of water to drown, and being tired himself from hunting all day over the mountains and hills of Erin, he went to sleep.

That minute his youngest daughter came, took the king's son out of the tank, placed plenty to eat and to drink before him, and gave him a good bed to sleep on that night.

The giant's daughter watched till she heard her father stirring before daybreak; then she roused the king's son, and put him in the tank again.

Soon the giant came to the tank and called out: "Are you here, son of the king of Erin?"

"I am," said the king's son.

"Well, come out now. There is a great work for you today. I have a stable outside, in which I keep five hundred horses, and that stable has not been cleaned these seven hundred years. My great-grandmother when a girl lost a slumber-pin (*bar an suan*) somewhere in that stable, and never could find it. You must have that pin for me when I come home tonight; if you don't, your head will be on the seven hundredth spike tomorrow."

Then two shovels were brought for him to choose from to clean out the stable, an old and a new one. He chose the new shovel, and went to work.

For every shovelful he threw out, two came in; and soon the door of the stable was closed on him. When the stable-door was closed, the giant's daughter called from outside: "How are you thriving now, king's son?"

"I'm not thriving at all," said the king's son; "for as much as I throw out, twice as much comes in, and the door is closed against me."

"You must make a way for me to come in, and I'll help you," said she.

"How can I do that?" asked the king's son.

However, she did it. The giant's daughter made her way into the stable, and she wasn't long inside till the stable was cleared, and she saw the *bar an suan*.

"There is the pin over there in the corner," said she to the king's son, who put it in his bosom to give to the giant.

Now he was happy, and the giant's daughter had good meat and drink put before him.

When the giant himself came home, he asked: "How did you do your work today?"

"I did it well; I thought nothing of it."

"Did you find the *bar an suan*?"

"I did indeed; here 'tis for you."

"Oh! then," said the giant, "it is either the devil or my daughter that helped you to do that work, for I know you never did it alone."

"It's neither the devil nor your daughter, but my own strength that did the work," said the son of the king of Erin.

"You have done the work; now you must have your meat."

"I want no meat today; I am well satisfied as I am," said the king's son.

"Well," said the giant, "since you'll have no meat, you must go to sleep in the tank."

He went into the tank. The giant himself was soon snoring, for he was tired from hunting over Erin all day.

The moment her father was away, Yellow Lily came, took the king's son out of the tank, gave him a good supper and bed, and watched till the giant was stirring before daybreak. Then she roused the king's son and put him in the tank.

"Are you alive in the tank?" asked the giant at daybreak.

"I am," said the king's son.

"Well, you have a great work before you today. That stable you cleaned yesterday hasn't been thatched these seven hundred years, and if you don't have it thatched for me when I come home tonight, with birds' feathers, and not two feathers of one colour or kind, I'll have your head on the seven hundredth spike tomorrow."

"Here are two whistles – an old, and a new one; take your choice of them to call the birds."

The king's son took the new whistle, and set out over the hills and valleys, whistling as he went. But no matter how he whistled, not a bird came near him. At last, tired and worn out with travelling and whistling, he sat down on a hillock and began to cry.

That moment Yellow Lily was at his side with a cloth, which she spread out, and there was a grand meal before him. He hadn't finished eating and drinking before the stable was thatched with birds' feathers, and no two of them of one colour or kind.

When he came home that evening the giant called out: "Have you the stable thatched for me tonight?"

"I have indeed," said the king's son; "and small trouble I had with it."

"If that's true," said the giant, "either the devil or my daughter helped you."

"It was my own strength, and not the devil or your daughter that helped me," said the king's son.

He spent that night as he had the two nights before.

Next morning, when the giant found him alive in the tank, he said: "There is great work before you today, which you must do, or your head'll be on the spike tomorrow. Below here, under my castle, is a tree nine hundred feet high, and there isn't a limb on that tree, from the roots up, except one small limb at the very top, where there is a crow's nest. The tree is covered with glass from the ground to the crow's nest. In the nest is one egg: you must have that egg before me here for my supper tonight, or I'll have your head on the seven hundredth spike tomorrow."

The giant went hunting, and the king's son went down to the tree, tried to shake it, but could not make it stir. Then he tried to climb; but no use, it was all slippery glass. Then he thought, "Sure I'm done for now; I must lose my head this time."

He stood there in sadness, when Yellow Lily came, and said: "How are you thriving in your work?"

"I can do nothing," said the king's son.

"Well, all that we have done up to this time is nothing to climbing this tree. But first of all let us sit down together and eat, and then we'll talk," said Yellow Lily.

They sat down, she spread the cloth again, and they had a splendid feast. When the feast was over she took out a knife from her pocket and said: –

"Now you must kill me, strip the flesh from my bones, take all the bones apart, and use them as steps for climbing the tree. When you are climbing the tree, they will stick to the glass as if they had grown out of it; but when you are coming down, and have put your foot on each one, they will drop into your hand when you touch them. Be sure and stand on each bone, leave none untouched; if you do, it will stay behind. Put all my flesh into this clean cloth by the side of the spring at the roots of the tree. When you come to the earth, arrange my bones together, put the flesh over them, sprinkle it with water from the spring, and I shall be alive and well before you. But don't forget a bone of me on the tree."

"How could I kill you," asked the king's son, "after what you have done for me?"

"If you won't obey, you and I are done for," said Yellow Lily. "You must climb the tree, or we are lost; and to climb the tree you must do as I say."

The king's son obeyed. He killed Yellow Lily, cut the flesh from her body, and unjointed the bones, as she had told him.

As he went up, the king's son put the bones of Yellow Lily's body against the side of the tree, using them as steps, till he came under the nest and stood on the last bone.

Then he took the crow's egg; and coming down, put his foot on every bone, then took it with him, till he came to the last bone, which was so near the ground that he failed to touch it with his foot.

He now placed all the bones of Yellow Lily in order again at the side of the spring, put the flesh on them, sprinkled it with water from the spring. She rose up before him, and said: "Didn't I tell you not to leave a bone of my body without stepping on it? Now I am lame for life! You left my little toe on the tree without touching it, and I have but nine toes."

When the giant came home that night, the first words he had were, "Have you the crow's egg for my supper?"

"I have," said the king's son.

"If you have, then either the devil or my daughter is helping you."

"It is my own strength that's helping me," said the king's son.

"Well, whoever it is, I must forgive you now, and your head is your own."

So the king's son was free to go his own road, and away he went, and never stopped till he came home to his own father and mother, who had a great welcome before him; and why not? For they had thought he was dead.

When the son was at home a time, the king called up the old blind sage, and asked, "What must I do with my son now?"

"If you follow my advice," said the old blind sage, "you'll find a wife for him; and then he'll not go roaming away again, and leave you as he did before."

The king was pleased with the advice, and he sent a message to the king of Lochlin to ask his daughter in marriage.

The king of Lochlin came with the daughter and a ship full of attendants, and there was to be a grand wedding at the castle of the king of Erin. Now, the king's son asked his father to invite the Giant of Loch Léin and Yellow Lily to the wedding. The king sent messages for them to come.

The day before the marriage there was a great feast at the castle. As the feast went on, and all were merry, the Giant of Loch Léin said: "I never was at a place like this but one man sang a song, a second told a story, and the third played a trick."

Then the king of Erin sang a song, the king of Lochlin told a story, and when the turn came to the giant, he asked Yellow Lily to take his place.

She threw two grains of wheat in the air, and there came down on the table two pigeons. The cock pigeon pecked at the hen and pushed her off the table. Then the hen called out to him in a human voice, "You wouldn't do that to me the day I cleaned the stable for you."

Next time Yellow Lily put two grains of wheat on the table. The cock ate the wheat, pecked the hen, and pushed her off the table to the floor. The hen said: "You would not do that to me the day I thatched the stable for you with birds' feathers, and not two of one colour or kind."

The third time Yellow Lily put two more grains of wheat on the table. The cock ate both, and pushed the hen off to the floor. Then the hen called out: "You wouldn't do that to me the day you killed me and took my bones to make steps up the glass tree nine hundred feet high to get the crow's egg for the supper of the Giant of Loch Léin, and forgot my little toe when you were coming down, and left me lame for life."

"Well," said the king's son to the guests at the feast, "when I was a little younger than I am now, I used to be everywhere in the world sporting and gaming; and once when I was away, I lost the key of a casket that I had. I had a new key made, and after it was brought to me I found the old one. Now, I'll leave it to anyone here to tell what am I to do – which of the keys should I keep?"

"My advice to you," said the king of Lochlin, "is to keep the old key, for it fits the lock better, and you're more used to it."

Then the king's son stood up and said: "I thank you, king of Lochlin, for a wise advice and an honest word. This is my bride, the daughter of the Giant of Loch Léin. I'll have her, and no other woman. Your daughter is my father's guest, and no worse, but better, for having come to a wedding in Erin."

The king's son married Yellow Lily, daughter of the Giant of Loch Léin, the wedding lasted long, and all were happy.

Assipattle and the Mester Stoorworm

IN FAR BYGONE DAYS, in the north, there lived a well-to-do farmer, who had seven sons and one daughter. And the youngest of these seven sons bore a very curious name; for men called him Assipattle, which means, 'He who grovels among the ashes.'

Perhaps Assipattle deserved his name, for he was rather a lazy boy, who never did any work on the farm as his brothers did, but ran about the doors with ragged clothes and unkempt hair, and whose mind was ever filled with wondrous stories of Trolls and Giants, Elves and Goblins.

When the sun was hot in the long summer afternoons, when the bees droned drowsily and even the tiny insects seemed almost asleep, the boy was content to throw himself down on the ash-heap amongst the ashes, and lie there, lazily letting them run through his fingers, as one might play with sand on the seashore, basking in the sunshine and telling stories to himself.

And his brothers, working hard in the fields, would point to him with mocking fingers, and laugh, and say to each other how well the name suited him, and of how little use he was in the world.

And when they came home from their work, they would push him about and tease him, and even his mother would make him sweep the floor, and draw water from the well, and fetch peats from the peat-stack, and do all the little odd jobs that nobody else would do.

So poor Assipattle had rather a hard life of it, and he would often have been very miserable had it not been for his sister, who loved him dearly, and who would listen quite patiently to all the stories that he had to tell; who never laughed at him or told him that he was telling lies, as his brothers did.

But one day a very sad thing happened – at least, it was a sad thing for poor Assipattle.

For it chanced that the King of these parts had one only daughter, the Princess Gemdelovely, whom he loved dearly, and to whom he denied nothing. And Princess Gemdelovely was in want of a waiting-maid, and as she had seen Assipattle's sister standing by the garden gate as she was riding by one day, and had taken a fancy to her, she asked her father if she might ask her to come and live at the Castle and serve her.

Her father agreed at once, as he always did agree to any of her wishes; and sent a messenger in haste to the farmer's house to ask if his daughter would come to the Castle to be the Princess's waiting-maid.

And, of course, the farmer was very pleased at the piece of good fortune which had befallen the girl, and so was her mother, and so were her six brothers, all except poor Assipattle, who looked with wistful eyes after his sister as she rode away, proud of her new clothes and of the rivlins which her father had made her out of cowhide, which she was to wear in the Palace when she waited on the Princess, for at home she always ran barefoot.

Time passed, and one day a rider rode in hot haste through the country bearing the most terrible tidings. For the evening before, some fishermen, out in their boats, had caught sight of the Mester Stoorworm, which, as everyone knows, was the largest, and the first, and the greatest of all Sea-Serpents. It was that beast which, in the Good Book, is called the Leviathan, and if it had been measured in our day, its tail would have touched Iceland, while its snout rested on the North Cape.

And the fishermen had noticed that this fearsome Monster had its head turned towards the mainland, and that it opened its mouth and yawned horribly, as if to show that it was hungry, and that, if it were not fed, it would kill every living thing upon the land, both man and beast, bird and creeping thing.

For 'twas well known that its breath was so poisonous that it consumed as with a burning fire everything that it lighted on. So that, if it pleased the awful creature to lift its head and put forth its breath, like noxious vapour, over the country, in a few weeks the fair land would be turned into a region of desolation.

As you may imagine, everyone was almost paralyzed with terror at this awful calamity which threatened them; and the King called a solemn meeting of all his Counsellors, and asked them if they could devise any way of warding off the danger.

And for three whole days they sat in Council, these grave, bearded men, and many were the suggestions which were made, and many the words of wisdom which were spoken; but, alas! no one was wise enough to think of a way by which the Mester Stoorworm might be driven back.

At last, at the end of the third day, when everyone had given up hope of finding a remedy, the door of the Council Chamber opened and the Queen appeared.

Now the Queen was the King's second wife, and she was not a favourite in the Kingdom, for she was a proud, insolent woman, who did not behave kindly to her step-daughter, the Princess Gemdelovely, and who spent much more of her time in the company of a great Sorcerer, whom everyone feared and dreaded, than she did in that of the King, her husband.

So the sober Counsellors looked at her disapprovingly as she came boldly into the Council Chamber and stood up beside the King's Chair of State, and, speaking in a loud, clear voice, addressed them thus:

"Ye think that ye are brave men and strong, oh, ye Elders, and fit to be the Protectors of the People. And so it may be, when it is mortals that ye are called on to face. But ye be no match for the foe that now threatens our land. Before him your weapons be but as straw. 'Tis not through strength of arm, but through sorcery, that he will be overcome. So listen to my words, even though they be but those of a woman, and take counsel with the great Sorcerer, from whom nothing is hid, but who knoweth all the mysteries of the earth, and of the air, and of the sea."

Now the King and his Counsellors liked not this advice, for they hated the Sorcerer, who had, as they thought, too much influence with the Queen; but they were at their wits' end, and knew not to whom to turn for help, so they were fain to do as she said and summon the Wizard before them.

And when he obeyed the summons and appeared in their midst, they liked him none the better for his looks. For he was long, and thin, and awesome, with a beard that came down to his knee, and hair that wrapped him about like a mantle, and his face was the colour of mortar, as if he had always lived in darkness, and had been afraid to look on the sun.

But there was no help to be found in any other man, so they laid the case before him, and asked him what they should do. And he answered coldly that he would think over the matter, and come again to the Assembly the following day and give them his advice.

And his advice, when they heard it, was like to turn their hair white with horror.

For he said that the only way to satisfy the Monster, and to make it spare the land, was to feed it every Saturday with seven young maidens, who must be the fairest who could be found; and if, after this remedy had been tried once or twice, it did not succeed in mollifying the Stoorworm and inducing him to depart, there was but one other measure that he could suggest, but that was so horrible and dreadful that he would not rend their hearts by mentioning it in the meantime.

And as, although they hated him, they feared him also, the Council had e'en to abide by his words, and pronounced the awful doom.

And so it came about that, every Saturday, seven bonnie, innocent maidens were bound hand and foot and laid on a rock which ran into the sea, and the Monster stretched out his long, jagged tongue, and swept them into his mouth; while all the rest of the folk looked on from the top of a high hill – or, at least, the men looked – with cold, set faces, while the women hid theirs in their aprons and wept aloud.

"Is there no other way," they cried, "no other way than this, to save the land?"

But the men only groaned and shook their heads. "No other way," they answered; "no other way."

Then suddenly a boy's indignant voice rang out among the crowd. "Is there no grown man who would fight that Monster, and kill him, and save the lassies alive? I would do it; I am not feared for the Mester Stoorworm."

It was the boy Assipattle who spoke, and everyone looked at him in amazement as he stood staring at the great Sea-Serpent, his fingers twitching with rage, and his great blue eyes glowing with pity and indignation.

"The poor bairn's mad; the sight hath turned his head," they whispered one to another; and they would have crowded round him to pet and comfort him, but his elder brother came and gave him a heavy clout on the side of his head.

"Thou fight the Stoorworm!" he cried contemptuously. "A likely story! Go home to thy ash-pit, and stop speaking havers"; and, taking his arm, he drew him to the place where his other brothers were waiting, and they all went home together.

But all the time Assipattle kept on saying that he meant to kill the Stoorworm; and at last his brothers became so angry at what they thought was mere bragging, that they picked up stones and pelted him so hard with them that at last he took to his heels and ran away from them.

That evening the six brothers were threshing corn in the barn, and Assipattle, as usual, was lying among the ashes thinking his own thoughts, when his mother came out and bade him run and tell the others to come in for their supper.

The boy did as he was bid, for he was a willing enough little fellow; but when he entered the barn his brothers, in revenge for his having run away from them in the afternoon, set on him and pulled him down, and piled so much straw on top of him that, had his father not come from the house to see what they were all waiting for, he would, of a surety, have been smothered.

But when, at supper-time, his mother was quarrelling with the other lads for what they had done, and saying to them that it was only cowards who set on bairns littler and younger than themselves, Assipattle looked up from the bicker of porridge which he was supping.

"Vex not thyself, Mother," he said, "for I could have fought them all if I liked; ay, and beaten them, too."

"Why didst thou not essay it then?" cried everybody at once.

"Because I knew that I would need all my strength when I go to fight the Giant Stoorworm," replied Assipattle gravely.

And, as you may fancy, the others laughed louder than before.

Time passed, and every Saturday seven lassies were thrown to the Stoorworm, until at last it was felt that this state of things could not be allowed to go on any longer; for if it did, there would soon be no maidens at all left in the country.

So the Elders met once more, and, after long consultation, it was agreed that the Sorcerer should be summoned, and asked what his other remedy was. "For, by our troth," said they, "it cannot be worse than that which we are practicing now."

But had they known it, the new remedy was even more dreadful than the old. For the cruel Queen hated her step-daughter, Gemdelovely, and the wicked Sorcerer knew that she did, and that she would not be sorry to get rid of her, and, things being as they were, he thought that he saw a way to please the Queen. So he stood up in the Council, and, pretending to be very sorry, said that the only other thing that could be done was to give the Princess Gemdelovely to the Stoorworm, then would it of a surety depart.

When they heard this sentence a terrible stillness fell upon the Council, and everyone covered his face with his hands, for no man dare look at the King.

But although his dear daughter was as the apple of his eye, he was a just and righteous Monarch, and he felt that it was not right that other fathers should have been forced to part with their daughters, in order to try and save the country, if his child was to be spared.

So, after he had had speech with the Princess, he stood up before the Elders, and declared, with trembling voice, that both he and she were ready to make the sacrifice.

"She is my only child," he said, "and the last of her race. Yet it seemeth good to both of us that she should lay down her life, if by so doing she may save the land that she loves so well."

Salt tears ran down the faces of the great bearded men as they heard their King's words, for they all knew how dear the Princess Gemdelovely was to him. But it was felt that what he said was wise and true, and that the thing was just and right; for 'twere better, surely, that one maiden should die, even although she were of Royal blood, than that bands of other maidens should go to their death week by week, and all to no purpose.

So, amid heavy sobs, the aged Lawman – he who was the chief man of the Council – rose up to pronounce the Princess's doom. But, ere he did so, the King's Kemper – or Fighting-man – stepped forward.

"Nature teaches us that it is fitting that each beast hath a tail," he said, "and this Doom, which our Lawman is about to pronounce, is in very sooth a venomous beast. And, if I had my way, the tail which it would bear after it is this, that if the Mester Stoorworm doth not depart, and that right speedily, after he have devoured the Princess, the next thing that is offered to him be no tender young maiden, but that tough, lean old Sorcerer."

And at his words there was such a great shout of approval that the wicked Sorcerer seemed to shrink within himself, and his pale face grew paler than it was before.

Now, three weeks were allowed between the time that the Doom was pronounced upon the Princess and the time that it was carried out, so that the King might send Ambassadors to all the neighbouring Kingdoms to issue proclamations that, if any Champion would come forward who was able to drive away the Stoorworm and save the Princess, he should have her for his wife.

And with her he should have the Kingdom, as well as a very famous sword that was now in the King's possession, but which had belonged to the great god Odin, with which he had fought and vanquished all his foes.

The sword bore the name of Sickersnapper, and no man had any power against it.

The news of all these things spread over the length and breadth of the land, and everyone mourned for the fate that was like to befall the Princess Gemdelovely. And the farmer, and his wife, and their six sons mourned also; – all but Assipattle, who sat amongst the ashes and said nothing.

When the King's Proclamation was made known throughout the neighbouring Kingdoms, there was a fine stir among all the young Gallants, for it seemed but a little thing to slay a Sea-Monster; and a beautiful wife, a fertile Kingdom, and a trusty sword are not to be won every day.

So six-and-thirty Champions arrived at the King's Palace, each hoping to gain the prize.

But the King sent them all out to look at the Giant Stoorworm lying in the sea with its enormous mouth open, and when they saw it, twelve of them were seized with sudden illness, and twelve of them were so afraid that they took to their heels and ran, and never stopped till they reached their own countries; and so only twelve returned to the King's Palace, and as for them, they were so downcast at the thought of the task that they had undertaken that they had no spirit left in them at all.

And none of them dare try to kill the Stoorworm; so the three weeks passed slowly by, until the night before the day on which the Princess was to be sacrificed. On that night the King, feeling that he must do something to entertain his guests, made a great supper for them.

But, as you may think, it was a dreary feast, for everyone was thinking so much about the terrible thing that was to happen on the morrow, that no one could eat or drink.

And when it was all over, and everybody had retired to rest, save the King and his old Kemperman, the King returned to the great hall, and went slowly up to his Chair of State, high up on the dais. It was not like the Chairs of State that we know nowadays; it was nothing but a massive Kist, in which he kept all the things which he treasured most.

The old Monarch undid the iron bolts with trembling fingers, and lifted the lid, and took out the wondrous sword Sickersnapper, which had belonged to the great god Odin.

His trusty Kemperman, who had stood by him in a hundred fights, watched him with pitying eyes.

"Why lift ye out the sword," he said softly, "when thy fighting days are done? Right nobly hast thou fought thy battles in the past, oh, my Lord! when thine arm was strong and sure. But when folk's years number four score and sixteen, as thine do, 'tis time to leave such work to other and younger men."

The old King turned on him angrily, with something of the old fire in his eyes. "Wheest," he cried, "else will I turn this sword on thee. Dost thou think that I can see my only bairn devoured by a Monster, and not lift a finger to try and save her when no other man will? I tell thee – and I will swear it with my two thumbs crossed on Sickersnapper – that both the sword and I will be destroyed before so much as one of her hairs be touched. So go, an' thou love me, my old comrade, and order my boat to be ready, with the sail set and the prow pointed out to sea. I will go myself and fight the Stoorworm; and if I do not return, I will lay it on thee to guard my cherished daughter. Peradventure, my life may redeem hers."

Now that night everybody at the farm went to bed betimes, for next morning the whole family was to set out early, to go to the top of the hill near the sea, to see the Princess eaten by the Stoorworm. All except Assipattle, who was to be left at home to herd the geese.

The lad was so vexed at this – for he had great schemes in his head – that he could not sleep. And as he lay tossing and tumbling about in his corner among the ashes, he heard his father and mother talking in the great box-bed. And, as he listened, he found that they were having an argument.

"'Tis such a long way to the hill overlooking the sea, I fear me I shall never walk it," said his mother. "I think I had better bide at home."

"Nay," replied her husband, "that would be a bonny-like thing, when all the country-side is to be there. Thou shalt ride behind me on my good mare Go-Swift."

"I do not care to trouble thee to take me behind thee," said his wife, "for methinks thou dost not love me as thou wert wont to do."

"The woman's havering," cried the Goodman of the house impatiently. "What makes thee think that I have ceased to love thee?"

"Because thou wilt no longer tell me thy secrets," answered his wife. "To go no further, think of this very horse, Go-Swift. For five long years I have been begging thee to tell me how it is that, when thou ridest her, she flies faster than the wind, while if any other man mount her, she hirples along like a broken-down nag."

The Goodman laughed. "'Twas not for lack of love, Goodwife," he said, "though it might be lack of trust. For women's tongues wag but loosely; and I did not want other folk to ken my secret. But since my silence hath vexed thy heart, I will e'en tell it thee.

"When I want Go-Swift to stand, I give her one clap on the left shoulder. When I would have her go like any other horse, I give her two claps on the right. But when I want her to fly like the wind, I whistle through the windpipe of a goose. And, as I never ken when I want her to gallop like that, I aye keep the bird's thrapple in the left-hand pocket of my coat."

"So that is how thou managest the beast," said the farmer's wife, in a satisfied tone; "and that is what becomes of all my goose thrapples. Oh! but thou art a clever fellow, Goodman; and now that I ken the way of it I may go to sleep."

Assipattle was not tumbling about in the ashes now; he was sitting up in the darkness, with glowing cheeks and sparkling eyes.

His opportunity had come at last, and he knew it.

He waited patiently till their heavy breathing told him that his parents were asleep; then he crept over to where his father's clothes were, and took the goose's windpipe out of the pocket of his coat, and slipped noiselessly out of the house. Once he was out of it, he ran like lightning to the stable. He saddled and bridled Go-Swift, and threw a halter round her neck, and led her to the stable door.

The good mare, unaccustomed to her new groom, pranced, and reared, and plunged; but Assipattle, knowing his father's secret, clapped her once on the left shoulder, and she stood as still as a stone. Then he mounted her, and gave her two claps on the right shoulder, and the good horse trotted off briskly, giving a loud neigh as she did so.

The unwonted sound, ringing out in the stillness of the night, roused the household, and the Goodman and his six sons came tumbling down the wooden stairs, shouting to one another in confusion that someone was stealing Go-Swift.

The farmer was the first to reach the door; and when he saw, in the starlight, the vanishing form of his favourite steed, he cried at the top of his voice:

"Stop thief, ho!
Go-Swift, whoa!"

And when Go-Swift heard that she pulled up in a moment. All seemed lost, for the farmer and his sons could run very fast indeed, and it seemed to Assipattle, sitting motionless on Go-Swift's back, that they would very soon make up on him.

But, luckily, he remembered the goose's thrapple, and he pulled it out of his pocket and whistled through it. In an instant the good mare bounded forward, swift as the wind, and was over the hill and out of reach of its pursuers before they had taken ten steps more.

Day was dawning when the lad came within sight of the sea; and there, in front of him, in the water, lay the enormous Monster whom he had come so far to slay. Anyone would have said that he was mad even to dream of making such an attempt, for he was but a slim, unarmed youth, and the Mester Stoorworm was so big that men said it would reach the fourth part round the world. And its tongue was jagged at the end like a fork, and with this fork it could sweep whatever it chose into its mouth, and devour it at its leisure.

For all this, Assipattle was not afraid, for he had the heart of a hero underneath his tattered garments. "I must be cautious," he said to himself, "and do by my wits what I cannot do by my strength."

He climbed down from his seat on Go-Swift's back, and tethered the good steed to a tree, and walked on, looking well about him, till he came to a little cottage on the edge of a wood.

The door was not locked, so he entered, and found its occupant, an old woman, fast asleep in bed. He did not disturb her, but he took down an iron pot from the shelf, and examined it closely.

"This will serve my purpose," he said, "and surely the old dame would not grudge it if she knew 'twas to save the Princess's life."

Then he lifted a live peat from the smouldering fire, and went his way.

Down at the water's edge he found the King's boat lying, guarded by a single boatman, with its sails set and its prow turned in the direction of the Mester Stoorworm.

"It's a cold morning," said Assipattle. "Art thou not well-nigh frozen sitting there? If thou wilt come on shore, and run about, and warm thyself, I will get into the boat and guard it till thou returnest."

"A likely story," replied the man. "And what would the King say if he were to come, as I expect every moment he will do, and find me playing myself on the sand, and his good boat left to a smatchet like thee? 'Twould be as much as my head is worth."

"As thou wilt," answered Assipattle carelessly, beginning to search among the rocks. "In the meantime, I must be looking for a wheen mussels to roast for my breakfast." And after he had gathered the mussels, he began to make a hole in the sand to put the live peat in. The boatman watched him curiously, for he, too, was beginning to feel hungry.

Presently the lad gave a wild shriek, and jumped high in the air. "Gold, gold!" he cried. "By the name of Thor, who would have looked to find gold here?"

This was too much for the boatman. Forgetting all about his head and the King, he jumped out of the boat, and, pushing Assipattle aside, began to scrape among the sand with all his might.

While he was doing so, Assipattle seized his pot, jumped into the boat, pushed her off, and was half a mile out to sea before the outwitted man, who, needless to say, could find no gold, noticed what he was about.

And, of course, he was very angry, and the old King was more angry still when he came down to the shore, attended by his Nobles and carrying the great sword Sickersnapper, in the vain hope that he, poor feeble old man that he was, might be able in some way to defeat the Monster and save his daughter.

But to make such an attempt was beyond his power now that his boat was gone. So he could only stand on the shore, along with the fast assembling crowd of his subjects, and watch what would befall.

And this was what befell!

Assipattle, sailing slowly over the sea, and watching the Mester Stoorworm intently, noticed that the terrible Monster yawned occasionally, as if longing for his weekly feast. And as it yawned a great flood of sea-water went down its throat, and came out again at its huge gills.

So the brave lad took down his sail, and pointed the prow of his boat straight at the Monster's mouth, and the next time it yawned he and his boat were sucked right in, and, like Jonah, went straight down its throat into the dark regions inside its body. On and on the boat floated; but as it went the water grew less, pouring out of the Stoorworm's gills, till at last it stuck, as it were, on dry land. And Assipattle jumped out, his pot in his hand, and began to explore.

Presently he came to the huge creature's liver, and having heard that the liver of a fish is full of oil, he made a hole in it and put in the live peat.

Woe's me! but there was a conflagration! And Assipattle just got back to his boat in time; for the Mester Stoorworm, in its convulsions, threw the boat right out of its mouth again, and it was flung up, high and dry, on the bare land.

The commotion in the sea was so terrible that the King and his daughter – who by this time had come down to the shore dressed like a bride, in white, ready to be thrown to the Monster – and all his Courtiers, and all the country-folk, were fain to take refuge on the hill top, out of harm's way, and stand and see what happened next.

And this was what happened next.

The poor, distressed creature – for it was now to be pitied, even although it was a great, cruel, awful Mester Stoorworm – tossed itself to and fro, twisting and writhing.

And as it tossed its awful head out of the water its tongue fell out, and struck the earth with such force that it made a great dent in it, into which the sea rushed. And that dent formed the crooked Straits which now divide Denmark from Norway and Sweden.

Then some of its teeth fell out and rested in the sea, and became the Islands that we now call the Orkney Isles; and a little afterwards some more teeth dropped out, and they became what we now call the Shetland Isles.

After that the creature twisted itself into a great lump and died; and this lump became the Island of Iceland; and the fire which Assipattle had kindled with his live peat still burns on underneath it, and that is why there are mountains which throw out fire in that chilly land.

When at last it was plainly seen that the Mester Stoorworm was dead, the King could scarce contain himself with joy. He put his arms round Assipattle's neck, and kissed him, and called him his son. And he took off his own Royal Mantle and put it on the lad, and girded his good sword Sickersnapper round his waist. And he called his daughter, the Princess Gemdelovely, to him, and put her hand in his, and declared that when the right time came she should be his wife, and that he should be ruler over all the Kingdom.

Then the whole company mounted their horses again, and Assipattle rode on Go-Swift by the Princess's side; and so they returned, with great joy, to the King's Palace.

But as they were nearing the gate Assipattle's sister, she who was the Princess's maid, ran out to meet him, and signed to the Princess to lout down, and whispered something in her ear.

The Princess's face grew dark, and she turned her horse's head and rode back to where her father was, with his Nobles. She told him the words that the maiden had spoken; and when he heard them his face, too, grew as black as thunder.

For the matter was this: The cruel Queen, full of joy at the thought that she was to be rid, once for all, of her step-daughter, had been making love to the wicked Sorcerer all the morning in the old King's absence.

"He shall be killed at once," cried the Monarch. "Such behaviour cannot be overlooked."

"Thou wilt have much ado to find him, Your Majesty," said the girl, "for 'tis more than an hour since he and the Queen fled together on the fleetest horses that they could find in the stables."

"But I can find him," cried Assipattle; and he went off like the wind on his good horse Go-Swift.

It was not long before he came within sight of the fugitives, and he drew his sword and shouted to them to stop.

They heard the shout, and turned round, and they both laughed aloud in derision when they saw that it was only the boy who grovelled in the ashes who pursued them.

"The insolent brat! I will cut off his head for him! I will teach him a lesson!" cried the Sorcerer; and he rode boldly back to meet Assipattle. For although he was no fighter, he knew that no ordinary weapon could harm his enchanted body; therefore he was not afraid.

But he did not count on Assipattle having the Sword of the great god Odin, with which he had slain all his enemies; and before this magic weapon he was powerless. And, at one thrust, the young lad ran it through his body as easily as if he had been any ordinary man, and he fell from his horse, dead.

Then the Courtiers of the King, who had also set off in pursuit, but whose steeds were less fleet of foot than Go-Swift, came up, and seized the bridle of the Queen's horse, and led it and its rider back to the Palace.

She was brought before the Council, and judged, and condemned to be shut up in a high tower for the remainder of her life. Which thing surely came to pass.

As for Assipattle, when the proper time came he was married to the Princess Gemdelovely, with great feasting and rejoicing. And when the old King died they ruled the Kingdom for many a long year.

How Ian Direach Got the Blue Falcon

LONG AGO A KING AND QUEEN ruled over the islands of the west, and they had one son, whom they loved dearly. The boy grew up to be tall and strong and handsome, and he could run and shoot, and swim and dive better than any lad of his own age in the country. Besides, he knew how to sail about, and sing songs to the harp, and during the winter evenings, when everyone was gathered round the huge hall fire shaping bows or weaving cloth, Ian Direach would tell them tales of the deeds of his fathers.

So the time slipped by till Ian was almost a man, as they reckoned men in those days, and then his mother the queen died. There was great mourning throughout all the isles, and the boy and his father mourned her bitterly also; but before the new year came the king had married another wife, and seemed to have forgotten his old one. Only Ian remembered.

On a morning when the leaves were yellow in the trees of the glen, Ian slung his bow over his shoulder, and filling his quiver with arrows, went on to the hill in search of game. But not a bird was to be seen anywhere, till at length a blue falcon flew past him, and raising his bow he took aim at her. His eye was straight and his hand steady, but the falcon's flight was swift, and he only shot a feather from her wing. As the sun was now low over the sea he put the feather in his game bag, and set out homewards.

"Have you brought me much game today?" asked his stepmother as he entered the hall.

"Nought save this," he answered, handing her the feather of the blue falcon, which she held by the tip and gazed at silently. Then she turned to Ian and said:

"I am setting it on you as crosses and as spells, and as the fall of the year! That you may always be cold, and wet and dirty, and that your shoes may ever have pools in them, till you bring me hither the blue falcon on which that feather grew."

"If it is spells you are laying I can lay them too," answered Ian Direach; "and you shall stand with one foot on the great house and another on the castle, till I come back again, and your face shall be to the wind, from wheresoever it shall blow." Then he went away to seek the bird, as his stepmother bade him; and, looking homewards from the hill, he saw the queen standing with one foot on the great house, and the other on the castle, and her face turned towards whatever tempest should blow.

On he journeyed, over hills, and through rivers till he reached a wide plain, and never a glimpse did he catch of the falcon. Darker and darker it grew, and the small birds were seeking their nests, and at length Ian Direach could see no more, and he lay down under some bushes and sleep came to him. And in his dream a soft nose touched him, and a warm body curled up beside him, and a low voice whispered to him:

"Fortune is against you, Ian Direach; I have but the cheek and the hoof of a sheep to give you, and with these you must be content." With that Ian Direach awoke, and beheld Gille Mairtean the fox.

Between them they kindled a fire, and ate their supper. Then Gille Mairtean the fox bade Ian Direach lie down as before, and sleep till morning. And in the morning, when he awoke, Gille Mairtean said:

"The falcon that you seek is in the keeping of the Giant of the Five Heads, and the Five Necks, and the Five Humps. I will show you the way to his house, and I counsel you to do his bidding, nimbly and cheerfully, and, above all, to treat his birds kindly, for in this manner he may give you his falcon to feed and care for. And when this happens, wait till the giant is out of his house; then throw a cloth over the falcon and bear her away with you. Only see that not one of her feathers touches anything within the house, or evil will befall you."

"I thank you for your counsel," spake Ian Direach, "and I will be careful to follow it." Then he took the path to the giant's house.

"Who is there?" cried the giant, as someone knocked loudly on the door of his house.

"One who seeks work as a servant," answered Ian Direach.

"And what can you do?" asked the giant again.

"I can feed birds and tend pigs; I can feed and milk a cow, and also goats and sheep, if you have any of these," replied Ian Direach.

"Then enter, for I have great need of such a one," said the giant.

So Ian Direach entered, and tended so well and carefully all the birds and beasts, that the giant was better satisfied than ever he had been, and at length he thought that he might even be trusted to feed the falcon. And the heart of Ian was glad, and he tended the blue falcon till his fathers shone like the sky, and the giant was well pleased; and one day he said to him:

"For long my brothers on the other side of the mountain have besought me to visit them, but never could I go for fear of my falcon. Now I think I can leave her with you for one day, and before nightfall I shall be back again."

Scarcely was the giant out of sight next morning when Ian Direach seized the falcon, and throwing a cloth over her head hastened with her to the door. But the rays of the sun pierced through the thickness of the cloth, and as they passed the doorpost she gave a spring, and the tip of one of her feathers touched the post, which gave a scream, and brought the giant back in three strides. Ian Direach trembled as he saw him; but the giant only said:

"If you wish for my falcon you must first bring me the White Sword of Light that is in the house of the Big Women of Dhiurradh."

"And where do they live?" asked Ian. But the giant answered:

"Ah, that is for you to discover." And Ian dared say no more, and hastened down to the waste. There, as he hoped, he met his friend Gille Mairtean the fox, who bade him eat his supper and lie down to sleep. And when he had wakened next morning the fox said to him:

"Let us go down to the shore of the sea." And to the shore of the sea they went. And after they had reached the shore, and beheld the sea stretching before them, and the isle of Dhiurradh in the midst of it, the soul of Ian sank, and he turned to Gille Mairtean and asked why he had brought him thither, for the giant, when he had sent him, had known full well that without a boat he could never find the Big Women.

"Do not be cast down," answered the fox, "it is quite easy! I will change myself into a boat, and you shall go on board me, and I will carry you over the sea to the Seven Big Women of Dhiurradh. Tell them that you are skilled in brightening silver and gold, and in the end they will take you as servant, and if you are careful to please them they will give you the White Sword of Light to make bright and shining. But when you seek to steal it, take heed that its sheath touches nothing inside the house, or ill will befall you."

So Ian Direach did all things as the fox had told him, and the Seven Big Women of Dhiurradh took him for their servant, and for six weeks he worked so hard that his seven mistresses said to each other: "Never has a servant had the skill to make all bright and shining like this one. Let us give him the White Sword of Light to polish like the rest."

Then they brought forth the White Sword of Light from the iron closet where it hung, and bade him rub it till he could see his face in the shining blade; and he did so. But one day, when the Seven Big Women were out of the way, he bethought him that the moment had come for him to carry off the sword, and, replacing it in its sheath, he hoisted it on his shoulder. But just as he was passing through the door the tip of the sheath touched it, and the door gave a loud shriek. And the Big Women heard it, and came running back, and took the sword from him, and said:

"If it is our sword you want, you must first bring us the bay colt of the King of Erin."

Humbled and ashamed, Ian Direach left the house, and sat by the side of the sea, and soon Gille Mairtean the fox came to him.

"Plainly I see that you have taken no heed to my words, Ian Direach," spoke the fox. "But eat first, and yet once more will I help you."

At these words the heart returned again to Ian Direach, and he gathered sticks and made a fire and ate with Gille Mairtean the fox, and slept on the sand. At dawn next morning Gille Mairtean said to Ian Direach:

"I will change myself into a ship, and will bear you across the seas to Erin, to the land where dwells the king. And you shall offer yourself to serve in his stable, and to tend his horses, till at length so well content is he that he gives you the bay colt to wash and brush. But when you run away with her see that nought except the soles of her hoofs touch anything within the palace gates, or it will go ill with you."

After he had thus counselled Ian Direach, the fox changed himself into a ship, and set sail for Erin. And the king of that country gave into Ian Direach's hands the care of his horses, and never before did their skins shine so brightly or was their pace so swift. And the king was well pleased, and at the end of a month he sent for Ian and said to him:

"You have given me faithful service, and now I will entrust you with the most precious thing that my kingdom holds." And when he had spoken, he led Ian Direach to the stable where stood the bay colt. And Ian rubbed her and fed her, and galloped with her all round the country, till he could leave one wind behind him and catch the other which was in front.

"I am going away to hunt," said the king one morning while he was watching Ian tend the bay colt in her stable. "The deer have come down from the hill, and it is time for me to give them chase." Then he went away; and when he was no longer in sight, Ian Direach led the bay colt out of the stable, and sprang on his back. But as they rode through the gate, which stood between the palace and the outer world, the colt swished her tail against the post, which shrieked loudly. In a moment the king came running up, and he seized the colt's bridle.

"If you want my bay colt, you must first bring me the daughter of the king of the Franks."

With slow steps went Ian Direach down to the shore where Gille Mairtean the fox awaited him.

"Plainly I see that you have not done as I bid you, nor will you ever do it," spoke Gille Mairtean the fox; "but I will help you yet again for a third time; I will change myself into a ship, and we will sail to France."

And to France they sailed, and, as he was the ship, the Gille Mairtean sailed where he would, and ran himself into the cleft of a rock, high on to the land. Then, he commanded Ian Direach to go up to the king's palace, saying that he had been wrecked, that his ship was made fast in a rock, and that none had been saved but himself only.

Ian Direach listened to the words of the fox, and he told a tale so pitiful that the king and queen, and the princess their daughter, all came out to hear it. And when they had heard, nought would please them except to go down to the shore and visit the ship, which by now was floating, for the tide was up. Torn and battered was she, as if she had passed through many dangers, yet music of a wondrous sweetness poured forth from within.

"Bring hither a boat," cried the princess, "that I may go and see for myself the harp that gives forth such music." And a boat was brought, and Ian Direach stepped in to row it to the side of the ship.

To the further side he rowed, so that none could see, and when he helped the princess on board he gave a push to the boat, so that she could not get back to it again. And the music sounded always sweeter, though they could never see whence it came, and sought it from one part of the vessel to another. When at last they reached the deck and looked around them, nought of land could they see, or anything save the rushing waters.

The princess stood silent, and her face grew grim. At last she said:

"An ill trick have you played me! What is this that you have done, and whither are we going?"

"It is a queen you will be," answered Ian Direach, "for the king of Erin has sent me for you, and in return he will give me his bay colt, that I may take him to the Seven Big Women of Dhiurradh, in exchange for the White Sword of Light. This I must carry to the giant of the Five Heads and Five Necks and Five Humps, and, in place of it, he will bestow on me the blue falcon, which I have promised my stepmother, so that she may free me from the spell which she has laid on me."

"I would rather be wife to you," answered the princess.

By-and-by the ship sailed into a harbour on the coast of Erin, and cast anchor there. And Gille Mairtean the fox bade Ian Direach tell the princess that she must bide yet a while in a cave amongst the rocks, for they had business on land, and after a while they would return to her. Then they took a boat and rowed up to some rocks, and as they touched the land Gille Mairtean changed himself into a fair woman, who laughed, and said to Ian Direach, "I will give the king a fine wife."

Now the king of Erin had been hunting on the hill, and when he saw a strange ship sailing towards the harbour, he guessed that it might be Ian Direach, and left his hunting, and ran down the hill to the stable. Hastily he led the bay colt from his stall, and put the golden saddle on his back, and the silver bridle over his head, and with the colt's bridle in his hand, he hurried to meet the princess.

"I have brought you the king of France's daughter," said Ian Direach. And the king of Erin looked at the maiden, and was well pleased, not knowing that it was Gille Mairtean the fox. And he bowed low, and besought her to do him the honour to enter the palace; and Gille Mairtean, as he went in, turned to look back at Ian Direach, and laughed.

In the great hall the king paused and pointed to an iron chest which stood in a corner.

"In that chest is the crown that has waited for you for many years," he said, "and at last you have come for it." And he stooped down to unlock the box.

In an instant Gille Mairtean the fox had sprung on his back, and gave him such a bite that he fell down unconscious. Quickly the fox took his own shape again, and galloped away to the seashore, where Ian Direach and the princess and the bay colt awaited him.

"I will become a ship," cried Gille Mairtean, "and you shall go on board me." And so he did, and Ian Direach let the bay colt into the ship and the princess went after them, and they set sail for Dhiurradh. The wind was behind them, and very soon they saw the rocks of Dhiurradh in front. Then spoke Gille Mairtean the fox:

"Let the bay colt and the king's daughter hide in these rocks, and I will change myself into the colt, and go with you to the house of the Seven Big Women."

Joy filled the hearts of the Big Women when they beheld the bay colt led up to their door by Ian Direach. And the youngest of them fetched the White Sword of Light, and gave it into the hands of Ian Direach, who took off the golden saddle and the silver bridle, and went down the hill with the sword to the place where the princess and the real colt awaited him.

"Now we shall have the ride that we have longed for!" cried the Seven Big Women; and they saddled and bridled the colt, and the eldest one got upon the saddle. Then the second sister sat on the back of the first, and the third on the back of the second, and so on for the whole seven. And when they were all seated, the eldest struck his side with a whip and the colt bounded forward. Over the moors he flew, and round and round the mountains, and still the Big Women clung to him and snorted with pleasure. At last he leapt high in the air, and came down on top of Monadh the high hill, where the crag is. And he rested his forefeet on the crag, and threw up his hind legs, and the Seven Big Women fell over the crag, and were dead when they reached the bottom. And the colt laughed, and became a fox again and galloped away to the seashore, where Ian Direach, and the princess and the real colt and the White Sword of Light were awaiting him.

"I will make myself into a ship," said Gille Mairtean the fox, "and will carry you and the princess, and the bay colt and the White Sword of Light back to the land." And when the shore was reached, Gille Mairtean the fox took back his own shape, and spoke to Ian Direach in this wise:

"Let the princess and the White Sword of Light, and the bay colt remain among the rocks, and I will change myself into the likeness of the White Sword of Light, and you shall bear me to the giant, and, instead, he will give you the blue falcon." And Ian Direach did as the fox bade him, and set out for the giant's castle. From afar the giant beheld the blaze of the White Sword of Light, and his heart rejoiced; and he took the blue falcon and put it in a basket, and gave it to Ian Direach, who bore it swiftly away to the place where the princess, and the bay colt, and the real Sword of Light were awaiting him.

So well content was the giant to possess the sword he had coveted for many a year, that he began at once to whirl it through the air, and to cut and slash with it. For a little while Gille Mairtean let the giant play with him in this manner; then he turned in the giant's hand, and cut through the Five Necks, so that the Five Heads rolled on the ground. Afterwards he went back to Ian Direach and said to him:

"Saddle the colt with the golden saddle, and bridle him with the silver bridle, and sling the basket with the falcon over your shoulders, and hold the White Sword of Light with its back against your nose. Then mount the colt, and let the princess mount behind you, and ride thus to your father's palace. But see that the back of the sword is ever against your nose, else when your stepmother beholds you, she will change you into a dry fagot. If, however, you do as I bid you, she will become herself a bundle of sticks."

Ian Direach hearkened to the words of Gille Mairtean, and his stepmother fell as a bundle of sticks before him; and he set fire to her, and was free from her spells for ever. After that he married the princess, who was the best wife in all the islands of the west. Henceforth he was safe from harm, for had he not the bay colt who could leave one wind behind him and catch the other wind, and the blue falcon to bring him game to eat, and the White Sword of Light to pierce through his foes?

And Ian Direach knew that all this he owed to Gille Mairtean the fox, and he made a compact with him that he might choose any beast out of his herds whenever hunger seized him, and that henceforth no arrow should be let fly at him or at any of his race. But Gille Mairtean the fox would take no reward for the help he had given to Ian Direach, only his friendship. Thus all things prospered with Ian Direach till he died.

The Brave Little Tailor

ONE SUMMER'S DAY a little tailor sat on his table by the window in the best of spirits, and sewed for dear life. As he was sitting thus a peasant woman came down the street, calling out: "Good jam to sell, good jam to sell." This sounded sweetly in the tailor's ears; he put his frail little head out of the window, and shouted: "Up here, my good woman, and you'll find a willing customer." The woman climbed up the three flights of stairs with her heavy basket to the tailor's room, and he made her spread out all the pots in a row before him. He examined them all, lifted them up and smelled them, and said at last: "This jam seems good, weigh me four ounces of it, my good woman; and even if it's a quarter of a pound I won't stick at it." The woman, who had hoped to find a good market, gave him what he wanted, but went away grumbling wrathfully. "Now heaven shall bless this jam for my use," cried the little tailor, "and it shall sustain and strengthen me." He fetched some bread out of a cupboard, cut a round off the loaf, and spread the jam on it. "That won't taste amiss," he said, "but I'll finish that waistcoat first before I take a bite." He placed the bread beside him, went on sewing, and out of the lightness of his heart kept on making his stitches bigger and bigger. In the meantime the smell of the sweet jam rose to the ceiling, where heaps of flies were sitting, and attracted them to such an extent that they swarmed on to it in masses. "Ha! who invited you?" said the tailor, and chased the unwelcome guests away. But the flies, who didn't understand English, refused to let themselves be warned off, and returned again in even greater numbers. At last the little tailor, losing all patience, reached out of his chimney corner for a duster, and exclaiming: "Wait, and I'll give it to you," he beat them mercilessly with it. When he left off he counted the slain, and no fewer than seven lay dead before him with outstretched legs. "What a desperate fellow I am!" said he, and was filled with admiration at his own courage. "The whole town must know about this"; and in great haste the little tailor cut out a girdle, hemmed it, and embroidered on it in big letters, "Seven at a blow." "What did I say, the town? No, the whole world shall hear of it," he said, and his heartbeat for joy as a lamb wags his tail.

The tailor strapped the girdle round his waist and set out into the wide world, for he considered his workroom too small a field for his prowess. Before he set forth he looked round about him, to see if there was anything in the house he could take with him on his journey; but he found nothing except an old cheese, which he took possession of. In front of the house he observed a bird that had been caught in some bushes, and this he put into his wallet beside the cheese. Then he went on his way merrily, and being light and agile he never felt tired. His way led up a hill, on the top of which sat a powerful giant, who was calmly surveying the landscape. The little tailor went up to him, and greeting him cheerfully said: "Good day, friend; there you sit at your ease viewing the whole wide world. I'm just on my way there. What do you say to accompanying me?" The giant looked contemptuously at the tailor, and said: "What a poor wretched little creature you are!" "That's a good joke," answered the little tailor, and unbuttoning his coat he showed the giant the girdle. "There now, you can read what sort of a fellow I am." The giant read: "Seven at a blow"; and thinking they were human beings the tailor had slain, he conceived a certain respect for the little man. But first he thought he'd test him, so taking up a stone in his hand, he squeezed it till some drops of water ran out. "Now you do the same," said the giant, "if you really wish to be thought strong." "Is that all?" said the little tailor; "that's child's play to me," so he dived into his wallet, brought out the cheese, and pressed it till the whey ran out. "My squeeze was in sooth better than yours," said he. The giant didn't know what to say, for he couldn't have believed it of the little fellow. To prove him again, the giant lifted a stone and threw it so high that the eye could hardly follow it. "Now, my little pigmy, let me see you do that." "Well thrown," said the tailor; "but after all, your stone fell to the ground; I'll throw one that won't come down at all." He dived into his wallet again, and grasping the bird in his hand, he threw it up into the air. The bird, enchanted to be free, soared up into the sky, and flew away never to return. "Well, what do you think of that little piece of business, friend?" asked the tailor. "You can certainly throw," said the giant; "but now let's see if you can carry a proper weight." With these words he led the tailor to a huge oak tree which had been felled to the ground, and said: "If you are strong enough, help me to carry the tree out of the wood." "Most certainly," said the little tailor: "just you take the trunk on your shoulder; I'll bear the top and branches, which is certainly the heaviest part." The giant laid the trunk on his shoulder, but the tailor sat at his ease among the branches; and the giant, who couldn't see what was going on behind him, had to carry the whole tree, and the little tailor into the bargain. There he sat behind in the best of spirits, lustily whistling a tune, as if carrying the tree were mere sport. The giant, after dragging the heavy weight for some time, could get on no further, and shouted out: "Hi! I must let the tree fall." The tailor sprang nimbly down, seized the tree with both hands as if he had carried it the whole way and said to the giant: "Fancy a big lout like you not being able to carry a tree!"

They continued to go on their way together, and as they passed by a cherry tree the giant grasped the top of it, where the ripest fruit hung, gave the branches into the tailor's hand, and bade him eat. But the little tailor was far too weak to hold the tree down, and when the giant let go the tree swung back into the air, bearing the little tailor with it. When he had fallen to the ground again without hurting himself, the giant said: "What! do you mean to tell me you haven't the strength to hold down a feeble twig?" "It wasn't strength that was wanting," replied the tailor; "do you think that would have been anything for a man who has killed seven at a blow? I jumped over the tree because the huntsmen are shooting among the branches near us. Do you do the like if you dare." The giant made an attempt, but couldn't get over the tree, and stuck fast in the branches, so that here too the little tailor had the better of him.

"Well, you're a fine fellow, after all," said the giant; "come and spend the night with us in our cave." The little tailor willingly consented to do this, and following his friend they went on till they reached a cave where several other giants were sitting round a fire, each holding a roast sheep in his hand, of which he was eating. The little tailor looked about him, and thought: "Yes, there's certainly more room to turn round in here than in my workshop." The giant showed him a bed and bade him lie down and have a good sleep. But the bed was too big for the little tailor, so he didn't get into it, but crept away into the corner. At midnight, when the giant thought the little tailor was fast asleep, he rose up, and taking his big iron walking-stick, he broke the bed in two with a blow, and thought he had made an end of the little grasshopper. At early dawn the giants went off to the wood, and quite forgot about the little tailor, till all of a sudden they met him trudging along in the most cheerful manner. The giants were terrified at the apparition, and, fearful lest he should slay them, they all took to their heels as fast as they could.

The little tailor continued to follow his nose, and after he had wandered about for a long time he came to the courtyard of a royal palace, and feeling tired he lay down on the grass and fell asleep. While he lay there the people came, and looking him all over read on his girdle: "Seven at a blow." "Oh!" they said, "what can this great hero of a hundred fights want in our peaceful land? He must indeed be a mighty man of valour." They went and told the King about him, and said what a weighty and useful man he'd be in time of war, and that it would be well to secure him at any price. This counsel pleased the King, and he sent one of his courtiers down to the little tailor, to offer him, when he awoke, a commission in their army. The messenger remained standing by the sleeper, and waited till he stretched his limbs and opened his eyes, when he tendered his proposal. "That's the very thing I came here for," he answered; "I am quite ready to enter the King's service." So he was received with all honour, and given a special house of his own to live in.

But the other officers resented the success of the little tailor, and wished him a thousand miles away. "What's to come of it all?" they asked each other; "if we quarrel with him, he'll let out at us, and at every blow seven will fall. There'll soon be an end of us." So they resolved to go in a body to the King, and all to send in their papers. "We are not made," they said, "to hold out against a man who kills seven at a blow." The King was grieved at the thought of losing all his faithful servants for the sake of one man, and he wished heartily that he had never set eyes on him, or that he could get rid of him. But he didn't dare to send him away, for he feared he might kill him along with his people, and place himself on the throne. He pondered long and deeply over the matter, and finally came to a conclusion. He sent for the tailor and told him that, seeing what a great and warlike hero he was, he was about to make him an offer. In a certain wood of his kingdom there dwelled two giants who did much harm; by the way they robbed, murdered, burned, and plundered everything about them; "no one could approach them without endangering his life. But if he could overcome and kill these two giants he should have his only daughter for a wife, and half his kingdom into the bargain; he might have a hundred horsemen, too, to back him up." "That's the very thing for a man like me," thought the little tailor; "one doesn't get the offer of a beautiful princess and half a kingdom every day." "Done with you," he answered; "I'll soon put an end to the giants. But I haven't the smallest need of your hundred horsemen; a fellow who can slay seven men at a blow need not be afraid of two."

The little tailor set out, and the hundred horsemen followed him. When he came to the outskirts of the wood he said to his followers: "You wait here, I'll manage the giants by myself"; and he went on into the wood, casting his sharp little eyes right and left about him. After a while he spied the two giants lying asleep under a tree, and snoring till the very boughs bent with the breeze. The little tailor lost no time in filling his wallet with stones, and then climbed up the tree under which they lay. When he got to about the middle of it he slipped along a branch till he sat just above the sleepers, when he threw down one stone after the other on the nearest giant. The giant felt nothing for a long time, but at last he woke up, and pinching his companion said: "What did you strike me for?" "I didn't strike you," said the other, "you must be dreaming." They both lay down to sleep again, and the tailor threw down a stone on the second giant, who sprang up and cried: "What's that for?

Why did you throw something at me?" "I didn't throw anything," growled the first one. They wrangled on for a time, till, as both were tired, they made up the matter and fell asleep again. The little tailor began his game once more, and flung the largest stone he could find in his wallet with all his force, and hit the first giant on the chest. "This is too much of a good thing!" he yelled, and springing up like a madman, he knocked his companion against the tree till he trembled. He gave, however, as good as he got, and they became so enraged that they tore up trees and beat each other with them, till they both fell dead at once on the ground. Then the little tailor jumped down. "It's a mercy," he said, "that they didn't root up the tree on which I was perched, or I should have had to jump like a squirrel on to another, which, nimble though I am, would have been no easy job." He drew his sword and gave each of the giants a very fine thrust or two on the breast, and then went to the horsemen and said: "The deed is done, I've put an end to the two of them; but I assure you it has been no easy matter, for they even tore up trees in their struggle to defend themselves; but all that's of no use against one who slays seven men at a blow." "Weren't you wounded?" asked the horsemen.

"No fear," answered the tailor; "they haven't touched a hair of my head." But the horsemen wouldn't believe him till they rode into the wood and found the giants weltering in their blood, and the trees lying around, torn up by the roots.

The little tailor now demanded the promised reward from the King, but he repented his promise, and pondered once more how he could rid himself of the hero. "Before you obtain the hand of my daughter and half my kingdom," he said to him, "you must do another deed of valour. A unicorn is running about loose in the wood, and doing much mischief; you must first catch it." "I'm even less afraid of one unicorn than of two giants; seven at a blow, that's my motto." He took a piece of cord and an axe with him, went out to the wood, and again told the men who had been sent with him to remain outside. He hadn't to search long, for the unicorn soon passed by, and, on perceiving the tailor, dashed straight at him as though it were going to spike him on the spot. "Gently, gently," said he, "not so fast, my friend"; and standing still he waited till the beast was quite near, when he sprang lightly behind a tree; the unicorn ran with all its force against the tree, and rammed its horn so firmly into the trunk that it had no strength left to pull it out again, and was thus successfully captured. "Now I've caught my bird," said the tailor, and he came out from behind the tree, placed the cord round its neck first, then struck the horn out of the tree with his axe, and when everything was in order led the beast before the King.

Still the King didn't want to give him the promised reward and made a third demand. The tailor was to catch a wild boar for him that did a great deal of harm in the wood; and he might have the huntsmen to help him. "Willingly," said the tailor; "that's mere child's play." But he didn't take the huntsmen into the wood with him, and they were well enough pleased to remain behind, for the wild boar had often received them in a manner which did not make them desire its further acquaintance. As soon as the boar perceived the tailor it ran at him with foaming mouth and gleaming teeth, and tried to knock him down; but our alert little friend ran into a chapel that stood near, and got out of the window again with a jump. The boar pursued him into the church, but the tailor skipped round to the door, and closed it securely. So the raging beast was caught, for it was far too heavy and unwieldy to spring out of the window. The little tailor summoned the huntsmen together, that they might see the prisoner with their own eyes. Then the hero betook himself to the King, who was obliged now, whether he liked it or not, to keep his promise, and hand him over his daughter and half his kingdom. Had he known that no hero-warrior, but only a little tailor stood before him, it would have gone even more to his heart. So the wedding was celebrated with much splendour and little joy, and the tailor became a king.

After a time the Queen heard her husband saying one night in his sleep: "My lad, make that waistcoat and patch these trousers, or I'll box your ears." Thus she learned in what rank the young gentleman had been born, and next day she poured forth her woes to her father, and begged him to help her to get rid of a husband who was nothing more nor less than a tailor. The King comforted her, and said: "Leave your bedroom door open tonight, my servants shall stand outside, and when your husband is fast asleep they shall enter, bind him fast, and carry him on to a ship, which shall sail away out into the wide ocean." The Queen was well satisfied with the idea, but the armour-bearer, who had overheard everything, being much attached to his young master, went straight to him and revealed the whole plot. "I'll soon put a stop to the business," said the tailor. That night he and his wife went to bed at the usual time; and when she thought he had fallen asleep she got up, opened the door, and then lay down again. The little tailor, who had only pretended to be asleep, began to call out in a clear voice: "My lad, make that waistcoat and patch those trousers, or I'll box your ears. I have killed seven at a blow, slain two giants, led a unicorn captive, and caught a wild boar, then why should I be afraid of those men standing outside my door?" The men, when they heard the tailor saying these words, were so terrified that they fled as if pursued by a wild army, and didn't dare go near him again. So the little tailor was and remained a king all the days of his life.

Brabo and the Giant

AGES AGO, when the giants were numerous on the earth, there lived a big fellow named Antigonus. That was not what his mother had called him, but someone told him of a Greek general of that name; so he took this for his own. He was rough and cruel. His castle was on the Scheldt River, where the city of Antwerp now stands. Many ships sailed out of France and Holland down this stream. They were loaded with timber, flax, iron, cheese, fish, bread, linen and other things made in the country. It was by this trade that many merchants grew rich, and their children had plenty of toys to play with. The river was very grand, deep and wide. The captains of the ships liked to sail on it because there was no danger from rocks, and the country through which it flowed was so pretty.

So every day, one could see hundreds of white-sailed craft moving towards the sea, or coming in from the ocean. Boys and girls came down to stand in their wooden shoes on the banks, to see the vessels moving to and fro. The incoming ships brought sugar, wine, oranges, lemons, olives and other good things to eat, and wool to make warm clothes. Often craftsmen came from the wonderful countries in the south to tell of the rich cities there, and help to build new and fine houses, and splendid churches, and town halls. So all the Belgian people were happy.

But one day, this wicked giant came into the country to stop the ships and make them pay him money. He reared a strong castle on the riverbanks. It had four sides and high walls, and deep down in the earth were dark, damp dungeons. One had to light a candle to find his way to the horrid places.

What was it all for? the people wondered, but they soon found out. The giant, with a big knotted club, made out of an oak tree, strode through the town. He cried out to all the people to assemble in the great open square.

"From this day forth," he roared, "no ship, whether up or down the river, shall pass by this place without my permission. Every captain must pay me toll, in money or goods. Whoever refuses shall have both his hands cut off and thrown into the river.

"Hear ye all and obey. Anyone caught in helping a ship go by without paying toll, whether it be night, or whether it be day, shall have his thumbs cut off and be put in the dark dungeon for a month. Again I say, obey!"

With this, the giant swung and twirled his club aloft and then brought it down on a poor countryman's cart, smashing it into flinders. This was done to show his strength.

So every day, when the ships hove in sight, they were hailed from the giant's castle and made to pay heavy toll. Poor or rich, they had to hand over their money. If any captain refused, he was brought ashore and made to kneel before a block and place one hand upon the other. Then the giant swung his axe and cut off both hands, and flung them into the river. If a ship master hesitated because he had no money, he was cast into a dungeon until his friends paid his ransom.

Soon, on account of this, the city got a bad name. The captains from France kept in, and the ship men from Spain kept out. The merchants found their trade dwindling, and they grew poorer every day. So some of them slipped out of the city and tried to get the ships to sail in the night, and silently pass the giant's castle.

But the giant's watchers, on the towers, were as wide awake as owls and greedy as hawks. They pounced on the ship captains, chopped off their hands and tossed them into the river. The townspeople, who were found on board, were thrown into the dungeons and had their thumbs cut off.

So the prosperity of the city was destroyed, for the foreign merchants were afraid to send their ships into the giant's country. The reputation of the city grew worse. It was nicknamed by the Germans *Hand Werpen*, or Hand Throwing; while the Dutchmen called it Antwerp, which meant the same thing. The Duke of Brabant, or lord of the land, came to the big fellow's fortress and told him to stop. He even shook his fist under the giant's huge nose, and threatened to attack his castle and burn it. But Antigonus only snapped his fingers and laughed at him. He made his castle still stronger and kept on hailing ships, throwing some of the crews into dungeons and cutting off the hands of the captains until the fish in the river grew fat.

Now there was a brave young fellow named Brabo, who lived in the province of Brabant. He was proud of his country and her flag of yellow, black and red, and was loyal to his lord. He studied the castle well and saw a window, where he could climb up into the giant's chamber.

Going to the Duke, Brabo promised if his lord's soldiers would storm the gates of the giant's castle, that he would seek out and fight the ruffian. While they battered down the gates, he would climb the walls. "He's nothing but a *bulle-wak*" (a bully and a boaster), said Brabo, "and we ought to call him that, instead of Antigonus."

The Duke agreed. On a dark night, one thousand of his best men-at-arms were marched with their banners, but with no drums or trumpets, or anything that could make a noise and alarm the watchmen.

Reaching a wood full of big trees near the castle, they waited till after midnight. All the dogs in the town and country, for five miles around, were seized and put into barns, so as not to bark and wake the giant up. They were given plenty to eat, so that they quickly fell asleep and were perfectly quiet.

At the given signal, hundreds of men holding ship's masts, or tree trunks, marched against the gates. They punched and pounded and at last smashed the iron-bound timbers and rushed in. After overcoming the garrison, they lighted candles, and unlocking the dungeons, went down and set the poor half-starved captives free. Some of them, pale, haggard and thin as hop poles, could hardly stand. About the same time, the barn doors where the dogs had been kept were thrown open. In full cry, a regiment of the animals, from puppies to hounds, were at once out, barking, baying and yelping, as if they knew what was going on and wanted to see the fun.

But where was the giant? None of the captains could find him. Not one of the prisoners or the garrison could tell where he had hid.

But Brabo knew that the big fellow, Antigonus, was not at all brave, but really only a bully and a coward. So the lad was not afraid. Some of his comrades outside helped him to set up a tall ladder against the wall. Then, while all the watchers and men-at-arms inside had gone away to defend the gates, Brabo climbed into the castle through a slit in the thick wall. This had been cut out, like a window, for the bow and arrow men, and was usually occupied by a sentinel. Sword in hand, Brabo made for the giant's own room. Glaring at the youth, the big fellow seized his club and brought it down with such force that it went through the wooden floor. But Brabo dodged the blow and, in a trice, made a sweep with his sword. Cutting off the giant's head, he threw it out the window. It had hardly touched the ground before the dogs arrived. One of the largest of these ran away with the trophy and the big, hairy noddle of the bully was never found again.

But the giant's huge hands! Ah, they were cut off by Brabo, who stood on the very top of the highest tower, while all below looked up and cheered. Brabo laid one big hand on top of the other, as the giant used to do, when he cut off the hands of captains. He took first the right hand and then the left hand and threw them, one at a time, into the river.

A pretty sight now revealed the fact that the people knew what had been going on and were proud of Brabo's valour. In a moment, every house in Antwerp showed lighted candles, and the city was illuminated. Issuing from the gates came a company of maidens. They were dressed in white, but their leader was robed in yellow, red and black, the colours of the Brabant flag. They all sang in chorus the praises of Brabo their hero.

"Let us now drop the term of disgrace to the city – that of the Hand-Throwing and give it a new name," said one of the leading men of Antwerp.

"No," said the chief ruler, "let us rather keep the name, and, more than ever, invite all peaceful ships to come again, 'an-'t-werf' (at the wharf), as of old. Then, let the arms of Antwerp be two red hands above a castle."

"Agreed," cried the citizens with a great shout. The Duke of Brabant approved and gave new privileges to the city, on account of Brabo's bravery. So, from high to low, all rejoiced to honour their hero, who was richly rewarded.

After this, thousands of ships, from many countries, loaded or unloaded their cargoes on the wharves, or sailed peacefully by. Antwerp excelled all seaports and became very rich again. Her people loved their native city so dearly that they coined the proverb "All the world is a ring, and Antwerp is the pearl set in it."

To this day, in the great square, rises the splendid bronze monument of Brabo the Brave. The headless and handless hulk of the giant Antigonus lies sprawling, while on his body rests Antwerp Castle. Standing over all, at the top, is Brabo high in the air. He holds one of the hands of Antigonus, which he is about to toss into the Scheldt River.

No people honour valour more than the Belgians. Themselves are today, as of old, among the bravest.

Sponsken and the Giant

THERE WAS ONCE A LAD whose face was so badly pitted by the smallpox that everybody called him Sponsken, which means little sponge. From the very day of his birth Sponsken had been a cause of great anxiety to his parents, and as he grew older he became more trouble still, for he was so full of whims and mischief that one never knew where one had him. He would not learn his lessons, nor work at any serious task for ten minutes on end. All he seemed to think of was cutting capers and playing practical jokes on people. At last, in despair, his parents told their trouble to the village sexton, who was a great friend of the family, and often came to smoke his pipe with Sponsken's father in the chimney corner.

"Don't worry, my friends," said the sexton. "I've seen young men like your son before, and they are quite easy to manage if one only goes about it the right way. Just leave him to me. What he wants is a good fright, and I'll make it my business to see that he gets it."

So far so good. Sponsken's parents were only too glad to fall in with any plan which seemed likely to reform their unruly son, so the sexton went off to make his arrangements. That night he whitened his face with flour, covered himself in a white sheet, and hid behind a tree on a road along which he knew Sponsken would have to pass.

It was the dark of the moon, and the place the sexton had chosen was very lonely. For a long time he waited; then, hearing Sponsken coming along whistling a merry tune, he sprang out suddenly from behind his tree and waved his arms in a terrifying manner.

"Hallo!" said Sponsken. "Who are you?"

The sexton uttered a hollow groan.

"What's the matter?" said the boy. "Are you ill? If you can't speak, get out of my way, for I am in a hurry."

The sexton groaned again, louder than before, and waved his arms wildly.

"Come, come," cried Sponsken, "I can't stay here all night. Tell me what you want at once and let me pass." Then, as the ghostly figure made no answer, he struck it a blow with the stout ash-stick which he carried, and the poor sexton fell, stunned, to the ground. Sponsken stayed long enough to take a glimpse of the ghost's face and to recognize the features of the sexton beneath the flour; then he went on his way homeward, whistling as merrily as before.

When he reached home his parents gazed at him uneasily. They were very anxious about the success of their friend's plan, but Sponsken did not look at all like a lad who had been frightened – quite the contrary in fact, for he drew his chair up to the table and set to work upon his supper with an excellent appetite.

"A funny thing happened to me tonight," he said carelessly between two bites of an onion. "As I was walking along the lonely road by the cemetery a white figure jumped out at me."

"A wh-white figure!" stammered his father. "How terrifying! And what did you do, my son?"

"Do?" said Sponsken cheerfully. "Why, I fetched him a crack on the skull with my staff. He went down like a ninepin, and I warrant he won't try to frighten travellers again!"

"Base, ungrateful boy!" cried his father, rising to his feet. "It was my dear friend Jan the sexton you struck. All I hope is that you have not killed him."

"Well, if I have, it is his own fault," answered Sponsken. "He should not play tricks on me." But his father continued to rage and grumble so long that Sponsken got tired of hearing him at last, and flung off to bed in a sulk.

"I'll stand no more of this," he said to himself. "Since my own people do not appreciate me, I'll go out and seek my own fortune in the world, and they may go on as best they can."

The next morning, therefore, having packed a loaf of bread and a piece of cheese in a bag, Sponsken set off on his travels, telling nobody where he was going, and taking nothing else with him except a sparrow which he had tamed and kept since it was a fledgling. After walking for a long time he came to a forest, and feeling rather tired he sat down on the trunk of a fallen tree to rest.

Now in this forest lived a giant who was the most hideous creature one could possibly imagine. From his forehead jutted a pair of horns; his features were more like those of a beast than a man, and his fingernails grew long and curved like the claws of a wild animal. The giant considered himself lord of the whole wood, and was very jealous lest anybody should enter his domain. When, therefore, he saw Sponsken he was very angry, and having pulled up a young tree by the roots to serve him as a club, he approached the young man, who was sitting with his eyes closed, and struck him a heavy blow on the shoulder.

In spite of appearances, Sponsken was not asleep; he was far too wary a person to be caught napping under such conditions. As a matter of fact, he had seen the giant before the giant saw him, and he knew that his only chance of escape was to remain unperturbed and calm. When, therefore, the giant struck him on the shoulder, he opened his eyes sleepily, rubbed the place, and said with a yawn: "A pest on these flies! They bite so hard that a fellow can't sleep for them."

"You shall sleep soundly enough in a minute!" muttered the giant, who was enraged at Sponsken's nonchalance. "See how you like this!" And he gave the lad a blow on the other shoulder, harder than before.

"There they are again!" cried Sponsken, rubbing the place. "My word! They bite even harder on this side than on the other. It is time I was going!" And he rose from his seat, starting back with surprise as he affected to see the giant for the first time.

"So it's you, is it?" he cried. "What do you mean by tickling me when I am trying to sleep? If I were not so kind-hearted I'd break your neck for you!"

"Have a care what you say," cried the giant. "Do you know that I have the strength of twenty men and could crush you between my hands like a kitten?"

"Pooh!" said Sponsken. "Words are windy things. I have no doubt you could kill a whole regiment with your breath. But words won't go with me, my man; you must give me some proof of your prowess."

"Proof!" roared the giant. "See here! I can throw a stone so high into the air that it will not come down for a quarter of an hour." And he was as good as his word, for, picking up a large stone, he flung it with all his strength, and it was more than a quarter of an hour before it fell again at their feet.

"Can you match that?" asked the giant with a grin.

"Easily," said Sponsken. "I will throw a stone so high that it will not come down at all!" Bending to the ground he picked up a pebble and showed it to the giant, but very cleverly he managed at the last moment to exchange it for the sparrow which he carried in his pocket, and this he was able to do because the giant was rather short-sighted, and, if truth be told, slow-witted as well.

"One, two, three!" cried Sponsken, and he tossed the bird into the air, and of course it flew up and up and never came down at all.

"Well, well," said the giant, "I never saw such a thing as that in my life before. You are certainly a wonderful stone-thrower, little man. But can you do this?" And picking up another stone, he squeezed it so hard between his immense fists that he crushed it into a fine powder.

"Yes, that is hard to do," said Sponsken, "but I think I can go one better. Any oaf, if he be strong enough, can crush a stone to powder, but it requires skill as well as strength to wring the juice out of one. Watch me!" So saying, Sponsken adroitly slipped out his piece of cheese, and squeezed it until the whey dripped from between his fingers.

"Marvellous!" said the giant. "I confess myself beaten. Let us go into partnership, for there cannot be two others like us in the whole world."

"Willingly," answered Sponsken, "but what are we to do?"

"Why, as for that," said the giant, "the King of this country has promised his daughter's hand in marriage, and a great treasure besides, to anybody who can destroy three ferocious beasts which are devastating his realm. It seems to me that this is a task we can quite well do together. You, with your quickness and skill, can trap the beasts, and I can kill them with my club. That done, we will divide the spoils."

So it was agreed, and without wasting a moment the two took the wood together. Before very long they reached the King's palace, and sent up a message by one of the lords in waiting that they would like to see His Majesty.

"And do you mean to tell me," asked the King, when he had heard the giant's tale, "that you can overcome the three fierce animals by the help of this ugly little pock-marked fellow."

"Hush! Not so loud, for the love of heaven!" whispered the giant. "My friend is very touchy about his appearance, and if he hears you making such slighting remarks it is very likely he will bring the whole of your palace down about your head!"

"You don't say so!" whispered the King in reply, glancing fearfully at the terrible little man. "Well, you are at liberty to try your luck. The three animals are a bear, a unicorn and a wild boar, and at present they are hidden in the wood close by. There you will find them, but take care of yourselves, for they have already killed scores of my men."

"Don't be afraid," answered the giant, "for us this is as easy as playing a game."

After having partaken of a good meal the two made their way towards the wood in which the animals were hidden.

"We must make a plan," said Sponsken. "Listen to what I propose. You go into the middle of the wood while I remain here on the outskirts; then when you drive the beasts out I will see that they do not escape."

So it was arranged. The giant went forward into the wood, while Sponsken remained outside, waiting to see what would happen. He had not to wait long, for presently there was a crashing and a tearing of undergrowth and a great bear came lumbering towards him. Sponsken did not like the look of the creature at all, and decided to put as much space between them as possible. Looking here and there for a refuge, he spied a big oak-tree, and quickly climbed its trunk and ensconced himself among the branches. Unfortunately the bear had already seen him, and, raising himself on his hind legs with a dreadful roar, he rushed to the tree and began to climb. In another moment Sponsken would have been lost, but by good chance the tree happened to be hollow, so without hesitation the lad let himself down into the trunk, and finding at the bottom a small hole which led to the open air, he was just able to wriggle through it and escape. The bear followed him into the hollow trunk, but the hole at the bottom was too small for him to get out by, and as there was hardly room to move inside the trunk, the angry creature had to stay where he was, waking all the echoes in the forest with his growling.

The next minute the giant came running out of the forest. "Have you seen the bear?" he cried. "I drove him towards you!"

"Don't worry," answered Sponsken coolly; "I've shut him up in the tree there to keep him safe."

The giant rushed to the tree and dispatched the bear with one blow of his great club. Then, pulling out the carcass, he shouldered it, and the two went back to the palace, congratulating each other on the excellent beginning of their enterprise.

There remained now the unicorn and the wild boar. Next day Sponsken and the giant went to the forest again, and since their first plan had been so successful, it was arranged that they should follow exactly the same course. The giant went into the depths of the wood to find the unicorn and drive him out, while Sponsken remained on the borders to capture the animal when he came.

This time the period of waiting was longer, and Sponsken, leaning against the oak-tree, had almost fallen asleep when a clattering of hoofs awakened him, and he sprang aside just in time to escape the unicorn, who, breathing fire from his nostrils, charged down upon him. So great was the impetus of the beast's charge that he could not stop himself, and with a mighty crash he ran full tilt into the tree, driving his horn so far into the trunk that, although he pulled and struggled, he could not wrench himself free.

When the giant came up, Sponsken showed him the animal, which was quickly killed with a single blow of the club.

"Didn't I manage that affair well?" asked Sponsken as they went back to the palace.

"You are a wonder!" answered the giant, and he really believed what he said.

Now only the wild boar remained, and on the following day the two went to the forest to capture him also. Once again the same plan was followed, but this time Sponsken kept his eyes wide open, and when the ferocious beast broke cover he ran as fast as he could in the direction of the royal chapel. The wild boar followed him, and a fearsome creature he looked, I assure you, with his wicked little eyes and his great curved tusks and the hair on his back bristling like the quills of a porcupine.

Through the open door of the chapel Sponsken ran, and the boar, snorting with fury, followed him. Then began a fine chase, round and round the aisles, over the pews, and in and out of the vestries. At last Sponsken seized a chair, and dashing it against a window broke several panes, and so made good his escape. While the boar was still standing stupidly staring at the hole through which he had gone out, Sponsken ran round to the door, which he closed and locked. Then, having broken one or two more panes of glass, he sat down quietly by the chapel wall and began to pare his nails.

A short time afterwards the giant came rushing up.

"Where is the boar? Have you let him get away?" he cried.

"Don't get so excited," answered Sponsken. "The boar is safe enough. He's in the chapel there. I had no other place to put him, so I flung him through the window!"

"What a wonderful little man you are!" said the giant gleefully, and he ran off to kill the boar with one blow of his club. This done, he hoisted the carcass on to his shoulders and took the road to the palace. Halfway there the weight of the boar began to tell, for it was a massive beast, and the giant was forced to stay and rest.

"It is all very well," said he, mopping his streaming brow, "but I think you ought to take a turn with me in carrying this carcass."

"Not I," answered Sponsken. "We made an agreement that my work was done when I captured the beast, and I intend to keep to it."

So the giant had to struggle on as best he could for the rest of the way, grumbling at every step, while Sponsken followed, laughing up his sleeve, and exceedingly thankful that he had escaped the task.

When they reached the palace the two presented themselves before the King and claimed the promised reward. But now a difficulty arose. It was quite easy to divide the treasure, but which of them was to have the Princess?

"I think it should be I," said the giant, "for I killed the three animals."

"Not at all," said Sponsken. "The Princess should be given to me, for I captured the beasts."

"A lot of good your capturing them would have been if I had not killed them!" said the giant.

"How could you have killed them if I had not caught them first?" answered Sponsken. And so the two began to quarrel, and neither would give way, and high words passed between them. Truth to tell, the King was not at all sorry that the dispute had arisen, for he did not very much relish the idea of his daughter marrying either the bestial giant or the pock-marked, ugly little fellow who was his companion.

"There is only one way out of the difficulty," said the King at last. "We must let fate decide. Listen to the plan I propose. You shall both of you sleep in the Princess's chamber tonight – the giant in a bed on one side of her couch, and Sponsken on the other. I also will remain in her chamber and watch her carefully. If she spends most of the night with her face turned towards Sponsken, it shall be a sign that she is to marry him; if, on the other hand, she favours the giant, he shall be her husband; but if she sleeps all night with her face towards neither of you, then you must both give her up, and be satisfied with the treasure."

So it was agreed, and that night the trial took place. Sponsken, however, did not by any means intend that blind chance should settle so important a matter, and he spent the intervening time in making certain preparations. First of all he went to the palace gardens, from which he gathered certain herbs having an aromatic and beautiful perfume; these he placed in a bag and hid under his clothes. Then from the woods he gathered all the herbs he could find which had a disagreeable smell, such as garlic and stinkwort and poisonous fungus; these also he placed in a bag, and seized an early opportunity, when they came to the Princess's chamber, of hiding the bag under the pillow on which the giant's head was to rest.

The Princess well knew the fateful issue which was to be decided in the night, and as she had firmly made up her mind not to marry either the one or the other of her suitors, she determined to remain awake all night and to take care to keep her face turned towards the ceiling. For a time she managed to do so, but before long drowsiness overcame her, and she slept. Presently she turned over on her left side and lay with her face turned towards the giant, who began to chuckle to himself.

"Wait a minute," thought Sponsken. "I don't think the Princess will keep that position long!" And sure enough, the horrible stench of the herbs in the bag beneath the giant's pillow penetrated even to her dreams, and the Princess turned over hurriedly on the other side. What a change was there! Instead of a disgusting smell which made her dream of gloomy caverns and noisome things, she found now a delicious perfume that brought pictures of sunlit gardens all glowing with flowers and bright-winged butterflies flitting over them. The Princess gave a little sigh of content, and for the rest of the night she remained with her face turned towards Sponsken, so that the King had no choice but to declare the little man the winner.

The Princess, however, refused to abide by the judgment. "I will *not* marry that vulgar fellow," she cried. "I will die first! Oh, Father, if you love me, think of a means of escape!"

"Do not be afraid, my child," answered the King. "I will arrange something." And the next day he took the giant aside and proposed to him that he should rid him of Sponsken, promising a rich reward for the service. The giant's greed was aroused, and being very jealous of his companion's success, he was the more ready to fall in with the King's suggestion.

Fortunately for himself, Sponsken's quick wits made him suspicious. He guessed that some treachery was afoot, and in order to be prepared for emergencies he took a heavy hammer with him when he retired to bed at night. His suspicions were justified, for towards midnight the door of his room opened and the giant entered on tiptoe, carrying a heavy axe with which he intended to dispatch our friend. No sooner was his foot inside the door, however, than Sponsken jumped out of bed and sprang at him, looking so fierce that the giant, who was a coward at heart, and had besides a healthy respect for his companion's powers, turned and fled in dismay. Then Sponsken lifted his heavy hammer and struck three resounding blows upon the floor. The noise awoke everybody in the palace, and servants, guards and lords-in-waiting came flocking to the room to discover the cause. The King came last of all, a little anxious about the success of his fine plot, and when he found Sponsken sitting up in bed, quite unharmed, his face fell.

"What is the matter?" he stammered.

"Matter?" answered Sponsken. "Nothing very much! Some person wandered into my room, so I just gave three taps with my fingers on the wall. It is lucky for you all that I did not strike the blows with my fist, for had I done so I am afraid there would have been nothing left of your palace but a heap of dust!"

At these words everybody turned pale, and the King made haste to protest his undying friendship for his terrible guest.

As for the giant, he was in such fear of encountering Sponsken's resentment that he fled, and nobody ever saw him again.

Now the poor King did not know what to do, for his daughter still persisted in her refusal to marry Sponsken, and he was torn two ways by love and fear. Just at that time, however, a neighbouring monarch, who was an old enemy of the King's, declared war upon him, and this offered another opportunity for delay. Calling Sponsken before him, the King proposed that he should prove his valour by challenging the enemy king to mortal combat. Sponsken agreed; but his fame had already been noised abroad, and the challenge was refused.

"Very well," said the King, who was at the end of his resources. "As my prospective son-in-law you ought to lead my armies into battle. I will place my own charger at your disposal, and I look to you to save my country from defeat."

Here was a pretty kettle of fish! Sponsken had never ridden a horse in his life, and he had not the slightest knowledge of warfare. To make matters worse, the steed in question was a notoriously vicious brute who would allow nobody but his own master to mount him. Already he had accounted for several grooms and stablemen, whom he had kicked to death.

Sponsken commanded that the steed should be led to the borders of the forest and tied by the bridle to a tree. He had not the slightest intention of trying to mount the brute, and his plan was to wait until the attendants had gone away and then to slip off unobserved. Fate, however, was too much for him, for hardly was the horse safely tied up than couriers came spurring along the road to say that the enemy king was advancing at the head of his army, and was at that very moment less than half a mile away.

All the attendants fled at once, and Sponsken himself was so overcome by terror that, without thinking what he was doing, he jumped upon the back of the steed, and, forgetting that it was tied to the tree, dug his sharp spurs into its side. The horse plunged and reared, champing at the bit and doing its best to dislodge Sponsken from the saddle, but the lad clung on for dear life. At last, finding all its efforts unavailing, the horse dragged the tree up by the roots and charged forward in a straight line towards the advancing enemy. Almost dislodged from his seat by the sudden jerk, Sponsken stretched out his hand and grasped the branches of the tree, which swung in a terrifying manner at his side, promising every moment to hurl him from the saddle, and the result was that to the enemy army it appeared as though he were charging down upon them at full speed, bearing a tree as a club. Filled with dismay at the terrifying sight, the soldiers of the enemy king fled in all directions and hid themselves in the woods and in the crevices of the rocks. Sponsken rode on for the simple reason that he could do nothing else, right into the enemy's camp, where the steed came to a standstill and our hero was able to jump down from its back. Entering the king's tent, he helped himself to all the documents and articles of value he could find; then, having cut the tree from the bridle, he remounted the horse, which was now quite tame and docile, and rode back to the palace.

When the King heard that the enemy was routed he was overjoyed, and he recognized that a man who could perform such a feat single-handed was not to be treated lightly. His daughter, however, was still firm in her refusal to marry Sponsken, and so the King made him an offer of half his kingdom if he would release him from his promise and allow the Princess to go free. Sponsken accepted his terms and married a girl who, although she was not a princess, was nevertheless very pretty. Their wedding was celebrated with great pomp and they lived together very happily for the rest of their lives.

The Tailor and the Giant

ALL GIANTS BEHAVE IN ABOUT THE SAME WAY in every country; so each one of the big-boned fellows in Switzerland was like his relations in other lands. He had two legs, each as thick as a telegraph pole, arms like crowbars, and a body that made one think of a hogshead. His bone box, called a skull, had only a spoonful or two of brains inside of it, for his head was no bigger than a coconut. Usually he went about roaring like a bull, and carried a club in his right hand, as long and thick as a young fir tree. Although he was as strong as an ox, he could hardly run as fast as an elephant, and any smart dog could move around more quickly than he. That is the reason why a nimble princess with a needle could outwit him, or any clever young fellow could trap him in a pit, and then crack his skull with a pickaxe.

The monstrous fellow had a stomach equal to that of a rhinoceros. At one meal, he could chew up a sirloin of beef, eat a half bushel of rice, and gulp down a firkin of milk. With his club, he could smash a hay wagon; but, besides eating and bullying, he was not good for much. In fact, when it came to a game of hard thinking, and using his two spoonfuls of brains, any clever boy or girl twelve years old could beat him. Some giants, of course, were more intelligent than others, but as a rule, a giant got very soon and very much tired out when he had to use his mind.

They do say that the reason why giants are so stupid is because when they were quite little babies, their skull bones closed tight too soon, so that their brains never grew any larger, while the bone became thicker and thicker. That is the reason why some people usually called the big lout 'Mr. Bone Head with the big club'.

There were other people, however, who believed that the heads of the giants were made of wood, and some always thought of the big clumsy fellows as belonging to the tribe of Wooden Heads.

One exception, to the general run of Swiss giants, was a bulky fellow named Kisher, who served the great Charlemagne when this mighty general was fighting the savages, called Huns and Avars. This giant could wade all rivers, no matter how deep. If his horse, which was bigger than a hippopotamus, was afraid to step in and cross over, Kisher would grab hold of his tail and pull him backward through the deep water and over to the other shore. When fighting with his long sword in front of Charlemagne's army, one would think, from the way he cut down the enemy and left their corpses in swathes, that he was a sort of mowing machine.

After the battle, Kisher poked his spear into eight or ten of the carcasses of the defunct savages. Then, stringing them on his spear shaft, like a pile of pretzels, he threw the load over his shoulders. Trudging to his general's tent, he shook off the dead savages on the ground, as though he was dropping sausages from a fork.

Thereupon, his general rewarded him by naming him Einheer, which means that the giant was a whole army in himself. He also ordered that the big fellow should have all the sausages and barley cakes and dried apples that he wanted.

In fact, it was necessary to have plenty of eatables ready for the giant, for fear that when very hungry, he might swallow the dishes, chew up the napkins, eat up the tablecloth, and gulp down the table, legs and all. So terrible was his appetite that the mothers, when they saw Einheer coming down the hill, or up the street, called all their children inside the house, for fear that a pretty plump girl or a nice fat boy should be seized to fill up the mammoth cave that he kept under his belt.

When no food was at hand, and the giant had to do without his dinner, he set up a roar like a lion, until people thought it was distant thunder echoing among the far off mountains. Then old Kisher – for the people often forgot his new title – used to pull his belt tighter. He would even let the buckle tongue go into two or three holes further back in the strap. This took off the edge of his appetite for a while, but only for a few hours. Then he began to roar once more. Again the mothers clasped their babies in their arms and locked the doors, for fear he might get in and eat them out of house and home. The farmers took the harness off the horses, so that even if he broke into the stables, he would help himself only to the animals and not devour also the traces and horse collars. But after all this, the giant never knew enough to pick a lock, or get into barns when the doors were properly barred. Even a trained monkey could beat him at this sort of smartness.

Now there was a young tailor who was tired of this giant's boasting. Although the people often laughed at this man of shears and measuring tape, and called him 'one-ninth,' and the boys at times shouted 'Cabbage' at him, he was really a brave fellow. Besides being an expert with needle and thread, he was really as clever as anyone in town. Indeed, he thought himself in this respect equal even to the judges in the court who put big wigs on their heads to look as if theirs contained more brains than common people have. He read stories of famous heroes and dragon slayers and wanted to be like them and even excel. He boasted that, with a bag and a pair of scissors, he could get the better of any giant living. But when he declared he would some day show them the giant's carcass, they laughed and said, "That's only a tailor's promise." Yet he always retorted, "You'll see."

At any rate, the tailor made up his mind that cunning could accomplish as much as force. So he studied the habits and tastes of giants, to see what they liked best to eat. He soon found that this monster in human shape was very fond of rice pudding, with plenty of sauce and sugar on it. But the tailor never said a word to the giant about knowing this special weakness of his.

One day, while walking on the road to the next town to take home a suit of clothes to a customer, he suddenly came upon the giant, who at this time was, as usual, very hungry. They both glared at each other, but the giant, speaking first, roared out:

"Here, you fraction of a fellow, come now let us have a trial of strength. I'll hang you on a tree if I beat you, and you can skin me alive if you win."

At first, the little tailor was so frightened that his knees knocked together and his hat fell off, but, quickly feeling brave again, he answered:

"All right, I'm not afraid of you. Come on, we'll try."

The tailor knew that a brainy fellow with a clear head and a sharp tongue was more than a match for the big bonehead, any day. So, when the giant picked up a boulder, weighing a ton or so, and threw it into the lake, and then dared the man to do likewise, the tailor answered:

"Bah! that's nothing. Why don't you give me something that's hard to do? I can pick up the hardest pebble and squeeze water out of it with my hands. I'll wager a gold coin you can't do it."

Thus dared, the giant picked up a bit of hard rock and nearly broke his finger bones trying to crush it, or make it yield water. Mad as fire, he called the tailor a rascal, and said he told fibs. Then he dared him to try his hand at it. He got his club ready to smash the man into a jelly if he failed.

Now the tailor, not expecting to get home until night, had brought a fresh cheese ball and some crackers to eat on the way. He turned his back to the giant and bent over, pretending to pick up a hard, round stone from the ground. Then he pressed this cheese between his two hands so hard that a drop or two of what looked like water came out. As the moisture glistened in the sun, the astonished giant dropped his club. Then, rushing up to the tailor, he grasped his hand and cried out:

"Comrade and brother you are. Don't skin me. Come along with me; we'll skin other people, and I'll make you rich and famous."

The tailor, pretending to be as merciful as he thought himself brave, and being very ambitious, walked along with the giant until they came to a castle. The tailor wanted to get rich quick and marry a princess, or at least an heiress.

Strange to say, they found everybody inside the castle shedding tears, so that there were barely handkerchiefs enough to go round. Even the sentinel at the castle gate was weeping and had already used up four. Secretly, the tailor wished he had brought along his whole stock of linen, for here he might have driven a good bargain and made large sales at a high profit. But he told no one his thoughts.

In one breath, both the tailor and the giant asked, "What's the matter?"

Then the man-at-arms told them the trouble. A dragon living up in the mountains in a cave had been roaring all night for food. The citizens wanted to feed the criminals, then in prison, to the monster, but he refused such common nourishment. In fact, he was the most particular dragon, as to his diet, that ever came to Switzerland. He required one maiden a day to appease his hunger. He never would be satisfied with boys, or men, or even with ladies, that were either slender or bony.

Now the supply of plump and beautiful girls had actually run so low that the new victims had to draw lots. This very day, the lot had fallen on the king's only daughter, and at sunrise the next day, she was to be swallowed up.

As soon as the news had spread abroad in the city after sunrise, the stock on hand in all the shops that kept mourning goods, or black silk, or muslin, or grief-bordered handkerchiefs, was sold out before noon, and there was not time enough to import a fresh supply of crêpe from Paris. So everybody was sighing and groaning, and the sounds were appalling. Some were shedding tears copiously for real grief, but others because their old mourning garments were out of fashion. With others, it was a case of economy rather than grief, for black goods saved their best clothes.

But the tailor, though feeling sad at first, saw a chance of coining wealth and getting into society, for he had quickly learned that the king had offered his daughter in marriage to anyone who would fight and kill the dragon, besides making a gift outright of a thousand pounds of gold.

So when the pair of heroes, the tailor and giant, proffered their services, the monarch gave the monstrous fellow an iron bar as big as the rail for a locomotive to run on.

But when the king saw that the little tailor had only a pair of scissors, he laughed until he forgot his grief. Then he offered the little man a battle-axe. It was as sharp as a razor and heavy enough to chop open a knight clothed in steel. Thus armed, the two were all ready to set out together to the dragon's cave.

Pretending that one of his shoelaces had broken and he needed to tie it up, the tailor told the giant to go on and carry both axe and iron club, and he would catch up with him. When the two were together, the giant was about to hand his companion the battle-axe, when the tailor began at once to talk about rice pudding. He smilingly asked the giant whether he liked raisins in it and would take it with grated nutmeg sprinkled over the top, or would he have it plain?

The subject was so interesting to the giant that his eyes sparkled at once. He forgot that he was carrying both of the two heavy things, axe and bar. He never dropped them until they reached the dragon's lair.

But while they were arguing which should go in first, the dragon rushed out and swallowed the little tailor at a gulp, without chewing him up.

The giant noticed that not a bit of butter nor drop of gravy was necessary, for the tailor had slid down and disappeared in a jiffy. Thereupon, the giant gave the monster a mighty wallop upon the head with the iron bar. It was so terrific that he fell dead and stiffened out, ten yards long. The giant waited to be sure he was defunct. Then, opening the monster's wide mouth, he thrust his big fist down the dragon's throat, pulled up the little tailor, and stood him on his feet.

The tailor was out of breath for a moment, but, quickly regaining both his wind and his wits, he took off his cap and began to rub his head.

"What's the matter?" asked the giant. "Don't you feel all right?"

"Why, no! You nearly dented my skull when you struck the dragon with your club. Why are you not more skilful? I can handle such monsters better than you. Can't you see that I just leaped into the dragon's mouth in order to cut his throat with my scissors?" With this, he flourished his shears, which were all bloody.

The stupid giant was dumbfounded, but he did not know enough to contradict the tailor, who told the big fellow to shoulder the dragon and they would both go back to the king's court and demand the promised reward. So, with much pulling and hauling, lifting and dragging, the giant did all the work. The clumsy carcass was laid before the royal throne. The princess, looking on, wondered which one of the two heroes was to be her husband.

She did not feel, just then, like marrying either of them, big or little. When, however, she thought it over, she believed she could live on her income better with the tailor than with the giant, who was already beginning to ask when dinner would be ready.

As for the king, he could not decide which was the hero, for both laid claims to the princess and to the gold. So, for the time being, the giant was fed all the beans and pork and barley and turnips he could eat; but even then, the tailor saw that the big fellow was not satisfied, and would rather have rice pudding.

The king and his wise men kept on debating for several days, for neither would give in. Then they became alarmed when the steward whispered in the royal ear that provisions were running low. In fact, both the larder and the cellar were nearly empty. This was on account of the giant's enormous appetite. By the following Sunday, nothing would be left except a hogshead of rice.

The tailor overheard the steward's talk, and at once he proposed a plan, by which the contest between the two claimants could be settled. Let that hogshead of rice be made into one enormous pudding. It must be well sweetened, and with plenty of raisins and powdered nutmeg on top, and then divided into two parts, or piles. Whichever ate up his portion the quickest should be hailed as the hero, marry the princess, get the money, and be publicly announced by the trumpeters as the royal son-in-law and successor to the throne.

"Now I'll keep my promise," said the tailor to himself, "as to what I could do with only a pair of scissors and a bag."

So, when the boiled rice, smoking hot, was piled on trenchers and served on a long table with a small shovel beside each large wooden plate, the trial began. The giant went at his mess as if he were himself a dragon. To his astonishment, however, the tailor made the rice pudding disappear as fast as he himself could. Even after unbuckling his belt, and letting out first two, and then four holes in the leather, the tailor kept on.

Finally the giant had to stop. He rolled over on the floor and cried out:

"I'm beaten. Give the tailor the princess and the money, but don't let him skin me alive."

All the while, the tailor, who had a pal under the table to hand him bag after bag as he dropped into them the shovelfuls of rice pudding, filled first one big bag strapped to his bosom, and when that was full, he put on another. The giant was so occupied with gorging himself that he did not notice anything but the rice before him.

Meanwhile the man whom the tailor had paid to do it kept on handing fresh bags to the tailor. When all of these, except several towards the last, were used up, he took the tailor's scissors and cut open the bags at the bottom of the pile, for fear the supply of bags might run out. Meanwhile, he filled a tub nearby. So the castle people were saved from starvation, but they all, from king to scullion, had only cold rice to eat the next day.

When the tailor explained to the giant that he had an extra stomach, and cut open the first one after enjoying the taste of the rice pudding, and then filled the second one, the giant, foolishly hoping still to eat more, and thinking it was the proper thing to do, cut open his big stomach with a sword. But that was too much even for a giant.

So on Monday, the next day, the giant's funeral took place, and on Tuesday, the day after, the tailor married the princess, and they lived happily ever after. He had several sons and daughters, and people said his boys and girls looked like their father, on whose coat of arms was a leather wallet and a pair of scissors.

Bedik and the Invulnerable Giant

MANY YEARS AGO there was a king who had seven sons. As soon as each one of the princes was of age his father sent him on an expedition, that he might display his bravery and marry the maiden whom he preferred. Thus six of the princes acquired wives, but Heaven only knows whether they displayed real bravery or not. It was now the turn of the seventh son, whose name was Bedik. His father gave him a horse of lightning, a magic sword and a bow and arrow, saying:

"Go, my son, and may Heaven grant you good luck."

Bedik started and travelled through the length and breadth of the world, visiting the land of darkness, the land of light, the land of fairies, the land of giants. He did battle with men, beasts, genii, and all kinds of creatures which he encountered on the way, and overcame them all, but in his wars he lost all his servants and his wealth. He was alone one day when he came to a magnificent castle built of marble, decorated with gold and jewels and surrounded with orchards and flower gardens. He walked about the building and gazed everywhere, but could see no human being, man or woman. He waited all the day, concealed behind some bushes. Towards evening there came a Giant covered all over with armour, brandishing his bow and arrows, which were of heavy steel. When he walked the earth trembled. When he came near the castle, becoming aware of the presence of a human being, he exclaimed:

"Aha! I smell a human being. I go a-hunting to the mountains, and lo! the prey has come to my home. Ho! human being, disclose yourself; else I will make a morsel of you."

The lad was looking at the Giant from his place of concealment. He was the strangest creature that he had ever seen; neither a sword nor an arrow could pierce him. Nevertheless he decided to face him, and coming out from behind the bushes, he stood before him.

"Who are you?" asked the Giant. "The bird with its wing, and the snake on its belly could not approach this castle of mine; and how could you venture to come? Have you not heard of the fame of the Invulnerable Giant?"

"I have," said the lad bravely, "and my name is no less famous than yours; I am Bedik; I have travelled all over the world, and having heard of you, I came to measure swords with you."

The Giant gazed at the lad for a moment and suddenly sneezed. The burst of air through his nostrils caused the lad to leap ten rods away.

"Halloo!" exclaimed the Giant, laughing, "you do not seem to be very well able to fight me, do you? Nay, come here again; do not be afraid, I will not hurt you. I have heard about you; you are a brave little fellow. But you see you can do no harm to me, because I am invulnerable. Come, be my servant, for I need a skilful human servant, and I do not think I can find a better one than you. Bring your sword and bow and arrows. You see they are not available to pierce me; we may need them for hunting and other purposes."

The lad consented, and they lived together for a time. One day the Giant said to the youth:

"You see I am immortal, but I have an anxiety which gnaws my heart day and night. The King of the East has a daughter, and there is no beauty like hers under the sun. I have made seven expeditions to carry her away, but so far have not succeeded. If you can bring her here I will bestow upon you a kingly reward."

"I will bring her for you," said the lad.

"But do you promise it upon your soul?" said the Giant.

"I do," answered the lad, and at once started on the expedition.

After a long journey he came to the city of the King of the East, changed his clothes, took the shape of a farmer boy, and became the apprentice of the King's gardener. He saw the king's daughter sitting in her window and working with her needle. She was so beautiful that she seemed to say to the sun, "Sun, you need not shine, since I am shining." The lad fell in love with her and began to curse the hour when he made the solemn promise to convey her to the Giant. One day, taking advantage of the absence of his master, the lad stripped off his humble clothes, and putting on his princely garments, mounted his horse of lightning and rode in the King's garden. The maiden was looking from her window and saw him. She had never seen a young man so perfect, and she fell in love with him. On the following day she sent two of her maids to the youth, informing him of her love. The lad sent her word who he was, how he had heard of her wondrous beauty, and now he was waiting to do anything that she might order. The city was surrounded by high walls, through fear of the Invulnerable Giant, who assaulted it every year with the intention of carrying off the maiden; but the people of the city, being brave fighters, would not let the maiden be borne away. So the lad had a hard task to perform. One day the girl sent to him, through her maids, the following message:

"Tomorrow is the feast of the Navasard, when all the maidens of the city go out for recreation and merriment, but I am not allowed to go forth because it is the day when the Invulnerable Giant makes his annual assault to seize me. I will, however, go to the garden by the riverside, which is surrounded by high walls; there I will wait for you to see you display your bravery."

Having received this message, on the next day the youth put on his princely garments, girded his magic sword, and taking his bow and arrows, mounted his horse of lightning. Once or twice he coursed the steed near the garden wall, until it began to gallop as fast as if it had wings. One stroke of the whip, and lo! it jumped over the wall like an eagle, and instantly the horse and its rider alighted in the middle of the garden. In the twinkling of an eye the lad put his arm around the maiden's waist, and placing her behind him on the saddle, gave another stroke of the whip, which made the horse leap over the garden wall, and in a second they were on safe ground outside the city galloping like a flash of lightning. The maids in attendance were horror-stricken, thinking that it was a hurricane which had taken their lady from them. It was a long time before they understood what had taken place; then they informed the King, who sent out his bravest horsemen in pursuit of the fugitives. But it was too late. The couple on the back of the horse of lightning passed over the mountains and valleys until they came to the border of the deep river. A stroke of the whip and the steed swam the deep waters and emerged on the other side. The King's horsemen came as far as the river, but seeing that the couple had crossed the frontier, they returned. As soon as the maiden and the youth had crossed the water, and the Invulnerable Giant's castle appeared in the distance, the maiden said to the lad:

"Bedik, dearest, we have come so far and you have not yet spoken a single word to me; you have shown no sign of love. For Heaven's sake, tell me; did you kidnap me for yourself or for another?"

"You said, 'For Heaven's sake,'" replied the lad, "I will therefore tell you the truth; I have kidnapped you for the Invulnerable Giant; I have promised to deliver you to him."

"Alas!" exclaimed the maiden. "May Heaven's curse rest upon the Invulnerable! He could not get me for all the world. You do not reflect that it was by your skill and valour that you secured me. Woe be to frail womanhood! Maidens are the slaves of their hearts. For you, only for you, I eloped. If you reject me, here is the deep water, and here the high precipice; I would better be food for fishes and birds. May Heaven's fire burn and consume the hard hearts of men!" So saying, she prepared to throw herself down the abyss into the deep water. The lad's heart began to burn like a furnace, and he took hold of her, crying:

"Nay, dearest, do not harm yourself. It was because of the vow I made upon my soul that I am taking you to the Giant, and the day you become his wife I will put an end to my life with this sword, for without you life for me would be a curse."

Then they exchanged vows that they would use every means to put a speedy end to the Invulnerable Giant, and then be married; because they could not marry without destroying the Giant. Thereupon, they mounted the horse and began to proceed towards the castle. The Giant, who from the tower of the castle was looking their way, seeing them at a distance, immediately came down and ran to meet them. He expressed his gratitude to the lad, and his excess of love to the maiden. He treated her with extreme kindness, fearing that he might hurt her tender feelings with his unpolished manners.

"Are you pleased with this place?" he asked her. "What do you want me to do in order to make you as happy as possible?"

"I am very well, thank you; you are everything for me," said the maiden, suppressing her bitter hatred towards him. "But my parents consented to send me to you only under the condition that I should keep myself a virgin seven years longer. I have given an oath that I will do so; otherwise the love with which they have cherished me would turn into poison and defile my whole life. Do you accept this condition?"

"I do," said the Giant. "As you are now in my hand, I am willing to wait not only seven years, but, if necessary, seven times seven years."

They exchanged solemn vows, and decided that Bedik should live with them, and be the best man at their wedding. The maiden occupied one apartment of the castle, the youth and the Giant the other apartments, and so they lived for a time. But the lad and the maiden were uneasy. It was in vain to think of killing the Giant – he was invulnerable. If they eloped he would certainly overtake them, and there was no escaping from his wrath. One day as the Giant was lying on the couch, with his head on the maiden's lap, she said to him:

"In former times, how did you live alone, without any companions? And how is it that you are invulnerable, when so many arrows and swords are thrown at you? What is the secret of your immortality?"

At first the Giant refused to tell, but the maiden importuned him, saying: "If you will not inform me, then you do not love me. Tell me in plain words that you love me not, and I will cease to live."

The Giant was at last persuaded to give up his secret, and he said:

"Seven days' journey from this castle there is a white mountain, where lives an unsubduable white bull which neither man nor beast dares to approach. Once in seven days he becomes thirsty and goes to the top of the white mountain, where there is a white fountain with seven white marble reservoirs full of water, which he drains at a single draught. The bull has in his belly a white fox, which in its turn has in its belly a white box made of mother-of-pearl. In that box are seven white sparrows. Those are my spirits, and those are my seven secrets. The bull cannot be subdued, the fox cannot be caught, the box cannot be opened, the sparrows cannot be seized. If any of them is taken, the others will escape. So I remain unconquerable and invulnerable and immortal."

The maiden told the secret to Bedik, adding:

"I have done what I could; now it remains for you to do the rest."

After a few days the lad girded on his sword, and bearing his bow and arrow, took leave of the Giant, saying that he would go on a month's journey. He started and went directly to the convent of the seven wise monks, who were renowned all over the world for their great erudition and learning. After performing his religious duties before the holy altar, he asked the monks:

"How is the unconquerable man conquered, and the unsubduable beast subdued?"

And he received the following answer:

"Man by woman; beast by wine."

On the following day he loaded seven horses with seven skinfuls of seven-year-old wine and took them to the white mountain. He emptied the water out of the seven marble reservoirs and filled them with wine, turning the water of the fountain elsewhere. Nearby he dug a trench, and hiding himself, waited for the result. At the end of seven days the white bull came to drink, and smelling the wine, he was so much terrified that he leaped as high as the height of seven poplar trees, and ran back roaring and bellowing. On the following day he returned, and being thirsty, drank the wine and was overcome. He leaped once or twice and fell down senseless. The lad drew his sword and approached and cut off the bull's head.

* * *

Let us return a moment to the palace of the Giant. It was the last day of the seven years during which he had waited for the maiden. He had gone to the hunt, that they might have noble game for their wedding dinner. When the bull was overcome and fell, the giant began to grow drowsy. As soon as the youth cut off the bull's head, the Giant turned dizzy, and a tremor ran through his frame.

"Alas!" cried the Giant. "Someone has killed the white bull. I know it is my fault. I gave my secret to the maiden, and she has told it to Bedik or to some other lover. The bull is killed, and I must die. I will go and kill the maiden. She is not to be for me; why shall she be for another?" So saying, he began to run towards the castle.

Bedik cut the bull's belly open; the fox also was drunk and stupid, and he cut off his head. The Giant lost his senses, and the blood began to gush out of his nostrils. The youth, opening the stomach of the fox, obtained the pearl box and put it in warm blood. The lid was opened, and the lad seized the seven sparrows. Thereupon streams of blood began to run from the Giant's mouth and ears, and his two eyeballs started from their sockets, like two great pomegranates. But still he was running towards the castle, sword in hand, and roaring like a mad beast. The maiden was horror-stricken, and quickly ran up to the top of the tower, determined to throw herself thence and kill herself, rather than fall into the hands of the Giant. The Giant had barely reached the castle door, when Bedik killed two of the sparrows; with that the two knees of the Giant were broken. He killed two more sparrows, and the Giant's two arms withered. He killed two more, and the lungs and heart of the Giant ceased to breathe and beat. He killed the last sparrow; the Giant knocked his head against the threshold of the castle, his skull was broken, and his brains oozed out. A black smoke rose from his mouth and nostrils, and he lay dead as a stone. Thereupon Bedik came on horseback like a flash of lightning. The maiden descended from the tower, and they embraced one another. At once they decided to go to the maiden's parents and celebrate their wedding. They collected all the wealth of the Invulnerable Giant, and mounting the horse of lightning, began to proceed towards the east.

The maiden being the only child of the King of the East, he was greatly grieved at her loss, seeing that he was getting old, and there was no successor to his throne. On the day following the maiden's disappearance, the King had sent his servants to the seven wise monks, asking their advice, and he had received the following message:

> *'The hero who carried off your daughter is a prince. At the end of seven years your daughter will be restored to you by the same hero, as pure and chaste as before.'*

The anxious father waited for seven long years. It was the last day of the seventh year; the King and his subjects had made great preparations for the reception of the returning princess and her hero. Towards evening the King and his peers were looking anxiously from the seven towers of the city wall. The sun was just going down, when a flash as of lightning was seen on the western horizon, and in the twinkling of an eye Bedik and the maiden reached the city gate on the back of their fiery steed. They were received amid the wild acclamations of the crowd, and were led to the King's palace. There they knelt before the King and told their story. The King blessed them, and for forty days and forty nights the wedding feast was celebrated.

They attained their wish. May Heaven grant that you may attain your wishes!

Three apples fell from heaven; one for me, one for the storyteller, and one for him who entertained the company.

Sir Peppercorn

THREE BROTHERS ONCE UPON A TIME went out into the neighbouring forest to choose some trees fit for building. Before going, however, they told their mother not to forget to send their sister into the wood after them with their dinners. The mother sent the girl as she had been told to do; but as the girl was on her way a giant met her in the wood, and carried her off to a cave, where he lived.

All day long the brothers waited, expecting their sister, and wondering why their mother had forgotten to send them food. At length, after remaining two days in the forest, and becoming anxious and angry at the delay, they went home. When they arrived there they asked their mother why she had not sent their sister with their food, as she had promised to do; she replied that she had sent the girl three days ago, and had been wondering greatly why she had not come back.

When the three brothers heard this they were exceedingly troubled, and the eldest said, "I will go back into the forest and look for my sister." Accordingly he went. After wandering about some time he came to a shepherdess, who was minding a flock of sheep. He asked her anxiously if she had seen his sister in the wood, or whether she could tell him anything about her. The shepherdess replied that she had indeed seen a girl carrying food, but a giant had met her and carried her off to his cave. Then the young man asked her to tell him the way to the giant's cave, which she did. The cave was hidden in a deep ravine. The brother at once went down, and called aloud on his sister by name. In a short time the girl came to the mouth of the cave, and, seeing her eldest brother, invited him to come in. This he did, and was exceedingly surprised to see that the seeming cave was in reality a magnificent palace. Whilst he stood there talking to his sister and enquiring how she liked her new home, he heard a loud whirring in the air overhead, and, immediately afterwards, saw a heavy mace fall on the ground just in front of the cave. Greatly terrified and astonished, he asked his sister what this meant, and she told him not to be afraid, for it was only the way the giant let her know of his return three hours before he came, that she might begin to prepare his supper.

When it grew dark the giant came home, and was at once aware that a stranger was in his place. In reply to his angry questions, his wife told him it was "only her brother, who had come to visit them." When the giant heard this he went to the mouth of the cave, and, calling a shepherd, ordered him to kill the largest sheep in his flock and roast it.

When the meat was ready the giant called his brother-in-law and said, as he cut the sheep in two equal parts, "My dear brother-in-law, listen well to what I say; if you eat your half of the meat sooner than I eat mine, I will give you leave to kill me; but if I eat my half quicker than you eat yours, I shall certainly kill you."

Thereupon the poor brother-in-law began to shake all over with fright; and, fearing the worst, tried to eat as fast as he could. But he had hardly swallowed three mouthfuls before the giant finished his share of the sheep, and killed him, according to his threat.

For some time the other two brothers and their old mother waited impatiently to see if the elder brother would come back. At last, hearing nothing either of the brother or of the sister, the second son said, "I will go and look after them." So he went into the same forest where his brother had gone, and, meeting there the same shepherdess minding her sheep, he enquired if she had seen his brother or sister. The shepherdess answered him as she had answered the elder brother, and he, too, asked the way to the giant's cave, and, on being told, went down the ravine until he reached the place. There he called on his sister by name, and she came out and invited him to enter the cave. This he did, and shared the fate of his brother; for, being unable to eat his part of the sheep as quickly as the giant ate his, he also was killed.

Not long after the third brother went forth the same road, to look after his two elder brothers and sister, and having found the giant's cave, was likewise invited to eat half a sheep, or be put to death. He, however, failed like his brothers had done before him, and, being unable to eat his part of the sheep as quickly as the giant ate his, he was also killed.

Now the parents, being alone in their house, prayed that God would give them another son, even were he no bigger than a peppercorn. As they prayed so it came to pass, and not very long after a little boy was born to them, who was so extremely small that they christened him 'Peppercorn.'

When the boy was old enough he went out to play with other boys; and one day, in a quarrel, one of these said to him, "May you share the fate of your elder brothers." Hearing this, Peppercorn ran off home at once, and asked his mother what these words meant. So the mother was forced to tell him how his three brothers had gone into the forest to look after their lost sister, and had never come back again. As soon as he heard this, Peppercorn began to search the house for pieces of old iron, and, having found some scraps, carried them off in the evening to a blacksmith, that with them he might make him a mace. Next morning Peppercorn went to the smith to ask for his mace, which the man gave him, saying at the same time, "Now pay me for making it." To this Peppercorn replied, "First let me see if it is strong enough"; and he threw it up in the air and held his head so that the mace might fall upon it. As soon as the mace struck his head, it broke into pieces; and Peppercorn, seeing how badly it was made, fell into a passion and killed the smith. Then he gathered up the pieces of iron and went off to look for a better workman. He soon found another blacksmith who was willing to make him a mace, but demanded a ducat for the work. Peppercorn said he would willingly pay the ducat if the smith made him a really strong, serviceable mace. So next morning he went to ask if it was ready, and the smith said, "Yes; but you must first pay me the ducat, and then I will give it you." Peppercorn, however, answered, "The ducat is ready in my pocket, but I must first see if the mace is good before I pay for it." Thereupon he caught it, flung it up in the air, and held his head under it as it fell. As soon as the mace struck his head it broke into pieces; and he, again falling into a great passion, killed this smith also.

Gathering up the pieces of iron, he now carried them to a third smith, who undertook to make him a good strong mace, and demanded a ducat for doing so. Next morning Peppercorn went for the mace and, after trying it three times, each time throwing it up higher in the air and letting it fall on his head, where it raised great bumps, he owned that he was satisfied with it, and accordingly paid the smith the ducat as he had promised.

Having now a good strong mace, Peppercorn started off at once for the forest, in which his three elder brothers and his sister had been lost. After wandering about for some time, he came to the place where the shepherdess sat watching her sheep, and, in reply to his questions, she told him that she had seen his three brothers go down the ravine in search of their sister, but had never seen them come up again.

Notwithstanding this, Peppercorn went resolutely down the ravine, calling aloud upon his sister by name. When she heard this she was exceedingly surprised, and said to herself, "Who can this be calling me by name, now that all my brothers are killed? I have no other relations to come and look for me." Then she went to the entrance of the cave and called out, "Who is it that calls me; I have no longer any brothers?"

Peppercorn said to her, "I am your brother who was born after you left home, and my name is Peppercorn."

On hearing this, his sister led him into the palace, but he had hardly had time to say a few words to her before a loud whirring was heard in the air, and the giant's mace fell to the ground. For a moment Peppercorn was terrified at this, but he recovered himself quickly, and, pulling the mace out of the ground, flung it back to the giant, who, in astonishment, said to himself, "Who is this who throws my mace back to me? Methinks I have at last found someone able to fight with me."

When the giant came home he immediately asked his wife who had been in the cave, and she answered him, "It is my youngest brother." Thereupon the giant ordered the shepherd to bring the largest sheep in his flock. When this was brought the giant killed it himself, and, whilst preparing it for roasting, said to Peppercorn, "Will you turn the meat, or will you take care of the fire?" Peppercorn said he would rather gather wood and make the fire; so he went out and tumbled down some large trees with his mace. These he carried to the mouth of the cave, and made a large fire ready for the meat.

When the sheep was roasted the giant cut it in two parts, and gave one half to Peppercorn, saying, "Take this half, and if you eat it before I eat my half you are free to kill me; but if you don't, I shall surely kill you." So Peppercorn and the giant began to eat as fast as they could, swallowing down large pieces of meat, and, in their haste, almost choking themselves. At last Peppercorn, by trickery, managed to get rid of his share of the sheep, and, according to the arrangement, killed the giant. This done, with the help of his sister, he collected all the treasures the giant had heaped up in his palace, and, taking them with him, returned home with his sister, to the great joy of their parents.

Peppercorn remained some time after this with his father, mother, and sister, and they lived very merrily on the treasures he had brought from the giant's cave. At length, however, he saw that the riches were coming to an end, so he resolved to go into the world to seek his fortune.

After travelling about a good while he came one day to a large city, where he saw a great crowd gathered about a man who held an iron pike in his hand, and every now and then squeezed drops of water out of the iron. Whilst the people watched, wondering and admiring his great strength, Peppercorn went up and asked him, "Do you think there is any man in the world stronger than yourself?"

"There is only one man alive who is stronger than myself, and that one is a certain person called Peppercorn," answered he. "Peppercorn can receive a mace on his head without being hurt."

Thereupon Peppercorn told the man who he was, and proposed to him that they should travel about the world together.

"That will I right gladly," said the Pikeman. "How can I help being glad to go with a trusty fellow like you!"

Travelling together they came one day to a certain city, and, finding a concourse of people assembled, they went to see what was the matter. They found a man sitting on the bank of a river turning the wheels of nine mills with his little finger. So they said to him, "Is there anyone stronger than you in the world?"

And he answered them, "There are only two men stronger than I am – a certain person named Peppercorn and a certain Pikeman." Hearing this, Peppercorn and the Pikeman told him who they were, and proposed that he should join them in their travels about the world.

The Mill-turner very gladly accepted the offer, and so all three continued their journey together.

After travelling some time they came to a city where they found all the people greatly excited because someone had stolen the three daughters of the king, and, notwithstanding the immense rewards His Majesty had offered, no one had as yet dared to go out to look for the princesses. As soon as Peppercorn and his two comrades heard this they went to the king and offered to search for his three daughters. But in order to accomplish the task they demanded that the king should give them a hundred thousand loads of wood. The king gave them what they wanted, and they made a fence all around the city with the timber. This done they began to watch.

The first morning they prepared a whole ox for their dinners, and discussed the question which of the three should stay behind to mind the meat whilst the other two watched the fence. The Pikeman said, "I think I will stay here and take care of the meat, and I will have dinner ready for you when you come back from looking after the fence." So it was thus settled. Just, however, as the Pikeman thought the ox was well roasted he was frightened by the sudden approach of a man with a forehead a yard high and a beard a span long. This man said to the Pikeman, "Good morning!" but the latter ran away instead of answering, he was so shocked by the strange appearance of the man.

Yard-high-forehead-and-span-long-beard was quite content at this, and, sitting down, soon finished the whole ox. When he had ended his dinner he got up and went away.

Shortly afterwards Sir Peppercorn and the Mill-turner came for their dinners, and, being very hungry, shouted from afar to the Pikeman, "Let us dine at once!" But the Pikeman, keeping himself hidden among the bushes, called out to them, "There is nothing left for us to eat! A little while ago Yard-high-forehead-and-span-long-beard came up and ate up the whole ox to the very last morsel! I was afraid of him, and so I did not say one word against it."

Peppercorn and the Mill-turner reproached their companion bitterly for allowing all their dinner to be stolen without once trying to prevent it, and the Mill-turner said scornfully, "Well, I will stop tomorrow and look after the meat, and Yard-high-forehead-and-span-long-beard may come if he likes!"

So the next day the Mill-turner stayed to roast the ox, and his two comrades went to look after the fence they had built round about the city.

Just before dinner-time Yard-high-forehead-and-span-long-beard came out of the forest and walked straight up to the ox, and stretched his hands out greedily to grasp it. The Mill-turner was so frightened by his strange appearance that he ran off as hard as he could to look for a place to hide in.

By-and-by Peppercorn and the Pikeman came for their dinners and asked angrily where the meat was. Whereupon the Mill-turner answered, "There is no meat! It has all been eaten by that horrible Yard-high-forehead-and-span-long-beard, and his looks frightened me so that I dared not say a single word to him."

It was no use complaining, so Peppercorn only said, "Tomorrow I will stay to mind the ox, and you two shall go and look after the fence. I will see if we are to remain the third day without dinner."

The next morning the Pikeman and the Mill-turner went to see if all was right round about the city, and Peppercorn remained to roast the ox. Exactly as on the two former days, just before dinner was ready, Yard-high-forehead-and-span-long-beard made his appearance, and went up to seize the meat. But Peppercorn pushed him roughly back, saying, "Two days I have been dinnerless on your account, but the third day I will not be so, as long as my head stands on my shoulders!"

Much astonished at his boldness, Yard-high-forehead-and-span-long-beard exclaimed, "Take care you don't begin to quarrel with me. There is no one in all the world who can conquer me, except a fellow called Peppercorn!"

Peppercorn was very pleased to hear this, and, without more hesitation, sprang at once on Yard-high-forehead-and-span-long-beard, and, after some struggling, pulled him down to the earth and bound him. This done, he tied him fast to a tall pine-tree. Now the Pikeman and Mill-turner came up and were exceedingly glad to find their dinners safe. Just as they were in the middle of their dinners, however, Yard-high-forehead-and-span-long-beard, with a sudden jerk, pulled up the pine-tree by the roots and ran off with tree and all, making furrows in the earth with it just as if three ploughs had been passing over the ground.

Seeing him run off, the Pikeman and Mill-turner jumped up quickly and ran after him, but Peppercorn called them back and told them to finish their dinners first, for there would be plenty of time to catch him after they had dined! So they all three went on eating, and when they had done they followed the furrows which Yard-high-forehead-and-span-long-beard had made in the ground. After a while they came to a deep dark hole in the earth, and when they had examined it all round and tried in vain on account of the darkness to look down into it, they returned to the king and asked him to give them a thousand miles of strong rope so that they could go down into the pit.

The king at once ordered his servants to give them what they required, and when they had got the great cable they went back to the hole. On the way, as they were going, they discussed which of the three should venture down first, and it was at last settled that the Pikeman should be let down. However, he made them solemnly promise him that they should pull him up again the instant he shook the rope.

He had been let down but a very little way before he shook the rope, and so they pulled him up as they had promised.

Then the Mill-turner said, "Let *me* go down." And so the other two lowered him, but in a moment or two he shook the rope violently; and so he, too, was pulled up.

Now Peppercorn grew angry, and exclaimed, "I did not think you were such cowards as to be afraid of a dark hole! Now let *me* down!" So they let him down and down until his foot touched solid ground. Finding that he had reached the bottom, he looked round him, and saw that he stood just in the very middle of a most beautiful green plain – a plain so beautiful that it was a real pleasure to look on it.

At one end of the plain stood a large handsome palace, and Peppercorn went nearer to look at it. There, in the gardens, walking, he met two young girls, and asked them if they were not the daughters of the king. When they said that they were, he enquired what had become of the other sister; and the princesses told him that their youngest sister was in the palace very busy binding up the wounds that Yard-high-forehead-and-span-long-beard had lately received from a certain knight called Peppercorn.

Then Peppercorn told them who he was, and that he had come down on purpose to release them, and to take them back to the king, their father. On hearing this good news, the two princesses rejoiced greatly, and told Peppercorn where he would find Yard-high-forehead-and-span-long-beard and their youngest sister. But they warned him not to rush in on the giant, but rather to go softly, and first try to get hold of the sabre which hung on the wall over his bed, for this sabre possessed the wonderful power of killing a man when he was a whole day's journey from it.

Peppercorn took care to do as the princesses had told him. He stole very quietly into the room where Yard-high-forehead-and-span-long-beard was lying, and when he was near the bed he sprang up suddenly and seized the sword. The moment the wounded giant saw his sabre in the hands of Peppercorn he jumped up quickly and ran out of the palace. Peppercorn followed him some time before he remembered what the two princesses had told him of the wonderful properties of the sword, but as soon as he recollected this he made a sharp cut with it in the air, as if he were cutting off a man's head, and the moment he did so Yard-high-forehead-and-span-long-beard fell down dead.

Then Peppercorn went back to the palace, and, taking with him the three princesses, prepared to return to the upper world.

When he came to the place where the rope was hanging he took a large basket, and, placing the eldest princess in it, fastened it to the rope, then, giving her a note, in which he said that he sent her for the Pikeman, he made the signal agreed upon for the rope to be drawn up. So his comrades pulled up the rope, and when it came down again with the empty basket, Peppercorn sent up the second princess, after giving her a paper, in which he had written, "This one is for the Mill-turner."

When the rope descended the third time he sent up the youngest princess, who was by far the most beautiful of the three. He gave her a paper which said that this one he meant to keep for himself. Just as the Pikeman and the Mill-turner began to pull up the rope the princess gave Peppercorn a little box, saying, "Open it when you have need of anything!"

Now, when the Pikeman and Mill-turner drew up the youngest princess, and saw how very beautiful she was, they determined to leave Peppercorn down in the pit, and go back without delay to the king's palace, and there see which of them could get the youngest princess for his wife.

Peppercorn waited patiently some time for the rope to be let down that he might be drawn up, but no rope appeared. At last he was obliged to own to himself that his two comrades had deceived and deserted him, and, seeing how useless it was to remain standing still any longer, he walked off without knowing where the road would take him. Walking on, after a long time, he came to the shore of a large lake, and heard a great noise of crying and shouting. Very soon a multitude of people, looking like a wedding party, made their appearance. After placing a young girl in bridal attire on the shore of the lake, the people left her there alone and went away.

Peppercorn, seeing the girl left by herself, and noticing how sad she looked, went up to her, and asked her why her friends had left her there, and why she was so sad? The girl answered, "In this lake is a dragon who, every year, swallows up a young girl. It is now my turn; and our people have brought me as a bride to the dragon, and left me to be swallowed up."

Peppercorn, on hearing this, asked her to let him rest near her a little, because he was very tired, but she answered, "You had far better fly away, my good knight; if it is necessary that I should die, it is not needful that you should die also."

But Peppercorn said to her, "Don't trouble yourself about me, only let me rest near you a little, for I am very tired. It will be time enough for me to run away when the dragon comes." Having said this he sat down near the girl, and in a little while fell asleep. He had not slept long before the surface of the lake became agitated, and the water rose up in large waves; presently the dragon lifted its head, and swam straight to the shore where the girl sat, evidently intending to swallow her at once. The maiden cried bitterly, and a tear falling on Peppercorn's face, awakened him. He sprang up quickly, grasped his sword, and, smiting fiercely, with one stroke, cut off the dragon's head.

Then he took the girl by the hand, and led her back to the city, where he found that she was the only daughter of the king of that country. The king was overjoyed at hearing that the dragon was killed, and also at seeing his daughter brought back to him safe and sound. So he insisted that Peppercorn should marry the princess, which he did, and they all lived together very happily for a long time.

After a while, however, Peppercorn began to long greatly for the other world, and grew sadder and sadder every day. When his wife noticed this change in his appearance she asked him very often what ailed him, but he would not tell her for a long time, because he did not wish to trouble her. At last, however, he could keep his secret no longer, and confessed to the princess how much he longed to go back to the upper world. Though she was very sorry to hear this, she promised him that she herself would beg the king to let him go, since he so greatly wished it. This she did; and when the king objected, not wishing to lose so good a son-in-law, the princess said, "Let him go; he has saved my life, and why should we keep him against his will? My three sons will still remain to comfort us!"

Then the king consented, saying, "Very well; let it be as he wishes, since you have nothing to say against it. Tell your benefactor to go to the lake-shore, and to say to the giant-bird he will find there, that the king sends her his greetings, and desires her to take the bearer of them up to the other world."

The princess returned to her husband and told him what her father had said, and then began to prepare some provisions for the journey. When these were ready, and the king had sent the letter for the bird, Peppercorn took a kind leave of his wife, and went down to the lake-shore, where he soon found the nest of the giant-bird and her little ones in it, though she herself was not there. So he sat down to wait under the tree where the nest was. As he sat there, he heard the little birds chirping very restlessly and anxiously. Then he saw that the lake was beginning to throw up high waves, and soon a monster came out of the water and made straight for the nest to swallow the young birds.

Peppercorn, however, did not stop long to think about the matter, but quickly drew his wonderful sword and killed the monster. It happened that the giant-bird was just coming back, and when she saw Peppercorn under the tree, she shrieked as she ran up to kill him, "Now I have caught you – you who have been killing all my little ones for so many years! Now you shall pay me for it, for I will kill you!" But the little birds from their nest high in the tree, cried out to her, "Don't do him any harm! he has saved us from being swallowed by a monster who came out of the lake to kill us."

Meanwhile, Peppercorn went to her, and presented the king's letter. The giant-bird read it through carefully, and then said to him, "Go home and kill twelve sheep. Fill their skins with water, and bring them here, together with the flesh of the sheep."

Peppercorn went back to the king, who at once ordered that he should be supplied with the flesh of twelve sheep, as well as with twelve sheep-skins full of fresh water. With this provision Peppercorn returned to the shore of the lake.

Then the giant-bird placed the twelve skins full of water under her left wing, and the flesh of the twelve sheep under her right, and took Peppercorn on her back. This done, she told him that he must watch well her movements, and when she turned her beak to the left side, he must give her water, and when she turned it to the right he must give her meat. After impressing these directions upon Peppercorn, the giant-bird rose with her triple load in the air, and flew straight up towards the other world. As she flew she turned, from time to time, her beak, now to the left and then to the right, and Peppercorn gave her water or meat, as she had directed him to do. At last, however, all the meat disappeared. So, when the giant-bird turned her beak once more to the right, Sir Peppercorn, having no more meat to give her, and fearing some evil might happen if he did not satisfy her, took out his knife, and, cutting a piece of flesh from the sole of his right foot, gave it to her.

But the bird knew by the taste that he had cut it from his own foot, so she did not swallow it, but hid it under her tongue, and held it there until she reached the other world.

Then she set Peppercorn down on the earth and told him to walk, and when he tried to do so he was forced to limp, because of the loss of part of his foot. When the giant-bird noticed this, she asked him, "Why do you limp so?" To this Peppercorn answered, "Oh, it is nothing! Do not trouble yourself about it!" But the bird told him to lift his right foot, and when he did so, she took the piece of flesh she had kept hidden under her tongue, and laid it on the place where he had cut it from. Then she tapped it two or three times with her beak to make it grow to the rest of the foot.

Peppercorn walked on some time before he remembered the little box which the youngest of the three daughters of the king had given him. Now, however, he opened it, and a bee and a fly flew out and asked him what he desired. He said, "I want a good horse to carry me to the king's residence, and a decent suit of clothes to wear." Next moment a suit of good clothes lay before him, and a handsome horse stood ready saddled for him to mount. Then he took the clothes, and, mounting the horse, rode off to the city where the king dwelt. Before entering the city, however, he opened his little box, and said to the fly and the bee, "I do not want the horse any more at present." Accordingly they took it with them into their little box.

Peppercorn went to live in the house of an old woman in the city. Next morning he heard the public crier shouting in the street, "Is there anyone bold enough to fight with the mighty Pikeman, the king's son-in-law?"

Peppercorn was very pleased to hear this challenge, and, opening his box without delay, told the bee and fly, who flew out to receive his orders, that he wanted at once a fine suit of clothes and a strong charger, so that he might go to fight with the Pikeman. The bee and fly instantly gave him what he required, and he dressed himself and rode off to the field, where he found the Pikeman proudly awaiting anyone who might presume to accept his challenge.

So Peppercorn and the Pikeman fought, and before very long the first son-in-law of the king was slain. Then Peppercorn returned home quickly, and opening his box, bade the bee and fly take away the horse and the fine clothes.

The king sought everywhere for the stranger who had killed his son-in-law, but no one knew anything about him. So, after some days, the city crier went round again, proclaiming that the Mill-turner, the second son-in-law of the king, would fight anyone who dared to meet him.

Peppercorn again let out his bee and his fly, and asked for a finer horse and handsomer clothes than the last. So they brought him a very gorgeous suit, and a most beautiful coal-black charger, and with these he went on the field to meet the Mill-turner. They fought, but Peppercorn soon killed the king's second son-in-law, and again went to his lodgings, where he ordered the bee and fly to take the horse and clothes with them into their little box.

Now, not only the king, but all his people were very much puzzled as to who the powerful knight could be who had killed the two valiant sons-in-law of the king. So a strict search was made, and he was sought everywhere. But no one could tell anything about him; while such horses as he rode and such clothes as he wore were not to be found in the whole kingdom.

Some time had passed since the king's sons-in-law had been killed, and people had begun to be a little quieter and had given up all hope of finding out who the stranger knight might be. Then Peppercorn wrote a letter to the king's youngest daughter, and sent it to her by the old woman in whose house he lived. In the letter he told the princess everything that had happened to him since he had sent her up in the basket to his false comrades, and told her also that he himself had slain both of the traitors in fair fight.

The young princess, as soon as she had read the letter, quickly ran to her father and begged him to pardon Peppercorn. The king saw he could not justly deny her this favour, since the two men who had been killed had deceived and deserted their friend, without whose superior courage they would never have been themselves his sons-in-law, seeing that all the three princesses, but for Peppercorn, must have remained in the other world where Yard-high-forehead-and-span-long-beard had carried them.

So, after thinking all this over in his mind, the king told his daughter that he willingly forgave Peppercorn, and that she might invite him to the palace. This the princess did at once, and very soon after, Peppercorn made his appearance before the king in splendid attire and was received very kindly.

Not long afterwards, the marriage of Peppercorn with the beautiful princess, the king's youngest daughter, was celebrated with great rejoicings, and the king built them a fine house near his palace to live in.

There Peppercorn and his princess lived long and happily, and he never had any wish to wander again about the world.

The Dragon-Giant and his Stone Steed

NOT ONE AMONGST THE NUMEROUS WIVES of Vladimir the Great was comparable in beauty to the Bulgarian Princess Milolika. Her eyes resembled those of the falcon; the fur of the sable was not more glossy than her eyebrows, and her breast was whiter than snow.

She had been carried off by robbers of the Volga, from the vicinity of Boogord, the capital of her native country, and on account of her rare beauty they deemed her worthy to be a wife of the great monarch. They therefore conducted her to Kiev, the residence of the mighty Vladimir, and presented her to him. Vladimir, a good judge of female charms, the moment he beheld her, was enchanted by the surpassing beauty of the Bulgarian princess, and in a short time his love for her became so great that he made her his consort, and dismissed all his other wives. The proud heart of the king's daughter was touched by this proof of his affection, and she rewarded his tenderness with reciprocal and true love.

The life of Vladimir was now one of great happiness. His conquests had procured him riches in superfluity; a long period of peace had augmented the prosperity of his country; his subjects loved him as their father; and the tenderness of Milolika made earth seem to him as heaven.

One day as in company with his consort and his Bojars, he sat in the golden chamber by his oaken table, holding a festival in memory of a victory over the Greeks, the sound of a warrior's horn was heard at a distance. The rejoicings in the lofty hall suddenly ceased. The monarch and the Bojars cast their eyes to the ground, full of thought and heaviness. Swâtorad alone, the spirited Voivode of Kiev, started up from the table, and leaving his goblet undrained, approached the great monarch. "Thou art," spake he, as he bent low before him, "thou art our father and our lord, thou art the child of renown: wherefore sinks thy head? Why does the sound of the warrior's horn make thy heart heavy? Even if it be a hostile knight who now appears before the capital, hast thou not enough brave heroes to confront any foe? Away then! Send forth thy heralds to demand who dares to defy the country of the Russians!"

Vladimir looked friendly upon the gallant Swâtorad, and thus replied to his address: "I thank thee for thy zeal, good Swâtorad; but my anxiety does not arise from fear. I have defeated hosts, made myself master of fortified cities, and overthrown kings: how should I know fear? But it was my desire henceforth to preserve to my subjects the blessing of peace, and that alone is the cause that this challenge to combat makes me sorrowful. If however it must be so, I will defend my country and myself. Go and send heralds to demand who dares to come forth against Kiev, to challenge Vladimir to battle!"

The brave Swâtorad immediately sent forth two heralds, who sprang upon their horses and rushed to the open plain, where they at once beheld a monstrous tent, before which a horse of unusual size was grazing. As soon as the horse perceived them, he stamped upon the ground, and cried aloud in a human voice: "Awake powerful son of the dragon, Tugarin awake! Kiev sends heralds to thee."

This marvel considerably astounded the heralds, and their amazement was increased when they beheld issuing from the tent a giant of the most monstrous kind, beneath whose footsteps the earth resounded. Yet they did not lose their composure, but discharged their commission as beseemed them well. "Who art thou?" cried they, after they had courteously bent before him. "Who art thou, bold youth from a foreign land? What is thy name, and how stands thy report in thy fatherland? Art thou a Czar, or a Czarewitsch? A king or a king's son? We are sent by the invincible prince of Kiev, the son of renown, by Vladimir, to ask thee why thou darest to advance against Kiev? – how thou darest to challenge him to combat?"

The questions displeased the giant, and he fell into fierce wrath. Lightning flashed from his eyes, his nose sent forth sparks, and he addressed the heralds in a voice of thunder: "Contemptible wights, how dare ye to put such questions to me? The herald's staff alone protects you from my fury. Return, and tell your prince that I am come to fetch his head, in order to carry it to the great king, Trewul of Bulgaria, who is wrath with him, for the abduction of his sister Milolika. Tell him that nought can save him: neither the summit of the mountain, nor the darkness of the forest; and that he cannot redeem his head by gold, nor by silver, by jewels, nor by pearls. What I am called, and what my report is in my country, it needs not that you should know; sufficient that I show you what I can perform." At these words, he grasped an enormous stone that lay near the tent, and flung it with such force into the air that it resembled a little speck.

Full of terror, the heralds returned to Kiev, and presenting themselves before the monarch, related what they had seen and heard. When Milolika heard that the horse had called the stranger knight Tugarin, Son of the Dragon, she grew pale, and a stream of tears bedewed her cheeks. "Ah," cried she, "beloved husband, we are lost! Nought can save us, but our flight to the sacred Bug. Tugarin is an invincible enchanter. His magic power ceases only on the shores of the Bug. Thither let us fly."

Vladimir endeavoured to re-assure his consort. He represented to her that the brave warriors, and the walls of the impregnable Kiev, would afford them sufficient protection; but Milolika was not to be comforted. "Thou knowest not, beloved husband," said she, sobbing and crying, "how dangerous is this giant, Tugarin, to me and my family, and how bitterly he must hate thee, since he was my betrothed, and awaited my hand." Vladimir besought Milolika to explain to him this enigma, and she related the following: –

"I am the daughter of the Bulgarian king, Bogoris, and of the princess Kuridana. My birthplace is the city Shikotin, where my parents were wont to pass the summer months. As this city lies on the banks of the Volga, it offers great facilities for fishing, a diversion to which my mother was extremely partial.

"Once, when my father was fighting against a neighbouring nation, my mother endeavoured to while away her grief at his absence by her accustomed diversion, and caused the nets to be spread in the Volga. The fish were very plentiful, and a great number of barks and boats covered the river, amongst which, the vessel in which my mother was embarked, was distinguishable by its magnificence and elegance. Surrounded by her ladies and her bodyguard, Kuridana stood in the centre of the vessel and beheld with pleasure the spectacle of the fishery, when suddenly a mountain, that was situated on the other side of the river, burst with a tremendous crash. Every eye was directed to the spot, and they saw issue from the aperture, a man of rude, and terrific aspect, seated on a car of shining steel drawn by two winged horses. He directed his course towards the river, and when he reached the water, the steel car rolled over the waves, as if they had been firm land. When it was perceived that he was bending his way to my mother's bark, heralds were dispatched in a boat, to enquire why he presumed to approach the princess without permission. But the fierce being, who was a powerful and malignant enchanter, did not permit the unfortunate heralds to discharge their commission. As they began to speak, he blew upon their boat, overset it, and all who were in it were buried beneath the waves. At this melancholy sight, my mother's attendants seized their bows and discharged a shower of arrows against the intruder; but in vain, for the arrows rebounded from him, and fell into the water.

"The greatest amazement now seized all present, for they became petrified when the magician with a single word bound every boat with its crew, so that they stood motionless, whilst he, with outstretched arms, hastened towards my mother and endeavoured to remove her into his car. But some unseen power crippled all his efforts. Each time he endeavoured to seize Kuridana, his arms sank powerless, and he was, at length, obliged to desist from the vain enterprise. He then sprang into the bark, cast himself on his knees before her, and in the most moving and earnest expressions, besought her love. He promised her all the treasures of the world, and the highest earthly happiness, if she would reward his vehement love with reciprocal affection, or only lay aside the talisman which she wore upon her breast. This talisman, which now preserved her, she had received at her birth from a beneficent enchantress, and as she well knew its force, she had drawn it out of the case where she usually concealed it, and held it before his eyes.

"Then the evil one trembled so violently, that at last, as if stricken by lightning, he fell to the ground, and not until Kuridana had again enclosed the talisman did he recover from his insensibility. He then sprang up and mounted his steel car, uttering the most fearful threats. 'Think not,' cried he, foaming with shame and rage, 'think not to escape my hands; I will possess thee, and will force Bogoris himself, by the most dreadful devastation of his country, to yield thee to me. Behold, I swear by Tschernobog, that I will either slay or gain possession of thee. Thou shalt see me soon again,' With these words he disappeared.

"Kuridana then left the spot, and not believing herself secure in Shikotin, retired to the strong city of Boogord, where she awaited, in great anxiety, the result of this alarming adventure.

"The very next morning appeared on the plain before the capital city a dreadful two-headed monster, of that dragon species which, in the language of my country, is called Sylant. It devoured herbs, and flocks, and men, and devastated the surrounding country with its poisonous breath. In a short time, the region round Boogord became a desert, and many brave warriors, who sought to free their country of this demon, fell victims to their patriotism and valour. The Sylant appeared each morning before the walls, and bellowed out with a fearful voice, 'Bogoris, give me Kuridana, or I will make thy country a desert!'

"No sooner did my father hear of the misfortune which menaced his people and his beloved Kuridana than he left his career of victory and hastened to the capital. What were his feelings when he beheld the misery which the monster had spread over his land! But greater bitterness still awaited him, for when the first tempest of joy and grief, which his return had excited in the hearts of all, and especially in that of Kuridana, had subsided, this noble-minded princess proposed herself as a willing sacrifice for the king, and the good Bulgarians. 'No!' cried Bogoris, 'sooner will I perish than lose thee. I will combat the dragon. Perhaps the gods will grant me victory, and if I am vanquished in the fight, at least I shall die for thee, and for my country,' The most generous dispute now arose between the magnanimous pair, and finally they agreed to appeal to the decision of the magnates of the empire who should decide the dispute.

"The king assembled them, and when they had heard Kuridana's resolution, they loaded her with panegyrics and expressions of gratitude. 'Thy magnanimous sacrifice alone, Kuridana,' said the eldest of the assembly, an aged man, of a hundred years, 'can rescue us and Bulgaria. For, supposing that Bogoris were to fight with the Sylant, and fall, would not our misfortune be greater still? No, Prince! Thou must preserve thyself for thy people, in order to heal the wounds which the dragon has inflicted. Kuridana alone can save us.' All the magnates coincided with the old man, and Bogoris was in despair.

"It was morning, and the dreadful words: 'Bogoris, give me thy wife!' at that moment resounded round the palace. Kuridana courageously arose, embraced her speechless husband, and bade him an eternal farewell.

"At the words *'for ever,'* Bogoris sank senseless on the ground. Manly as his heart had been up to that hour, it could not endure separation from the beloved Kuridana. The high-minded wife bedewed him with her tears, but at length, turning to the nobles, who stood round her weeping, she said: 'Lead me where you will. I am prepared to endure everything for my husband and my country,' They now reverentially supported her trembling steps, and conducted her as rapidly as her weak state permitted to the front of the city.

"Meanwhile the altars smoked with incense, and both priests and people supplicated for the deliverance of their noble princess.

"Shortly after the magnates had left the palace with Kuridana, Bogoris came to himself, and when he perceived that he was alone, he guessed his misfortune, and his despair knew no bounds. He drew his sword, and was in the act of piercing his breast with it in order not to survive Kuridana, when a matron of beautiful and majestic aspect stood before him, staid his hand, and thus addressed him:

"'What, Bogoris! Dost thou despair? – Be tranquil; the Sylant has no power to harm Kuridana. The talisman which she wears on her breast, will, at all times, and under all circumstances, mock his power. I am the enchantress Dobrada, the protectress of thy wife, she who, as thou knewest, hung the talisman around her immediately on her birth. But it is not now requisite that I should reveal to thee the causes which induced me to provide her with that shield against danger. Enough, that I foresaw at her birth that she would have much to fear from the love of a powerful sorcerer called Sarragur. And because I am ever willing to do all the good I can, I hung around her this talisman, which protects her from his utmost power, and will now defend her from the Sylant, who is no other than

Sarragur himself. For, when he perceived that I was opposed to his passion, and had taken Kuridana under my protection, he sought to avenge himself on me by every kind of secret mischief, so that I was at length obliged to chastise him. By my superior power, I enclosed him within a mountain by the Volga, and bound his fate by the most awful spell, which even Tschernobog respects, to a golden fish, which I sank in the depths of the Volga. By this spell, Sarragur was to remain in his subterranean prison until some mortal should draw up the golden fish; and should he ever thus obtain his freedom, he could then never transform himself into an evil and noxious animal, except on the condition that he should never again resume his own form, and should perish shortly after the transformation. It chanced that a sturgeon swallowed the golden fish, and this sturgeon was caught on the very day when Kuridana was diverting herself with the fishery. Sarragur thus became free, and the first use he made of his freedom was to endeavour to carry off Kuridana, whom he still loved with unabated passion.

"'When this attempt was baffled by the power of the talisman, and still more when he perceived Kuridana's aversion for him, he became furious, and transformed himself into the Sylant, although he knew what must be the consequences. Madman, his hour is come, and thou, Bogoris, art destined to destroy him. Receive from my hands the sword of the renowned Egyptian king, Sesostris. It possesses the wonderful power of destroying every spell, and with it thou wilt overpower the sorcerer, though he should summon all the powers of hell to succour him. Only, mark what I am now about to say. In order to extirpate Sarragur, and every remembrance of him from the earth, thou must cut off both the heads of the Sylant by one stroke. If thou succeed not in doing this, and hewest off but one head, the sorcerer, it is true, will lose his life, but he will escape to his cavern, where, before he expires, he will lay an egg, in which will be enclosed all his magic power, and from the head hewn off, will arise a horse of stone, which shall receive life at the moment the bad spirits shall have hatched the egg, and from this egg will issue the giant Tugarin, who, one day, will be formidable to thy children. For, not only will he inherit from his father the entire power to work evil, whereby so much misery has befallen thee and thy land, but he will also love thy daughter as fiercely as Sarragur loves thy wife. Thy son Trewul will refuse him his sister's hand, and then he will desolate the country, until Milolika's hand is promised to him. He also is to be conquered by no other weapon than the sword of the wise Sesostris, and a knight who shall live without having been born is destined to slay him. After thy victory over the Sylant, hang up the sword in thy armoury amongst the other swords there, and at the appointed time Fate will give it into the hands destined wield it. Of that which I have now told thee, reveal not a word, except to thy wife, and she may hereafter repeat it to her daughter.'

"Having uttered these words, Dobrada shrouded herself in a rose-coloured cloud, and disappeared. Heavenly perfumes filled the chamber, and Bogoris felt that all sorrow had vanished from his soul. Hastily he vaulted on his horse, and rushed to deliver his wife and his country from the fell sorcerer.

"When he reached the plain, he beheld the efforts of the Sylant to grasp Kuridana, and how he was impeded by the talisman from coming close to her. Bogoris immediately unsheathed his sword and flew upon the monster. When the Sylant perceived his antagonist, he sent forth fire streams from both his jaws, which, however, were rendered innocuous by the sword of Sesostris. In order to bring the combat to a speedy conclusion, Bogoris aimed a powerful stroke at the heads of the monster, which would assuredly have separated both from the trunk, and so have extirpated the sorcerer and all remembrance of him from the earth, if the Sylant, at the very moment the stroke fell, had not soared into the air. By this movement, he saved one head. The other rolled on the ground and immediately became stone. Awfully bellowing, the impure being flew to his cavern. Bogoris pursued, but in vain; the Sylant disappeared in the mountain by the Volga, which immediately closed on him.

"My father regretted that he had not succeeded in entirely annihilating the sorcerer and all his brood; but joy at having delivered his beloved wife and his country soon prevailed over sorrow. He committed the future to the gods, and after he had revealed to my mother the predictions of the good enchantress, he hung up the sword of Sesostris in his armoury.

"My parents passed the remainder of their lives in uninterrupted peace and contentment. When I was grown up, my mother related to me her history, and at the same time revealed to me what awaited me through the giant Tugarin. She then hung round me the talisman which she had received from Dobrada. Shortly after this both my parents died. After their death I lived several years with my brother in undisturbed tranquillity, till one day the report arose of a wonderful phenomenon of nature, which was to be seen in the vicinity of the capital. The king, my brother, went thither, and I accompanied him. They showed us a stone which daily increased in size, and was assuming the form of an enormous horse. Everybody marvelled at this sport of Nature, as they called it; but I remembered Dobrada's predictions, and doubted not that the hour of Tugarin's birth, and of my misfortunes, was arrived. Whilst I was still thinking on it, we were alarmed by an earthquake. The neighbouring Sylant Mount – for from the time the Sylant had escaped thither, it had borne that name – opened, and a giant of monstrous size stepped forth. He strode across the Volga, and went straight to the stone horse. The moment he laid his hand on it, it became animated. The giant sprang upon it and dashed towards me. He tried to seize me, but quickly drew back his robber hands as if they had been burnt. The power of the talisman withstood him. He then turned towards my brother, and cried out in dreadful tones: – 'Hear, Trewul! I see that thy sister cannot be carried off by force, and therefore I require of thee to persuade her to give me her hand voluntarily. I give thee three days for consideration, and when they are expired, I either receive Milolika from thy hands or I make thy country desolate.' After these terrible words he departed on his colossal steed, with the rapidity of lightning.

"We returned heavy-hearted to the city, where my brother immediately assembled the council, and laid before it the giant's demand, and his threats. The counsellors were unanimously of opinion, that, as the princess was averse to giving her hand to the giant, an army must be sent against him, of sufficient force to set his menaces at nought. Ten thousand archers, and two thousand horsemen, in armour, were hastily collected, and on the dawn of the third day, were drawn out on the plain before the city, to await the giant. Tugarin soon appeared, and the Bulgarians at once discharged their arrows and darts at him, but they proved as powerless against him as formerly against his father. They rebounded from him as from a rock. At this attack, the giant broke forth with mingled rage and scorn: – 'What,' bellowed he, 'does Trewul send troops against me? Must I then become his enemy? Woe to the helpless being!' And without further delay, he seized the horsemen and archers by the dozen, and swallowed them a dozen at a time, till not a man was left.

"He then began to lay waste and destroy everything round the city. Men and cattle were all engulfed in the monster's insatiable maw. He shattered the dwellings of the inhabitants with his gigantic fists. Whole forests were uprooted by him, and the hoofs of his enormous horse trod down fields and meadows. At length, my brother, in order to put a stop to the universal misery, resolved to sacrifice me. With bitter tears he announced to me that he knew no other means of saving himself and his country from destruction than to promise my hand to the giant. I replied to him only by my tears, and he reluctantly sent an embassy to invite Tugarin to Boogord. He came. Proudly he advanced to the gate where Trewul and the nobles of the land awaited him. I was in despair. At length I bethought me of a means of escape. I agreed to bestow my hand on the giant, on condition that, through some beneficent power, he should first obtain the form and stature of an ordinary man. I trusted that this would not easily be done, and in the meantime I might be able to effect my escape. Tugarin, blinded by his love for me, did not hesitate to accept the condition, and swore by Tschernobog that he would not require me to be delivered to him until my requisition was satisfied. He established himself in Boogord, and served my brother with great zeal. I soon found an opportunity of making my escape, and wandering a whole day without food, was at last taken by the robbers of the Volga and brought to thy court.

"You will now, my beloved husband," said Milolika, as she concluded her narration, "easily comprehend the danger which threatens you. Tugarin must hate thee, since thou art my husband. His power is great, and no one can vanquish him except the knight who came unborn into the world, and no weapon can slay him, but the sword of the wise Sesostris. Thou and all thy brave heroes are powerless against him. Therefore, dear husband, let us flee. On the banks of the sacred Bug we shall be safe; no magic can operate there."

This narration made the deepest impression on the heart of the prince; he could not, however, resolve to abandon his country in the hour of need, and besides, to fly before a single warrior, great as he might be, seemed still not a very honourable proceeding. "What!" exclaimed he, "shall the monarch before whom the east trembles, whose courage the whole world admires, shall he shrink in the moment of danger – shall he, with all his might, flee before a single foe? No: sooner a hundred times will I die the most cruel death!" But with all this how was he to comfort Milolika? How was he to withstand the dreadful giant, seeing that he had not, unborn, beheld the light, neither did he possess the sword of the Egyptian king Sesostris? These difficulties weighed upon his soul. The first, however, he soon disposed of. He bethought himself that the lime with which the walls of Kiev were constructed, had been tempered with water from the sacred Bug, and consequently would prevent the giant from entering the city. This sufficed to tranquilise Milolika, who no longer insisted on flight, as she perceived that her beloved Vladimir was just as secure in Kiev as he would be on the shores of the Bug. As far as she herself was concerned, the giant could avail nothing, since the power of the talisman would shield her from every danger. But still the thought of the combat with this giant greatly disturbed the prince. "Where," said he, "is the unborn mortal who is destined, with the sword of Sesostris, to destroy the fell Tugarin?"

Lo! suddenly a knight of bold and noble aspect, armed with a costly sword, and cased in shining armour, but without shield or lance, rode at full speed into the court of the palace. He sprang from his spirited steed and gave him to his lusty squire. Then he proudly advanced up the steps to the golden chamber of the great monarch, and addressed Vladimir as follows: – "My name is Dobrünä Mikilitsch, and I come to serve thee."

"Thou art welcome," replied Vladimir, "but how is it possible that thou hast escaped the giant Tugarin, who holds the road to Kiev in blockade?"

"Tugarin!" rejoined the knight, "*I* fear him! – already would I have laid his great head at thy feet, but that I desired to achieve that deed in thy presence."

The monarch marvelled at the boldness of the stranger-youth, and enquired if he seriously intended to combat the giant.

"Assuredly," said Dobrünä, "and with that object am I come to Kiev."

"But knowest thou not, that none can vanquish the giant, except only a knight who came into the world unborn?"

"I know it," replied Dobrünä, "and that knight am I!"

"Hast thou, then, the sword of Sesostris?"

"Behold it," said Dobrünä, as he drew the sword from its scabbard, "and if thou wilt permit me, mighty prince, to relate to thee my history, thou wilt know that it is I who am appointed by destiny to rid the earth of the monster Tugarin."

The monarch joyfully granted him permission, and Dobrünä thus commenced: –

"It is true that I had both a father and a mother, but not the less did I behold the light of the world without going through the process of being born. Shortly before my mother would have brought me forth, she was slain by robbers during a journey she was making with my father, to visit a relation. My father being also killed, I must doubtless have perished, if the beneficent enchantress Dobrada, who was just then passing by, had not rescued me and taken me under her protection. She carried me to the beautiful island in the ocean, where she usually dwells, and brought me up with the greatest care. She nourished me with the milk of a lioness, bathed me several times a day in the waves of the ocean, and inured me by day and night to labour and privation. This mode of education rendered my body so strong that in my tenth year, I was already able to tear up the strongest trees by the root. Six ancient men instructed me in all the six-and-twenty known languages, and in arms, wherein I made such progress, that in my fifteenth year I was able to parry at once all the six swords of my teachers. Dobrada recompensed me for my diligence with the shining armour I now wear, which possesses the virtue of protecting my body from every danger.

"Shortly after that time, the enchantress whom I loved and honoured as a mother thus addressed me: – 'Dobrünä Mikilitsch, thy education is completed, and it is time that in foreign lands thou shouldst by knightly deeds acquire renown and honour. Go forth: thou art destined for great things. It is not permitted to me to reveal all the future to thee; but thus much thou mayst know: thou wilt obtain possession of the wondrous sword of the wise Sesostris of Egypt. As soon as thou approachest it, the sword thou now wearest will fall of itself to the earth, and that of Sesostris will become agitated. Take possession of it in peace, for thou wilt require it, for a great service thou must render to him in whose armoury thou wilt find it; for with it thou wilt destroy a mighty sorcerer and giant, who has worked him much woe. Whatever else thou mayst require during thy travels,' continued she, 'this ring will supply. Thou hast but to turn it three times on thy finger, in order to see every reasonable wish fulfilled.'

"She then bade me enter a boat into which she followed me. The boat shot through the waves like an arrow, and I presently sank into a profound sleep. How long our journey was I know not; for when I awoke I found myself alone on a vast plain, not far from a large city. But Dobrada could not have long quitted me, for the heavenly perfumes which ordinarily surrounded her yet floated round me, and far in the eastern horizon I saw the rose-coloured cloud which always shrouded her. My soul was now filled with sadness at the thought that I was now separated from the wise and kind Dobrada, whom I loved as my mother.

"At length I regained my composure. I wished that I had a horse and squire that I might ride into the city that lay near me, and as at the same time I accidentally turned on my finger three times the ring, whose virtue I scarcely recollected, I saw at once before me a squire with two horses, of which I selected the finest and the most richly adorned for myself and left the other for my squire; and thus I rode into the city.

"At the gate I was informed that the city was called Boogord, and was the capital of the Bulgarian empire. Trewul reigned in Boogord, and the giant Tugarin was at his court. The king had been obliged to promise him the hand of his sister in order to avert the total ruin of his country, which the giant had devastated until Trewul had acceded to his desire. When I appeared in the king's presence, I made a very favourable impression on him, and he not only received me into his service, but made me keeper of the armoury, the first dignity at the Bulgarian court.

"From the first moment that Tugarin beheld me, he manifested the bitterest hate towards me; and when I heard what evil he had brought on Trewul and his land, I doubted not that he was the sorcerer and giant I was destined to overthrow. But the sword of Sesostris was still wanting to me. It was however not long before this invaluable weapon came into my possession.

"I entered the royal armoury in order to inspect the weapons entrusted to my care, and I had scarcely crossed the threshold when the sword I wore fell to the ground, and amongst the numerous others that hung there, I observed one moving to and fro. I could not doubt that this was the wonderful sword of the Egyptian king with which I was to slay the giant. I took possession of it with the greater confidence, from the knowledge that by its aid I should rid Trewul of so dangerous an enemy to himself and his family. I girded it upon me, and hung mine in its place.

"From that moment the giant avoided me, knowing most likely by his magic art that I was in possession of the sword that was to be fatal to him, and ere long he disappeared from Boogord, telling the king he was going in search of Milolika.

"I immediately took leave of the king, and set out in pursuit of the giant. I gained information on my way that he had gone to Kiev, where Milolika resided as thy wife. I hastened after him, and am come, as I see, at the right moment to prevent misfortune. I now await thy permission, mighty prince, to engage in combat thine enemy and mine."

As he concluded Dobrünä bent one knee before the monarch, who rose from his seat, and taking the golden chain from his own neck, threw it round the knight's with the following words: "Let this mark of my favour prove to thee, Dobrünä Mikilitsch, how greatly I rejoice to have so brave a knight in my service. Tomorrow thou shalt engage the giant, and I doubt not that thou wilt conquer." He then commanded that an apartment should be prepared for him in the palace, and all due honour be paid to him. Dobrünä returned thanks to the monarch for the favours shown him, and took leave in order to repose after his journey, and to gather strength for the approaching fight.

In the meantime the heralds by Vladimir's command went round the city, and summoned the people to assemble on the walls the following morning, to witness the combat between the knight and the sorcerer, and the priests offered up solemn sacrifices to implore blessings on Kiev and the knight against the malignant sorcerer and the powers which aided him.

Scarcely had the purple-tinted Simzerla spread her glowing mantle over the sky, and decked the path of the great light of the world with her thousand coloured rays, before the vast population of Kiev impatiently thronged to the walls in order not to delay the grand spectacle. The monarch, attended by his consort and all the magnates of the empire, ascended a tribunal which had been hastily erected over the principal gate of the city for this great event.

The clangour of trumpets and horns at length announced the arrival of the knight. Ten thousand corsletted warriors rode with uplifted lances before him, and drew up in two lines before the gate. After them, on a richly caparisoned charger, rode the knight in his shining armour, bearing in his hand the precious sword of Sesostris. The people welcomed him with a cry of joy, and the warriors clashed their arms as he appeared before the gate. With noble bearing and knightly aspect he turned his horse and saluted the monarch by thrice lowering his sword. "Great ruler of Russia," he began, "at thy command I go forth to fight the sorcerer and giant Tugarin, who has presumed to challenge thee to combat." "Go forth," replied Vladimir, "go forth, valiant youth, and fight in my name the vile sorcerer: may the gods give thee victory!" Dobrünä then dashed at full speed through the lines of warriors to the white tent, followed by the acclamations and the blessings of the spectators.

The giant, who had been awakened by the unusual noise of the trumpets and horns, and the joyful cries of the people, had already mounted his horse, and was in the act of riding towards the city to ascertain the cause when he beheld the knight approaching. When he recognized in him the dreaded keeper of the Bulgarian monarch's armoury, who was in possession of the wonderful sword, he set up a fearful yell. Foaming with rage he rushed with outspread arms against the knight to grasp him; but Dobrünä laughed at his impotent fury, and in order better to overcome him, he first touched with his sword the enchanted horse, which immediately crumbled into dust. He then caused the magic-destroying weapon of the wise Sesostris to gleam over the head of the sorcerer, who, by the sudden crumbling of his horse, had fallen to the earth. Tugarin's destruction seemed inevitable, and the beholders from the walls already shouted forth their plaudits to the victor, when at once all the powers of hell broke forth to aid their beloved son. A stream of fire crackled between the combatants, fiery serpents hissed around the knight, and a thick cloud of smoke enveloped the giant. But short was this infernal display. Dobrünä touched the stream with his sword, made a few strokes with it in the air, and the fiery flood and the hissing serpents vanished. He then approached the smoke which concealed the giant, but scarcely had he thrust his sword into it when like the enchantments that also disappeared. The giant was seen outstretched on the ground, and heard to roar with terror. No sooner did he perceive that the smoke which concealed him had vanished than he sprang up and rushed, as if in madness, on the knight. Dobrünä awaited him unmoved, and as the giant stretched forth his monstrous hands for the second time to seize him, he cut them both off with a single stroke. The second stroke of that wondrous sword, wielded by the strong hand of the knight, severed the vile head from the shoulders. The colossus fell, and the earth shook beneath his weight.

Then the people lifted up a cry of joy. A hundred thousand voices shouted, "Long live our monarch, and the conqueror of the giant, Dobrünä Mikilitsch!"

The knight, who had dismounted to raise the fallen enemy's head on the point of his sword in sign of victory, was about to remount in order to give the monarch an account of his combat when he beheld him coming towards him, accompanied by his consort and the magnates of the empire. The courteous knight hastened forward and laid the giant's head at his feet. The great prince embraced him in presence of the assembled people, and placed on his finger a gold ring, whilst Milolika hung around him a gold-embroidered scarf. Dobrünä bent his knee and thanked the royal pair in graceful and courteous words for these marks of favour. They then all returned full of joy to the city, where the festivities and rejoicings in honour of the knight lasted many weeks.

Vladimir also despatched messengers to his brother-in-law, Trewul, to inform him of his marriage with the beautiful Milolika, and the overthrow of their common enemy, the giant Tugarin. Dobrünä however remained at the court of Vladimir, and performed many more great and valiant deeds, which procured him great fame and honour, and rendered great service to the monarch, and he became the most beloved and most esteemed, both by prince and people, of all the knights in Vladimir's court.

The Man Who Lost His Legs

THERE WAS A MERCHANT IN CHONG-JU who used to go to Quelpart to buy seaweed. One time when he drew upon the shore he saw a man shuffling along on the ground towards the boat. He crept nearer, and at last took hold of the side with both his hands and pulled himself in.

"When I looked at him," said the merchant, "I found he was an old man without any legs. Astonished, I asked, saying, 'How is it, old man, that you have lost your legs?'

"He said in reply, 'I lost my legs on a trip once when I was shipwrecked, and a great fish bit them off.'"

"However did that happen?" enquired the merchant.

And the old man said:

"We were caught in a gale and driven till we touched on some island or other. Before us on the shore stood a high castle with a great gateway. The twenty or so of us who were together in the storm-tossed boat were all exhausted from cold and hunger, and lying exposed. We landed and managed to go together to the castle.

"There was in it one man only, whose height was terrible to behold, and whose chest was many spans round. His face was black and his eyes large and rolling. His voice was like the braying of a monster donkey.

"Our people made motions showing that they wanted something to eat. The man made no reply, but securely fastened the front gate. After this he brought an armful of wood, put it in the middle of the courtyard, and there made a fire. When the fire blazed up he rushed after us and caught a young lad, one of our company, cooked him before our eyes, pulled him to pieces and ate him. We were all reduced to a state of horror, not knowing what to do. We gazed at each other in dismay and stupefaction.

"When he had eaten his fill, he went up into a verandah and opened a jar, from which he drank some kind of spirit. After drinking it he uttered the most gruesome and awful noises; his face grew very red and he lay down and slept. His snorings were like the roarings of the thunder.

"We planned then to make our escape, and so tried to open the great gate; but one leaf was about twenty-four feet across, and so thick and heavy that with all our strength we could not move it. The walls, too, were a hundred and fifty feet high, and so we could do nothing with them. We were like fish in a pot – beyond all possible way of escape. We held each other's hands and cried.

"Among us one man thought of this plan: We had a knife and he took it, and while the monster was drunk and asleep, decided to stab his eyes out, and cut his throat. We said in reply, 'We are all doomed to death anyway; let's try'; and we made our way up on the verandah and stabbed his eyes. He gave an awful roar, and struck out on all sides to catch us. We rushed here and there, making our escape out of the court back into the rear garden. There were in this enclosure pigs and sheep, about sixty of them in all. There we rushed, in among the pigs and sheep.

"He floundered about, waving his two arms after us, but not one of us did he get hold of; we were all mixed up – sheep, pigs, and people. When he did catch anything it was a sheep; and when it was not a sheep it was a pig. So he opened the front gate to send all the animals out.

"We then each of us took a pig or sheep on the back and made straight for the gate. The monster felt each, and finding it a pig or a sheep, let it go. Then we all got out and rushed for the boat.

"A little later he came and sat on the bank and roared his threatenings at us. A lot of other giants came at his call. They took steps of thirty feet or so, came racing after us, caught the boat and made it fast; but we took axes and struck at the hands that held it, and so got free at last and out to the open sea.

"Again a great wind arose, and we ran on to the rocks and were all destroyed. Everyone was engulfed in the sea and drowned; I alone got hold of a piece of boat-timber and lived. Then there was a horrible fish from the sea that came swimming after me and bit off my legs. At last I drifted back home and here I am.

"When I think of it still, my teeth are cold and my bones shiver. My Eight Lucky Stars are very bad, that's why it happened to me."

Mirza

A KING, ON SUSPICION OF AN ATTEMPT TO USURP THE THRONE, had put his brother in chains and suspended him between heaven and earth. The King was old, and the day of his death being near, he called his three sons, and advised them not to leave the throne empty, lest their uncle should usurp it and put them to death. After giving the young Princes other important counsel, the old King died. The oldest son, who succeeded his father on the throne, one day went fowling. The youngest brother, whose name was Mirza, remembering their father's advice, immediately leaped up and sat on the throne. In the evening the oldest brother returned and began to scold Mirza, saying:

"How now, rogue! Have you a mind to usurp my throne?"

"No, Your Majesty," replied Mirza; "I sat on the throne lest our uncle, finding it empty, should usurp it. But if it displeases you I will not do it again."

On the following day the King again went fowling, and the throne was left empty. Suddenly a loud jangling of chains was heard, and lo! the uncle, having broken the fetters, descended from the skies and seated himself on the empty throne. Forthwith he ordered his men to put the three brothers to death, but his officials interceded and begged the King not to kill his nephews, but to banish them from the country. The King consented, and the three brothers were banished.

The lot of the three Princes was now to lead a sad, wandering life in the dreary desert. After a long journey, they came to a ruined mill just at the time when the sun was going down. The elder brothers at once dismounted to spend the night in the ruined mill, but Mirza implored them not to do so, saying:

"Brothers, when our father died he advised us that in case our uncle usurped the throne and banished us, we must take heed not to lodge in a ruined mill, not to camp on a green meadow, and not to resort to the Black Mountain. Come, be advised, lest worse trouble befall us."

"Hush, coward!" said the elder brothers, and they prepared to lodge in the mill. The oldest brother said:

"Let us turn the horses out to pasture, and do you two go to bed; I will keep watch all night."

After eating their meal the two younger brothers went to bed, while the oldest began his watch. Mirza shut his eyes and pretended to sleep, peeping, however, through his eyelashes to see what his oldest brother was doing. After watching a while the latter was tired, withdrew and went to bed. By the snoring of his brothers, Mirza understood that they had fallen into sound sleep. He rose, girded on his magic sword, and taking his bow and arrow, began to walk about and to keep watch. In the middle of the night he saw, at a distance, the gleaming of a light which drew nearer and nearer, and soon, to his terror, he saw a horrible dragon with seven heads, on each of which was an enormous jewel burning like a torch. It approached his brothers and was about to devour them, when Mirza took aim and shot all its seven heads with a single arrow. The monster stretched itself on the ground, hissing and wheezing. The lad drew his magic sword, and cutting the dragon to pieces put the seven jewels in his pocket. He spent the rest of the night watching, and towards morning went to bed and pretended to sleep. On the morrow the oldest brother awoke and nudged Mirza in the side, saying:

"Get up, ho! Have you not slept enough? I was guarding your repose all night long."

All three rose and started upon their journey. They travelled until they came to a green meadow, at the sight of which the two elder brothers dismounted and began to pitch their tents to spend the night, in spite of the entreaties of Mirza, who reminded them of the advice of their father to avoid the green meadow.

"What a coward you are!" exclaimed the second brother. "You need not be so much afraid; I will keep guard tonight," and dismounting, all three pitched their tents on the green meadow. The second brother kept watch till midnight, and then went to bed. Mirza, who was only pretending to sleep, hearing his second brother snore soundly, got up, girded on his magic sword, and taking his bow and arrows, began to keep watch. Soon he saw something approaching the tents. As it drew nearer, he could see that it was a terrible giantess, with one of her lips reaching the skies, and the other sweeping the ground. He at once took ambush in a neighbouring trench, and aimed an arrow towards her, saying to himself:

"If she does no harm to my brothers I will not shoot her."

The giantess arrived and was apparently surprised to find three tents, and three horses, but only two men. However, she came to the conclusion that the third human being had been devoured by the wild beasts. She then approached the two sleeping lads and hung a sleep-ring on an ear of each, saying:

"Sleep now, until I send my seven sons to devour you."

Mirza followed her until she came to a large rock, which was the gate of an underground cave. She turned the rock over, and entering the cave, exclaimed to her sons:

"Get up, boys! I have found a good meal for you. Go make your repast on the two human beings, and save a portion for me." Mirza stood at the cave's entrance with his magic sword, and cut off the head of each giant as they came out one by one. Then he entered the cave, and taking hold of the giantess, said:

"Ugly hag! did you dare to send your sons to devour my brothers! Here! share the fate of your younglings." So speaking, he cut her head off too. He came back and found his brothers snoring as before. He took the sleep-rings from their ears, and at daybreak went to bed and feigned sleep. In the morning the second brother jogged Mirza, saying:

"Get up, ho! Will you sleep till noon? Have a little mercy on me, who have watched all the night."

They all rose and mounted their horses. That day they came to the Black Mountain, where the two elder brothers desired to camp. Mirza began again to implore them, saying:

"This time, at least, let us follow the advice of our father and not halt on this enchanted ground; let us avoid a third disaster which may perhaps be fatal."

"What a coward you are!" exclaimed his brothers. "What danger was there in lodging in the mill or in camping on the green meadows? As it is your turn to watch tonight, you grumble. Be silent! We will camp here tonight, and you must keep watch."

They pitched their tents, and after a meal, the two elder brothers soon went to bed. Mirza girded on his magic sword, took his bow and arrows, and began his watch. The first part of the night was quiet. After midnight he sat down to take a little rest, and on account of his sleeplessness on the two previous nights, he soon fell asleep. When he opened his eyes it was near daybreak. He rose, and to his great dismay he found the fire was out. It was a sign that he had slept and this would disgrace him. He could not start the fire anew because the flint and steel were in the pockets of the other brothers. He ran to the top of the neighbouring hill, whence he saw a light gleaming at a distance. He determined to fetch embers from that light, and make his own fire. On the hilltop he met an old man winding a ball of black thread, while another ball of white thread lay near him.

"Good day to you, father!" said the lad.

"God's blessing rest upon you!" answered the old man.

"Who are you, and what are these balls?" asked Mirza.

"I am Time," answered the old man; "this black ball signifies the night, which as you see, is near its end. As soon as it finishes, the morning breaks. Then I will roll this white ball, which represents the day, down the hill, and it will go on unwrapping until it is noon. I shall then wrap it again, and finish just when it is evening."

Mirza snatched the black ball from the old man's hand, and rolling it down the hill, unwrapped it, saying:

"Now, Father, wrap it up again. I wish this night to be a little longer, for I have much to do."

So saying, he proceeded towards the gleaming light. On arriving he saw that it came from a cave, with a fireplace over which there was a great cauldron with forty handles. The meat of seven oxen was cooking in the cauldron, around which forty giants were lying asleep. The youth approached the fireplace, seized the cauldron, put it down, taking some embers from under, replaced it and started back on his way. It chanced that one of the giants was watching, and saw what the lad did. As soon as Mirza disappeared, he woke his brothers and told them what the human being had done. All the forty were surprised, and bit their lips upon hearing this marvellous news in regard to a human being, who had displayed a strength surpassing the united force of the forty brothers. At once they decided to make that human hero their partner; so accordingly they ran after him, and overtaking him, proposed to him to be their brother. The lad consented, and they adopted each other as brothers, exchanging promises to go to one another's assistance in case of need. Mirza returned to the camp, and after starting the fire, lay down to take a morning nap. By that time his brothers awakened, and jogged him in the side, saying:

"Get up! We have been watching this night also, and do you still sleep?"

He did not utter a word. They all mounted their horses and went their way until they came to the city of the King of the Black Mountain, and camped in a meadow outside the city. In the middle of the night as Mirza was keeping watch around the camp, he saw giants proceeding towards the palace of the King. Coming nearer he perceived that they were his adopted brothers each carrying a large iron nail as long as a man is high.

"God speed!" said Mirza.

"Well met!" answered the giants; "come and help us in our enterprise tonight, and here are three golden apples as a present for you. The King has three daughters whom we have been hunting for seven years, but cannot find. We have prepared these three golden apples for their love, but we will give them to you if you help us. We have made these iron nails to use in climbing the walls."

Mirza's anger began to boil, but he carefully concealed his feeling.

"Very well," he said, at last, "this very night you will attain your desires, but you must obey me."

He walked at their head and the giants followed until they came to the foot of the palace wall. He took the iron nails, and thrusting them into the wall with his thumb, formed a row of steps by which he could ascend to the top of the wall. He then ordered the giants to mount, and as they went up one by one, he cut off their heads with his magic sword, throwing their bodies into a trench on the other side. Then cutting off the ears of each, he put them in his pocket, and arranged their heads in a row on the top of the wall. After that he jumped over and entered the palace. In the King's bedchamber he saw a golden candlestick burning at the head of the King's bed, and a silver candlestick burning at the foot. Mirza changed the places of the candlesticks, and drank the syrup which was in the golden cup near the King. As he was going out, he saw a dragon coiled around the pillar ready to devour the King. At once he drew his dagger, and stabbed the dragon, nailing it to the pillar. Next he took the King's dagger from under his pillow and put it in his belt. Then he entered the bedchamber of the three maidens, drank the syrup in their golden cups and placed a golden apple on the pillow of each, thus betrothing the oldest to his oldest brother, the middle one to his middle brother, and the youngest to himself. He also placed on the pillow of the youngest maiden a necklace made of the seven jewels which he had taken by killing the seven-headed dragon in the ruined mill. Then he came back to his tent, and at daybreak went to bed.

When morning came there was a great tumult among the people of the city, who had seen the heads of the forty giants who had been butchered. Informants ran to the King bearing the glad tidings that his forty troublesome enemies had all been killed, that their bodies were lying in the trench and their heads were on the top of the wall. The King, who by that time had discovered what had happened in his palace, was filled with amazement. His peers and subjects came to congratulate him. Upon this the King sent out heralds to proclaim that the one who did all these things, whoever he might be, must present himself. Not only should he become the son-in-law of the King by marrying the most beautiful of the three maidens, but the King would gladly bestow on him any gift which he might ask. Thousands appeared before the King claiming to be the hero, but none could prove it. No man was left in the city who did not make his appearance before the sovereign. Then the King bade his men call the strangers who were camping without the walls. Mirza feigned sickness, and at first did not go. His two brothers feared that they were to be fined for trampling upon the King's ground, but as soon as they were told wherefore they were called, they began to boast that they had done the heroic deed, yet upon trial they also were turned back in shame.

"Is there no one else left?" enquired the King.

"Nobody," answered the attendant, "except a sickly boy lying in the tent of these strangers."

"Bring him hither," ordered the King.

Mirza, seeing the King's attendant about to force him to go, rose, and leaping on the back of his horse, made his appearance before the King. He put before him the ears of the forty giants and told the King how he slew them, how he changed the places of the candlesticks, how he stabbed the dragon, and betrothed the King's daughters to his brothers and to himself. He gave to the King the dagger, and drew out from the pillar his own dagger which neither the King nor his peers had been able to withdraw. The King sprang from his throne and kissed Mirza on the forehead, exclaiming:

"May Heaven bless you, worthy hero! You are my beloved son-in-law, and after my death my throne is yours."

His brothers bowed down before Mirza, saying:

"Pardon our harshness; hereafter you are our elder brother and we are your subordinates."

After that there was a great wedding festival for forty days and forty nights, and the three maidens were given in marriage to the three brothers. At the nuptials, however, the brides said to the bridegrooms:

"We are not for you, such frail men as you are. Do you think killing forty dwarfish giants a heroic act? Not so. We have our lover, upon whose breast roses and lilies grow. If you are men of valour, go fight the Roaring Giant, our lover; if you can overcome him we are yours, but not until you do so."

On the following morning, Mirza advised his brothers to keep silent and not reveal their secret, lest they should be the laughing-stock of the people. He took leave of the King, saying that he had important work to do, and would be absent for two months. He started, and after a long journey came to a white castle. A maiden as beautiful as the moon was sitting in the window working with her needle. Seeing the lad, she said to him:

"Human being, neither the snake on its belly nor the bird with its wing could come here! How could you venture to come?"

"Your love brought me hither, fair maiden," answered the lad.

"Here is food for you," said the maiden, letting down from the window a basket; "eat, and go your way. This castle belongs to the White Giant. Go away before he comes, lest he devour you."

"Who are you, fair maiden? Who has brought you hither?" enquired the lad.

"My father is the King of India. We were three sisters, but the White Giant, the Red Giant and the Black Giant stole us and brought us into this lonely country. It has been seven years since I have seen a human being."

Mirza asked if she knew where the Roaring Giant lived.

"You must pass the lands of the Red Giant and the Black Giant before you arrive," said the maiden.

"Farewell!" said Mirza.

"Farewell!" said the fair maiden, sighing.

Mirza continued on his way. Towards evening he saw the White Giant returning from hunting. He detected his presence by the human smell, and seeing Mirza, exclaimed:

"What luck! I have not tasted human flesh for a long time;" and he assailed Mirza, to devour him.

"Halt!" exclaimed the lad, preparing his bow and arrow. "I shall prove a hard nut for you to crack. My name is Mirza. I have so far butchered forty-seven giants; you are the forty-eighth."

He shot his arrow, which passed through the giant's heart and nailed him to the ground. Drawing his magic sword, he cut off his head, and thrusting it on his sword's point took it to the white castle and called to the maiden:

"Fair Princess, here is the head of the White Giant, whom I have sacrificed to your love."

The maiden seeing it from the window, ran wild with joy. At once she opened the door of the castle, saying:

"Enter, and may Heaven bless you, who came to deliver me from my bondage!"

The lad entered, and that night lodged in the castle. On the morning, when departing, he put on the maiden's finger a ring, saying:

"Now you are the betrothed of my oldest brother. After fighting the other giants I will come back and carry you with me."

And he took leave of her. After a long journey he came to a black castle with a beautiful maiden sitting in the window, who gave him refreshment as the former had done. Leaving her, he met the Black Giant, and killing him as he had the former one, brought his head to the maiden. He spent the night there, and on the following morning, putting a ring on the finger of the maiden, betrothed her to his second brother. Another long journey brought him to a red castle. A maiden as beautiful as the sun was sitting in the window and working with her needle. The lad at first glance fell in love with her. She also had fallen in love with him at first sight, and said to him:

"Human being, for Heaven's sake, beware of the Red Giant!"

"I have come on purpose to fight with him, fair creature," answered the lad. "I have already killed the White Giant and the Black Giant and freed your sisters."

"But the Red Giant is a sorcerer," said the maiden, "and when brought to bay, changes himself into a mound of earth, with a hole at the top, whence he pours out smoke and flames, and devours everyone who ventures to go near."

He had hardly departed from the maiden, when lo! the Red Giant appeared, brandishing his terrible mace.

"Aha!" exclaimed the giant, seeing the lad, "a delicious morsel indeed is this which has come to me of its own free will."

"Nay, come, let us fight," said the lad, "and see who shall be the morsel, I or you!" and he prepared his bow and arrow.

"Dwarfish human being!" exclaimed the giant, "how can you oppose me?"

Saying this, he threw his mace at the lad, who took hold of it, exclaiming:

"I have killed forty-nine giants, your White and Black brothers included. Mirza is my name; do you think you will escape from my hand?"

When the giant heard that this was Mirza, the terror of the giants, he was so frightened that he at once changed himself into a red mound with smoke and flames shooting out from the hole in its top. Immediately the lad jumped on the mound, drew his magic sword and thrusting it into the smoking hole, began quickly to stir it until the heart and intestines of the giant were cut to pieces and were thrown out of the orifice. The youth then jumped down, and lo! the mound fell and was ruined. Mirza then went back to the red castle and called to the maiden.

"Fair Princess," he said, showing her his sword dyed with blood and the pieces of the giant's heart and intestines still clinging to it, "I have sacrificed the Red Giant to your love."

The maiden was almost wild with joy. She opened the door, and embracing Mirza's feet, exclaimed:

"Hero! you have saved me; I owe you my life and all my being. I am still a virgin, and though unworthy to be your wife, for Heaven's sake accept me as your handmaid!"

"Nay, fair maiden, you are my love, you are my betrothed if you do love me," said the lad, putting a ring on her finger.

Then the lad asked her concerning the place where lived the Roaring Giant.

"Be advised, do not go," said the maiden. "The Roaring Giant is a cruel tyrant; you will not come back alive; do not go. He is vulnerable only by his own bow and arrows, and who shall give them to you that you may shoot him with them? It is impossible. For the sake of the love you bear to me, do not go, or take me with you that I may die with you," and the maiden began to sob.

"Nay, love, do not cry," said the lad, "I must go at any risk."

And he started. After a long journey he came to a magnificent castle decorated with gold and jewels. It was the castle of the Roaring Giant. It was towards evening when the lad arrived. At once he took the shape of a servant, sprinkled water about the palace, swept all clean, and hid himself behind the trees and bushes. Soon a noise like that of thunder was heard, from the distant mountains. It was the Roaring Giant who was coming from fowling. Every bird, every beast of the forest hid itself on hearing the noise of the giant. Mirza's hair stood on end, and he felt what a terrible task it was which he had undertaken. The giant, seeing the courtyard round the palace swept and cleaned was pleased, and soliloquized to himself:

"This must be the work of a human being; I must find him out; it would be pleasant to have a human servant." And he exclaimed:

"Where are you, human being? Who are you? Come out from your hiding place. I will not hurt you, but give you what you desire."

Mirza leaped out from his place of concealment, and stood before the Roaring Giant, saying in a humble voice:

"My lord, I have lost my companions and gone astray. Heaven was kind enough to guide me until I came to your door. Will you accept me as your servant?"

The giant accepted him, and the lad served so diligently and devotedly that the giant was greatly pleased, and held him in high esteem. One day the giant and the lad entered the flower garden. Roses, violets and other flowers of every colour and perfume grew there luxuriously. Nightingales, birds of paradise, and all kinds of birds and beasts of the forest were there. In the middle of the orchard a fountain gushed out its crystal waters, and formed a pond amid overhanging verdure. It was, throughout, a paradise.

"Bring those flower pots and put them around this pond," said the giant to the lad. "Bring here all kinds of delicious foods, which you have prepared. Every day this week we shall have company, and we must prepare for them."

The lad made the necessary preparations meditating to himself that the expected guests were no doubt the three sisters, the wives of himself and his brothers. Near the pond there was a tree on which the giant had hung his bow and arrows. The lad took them down.

"Halloo! what are you doing?" exclaimed the giant.

"Master, I wish to take the cloth and clean them," answered the lad.

Soon the arrow fell down.

"Bring it to me," said the giant, and putting the arrow in the bow handed it over to the lad. He took it and went backward as if to hang it up. He had scarcely come to the tree when he turned to the giant and took aim at his heart.

"Alas!" exclaimed the giant.

"Nay, I have come expressly to take your life," said Mirza. "I am Mirza. I have killed fifty giants; you are the fifty-first."

Whiz! and the arrow was flung and pierced the Roaring Giant through the heart and nailed him to the ground. He uttered his last roar, and then lay dead as a stone. The lad thereupon hid himself behind a tree near the pond to see what might happen.

Soon three turtledoves came from the sky flapping their wings and perched gently on the border of the pond. At once they dived into the water and were changed into three maidens. The lad saw that they were his own wife and the wives of his brothers. He kept silent and did not stir. The maidens, putting on the human dresses which they had brought with them, went to embrace the Roaring Giant, who they supposed was asleep. But seeing him nailed to the ground with an arrow through his heart and dead, they were horror-stricken. They ran back to the pond, and undressing themselves, leaped into the water. Just at that time, Mirza came up and stood on the brink of the pond.

"For shame!" he exclaimed. "How now! did you see your lover? Did you enjoy the roses and the lilies growing on his breast?"

They were horror-stricken and mute, hiding their faces with their hands. Mirza cut pieces from the skirts of their dresses, and let them go. They were turned to turtledoves, and flew away with drooping wings. Thereupon Mirza, entering the palace of the Roaring Giant, gathered all the riches and loaded them on forty camels. He then went and took the three Princesses whom he had betrothed to himself and his brothers, also the wealth of the Red, Black and White Giants. Then he drove back and came again to the city of the King of the Black Mountain. The king, hearing that Mirza had come, bringing inestimable wealth, hastened to meet him at the city gate, all his noblemen and peers accompanying him. As soon as they met, Mirza said to the King:

"I cannot talk with you until you convoke a meeting of all the noblemen and wise men of your realm to try your three daughters."

"What!" said the King, "is it not a shame to bring maidens to trial?"

"Nay," said the lad, "your daughters are false, and shameless; they must be tried and punished as an example to the womanhood of the realm. If you do not call a meeting as I have requested, I will leave you and go elsewhere."

Now the King loved Mirza as his very life, and could not part with him. So he gave the order and all the peers and wise men of his realm were summoned to a parliament. The three maidens were brought before the court. Mirza recited his adventures, and placed before the court the pieces which he had cut from the dresses of the maidens. On being put in their respective places they fitted. Thus everything being proved, the maidens could not deny it. The court gave its decision, which the King sanctioned. Thereupon the three daughters of the King were bound by their hair to the tails of three wild horses, which were whipped up and carried them away to the wilderness, dashing them from stone to stone until they were cut into pieces.

Then the King adopted the three Princesses whom Mirza had brought with him. A wedding festival for forty days and nights was celebrated, and the three maidens were given in marriage to the three brothers.

Three apples fell from heaven; one for me, one for the storyteller, and one for him who entertained the company.

The Forest Lad and the Wicked Giant

ONCE UPON A TIME there was a man who took his wife and tiny baby son into the deep forest to make their home. With his own hands he built the house out of mud, and he made for it a thatched roof from the grass of the forest. For food they depended upon the fruits of the forest and the beasts which they killed in the hunt. They lived like hermits, seeing no one.

As the baby son grew into a large strong boy he learned from his father all the secrets of the forest. He grew wise as well as strong. From his mother he heard stories of their former life in the great city which had been their home before they went to live in the forest. These were the tales he loved to hear best of all. Very often when his father went out into the forest to hunt, the boy would beg to remain at home with his mother. While his father was away she would sit on the ground before their hut and unfold to the boy all her memories of their old life.

"Father," said the lad one day after his father had returned from his hunting trip, "I am tired of living here in the forest all by ourselves. Let us return to the city to live."

"Your mother has been telling tales to you," replied his father. "I will see to it that she never mentions the city to you again. We left the city to save our lives. Let me never hear from you another word about returning to the city."

After that the lad was made to accompany his father when he went out hunting. There was no more opportunity to hear the tales he loved from his mother's lips. Nevertheless he hid away in his mind all that his mother had told him of their old life; and at night, when the fierce storms in the forest or the sound of the wild beasts would not let him sleep, he often lay awake upon his mat on the floor of the hut, pondering over the stories she had told.

At last the father grew sick of a fever and died. Now that the lad and his mother were left alone in the forest the lad said, "Come, let us return to our home in the city. Let us not stay here alone in the forest any longer. I must live in my own life the tales you have told me of the *festas* and the dancing, the great tournaments, and the songs at night under the balconies of the fair maidens."

The lad's request was so urgent that his mother could not have refused him, even if she, in her own heart, was not longing for a return to the life of the city. Accordingly, they took all their possessions, which consisted only of a horse and a sword, and set out for the city.

The lad and his mother reached the city at nightfall. They went from one street to another, but saw no living being. They knocked and clapped their hands before all the doors of the city, but no one responded. At last they reached the street where their old home had been. The lad was delighted to see what a big handsome house it was. "No wonder my mother longed to return to a home like this," he thought. "How could she ever have endured the rude hut in the depths of the forest?"

The doors of the beautiful house stood wide open. The lad and his mother entered, and passed from one room to another. His mother saw one room after another with everything unchanged. She recognized one object after another just as she had left it. There was one room in the house which was securely barred on the inside, however.

The lad and his mother spent the night in their old home. In the morning they again walked about the deserted streets of the city. They saw no one and heard no living sound. It was like a city of the dead. They grew hungry at length; and the lad went outside the city to seek for food in the forest, according to the custom which he had known all his life.

The mother returned to her old home to await the coming of her son. As soon as she went upstairs she saw that the barred door was wide open. There in the hall stood the most enormous giant she had ever seen. The great halls of the house were high, but the giant could not stand up in them without stooping.

"Who are you and what are you doing in my house?" roared the giant in such a terrible voice that the house trembled.

The woman who had lived so many years in the forest was not easily frightened. "Who are you and what are you doing in my house?" she shouted at the giant in the loudest tones she could muster.

One might have expected that the giant would have killed her instantly, but on the contrary her bold answer pleased him exceedingly. He laughed so hard that he had to lean against the wall to keep from falling.

"So you think that this is your house, do you?" said the giant as soon as he could regain his voice. "Well, I'll tell you what we can do. I like you, and we can share this house if you will consent to be my wife."

"I am not alone," said the lad's mother as soon as she could recover from her surprise sufficiently to find words. "My son is with me and I am expecting him any moment to return from the forest whither he has gone to procure food for us."

"I can dispose of your son very quickly, just as I have destroyed all the inhabitants of this city," said the giant with a frown.

"You cannot dispose of my son so easily as you may think," replied his mother. "He has grown in the deep forest and is very strong, far stronger than the city dwellers. Besides his great strength, he is surrounded by the magic circle of his mother's love."

"I do not know what the magic circle of a mother's love is like," said the giant. "I don't remember having seen one anywhere. Nevertheless I like you, and because I like you I will endeavour to dispose of your son as painlessly as possible. I believe you say you are expecting him any moment. Just lie down here and pretend that you are sick. When the boy comes in tell him that you have a terrible pain in your eyes. As you have lived long in the forest you will know that the best remedy for a pain in your eyes is the oil of the deadly cobra of the jungle. Send the lad out into the jungle to obtain this oil for you, and I promise you he will never return alive. I'll go back into my room and bar the door so the boy will never see me, but I shall listen through the wall to know whether you carry out my command."

At that very moment they heard the lad's footsteps and his gay voice at the door. The giant went inside his room and barred the door. The lad's mother lay down with a cloth over her eyes, moaning in loud tones. "The giant little knows the strength and skill of the lad whose mother I am," she said to herself as she smiled amidst her moans and groans.

"O dear little Mother, what evil has befallen you during my absence?" asked the boy as he entered the room.

His mother complained of the pain in her eyes just as the giant had instructed. "The only thing which will cure me of this terrible affliction is the oil of the cobra," she said.

The boy well knew the dangers which attended securing the oil from the deadly cobra of the jungle, but never in his life had he disregarded a request from his mother. He at once set out for the jungle; and, in spite of the perils of the deed, he succeeded in obtaining the oil which his mother had requested.

On the way back to the city, the boy met a little old woman carrying a pole over her shoulder from which there hung, head downward, several live fowls which she was taking to market. It was really the Holy Mother herself who had come to aid the lad in answer to his mother's prayer.

"Where are you going, my lad?" asked the old woman. The boy told his story and showed the precious oil which he had obtained from the cobra. "The day is coming, the day is coming, my lad, when you will, in truth, need the cobra's oil," said the little old woman. "But that day is not today. Today hen's oil will serve your purpose just as well. You may kill one of my hens and use the hen's oil, but leave the cobra's oil with me so that I may keep it safely for you until the day when you will require it."

The boy heeded the advice of the little old woman and killed one of her hens. He left the cobra's oil with her and took the hen's oil in its place to his mother. Because his mother had nothing at all the matter with her eyes, the hen's oil cured them just as well as the cobra's oil. There was no one who knew the difference, except the boy and the little old woman.

When the boy had gone out the giant came in from his own room and said, "In truth your son is a brave lad. I did not dream that he would have the courage to go in search of the oil of the deadly cobra, much less succeed in his quest."

"You do not know the great love we bear each other," said the lad's mother.

"I am going to demand a new proof of your son's strength and skill," said the giant. "Tomorrow you must complain of the pain in your back and send the boy in search of the oil of the porcupine to cure it. This is my command."

The next day the woman had to complain of a pain in her back just as the giant had commanded. There was nothing else which she could do. The boy at once went in search of a porcupine, and succeeded in slaying one and getting the oil.

On his way back to the city the lad again met the little old woman who was really Nossa Senhora. "Leave the oil of the porcupine with me, my son," said she when she had heard his story. "I will keep it for you until the morrow when you will have great need of it. Today hen's oil will serve your purpose just as well."

Because the boy's mother had nothing at all the matter with her back she was cured with the hen's oil which the boy brought, just as easily as if it had been the porcupine's oil. The giant came out of his room and said, "In truth, lad, you are a boy of great skill and strength."

The boy had not seen the giant before and he was very much surprised. Before he even had time to recover from his amazement the giant had seized him and bound him securely with a great rope. "If you are really a strong boy you will break this rope," said the giant. "If you are not strong enough to break it I shall cut you into five pieces with my sword."

The boy struggled with all his might to break the great rope. It was no use. He was not strong enough. The giant stood by laughing.

When the lad's mother saw that he could not break the rope she fell upon her knees before the giant and cried, "Do what you will to me, but spare my son!"

The cruel giant laughed at her request. When she saw that she could not keep him from slaying the boy, she said, "If you will not grant my large request I beg that you will listen to just a tiny, tiny, little one. When you cut my son into five pieces do it with his father's sword which he has brought with him from the little hut in the forest where we used to live. Then bind his body upon the back of his father's horse which he brought with him out of the forest and turn the horse loose, so it may travel, perchance, back to the forest from which I brought my lad to meet this terrible death."

The giant did as she requested, and the horse bore the slain boy's body along the road to the forest. Outside the city they met the little old woman who was really Nossa Senhora. She took the parts of the lad's body and anointed them with the porcupine's oil. Then she held them tight together. They stayed securely joined. "Are you lacking anything?" she asked the boy.

The boy felt of his legs, his arms, his ears, his nose, his hair. "I am all here except my eyesight," he said. The little old woman anointed his eyes with the cobra's oil. His sight was immediately restored. Then he knew that the little old woman was indeed the Holy Mother. She vanished as he knelt to receive her blessing.

The boy in his new strength quickly hastened back to the city. It was night and the giant was asleep. He seized his father's sword and plunged it into the giant's body. The giant turned over without awakening. "The mosquitoes are biting me," he muttered in his sleep.

The boy saw the giant's own enormous sword lying on the floor. It was so heavy he could barely lift it, but mustering all his strength he drove it into the giant's body. The giant died immediately.

"The magic circle of a mother's love, with the Holy Mother's help, will guard a lad against all perils," said the boy's mother when she heard her son's story and saw the giant lying dead.

The Magical & the Supernatural

Introduction

"I AM NOT AFRAID of these Frost Giants from the North Pole.... Let our Fairy Queen change me into a flower, and clothe me warm enough, and I'll defy even the Frost King to hurt me." Thus the valiant spirit in the Swiss story becomes 'The Fairy of the Edelweiss' and the eternal protector of the Alpine country. Giants are just about by definition formidable opponents. They are scarcely to be defeated by ordinary means, and certainly not by regular mortal humans – though, as we've seen, heroic status can reduce the odds, especially when backed up by divine assistance.

But supernatural help can come in many different forms. Sympathetic spirits intervene in several of these stories, like the magic women who help the boy along his way in the Swedish tale 'The Mount of the Golden Queen', or the frog who helps free the captured queen in the French story 'The Frog and the Lion Fairy'. Some of the most rewarding tales show the power of enchantment and regular human resourcefulness and courage combining. In the Serbian story 'The Biter Bit', for instance, a giant kidnaps a boy and trains him in magic. He gets his comeuppance when, with his father's support, the boy turns his tutor's spells against him.

The Strong Prince

ONCE UPON A TIME there lived a king who was so fond of wine that he could not go to sleep unless he knew he had a great flaskful tied to his bed-post. All day long he drank till he was too stupid to attend to his business, and everything in the kingdom went to rack and ruin. But one day an accident happened to him, and he was struck on the head by a falling bough, so that he fell from his horse and lay dead upon the ground.

His wife and son mourned his loss bitterly, for, in spite of his faults, he had always been kind to them. So they abandoned the crown and forsook their country, not knowing or caring where they went.

At length they wandered into a forest, and being very tired, sat down under a tree to eat some bread that they had brought with them. When they had finished the queen said: "My son, I am thirsty; fetch me some water."

The prince got up at once and went to a brook which he heard gurgling near at hand. He stooped and filled his hat with the water, which he brought to his mother; then he turned and followed the stream up to its source in a rock, where it bubbled out clear and fresh and cold. He knelt down to take a draught from the deep pool below the rock, when he saw the reflection of a sword hanging from the branch of a tree over his head. The young man drew back with a start; but in a moment he climbed the tree, cutting the rope which held the sword, and carried the weapon to his mother.

The queen was greatly surprised at the sight of anything so splendid in such a lonely place, and took it in her hands to examine it closely. It was of curious workmanship, wrought with gold, and on its handle was written: 'The man who can buckle on this sword will become stronger than other men.' The queen's heart swelled with joy as she read these words, and she bade her son lose no time in testing their truth. So he fastened it round his waist, and instantly a glow of strength seemed to run through his veins. He took hold of a thick oak tree and rooted it up as easily as if it had been a weed.

This discovery put new life into the queen and her son, and they continued their walk through the forest. But night was drawing on, and the darkness grew so thick that it seemed as if it could be cut with a knife. They did not want to sleep in the wood, for they were afraid of wolves and other wild beasts, so they groped their way along, hand in hand, till the prince tripped over something which lay across the path. He could not see what it was, but stooped down and tried to lift it. The thing was very heavy, and he thought his back would break under the strain. At last with a great heave he moved it out of the road, and as it fell he knew it was a huge rock. Behind the rock was a cave which it was quite clear was the home of some robbers, though not one of the band was there.

Hastily putting out the fire which burned brightly at the back, and bidding his mother come in and keep very still, the prince began to pace up and down, listening for the return of the robbers. But he was very sleepy, and in spite of all his efforts he felt he could not keep awake much longer, when he heard the sound of the robbers returning, shouting and singing as they marched along. Soon the singing ceased, and straining his ears he heard them discussing anxiously what had become of their cave, and why they could not see the fire as usual. "This must be the place," said a voice, which the prince took to be that of the captain. "Yes, I feel the ditch before the entrance. Someone forgot to pile up the fire before we left and it has burnt itself out! But it is all right. Let every man jump across, and as he does so cry out 'Hop! I am here.' I will go last. Now begin."

The man who stood nearest jumped across, but he had no time to give the call which the captain had ordered, for with one swift, silent stroke of the prince's sword, his head rolled into a corner. Then the young man cried instead, "Hop! I am here."

The second man, hearing the signal, leapt the ditch in confidence, and was met by the same fate, and in a few minutes eleven of the robbers lay dead, and there remained only the captain.

Now the captain had wound round his neck the shawl of his lost wife, and the stroke of the prince's sword fell harmless. Being very cunning, however, he made no resistance, and rolled over as if he were as dead as the other men. Still, the prince was no fool, and wondered if indeed he was as dead as he seemed to be; but the captain lay so stiff and stark, that at last he was taken in.

The prince next dragged the headless bodies into a chamber in the cave, and locked the door. Then he and his mother ransacked the place for some food, and when they had eaten it they lay down and slept in peace.

With the dawn they were both awake again, and found that, instead of the cave which they had come to the night before, they now were in a splendid castle, full of beautiful rooms. The prince went round all these and carefully locked them up, bidding his mother take care of the keys while he was hunting.

Unfortunately, the queen could not bear to think that there was anything which she did not know. So the moment that her son had turned his back, she opened the doors of all the rooms, and peeped in, till she came to the one where the robbers lay. But if the sight of the blood on the ground turned her faint, the sight of the robber captain walking up and down was a greater shock still. She quickly turned the key in the lock, and ran back to the chamber she had slept in.

Soon after her son came in, bringing with him a large bear, which he had killed for supper. As there was enough food to last them for many days, the prince did not hunt the next morning, but, instead, began to explore the castle. He found that a secret way led from it into the forest; and following the path, he reached another castle larger and more splendid than the one belonging to the robbers. He knocked at the door with his fist, and said that he wanted to enter; but the giant, to whom the castle belonged, only answered: "I know who you are. I have nothing to do with robbers."

"I am no robber," answered the prince. "I am the son of a king, and I have killed all the band. If you do not open to me at once I will break in the door, and your head shall go to join the others."

He waited a little, but the door remained shut as tightly as before. Then he just put his shoulder to it, and immediately the wood began to crack. When the giant found that it was no use keeping it shut, he opened it, saying: "I see you are a brave youth. Let there be peace between us."

And the prince was glad to make peace, for he had caught a glimpse of the giant's beautiful daughter, and from that day he often sought the giant's house.

Now the queen led a dull life all alone in the castle, and to amuse herself she paid visits to the robber captain, who flattered her till at last she agreed to marry him. But as she was much afraid of her son, she told the robber that the next time the prince went to bathe in the river, he was to steal the sword from its place above the bed, for without it the young man would have no power to punish him for his boldness.

The robber captain thought this good counsel, and the next morning, when the young man went to bathe, he unhooked the sword from its nail and buckled it round his waist. On his return to the castle, the prince found the robber waiting for him on the steps, waving the sword above his head, and knowing that some horrible fate was in store, fell on his knees and begged for mercy. But he might as well have tried to squeeze blood out of a stone. The robber, indeed, granted him his life, but took out both his eyes, which he thrust into the prince's hand, saying brutally:

"Here, you had better keep them! You may find them useful!"

Weeping, the blind youth felt his way to the giant's house, and told him all the story.

The giant was full of pity for the poor young man, but enquired anxiously what he had done with the eyes. The prince drew them out of his pocket, and silently handed them to the giant, who washed them well, and then put them back in the prince's head. For three days he lay in utter darkness; then the light began to come back, till soon he saw as well as ever.

But though he could not rejoice enough over the recovery of his eyes, he bewailed bitterly the loss of his sword, and that it should have fallen to the lot of his bitter enemy.

"Never mind, my friend," said the giant, "I will get it back for you." And he sent for the monkey who was his head servant.

"Tell the fox and the squirrel that they are to go with you, and fetch me back the prince's sword," ordered he.

The three servants set out at once, one seated on the back of the others, the monkey, who disliked walking, being generally on top. Directly they came to the window of the robber captain's room, the monkey sprang from the backs of the fox and the squirrel, and climbed in. The room was empty, and the sword hanging from a nail. He took it down, and buckling it round his waist, as he had seen the prince do, swung himself down again, and mounting on the backs of his two companions, hastened to his master. The giant bade him give the sword to the prince, who girded himself with it, and returned with all speed to the castle.

"Come out, you rascal! Come out, you villain!" cried he, "and answer to me for the wrong you have done. I will show you who is the master in this house!"

The noise he made brought the robber into the room. He glanced up to where the sword usually hung, but it was gone; and instinctively he looked at the prince's hand, where he saw it gleaming brightly. In his turn he fell on his knees to beg for mercy, but it was too late. As he had done to the prince, so the prince did to him, and, blinded, he was thrust forth, and fell down a deep hole, where he is to this day. His mother the prince sent back to her father, and never would see her again. After this he returned to the giant, and said to him:

"My friend, add one more kindness to those you have already heaped on me. Give me your daughter as my wife."

So they were married, and the wedding feast was so splendid that there was not a kingdom in the world that did not hear of it. And the prince never went back to his father's throne, but lived peacefully with his wife in the forest, where, if they are not dead, they are living still.

The Three Treasures of the Giants

LONG, LONG AGO, there lived an old man and his wife who had three sons; the eldest was called Martin, the second Michael, while the third was named Jack.

One evening they were all seated round the table, eating their supper of bread and milk.

"Martin," said the old man suddenly, "I feel that I cannot live much longer. You, as the eldest, will inherit this hut; but if you value my blessing, be good to your mother and brothers."

"Certainly, father; how can you suppose I should do them wrong?" replied Martin indignantly, helping himself to all the best bits in the dish as he spoke. The old man saw nothing, but Michael looked on in surprise, and Jack was so astonished that he quite forgot to eat his own supper.

A little while after, the father fell ill, and sent for his sons, who were out hunting, to bid him farewell. After giving good advice to the two eldest, he turned to Jack.

"My boy," he said, "you have not got quite as much sense as other people, but if Heaven has deprived you of some of your wits, it was given you a kind heart. Always listen to what it says, and take heed of the words of your mother and brothers, as well as you are able!" So saying, the old man sank back on his pillows and died.

The cries of grief uttered by Martin and Michael sounded through the house, but Jack remained by the bedside of his father, still and silent, as if he were dead also. At length he got up, and going into the garden, hid himself in some trees, and wept like a child, while his two brothers made ready for the funeral.

No sooner was the old man buried than Martin and Michael agreed that they would go into the world together to seek their fortunes, while Jack stayed at home with their mother. Jack would have liked nothing better than to sit and dream by the fire, but the mother, who was very old herself, declared that there was no work for him to do, and that he must seek it with his brothers.

So, one fine morning, all three set out; Martin and Michael carried two great bags full of food, but Jack carried nothing. This made his brothers very angry, for the day was hot and the bags were heavy, and about noon they sat down under a tree and began to eat. Jack was as hungry as they were, but he knew that it was no use asking for anything; and he threw himself under another tree, and wept bitterly.

"Another time perhaps you won't be so lazy, and will bring food for yourself," said Martin, but to his surprise Jack answered:

"You are a nice pair! You talk of seeking your fortunes so as not to be a burden on our mother, and you begin by carrying off all the food she has in the house!"

This reply was so unexpected that for some moments neither of the brothers made any answer. Then they offered their brother some of their food, and when he had finished eating they went their way once more.

Towards evening they reached a small hut, and knocking at the door, asked if they might spend the night there. The man, who was a woodcutter, invited them him, and begged them to sit down to supper. Martin thanked him, but being very proud, explained that it was only shelter they wanted, as they had plenty of food with them; and he and Michael at once opened their bags and began to eat, while Jack hid himself in a corner. The wife, on seeing this, took pity on him, and called him to come and share their supper, which he gladly did, and very good he found it. At this, Martin regretted deeply that he had been so foolish as to refuse, for his bits of bread and cheese seemed very hard when he smelt the savoury soup his brother was enjoying.

"He shan't have such a chance again," thought he; and the next morning he insisted on plunging into a thick forest where they were likely to meet nobody.

For a long time they wandered hither and thither, for they had no path to guide them; but at last they came upon a wide clearing, in the midst of which stood a castle. Jack shouted with delight, but Martin, who was in a bad temper, said sharply:

"We must have taken a wrong turning! Let us go back."

"Idiot!" replied Michael, who was hungry too, and, like many people when they are hungry, very cross also. "We set out to travel through the world, and what does it matter if we go to the right or to the left?" And, without another word, took the path to the castle, closely followed by Jack, and after a moment by Martin likewise.

The door of the castle stood open, and they entered a great hall, and looked about them. Not a creature was to be seen, and suddenly Martin – he did not know why – felt a little frightened. He would have left the castle at once, but stopped when Jack boldly walked up to a door in the wall and opened it. He could not for very shame be outdone by his younger brother, and passed behind him into another splendid hall, which was filled from floor to ceiling with great pieces of copper money.

The sight quite dazzled Martin and Michael, who emptied all the provisions that remained out of their bags, and heaped them up instead with handfuls of copper.

Scarcely had they done this when Jack threw open another door, and this time it led to a hall filled with silver. In an instant his brothers had turned their bags upside down, so that the copper money tumbled out on to the floor, and were shovelling in handfuls of the silver instead. They had hardly finished, when Jack opened yet a third door, and all three fell back in amazement, for this room was a mass of gold, so bright that their eyes grew sore as they looked at it. However, they soon recovered from their surprise, and quickly emptied their bags of silver, and filled them with gold instead. When they would hold no more, Martin said:

"We had better hurry off now lest somebody else should come, and we might not know what to do"; and, followed by Michael, he hastily left the castle. Jack lingered behind for a few minutes to put pieces of gold, silver, and copper into his pocket, and to eat the food that his brothers had thrown down in the first room. Then he went after them, and found them lying down to rest in the midst of a forest. It was near sunset, and Martin began to feel hungry, so, when Jack arrived, he bade him return to the castle and bring the bread and cheese that they had left there.

"It is hardly worth doing that," answered Jack; "for I picked up the pieces and ate them myself."

At this reply both brothers were beside themselves with anger, and fell upon the boy, beating him, and calling him names, till they were quite tired.

"Go where you like," cried Martin with a final kick; "but never come near us again." And poor Jack ran weeping into the woods.

The next morning his brothers went home, and bought a beautiful house, where they lived with their mother like great lords.

Jack remained for some hours in hiding, thankful to be safe from his tormentors; but when no one came to trouble him, and his back did not ache so much, he began to think what he had better do. At length he made up his mind to go to the castle and take away as much money with him as would enable him to live in comfort for the rest of his life. This being decided, he sprang up, and set out along the path which led to the castle. As before, the door stood open, and he went on till he had reached the hall of gold, and there he took off his jacket and tied the sleeves together so that it might make a kind of bag. He then began to pour in the gold by handfuls, when, all at once, a noise like thunder shook the castle. This was followed by a voice, hoarse as that of a bull, which cried:

"I smell the smell of a man." And two giants entered.

"So, little worm! It is you who steal our treasures!" exclaimed the biggest. "Well, we have got you now, and we will cook you for supper!" But here the other giant drew him aside, and for a moment or two they whispered together. At length the first giant spoke:

"To please my friend I will spare your life on condition that, for the future, you shall guard our treasures. If you are hungry take this little table and rap on it, saying, as you do so: 'The dinner of an emperor!' and you will get as much food as you want."

With a light heart Jack promised all that was asked of him, and for some days enjoyed himself mightily. He had everything he could wish for, and did nothing from morning till night; but by-and-by he began to get very tired of it all.

"Let the giants guard their treasures themselves," he said to himself at last; "I am going away. But I will leave all the gold and silver behind me, and will take nought but you, my good little table."

So, tucking the table under his arm, he started off for the forest, but he did not linger there long, and soon found himself in the fields on the other side. There he saw an old man, who begged Jack to give him something to eat.

"You could not have asked a better person," answered Jack cheerfully. And signing to him to sit down with him under a tree, he set the table in front of them, and struck it three times, crying:

"The dinner of an emperor!" He had hardly uttered the words when fish and meat of all kinds appeared on it!

"That is a clever trick of yours," said the old man, when he had eaten as much as he wanted. "Give it to me in exchange for a treasure I have which is still better. Do you see this cornet? Well, you have only to tell it that you wish for an army, and you will have as many soldiers as you require."

Now, since he had been left to himself, Jack had grown ambitious, so, after a moment's hesitation, he took the cornet and gave the table in exchange. The old man bade him farewell, and set off down one path, while Jack chose another, and for a long time he was quite pleased with his new possession. Then, as he felt hungry, he wished for his table back again, as no house was in sight, and he wanted some supper badly. All at once he remembered his cornet, and a wicked thought entered his mind.

"Two hundred hussars, forward!" cried he. And the neighing of horses and the clanking of swords were heard close at hand. The officer who rode at their head approached Jack, and politely enquired what he wished them to do.

"A mile or two along that road," answered Jack, "you will find an old man carrying a table. Take the table from him and bring it to me."

The officer saluted and went back to his men, who started at a gallop to do Jack's bidding.

In ten minutes they had returned, bearing the table with them.

"That is all, thank you," said Jack; and the soldiers disappeared inside the cornet.

Oh, what a good supper Jack had that night, quite forgetting that he owed it to a mean trick. The next day he breakfasted early, and then walked on towards the nearest town. On the way thither he met another old man, who begged for something to eat.

"Certainly, you shall have something to eat," replied Jack. And, placing the table on the ground he cried:

"The dinner of an emperor!" when all sorts of food dishes appeared. At first the old man ate quite greedily, and said nothing; but, after his hunger was satisfied, he turned to Jack and said:

"That is a very clever trick of yours. Give the table to me and you shall have something still better."

"I don't believe that there is anything better," answered Jack.

"Yes, there is. Here is my bag; it will give you as many castles as you can possibly want."

Jack thought for a moment; then he replied: "Very well, I will exchange with you." And passing the table to the old man, he hung the bag over his arm.

Five minutes later he summoned five hundred lancers out of the cornet and bade them go after the old man and fetch back the table.

Now that by his cunning he had obtained possession of the three magic objects, he resolved to return to his native place. Smearing his face with dirt, and tearing his clothes so as to look like a beggar, he stopped the passersby and, on pretence of seeking money or food, he questioned them about the village gossip. In this manner he learned that his brothers had become great men, much respected in all the country round. When he heard that, he lost no time in going to the door of their fine house and imploring them to give him food and shelter; but the only thing he got was hard words, and a command to beg elsewhere. At length, however, at their mother's entreaty, he was told that he might pass the night in the stable. Here he waited until everybody in the house was sound asleep, when he drew his bag from under his cloak, and desired that a castle might appear in that place; and the cornet gave him soldiers to guard the castle, while the table furnished him with a good supper. In the morning, he caused it all to vanish, and when his brothers entered the stable they found him lying on the straw.

Jack remained here for many days, doing nothing, and – as far as anybody knew – eating nothing. This conduct puzzled his brothers greatly, and they put such constant questions to him, that at length he told them the secret of the table, and even gave a dinner to them, which far outdid any they had ever seen or heard of. But though they had solemnly promised to reveal nothing, somehow or other the tale leaked out, and before long reached the ears of the king himself. That very evening his chamberlain arrived at Jack's dwelling, with a request from the king that he might borrow the table for three days.

"Very well," answered Jack, "you can take it back with you. But tell His Majesty that if he does not return it at the end of the three days I will make war upon him."

So the chamberlain carried away the table and took it straight to the king, telling him at the same time of Jack's threat, at which they both laughed till their sides ached.

Now the king was so delighted with the table, and the dinners it gave him, that when the three days were over he could not make up his mind to part with it. Instead, he sent for his carpenter, and bade him copy it exactly, and when it was done he told his chamberlain to return it to Jack with his best thanks. It happened to be dinner time, and Jack invited the chamberlain, who knew nothing of the trick, to stay and dine with him. The good man, who had eaten several excellent meals provided by the table in the last three days, accepted the invitation with pleasure, even though he was to dine in a stable, and sat down on the straw beside Jack.

"The dinner of an emperor!" cried Jack. But not even a morsel of cheese made its appearance.

"The dinner of an emperor!" shouted Jack in a voice of thunder. Then the truth dawned on him; and, crushing the table between his hands, he turned to the chamberlain, who, bewildered and half-frightened, was wondering how to get away.

"Tell your false king that tomorrow I will destroy his castle as easily as I have broken this table."

The chamberlain hastened back to the palace, and gave the king Jack's message, at which he laughed more than before, and called all his courtiers to hear the story. But they were not quite so merry when they woke next morning and beheld ten thousand horsemen, and as many archers, surrounding the palace. The king saw it was useless to hold out, and he took the white flag of truce in one hand, and the real table in the other, and set out to look for Jack.

"I committed a crime," said he; "but I will do my best to make up for it. Here is your table, which I own with shame that I tried to steal, and you shall have besides my daughter as your wife!"

There was no need to delay the marriage when the table was able to furnish the most splendid banquet that ever was seen, and after everyone had eaten and drunk as much as they wanted, Jack took his bag and commanded a castle filled with all sorts of treasures to arise in the park for himself and his bride.

At this proof of his power the king's heart died within him.

"Your magic is greater than mine," he said, "and you are young and strong, while I am old and tired. Take, therefore, the sceptre from my hand, and my crown from my head, and rule my people better than I have done."

So at last Jack's ambition was satisfied. He could not hope to be more than king, and as long as he had his cornet to provide him with soldiers he was secure against his enemies. He never forgave his brothers for the way they had treated him, though he presented his mother with a beautiful castle, and everything she could possibly wish for. In the centre of his own palace was a treasure chamber, and in this chamber the table, the cornet, and the bag were kept as the most prized of all his possessions, and not a week passed without a visit from King John to make sure they were safe. He reigned long and well, and died a very old man, beloved by his people. But his good example was not followed by his sons and his grandsons. They grew so proud that they were ashamed to think that the founder of their race had once been a poor boy; and as they and all the world could not fail to remember it, as long as the table, the cornet and the bag were shown in the treasure chamber, one king, more foolish than the rest, thrust them into a dark and damp cellar.

For some time the kingdom remained, though it became weaker and weaker every year that passed. Then, one day, a rumour reached the king that a large army was marching against him. Vaguely he recollected some tales he had heard about a magic cornet which could provide as many soldiers as would serve to conquer the earth, and which had been removed by his grandfather to a cellar. Thither he hastened that he might renew his power once more, and in that black and slimy spot he found the treasures indeed. But the table fell to pieces as he touched it, in the cornet there remained only a few fragments of leathern belts which the rats had gnawed, and in the bag nothing but broken bits of stone.

And the king bowed his head to the doom that awaited him, and in his heart cursed the ruin wrought by the pride and foolishness of himself and his forefathers.

The Blue Belt

A BEGGAR WOMAN AND HER SON were walking along through the country, and they came to a crossroad, and there, right in the dust of the road, lay a handsome belt of blue leather. The lad asked his mother's leave to pick it up and wear it.

"Let it alone," said the woman crossly. "For all we know, there may be some magic about it. Indeed, I am almost sure there is, for I don't like the looks of it."

The lad begged and pleaded to be allowed to pick it up, but the old woman would not hear of it, and so in the end he was obliged to go on without it. But all the same, as they trudged along, he kept thinking and thinking about the belt, and the farther they went the more he wished he had it.

After a while they came to where the road led through a forest, and the lad made some excuse to step aside for a moment. He slipped along from one tree to another until he was out of his mother's sight; and then he ran back to where the blue belt was lying. He picked it up and buckled it around him under his shirt where it could not be seen.

No sooner had he done this, than he felt as though the strength of ten men had passed into him. It seemed to him as though he could tear up trees by the roots if he chose, or carry a mountain on his shoulders and think nothing of it.

When he came back, his mother was in a fine rage. "I ought to beat you for keeping me waiting all this time," she cried, "and I would do it, too, if I were not so tired. Wherever we're to sleep I'm sure I don't know, for it's too late now to get on to the next village."

The boy answered nothing, but he trudged along at his mother's side, and all the while he was feeling stronger and stronger.

After a while the old woman said she was tired, and she would have to sit down and rest a bit.

The lad asked leave to go to the top of a cliff close by, so as to look about and see whether he could not see a house somewhere near.

"Go if you choose," said his mother, "but if you stay away as you did before, I'll give you a good beating when you get back, however tired I am."

The lad ran quickly to the top of the cliff and looked about him, and there, sure enough, off towards the north, he saw the light of a house, and it was not so very far away, either.

He ran down and told his mother what he had seen. "Mother, let us go there and ask for a bite to eat, for if we don't, we'll have to go hungry till tomorrow," he cried. "And maybe the people who live there will let us spend the night there, too."

The mother began to groan and lament. "Never in the world could I climb up that cliff and over," said she. "I'm so tired I can scarce put one foot before the other, and that's the truth of the matter."

"Never bemoan yourself about that," cried the lad, "for I'll carry you over"; and so saying, he caught her up as though she weighed no more than a feather, and ran up the cliff and over, and down on the other side with her; and when he put her down he was not even breathing fast from carrying her.

"You've grown to be a strong, stout lad, and there's no doubt about that," said his mother.

After that they went along again until they came to the house with the light in it, and when they got up close to it, the mother began to shake and tremble.

"Come away! Come away!" said she. "This is a Troll's house, and it would be a bad thing for us if he were to get hold of us."

But the lad was not one whit afraid. He knocked at the door, and then, before anyone could answer the knock, he opened the door and stepped inside, dragging his mother with him.

There, on a great settle by the fire, sat a man at least twenty feet high, and it was easy enough to tell by the look of him that he was a Troll.

The mother almost fainted with terror, but the lad spoke up as bold as bold could be, for he felt the strength inside of him and feared nobody. He told the Troll that he and his mother were footsore and weary, and he asked whether they might come in and rest a bit.

The Troll told him he and his mother were welcome, and then he made the lad sit down and they talked of one thing and another, but the woman was so frightened she just crept into a corner and groaned every time the Troll looked at her.

After a while the lad asked the Troll whether he could not give him and his mother a bite of supper, for they were hungry as well as weary.

Yes, the Troll could do that, too.

He went outside and came back with a whole load of wood in his arms, as much as two horses could haul. This he threw upon the fire and stirred it up into a blaze.

And now the woman began to shake and shiver as though she would fall to pieces, for she thought for sure the Troll was making ready to cook her and her son for supper; but instead he brought in a whole ox and put it over the fire to roast. When it was done, he took out a great silver platter from the cupboard, and the platter was so large that when he put the ox on it, not any part of the ox hung over the edge. He also set out on the table knives and forks, each six feet long, and a great hogshead for a drinking cup.

When all this was done, he said to the lad, "Draw up and eat and drink as you are able."

The lad bade his mother come, too, but she would not, so he took up the knife and fork with no trouble at all to himself and cut a slice from the ox and carried it to her. After she had eaten, he lifted the hogshead down from the table, and then he carried her over to it and lowered her down into it so she could drink.

He himself, after he had eaten, climbed to the edge of the hogshead and hung himself over into it head downward, and drank till he was satisfied. After a while the Troll said he might as well have a bite of supper himself. So he went to the table and ate all that was left of the ox – the meat and the bones and the horns and hoofs of it – and drained off all that was in the hogshead at one draught.

Not long afterward it was time to go to bed, and the Troll did not know how to manage that.

"There's only the bed I sleep in, and a cradle," said the Troll.

But when the lad came to look at the cradle, it was as long and wide as any bed he had ever seen.

"This will do for me," said he.

So it was settled that he should sleep in the cradle and his mother in the bed, though it was so enormous that she shook and shivered at the very thought of getting into it, and if she had had her choice, she would have stayed all night in the corner.

After they were all settled, the lad thought to himself, "I'd best stay awake and listen how things go on through the night, for there's no knowing what this Troll may intend to do to us before morning." But he lay there very quiet and kept his eyes shut, and now and then he snored a bit, so the Troll thought he was asleep.

Presently the Troll began to talk to the woman. "Do you think that lad of yours is asleep?" he asked of her.

"He must be from the way he's snoring," she answered.

"Then, listen," said the Troll. "It has come into my head that you and I could live here very happily together if we could only get rid of him, for to tell you the truth I have no liking for the way he goes about things."

"I'm sure I don't know how you can do anything with him," said the woman, "for he seems to have grown very strong all of a sudden."

Oh, the Troll had a plan that would do for the lad. The next morning he would ask the woman and her son to stay there with him for a day or so, and she was to agree. Then sometime in the morning he would take the lad out to the quarry with him to get out some cornerstones, and once there, it would be easy enough in one way or another to send him down to the bottom of the quarry, and then roll a rock down on him and crush him.

To this plan the woman consented, and all the while they talked the boy lay there and listened, though he breathed with his mouth open as though he were still sleeping.

The next day the woman got up early and cooked breakfast for them, and after they had all eaten, the Troll said, wouldn't she stay there and keep house for him for a day or so.

"There's nothing to take me elsewhere," answered the woman.

Not long after, the Troll took up a crowbar that he kept over in a corner.

"I'll just go over to the quarry and get out a few cornerstones while you are cooking the dinner," said he. He then asked the lad whether he would go along with him.

"Yes, and gladly," answered the lad; so the two set out together.

They worked for a while at the top of the quarry, and then the Troll told the lad to go down to the bottom of it and see whether there were any loose stones lying around down there.

The lad was willing to do that, too. He went on down towards the bottom of the quarry. No sooner was he gone than the Troll set to work with his crowbar. He worked so hard that he groaned and sweated, and presently he loosened a whole crag and sent it rolling down on the boy.

But the lad saw it coming and was ready for it. He put out his hands and stopped it until he could get out of the way, and then he let it roll on to the bottom. After that he went back to where the Troll was.

"I couldn't find any loose rocks down there so now do you go down and look for some," he said.

The Troll was frightened when he saw the lad had come back to the top of the quarry unharmed. He thought he would certainly have been crushed under the crag that had rolled down on him. Neither did the Troll want to go down there below, but he had to.

Then the lad took up the crowbar and pried out another crag, and it rolled down on the Troll and hurt him so that he could not move, but lay where he was groaning. The boy had to go down and roll the crag off him and pick him up and carry him back to the house, and all the while the Troll kept on groaning most terribly. When they got home, the lad put the Troll to bed and he was hurt so badly he had to lie there.

That night the lad stayed awake again and listened, and presently the Troll and the woman began to talk things over again.

"I tell you he's a dangerous one," said the woman, "and I'm sure I don't see how you're ever to get rid of him."

"I have a brother," said the Troll, "and he has a walled-in garden, and in the garden are twelve fierce lions. If we could find some excuse for getting the lad there, they would very quickly tear him to pieces."

"Then I will find the excuse," said the woman. "Tomorrow I will say that I am very poorly, and that nothing in the world will cure me except a few drops of lions' milk. Then you must tell about the lions in your brother's garden, and I'll beg and entreat him until he'll agree to go off there to get some for me."

This plan pleased the Troll, and it was settled between them that as she said so they would do.

The next morning the woman did not get up to cook the breakfast, but lay in bed, moaning.

"What ails you, mother?" asked the lad.

"Oh, I'm ill. I'm very ill," replied the woman.

"I'm sorry for that," said her son, "but I'm sure I don't know what would make you better."

"If I had but a few drops of lions' milk, that would cure me," groaned the woman.

"That's a hard thing to get," replied the lad; "and if that's the only thing to cure you, I fear you'll be ailing a long time."

Then the Troll spoke up and said he knew where such milk was to be had. "But it takes a brave heart and a strong arm to get it, and that's the truth," said the Troll. He then told about his brother's walled-in garden and the lions that were in it, and he said that if anyone had the courage to go for it, 'twas there the milk was to be had.

The woman at once began to beg and entreat the lad to go and get it for her. He did not say no. "Though," said he, "I think it is but little good the milk will do you, and that's the truth."

The Troll told him exactly where the garden was, and he gave him a key to the gate of it, so he would have no trouble in getting in. The lad took the key and a milking pail, and off he set. The Troll and the woman had no other thought than that was the end of him.

On and on he went, one foot before the other, and after a while he came to the garden, and then he took out the key and unlocked the door and stepped inside.

No sooner had he done this than he saw twelve great lions, each one fiercer and larger than the other, and they came at him ramping and roaring so that he was almost deafened by the noise of it, and their teeth were terrible to see.

But the lad was no whit frightened. He caught hold of the foremost lion, and tore it in two, and scattered it in pieces all about him.

When the other lions saw that, all the fierceness went out of them, and they crawled to his feet, and fawned on him, and became as tame as dogs.

The lad patted them, and then he milked a few drops into the milk pail and started for home with it, but the lions would not be left behind. They followed after him close at his heels, as dogs follow their master.

After a while he came within sight of the Troll's house, and at that very moment the woman happened to be looking out of the window, and there she saw him coming along, with the eleven lions following after him. Then she was terribly frightened, and she called to the Troll, and together they barred all the doors and windows, so the lions could not get in at them.

The lad came to the door and tried to open it, and when he found it was fastened, he called to them to let him in, but they would not until he made the lions lie down outside, and promised they should stay there.

When he went in, there stood his mother shaking and trembling.

"Well, mother, here is the lions' milk," he said, "and I'm sure I hope it may make you well again."

The woman was obliged to drink the milk, though she did not want it.

That night the Troll and she began talking together after they thought the lad was sleeping. But he was wide awake and heard all they said between them, though they spoke in whispers.

"This son of yours is so strong I don't see how we're ever to get rid of him," said the Troll.

"Well, if you don't know, I'm sure I don't," replied the woman.

"There's one other plan we might try," said the Troll. "I have two more brothers who live not so very far away from here in a castle, and they are very strong and terrible. Round about the castle is an orchard that bears apples all the year round, and anyone who so much as tastes of those apples at once falls into a deep sleep, and nothing can waken him till he has had his sleep out, and the sleep lasts for three days and three nights. If we could but send the lad there after the apples, he would be sure to eat of them, and fall asleep, and then my brothers would find him there and tear him to pieces for they come out every day to walk in the garden and so would be sure to find him."

"If that is the way of it, we've no need to worry," said the woman, "for I'll find a way to send him there."

The next day the woman said she still was not able to get up. She lay there in the bed, moaning and groaning.

"I'm sorry to see you so ailing, mother, but I'm sure I don't know what to do about it."

"If I but had some apples from the orchard that belongs to the Troll's brothers, I'd be well enough," said the woman, "and if you were but the good son you pretend to be, I know you'd fetch them for me."

"I'll fetch you the apples soon enough," replied her son. "No trouble about that. Though to tell you the truth, I doubt whether they'll cure you."

The lad made no more ado about it, but off he set for the orchard, and the eleven lions followed close at his heels.

When he came to where the apple trees were, he climbed up into the one that bore the finest fruit, and ate and ate until he could eat no more. Then he came down and stretched himself out on the soft grass and fell into a deep sleep.

The eleven lions gathered about him and guarded him while he slept.

Now not long after this, the Troll's two brothers came out into the orchard for a stroll, and there, the first thing they saw, was the lad lying under the finest of the apple trees fast asleep, with the apples lying all about him and one in his hand.

At that sight they flew into a fine rage, and they turned themselves into fierce man-eating steeds, and rushed at him to destroy him.

But before they had a chance even so much as to touch him, the eleven lions rose up and rushed at the two steeds and fought them, and tore them into small pieces and scattered them around like dung.

At the end of three days and three nights, the lad awoke and looked about him, and there were the lions still guarding him, but the ground was all dug up as though a battle had been fought there, and there were deep hoof marks, and pieces of the steeds were scattered all about the orchard. The lad looked and wondered, and he could not think what had been happening, but he was not a bit afraid, and he thought as long as he was there, he might as well go and have a look at the castle.

When he drew near to it, he saw a most beautiful maiden looking out from one of the windows, and at the sight of her the lad's heart melted within him for love of her, she was so beautiful.

"It is lucky for you that you had your lions with you just now," said the maiden.

"Why is that?" asked the lad.

Then the maiden told him how the Trolls had gone out into the orchard a bit ago, when he was asleep under the apple tree, and how they had changed themselves into man-eating steeds and come at him to destroy him, and how the lions had then risen up and torn the Trolls to pieces.

The lad listened to her until she had made an end of the story, and then he said, "That is as it should be, and it was to guard me that I brought them hither." Then he asked the maiden whether he might come in, and at first she would not let him, because she was afraid of the lions, but when he promised they should not harm her, but would lie down at the threshold as quiet as house cats, she opened the door to him.

The lad looked about him, and it seemed to him the castle was but a rough place for such a beauty to live in.

"I wonder," said he, "that such a one as you should be living here with no better company than those two Trolls were."

"It is not of my own will I am living here," replied the maiden. Then she told him she was the daughter of the King of Arabia, and that she had been walking in her father's garden one day, and the Trolls had appeared out of a forest nearby, and carried her away with them, and she had been well-nigh scared out of her wits by it. But they had done her no harm, though they had kept her a prisoner here, and they intended that after a while one or other of them should take her as a wife. Then she asked the lad who he was, and where he had come from, and he told her all about it.

"You may be the son of a beggar, but all the same it seems to me you are something of a hero," said the Princess, "and now we will see whether I am right about it."

Then she led him into another room and showed him where two great swords were hanging on the wall.

"Those are the Trolls' swords," said the Princess, "and they are very heavy to handle. Now try whether you can lift one of them down from the wall, though I doubt whether you are strong enough."

"That is an easy task you are setting me," said the lad. He took a chair and set it on a table, and another chair on top of that; and then he climbed up on them, for the swords were so high on the wall that only in that way could he reach the place where they were hanging. Then he reached out and set one finger under the point of one of the swords, and tossed it up in the air and caught it, and he leaped down and flourished the sword about him, so that it whistled.

"Yes, I can see that you are indeed a hero," said the Princess; "so now tell me: shall I go home to my father, the King of Arabia, or shall I stay here and be your wife?"

It did not take the lad long to make his choice in that matter.

"You shall stay here and be my wife," said he, "for indeed I love you so dearly that if I cannot marry you, then I shall never marry anyone."

So the Princess stayed on in the castle, and she and the lad were very happy together.

But after some time had passed, the Princess said she ought to go back and see her father, for he did not know what had become of her, and no doubt he had grieved bitterly, thinking she was dead.

This reminded the lad that he had promised to take back the apples to his mother, and it was agreed between them that she should go back to Arabia, and that he should take the apples to his mother, and that then he should come after her to her father's kingdom and claim her.

So the next day they set out, and the Princess went to the nearest seaport, and hired a vessel with some of the jewels she wore, and sailed back to Arabia. But the lad set out for the Troll's house with the bosom of his shirt full of apples, and the lions following close at his heels.

When he came near the Troll's house, his mother was looking out of the window, and no sooner did she see him than she began to shake and shiver.

"There is my son back again," said she, "and indeed I feel terribly frightened."

"He's a strong one, and that's the truth," said the Troll, "and I wish we could find out what makes him so, for it's not in nature for anyone to be as strong as he is."

"Perhaps there is indeed some secret about it," said the woman, "and if there is, I may be able in some way to wheedle it out of him. At least I can do no better then try."

So she made haste to open the door and welcome the lad back to his home again, but the lions had to stay outside, because both she and the Troll were afraid of them.

"And did you get the apples?" she asked of him.

Yes, he had the apples. "And I hope they'll cure you, mother," said he, "though I think you have little need of them, for I never saw you looking better."

"Oh I'm still very ailing," said she, "and I'll eat the apples after a bit; but first do you sit down and have a bite of the good supper I've cooked for you."

So the lad sat down, and the mother gave him his supper, and while he ate it, she sat beside him and talked to him.

"You're a strong one," said she, "and there's no doubt about that."

"Strong enough," replied her son, still eating.

"And how did it all come about?" asked the woman. "For only a while ago you were a weakling, and it was I who had to help you over the rough places."

"Now I'll tell you," said the lad, for he was sleepy from eating so much supper and scarce knew what he was saying. "It's all because of that blue belt that we saw at the crossroads and that I wanted to pick up, and you forbade me."

Then he told his mother the whole story, and the woman sat and listened, and the Troll listened, too, only he was hidden behind a door and the lad did not see him.

"And that's the way the strength came to me," said the lad, when he had made an end of the telling.

"And have you the belt on you now?" asked the woman.

"Yes, I have," said the lad, and he opened his shirt and showed it to her.

Then, before he could stop her, the woman caught hold of the belt and tore it from him, and at once all his strength went out of him, so that he was helpless before her.

Then the Troll came from behind the door, and he and the woman made merry together because the lad was so helpless, and they talked together about what they should do with the lad to get rid of him. The woman was for taking him out to a high cliff and throwing him over, but the Troll said no, that was not bad enough for him. In the end the Troll put out the lad's eyes, and set him adrift in a boat on the sea, and he and the woman thought that was the end of him.

But it was not, for the lions were faithful, and they had followed after, and when they saw the boat drifting away, they swam after it and caught the edge of the boat with their teeth, and brought it ashore on an island.

There they and the lad lived, and the lions took care of him, for the lad was helpless because he was blind. The lions found a cave for him to live in and caught birds and wild animals for him to eat, and the lad picked the feathers off the birds, and took the skins of the animals, and made a soft bed for himself, and always, while some of the lions were out hunting, others stayed with him to guard him and see that no harm came to him.

One day the oldest lion went out hunting, and he went a long way before he found anything. Then, after a while, he startled up a hare, and it was blind. The lion chased the hare, and it went leaping along, and presently, because it was blind, it fell into a pool of water. As soon as the water touched its eyes, it could see again, and it scrambled out from the pool and escaped the lion.

The lion went back to where the lad was sitting in his cave, and took hold of his clothes, and began to pull at them. The lad did not know what the lion wanted of him, but he got up and allowed the lion to lead him. It led him on and on, until they came to the edge of the pool, and then the lion loosed his clothing and gave the lad such a push that he fell head over heels into the water. No sooner did the water touch his eyes than the blindness was all gone, and he could see again even better than before.

Then the lad rejoiced greatly, and he got into the boat and went back to the place where the Troll lived, and the lions swam after.

After he landed, he crept up towards the house very carefully, so that no one saw him, and peeped in at the door. The woman was busy at the dough-trough making up bread, and her back was towards him, and there was the blue belt hanging from a nail in the wall.

The lad crept in and seized it and put it around him, and then he began to shout and stamp about, and call to the woman and the Troll to come and catch hold of him.

The woman turned about, and when she saw the lad was there and the belt gone from the wall, she knew what had happened. She was terribly frightened, and began to coax and cajole him, and beg him to let her have the belt again.

But the lad would not listen to her. He threw open the door and called in the lions, and they soon made an end of her. Then they ran out and found the Troll, too, and tore him to pieces in spite of all his cries and prayers for mercy.

That was the end of them, and after that the lad was ready to set out for Arabia to claim the Princess as his wife, but he would not let the lions go with him for there was no need for them in that business.

The lad journeyed on and on, and after a while he came to Arabia, and there he heard a story of how the daughter of the King of that country had been stolen away by Trolls, and kept a prisoner for a long time but now she was home, and the King was so glad to have her back he said he would never let her leave him again. He had hidden her away, no one knew where, and when anyone came to ask her hand in marriage the King said no one might have her but he who could find her, and if anyone tried to find her and failed, he should have his head cut off.

Many kings and princes had lost their lives in this manner.

The lad listened and listened to everything that was said, and he thought to himself that he would be the next to have a try at finding the Princess, but he said nothing about it to anyone.

One day the lad met a man who was selling white bearskins, and the lad stopped him and began talking to him. "I will tell you what we will do," said he. "I will put on one of those bearskins, and then do you fasten a collar around my neck and lead me through the town by a chain, and I will dance and perform tricks."

This plan pleased the man, and he readily agreed to it; so the lad put on the bearskin, and the man led him about by a chain, and everywhere the lad danced and performed in such a wonderful way that the people were amazed.

After a while it came to the King's ears that such a beast was in the town, and that not only could it dance and perform tricks, but it could understand everything that was said to it.

The King became very curious to see the animal, and he sent word for the man to come to the palace and bring the bear with him.

The man at once set out for the palace, and on the way he said to the lad, "Now you must do your best, for if you can succeed in pleasing the King, he will be sure to pay us well."

"Yes," said the lad, "but when we come to the palace, you must warn everybody that they are not to laugh at me, for if the people there laugh at me, I may become so enraged that I will tear them to pieces before I know what I am doing."

So as soon as the man came to the palace, he said that no one was to laugh at the bear, whatever happened, and the King promised that no one should.

Then the lad began to perform his tricks, but in the very midst of things one of the maids began to laugh, and at once the pretended bear flew at her and tore her to pieces before anyone could stop him.

The man was terrified, but the King said, "It does not matter; she was only a maid, after all."

After that the King said the man and the bear must spend the night at the castle. The man might sleep in the kitchen, but the bear should stay in the little room that opened out from the King's own chamber. The man had nothing to sleep on but hard boards, but the bear was given a bed made of feathers and soft cushions to lay his head on.

That night, when all the palace was still, and no one awake to see him, the King came to the room where the pretended bear was lying, and roused him and bade him come with him, for the King had a mind to show the bear to his daughter, and have her see the tricks and the dancing.

The King led the pretended bear upstairs and downstairs, and through cellars and long galleries and around corners, and all the while the lad kept his eyes open, and watched carefully just where they were going, so that he might know how to come the next time.

After a while, the King still leading him, they came out on a long pier with the water washing about it. Here the King pulled and pushed at different posts and wooden pegs, and all the while the lad watched him carefully. Presently a little house came floating, floating across the water until it lay close up against the pier, and then the King took out a bunch of keys and unlocked the door and led the bear inside, and there, in a little golden room, sat the beautiful Princess.

The Princess started up when the King entered, and when she saw the bear she cried aloud with terror. But the King bade her not to fear it, for it was a trained bear, and there was no danger from it unless someone laughed at it.

The Princess promised she would not laugh, and then the King bade the bear perform its tricks. All went well until the Princess's waiting-maid quite forgot the warning the King had given, and began to laugh. At once the pretended bear flew at her and tore her in pieces.

The Princess screamed, but the King said, "Why should you be troubled? It was her own fault, for I warned her. Besides, she was nothing but a waiting-maid."

Then he said he would leave the bear there until morning, for he had no mind to lead it back through all those galleries and cellars and windings at that time of night.

The Princess was very unwilling to have the beast left there, and so she told the King, but while she and her father were talking, the bear curled down in the corner and pretended to go to sleep. So then the Princess agreed that it might stay there, but she made the King promise to come back and get it the first thing in the morning.

Then the King went away, locking the door behind him, and as soon as he had gone, the bear rose up and came over to the Princess, and begged her to undo his collar. The Princess was like to die of terror at this, but the bear spoke so gently and pleaded with her so piteously that at last she took courage and felt in among his fur and unfastened the collar.

At once the lad threw off the bearskin, and there the Princess saw her own dear husband standing before her. Then there was great joy between them, and the lad told the Princess all that had happened to him since they had parted, and they spent the night together very happily.

But at earliest dawn the lad put on the bearskin again, and made the Princess fasten the collar, for so he would have it, and when the King came again, there was the bear still slumbering in his corner, and the Princess asleep among her pillows.

The King took hold of the chain that was fastened to the bear's collar, and made it get up and follow, and he led it out of the house to the pier. Then he pulled and pushed at the posts and pivots, and the little house floated away across the water, to some place where no one could see it. After that the King led the bear back to its master, and gave the man a handful of gold as a reward, and bade him be off with it.

As soon as the man and the lad were back where they lived, the lad made him undo the collar, and he took off the bearskin. Then it was not long before he was back at the palace and asking to see the King, for he said he had come there to have a hunt for the Princess.

When the King saw the lad he had pity on him because he was so young and handsome.

"This is a very foolish thing that you would do," said he. "Do you not know how many kings and nobles have lost their lives in searching for the Princess? Why should you wish to perish also?"

But the lad would not listen to him. Hunt for the Princess he must and would.

"Very well", said the King at last. "Since your heart is set on it, you must go your own way, but remember you will be allowed only twenty-four hours in which to find her."

Very well! That suited the lad well enough.

Now there were many pretty girls in the palace, and music and dancing, and the lad joined in and danced and laughed with the best of them. He amused himself all day, and at last only one hour was left of all the twenty-four in which he was to search for the Princess.

"There!" said the King. "Now you have danced your life away, and it is time for the headsman."

"Not so," said the lad, "for I have still one hour left, and now I will go and look for the Princess."

With that he set out, and the King and the court were obliged to follow. The lad went upstairs and downstairs, through cellars and along galleries, along the way the King had led him the night before, and all the while the King kept saying, "This is not the way to go. You are all wrong, and you will never find her this way."

When they came out on the pier, the lad began pulling and pushing at posts and pivots, and the King did not dare to stop him.

Presently the little house came floating up to the pier, and there were only two minutes left of all the twenty-four hours.

"And now unlock the door," cried the lad, "for within here sits the Princess."

The King took out his keys, and he fumbled and fumbled, and then he said he had no key there to unlock it.

"Then if you have not, I have," said the lad, and he raised his fist and with one blow the door was shattered and burst open, and he stepped inside – and there was the Princess.

Then she rose up and threw her arms about him and kissed him, and she told her father the lad was her own true love who had saved her from the Trolls and had come all this way to find her, and how if she might not have him for her husband, she would pine away with grief and longing.

When the King heard this, he could no longer refuse to let her marry the lad, and indeed he was well enough pleased to have such a clever fellow for a son-in-law, for the lad soon told him of the trick he had played upon him.

So he and the Princess were married and with much rejoicing, and the lad sent back to the Troll's house for the lions that had been waiting for him there all this time. And when they came, they were given a whole park to roam about in, and the lad and the Princess lived happy for ever after, with no misfortunes to trouble them.

The Feast of the Dwarfs

NOT VERY FAR FROM DRONTHEIM, in Norway, dwelt a powerful man, blessed with all the gifts of fortune. A considerable portion of the land around belonged to him; numerous herds grazed in his pastures, and a numerous establishment of domestics contributed to the grandeur of his dwelling. He had an only daughter called Aslog, whose beauty was celebrated far and near. The most illustrious of her countrymen sought to obtain her hand, but without success; and those who arrived gay and full of hope rode away in silence and with heavy hearts. Her father, who thought that his daughter's rejection of so many suitors proceeded from her anxiety to make a prudent choice, did not interfere, and rejoiced to think that she was so discreet. At length, however, when he perceived that the noblest and the most wealthy of the land were rejected equally with all others, he grew angry, and thus addressed her: –

"Hitherto I have left you at full liberty to make your own selection; but, as I observe that you reject all indiscriminately, and that the most eligible suitors are yet in your opinion not good enough for you, I shall no longer permit such conduct. Is my race, then, to be extinguished, and are my possessions to fall into the hands of strangers? I am resolved to bend your stubborn will. I give you time for consideration until the great winter nights' festival; if you shall not then have made your election, be prepared to accept him whom I determine upon for you."

Aslog loved a handsome, brave and noble youth, whose name was Orm. She loved him with her whole soul, and would have preferred death to giving her hand to anyone but him. But Orm was poor, and his poverty compelled him to take service in her father's house. Aslog's love for him was therefore kept secret, for her haughty father would never have consented to an alliance with a man in so subordinate a position. When Aslog beheld his stern aspect and heard his angry words, she became deathly pale, for she knew his disposition, and was well aware that he would put his threat in action. Without offering a word in reply, she withdrew to her chamber, there to consider how to escape the storm that menaced her.

The great festival drew near, and her anxiety increased daily.

At length the lovers resolved to fly. "I know a hiding place," said Orm, "where we can remain undiscovered till we find an opportunity of quitting the country."

During the night, whilst all were asleep, Orm conducted the trembling Aslog across the snow and fields of ice to the mountains. The moon and stars, which always seem brightest in the cold winter's night, lighted them on their way. They had brought with them some clothes and furs, but that was all they could carry.

They climbed the mountains the whole night long, till they arrived at a solitary spot completely encircled by rock. Here Orm led the weary Aslog into a cave, the dark and narrow entrance to which was scarcely perceptible; it soon widened, however, into a spacious chamber that penetrated far into the mountain. Orm kindled a fire and they sat beside it, leaning against the rock, shut out from the rest of the world.

Orm was the first who had discovered this cavern, which is now shown as a curiosity; and, as at that time no one knew of its existence, they were secure from the pursuit of Aslog's father. Here they passed the winter. Orm went out to chase the wild animals of the lonely region, and Aslog remained in the cave, attended to the fire, and prepared their necessary food. She frequently climbed to the summit of the rock, but far as her eye could reach, it beheld only the sparkling snow-fields.

Spring arrived, the woods became green, the fields arrayed themselves in bright colours, and Aslog dared now only seldom, and with great precaution, to emerge from her cavern.

One evening Orm returned home bringing news that he had recognized, at a distance, her father's people, and that they had no doubt also descried him, as they could see as clearly as himself. "They will surround this place," continued he, "and not rest till they have found us; we must therefore instantly be off."

They immediately descended the mountain on the other side, and reached the seashore, where they fortunately found a boat. Orm pushed off, and the boat was driven into the open sea. They had, it is true, escaped their pursuers, but they were now exposed to perils of another kind. Whither should they turn? They dared not land, for Aslog's father was lord of the whole coast, and they would so fall into his hands. Nothing remained, therefore, for them, but to commit the boat to the winds and waves, which pursued its way all night, so that at daybreak the coast had disappeared, and they saw only sky and water; they had not brought any provisions with them, and hunger and thirst began to torture them. Thus they drove on for three days, and Aslog, weak and exhausted, foresaw their certain destruction.

At length, on the evening of the third day, they beheld an island of considerable size, surrounded by a multitude of lesser islets. Orm immediately steered towards it, but, as they approached it, a gale arose and the waves swelled higher and higher; he turned the boat in hopes to be able to land on some other side, but equally without success. Whenever the bark approached the island, it was driven back as if by some invisible force.

Orm, gazing on the unhappy Aslog, who seemed dying from exhaustion, crossed himself, and uttered an exclamation, which had scarcely passed his lips when the storm ceased, the waves sank, and the little bark landed without further obstruction. He then sprang on shore, and a few mussels which he collected so revived and strengthened the exhausted Aslog that in a short time she also was able to quit the boat.

The island was entirely covered with dwarf mushrooms, and appeared to be uninhabited; but when they had penetrated nearly to the centre of it they perceived a house, half of which only was above the ground, and the other half under it. In the hope that they might find human help, they joyfully approached it; they listened for some sound, but the deepest silence prevailed all around. At length Orm opened the door and entered with his companion; great was their astonishment, however, when they perceived everything prepared as if for inhabitants, but no living being visible. The fire burnt in the hearth in the middle of the room, and a kettle with fish hung over it, waiting, probably, for someone to make a meal of its contents; beds were ready prepared for the reception of sleepers. Orm and Aslog stood for a time doubtful, and looked fearfully about; at length, impelled by hunger, they took the food and ate it. When they had satisfied their hunger, and, by the last rays of the sun, could not discover anyone far and wide, they yielded to fatigue and lay down on the beds, a luxury which they had so long been deprived of.

They had fully expected to be awakened in the night by the return of the owners of the house, but they were deceived in their expectation; throughout the following day, also, no one appeared, and it seemed as if some invisible power had prepared the house for their reception. Thus did they pass the whole summer most happily; it is true they were alone, but the absence of mankind was not felt by them. The eggs of wild fowl and the fish which they caught afforded them sufficient provision.

When autumn approached, Aslog bore a son, and in the midst of their rejoicing at his arrival they were surprised by a wonderful apparition – the door opened suddenly, and an old woman entered; she wore a beautiful blue garment, and in her form and manner was something dignified, and at the same time unusual and strange.

"Let not my sudden appearance alarm you," said she. "I am the owner of this house, and I thank you for having kept it so clean and well, and that I now find everything in such good order. I would willingly have come sooner, but I could not until the little heathen there," – pointing to the infant – "had established himself here. Now I have free access; but do not, I pray you, fetch a priest here from the mainland to baptise him, for then I shall be obliged to go away again. If you fulfil my wish, not only may you remain here, but every good you can desire I will bestow on you; whatever you undertake shall succeed; good fortune shall attend you wherever you go. But if you break this condition, you may assure yourselves that misfortune on misfortune shall visit you, and I will even avenge myself on the child. If you stand in need of anything, or are in danger, you have only to pronounce my name thrice: I will appear and aid you. I am of the race of the ancient giants, and my name is Guru. Beware, however, of pronouncing, in my presence, the name that no giant likes to hear, and never make the sign of the cross, nor cut it in any of the boards in the house. You may live here the year round; only on Yule evening be so kind as to leave the house to me as soon as the sun goes down. Then we celebrate our great festival, the only occasion on which we are permitted to be merry. If, however, you do not like to quit the house, remain as quietly as possible underground, and, as you value your lives, do not look into the room before midnight; after that hour you may again take possession of all."

When the old woman had thus spoken, she disappeared, and Aslog and Orm, thus rendered easy as to their position, lived on without disturbance contented and happy. Orm never cast his net without a good draught – never shot an arrow that did not hit – in short, whatever he undertook, however trifling it might be, prospered visibly.

When Christmas came they made the house as clean as possible, set everything in order, kindled a fire on the hearth, and on the approach of twilight descended to the under part of the house, where they remained quiet and silent. At length it grew dark, and they fancied they heard a rustling and snorting in the air, like that which the swans make in the winter season. In the wall over the hearth was an aperture that could be opened and shut to admit light, or to let out smoke. Orm raised the lid, which was covered with a skin, and put out his head, when a wonderful spectacle presented itself. The little surrounding islets were illuminated by countless little blue lights, which moved incessantly, danced up and down, then slid along the shore, collected together, and approached nearer and nearer to the island in which Orm and Aslog dwelt. When they reached it they arranged themselves in a circle round a great stone, which stood not very far from the shore, and which was well known to Orm. But how great was his astonishment when he saw that the stone had assumed a perfectly human form, although of gigantic stature. He could now clearly distinguish that the lights were carried by dwarfs, whose pale, earth-coloured faces, with large noses and red eyes, in the form of birds' beaks and owls' eyes, surmounted mis-shapen bodies. They waddled and shuffled here and there, and seemed to be sad and gay at the same time. Suddenly the circle opened, the little people drew back on either side, and Guru, who now appeared as large as the stone, approached with giant steps. She threw her arms around the stony figure, which at that moment received life and movement. At the first indication of this, the little people set up, accompanied by extraordinary grimaces and gestures, such a song, or rather howl, that the whole island resounded and shook with the noise. Orm, quite terrified, drew in his head, and he and Aslog now remained in the dark so quiet that they scarcely dared to breathe.

The procession arrived at the house, as was clearly perceived by the nearer approach of the howl. They now all entered. Light and active, the dwarfs skipped over the benches; heavy and dull sounded the steps of the giants among them. Orm and his wife heard them lay out the table and celebrate their feast with the clattering of plates and cries of joy. When the feast was over and midnight was approaching, they began to dance to that magic melody which wraps the soul in sweet bewilderment, and which has been heard by some persons in the valleys and amid the rocks, who have thus learnt the air from subterranean musicians.

No sooner did Aslog hear the melody than she was seized with an indescribable longing to witness the dance. Orm was unable to restrain her. "Let me look," said she, "or my heart will break." She took her infant and placed herself at the furthest extremity of the chamber, where she could see everything without being herself seen. Long did she watch, without turning away her eyes, the dance, and the agile and wonderful steps and leaps of the little beings, who seemed to float in the air and scarcely to touch the ground, whilst the enchanting music of the elves filled her soul.

In the meantime the infant on her arm grew sleepy and breathed heavily, and, without remembering the promise she had made to the old woman, she made the sign of the cross (as is the custom) over the child's mouth, and said, "Christ bless thee, my child!" She had scarcely uttered the words when a fearful piercing cry arose. The sprites rushed headlong out of the house, their lights were extinguished, and in a few minutes they had all left the house. Orm and Aslog, terrified almost to death, hid themselves in the remotest corner of the house. They ventured not to move until daybreak, and not until the sun shone through the hole over the hearth did they find courage to come out of their hiding-place.

The table was still covered as the sprites had left it, with all their precious and wonderfully wrought silver vessels. In the middle of the room stood, on the ground, a high copper vessel half filled with sweet metheglin, and by its side a drinking-horn of pure gold. In the corner lay a stringed instrument, resembling a dulcimer, on which, as it is believed, the female giants play. They gazed with admiration on all, but did not venture to touch anything. Greatly were they startled, however, when, on turning round, they beheld, seated at the table, a monstrous form, which Orm immediately recognized as the giant whom Guru had embraced. It was now a cold hard stone. Whilst they stood looking at it, Guru herself, in her giant form, entered the room. She wept so bitterly that her tears fell on the ground, and it was long before her sobs would allow her utterance; at length she said: –

"Great sorrow have you brought upon me; I must now weep for the remainder of my days. As, however, I know that you did it not from any evil intention, I forgive you, although it would be easy for me to crumble this house over your heads like an eggshell.

"Ah!" exclaimed she, "there sits my husband, whom I loved better than myself, turned for ever into stone, never again to open his eyes. For three hundred years I lived with my father on the island of Kuman, happy in youthful innocence, the fairest amongst the virgins of the giant race. Mighty heroes were rivals for my hand; the sea that surrounds that island is full of fragments of rock which they hurled at each other in fight. Andfind won the victory, and I was betrothed to him. But before our marriage came the abhorred Odin into the country, conquered my father, and drove us off the island. My father and sister fled to the mountains, and my eyes have never since beheld them. Andfind and I escaped to this island, where we lived for a long time in peace, and began to hope that we should never be disturbed. But Destiny, which no one can escape, had decreed otherwise; Oluf came from Britain. They called him the Holy, and Andfind at once discovered that his journey would be fatal to the giant race. When he heard Oluf's ship dashing through the waves, he went to the shore and blew against it with all his strength. The waves rose into mountains. But Oluf was mightier than he; his vessel flew unharmed through the waves, like an arrow from the bow. He steered straight to our island. When the ship was near enough for Andfind to reach it, he grasped the prow with his right hand, and was in the act of sending it to the bottom, as he had often done with other ships. But Oluf, the dreadful Oluf, stepped forward, and crossing his hands, cried out with a loud voice: – 'Stand there, a stone, until the last day!' and in that moment my unhappy husband became a mass of stone. The ship sailed on unhindered towards the mountain, which it severed, and separated from it the little islands that lie around it.

"From that day all my happiness was annihilated, and I have passed my life in loneliness and sorrow. Only on Yule evening can a petrified giant recover life for seven hours, if one of the race embraces him, and is willing to renounce a hundred years of life for this purpose. It is seldom that a giant does this. I loved my husband too tenderly not to recall him to life as often as I could, at whatever cost to myself. I never counted how often I had done it, in order that I might not know when the time would come when I should share his fate, and in the act of embracing him become one with him. But ah! even this consolation is denied me. I can never again awaken him with an embrace, since he has heard the name which I may not utter, and never will he again see the light until the dawn of the last day.

"I am about to quit this place. You will never again behold me. All that is in the house I bestow on you. I reserve only my dulcimer. Let no one presume to set foot on the little surrounding islands. There dwells the little subterranean race, whom I will protect as long as I live."

With these words she vanished. The following spring, Orm carried the golden horn and the silver vessels to Drontheim, where no one knew him. The value of these costly utensils was so great that he was enabled to purchase all that a rich man requires. He loaded his vessel with his purchases, and returned to the island, where he lived for many years in uninterrupted happiness. Aslog's father soon became reconciled to his wealthy son-in-law.

The stone figure remained seated in the house. No one was able to remove it thence. The stone was so hard that axe and hammer were shivered against it, without making the slightest impression on it. There the giant remained till a holy man came to the island, and with one word restored it to its former place, where it still is to be seen.

The copper vessel which the subterranean people left behind them, is preserved as a memorial on the island, which is still called the Island of the Hut.

The Giantess and the Granite Boat

ONCE UPON A TIME, there lived a king and queen who were greatly beloved by all their people. They had only one son, named Sigurd, who, even as a boy, was distinguished for his marvellous skill and dexterity in all manly sports and pastimes, whilst his strength was only equalled by his wisdom and his handsome person.

Years passed on. Sigurd had become a man, when one day the king called him to him.

"My son," he said, "it is now time for you to choose a fitting bride. I am getting old, and cannot expect to live much longer. You must take my place in a few years, and must try to gain men's respect and esteem by showing yourself capable of winning a princess worthy to share your throne. Visit first the country of Hardrada, my friend. His daughter is indeed, I hear, a marvel of beauty and goodness."

Sigurd at once prepared to start on his journey. With a few chosen companions, he set sail in his noble galley, the high prow breasting the waves, and the stern, all gorgeous with carving and gilding, glittering in the sun. After sailing for some days over the tossing waters, the vessel at length reached Hardrada's country. It was night, one of those glorious summer nights of the north, when the moon is almost as brilliant as the sun. The bold shore, with its strange, grotesque crags and peaks, seemed utterly unapproachable, till suddenly a large creek or fiord was seen, at the head of which rose the king's palace. The windows were all ablaze with light, and the sounds of music and revelry told the travellers that some banquet was in progress.

Leaving their ship, Sigurd and his companions proceeded towards the palace, where they received the warmest of welcomes from the king and his daughter Helga. The princess was indeed all she had been pictured, tall and beautiful, and so gentle and charming that Sigurd made up his mind to win her. Next morning he acquainted the king with the object of his journey, and gained his consent. Hardrada was indeed anxious to have a son-in-law to share the cares of his kingdom, which, now that he was an old man, weighed heavily upon him. As a condition of his remaining with Hardrada, Sigurd only stipulated that he should return to his own country directly his father sent for him.

So the marriage of Sigurd the brave with Helga the fair took place with great pomp and rejoicing, thanes and nobles coming from all parts to bring presents to the young people.

Sigurd and his wife loved each other very dearly, and their happiness was completed when, after the lapse of a year, a son was born to them, inheriting the beauty of the mother, and the strength and handsome form of the father. Three happy years thus passed, little

Kurt being two years old, when Sigurd received the news of his father's death and a recall to his native land.

It was a sad parting between Helga and her father; but Sigurd dared not linger, and once more the beautiful Viking ship started on its voyage through the sun-tipped waves, bearing the young king and his wife and child.

For several days the wind was favourable; but when within a day's sail of Sigurd's country the vessel ran into an extraordinary calm. Day after day the sun blazed down fierce and strong; not a breath of air was to be felt. In the forepart of the vessel, the men had all gone below. Sigurd's companions were also asleep, while he and his wife remained on deck, beneath the awning, talking quietly, with little Kurt playing at their feet. After a little, a strange drowsiness seemed to overpower Sigurd himself, and, declaring he could no longer keep awake, he too went below, and fell asleep like the others.

Helga was now quite alone on deck with her boy. Suddenly, as she was playing with him, she saw a strange object moving slowly along the smooth surface of the water. Shading her eyes with her hands, she watched it, and as it came nearer she made out that it was a boat, with a curious, ungainly form seated in it rowing.

Nearer and nearer it came, with silent, swift strokes, and as it touched the vessel with a hard sound the queen saw that it was very large and cut out of granite. With one spring the terrible giantess who had been rowing it was on deck. Like one in a dream, the queen could neither move nor utter a sound to arouse the king or the ship's crew. She seemed held by an invisible power. The giantess came up to her, and, snatching away the child, placed him behind her; then she proceeded to take off all the young queen's beautiful embroidered robes, leaving her only a single linen garment, and as she herself put on Helga's clothes, she gradually also assumed her shape and likeness. Lastly, she seized the queen and placed her in the granite boat, saying as she did so, in a terrible voice –

"Obey my words and my magic spell. Thou must neither rest nor pause on the way, till thou reachest my brother in the lower regions."

The poor queen, half fainting and utterly powerless, sat still and silent in the boat like a statue. With a strong push the giantess sent the boat from the vessel's side, and it was speedily lost to sight. Then little Kurt began to cry. In vain the giantess tried to soothe him; the more she attempted it the worse he became, till at length, losing all patience, she snatched him up and carried him down to the king.

Waking him roughly, she upbraided him loudly for leaving her alone on deck with the child.

"It was most careless and negligent of you," she went on. "Someone ought to have been left on guard while you were asleep. No one can tell what may happen when one is thus left alone. As it is, I found it impossible to quiet the child; I have therefore brought him down here, which is the proper place for him. It is high time you roused your lazy crew. A favourable wind has at last sprung up, and we can have a chance of getting off this wretched ship."

Sigurd was astonished at being addressed by his queen in such terms. In all their married life he had never heard her speak like that. He, however, decided to take no notice of it; she must be overtired with the heat, he thought, and, answering her very gently, he endeavoured to quiet the child. The little fellow, however, sobbed and cried as much as ever.

By this time the crew were aroused, the sails hoisted and, the wind freshening splendidly, they reached land the following day. Here the whole country was still in mourning for the late king. But the people rejoiced greatly when it became known that Sigurd had returned in safety. He was crowned amid universal acclamations, and at once took the reins of government into his hands.

But ever since the strange calm at sea the king's little son had never ceased crying and sobbing, especially in the presence of his supposed mother, while before that time he had been a remarkably happy, affectionate child. The king, therefore, chose a nurse for him from among the people at his court, and when he was with her the little fellow seemed to be once more the bright, happy child he had been.

The king could not, however, understand the change that had come over the queen ever since their journey. She who formerly had always been so good and gentle, was now obstinate, cross and untruthful. And ere long others began to notice the disagreeable, quarrelsome nature of the king's wife.

Now, there were at the court two young men who were so devoted to playing chess that they would sit for hours over their game, instead of joining in the outdoor sports of the other young courtiers. As they were the king's cousins, their room was in the palace, and it happened to be next to that of the queen. She had been particularly rude and disagreeable to them ever since she came, and they would have been glad to revenge themselves upon her in any way.

One day, hearing her moving about and talking angrily, they looked through a slit in the door, and distinctly heard her say –

"When I yawn slightly, I grow small and dainty, like a young maiden; when I give a bigger yawn, I grow into half a giantess; but when I stretch out my arms and yawn with all my might, I return to my original size, and become a mighty giantess."

And as she said these words, she stretched herself, yawned frightfully, as if her jaws would break, and suddenly grew into a monstrous and terrible giantess. Then, stamping her foot, the floor opened, and up came a three-headed giant, bearing a huge trough of raw meat. Greeting the queen as his sister, he placed the trough before her, and she devoured the contents, never resting till she had emptied it.

The two young courtiers watched this strange scene, though they could not hear all that the giantess and her brother said to one another. They were horrified to see how greedily she devoured the raw meat, and amazed at the quantity she ate, for at the king's table she only picked daintily at the dishes. As soon as she had emptied the trough, the three-headed giant disappeared in the same manner as he had come, and the queen, giving a slight yawn, at once assumed her human figure again. The young princes then returned to their game, discussing the mystery in undertones.

And what of the king's little son all this time? One evening, when the nurse had lighted her lamp, and was playing with the child in her arms, some of the boards in the centre of the floor opened, and a most lovely lady, wearing only a single white linen garment, stepped forth. Her waist was encircled by a heavy iron ring, to which was attached a chain, which descended right down through the hole in the floor.

With a soft little cry, she ran up to the nurse, took the little boy in her arms, kissed him and fondled him, and, after lavishing no end of caresses on him, gently placed him back in his nurse's arms and disappeared in the same way as she had come, the floor closing over her again. All this time she never spoke a single word.

The nurse was greatly amazed at the incident, but, startled though she was, she did not say a word to anyone. The next evening the same thing occurred. The white-robed lady came up through the floor, took the child, kissed and caressed him lovingly, and then replaced him in his nurse's arms. But this time, when she prepared to descend, she murmured, in sorrowful tones, "Twice this happiness has been permitted. Once more, and then all will be over."

Then she disappeared, and the floor closed over her as before.

The nurse became greatly alarmed when she heard the white lady say those words. She feared that some danger must threaten the child, and yet she had been much taken with the stranger, who had caressed the boy as if he were her own. She therefore thought it best to speak to the king, tell him what had happened, and beg him to be present at the time when the white-robed lady was wont to appear. The king listened attentively to the woman's story, and, suspecting foul play, promised he would be there.

The following evening, therefore, found him betimes in the nursery, seated in a chair, with his sword drawn, close to the spot where the stranger had always appeared. He had not long to wait. With a faint grating noise the boards opened, and forth stepped the beautiful white-robed figure, with the iron ring round her waist, and the long trailing chain.

In an instant Sigurd recognized in her his own beloved wife, Helga, and quick as lightning he seized her in his arms, and with one stroke of his sword cut the chain that fastened her. Immediately the most terrible groans and rumblings issued from the earth, the whole castle rocked and trembled, and everyone thought that an earthquake was taking place. But in a short time the unearthly sounds ceased without any damage having been done.

Then Helga related to her dear lord all that had befallen her – how the wicked giantess had come to the ship in her granite boat when they were all asleep, and with her magic power had taken away all her clothes and put them on herself.

"When she had placed me in the granite boat, it floated on by itself, until the ship was quite out of sight," she continued, "and then I perceived we were going towards a large dark object, which, as we came near to land, I saw was a huge three-headed giant. He wanted me to marry him, but I steadfastly refused to be his wife, whereupon he chained me up in a big lonely cave, telling me I should never be free unless I consented. Every second day he came, repeating the same request and the same threats. Then, as time went on and I saw no hope of help, I began to think how I could escape his hands. At last I told him that I would be his wife if he would allow me to visit my son on the earth for three days running. At first he would not consent, but when I persisted he gave in; but I had to promise that I would not say who I was. He then placed this iron ring round my waist, to which he attached a chain, the other end being fastened to himself. I hoped that perhaps one evening you might be there when I came to see our little Kurt. How sadly my heart failed me when the second evening passed without my seeing you! But my prayers never ceased, and now my reward has come. The terrible groans when you cut the chain must have been the giant. He would fall when the strain was suddenly taken off the chain, for he lives right under the castle. He probably broke his neck when he fell, and the terrible shock must have been his death throes."

Now the king saw clearly why he could not reconcile the behaviour of the giantess with that of the gentle Helga, his own dear queen. The hideous impostor, who had now reverted to her original form, was summoned before the State Council, and, as additional evidence against her, the two young princes related what they had heard and seen. She was condemned to be stoned to death, and her body was put into a sack and torn to pieces by wild horses.

Then the real queen was invested with all her rightful honours, and soon won the hearts of her people. And little Kurt's nurse was not forgotten. She was married to a great nobleman, the king and queen giving her a rich dowry. She and her husband remained to the end of their days the friends of Sigurd and Helga.

Trouble and Care

FAR, FAR FROM HERE there once lived a king, who had three beautiful daughters. But he had no sons, and therefore he grew so fond of the three princesses that he granted their every wish. But in time the enemy invaded the country, and the king had to go to war. When he set out, the oldest princess begged him to buy her a ring that would prevent her dying as long as she wore it. The second princess asked him for a wreath that would make her happy whenever she looked at it, no matter how sad and troubled her heart might be. "Buy me trouble and care!" said the youngest. And the king promised everything.

When he had driven the enemy out of his own land, and out of the neighbouring land as well, and was about to set out for home, he remembered what he had promised the three princesses. The ring and the wreath were easy enough to obtain; but trouble and care were to be had neither in one place nor in another, for all the people were so happy that the enemy had been driven out that there was no sorrow nor care to be found in the entire kingdom. And since he could not buy it, it was not to be had at all, and he had to travel home without it, loath as he was to do so.

When he was not far from the castle, his way took him through a thick forest. And there sat a squirrel in a tree by the road. "Buy me! Buy me! My name is Trouble and Care!" it said. Thought the king to himself, It is better to have a squirrel than two empty hands, so he brought it along for his youngest daughter. And she was quite as well pleased with her present as her two sisters were with the ring and the wreath. The squirrel played about in her room, sometimes it balanced itself on the bed-posts, at others it would sit on the top of the wardrobe, and it always had a great deal to chatter about.

But as soon as it grew dark, it turned into a man. And he told her how an evil and malicious giantess dwelt in the golden forest, who had turned him into a squirrel because he would not marry her. During the night she had no power over him; but every morning at daybreak he had to slip back into his squirrel form.

And in the course of time the princess actually wanted to marry Trouble and Care; but when they were betrothed, he begged her earnestly, and as best he knew how, never to light a light at night, and try to look at him, "for then both of us would be unhappy," said he. No, said she, she would be quite sure not to do so.

And every evening, when the princess had lain down and blown out the light, she would hear a man go into Trouble and Care's room; but when morning dawned, the squirrel sat on her bed-post and greeted her, and chattered and babbled about all sorts of things.

Once, when she thought Trouble and Care had gone to sleep, she could not help herself; but stood up quietly, lit a light and crept softly into his room and to his bed, and when the ray of light fell on him, she saw that he was far, far handsomer than the most handsome prince. He was so surpassingly handsome that she bent over him in order to see more clearly, and finally she could not help herself, but had to kiss him. And then three drops of wax from the candle fell on his chest, and he awoke.

"But how could you have done this!" he cried, and was quite unhappy. "Had you only waited three days longer, I should have been free!" said he. "But now I must return to the evil giantess and marry her, and all is over between us." "Can I not follow you there?" asked the princess. "No, that is something you could not do in all your days, for if you rest or even so much as bend your knees to sit down, you will go back during the night as far as you came forward during the day," said he. He leaped to the door and disappeared.

Then the princess wept and wailed, and waited for him to return; but she heard and saw nothing more of him. After a few days she grew so restless and wretched that she could no longer remain at home, and implored her maid to go along with her to search for the golden forest. The girl finally allowed herself to be moved; but she would not agree to set out until she had gotten together a yard of drilling, a yard of ticking and a yard of fine linen; and she got them at once, as you may imagine, for there was no shortage of such things in the castle.

So they set out and wandered far, and ever farther, until their feet ached and their spirits fell. Towards evening they came into the middle of a thick, dark forest and climbed up into a high tree. The princess was so tired that the maid had to hold her in her arms while she slept a little. But during the night the ground about the tree grew alive with wolves, in the most sinister fashion, and they howled and cried, so that the princess did not venture to close her eyes another moment. But when daylight appeared in the skies, it seemed as though the wolves had suddenly all been blown away.

The following day they wandered far and ever farther, until their feet ached more and their spirits sank lower. Towards evening they again came to the middle of a thick, dark forest. And they once more climbed into a high, high tree; but the princess was so tired that the maid had to hold her in her arms while she slept a little. When it grew darker, a most alarming number of bears flocked together under the tree, and began to dance and turn in a circle with alarming speed, and all at once they tried to climb the tree. So the princess and her maid had to stand up in the treetop the whole night through, and could not close an eye; but when day came, it seemed as though the bears sank into the earth in a single moment.

The third day they wandered far and ever farther, and then a bit more. Towards evening they again came to a thick, dark forest. There they again climbed into a high, high tree; but no sooner were they up in the tree than the ground beneath the tree and the whole forest was alive with lions, and they all roared and howled together in such a gruesome way that the echoes came back from rock and woodland. Suddenly they began to dance and whirl around in such a terrible fashion that the earth trembled, and in between they would clutch the tree again, and try to shake and loosen it, as though they would pull it out root and branch. The princess and her maid had to stand up in the very treetop, and though they were so tired they could have fallen down from time to time, neither of them dared think of sleeping. But the moment day dawned, the lions all suddenly disappeared from the face of the earth, where they were, walking and standing.

Then they stumbled along, this way and that, the whole day long, until their feet ached harder than hard, and their spirits sank lower than low. They lost path and direction, and though they hunted north and south and east and west, they could not find the way out of the great, dark forest.

At last the princess grew tired and sad beyond all measure, and wanted to sit down every moment, in order to rest a little; but the maid held her and dragged her forward, and never let her bend her knees for a moment to sit down, because then they would have gone back just as far as they had come that day; for you must know that the giantess in the golden forest had so arranged matters.

In the evening they came to an enormous, horrible rock. "I will knock here," said the maid, and tapped and knocked. "O no," said the princess, "please don't knock here, you can see how ugly everything is here!" "Who is knocking there at my door?" cried the giantess in the rock, in a loud, harsh manner, opened the door, and stuck her nose – it was all of a yard long – out through the crack.

"The youngest princess and her maid, they want to get to a prince in the golden forest, whose name is Trouble and Care," was the maid's reply.

"O, faugh!" cried the giantess, "that is so far to the north that one can neither sail nor row there. But what do you want of Trouble and Care? Is this, perhaps, the princess who wanted to marry him?" asked the giantess. Yes, this was the princess. "Well, she will never get him as long as she lives," said the giantess, "for now he must marry the great giantess in the golden forest. You might just as well go back home now as later," said she. No, they would not turn back for anything, and the maid asked whether it would not be possible for her to take them in for the darkest part of the night. "I can take you in easily enough," said the giantess, "but when my husband comes home he will tear off your heads, and eat you up!" But there was no help for it, they could not go on in the middle of the night. Then the maid pulled out the yard of ticking, and gave it to the giantess for linen. "It can't be true! It can't be true!" cried she. "Here I have been married all of a hundred years, and have never yet had any ticking!" And she was so pleased that she invited the wanderers in, received them kindly, and took the best care of them. After a while, when they had strengthened themselves with food and drink, the giantess said to them: "Yes, he is a ferocious fellow, is my husband, and I will have to hide you in the anteroom. Perhaps he will not find you then." And she prepared a bed for them, as soft and comfortable as a bed can be; but they did not care to lie down in it, nor sit in it; no, they could not even close their eyes, for they had to watch to see that their knees did not bend. So they stood the whole night through, and took turns holding each other up, for by now the maid was so weary and wretched that she was ready to give in.

Towards midnight it began to thunder and rumble in a terrible manner. This was the troll coming home; and no sooner had he thrust his first head in at the door than he cried out loudly and harshly: "Faugh! faugh! I smell Christian bodies!" and he rushed about in so wild and furious a manner that the sparks flew. "Yes," said the giantess, "a bird flew past with a bone from a Christian, and he let it drop down the chimney. I threw it out again as quickly as I could, but perhaps one can smell it still." She soothed him again. And he was satisfied with her explanation. But the next morning the giantess told him that the youngest princess and her maid had come in search of a prince named Trouble and Care, in the golden forest. "O faugh! that is so far to the north that one can neither sail nor row there!" the troll at once cried. "It is the princess who wanted to marry him, I know, but she will never get him as long as she lives, for he has to marry the great giantess in three days' time. But the maidens shall not get away from me! Where are they, where are they?" he cried, and sniffed and snuffed about in every corner. "O no, you must not touch them," said the giantess. "They have given me a yard of ticking, and here I have been married now for more than a hundred years, and have never owned any ticking. Therefore you must lend them your seven-mile waistcoat to the nearest neighbour," said the giantess, and pleaded for the girls. And the troll was willing when he heard how kind they had been to his wife.

When they had eaten and were ready to travel, he put his seven-mile waistcoat on them: "And now you must repeat: 'Forward over willow bush and pine-tree, over hill and dale, to the nearest neighbour,'" said he. "And when you get there you must say: 'You are to be hung up this evening where you were put on this morning!'" The maidens did as he said, and were carried for miles, over hill and dale. In the evening, at dusk, they again came to a great, ugly rock. There they pulled off the seven-mile waistcoat and said: "You are to be hung up this evening where you were put on this morning," and then the waistcoat ran home by itself.

"I will knock here," said the maid, and knocked and thumped on the rock. "O no," said the princess, "please do not knock here. You can see how sinister everything is here!" "Who is thumping at my door?" cried the giantess inside the rock, more loudly and harshly than the first one, and she opened the door and thrust her nose, that was all of two yards long, right through the crack. "Here stand the youngest princess and her maid, and they are looking for a prince named Trouble and Care, who lives in the golden forest," answered the maid. And then this giantess also said it was so far north that one could neither sail nor row there, and wanted them to turn back by all means. "You might just as well turn back now as later," said she. But this the maidens did not want to do at all, and the maid asked whether she would not, perhaps, take them in for the night, and if it were only the darkest part of the night. "Yes, I can take you in easily enough," said the giantess, "but when my husband comes home tonight, he will tear off your heads and eat you up!" Then the maid pulled out a yard of drilling, and gave it to the giantess for linen. "It can't be true! It can't be true! Here I have been married now for over two hundred years, and I have never yet had any drilling in the house," cried the giantess, and she was so pleased that she invited them in, and received them kindly, and saw that they wanted for nothing. After a while, when they had strengthened themselves with food and drink, the giantess said: "Yes, he is a ferocious fellow, is my husband, and he eats up every Christian who comes here, root and branch. I'll have to put you in the anteroom, perhaps he will not find you there," and she prepared a bed for the maidens. But they did not dare either to lie down nor sit on it, not for a single moment, for they had to watch to see that they did not bend their knees. So they stood there the whole night through, and took turns holding each other up, while each snatched a little sleep.

Towards midnight it began to rumble and thunder in such a terrible manner that they could feel the earth tremble beneath them. Then the troll came rushing in. "Faugh! faugh! I smell Christian bodies!" he cried out loudly and harshly, and thrashed about in such a furious way that the sparks flew from him as from a fire. "Yes," said the giantess, "a bird flew by, and let a bone from a Christian fall through the chimney. I threw it out again as quickly as I could, but it may well be the case that the smell still lingers," said she, and quieted her husband. And he was satisfied with her explanation. But when he got up in the morning, she told him that the youngest princess and her maid had come in search of a prince named Trouble and Care, in the golden forest. When the troll heard that, he also said that it was so far north that one could neither sail nor row there. "That is the princess who wanted to marry him. Yes, I know; but she will never get him as long as she lives, for he must marry the great giantess herself in two days' time," said the troll. "And where are they, these maidens? They shall not escape from me with their lives!" he shouted, and sniffed and snuffed about everywhere. "O no, you must not harm them!" said the giantess, and told him that they had given her a yard of drilling for linen. "Therefore you must lend them your seven-mile waistcoat to the nearest neighbour," said she. And he was willing at once, when he heard how kind they had been to his giantess. When they had eaten in the morning, he put his seven-mile waistcoat on them. "When you reach your goal, you need only say: 'Where you were put on this morning, there you are to hang again tonight!' and then the seven-mile waistcoat will travel home by itself," said the troll. Then they were carried for miles, over hill and dale, on and on. In the evening, at dusk, they again came to a great, ugly rock.

"I will knock here!" said the maid, and knocked and thumped on the rock. "O no," said the princess, "please do not knock here, you can see how sinister everything looks here!" "Who is thumping at my door?" the giantess cried inside the rock, in a ruder and harsher manner than the other two giantesses, and she opened the door just far enough so that she could thrust her nose, which was all of three yards long, through the crack. "Here stand the youngest princess and her maid, in search of a prince named Trouble and Care, who lives in the golden forest," was the maid's reply. "O faugh!" cried the giantess, "that is so far to the north that one can neither sail nor row there. But what do you want of Trouble and Care? Is this, perhaps, the princess who wanted to marry him?" asked the giantess. Yes, this was the princess, was the maid's reply. Then this giantess said in turn: "He must marry the great giantess in the golden forest, so you might just as well turn back home now as later!" But this the maidens did not want to do at all, and the maid asked whether, perhaps, she would not take them in for the night, and if it were only for the very darkest part of the night.

"Yes, I can take you in easily enough," said the giantess, "but when my husband comes home tonight he will tear off your heads and eat you up!" But there was nothing else to do; they could not travel on through the wood and wilderness, in the very darkest part of the night. Then the maid pulled out the yard of linen and made the giantess a present of it. "It can't be true! It can't be true!" cried she. "Here I have been married now for more than three hundred years, and have never yet had a bit of linen!" And she was so pleased that she invited the maidens in, and received them kindly, and let them want for nothing. "He is a ferocious fellow, is my husband, and he does away with every Christian soul that strays here," she said, when her guests had eaten. "But I will hide you in the anteroom. Perhaps he will not find you there." Then she carefully made up a soft bed for them, as fine as the finest in the world. But now the princess was weary and wretched and sleepy beyond all measure. She could no longer stand up at all, and finally had to lie down and sleep a little, and even though it were but a tiny little while. The maid was also so weary and wretched that she fell asleep standing, and fell over from time to time. Yet she still managed to keep her wits about her to the extent of seizing the princess, and holding her up, so that she did not bend her knees. Towards midnight it began to rumble and thunder so that the whole house shook, and it seemed as though the roof and walls would fall in. This was the great troll, who was coming home. When he thrust his first nose in at the door, he at once cried out in a manner so wild and harsh that the like had never been heard before: "Faugh! faugh! I smell Christian bodies!" and he fell into a white rage, so that sparks and flame flew from him. "Yes, a bird flew by, and let a bone from a Christian fall through the chimney. I threw it out as quickly as ever I could; but it may be that the smell still persists!" said the giantess, and tried to pacify her troll. And he was satisfied with her explanation. But when he awoke in the morning, she told him that the youngest princess and her maid had come in search of a prince named Trouble and Care, who lived in the golden forest. "O faugh! That is so far north that one can neither sail nor row there!" cried the great troll, just as the smaller trolls had. "But she will never get him as long as she lives, for tomorrow he must marry the great giantess. Where are they, these maidens? Hm, hm, hm, they will make tasty eating!" he cried, and danced around everywhere, and sniffed and snuffed with all his nine noses at once. "O no, you must not harm them!" cried the giantess. "They have given me a yard of linen, and here I have been married for more than three hundred years, and have never had a bit of linen yet. Therefore you must lend them your seven-mile waistcoat to the nearest neighbour." And when the super-troll heard that the maidens had been so kind, he was agreeable.

When they had strengthened themselves in the morning, he put his seven-mile waistcoat on them. "And now you must repeat: 'On, on! Over willow brush and pine tree, over hill and dale, to the nearest neighbour.' And when you reach your goal, you need only say: 'You must hang again tonight on the nail from which you were taken down this morning!'" said the great troll. They did as he had told them, and were carried farther and farther along, over hills and deep valleys.

At dusk they came to a large, large forest, where all the trees were black as coal. If one only so much as touched them, they made one look like a chimney-sweep. And in the middle of the forest was a clearing, and there stood a wretched hut, ready to fall apart; it was only held together by two beams, and looked more forlorn than the most wretched herdsman's hut. And in front of the door lay a rubbish heap of old shoes, dirty rags and other ugly stuff. Here the maid took off the seven-mile waistcoat, and said: "You must hang again tonight from the nail from which you were taken down this morning!" and the waistcoat wandered home all by itself.

"I will knock here!" said the maid. "O no, O no," wailed the princess, "please do not knock here, you can see how ugly everything is!" "If you do not do as I do, then it will be the worse for both of us!" said the maid; trampled through the rubbish-pile and knocked. An old, old troll-woman with a nose all of three yards long looked out through the crack in the door. "If you girls want to come in, then come in, and if you do not want to, you can stay out!" said she, and made as though to close the door in their faces. "Yes, indeed, we want to come in," replied the maid, and drew the princess in with her. "If you girls want to come through the door, then come through, but if you do not want to, you can stay out," the woman said once more. "Yes, thanks, we want to come in," said the maid, and tramped over the threshold through the dirt and rags. "Alas, alas!" wailed the princess, and tramped after her. All was black and ugly inside, and as grimy and dirty as a corn-loft. After a while the giantess went out, and fetched them some milk to drink. "If you girls want to drink, why, drink, and if you do not, why, do without!" said she, and was about to carry it out again. "Yes, thanks, we want to drink," said the maid, and drank. "Alas, alas!" wailed the princess, when it came her turn, for the milk was in a pig-trough, and dirt and clots of hair were swimming in it. Then the giantess gave them something to eat. "If you girls want to eat, why, eat, and if you do not, why, do without," said the giantess. "Yes, indeed, we will be glad to," said the maid, before the ugly nosey could take the food away again. The bread was mouldly, mice had been nibbling at the cheese, the meat was so old that one could smell it at a distance, and two dirty calves' tails were draped about the butter. "Alas, alas!" wailed the princess, and was ready to cry; but she had to do what her maid did, and taste the horrible dishes. Then they had to say they were much obliged. An old man, whom thus far they had not seen, lay on a bed covered with a few old odds and ends of fur and other rags. When they went up to him to thank him, he stood up, and when the princess gave him her hand he kissed it; and at that very moment he turned into a prince handsome beyond all measure, and the princess saw that he was Trouble and Care, for whom she had so greatly longed. "Now you have delivered me!" he said. "Woe to whoever has delivered you!" cried the giantess, and rushed out of the door; but on the doorstep she stood like a stone, for the forest was no longer black, and all the trees looked as though they had been gilded from root to crest, and glittered and sparkled more brightly than the sun at noon-day. The wretched, dirty hut had changed into a royal castle, immensely large and handsome. One might have thought that the roof and walls were made of the purest gold and silver, and so they were. "Now you may bend your knee again," said the prince, "and if you have hitherto known nothing but sorrow and care, you shall henceforth know all the more happiness."

The old giantess had brewed and baked, and prepared the whole wedding dinner. And when the next day dawned, the prince and the princess, and all the people in the castle, and in the whole country over which he was king, celebrated the wedding. And it lasted for four times fourteen days, so that the news spread through seven kingdoms, and reached the bride's father and her two sisters. And they would have celebrated it with them, had they not been so far away. I was invited to the feast myself, and the bridegroom made me chief cook, and I had to speak the toast for the bride and groom. But on the last day of the feast, I had to draw mead from a large, large cask that lay at the farthest end of the cellar. Before I sent off the filled jug, I took a taste myself, and the mead was so strong that it suddenly went to my head, and I flew through the air like a bird, and there I was, floating between heaven and earth for full nine years, and then I fell down here in the village, in front of the house up there on the hill. And out came Bertha Friendly, with a letter for me from the prince, who had become king in the meantime, and the letter said that he and the young queen were doing well, and that they sent me their greetings, and that I was to greet you for them, and that you and your sisters were invited to the castle on the Sunday after Michaelmas, and then you should see a pair of dear little princes, the golden forest and the old stone giantess, who stands before the door with her nose three yards long.

The Master-Maid

ONCE UPON A TIME there was a king who had many sons. I do not exactly know how many there were, but the youngest of them could not stay quietly at home, and was determined to go out into the world and try his luck, and after a long time the King was forced to give him leave to go. When he had travelled about for several days, he came to a giant's house, and hired himself to the giant as a servant. In the morning the giant had to go out to pasture his goats, and as he was leaving the house he told the King's son that he must clean out the stable. "And after you have done that," he said, "you need not do any more work today, for you have come to a kind master, and that you shall find. But what I set you to do must be done both well and thoroughly, and you must on no account go into any of the rooms which lead out of the room in which you slept last night. If you do, I will take your life."

"Well to be sure, he is an easy master!" said the Prince to himself as he walked up and down the room humming and singing, for he thought there would be plenty of time left to clean out the stable; "but it would be amusing to steal a glance into his other rooms as well," thought the Prince, "for there must be something that he is afraid of my seeing, as I am not allowed to enter them." So he went into the first room. A cauldron was hanging from the walls; it was boiling, but the Prince could see no fire under it. "I wonder what is inside it," he thought, and dipped a lock of his hair in, and the hair became just as if it were all made of copper. "That's a nice kind of soup. If anyone were to taste that his throat would be gilded," said the youth, and then he went into the next chamber. There, too, a cauldron was hanging from the wall, bubbling and boiling, but there was no fire under this either. "I will just try what this is like too," said the Prince, thrusting another lock of his hair into it, and it came out silvered over. "Such costly soup is not to be had in my father's palace," said the Prince; "but everything depends on how it tastes," and then he went into the third room. There, too, a cauldron was hanging from the wall, boiling, exactly the same as in the two other rooms, and the Prince took pleasure in trying this also, so he dipped a lock of hair in, and it came out so brightly gilded that it shone again. "Some talk about going from bad to worse," said the Prince; "but this is better and better. If he boils gold here, what can he boil in there?" He was determined to see, and went through the door into the fourth room. No cauldron was to be seen there, but on a bench someone was seated who was like a king's daughter, but whosoever she was, she was so beautiful that never in the Prince's life had he seen her equal.

"Oh! in heaven's name what are you doing here?" said she who sat upon the bench.

"I took the place of servant here yesterday," said the Prince.

"May you soon have a better place, if you have come to serve here!" said she.

"Oh, but I think I have got a kind master," said the Prince. "He has not given me hard work to do today. When I have cleaned out the stable I shall be done."

"Yes, but how will you be able to do that?" she asked again. "If you clean it out as other people do, ten pitchforksful will come in for everyone you throw out. But I will teach you how to do it; you must turn your pitchfork upside down, and work with the handle, and then all will fly out of its own accord."

"Yes, I will attend to that," said the Prince, and stayed sitting where he was the whole day, for it was soon settled between them that they would marry each other, he and the King's daughter; so the first day of his service with the giant did not seem long to him. But when evening was drawing near she said that it would now be better for him to clean out the stable before the giant came home. When he got there he had a fancy to try if what she had said were true, so he began to work in the same way that he had seen the stable-boys doing in his father's stables, but he soon saw that he must give up that, for when he had worked a very short time he had scarcely any room left to stand. So he did what the Princess had taught him, turned the pitchfork round, and worked with the handle, and in the twinkling of an eye the stable was as clean as if it had been scoured. When he had done that, he went back again into the room in which the giant had given him leave to stay, and there he walked backward and forward on the floor, and began to hum and sing.

Then came the giant home with the goats. "Have you cleaned the stable?" asked the giant.

"Yes, now it is clean and sweet, master," said the King's son.

"I shall see about that," said the giant, and went round to the stable, but it was just as the Prince had said.

"You have certainly been talking to my Master-maid, for you never got that out of your own head," said the giant.

"Master-maid! What kind of a thing is that, master?" said the Prince, making himself look as stupid as an ass; "I should like to see that."

"Well, you will see her quite soon enough," said the giant.

On the second morning the giant had again to go out with his goats, so he told the Prince that on that day he was to fetch home his horse, which was out on the mountainside, and when he had done that he might rest himself for the remainder of the day, "for you have come to a kind master, and that you shall find," said the giant once more. "But do not go into any of the rooms that I spoke of yesterday, or I will wring your head off," said he, and then went away with his flock of goats.

"Yes, indeed, you are a kind master," said the Prince; "but I will go in and talk to the Master-maid again; perhaps before long she may like better to be mine than yours."

So he went to her. Then she asked him what he had to do that day.

"Oh! not very dangerous work, I fancy," said the King's son. "I have only to go up the mountainside after his horse."

"Well, how do you mean to set about it?" asked the Master-maid.

"Oh! there is no great art in riding a horse home," said the King's son. "I think I must have ridden friskier horses before now."

"Yes, but it is not so easy a thing as you think to ride the horse home," said the Master-maid; "but I will teach you what to do. When you go near it, fire will burst out of its nostrils like flames from a pine torch; but be very careful, and take the bridle which is hanging by the door there, and fling the bit straight into his jaws, and then it will become so tame that you will be able to do what you like with it." He said he would bear this in mind, and then he again sat in there the whole day by the Master-maid, and they chatted and talked of one thing and another, but the first thing and the last now was how happy and delightful it would be if they could but marry each other, and get safely away from the giant; and the Prince would have forgotten both the mountainside and the horse if the Master-maid had not reminded him of them as evening drew near, and said that now it would be better if he went to fetch the horse before the giant came. So he did this, and took the bridle which was hanging on a crook, and strode up the mountainside, and it was not long before he met with the horse, and fire and red flames streamed forth out of its nostrils. But the youth carefully watched his opportunity, and just as it was rushing at him with open jaws he threw the bit straight into its mouth, and the horse stood as quiet as a young lamb, and there was no difficulty at all in getting it home to the stable. Then the Prince went back into his room again, and began to hum and to sing.

Towards evening the giant came home. "Have you fetched the horse back from the mountainside?" he asked.

"That I have, master; it was an amusing horse to ride, but I rode him straight home, and put him in the stable too," said the Prince.

"I will see about that," said the giant, and went out to the stable, but the horse was standing there just as the Prince had said. "You have certainly been talking with my Master-maid, for you never got that out of your own head," said the giant again.

"Yesterday, master, you talked about this Master-maid, and today you are talking about her; ah, heaven bless you, master, why will you not show her to me? For it would be a real pleasure to me to see her," said the Prince, who again pretended to be silly and stupid.

"Oh! you will see her quite soon enough," said the giant.

On the morning of the third day the giant again had to go into the wood with the goats. "Today you must go underground and fetch my taxes," he said to the Prince. "When you have done this, you may rest for the remainder of the day, for you shall see what an easy master you have come to," and then he went away.

"Well, however easy a master you may be, you set me very hard work to do," thought the Prince; "but I will see if I cannot find your Master-maid; you say she is yours, but for all that she may be able to tell me what to do now," and he went back to her. So, when the

Master-maid asked him what the giant had set him to do that day, he told her that he was to go underground and get the taxes.

"And how will you set about that?" said the Master-maid.

"Oh! you must tell me how to do it," said the Prince, "for I have never yet been underground, and even if I knew the way I do not know how much I am to demand."

"Oh! yes, I will soon tell you that; you must go to the rock there under the mountain-ridge, and take the club that is there, and knock on the rocky wall," said the Master-maid. "Then someone will come out who will sparkle with fire; you shall tell him your errand, and when he asks you how much you want to have you are to say: 'As much as I can carry.'"

"Yes, I will keep that in mind," said he, and then he sat there with the Master-maid the whole day, until night drew near, and he would gladly have stayed there till now if the Master-maid had not reminded him that it was time to be off to fetch the taxes before the giant came.

So he set out on his way, and did exactly what the Master-maid had told him. He went to the rocky wall, and took the club, and knocked on it. Then came one so full of sparks that they flew both out of his eyes and his nose. "What do you want?" said he.

"I was to come here for the giant, and demand the tax for him," said the King's son.

"How much are you to have then?" said the other.

"I ask for no more than I am able to carry with me," said the Prince.

"It is well for you that you have not asked for a horse-load," said he who had come out of the rock. "But now come in with me."

This the Prince did, and what a quantity of gold and silver he saw! It was lying inside the mountain like heaps of stones in a waste place, and he got a load that was as large as he was able to carry, and with that he went his way. So in the evening, when the giant came home with the goats, the Prince went into the chamber and hummed and sang again as he had done on the other two evenings.

"Have you been for the tax?" said the giant.

"Yes, that I have, master," said the Prince.

"Where have you put it then?" said the giant again.

"The bag of gold is standing there on the bench," said the Prince.

"I will see about that," said the giant, and went away to the bench, but the bag was standing there, and it was so full that gold and silver dropped out when the giant untied the string.

"You have certainly been talking with my Master-maid!" said the giant, "and if you have I will wring your neck."

"Master-maid?" said the Prince; "yesterday my master talked about this Master-maid, and today he is talking about her again, and the first day of all it was talk of the same kind. I do wish I could see her myself," said he.

"Yes, yes, wait till tomorrow," said the giant, "and then I myself will take you to her."

"Ah! master, I thank you – but you are only mocking me," said the King's son.

Next day the giant took him to the Master-maid. "Now you shall kill him, and boil him in the great big cauldron you know of, and when you have got the broth ready give me a call," said the giant; then he lay down on the bench to sleep, and almost immediately began to snore so that it sounded like thunder among the hills.

So the Master-maid took a knife, and cut the Prince's little finger, and dropped three drops of blood upon a wooden stool; then she took all the old rags, and shoe-soles, and all the rubbish she could lay hands on, and put them in the cauldron; and then she filled a chest with gold dust, and a lump of salt, and a water-flask which was hanging by the door, and she also took with her a golden apple, and two gold chickens; and then she and the Prince went away with all the speed they could, and when they had gone a little way they came to the sea, and then they sailed, but where they got the ship from I have never been able to learn.

Now, when the giant had slept a good long time, he began to stretch himself on the bench on which he was lying. "Will it soon boil?" said he.

"It is just beginning," said the first drop of blood on the stool.

So the giant lay down to sleep again, and slept for a long, long time. Then he began to move about a little again. "Will it soon be ready now?" said he, but he did not look up this time any more than he had done the first time, for he was still half asleep.

"Half done!" said the second drop of blood, and the giant believed it was the Master-maid again, and turned himself on the bench, and lay down to sleep once more. When he had slept again for many hours, he began to move and stretch himself. "Is it not done yet?" said he.

"It is quite ready," said the third drop of blood. Then the giant began to sit up and rub his eyes, but he could not see who it was who had spoken to him, so he asked for the Master-maid, and called her. But there was no one to give him an answer.

"Ah! well, she has just stolen out for a little," thought the giant, and he took a spoon, and went off to the cauldron to have a taste; but there was nothing in it but shoe-soles, and rags, and such trumpery as that, and all was boiled up together, so that he could not tell whether it was porridge or milk pottage. When he saw this, he understood what had happened, and fell into such a rage that he hardly knew what he was doing. Away he went after the Prince and the Master-maid so fast that the wind whistled behind him, and it was not long before he came to the water, but he could not get over it. "Well, well, I will soon find a cure for that; I have only to call my river-sucker," said the giant, and he did call him. So his river-sucker came and lay down, and drank one, two, three draughts, and with that the water in the sea fell so low that the giant saw the Master-maid and the Prince out on the sea in their ship. "Now you must throw out the lump of salt," said the Master-maid, and the Prince did so, and it grew up into such a great high mountain right across the sea that the giant could not come over it, and the river-sucker could not drink any more water. "Well, well, I will soon find a cure for that," said the giant, so he called to his hill-borer to come and bore through the mountain so that the river-sucker might be able to drink up the water again. But just as the hole was made, and the river-sucker was beginning to drink, the Master-maid told the Prince to throw one or two drops out of the flask, and when he did this the sea instantly became full of water again, and before the river-sucker could take one drink they reached the land and were in safety. So they determined to go home to the Prince's father, but the Prince would on no account permit the Master-maid to walk there, for he thought that it was unbecoming either for her or for him to go on foot.

"Wait here the least little bit of time, while I go home for the seven horses which stand in my father's stable," said he; "it is not far off, and I shall not be long away, but I will not let my betrothed bride go on foot to the palace."

"Oh! no, do not go, for if you go home to the King's palace you will forget me, I foresee that."

"How could I forget you? We have suffered so much evil together, and love each other so much," said the Prince; and he insisted on going home for the coach with the seven horses, and she was to wait for him there, by the seashore. So at last the Master-maid had to yield, for he was so absolutely determined to do it. "But when you get there you must not even give yourself time to greet anyone, but go straight into the stable, and take the horses, and put them in the coach, and drive back as quickly as you can. For they will all come round about you; but you must behave just as if you did not see them, and on no account must you taste anything, for if you do it will cause great misery both to you and to me," said she; and this he promised.

But when he got home to the King's palace one of his brothers was just going to be married, and the bride and all her kith and kin had come to the palace; so they all thronged round him, and questioned him about this and that, and wanted him to go in with them; but he behaved as if he did not see them, and went straight to the stable, and got out the horses and began to harness them. When they saw that they could not by any means prevail on him to go in with them, they came out to him with meat and drink, and the best of everything that they had prepared for the wedding; but the Prince refused to touch anything, and would do nothing but put the horses in as quickly as he could. At last, however, the bride's sister rolled an apple across the yard to him, and said: "As you won't eat anything else, you may like to take a bite of that, for you must be both hungry and thirsty after your long journey." And he took up the apple and bit a piece out of it. But no sooner had he got the piece of apple in his mouth than he forgot the Master-maid and that he was to go back in the coach to fetch her.

"I think I must be mad! What do I want with this coach and horses?" said he; and then he put the horses back into the stable, and went into the King's palace, and there it was settled that he should marry the bride's sister, who had rolled the apple to him.

The Master-maid sat by the seashore for a long, long time, waiting for the Prince, but no Prince came. So she went away, and when she had walked a short distance she came to a little hut which stood all alone in a small wood, hard by the King's palace. She entered it and asked if she might be allowed to stay there. The hut belonged to an old crone, who was also an ill-tempered and malicious troll. At first she would not let the Master-maid remain with her; but at last, after a long time, by means of good words and good payment, she obtained leave. But the hut was as dirty and black inside as a pigsty, so the Master-maid said that she would smarten it up a little, that it might look a little more like what other people's houses looked inside. The old crone did not like this either. She scowled, and was very cross, but the Master-maid did not trouble herself about that. She took out her chest of gold, and flung a handful of it or so into the fire, and the gold boiled up and poured out over the whole of the hut, until every part of it both inside and out was gilded. But when the gold began to bubble up the old hag grew so terrified that she fled as if the Evil One himself were pursuing her, and she did not remember to stoop down as she went through the doorway, and so she split her head and died. Next morning the sheriff came travelling by there. He was greatly astonished when he saw the gold hut shining and glittering there in the copse, and he was still more astonished when he went in and caught sight of the beautiful young maiden who was sitting there; he fell in love with her at once, and straightway on the spot he begged her, both prettily and kindly, to marry him.

"Well, but have you a great deal of money?" said the Master-maid.

"Oh! yes; so far as that is concerned, I am not ill off," said the sheriff. So now he had to go home to get the money, and in the evening he came back, bringing with him a bag with two bushels in it, which he set down on the bench. Well, as he had such a fine lot of money, the Master-maid said she would have him, so they sat down to talk.

But scarcely had they sat down together before the Master-maid wanted to jump up again. "I have forgotten to see to the fire," she said.

"Why should you jump up to do that?" said the sheriff; "I will do that!" So he jumped up, and went to the chimney in one bound.

"Just tell me when you have got hold of the shovel," said the Master-maid.

"Well, I have hold of it now," said the sheriff.

"Then you may hold the shovel, and the shovel you, and pour red-hot coals over you, till day dawns," said the Master-maid. So the sheriff had to stand there the whole night and pour red-hot coals over himself, and, no matter how much he cried and begged and entreated, the red-hot coals did not grow the colder for that. When the day began to dawn, and he had power to throw down the shovel, he did not stay long where he was, but ran away as fast as he possibly could; and everyone who met him stared and looked after him, for he was flying as if he were mad, and he could not have looked worse if he had been both flayed and tanned, and everyone wondered where he had been, but for very shame he would tell nothing.

The next day the attorney came riding by the place where the Master-maid dwelt. He saw how brightly the hut shone and gleamed through the wood, and he too went into it to see who lived there, and when he entered and saw the beautiful young maiden he fell even more in love with her than the sheriff had done, and began to woo her at once. So the Master-maid asked him, as she had asked the sheriff, if he had a great deal of money, and the attorney said he was not ill off for that, and would at once go home to get it; and at night he came with a great big sack of money – this time it was a four-bushel sack – and set it on the bench by the Master-maid. So she promised to have him, and he sat down on the bench by her to arrange about it, but suddenly she said that she had forgotten to lock the door of the porch that night, and must do it.

"Why should you do that?" said the attorney; "sit still, I will do it."

So he was on his feet in a moment, and out in the porch.

"Tell me when you have got hold of the door-latch," said the Master-maid.

"I have hold of it now," cried the attorney.

"Then you may hold the door, and the door you, and may you go between wall and wall till day dawns."

What a dance the attorney had that night! He had never had such a waltz before, and he never wished to have such a dance again. Sometimes he was in front of the door, and sometimes the door was in front of him, and it went from one side of the porch to the other, till the attorney was well-nigh beaten to death. At first he began to abuse the Master-maid, and then to beg and pray, but the door did not care for anything but keeping him where he was till break of day.

As soon as the door let go its hold of him, off went the attorney. He forgot who ought to be paid off for what he had suffered, he forgot both his sack of money and his wooing, for he was so afraid lest the house-door should come dancing after him. Everyone who met him stared and looked after him, for he was flying like a madman, and he could not have looked worse if a herd of rams had been butting at him all night long.

On the third day the bailiff came by, and he too saw the gold house in the little wood, and he too felt that he must go and see who lived there; and when he caught sight of the Master-maid he became so much in love with her that he wooed her almost before he greeted her.

The Master-maid answered him as she had answered the other two, that if he had a great deal of money, she would have him. "So far as that is concerned, I am not ill off," said the bailiff; so he was at once told to go home and fetch it, and this he did. At night he came back, and he had a still larger sack of money with him than the attorney had brought; it must have been at least six bushels, and he set it down on the bench. So it was settled that he was to have the Master-maid. But hardly had they sat down together before she said that she had forgotten to bring in the calf, and must go out to put it in the byre.

"No, indeed, you shall not do that," said the bailiff; "I am the one to do that." And, big and fat as he was, he went out as briskly as a boy.

"Tell me when you have got hold of the calf's tail," said the Master-maid.

"I have hold of it now," cried the bailiff.

"Then may you hold the calf's tail, and the calf's tail hold you, and may you go round the world together till day dawns!" said the Master-maid. So the bailiff had to bestir himself, for the calf went over rough and smooth, over hill and dale, and, the more the bailiff cried and screamed, the faster the calf went. When daylight began to appear, the bailiff was half dead; and so glad was he to leave loose of the calf's tail, that he forgot the sack of money and all else. He walked now slowly – more slowly than the sheriff and the attorney had done, but the slower he went, the more time had everyone to stare and look at him; and they used it too, and no one can imagine how tired out and ragged he looked after his dance with the calf.

On the following day the wedding was to take place in the King's palace, and the elder brother was to drive to church with his bride, and the brother who had been with the giant with her sister. But when they had seated themselves in the coach and were about to drive off from the palace one of the trace-pins broke, and, though they made one, two, and three to put in its place, that did not help them, for each broke in turn, no matter what kind of wood they used to make them of. This went on for a long time, and they could not get away from the palace, so they were all in great trouble. Then the sheriff said (for he too had been bidden to the wedding at Court): "Yonder away in the thicket dwells a maiden, and if you can get her to lend you the handle of the shovel that she uses to make up her fire I know very well that it will hold fast." So they sent off a messenger to the thicket, and begged so prettily that they might have the loan of her shovel-handle of which the sheriff had spoken that they were not refused; so now they had a trace-pin which would not snap in two.

But all at once, just as they were starting, the bottom of the coach fell in pieces. They made a new bottom as fast as they could, but no matter how they nailed it together, or what kind of wood they used, no sooner had they got the new bottom into the coach and were about to drive off than it broke again, so that they were still worse off than when they had broken the trace-pin. Then the attorney said, for he too was at the wedding in the palace: "Away there in the thicket dwells a maiden, and if you could but get her to lend you one-half of her porch-door I am certain that it will hold together." So they again sent a messenger to the thicket, and begged so prettily for the loan of the gilded porch-door of which the attorney had told them that they got it at once. They were just setting out again, but now the horses were not able to draw the coach. They had six horses already, and now they put in eight, and then ten, and then twelve, but the more they put in, and the more the coachman whipped them, the less good it did; and the coach never stirred from the spot. It was already beginning to be late in the day, and to church they must and would go, so everyone who was in the palace was in a state of distress. Then the bailiff spoke up and said: "Out there in the gilded cottage in the thicket dwells a girl, and if you could but get her to lend you her calf I know it could draw the coach, even if it were as heavy as a mountain." They all thought that it was ridiculous to be drawn to church by a calf, but there was nothing else for it but to send a messenger once more, and beg as prettily as they could, on behalf of the King, that she would let them have the loan of the calf that the bailiff had told them about. The Master-maid let them have it immediately – this time also she would not say "no."

Then they harnessed the calf to see if the coach would move; and away it went, over rough and smooth, over stock and stone, so that they could scarcely breathe, and sometimes they were on the ground, and sometimes up in the air; and when they came to the church the coach began to go round and round like a spinning-wheel, and it was with the utmost difficulty and danger that they were able to get out of the coach and into the church. And when they went back again the coach went quicker still, so that most of them did not know how they got back to the palace at all.

When they had seated themselves at the table the Prince who had been in service with the giant said that he thought they ought to have invited the maiden who had lent them the shovel-handle, and the porch-door, and the calf up to the palace, "for," said he, "if we had not got these three things, we should never have got away from the palace."

The King also thought that this was both just and proper, so he sent five of his best men down to the gilded hut, to greet the maiden courteously from the King, and to beg her to be so good as to come up to the palace to dinner at midday.

"Greet the King, and tell him that, if he is too good to come to me, I am too good to come to him," replied the Master-maid.

So the King had to go himself, and the Master-maid went with him immediately, and, as the King believed that she was more than she appeared to be, he seated her in the place of honour by the youngest bridegroom. When they had sat at the table for a short time, the Master-maid took out the cock, and the hen, and the golden apple which she had brought away with her from the giant's house, and set them on the table in front of her, and instantly the cock and the hen began to fight with each other for the golden apple.

"Oh! look how those two there are fighting for the golden apple," said the King's son.

"Yes, and so did we two fight to get out that time when we were in the mountain," said the Master-maid.

So the Prince knew her again, and you may imagine how delighted he was. He ordered the troll-witch who had rolled the apple to him to be torn in pieces between four-and-twenty horses, so that not a bit of her was left, and then for the first time they began really to keep the wedding, and, weary as they were, the sheriff, the attorney, and the bailiff kept it up too.

The Mount of the Golden Queen

ONCE UPON A TIME, a lad who tended the cattle in the wood was eating his noon-tide meal in a clearing in the forest. As he was sitting there he saw a rat run into a juniper bush. His curiosity led him to look for it; but as he bent over, down he went, head over heels, and fell asleep. And he dreamed that he was going to find the princess on the Mount of the Golden Queen, but that he did not know the way.

The following day he once more pastured his cattle in the wood when he came to the same clearing, and again ate his dinner there. And again he saw the rat and went to look for it, and again when he bent down he went head over heels, and fell fast asleep. And again he dreamed of the princess on the Mount of the Golden Queen, and that in order to get her he would need seventy pounds of iron and a pair of iron shoes. He awoke and it was all a dream; but by now he had made up his mind to find the Mount of the Golden Queen, and he went home with his herd. On the third day, when he led out his cattle, he could not reach the clearing of his happy dream too soon. Again the rat showed itself and when he went to look for it, he fell asleep as he had done each preceding day. And again he dreamed of the princess on the Mount of the Golden Queen, and that she came to him, and laid a letter and a band of gold in his pocket. Then he awoke and to his indescribable surprise, he found in his pocket both of the things of which he had dreamed, the letter and the band. Now he had no time to attend to the cattle any longer, but drove them straight home. Then he went into the stable, led out a horse, sold it, and bought seventy pounds of iron and a pair of iron shoes with the money. He made thole-pins out of the iron, put on his iron shoes, and set forth.

For a time he travelled by land; but at last he came to the lake which he had to row across. He saw naught but water before and behind him, and rowing so long and steadily that he wore out one thole-pin after another, he at length reached land, and a green meadow where no trees grew. He walked all around the meadow, and at last found a mound of earth from which smoke was rising. When he looked more closely, out came a woman who was nine yards tall. He asked her to tell him the way to the Mount of the Golden Queen, but she replied: "That I do not know. Go ask my sister, who is nine yards taller than I am and who lives in an earth-mound which you can find without any trouble." So he left her and came to a mound of earth that looked just like the first, and from which smoke was also rising. A woman at once came out who was tremendously tall, and of her he asked the way to the Mount of the Golden Queen. "That I do not know," said she. "Go ask my brother, who is nine yards taller than I am, and who lives in a hill a little further away."

So he came to the hill, from which smoke was also rising, and knocked. A man at once came out who was a veritable giant, for he was twenty-seven yards in height, and of him he asked the way to the Mount of the Golden Queen. Then the giant took a whistle and whistled in every direction, to call together all the animals to be found on the earth. And all the animals came from the woods, foremost among them a bear. The giant asked him about the Mount of the Golden Queen, but he knew nothing of it. Again the giant blew his whistle in every direction to call together all the fishes to be found in the waters. They came at once, and he asked them about the Mount of the Golden Queen, but they knew nothing of it. Once more the giant blew his whistle in every direction, and called together all the birds of the air. They came, and he asked the eagle about the Mount of the Golden Queen, and whether he knew where it might be.

The eagle said: "Yes!"

"Well then, take this lad there," said the giant "but do not treat him unkindly!"

This the eagle promised, allowed the youth to seat himself on his back, and then off they were through the air, over fields and forests, hill and dale, and before long they were above the ocean, and could see nothing but sky and water. Then the eagle dipped the youth in the ocean up to his ankles and asked: "Are you afraid?" "No," said the youth. Then the eagle flew on a while, and again dipped the youth into the water, up to his knees and said: "Are you afraid?" "Yes," answered the youth, "but the giant said you were not to treat me unkindly." "Are you really afraid?" asked the eagle once more. "Yes," answered the youth. Then the eagle said: "The fear you now feel is the very same fear I felt when the princess thrust the letter and the golden band into your pocket." And with that they had reached a large, high mountain in one side of which was a great iron door. They knocked, and a serving-maid appeared to open the door and admit them. The youth remained and was well received; but the eagle said farewell and flew back to his native land.

The youth asked for a drink, and he was at once handed a beaker containing a refreshing draught. When he had emptied it and returned the beaker, he let the golden band drop into it. And when the maid brought back the beaker to her mistress – who was the princess of the Mount of the Golden Queen – the latter looked into the beaker, and behold, there lay a golden band which she recognized as her own. So she asked: "Is there someone here?" and when the maid answered in the affirmative, the princess said: "Bid him come in!" And as soon as the youth entered she asked him if he chanced to have a letter. The youth drew out the letter he had received in so strange a manner, and gave it to the princess. And when she had read it she cried, full of joy: "Now I am delivered!" And at that very moment the mountain turned into a most handsome castle, with all sorts of precious things, servants, and every sort of convenience, each for its own purpose. (Whether the princess and the youth married the story does not say; yet we must take for granted that a wedding is the proper end for the fairy tale).

Nix Nought Nothing

THERE ONCE LIVED A KING AND A QUEEN as many a one has been. They were long married and had no children; but at last a baby boy came to the queen when the king was away in the far countries. The queen would not christen the boy till the king came back, and she said, "We will just call him *Nix Nought Nothing* until his father comes home." But it was long before he came home, and the boy had grown a nice little laddie. At length the king was on his way back; but he had a big river to cross, and there was a whirlpool, and he could not get over the water. But a giant came up to him, and said, "I'll carry you over." But the king said: "What's your pay?" "O give me Nix, Nought, Nothing, and I will carry you over the water on my back." The king had never heard that his son was called Nix Nought Nothing, and so he said: "O, I'll give you that and my thanks into the bargain." When the king got home again, he was very happy to see his wife again, and his young son. She told him that she had not given the child any name, but just Nix Nought Nothing, until he should come home again himself. The poor king was in a terrible case. He said: "What have I done? I promised to give the giant who carried me over the river on his back Nix Nought Nothing." The king and the queen were sad and sorry, but they said: "When the giant comes we will give him the hen-wife's boy; he will never know the difference." The next day the giant came to claim the king's promise, and he sent for the hen-wife's boy; and the giant went away with the boy on his back. He travelled till he came to a big stone, and there he sat down to rest. He said,

"Hidge, Hodge, on my back, what time of day is that?"

The poor little boy said: "It is the time that my mother, the hen-wife, takes up the eggs for the queen's breakfast."

The giant was very angry, and dashed the boy's head on the stone and killed him.

So he went back in a tower of a temper and this time they gave him the gardener's boy. He went off with him on his back till they got to the stone again when the giant sat down to rest. And he said:

"Hidge, Hodge, on my back, what time of day do you make that?"

The gardener's boy said: "Sure it's the time that my mother takes up the vegetables for the queen's dinner." Then the giant was right wild and dashed his brains out on the stone.

Then the giant went back to the king's house in a terrible temper and said he would destroy them all if they did not give him Nix Nought Nothing this time. They had to do it; and when he came to the big stone, the giant said: "What time of day is that?" Nix Nought Nothing said: "It is the time that my father the king will be sitting down to supper." The giant said: "I've got the right one now;" and took Nix Nought Nothing to his own house and brought him up till he was a man.

The giant had a bonny daughter, and she and the lad grew very fond of each other. The giant said one day to Nix Nought Nothing: "I've work for you tomorrow. There is a stable seven miles long and seven miles broad, and it has not been cleaned for seven years, and you must clean it tomorrow, or I will have you for my supper."

The giant's daughter went out next morning with the lad's breakfast, and found him in a terrible state, for always as he cleaned out a bit, it just fell in again. The giant's daughter said she would help him, and she cried all the beasts in the field, and all the fowls of the air, and in a minute they all came, and carried away everything that was in the stable and made it all clean before the giant came home. He said: "Shame on the wit that helped you; but I have a worse job for you tomorrow." Then he said to Nix Nought Nothing: "There's a lake seven miles long, and seven miles deep, and seven miles broad, and you must drain it tomorrow by nightfall, or else I'll have you for my supper." Nix Nought Nothing began early next morning and tried to lave the water with his pail, but the lake was never getting any less, and he didn't know what to do; but the giant's daughter called on all the fish in the sea to come and drink the water, and very soon they drank it dry. When the giant saw the work done he was in a rage, and said: "I've a worse job for you tomorrow; there is a tree, seven miles high, and no branch on it, till you get to the top, and there is a nest with seven eggs in it, and you must bring down all the eggs without breaking one, or else I'll have you for my supper." At first the giant's daughter did not know how to help Nix Nought Nothing; but she cut off first her fingers and then her toes, and made steps of them, and he climbed the tree and got all the eggs safe till he came just to the bottom, and then one was broken. So they determined to run away together and after the giant's daughter had tidied up her hair a bit and got her magic flask they set out together as fast as they could run. And they hadn't got but three fields away when they looked back and saw the giant walking along at top speed after them. "Quick, quick," called out the giant's daughter, "take my comb from my hair and throw it down." Nix Nought Nothing took her comb from her hair and threw it down, and out of every one of its prongs there sprung up a fine thick briar in the way of the giant. You may be sure it took him a long time to work his way through the briar bush and by the time he was well through Nix Nought Nothing and his sweetheart had run on a tidy step away from him. But he soon came along after them and was just like to catch 'em up when the giant's daughter called out to Nix Nought Nothing, "Take my hair dagger and throw it down, quick, quick." So Nix Nought Nothing threw down the hair dagger and out of it grew as quick as lightning a thick hedge of sharp razors placed criss-cross. The giant had to tread very cautiously to get through all this and meanwhile the young lovers ran on, and on, and on, till they were nearly out of sight. But at last the giant was through, and it wasn't long before he was like to catch them up. But just as he was stretching out his hand to catch Nix Nought Nothing his daughter took out her magic flask and dashed it on the ground. And as it broke out of it welled a big, big wave that grew, and that grew, till it reached the giant's waist and then his neck, and when it got to his head, he was drowned dead, and dead, and dead indeed. So he goes out of the story.

But Nix Nought Nothing fled on till…where do you think they came to? Why, to near the castle of Nix Nought Nothing's father and mother. But the giant's daughter was so weary that she couldn't move a step further. So Nix Nought Nothing told her to wait there while he went and found out a lodging for the night. And he went on towards the lights of the castle, and on the way he came to the cottage of the hen-wife whose boy had had his brains dashed out by the giant. Now she knew Nix Nought Nothing in a moment, and hated him because he was the cause of her son's death. So when he asked his way to the castle she put a spell upon him, and when he got to the castle, no sooner was he let in than he fell down dead asleep upon a bench in the hall. The king and queen tried all they could do to wake him up, but all in vain. So the king promised that if any lady could wake him up she should marry him. Meanwhile the giant's daughter was waiting and waiting for him to come back. And she went up into a tree to watch for him. The gardener's daughter, going to draw water in the well, saw the shadow of the lady in the water and thought it was herself, and said, "If I'm so bonny, if I'm so brave, why do you send me to draw water?" So she threw down her pail and went to see if she could wed the sleeping stranger. And she went to the hen-wife, who taught her an unspelling catch which would keep Nix Nought Nothing awake as long as the gardener's daughter liked. So she went up to the castle and sang her catch and Nix Nought Nothing was wakened for a bit and they promised to wed him to the gardener's daughter. Meanwhile the gardener went down to draw water from the well and saw the shadow of the lady in the water. So he looked up and found her, and he brought the lady from the tree, and led her into his house. And he told her that a stranger was to marry his daughter, and took her up to the castle and showed her the man: and it was Nix Nought Nothing asleep in a chair. And she saw him, and cried to him: "Waken, waken, and speak to me!" But he would not waken, and soon she cried:

"I cleaned the stable, I laved the lake, and I climbed the tree,
And all for the love of thee,
And thou wilt not waken and speak to me."

The king and the queen heard this, and came to the bonny young lady, and she said: "I cannot get Nix Nought Nothing to speak to me for all that I can do."

Then were they greatly astonished when she spoke of Nix Nought Nothing, and asked where he was, and she said: "He that sits there in the chair." Then they ran to him and kissed him and called him their own dear son; so they called for the gardener's daughter and made her sing her charm, and he wakened, and told them all that the giant's daughter had done for him, and of all her kindness. Then they took her in their arms and kissed her, and said she should now be their daughter, for their son should marry her. But they sent for the hen-wife and put her to death. And they lived happy all their days.

The History of Jack and the Beanstalk

IN THE DAYS OF KING ALFRED there lived a poor woman whose cottage was situated in a remote country village, a great many miles from London.

She had been a widow some years, and had an only child named Jack, whom she indulged to a fault. The consequence of her blind partiality was that Jack did not pay the least attention to anything she said, but was indolent, careless and extravagant. His follies were not owing to a bad disposition, but that his mother had never checked him. By degrees she disposed of all she possessed – scarcely anything remained but a cow.

The poor woman one day met Jack with tears in her eyes. Her distress was great, and, for the first time in her life, she could not help reproaching him, saying –

"O you wicked child! by your ungrateful course of life you have at last brought me to beggary and ruin. Cruel, cruel boy! I have not money enough to purchase even a bit of bread for another day. Nothing now remains to sell but my poor cow. I am sorry to part with her. It grieves me sadly, but we must not starve."

For a few minutes Jack felt a degree of remorse, but it was soon over, and he began teasing his mother to let him sell the cow at the next village so much, that she at last consented.

As he was going along he met a butcher, who enquired why he was driving the cow from home. Jack replied he was going to sell it. The butcher held some curious beans in his hat that were of various colours and attracted Jack's notice. This did not pass unnoticed by the butcher, who, knowing Jack's easy temper, thought now was the time to take advantage of it, and, determined not to let slip so good an opportunity, asked what was the price of the cow, offering at the same time all the beans in his hat for her. The silly boy could not conceal the pleasure he felt at what he supposed so great an offer. The bargain was struck instantly, and the cow exchanged for a few paltry beans. Jack made the best of his way home, calling aloud to his mother before he reached the house, thinking to surprise her.

When she saw the beans and heard Jack's account, her patience quite forsook her. She kicked the beans away in a passion – they flew in all directions – some were scattered in the garden. Not having anything to eat, they both went supperless to bed.

Jack awoke very early in the morning, and seeing something uncommon from the window of his bed-chamber, ran downstairs into the garden, where he soon discovered that some of the beans had taken root and sprung up surprisingly. The stalks were of an immense thickness, and had so entwined that they formed a ladder nearly like a chain in appearance.

Looking upwards, he could not discern the top. It appeared to be lost in the clouds. He tried the stalk, found it firm, and not to be shaken. He quickly formed the resolution of endeavouring to climb up to the top in order to seek his fortune, and ran to communicate his intention to his mother, not doubting but she would be equally pleased with him. She declared he should not go; said it would break her heart if he did; entreated and threatened, but all in vain.

Jack set out, and, after climbing for some hours, reached the top of the beanstalk, fatigued and quite exhausted. Looking around, he found himself in a strange country. It appeared to be a desert, quite barren, not a tree, shrub, house, or living creature to be seen. Here and there were scattered fragments of stone, and at unequal distances small heaps of earth were loosely thrown together.

Jack seated himself, pensively, upon a block of stone, and thought of his mother. He reflected with sorrow on his disobedience in climbing the beanstalk against her will, and concluded that he must die of hunger.

However, he walked on, hoping to see a house where he might beg something to eat and drink. Presently a handsome young woman appeared at a distance. As she approached Jack could not help admiring how beautiful and lively she looked. She was dressed in the most elegant manner, and had a small white wand in her hand, on the top of which was a peacock of pure gold.

While Jack was looking, with the greatest surprise, at this charming female, she came up to him, and, with a smile of the most bewitching sweetness, enquired how he came there. Jack related the circumstance of the beanstalk. She asked him if he recollected his father. He replied he did not, and added there must be some mystery relating to him, because if he asked his mother who his father was she always burst into tears and appeared to be violently agitated, nor did she recover herself for some days after. One thing, however, he could not avoid observing on these occasions, which was that she always carefully avoided answering him, and even seemed afraid of speaking, as if there were some secret connected with his father's history which she must not disclose.

The young woman replied –

"I will reveal the whole story. Your mother must not do so. But before I begin I require a solemn promise on your part to do what I command. I am a fairy, and, if you do not perform exactly what I desire, you will be destroyed."

Jack was frightened at her menaces, and promised to fulfil her injunctions exactly, and the fairy thus addressed him –

"Your father was a rich man. His disposition was very benevolent. He was very good to the poor, and constantly relieved them. He made it a rule never to let a day pass without doing good to some person. On one particular day in the week he kept open house, and invited only those who were reduced and had lived well. He always presided himself, and did all in his power to render his guests comfortable. The rich and the great were next invited. The servants were all happy and greatly attached to their master and mistress. Your father, though only a private gentleman, was as rich as a prince, and he deserved all he possessed, for he only lived to do good. Such a man was soon known and talked of. A giant lived a great many miles off. This man was altogether as wicked as your father was good. He was, in his heart, envious, covetous and cruel, but he had the art of concealing those vices. He was poor, and wished to enrich himself at any rate.

"Hearing your father spoken of, he formed the design of becoming acquainted with him, hoping to ingratiate himself into your father's favour. He removed quickly into your neighbourhood, and caused it to be reported that he was a gentleman who had just lost all he possessed by an earthquake and had found it difficult to escape with his life. His wife was with him. Your father gave credit to his story and pitied him. He gave him handsome apartments in his own house, and caused him and his wife to be treated like visitors of consequence, little imagining that the giant was undertaking a horrid return for all his favours.

"Things went on this way for some time, the giant becoming daily more impatient to put his plan into action. At last a favourable opportunity presented itself. Your father's house was at some distance from the seashore, but with a glass the coast could be seen distinctly. The giant was one day using the telescope; the wind was very high, and he saw a fleet of ships in distress off the rocks. He hastened to your father, mentioned the circumstance, and eagerly requested he would send all the servants he could spare to relieve the sufferers.

"Everyone was instantly despatched, except the porter and your nurse. The giant then joined your father in the study, and appeared to be delighted. He really was so. Your father recommended a favourite book, and was handing it down, when the giant, taking the opportunity, stabbed him, and he instantly fell down dead. The giant left the body, found the porter and nurse, and presently despatched them, being determined to have no living witnesses of his crimes.

"You were then only three months old. Your mother had you in her arms in a remote part of the house, and was ignorant of what was going on. She went into the study, but how was she shocked on discovering your father dead. She was stupefied with horror and grief, and was motionless. The giant, who was seeking her, found her in that state, and hastened to serve her and you as he had done your father, but she fell at his feet, and, in a pathetic manner, besought him to spare her life and yours.

"Remorse, for a moment, seemed to touch the barbarian's heart. He granted your lives, but first he made her take a most solemn oath never to inform you who your father was, or to answer any questions concerning him, assuring her that if she did he would certainly discover her and put both of you to death in the most cruel manner. Your mother took you in her arms and fled as quickly as possible. She was scarcely gone when the giant repented he had suffered her to escape. He would have pursued her instantly, but he had to provide for his own safety, as it was necessary he should be gone before the servants returned. Having gained your father's confidence he knew where to find all his treasure. He soon loaded himself and his wife, set the house on fire in several places, and, when the servants returned, the house was burnt quite down to the ground.

"Your poor mother, forlorn, abandoned and forsaken, wandered with you a great many miles from this scene of desolation. Fear added to her haste. She settled in the cottage where you were brought up, and it was entirely owing to her fear of the giant that she never mentioned your father to you.

"I became your father's guardian at his birth, but fairies have laws to which they are subject as well as mortals. A short time before the giant went to your father's I transgressed. My punishment was a suspension of power for a limited time – an unfortunate circumstance – for it totally prevented my succouring your father.

"The day on which you met the butcher, as you went to sell your mother's cow, my power was restored. It was I who secretly prompted you to take the beans in exchange for the cow.

"By my power the beanstalk grew to so great a height and formed a ladder. I need not add I inspired you with a strong desire to ascend the ladder.

"The giant lives in this country, and you are the person appointed to punish him for all his wickedness. You will have dangers and difficulties to encounter, but you must persevere in avenging the death of your father, or you will not prosper in any of your undertakings, but be always miserable.

"As to the giant's possessions, you may seize on all you can, for everything he has is yours though now you are unjustly deprived of it. One thing I desire. Do not let your mother know you are acquainted with your father's history till you see me again.

"Go along the direct road, and you will soon see the house where your cruel enemy lives. While you do as I order you I will protect and guard you, but remember, if you dare disobey my commands, a most dreadful punishment awaits you."

When the fairy had concluded, she disappeared, leaving Jack to pursue his journey. He walked on till after sunset when, to his great joy, he espied a large mansion. This agreeable sight revived his drooping spirits, and he redoubled his speed, and soon reached the house. A plain-looking woman was at the door, and Jack accosted her, begging she would give him a morsel of bread and a night's lodging.

She expressed the greatest surprise at seeing him, and said it was quite uncommon to see a human being near their house, for it was well known her husband was a large and very powerful giant, and that he would never eat anything but human flesh, if he could possibly get it; that he did not think anything of walking fifty miles to procure it, usually being out the whole day for that purpose.

This account greatly terrified Jack, but still he hoped to elude the giant, and therefore he again entreated the woman to take him in for one night only, and hide him where she thought proper. The good woman at last suffered herself to be persuaded, for she was of a compassionate and generous disposition, and took him into the house.

First they entered a large, fine hall, magnificently furnished. They then passed through several spacious rooms, all in the same style of grandeur, but they appeared to be quite forsaken and desolate.

A long gallery was next. It was very dark, with just light enough to show that, instead of a wall, on one side there was a grating of iron which parted off a dismal dungeon, from whence issued the groans of those poor victims whom the cruel giant reserved in confinement for his own voracious appetite.

Poor Jack was half dead with fear, and would have given the world to have been with his mother again, for he now began to fear that he should never see her more, and gave himself up for lost. He even mistrusted the good woman, and thought she had let him into the house for no other purpose than to lock him up among the unfortunate people in the dungeon.

At the further end of the gallery there was a spacious kitchen, and a very excellent fire was burning in the grate. The good woman bade Jack sit down, and gave him plenty to eat and drink. Jack, not seeing anything here to make him uncomfortable, soon forgot his fear, and was just beginning to enjoy himself when he was aroused by a loud knocking at the street-door, which made the whole house shake. The giant's wife ran to secure Jack in the oven and then went to let her husband in.

Jack heard him accost her in a voice like thunder, saying –

"Wife, I smell fresh meat."

"Oh, my dear," replied she, "it is nothing but the people in the dungeon."

The giant appeared to believe her, and walked into the very kitchen where poor Jack was concealed, who shook, trembled, and was more terrified than he had yet been.

At last the monster seated himself quietly by the fireside, whilst his wife prepared supper. By degrees Jack recovered himself sufficiently to look at the giant through a small crevice.

He was quite astonished to see what an amazing quantity he devoured, and thought he would never have done eating and drinking. When supper was ended the giant desired his wife to bring him his hen. A very beautiful hen was brought and placed on the table before him. Jack's curiosity was very great to see what would happen. He observed that every time the giant said, "Lay," the hen laid an egg of solid gold.

The giant amused himself a long while with his hen, and meanwhile his wife went to bed. At length the giant fell asleep by the fireside and snored like the roaring of a cannon. At daybreak Jack, finding the giant still asleep, and not likely to awaken soon, crept softly out of his hiding-place, seized the hen, and ran off with her.

He met with some difficulty in finding his way out of the house, but, at last, he reached the road in safety. He easily found his way to the beanstalk and descended it better and quicker than he had expected. His mother was overjoyed to see him. He found her crying bitterly, and lamenting his hard fate, for she concluded he had come to some shocking end through his rashness.

Jack was impatient to show his hen, and inform his mother how valuable it was.

"And now, Mother," said Jack, "I have brought home that which will make us rich, and I hope to make some amends for the affliction I have caused you through my idleness, extravagance and folly."

The hen produced as many golden eggs as they desired, which Jack and his mother sold, and so in a little time became possessed of as much riches as they wanted.

For some months Jack and his mother lived very happily together, but he, being very desirous of travelling, recollecting the fairy's commands, and fearing that if he delayed she would put her threats into action, longed to climb the beanstalk and pay the giant another visit, in order to carry away some more of his treasure, for, during the time that Jack was in the giant's mansion, while he lay concealed in the oven, he learned, from the conversation that took place between the giant and his wife, that he possessed some wonderful curiosities. Jack thought of his journey again and again, but still he could not summon resolution enough to break it to his mother, being well assured she would endeavour to prevent his going. However, one day he told her boldly that he must take a journey up the beanstalk. His mother begged and prayed him not to think of it, and tried all in her power to dissuade him. She told him that the giant's wife would certainly know him again, and the giant would desire nothing better than to get him into his power, that he might put him to a cruel death in order to be revenged for the loss of his hen.

Jack, finding that all his arguments were useless, pretended to give up this point, though he was resolved to go at all events. He had a dress prepared which would disguise him, and something to colour his skin, and he thought it impossible for anyone to recollect him in this dress.

In a few mornings after this, he rose very early, changed his complexion, and, unperceived by anyone, climbed the beanstalk a second time. He was greatly fatigued when he reached the top, and very hungry.

Having rested some time on one of the stones, he pursued his journey to the giant's mansion. He reached it late in the evening, and found the woman at the door as before. Jack addressed her, at the same time telling her a pitiful tale, and requesting she would give him some victuals and drink, and also a night's lodging.

She told him (what he knew very well before) about her husband's being a powerful and cruel giant and also how she one night admitted a poor, hungry, friendless boy, who was half dead with travelling, and that the ungrateful fellow had stolen one of the giant's treasures, ever since which her husband had been worse than before, had used her very cruelly, and continually upbraided her with being the cause of his loss.

Jack was at no loss to discover that he was attending to the account of a story in which he was the principal actor. He did his best to persuade the old woman to admit him, but found it a very hard task.

At last she consented, and as she led the way Jack observed that everything was just as he had found it before. She took him into the kitchen, and after he had done eating and drinking, she hid him in an old lumber closet. The giant returned at the usual time, and walked in so heavily that the house was shaken to the foundation. He seated himself by the fire, and, soon after, exclaimed –

"Wife, I smell fresh meat."

The wife replied it was the crows, which had brought a piece of raw meat and left it on the top of the house.

Whilst supper was preparing, the giant was very ill-tempered and impatient, frequently lifting up his hand to strike his wife for not being quick enough, but she was always so fortunate as to elude the blow. The giant was also continually upbraiding her with the loss of his wonderful hen.

The giant's wife, having set supper on the table, went to another apartment and brought from it a huge pie which she also placed before him.

When he had ended his plentiful supper and eaten till he was quite satisfied, he said to his wife –

"I must have something to amuse me, either my bags of money or my harp."

After a good deal of ill-humour, and after having teased his wife for some time, he commanded her to bring down his bags of gold and silver. Jack, as before, peeped out of his hiding place, and presently the wife brought two bags into the room. They were of a very large size. One was filled with new guineas, and the other with new shillings. They were placed before the giant, who began reprimanding his poor wife most severely for staying so long. She replied, trembling with fear, that they were so heavy she could scarcely lift them, and concluded by saying she would never again bring them downstairs, adding that she had nearly fainted owing to their weight.

This so exasperated the giant that he raised his hand to strike her, but she escaped and went to bed, leaving him to count over his treasure by way of amusement.

The giant took his bags, and after turning them over and over to see they were in the same state he had left them, began to count their contents. First the bag which contained the silver was emptied, and the contents placed upon the table. Jack viewed the glittering heaps with delight, and most heartily wished them in his own possession. The giant (little thinking he was so narrowly watched) reckoned the silver over several times, and then, having satisfied himself that all was safe, put it into the bags again, which he made very secure.

The other bag was opened next, and the guineas placed upon the table. If Jack was pleased at the sight of the silver, how much more delighted must he have felt when he saw such a heap of glittering gold? He even had the boldness to think of gaining both bags, but, suddenly recollecting himself, he began to fear that the giant would sham sleep, the better to entrap anyone who might be concealed.

When the giant had counted over the gold till he was tired, he put it up, if possible more securely than he had put up the silver before, and he then fell back on his chair by the fireside and fell asleep. He snored so loud that Jack compared his noise to the roaring of the sea in a high wind, when the tide is coming in. At last Jack concluded him to be asleep and therefore secure. He stole out of his hiding-place and approached the giant, in order to carry off the two bags of money. Just as he laid his hand upon one of the bags a little dog, which he had not observed before, started from under the giant's chair and barked at Jack most furiously, who now gave himself up for lost. Fear riveted him to the spot, and instead of endeavouring to escape he stood still, though expecting his enemy to awake every instant. Contrary, however, to his expectation the giant continued in a sound sleep, and the dog grew weary of barking. Jack now began to recollect himself, and, on looking around, saw a large piece of meat. This he threw to the dog, who instantly seized it, and took it into the lumber-closet which Jack had just left.

Finding himself delivered from a noisy and troublesome enemy, and seeing the giant did not awake, Jack boldly seized the bags, and, throwing them over his shoulders, ran out of the kitchen. He reached the street-door in safety, and found it quite daylight. On his way to the top of the beanstalk he found himself greatly incommoded with the weight of the money bags, and, really, they were so heavy he could scarcely carry them.

Jack was overjoyed when he found himself near the beanstalk. He soon reached the bottom and ran to meet his mother. To his great surprise the cottage was deserted. He ran from one room to another without being able to find anyone. He then hastened into the village, hoping to see some of his neighbours, who could inform him where he could find her.

An old woman at last directed him to a neighbouring house, where his mother was ill of a fever. He was greatly shocked on finding her apparently dying, and could scarcely bear his own reflections on knowing himself to be the cause of it.

On being informed of our hero's safe return, his mother, by degrees, revived, and gradually recovered. Jack presented her his two valuable bags, and they lived happy and comfortably. The cottage was rebuilt and well furnished.

For three years Jack heard no more of the beanstalk, but he could not forget it, though he feared making his mother unhappy. She would not mention the hated beanstalk, lest her doing so should remind him of taking another journey.

Notwithstanding the comforts Jack enjoyed at home, his mind continually dwelt upon the beanstalk, for the fairy's menaces in case of his disobedience were ever present to his mind and prevented him from being happy. He could think of nothing else. It was in vain he endeavoured to amuse himself. He became thoughtful, would arise at the first dawn of day, and would view the beanstalk for hours together.

His mother discovered that something preyed heavily upon his mind, and endeavoured to discover the cause, but Jack knew too well what the consequence would be should he disclose the cause of his melancholy to her. He did his utmost, therefore, to conquer the great desire he had for another journey up the beanstalk. Finding, however, that his inclination grew too powerful for him, he began to make secret preparations for his journey, and, on the longest day, arose as soon as it was light, ascended the beanstalk, and reached the top with some little trouble. He found the road, journey, etc., much as it was on the two former times. He arrived at the giant's mansion in the evening, and found his wife standing, as usual, at the door. Jack had disguised himself so completely that she did not appear to have the least recollection of him. However, when he pleaded hunger and poverty in order to gain admittance, he found it very difficult, indeed, to persuade her. At last he prevailed, and was concealed in the copper.

When the giant returned, he said –

"I smell fresh meat," but Jack felt composed, for the giant had said so before, and had been soon satisfied; however, the giant started up suddenly and searched all round the room. Whilst this was going forward Jack was exceedingly terrified, and ready to die with fear, wishing himself at home a thousand times, and when the giant approached the copper, and put his hand upon the lid, Jack thought his death was certain. The giant ended his search there without moving the lid, and seated himself quietly by the fireside.

The giant at last ate a hearty supper, and when he had finished, he commanded his wife to fetch down his harp. Jack peeped out from under the copper lid and soon saw the most beautiful harp that could be imagined. It was placed by the giant on the table, who said –

"Play," and it instantly played of its own accord, without being touched. The music was uncommonly fine. Jack was delighted, and felt more anxious to get the harp into his possession than either of the former treasures.

The giant's soul was not attuned to harmony, and the music soon lulled him into a sound sleep. Now, therefore, was the time to carry off the harp. As the giant appeared to be in a more profound sleep than usual, Jack, soon determined, got out of the copper and seized the harp. The harp, however, was enchanted by a fairy, and it called out loudly –

"Master, master!"

The giant awoke, stood up, and tried to pursue Jack, but he had drunk so much that he could hardly stand. Poor Jack ran as fast as he could, and, in a little time, the giant recovered sufficiently to walk slowly, or rather, to reel after him. Had he been sober he must have overtaken Jack instantly, but as he then was, Jack contrived to be first at the top of the beanstalk. The giant called after him in a voice like thunder, and sometimes was very near him.

The moment Jack got down the beanstalk he called out for a hatchet, and one was brought him directly. Just at that instant the giant was beginning to descend, but Jack with his hatchet cut the beanstalk close off at the root, which made the giant fall headlong into the garden. The fall killed him, thereby releasing the world from a barbarous enemy.

Jack's mother was delighted when she saw the beanstalk destroyed. At this instant the fairy appeared. She first addressed Jack's mother, and explained every circumstance relating to the journeys up the beanstalk. The fairy then charged Jack to be dutiful to his mother, and to follow his father's good example, which was the only way to be happy. She then disappeared. Jack heartily begged his mother's pardon for all the sorrow and affliction he had caused her, promising most faithfully to be very dutiful and obedient to her in the future.

The Weaver's Son and the Giant of the White Hill

THERE WAS ONCE A WEAVER IN ERIN who lived at the edge of a wood; and on a time when he had nothing to burn, he went out with his daughter to get fagots for the fire.

They gathered two bundles, and were ready to carry them home, when who should come along but a splendid-looking stranger on horseback. And he said to the weaver: "My good man, will you give me that girl of yours?"

"Indeed then I will not," said the weaver.

"I'll give you her weight in gold," said the stranger, and he put out the gold there on the ground.

So the weaver went home with the gold and without the daughter. He buried the gold in the garden, without letting his wife know what he had done. When she asked, "Where is our daughter?" the weaver said: "I sent her on an errand to a neighbour's house for things that I want."

Night came, but no sight of the girl. The next time he went for fagots, the weaver took his second daughter to the wood; and when they had two bundles gathered, and were ready to go home, a second stranger came on horseback, much finer than the first, and asked the weaver would he give him his daughter.

"I will not," said the weaver.

"Well," said the stranger, "I'll give you her weight in silver if you'll let her go with me;" and he put the silver down before him.

The weaver carried home the silver and buried it in the garden with the gold, and the daughter went away with the man on horseback.

When he went again to the wood, the weaver took his third daughter with him; and when they were ready to go home, a third man came on horseback, gave the weight of the third daughter in copper, and took her away. The weaver buried the copper with the gold and silver.

Now, the wife was lamenting and moaning night and day for her three daughters, and gave the weaver no rest till he told the whole story.

Now, a son was born to them; and when the boy grew up and was going to school, he heard how his three sisters had been carried away for their weight in gold and silver and copper; and every day when he came home he saw how his mother was lamenting and wandering outside in grief through the fields and pits and ditches, so he asked her what trouble was on her; but she wouldn't tell him a word.

At last he came home crying from school one day, and said: "I'll not sleep three nights in one house till I find my three sisters." Then he said to his mother: "Make me three loaves of bread, mother, for I am going on a journey."

Next day he asked had she the bread ready. She said she had, and she was crying bitterly all the time. "I'm going to leave you now, mother," said he; "and I'll come back when I have found my three sisters."

He went away, and walked on till he was tired and hungry; and then he sat down to eat the bread that his mother had given him, when a red-haired man came up and asked him for something to eat. "Sit down here," said the boy. He sat down, and the two ate till there was not a crumb of the bread left.

The boy told of the journey he was on; then the red-haired man said: "There may not be much use in your going, but here are three things that'll serve you – the sword of sharpness, the cloth of plenty, and the cloak of darkness. No man can kill you while that sword is in your hand; and whenever you are hungry or dry, all you have to do is to spread the cloth and ask for what you'd like to eat or drink, and it will be there before you. When you put on the cloak, there won't be a man or a woman or a living thing in the world that'll see you, and you'll go to whatever place you have set your mind on quicker than any wind."

The red-haired man went his way, and the boy travelled on. Before evening a great shower came, and he ran for shelter to a large oak-tree. When he got near the tree his foot slipped, the ground opened, and down he went through the earth till he came to another country. When he was in the other country he put on the cloak of darkness and went ahead like a blast of wind, and never stopped till he saw a castle in the distance; and soon he was there. But he found nine gates closed before him, and no way to go through. It was written inside the cloak of darkness that his eldest sister lived in that castle.

He was not long at the gate looking in when a girl came to him and said, "Go on out of that; if you don't, you'll be killed."

"Do you go in," said he to the girl, "and tell my sister, the woman of this castle, to come out to me." The girl ran in; out came the sister, and asked: "Why are you here, and what did you come for?"

"I have come to this country to find my three sisters, who were given away by my father for their weight in gold, silver, and copper; and you are my eldest sister."

She knew from what he said that he was her brother, so she opened the gates and brought him in, saying: "Don't wonder at anything you see in this castle. My husband is enchanted. I see him only at night. He goes off every morning, stays away all day, and comes home in the evening."

The sun went down; and while they were talking, the husband rushed in, and the noise of him was terrible. He came in the form of a ram, ran upstairs, and soon after came down a man.

"Who is this that's with you?" asked he of the wife.

"Oh! that's my brother, who has come from Erin to see me," said she.

Next morning, when the man of the castle was going off in the form of a ram, he turned to the boy and asked, "Will you stay a few days in my castle? You are welcome."

"Nothing would please me better," said the boy; "but I have made a vow never to sleep three nights in one house till I have found my three sisters."

"Well," said the ram, "since you must go, here is something for you." And pulling out a bit of his own wool, he gave it to the boy, saying: "Keep this; and whenever a trouble is on you, take it out, and call on what rams are in the world to help you." Away went the ram. The boy took farewell of his sister, put on the cloak of darkness, and disappeared. He travelled till hungry and tired, then he sat down, took off the cloak of darkness, spread the cloth of plenty, and asked for meat and drink. After he had eaten and drunk his fill, he took up the cloth, put on the cloak of darkness, and went ahead, passing every wind that was before him, and leaving every wind that was behind.

About an hour before sunset he saw the castle in which his second sister lived. When he reached the gate, a girl came out to him and said: "Go away from that gate, or you'll be killed."

"I'll not leave this till my sister who lives in the castle comes out and speaks to me."

The girl ran in, and out came the sister. When she heard his story and his father's name, she knew that he was her brother, and said: "Come into the castle, but think nothing of what you'll see or hear. I don't see my husband from morning till night. He goes and comes in a strange form, but he is a man at night."

About sunset there was a terrible noise, and in rushed the man of the castle in the form of a tremendous salmon. He went flapping upstairs; but he wasn't long there till he came down a fine-looking man.

"Who is that with you?" asked he of the wife. "I thought you would let no one into the castle while I was gone."

"Oh! this is my brother, who has come to see me," said she.

"If he's your brother, he's welcome," said the man.

They supped, and then slept till morning. When the man of the castle was going out again, in the form of a great salmon, he turned to the boy and said: "You'd better stay here with us a while."

"I cannot," said the boy. "I made a vow never to sleep three nights in one house till I had seen my three sisters. I must go on now and find my third sister."

The salmon then took off a piece of his fin and gave it to the boy, saying: "If any difficulty meets you, or trouble comes on you, call on what salmon are in the sea to come and help you."

They parted. The boy put on his cloak of darkness, and away he went, more swiftly than any wind. He never stopped till he was hungry and thirsty. Then he sat down, took off his cloak of darkness, spread the cloth of plenty, and ate his fill; when he had eaten, he went on again till near sundown, when he saw the castle where his third sister lived. All three castles were near the sea. Neither sister knew what place she was in, and neither knew where the other two were living.

The third sister took her brother in just as the first and second had done, telling him not to wonder at anything he saw.

They were not long inside when a roaring noise was heard, and in came the greatest eagle that ever was seen. The eagle hurried upstairs, and soon came down a man.

"Who is that stranger there with you?" asked he of the wife. (He, as well as the ram and salmon, knew the boy; he only wanted to try his wife.)

"This is my brother, who has come to see me."

They all took supper and slept that night. When the eagle was going away in the morning, he pulled a feather out of his wing, and said to the boy: "Keep this; it may serve you. If you are ever in straits and want help, call on what eagles are in the world, and they'll come to you."

There was no hurry now, for the third sister was found; and the boy went upstairs with her to examine the country all around, and to look at the sea. Soon he saw a great white hill, and on the top of the hill a castle.

"In that castle on the white hill beyond," said the sister, "lives a giant, who stole from her home the most beautiful young woman in the world. From all parts the greatest heroes and champions and kings' sons are coming to take her away from the giant and marry her. There is not a man of them all who is able to conquer the giant and free the young woman; but the giant conquers them, cuts their heads off, and then eats their flesh. When he has picked the bones clean, he throws them out; and the whole place around the castle is white with the bones of the men that the giant has eaten."

"I must go," said the boy, "to that castle to know can I kill the giant and bring away the young woman."

So he took leave of his sister, put on the cloak of darkness, took his sword with him, and was soon inside the castle. The giant was fighting with champions outside. When the boy saw the young woman he took off the cloak of darkness and spoke to her.

"Oh!" said she, "what can you do against the giant? No man has ever come to this castle without losing his life. The giant kills every man; and no one has ever come here so big that the giant did not eat him at one meal."

"And is there no way to kill him?" asked the boy.

"I think not," said she.

"Well, if you'll give me something to eat, I'll stay here; and when the giant comes in, I'll do my best to kill him. But don't let on that I am here."

Then he put on the cloak of darkness, and no one could see him. When the giant came in, he had the bodies of two men on his back. He threw down the bodies and told the young woman to get them ready for his dinner. Then he snuffed around, and said: "There's someone here; I smell the blood of an Erineach."

"I don't think you do," said the young woman; "I can't see anyone."

"Neither can I," said the giant; "but I smell a man."

With that the boy drew his sword; and when the giant was struck, he ran in the direction of the blow to give one back; then he was struck on the other side.

They were at one another this way, the giant and the boy with the cloak of darkness on him, till the giant had fifty wounds, and was covered with blood. Every minute he was getting a slash of a sword, but never could give one back. At last he called out: "Whoever you are, wait till tomorrow, and I'll face you then."

So the fighting stopped; and the young woman began to cry and lament as if her heart would break when she saw the state the giant was in. "Oh! you'll be with me no longer; you'll be killed now: what can I do alone without you?" and she tried to please him, and washed his wounds.

"Don't be afraid," said the giant; "this one, whoever he is, will not kill me, for there is no man in the world who can kill me." Then the giant went to bed, and was well in the morning.

Next day the giant and the boy began in the middle of the forenoon, and fought till the middle of the afternoon. The giant was covered with wounds, and he had not given one blow to the boy, and could not see him, for he was always in his cloak of darkness. So the giant had to ask for rest till next morning.

While the young woman was washing and dressing the wounds of the giant she cried and lamented all the time, saying: "What'll become of me now? I'm afraid you'll be killed this time; and how can I live here without you?"

"Have no fear for me," said the giant; "I'll put your mind at rest. In the bottom of the sea is a chest locked and bound, in that chest is a duck, in the duck an egg; and I never can be killed unless someone gets the egg from the duck in the chest at the bottom of the sea, and rubs it on the mole that is under my right breast."

While the giant was telling this to the woman to put her mind at rest, who should be listening to the story but the boy in the cloak of darkness. The minute he heard of the chest in the sea, he thought of the salmon. So off he hurried to the seashore, which was not far away. Then he took out the fin that his eldest sister's husband had given him, and called on what salmon were in the sea to bring up the chest with the duck inside, and put it out on the beach before him.

He had not long to wait till he saw nothing but salmon – the whole sea was covered with them, moving to land; and they put the chest out on the beach before him.

But the chest was locked and strong; how could he open it? He thought of the rams; and taking out the lock of wool, said: "I want what rams are in the world to come and break open this chest!"

That minute the rams of the world were running to the seashore, each with a terrible pair of horns on him; and soon they battered the chest to splinters. Out flew the duck, and away she went over the sea.

The boy took out the feather, and said: "I want what eagles are in the world to get me the egg from that duck."

That minute the duck was surrounded by the eagles of the world, and the egg was soon brought to the boy. He put the feather, the wool and the fin in his pocket, put on the cloak of darkness, and went to the castle on the white hill, and told the young woman, when she was dressing the wounds of the giant again, to raise up his arm.

Next day they fought till the middle of the afternoon. The giant was almost cut to pieces, and called for a cessation.

The young woman hurried to dress the wounds, and he said: "I see you would help me if you could: you are not able. But never fear, I shall not be killed." Then she raised his arm to wash away the blood, and the boy, who was there in his cloak of darkness, struck the mole with the egg. The giant died that minute.

The boy took the young woman to the castle of his third sister. Next day he went back for the treasures of the giant, and there was more gold in the castle than one horse could draw.

They spent nine days in the castle of the eagle with the third sister. Then the boy gave back the feather, and the two went on till they came to the castle of the salmon, where they spent nine more days with the second sister; and he gave back the fin.

When they came to the castle of the ram, they spent fifteen days with the first sister, and had great feasting and enjoyment. Then the boy gave back the lock of wool to the ram, and taking farewell of his sister and her husband, set out for home with the young woman of the white castle, who was now his wife, bringing presents from the three daughters to their father and mother.

At last they reached the opening near the tree, came up through the ground, and went on to where he met the red-haired man. Then he spread the cloth of plenty, asked for every good meat and drink, and called the red-haired man. He came. The three sat down, ate and drank with enjoyment.

When they had finished, the boy gave back to the red-haired man the cloak of darkness, the sword of sharpness, and the cloth of plenty, and thanked him.

"You were kind to me," said the red-haired man; "you gave me of your bread when I asked for it, and told me where you were going. I took pity on you; for I knew you never could get what you wanted unless I helped you. I am the brother of the eagle, the salmon and the ram."

They parted. The boy went home, built a castle with the treasure of the giant, and lived happily with his parents and wife.

The King of Lochlin's Three Daughters

THERE WAS A KING OVER LOCHLIN, once upon a time, who had a leash of daughters; they went out (on) a day to take a walk; and there came three giants, and they took with them the daughters of the king, and there was no knowing where they had gone. Then the king sent word for the sheanachy, and he asked him if he knew where his lot of daughters had gone. The sheanachy said to the king that three giants had taken them with them, and they were in the earth down below by them, and there was no way to get them but by making a ship that would sail on sea and land; and so it was that the king set out an order, anyone who would build a ship that would sail on sea and on land, that he should get the king's big daughter to marry. There was a widow there who had a leash of sons; and the eldest said to his mother on a day that was there, "Cook for me a bannock, and roast a cock; I am going away to cut wood, and to build a ship that will go to seek the daughters of the king." His mother said to him, "Which is better with thee, the big bannock with my cursing, or a little bannock with my blessing?"

"Give me a big bannock, it will be small enough before I build a ship." He got a bannock and he went away. He arrived where there was a great wood and a river, and there he sat at the side of the river to take the bannock. A great Uruisg came out of the river, and she asked a part of the bannock. He said that he would not give her a morsel, that it was little enough for himself. He began cutting the wood, and every tree he cut would be on foot again; and so he was till the night came.

When the night came, he went home mournful, tearful, blind sorrowful. His mother asked, "How went it with thee today, son?" He said, "That it went but black ill; every tree I would cut would be on foot again." A day or two after this the middle brother said that he himself would go; and he asked his mother to cook him a cake and roast him a cock; and in the very way as happened to his eldest brother, so it happened to him. The mother said the very same thing to the young one; and *he* took the little bannock. The Uruisg came, and she asked a part of the cake and the cock. He said to her, "That she should get that." When the Uruisg had eaten her own share of the cake and of the cock, she said to him, That she knew what had brought him there as well as he himself, but he was to go home; but to be sure to meet her there at the end of a day and year; and that the ship would be ready at the end.

It was thus it happened: At the end of a day and a year the widow's young son went, and he found that the Uruisg had the ship floating on the river, fully equipped. He went away then with the ship, and a leash of gentlemen, as great as were in the kingdom, that were to marry the daughters of the king. They were but a short time sailing when they saw a man drinking a river that was there. He asked him, "What art thou doing there?"

"I am drinking up this river."

"Thou hadst better come with me, and I will give thee meat and wages, and better work than that."

"I will do that," said he. They had not gone far forward, when they saw a man eating a stot in a park. "What art thou doing there?" said he.

"I am here going to eat all the stots in this park."

"Thou hadst better go with me, and thou wilt get work, and wages better than raw flesh."

"I will do that," said he. They went but a short distance when they saw another man with his ear to the earth.

"What art thou doing there?" said he.

"I am here hearing the grass coming through earth."

"Go with me, and thou wilt get meat, and better wages than to be there with thy ear to the earth." They were thus sailing back and forward, when the man who was listening said, "That this was the place in which were the king's daughters and the giants." The widow's son, and the three that had fallen in with them, were let down in a creel in a great hole that was there. They reached the house of the big giant. "Ha! ha!" said he, the giant, "I knew well what thou art seeking here. Thou art seeking the king's daughter, but thou wilt not get that, unless thou hast a man that wilt drink as much water as I." He set the man who was drinking the river to hold drinking against the giant; and before he was half satisfied the giant burst. Then they went where the second giant was. "Ho, both! ha, hath!" said the giant, "I know well what sent thee here;

thou art seeking the king's daughter; but thou shalt not get her, if thou hast not a man who will eat as much flesh as I." He set the man who was eating the stot to hold the eating of flesh against the giant; but before he was half satisfied the giant burst. Then he went where the third giant was. "Haio!" said the giant, "I know what set thee here; but thou wilt not get the king's daughter, by any means, unless thou stayest a day and a year by me a sgalag" (slave, servant).

"I will do that," said he; and he sent up in the basket, first the three men, and then the king's daughters. The three great men were waiting at the mouth of the hole till they should come up, and they went with them where the king was; and they told the king that they themselves had done all the daring deeds that there were.

When the end of a day and year had come, he said to the giant, "that he was going." The giant said, "That he had an eagle that would set him up to the top of the hole." The giant set the eagle away with him, and five stots and ten for a meal for her; but the eagle went not halfway up through the hole when she had eaten the stots, and she returned back again.

Then the giant said to him, "Thou must remain by me another day and year, and then I will send thee away." When the end of this year came he sent the eagle away with him, and ten stots and twenty. They went this time well further on than they went before, but she ate the stots and she turned back. "Thou must," said the giant, "stay by me another year, and then I will send thee away." The end of this year came, and the giant sent them away, and three score of stots for the eagle's meat; and when they were at the mouth of the hole the stots were expended, and she was going to turn back; but he took a steak out of his own thigh, and he gave this to the eagle, and with one spring she was on the surface of the earth.

At the time of parting the eagle gave him a whistle, and she said to him, "Any hard lot that comes on thee, whistle and I will be at thy side." He did not allow his foot to stop, or empty a puddle out of his shoe, till he reached the king's big town. He went where there was a smith who was in the town, and he asked the smith if he was in want of a gillie to blow the bellows. The smith said that he was. He was but a short time by the smith, when the king's big daughter sent word for the smith. "I am hearing," said she, "that thou art the best smith in the town; but if thou dost not make for me a golden crown, like the golden crown that I had when I was by the giant, the head shall be taken off thee."

The smith came home sorrowfully, lamentably; and his wife asked him his news from the king's house. "There is but poor news," said the smith; "the king's daughter is asking that a golden crown shall be made for her, like the crown that she had when she was under the earth by the giant; but what do I know what likeness was on the crown that the giant had." The bellows-blowing gillie said, "Let not that set thee thinking; get thou for me enough of gold, and I will not be long making the crown." The smith got of gold as he asked, with the king's order. The gillie went into the smithy, and he shut the door; and he began to splinter the gold asunder, and to throw it out of the window. Each one that came the way was gathering the gold, that the bellows lad was hurling out. Here, then, he blew the whistle, and in the twinkling of an eye the eagle came. "Go," said he to the eagle, "and bring here the golden crown that is above the big giant's door." The eagle went, and she was not long on the way, and the crown (was) with her. He gave the crown to the smith. The smith went so merrily, cheerily with the crown where the king's daughter was. "Well then," said she, "if I did not know that it could not be done, I would not believe that this is not the crown I had when I was with the big giant." The king's middle daughter said to the smith, "Thou wilt lose the head if thou dost not make for me, a silver crown, like the one I had when I was by the giant."

The smith took himself home in misery: but his wife went to meet him, expecting great news and flattery; but so it was, that the gillie said that he would make a silver crown if he could get enough of silver. The smith got plenty of silver with the king's order. The gillie went, and he did as he did before. He whistled: the eagle came. "Go," said he, "and bring hither here to me, the silver crown that the king's middle daughter had when she was by the giant."

The eagle went, and she was not long on the journey with the silver crown. The smith went merrily, cheerily, with the silver crown to the king's daughter. "Well, then," said she, "it is marvellously like the crown I had when I was by the giant." The king's young daughter said to the smith that he should make a copper crown for her, like the copper crown she had when she was by the giant. The smith now was taking courage, and he went home much more pleasantly this turn. The gillie began to splinter the copper, and to throw it out of each door and window; and now they were from each end of the town gathering the copper, as they were gathering the silver and gold. He blew the whistle, and the eagle was at his side.

"Go back," said he, "and bring here hither to me the copper crown that the king's young daughter had when she was by the giant," The eagle went, and she was not long going and coming. He gave the crown to the smith. The smith went merrily, cheerily, and he gave it to the king's young daughter. "Well, then!" said she, "I would not believe that this was not the very crown that I had when I was by the giant underground, if there were a way of getting it." Here the king said to the smith, that he must tell him where he had learned crown making, "for I did not know that the like of thee was in the kingdom."

"Well, then," said the smith, "with your leave, oh king, it was not I who made the crowns, but the gillie I have blowing the bellows."

"I must see thy gillie," said the king, "till he makes a crown for myself."

The king ordered four horses in a coach, and that they should go to seek the smith's gillie; and when the coach came to the smithy, the smith's gillie was smutty and dirty, blowing the bellows. The horse gillies came, and they asked for the man who was going to look on the king. The smith said, "That was he yonder, blowing the bellows."

"Oov! oov!" said they; and they (set) to catch him, and throw him head foremost into the coach, as if they had a dog.

They went not far on their journey when he blew the whistle. The eagle was at his side. "If ever thou didst good for me take me out of this, and fill it full of stones," said he. The eagle did this. The king was out waiting on the coach; and when the king opened the door of the coach, he was like to be dead with the stones bouncing on top of him. There was catching of the horse gillies, and hanging them for giving such an affront to the king,

Here the king sent other gillies with a coach and when they reached the smithy, "Oov! oov!" said they. "Is this, the black thing the king sent us to seek?" They caught him, and they cast him into the coach as if they had a turf peat. But they went not far on their way when he blew the whistle, and the eagle was at his side; and he said to her, "Take me out of this, and fill it with every dirt thou canst get." When the coach reached the king's palace, the king went to open the door. Each dirt and rubbish fell about the king's head. Then the king was in a great rage, and he ordered the horse gillies to be hanged immediately. Here the king sent his own confidential servant away; and when he reached the smithy, he caught the black bellows-blowing gillie by the hand. "The king," said he, "sent me to seek thee. Thou hadst better clean a little of the coal off thy face."

The gillie did this; he cleaned himself well, and right well; and the king's servant caught him by the hand, and he put him into the coach. They were but a short time going, when he blew the whistle. The eagle came; and he asked her to bring the gold and silver dress that was by the big giant here without delay, and the eagle was not long going and coming with the dress. He arrayed himself with the giant's dress. And when they came to the king's palace, the king came, and he opened the door of the coach, and there was the very finest man the king ever saw. The king took him in, and he told the king how it happened to him from first to last. The three great men who were going to marry the king's daughters were hanged, and the king's big daughter was given him to marry; and they made them a wedding the length of twenty nights and twenty days; and I left them dancing, and I know not but that they are cutting capers on the floor till the day of today.

Peerifool

THERE WAS ONCE A KING AND A QUEEN in Rousay who had three daughters. When the young Princesses were just grown up, the King died, and the Crown passed to a distant cousin, who had always hated him, and who paid no heed to the widowed Queen and her daughters.

So they were left very badly off, and they went to live in a tiny cottage, and did all the housework themselves. They had a kailyard in front of the cottage, and a little field behind it, and they had a cow that grazed in the field, and which they fed with the cabbages that grew in the kailyard. For everyone knows that to feed cows with cabbages makes them give a larger quantity of milk.

But they soon discovered that someone was coming at night and stealing the cabbages, and, of course, this annoyed them very much. For they knew that if they had not cabbages to give to the cow, they would not have enough milk to sell.

So the eldest Princess said she would take out a three-legged stool, and wrap herself in a blanket, and sit in the kailyard all night to see if she could catch the thief. And, although it was very cold and very dark, she did so.

At first it seemed as if all her trouble would be in vain, for hour after hour passed and nothing happened. But in the small hours of the morning, just as the clock was striking two, she heard a stealthy trampling in the field behind, as if some very heavy person were trying to tread very softly, and presently a mighty Giant stepped right over the wall into the kailyard.

He carried an enormous creel on his arm, and a large, sharp knife in his hand; and he began to cut the cabbages, and to throw them into the creel as fast as he could.

Now the Princess was no coward, so, although she had not expected to face a Giant, she gathered up her courage, and cried out sharply, "Who gave thee liberty to cut our cabbages? Leave off this minute, and go away."

The Giant paid no heed, but went on steadily with what he was doing.

"Dost thou not hear me?" cried the girl indignantly; for she was the Princess Royal, and had always been accustomed to be obeyed.

"If thou be not quiet I will take thee too," said the Giant grimly, pressing the cabbages down into the creel.

"I should like to see thee try," retorted the Princess, rising from her stool and stamping her foot; for she felt so angry that she forgot for a moment that she was only a weak maiden and he was a great and powerful Giant.

And, as if to show her how strong he was, he seized her by her arm and her leg, and put her in his creel on the top of the cabbages, and carried her away bodily.

When he reached his home, which was in a great square house on a lonely moor, he took her out, and set her down roughly on the floor.

"Thou wilt be my servant now," he said, "and keep my house, and do my errands for me. I have a cow, which thou must drive out every day to the hillside; and see, here is a bag of wool, when thou hast taken out the cow, thou must come back and settle thyself at home, as a good housewife should, and comb, and card it, and spin it into yarn, with which to weave a good thick cloth for my raiment. I am out most of the day, but when I come home I shall expect to find all this done, and a great bicker of porridge boiled besides for my supper."

The poor Princess was very dismayed when she heard these words, for she had never been accustomed to work hard, and she had always had her sisters to help her; but the Giant took no notice of her distress, but went out as soon as it was daylight, leaving her alone in the house to begin her work.

As soon as he had gone she drove the cow to the pasture, as he had told her to do; but she had a good long walk over the moor before she reached the hill, and by the time that she got back to the house she felt very tired.

So she thought that she would put on the porridge pot, and make herself some porridge before she began to card and comb the wool. She did so, and just as she was sitting down to sup them the door opened, and a crowd of wee, wee Peerie Folk came in.

They were the tiniest men and women that the Princess had ever seen; not one of them would have reached halfway to her knee; and they were dressed in dresses fashioned out of all the colours of the rainbow – scarlet and blue, green and yellow, orange and violet; and the funny thing was, that every one of them had a shock of straw-coloured yellow hair.

They were all talking and laughing with one another; and they hopped up, first on stools, then on chairs, till at last they reached the top of the table, where they clustered round the bowl, out of which the Princess was eating her porridge.

"We be hungry, we be hungry," they cried, in their tiny shrill voices. "Spare a little porridge for the Peerie Folk."

But the Princess was hungry also; and, besides being hungry, she was both tired and cross; so she shook her head and waved them impatiently away with her spoon,

"Little for one, and less for two,
And never a grain have I for you."

she said sharply, and, to her great delight, for she did not feel quite comfortable with all the Peerie Folk standing on the table looking at her, they vanished in a moment.

After this she finished her porridge in peace; then she took the wool out of the bag, and she set to work to comb and card it. But it seemed as if it were bewitched; it curled and twisted and coiled itself round her fingers so that, try as she would, she could not do anything with it. And when the Giant came home he found her sitting in despair with it all in confusion round her, and the porridge, which she had left for him in the pot, burned to a cinder.

As you may imagine, he was very angry, and raged, and stamped, and used the most dreadful words; and at last he took her by the heels, and beat her until all her back was skinned and bleeding; then he carried her out to the byre, and threw her up on the joists among the hens. And, although she was not dead, she was so stunned and bruised that she could only lie there motionless, looking down on the backs of the cows.

Time went on, and in the kailyard at home the cabbages were disappearing as fast as ever. So the second Princess said that she would do as her sister had done, and wrap herself in a blanket, and go and sit on a three-legged stool all night, to see what was becoming of them.

She did so, and exactly the same fate befell her that had befallen her elder sister. The Giant appeared with his creel, and he carried her off, and set her to mind the cow and the house, and to make his porridge and to spin; and the little yellow-headed Peerie Folk appeared and asked her for some supper, and she refused to give it to them; and after that, she could not comb or card her wool, and the Giant was angry, and he scolded her, and beat her, and threw her up, half dead, on the joists beside her sister and the hens.

Then the youngest Princess determined to sit out in the kailyard all night, not so much to see what was becoming of the cabbages, as to discover what had happened to her sisters.

And when the Giant came and carried her off, she was not at all sorry, but very glad, for she was a brave and loving little maiden; and now she felt that she had a chance of finding out where they were, and whether they were dead or alive.

So she was quite cheerful and happy, for she felt certain that she was clever enough to outwit the Giant, if only she were watchful and patient; so she lay quite quietly in her creel above the cabbages, but she kept her eyes very wide open to see by which road he was carrying her off.

And when he set her down in his kitchen, and told her all that he expected her to do, she did not look downcast like her sisters, but nodded her head brightly, and said that she felt sure that she could do it.

And she sang to herself as she drove the cow over the moor to pasture, and she ran the whole way back, so that she should have a good long afternoon to work at the wool, and, although she would not have told the Giant this, to search the house.

Before she set to work, however, she made herself some porridge, just as her sisters had done; and, just as she was going to sup them, all the little yellow-haired Peerie Folk trooped in, and climbed up on the table, and stood and stared at her.

"We be hungry, we be hungry," they cried. "Spare a little porridge for the Peerie Folk."

"With all my heart," replied the good-natured Princess. "If you can find dishes little enough for you to sup out of, I will fill them for you. But, methinks, if I were to give you all porringers, you would smother yourselves among the porridge."

At her words the Peerie Folk shouted with laughter, till their straw-coloured hair tumbled right over their faces; then they hopped on to the floor and ran out of the house, and presently they came trooping back holding cups of blue-bells, and foxgloves, and saucers of primroses and anemones in their hands; and the Princess put a tiny spoonful of porridge into each saucer, and a tiny drop of milk into each cup, and they ate it all up as daintily as possible with neat little grass spoons, which they had brought with them in their pockets.

When they had finished they all cried out, "Thank you! Thank you!" and ran out of the kitchen again, leaving the Princess alone. And, being alone, she went all over the house to look for her sisters, but, of course, she could not find them.

"Never mind, I will find them soon," she said to herself. "Tomorrow I will search the byre and the outhouses; in the meantime, I had better get on with my work." So she went back to the kitchen, and took out the bag of wool, which the Giant had told her to make into cloth.

But just as she was doing so the door opened once more, and a Yellow-Haired Peerie Boy entered. He was exactly like the other Peerie Folk who had eaten the Princess's porridge, only he was bigger, and he wore a very rich dress of grass-green velvet. He walked boldly into the middle of the kitchen and looked round him.

"Hast thou any work for me to do?" he asked. "I ken grand how to handle wool and turn it into fine thick cloth."

"I have plenty of work for anybody who asks it," replied the Princess; "but I have no money to pay for it, and there are but few folk in this world who will work without wages."

"All the wages that I ask is that thou wilt take the trouble to find out my name, for few folk ken it, and few folk care to ken. But if by any chance thou canst not find it out, then must thou pay toll of half of thy cloth."

The Princess thought that it would be quite an easy thing to find out the Boy's name, so she agreed to the bargain, and, putting all the wool back into the bag, she gave it to him, and he swung it over his shoulder and departed.

She ran to the door to see where he went, for she had made up her mind that she would follow him secretly to his home, and find out from the neighbours what his name was.

But to her great dismay, though she looked this way and that, he had vanished completely, and she began to wonder what she should do if the Giant came back and found that she had allowed someone, whose name she did not even know, to carry off all the wool.

And, as the afternoon wore on, and she could think of no way of finding out who the boy was, or where he came from, she felt that she had made a great mistake, and she began to grow very frightened.

Just as the gloaming was beginning to fall a knock came at the door, and, when she opened it, she found an old woman standing outside, who begged for a night's lodging.

Now, as I have told you, the Princess was very kind-hearted, and she would fain have granted the poor old Dame's request, but she dared not, for she did not know what the Giant would say. So she told the old woman that she could not take her in for the night, as she was only a servant, and not the mistress of the house; but she made her sit down on a bench beside the door, and brought her out some bread and milk, and gave her some water to bathe her poor, tired feet.

She was so bonnie, and gentle, and kind, and she looked so sorry when she told her that she would need to turn her away, that the old woman gave her her blessing, and told her not to vex herself, as it was a fine, dry night, and now that she had had a meal she could easily sit down somewhere and sleep in the shelter of the outhouses.

And, when she had finished her bread and milk, she went and laid down by the side of a green knowe, which rose out of the moor not very far from the byre door.

And, strange to say, as she lay there she felt the earth beneath her getting warmer and warmer, until she was so hot that she was fain to crawl up the side of the hillock, in the hope of getting a mouthful of fresh air.

And as she got near the top she heard a voice, which seemed to come from somewhere beneath her, saying, "TEASE, TEASENS, TEASE; CARD, CARDENS, CARD; SPIN, SPINNENS, SPIN; for PEERIFOOL PEERIFOOL, PEERIFOOL is what men call me." And when she got to the very top, she found that there was a crack in the earth, through which rays of light were coming; and when she put her eye to the crack, what should she see down below her but a brilliantly lighted chamber, in which all the Peerie Folk were sitting in a circle, working away as hard as they could.

Some of them were carding wool, some of them were combing it, some of them were spinning it, constantly wetting their fingers with their lips, in order to twist the yarn fine as they drew it from the distaff, and some of them were spinning the yarn into cloth.

While round and round the circle, cracking a little whip, and urging them to work faster, was a Yellow-Haired Peerie Boy.

"This is a strange thing, and these be odd on-goings," said the old woman to herself, creeping hastily down to the bottom of the hillock again. "I must e'en go and tell the bonnie lassie in the house yonder. Maybe the knowledge of what I have seen will stand her in good stead some day. When there be Peerie Folk about, it is well to be on one's guard."

So she went back to the house and told the Princess all that she had seen and heard, and the Princess was so delighted with what she had told her that she risked the Giant's wrath and allowed her to go and sleep in the hayloft.

It was not very long after the old woman had gone to rest before the door opened, and the Peerie Boy appeared once more with a number of webs of cloth upon his shoulder. "Here is thy cloth," he said, with a sly smile, "and I will put it on the shelf for thee the moment that thou tellest me what my name is."

Then the Princess, who was a merry maiden, thought that she would tease the little follow for a time ere she let him know that she had found out his secret.

So she mentioned first one name and then another, always pretending to think that she had hit upon the right one; and all the time the Peerie Boy jumped from side to side with delight, for he thought that she would never find out the right name, and that half of the cloth would be his.

But at last the Princess grew tired of joking, and she cried out, with a little laugh of triumph, "Dost thou by any chance ken anyone called PEERIFOOL, little Mannikin?"

Then he knew that in some way she had found out what men called him, and he was so angry and disappointed that he flung the webs of cloth down in a heap on the floor, and ran out at the door, slamming it behind him.

Meanwhile the Giant was coming down the hill in the darkening, and, to his astonishment, he met a troop of little Peerie Folk toiling up it, looking as if they were so tired that they could hardly get along. Their eyes were dim and listless, their heads were hanging on their breasts, and their lips were so long and twisted that the poor little people looked quite hideous.

The Giant asked how this was, and they told him that they had to work so hard all day, spinning for their Master that they were quite exhausted; and that the reason why their lips were so distorted was that they used them constantly to wet their fingers, so that they might pull the wool in very fine strands from the distaff.

"I always thought a great deal of women who could spin," said the Giant, "and I looked out for a housewife that could do so. But after this I will be more careful, for the housewife that I have now is a bonnie little woman, and I would be loath to have her spoil her face in that manner."

And he hurried home in a great state of mind in case he should find that his new servant's pretty red lips had grown long and ugly in his absence.

Great was his relief to see her standing by the table, bonnie and winsome as ever, with all the webs of cloth in a pile in front of her.

"By my troth, thou art an industrious maiden," he said, in high good humour, "and, as a reward for working so diligently, I will restore thy sisters to thee." And he went out to the byre, and lifted the two other Princesses down from the rafters, and brought them in and laid them on the settle.

Their little sister nearly screamed aloud when she saw how ill they looked and how bruised their backs were, but, like a prudent maiden, she held her tongue, and busied herself with applying a cooling ointment to their wounds, and binding them up, and by and by her sisters revived, and, after the Giant had gone to bed, they told her all that had befallen them.

"I will be avenged on him for his cruelty," said the little Princess firmly; and when she spoke like that her sisters knew that she meant what she said.

So next morning, before the Giant was up, she fetched his creel, and put her eldest sister into it, and covered her with all the fine silken hangings and tapestry that she could find, and on the top of all she put a handful of grass, and when the Giant came downstairs she asked him, in her sweetest tone, if he would do her a favour.

And the Giant, who was very pleased with her because of the quantity of cloth which he thought she had spun, said that he would.

"Then carry that creelful of grass home to my mother's cottage for her cow to eat," said the Princess. "'Twill help to make up for all the cabbages which thou hast stolen from her kailyard."

And, wonderful to relate, the Giant did as he was bid, and carried the creel to the cottage.

Next morning she put her second sister into another creel, and covered her with all the fine napery she could find in the house, and put an armful of grass on the top of it, and at her bidding the Giant, who was really getting very fond of her, carried it also home to her mother.

The next morning the little Princess told him that she thought that she would go for a long walk after she had done her housework, and that she might not be in when he came home at night, but that she would have another creel of grass ready for him, if he would carry it to the cottage as he had done on the two previous evenings. He promised to do so; then, as usual, he went out for the day.

In the afternoon the clever little maiden went through the house, gathering together all the lace, and silver, and jewellery that she could find, and brought them and placed them beside the creel. Then she went out and cut an armful of grass, and brought it in and laid it beside them.

Then she crept into the creel herself, and pulled all the fine things in above her, and then she covered everything up with the grass, which was a very difficult thing to do, seeing she herself was at the bottom of the basket. Then she lay quite still and waited.

Presently the Giant came in, and, obedient to his promise, he lifted the creel and carried it off to the old Queen's cottage.

No one seemed to be at home, so he set it down in the entry, and turned to go away. But the little Princess had told her sisters what to do, and they had a great can of boiling water ready in one of the rooms upstairs, and when they heard his steps coming round that side of the house, they threw open the window and emptied it all over his head; and that was the end of him.

The Frog and the Lion Fairy

ONCE UPON A TIME there lived a king who was always at war with his neighbours, which was very strange, as he was a good and kind man, quite content with his own country, and not wanting to seize land belonging to other people. Perhaps he may have tried too much to please everybody, and that often ends in pleasing nobody; but at any rate, he found himself, at the end of a hard struggle, defeated in battle, and obliged to fall back behind the walls of his capital city. Once there, he began to make preparations for a long siege, and the first thing he did was to plan how best to send his wife to a place of security.

The queen, who loved her husband dearly, would gladly have remained with him to share his dangers, but he would not allow it. So they parted, with many tears, and the queen set out with a strong guard to a fortified castle on the outskirts of a great forest, some two hundred miles distant. She cried nearly all the way, and when she arrived she cried still more, for everything in the castle was dusty and old, and outside there was only a gravelled courtyard, and the king had forbidden her to go beyond the walls without at least two soldiers to take care of her.

Now the queen had only been married a few months, and in her own home she had been used to walk and ride all over the hills without any attendants at all; so she felt very dull at her being shut up in this way. However, she bore it for a long while because it was the king's wish, but when time passed and there were no signs of the war drifting in the direction of the castle, she grew bolder, and sometimes strayed outside the walls, in the direction of the forest.

Then came a dreadful period when news from the king ceased entirely.

"He must surely be ill or dead," thought the poor girl, who even now was only sixteen. "I can bear it no longer, and if I do not get a letter from him soon I shall leave this horrible place and go back to see what is the matter. Oh! I do wish I had never come away!"

So, without telling anyone what she intended to do, she ordered a little low carriage to be built, something like a sledge, only it was on two wheels – just big enough to hold one person.

"I am tired of being always in the castle," she said to her attendants; "and I mean to hunt a little. Quite close by, of course," she added, seeing the anxious look on their faces. "And there is no reason that you should not hunt too."

All the faces brightened at that, for, to tell the truth, they were nearly as dull as their mistress; so the queen had her way, and two beautiful horses were brought from the stable to draw the little chariot. At first the queen took care to keep near the rest of the hunt, but gradually she stayed away longer and longer, and at last, one morning, she took advantage of the appearance of a wild boar, after which her whole court instantly galloped to turn into a path in the opposite direction.

Unluckily, it did not happen to lead towards the king's palace, where she intended to go, but she was so afraid her flight would be noticed that she whipped up her horses till they ran away.

When she understood what was happening, the poor young queen was terribly frightened, and, dropping the reins, clung to the side of the chariot. The horses, thus left without any control, dashed blindly against a tree, and the queen was flung out on the ground, where she lay for some minutes unconscious.

A rustling sound near her at length caused her to open her eyes; before her stood a huge woman, almost a giantess, without any clothes save a lion's skin, which was thrown over her shoulders, while a dried snake's skin was plaited into her hair. In one hand she held a club on which she leaned, and in the other a quiver full of arrows.

At the sight of this strange figure the queen thought she must be dead, and gazing on an inhabitant of another world. So she murmured softly to herself:

"I am not surprised that people are so loath to die when they know that they will see such horrible creatures." But low as she spoke, the giantess caught the words, and began to laugh.

"Oh, don't be afraid; you are still alive, and perhaps, after all, you may be sorry for it. I am the Lion Fairy, and you are going to spend the rest of your days with me in my palace, which is quite near this. So come along." But the queen shrank back in horror.

"Oh, Madam Lion, take me back, I pray you, to my castle; and fix what ransom you like, for my husband will pay it, whatever it is." But the giantess shook her head.

"I am rich enough already," she answered, "but I am often dull, and I think you may amuse me a little." And, so saying, she changed her shape into that of a lion, and throwing the queen across her back, she went down the ten thousand steps that led to her palace. The lion had reached the centre of the earth before she stopped in front of a house, lighted with lamps, and built on the edge of a lake of quicksilver. In this lake various huge monsters might be seen playing or fighting – the queen did not know which – and around flew rooks and ravens, uttering dismal croaks. In the distance was a mountain down whose sides waters slowly coursed – these were the tears of unhappy lovers – and nearer the gate were trees without either fruit of flowers, while nettles and brambles covered the ground. If the castle had been gloomy, what did the queen feel about this?

For some days the queen was so much shaken by all she had gone through that she lay with her eyes closed, unable either to move or speak. When she got better, the Lion Fairy told her that if she liked she could build herself a cabin, as she would have to spend her life in that place. At these words the queen burst into tears, and implored her gaoler to put her to death rather than condemn her to such a life; but the Lion Fairy only laughed, and counselled her to try to make herself pleasant, as many worse things might befall her.

"Is there no way in which I can touch your heart?" asked the poor girl in despair.

"Well, if you really wish to please me you will make me a pasty out of the stings of bees, and be sure it is good."

"But I don't see any bees," answered the queen, looking round.

"Oh, no, there aren't any," replied her tormentor; "but you will have to find them all the same." And, so saying, she went away.

"After all, what does it matter?" thought the queen to herself, "I have only one life, and I can but lose it." And not caring what she did, she left the palace and seating herself under a yew tree, poured out all her grief.

"Oh, my dear husband," wept she, "what will you think when you come to the castle to fetch me and find me gone? Rather a thousand times that you should fancy me dead than imagine that I had forgotten you! Ah, how fortunate that the broken chariot should be lying in the wood, for then you may grieve for me as one devoured by wild beasts. And if another should take my place in your heart – well, at least I shall never know it."

She might have continued for long in this fashion had not the voice of a crow directly overhead attracted her attention. Looking up to see what was the matter she beheld, in the dim light, a crow holding a fat frog in his claws, which he evidently intended for his supper. The queen rose hastily from the seat, and striking the bird sharply on the claws with the fan which hung from her side, she forced him to drop the frog, which fell to the ground more dead than alive. The crow, furious at his disappointment, flew angrily away.

As soon as the frog had recovered her senses she hopped up to the queen, who was still sitting under the yew. Standing on her hind legs, and bowing low before her, she said gently:

"Beautiful lady, by what mischance do you come here? You are the only creature that I have seen do a kind deed since a fatal curiosity lured me to this place."

"What sort of a frog can you be that knows the language of mortals?" asked the queen in her turn. "But if you do, tell me, I pray, if I alone am a captive, for hitherto I have beheld no one but the monsters of the lake."

"Once upon a time they were men and women like yourself," answered the frog, "but having power in their hands, they used it for their own pleasure. Therefore Fate has sent them here for a while to bear the punishment of their misdoings."

"But you, friend frog, you are not one of these wicked people, I am sure?" asked the queen.

"I am half a fairy," replied the frog; "but, although I have certain magic gifts, I am not able to do all I wish. And if the Lion Fairy were to know of my presence in her kingdom she would hasten to kill me."

"But if you are a fairy, how was it that you were so nearly slain by the crow?" said the queen, wrinkling her forehead.

"Because the secret of my power lies in my little cap that is made of rose leaves; but I had laid it aside for the moment, when that horrible crow pounced upon me. Once it is on my head I fear nothing. But let me repeat; had it not been for you I could not have escaped death, and if I can do anything to help you, or soften your hard fate, you have only to tell me."

"Alas," sighed the queen, "I have been commanded by the Lion Fairy to make her a pasty out of the stings of bees, and, as far as I can discover, there are none here; as how should there be, seeing there are no flowers for them to feed on? And, even if there were, how could I catch them?"

"Leave it to me," said the frog, "I will manage it for you." And, uttering a strange noise, she struck the ground thrice with her foot. In an instant six thousand frogs appeared before her, one of them bearing a little cap.

"Cover yourselves with honey, and hop round by the beehives," commanded the frog, putting on the cap which her friend was holding in her mouth. And turning to the queen, she added:

"The Lion Fairy keeps a store of bees in a secret place near to the bottom of the ten thousand steps leading into the upper world. Not that she wants them for herself, but they are sometimes useful to her in punishing her victims. However, this time we will get the better of her."

Just as she had finished speaking the six thousand frogs returned, looking so strange with bees sticking to every part of them that, sad as she felt, the poor queen could not help laughing. The bees were all so stupefied with what they had eaten that it was possible to draw their stings without hunting them. So, with the help of her friend, the queen soon made ready her pasty and carried it to the Lion Fairy.

"Not enough pepper," said the giantess, gulping down large morsels, in order to hide the surprise she felt. "Well, you have escaped this time, and I am glad to find I have got a companion a little more intelligent than the others I have tried. Now, you had better go and build yourself a house."

So the queen wandered away, and picking up a small axe which lay near the door she began with the help of her friend the frog to cut down some cypress trees for the purpose. And not content with that, the six thousand froggy servants were told to help also, and it was not long before they had built the prettiest little cabin in the world, and made a bed in one corner of dried ferns which they fetched from the top of the ten thousand steps. It looked soft and comfortable, and the queen was very glad to lie down upon it, so tired was she with all that had happened since the morning. Scarcely, however, had she fallen asleep when the lake monsters began to make the most horrible noises just outside, while a small dragon crept in and terrified her so that she ran away, which was just what the dragon wanted!

The poor queen crouched under a rock for the rest of the night, and the next morning, when she woke from her troubled dreams, she was cheered at seeing the frog watching by her.

"I hear we shall have to build you another palace," said she. "Well, this time we won't go so near the lake." And she smiled with her funny wide mouth, till the queen took heart, and they went together to find wood for the new cabin.

The tiny palace was soon ready, and a fresh bed made of wild thyme, which smelt delicious. Neither the queen nor the frog said anything about it, but somehow, as always happens, the story came to the ears of the Lion Fairy, and she sent a raven to fetch the culprit.

"What gods or men are protecting you?" she asked, with a frown. "This earth, dried up by a constant rain of sulphur and fire, produces nothing, yet I hear that *your* bed is made of sweet smelling herbs. However, as you can get flowers for yourself, of course you can get them for me, and in an hour's time I must have in my room a nosegay of the rarest flowers. If not—! Now you can go."

The poor queen returned to her house looking so sad that the frog, who was waiting for her, noticed it directly.

"What is the matter?" said she, smiling.

"Oh, how can you laugh!" replied the queen. "This time I have to bring her in an hour a posy of the rarest flowers, and where am I to find them? If I fail I know she will kill me."

"Well, I must see if I can't help you," answered the frog. "The only person I have made friends with here is a bat. She is a good creature, and always does what I tell her, so I will just lend her my cap, and if she puts it on, and flies into the world, she will bring back all we want. I would go myself, only she will be quicker."

Then the queen dried her eyes, and waited patiently, and long before the hour had gone by the bat flew in with all the most beautiful and sweetest flowers that grew on the earth. The girl sprang up overjoyed at the sight, and hurried with them to the Lion Fairy, who was so astonished that for once she had nothing to say.

Now the smell and touch of the flowers had made the queen sick with longing for her home, and she told the frog that she would certainly die if she did not manage to escape somehow.

"Let me consult my cap," said the frog; and taking it off she laid it in a box, and threw in after it a few sprigs of juniper, some capers and two peas, which she carried under her right leg; she then shut down the lid of the box, and murmured some words which the queen did not catch.

In a few moments a voice was heard speaking from the box.

"Fate, who rules us all," said the voice, "forbids your leaving this place till the time shall come when certain things are fulfilled. But instead, a gift shall be given you, which will comfort you in all your troubles."

And the voice spoke truly, for, a few days after, when the frog peeped in at the door she found the most beautiful baby in the world lying by the side of the queen.

"So the cap has kept its word," cried the frog with delight. "How soft its cheeks are, and what tiny feet it has got! What shall we call it?"

This was a very important point, and needed much discussion. A thousand names were proposed and rejected for a thousand silly reasons. One was another reminded the queen of somebody she did not like; but at length an idea flashed into the queen's head, and she called out:

"I know! We will call her Muffette."

"That is the very thing," shouted the frog, jumping high into the air; and so it was settled.

The princess Muffette was about six months old when the frog noticed that the queen had begun to grow sad again.

"Why do you have that look in your eyes?" she asked one day, when she had come in to play with the baby, who could now crawl.

The way they played their game was to let Muffette creep close to the frog, and then for the frog to bound high into the air and alight on the child's head, or back, or legs, when she always sent up a shout of pleasure. There is no play fellow like a frog; but then it must be a fairy frog, or else you might hurt it, and if you did, something dreadful might happen to you. Well, as I have said, our frog was struck with the queen's sad face, and lost no time in asking her what was the reason.

"I don't see what you have to complain of now; Muffette is quite well and quite happy, and even the Lion Fairy is kind to her when she sees her. What is it?"

"Oh! if her father could only see her!" broke forth the queen, clasping her hands. "Or if I could only tell him all that has happened since we parted. But they will have brought him tidings of the broken carriage, and he will have thought me dead, or devoured by wild beasts. And though he will mourn for me long – I know that well – yet in time they will persuade him to take a wife, and she will be young and fair, and he will forget me."

And in all this the queen guessed truly, save that nine long years were to pass before he would consent to put another in her place.

The frog answered nothing at the time, but stopped her game and hopped away among the cypress trees. Here she sat and thought and thought, and the next morning she went back to the queen and said:

"I have come, madam, to make you an offer. Shall I go to the king instead of you, and tell him of your sufferings, and that he has the most charming baby in the world for his daughter? The way is long, and I travel slowly; but sooner or later, I shall be sure to arrive. Only, are you not afraid to be left without my protection? Ponder the matter carefully; it is for you to decide."

"Oh, it needs no pondering," cried the queen joyfully, holding up her clasped hands, and making Muffette do likewise, in token of gratitude. "But in order that he may know that you have come from me I will send him a letter." And pricking her arm, she wrote a few words with her blood on the corner of her handkerchief. Then tearing it off, she gave it to the frog, and they bade each other farewell.

It took the frog a year and four days to mount the ten thousand steps that led to the upper world, but that was because she was still under the spell of a wicked fairy. By the time she reached the top, she was so tired that she had to remain for another year on the banks of a stream to rest, and also to arrange the procession with which she was to present herself before the king. For she knew far too well what was due to herself and her relations, if she were to appear at Court as if she was a mere nobody. At length, after many consultations with her cap, the affair was settled, and at the end of the second year after her parting with the queen they all set out.

First walked her bodyguard of grasshoppers, followed by her maids of honour, who were those tiny green frogs you see in the fields, each one mounted on a snail, and seated on a velvet saddle. Next came the water-rats, dressed as pages, and lastly the frog herself, in a litter borne by eight toads, and made of tortoiseshell. Here she could lie at her ease, with her cap on her head, for it was quite large and roomy, and could easily have held two eggs when the frog was not in it.

The journey lasted seven years, and all this time the queen suffered tortures of hope, though Muffette did her best to comfort her. Indeed, she would most likely have died had not the Lion Fairy taken a fancy that the child and her mother should go hunting with her in the upper world, and, in spite of her sorrows, it was always a joy to the queen to see the sun again. As for little Muffette, by the time she was seven her arrows seldom missed their mark. So, after all, the years of waiting passed more quickly than the queen had dared to hope.

The frog was always careful to maintain her dignity, and nothing would have persuaded her to show her face in public places, or even along the high road, where there was a chance of meeting anyone. But sometimes, when the procession had to cross a little stream, or go over a piece of marshy ground, orders would be given for a halt; fine clothes were thrown off, bridles were flung aside, and grasshoppers, water-rats, even the frog herself, spent a delightful hour or two playing in the mud.

But at length the end was in sight, and the hardships were forgotten in the vision of the towers of the king's palace; and, one bright morning, the cavalcade entered the gates with all the pomp and circumstance of a royal embassy. And surely no ambassador had ever created such a sensation! Door and windows, even the roofs of houses, were filled with people, whose cheers reached the ears of the king. However, he had no time to attend to such matters just then, as, after nine years, he had at last consented to the entreaties of his courtiers, and was on the eve of celebrating his second marriage.

The frog's heartbeat high when her litter drew up before the steps of the palace, and leaning forward she beckoned to her side one of the guards who were standing in his doorway.

"I wish to see His Majesty," said she.

"His Majesty is engaged, and can see no one," answered the soldier.

"His Majesty will see *me*," returned the frog, fixing her eye upon him; and somehow the man found himself leading the procession along the gallery into the Hall of Audience, where the king sat surrounded by his nobles arranging the dresses which everyone was to wear at his marriage ceremony.

All stared in surprise as the procession advanced, and still more when the frog gave one bound from the litter on to the floor, and with another landed on the arm of the chair of state.

"I am only just in time, sire," began the frog; "had I been a day later you would have broken your faith which you swore to the queen nine years ago."

"Her remembrance will always be dear to me," answered the king gently, though all present expected him to rebuke the frog severely for her impertinence. "But know, Lady Frog, that a king can seldom do as he wishes, but must be bound by the desires of his subjects. For nine years I have resisted them; now I can do so no longer, and have made choice of the fair young maiden playing at ball yonder."

"You cannot wed her, however fair she may be, for the queen your wife is still alive, and sends you this letter written in her own blood," said the frog, holding out the square of handkerchief as she spoke. "And, what is more, you have a daughter who is nearly nine years old, and more beautiful than all the other children in the world put together."

The king turned pale when he heard these words, and his hand trembled so that he could hardly read what the queen had written. Then he kissed the handkerchief twice or thrice, and burst into tears, and it was some minutes before he could speak. When at length he found his voice he told his councillors that the writing was indeed that of the queen, and now that he had the joy of knowing she was alive he could, of course, proceed no further with his second marriage. This naturally displeased the ambassadors who had conducted the bride to court, and one of them enquired indignantly if he meant to put such an insult on the princess on the word of a mere frog.

"I am not a 'mere frog,' and I will give you proof of it," retorted the angry little creature. And putting on her cap, she cried: "Fairies that are my friends, come hither!" And in a moment a crowd of beautiful creatures, each one with a crown on her head, stood before her. Certainly none could have guessed that they were the snails, water-rats, and grasshoppers from which she had chosen her retinue.

At a sign from the frog the fairies danced a ballet, with which everyone was so delighted that they begged to have to repeated; but now it was not youths and maidens who were dancing, but flowers. Then these again melted into fountains, whose waters interlaced and, rushing down the sides of the hall, poured out in a cascade down the steps, and formed a river found the castle, with the most beautiful little boats upon it, all painted and gilded.

"Oh, let us go in them for a sail!" cried the princess, who had long ago left her game of ball for a sight of these marvels, and, as she was bent upon it, the ambassadors, who had been charged never to lose sight of her, were obliged to go also, though they never entered a boat if they could help it.

But the moment they and the princess had seated themselves on the soft cushions, river and boats vanished, and the princess and the ambassadors vanished too. Instead the snails and grasshoppers and water-rats stood round the frog in their natural shapes.

"Perhaps," said she, "Your Majesty may now be convinced that I am a fairy and speak the truth. Therefore lose no time in setting in order the affairs of your kingdom and go in search of your wife. Here is a ring that will admit you into the presence of the queen, and will likewise allow you to address unharmed the Lion Fairy, though she is the most terrible creature that ever existed."

By this time the king had forgotten all about the princess, whom he had only chosen to please his people, and was as eager to depart on his journey as the frog was for him to go. He made one of his ministers regent of the kingdom, and gave the frog everything her heart could desire; and with her ring on his finger he rode away to the outskirts of the forest. Here he dismounted, and bidding his horse go home, he pushed forward on foot.

Having nothing to guide him as to where he was likely to find the entrance of the underworld, the king wandered hither and thither for a long while, till, one day, while he was resting under a tree, a voice spoke to him.

"Why do you give yourself so much trouble for nought, when you might know what you want to know for the asking? Alone you will never discover the path that leads to your wife."

Much startled, the king looked about him. He could see nothing, and somehow, when he thought about it, the voice seemed as if it were part of himself. Suddenly his eyes fell on the ring, and he understood.

"Fool that I was!" cried he; "and how much precious time have I wasted? Dear ring, I beseech you, grant me a vision of my wife and my daughter!" And even as he spoke there flashed past him a huge lioness, followed by a lady and a beautiful young maid mounted on fairy horses.

Almost fainting with joy he gazed after them, and then sank back trembling on the ground.

"Oh, lead me to them, lead me to them!" he exclaimed. And the ring, bidding him take courage, conducted him safely to the dismal place where his wife had lived for ten years.

Now the Lion Fairy knew beforehand of his expected presence in her dominions, and she ordered a palace of crystal to be built in the middle of the lake of quicksilver; and in order to make it more difficult of approach she let it float whither it would. Immediately after their return from the chase, where the king had seen them, she conveyed the queen and Muffette into the palace, and put them under the guard of the monsters of the lake, who one and all had fallen in love with the princess. They were horribly jealous, and ready to eat each other up for her sake, so they readily accepted the charge. Some stationed themselves round the floating palace, some sat by the door, while the smallest and lightest perched themselves on the roof.

Of course the king was quite ignorant of these arrangements, and boldly entered the palace of the Lion Fairy, who was waiting for him, with her tail lashing furiously, for she still kept her lion's shape. With a roar that shook the walls she flung herself upon him; but he was on the watch, and a blow from his sword cut off the paw she had put forth to strike him dead. She fell back, and with his helmet still on and his shield up, he set his foot on her throat.

"Give me back the wife and the child you have stolen from me," he said, "or you shall not live another second!"

But the fairy answered:

"Look through the window at that lake and see if it is in my power to give them to you." And the king looked, and through the crystal walls he beheld his wife and daughter floating on the quicksilver. At that sight the Lion Fairy and all her wickedness was forgotten. Flinging off his helmet, he shouted to them with all his might. The queen knew his voice, and she and Muffette ran to the window and held out their hands. Then the king swore a solemn oath that he would never leave the spot without taking them if it should cost him his life; and he meant it, though at the moment he did not know what he was undertaking.

Three years passed by, and the king was no nearer to obtaining his heart's desire. He had suffered every hardship that could be imagined – nettles had been his bed, wild fruits more bitter than gall his food, while his days had been spent in fighting the hideous monsters which kept him from the palace. He had not advanced one single step, nor gained one solitary advantage. Now he was almost in despair, and ready to defy everything and throw himself into the lake.

It was at this moment of his blackest misery that, one night, a dragon who had long watched him from the roof crept to his side.

"You thought that love would conquer all obstacles," said he; "well, you have found it hasn't! But if you will swear to me by your crown and sceptre that you will give me a dinner of the food that I never grow tired of, whenever I choose to ask for it, I will enable you to reach your wife and daughter."

Ah, how glad the king was to hear that! What oath would he not have taken so as to clasp his wife and child in is arms? Joyfully he swore whatever the dragon asked of him; then he jumped on his back, and in another instant would have been carried by the strong wings into the castle if the nearest monsters had not happened to awake and hear the noise of talking and swum to the shore to give battle. The fight was long and hard, and when the king at last beat back his foes another struggle awaited him. At the entrance gigantic bats, owls and crows set upon him from all sides; but the dragon had teeth and claws, while the queen broke off sharp bits of glass and stabbed and cut in her anxiety to help her husband. At length the horrible creatures flew away; a sound like thunder was heard, the palace and the monsters vanished, while, at the same moment – no one knew how – the king found himself standing with his wife and daughter in the hall of his own home.

The dragon had disappeared with all the rest, and for some years no more was heard or thought of him. Muffette grew every day more beautiful, and when she was fourteen the kings and emperors of the neighbouring countries sent to ask her in marriage for themselves or their sons. For a long time the girl turned a deaf ear to all their prayers; but at length a young prince of rare gifts touched her heart, and though the king had left her free to choose what husband she would, he had secretly hoped that out of all the wooers this one might be his son-in-law. So they were betrothed that same day with great pomp, and then with many tears, the prince set out for his father's court, bearing with him a portrait of Muffette.

The days passed slowly to Muffette, in spite of her brave efforts to occupy herself and not to sadden other people by her complaints. One morning she was playing on her harp in the queen's chamber when the king burst into the room and clasped his daughter in his arms with an energy that almost frightened her.

"Oh, my child! my dear child! why were you ever born?" cried he, as soon as he could speak.

"Is the prince dead?" faltered Muffette, growing white and cold.

"No, no; but – oh, how can I tell you!" And he sank down on a pile of cushions while his wife and daughter knelt beside him.

At length he was able to tell his tale, and a terrible one it was! There had just arrived at court a huge giant, as ambassador from the dragon by whose help the king had rescued the queen and Muffette from the crystal palace. The dragon had been very busy for many years past, and had quite forgotten the princess till the news of her betrothal reached his ears. Then he remembered the bargain he had made with her father; and the more he heard of Muffette the more he felt sure she would make a delicious dish. So he had ordered the giant who was his servant to fetch her at once.

No words would paint the horror of both the queen and the princess as they listened to this dreadful doom. They rushed instantly to the hall, where the giant was awaiting them, and flinging themselves at his feet implored him to take the kingdom if he would, but to have pity on the princess. The giant looked at them kindly, for he was not at all hard-hearted, but said that he had no power to do anything, and that if the princess did not go with him quietly the dragon would come himself.

Several days went by, and the king and queen hardly ceased from entreating the aid of the giant, who by this time was getting weary of waiting.

"There is only one way of helping you," he said at last, "and that is to marry the princess to my nephew, who, besides being young and handsome, has been trained in magic, and will know how to keep her safe from the dragon."

"Oh, thank you, thank you!" cried the parents, clasping his great hands to their breasts. "You have indeed lifted a load from us. She shall have half the kingdom for her dowry." But Muffette stood up and thrust them aside.

"I will not buy my life with faithlessness," she said proudly; "and I will go with you this moment to the dragon's abode." And all her father's and mother's tears and prayers availed nothing to move her.

The next morning Muffette was put into a litter, and, guarded by the giant and followed by the king and queen and the weeping maids of honour, they started for the foot of the mountain where the dragon had his castle. The way, though rough and stony, seemed all too short, and when they reached the spot appointed by the dragon the giant ordered the men who bore the litter to stand still.

"It is time for you to bid farewell to your daughter," said he; "for I see the dragon coming to us."

It was true; a cloud appeared to pass over the sun, for between them and it they could all discern dimly a huge body half a mile long approaching nearer and nearer. At first the king could not believe that this was the small beast who had seemed so friendly on the shore of the lake of quicksilver but then he knew very little of necromancy, and had never studied the art of expanding and contracting his body. But it was the dragon and nothing else, whose six wings were carrying him forward as fast as might be, considering his great weight and the length of his tail, which had fifty twists and a half.

He came quickly, yes; but the frog, mounted on a greyhound, and wearing her cap on her head, went quicker still. Entering a room where the prince was sitting gazing at the portrait of his betrothed, she cried to him:

"What are you doing lingering here, when the life of the princess is nearing its last moment? In the courtyard you will find a green horse with three heads and twelve feet, and by its side a sword eighteen yards long. Hasten, lest you should be too late!"

The fight lasted all day, and the prince's strength was well-nigh spent, when the dragon, thinking that the victory was won, opened his jaws to give a roar of triumph. The prince saw his chance, and before his foe could shut his mouth again had plunged his sword far down his adversary's throat. There was a desperate clutching of the claws to the earth, a slow flagging of the great wings, then the monster rolled over on his side and moved no more. Muffette was delivered.

After this they all went back to the palace. The marriage took place the following day, and Muffette and her husband lived happy for ever after.

The Fairy of the Edelweiss

EVERY CHILD IN SWITZERLAND has heard of the Golden Age, long, long ago, when no ice or snow covered the mountains. Then grass grew, and flowers bloomed, clear up on the highest summits. Those barren and rocky heights, such as we see now, where nothing can live, but the big horned woolly ibex, were unknown; for they were then clothed with forests and verdure. One could walk all the way up to the peak's top, amid beautiful trees, lovely shrubs and blossoming plants and sweet-smelling herbage.

Summer then reigned for at least ten months in the year. The cows grazed on the delicious aromatic grass that makes the breath of kine so sweet. Where now are only masses of snow and ice, and rivers called glaciers, were flowery meadows, full of birds and bright dragonflies, and musical with bees, crickets and singing insects. Then the cows were so big and fat that they gave their milk, that was rich in cream, three times a day. Pastures were everywhere, and nobody went hungry, for food was as cheap as leaves or pebbles.

The old people still tell us that, during this period, all that one had to do was to ladle out the milk from tanks, as large as ponds, or pick big red cherries by putting out your hands. Then the fairies were happy. On every moonlight night, they held dancing parties in the meadows.

But by and by, the terrible Frost Giants, that live up around the North Pole, heard of this Land of a Thousand Mountains, where the chief rivers of Europe were born and still have their cradles. Then these greedy fellows that in winter tie up all things fast, or freeze them solid, except for a few hours on warm days when the sun is shining, said one to the other:

"Come on, fellows, let us go down and conquer this mountain country, that is so rich in honey, and cream, and flowers. We shall pile up the snowflakes, leagues high, and freeze solid the falling snow and cold water. We shall turn these into sheets of ice that will cover the land thousands of yards thick, and kill all living things. We shall drive off all the flowers, blow the grass away, and chill the noses of the cows so that they cannot graze. That will prevent men from having houses, and milk churns, and stores of cheeses. We must drive off the hens, too, so the people can have no eggs. If the sun tries to stop our work, we'll laugh at him, so we will."

Thus spoke the Frost King, while the mists rolled out in clouds from his mouth as he boasted of what he could do.

"Yes, yes, indeed we shall," cried all the Frost Giants, and a shower of snowflakes and ice particles filled the air, for even their icy breath turned solid and was deadly to all plants.

When the North Wind blew down the news to the Swiss fairies, there was much sadness and even terror. Where could the fairies dance when the meadows were gone and the flowers dead?

How could they float in the air, clad only in gauzy garments? How could they see each other if mist and storm and darkness filled the air and ice covered the ground? And how could they live without the blossoms? One fairy actually wept tears in sympathy for the poor cows that were certain to starve. And as for the children, whom the fairies loved, where could they play, if there were no fields to play in, or roses or violets to pick?

One bold fairy looked defiant and spoke out loud in the meeting:

"I'm not afraid of these Frost Giants from the North Pole. They are nothing but big, boasting bullies. Let our Fairy Queen change me into a flower, and clothe me warm enough, and I'll defy even the Frost King to hurt me."

"Bravo, bravo!" cried all the fairies in chorus.

"But how could you stay all the time up there, with no living thing near you, and all alone? You will have no neighbours, except the rocks and crags, and even they will be all bare and swept by the fierce winds. Can you stand that?" asked an old fairy, doubtingly.

"Yes, if for nothing else, than to show that we fairies are not afraid of the Frost Giants, I should be willing to live alone. Besides, our fairy queen will see that, by and by, there will be others like me, and then I shall have company. The more of us, the merrier, I am sure. In a few thousand years, we'll make an army and a victorious one, too."

Seeing this brave one of her company so ready and willing, the Queen of the Fairies put on her thinking cap. She spent a whole night in planning how to turn this volunteer fairy into a flower. Then she would bundle her up in furs, and dress her so warmly that even the biggest and coldest of the Frost Giants could not kill her with his icy breath.

And this was the way this volunteer from the fairy ranks was clothed and made ready to fight, in the long war with cold and storm, so that for ages, this little thing has been able to live far up on the mountain heights and, all the time, to smile and be joyful, and laugh, in the face of the Frost Giants. In fact, so happy is she, among the rock crags and sunshiny crannies, and so amused at herself, in looking down over the terrible precipices to the rocks thousands of feet below, that she would not exchange places or climates with even the cloves and nutmegs; no, not even with the tea roses and coffee blossoms in the Spice Islands of the southern seas.

Now it is customary in all happy families, when father and mother are expecting the cradle soon to be filled, to choose a name for the baby, and to have its clothes ready. This is done so that the poor little thing, on coming into the world, will not get a chill, or sneeze, or have a cough, and die. Moreover, if it have a name, no one will mistake one baby for another, unless they arrive as twins, when some mark, such as a blue ribbon for a boy and a pink one for a girl, is necessary.

So the old fairies put their heads together to find a proper name for the new fairy flower-baby that was to live among the cold mountain tops and refuse to be frightened, or frozen, or be driven down lower, or to be cuddled up in meadows, near men's houses, where it was warm.

"What say you?" asked the Queen, the wisest of the fairies, who was considered a sort of sage or prophet, and who had a wonderfully long head. "What name do you give?"

With a loud voice, almost like a roar, this fairy, that wore clothes the colour of an old man's beard, called out "Anawphilis Margarita."

At this, every fairy looked at each other, as if to say, "What a mouthful," "How strange a name," or "So big for a little fairy!" or "Why does she talk Latin?"

There were questions in their eyes also, but none asked "What does the name mean?" for all fairies are very shy about confessing ignorance.

But the Fairy Queen, who knew almost everything, put on a look of great dignity, and discreetly enquired of the sage if her everyday talk was in Latin. She did not mean to be sarcastic, however.

"Why would you call me by the 'Pearly Lion's Foot,' if I were to volunteer?" asked a bright young fairy.

"For two reasons, Your Majesty," answered the old oracle, addressing, not the young volunteer, but the Queen, as was proper.

"First, to reward valour and virtue, by giving an august name; and second, to let the Frost Giants, the insolent fellows from the North Pole, know that when even one of us fairies puts her foot down, it is like a lion's. No one can move, or lift, or push or drive it away. We thrust forward this fairy flower as our banner, to say to the enemy, 'We shall not surrender, and we defy you!'"

The Fairy Queen, full of admiration, replied:

"We bow to your wisdom, and so it shall be written in our books. Nevertheless, both mortals and fairies must have also a short name for everyday use. How about the second, or personal part, Margarita?"

"As you will, Your Highness, but may I suggest even a better term, in the speech of the mortals of this mountain land? They will love anything that you may clothe and adorn, I am sure."

After this ending of her speech, the wise old fairy curtsied most politely.

The Fairy Queen looked very lovely, as thus flattered by the fine tact and the charming speech of this oldest member of the family; and, besides, as she loved the brave Swiss nation, she said.

"You are always wise. So please let me have a name that will be popular with the Swiss people."

"Well, Your highness, if it be your pleasure, we shall clothe your pet in purest white, like ermine, rivalling even the snow, without spot, or stain, or any dark tint. So we may justly call it the Edelweiss, that is, the Noble White."

At this, all the fairies shouted with delight. Even the Queen herself smiled, and then made answer.

"You have well spoken; 'Edelweiss' it shall be."

Now that the name was ready, the Queen called for the attendant maids of the brave fairy volunteer and, then and there, the custom was begun, which mortals always afterwards followed, of robing a princess who was to marry a husband in a foreign country. She must drop off all her former clothing, even to her glistening skin. Then, entering another room, in the new land, she must apparel herself in the garments that are fashionable in her new home – as in the case, for example, of the Belgian lady, who, long afterwards, came as a bride to the Castle of the Hawk, in the Land of the Swiss.

Stripped of all her pretty gauzy skirts, bodice and chemise, and standing forth as nude as a baby in the bath tub, the Queen bade her brave fairy look at her new wardrobe, which lay piled up and as white as any snowdrift. Then, before all the other fairies, the Queen put this question:

"Are you willing to leave the company of your fellows in fairy land and be a flower, to remain rooted in the rocks and amid the cold for ever?"

"Yes, truly, with all my heart," answered the brave one.

"And will you cast seed every year and multiply your family, that will bear your noble name?"

"Surely, for the more of us there are, and the more we can resist the cruel enemy, the Frost Giants, and make mortals glad, the happier we shall be."

"You have spoken wisely," said the Queen. "We shall clothe you very thickly, in white robes that look like flannel, but that are even warmer. So no giant can hurt you when he bites with frost, no snow storm chill you, or ice choke you, or North Wind make you shiver. We shall give you roots that dig their way down deep in the crannies and that will nourish your life. Besides, we have searched the world over, and, whatever of hair, or fur of arctic animals, or wool of sheep, or down of birds can show or suggest to us, we have used to weave a garment so warm that the biggest of the giants, with the iciest breath and a beard of icicles, cannot even give you a chill. With your long hair, and woolly coat, and roots that resist frost bites, you can tickle his nose when he comes too near and even laugh in his face."

"Indeed I will," answered the fairy defiantly.

"And will you do even more? Will you keep your eye on the cracks and crevices that hold the sun's warmth, so that your children can creep up higher every year?" asked the Queen.

"The sun in the heaven helping me, I will," replied this 'Fairy of the Vanguard,' as some of her sisters already spoke of her.

Then the Queen lifted her wand tipped with a star. She touched the forehead of the Fairy of the Lion's Foot, which was her war name; while in the talk of mortals, she was called Noble White, though still the fairies, quite often, use the name Margarita.

Then they stood fairy Edelweiss on a pile of rocks, filled in with sand and earth, to show the others where, and how, in the new world, Edelweiss was to live and grow and enlarge her kingdom.

It was a strange and wonderful transformation, as the fairy's pretty feet turned into rootlets, that quickly thrust themselves deeply downwards, gripping the rough rock and drinking in the moisture and juices in the soil. Grandly the Edelweiss showed her pride in belonging to the great family which a famous man first named after the Little Frogs, because they love moist, damp and soft places.

Yet all this was beneath.

Above, there first rose a stalk, a few inches high, until it reached half a foot. Then the arms multiplied and stretched out. They were densely covered, like sleeves of overcoats, with thick coverings, each resembling white flannel, or velvet, and as warm as the fur of an ermine.

"Looks as if she had on an ulster," said one of the many fairies, some of whom thought she looked too sweet for any use.

And yet, so far, there was no real flower, but only a defence, like armour, against those worst enemies of a plant, cold and frost.

"Now for beauty and for glory," said the Queen.

Out of, and on top of, the dense star-like mass of warmth and coziness, as if robed for a skiing or skating party, there blossomed forth many round-headed tufts, or rosettes, that were pearly white.

Now, not only thickly clothed, but beautiful and strong, the Noble White was given a home at once in a rock cranny. Like a newborn baby, that, as soon as it arrives, sticks its thumb in its mouth, as much as to say, "This world is all right; I am going to like it," the Edelweiss rooted itself at once and began to grow.

Years passed by, and the lovely white flower, flourishing where only the chamois and the ibex among animals lived, or the red Alpine rose could bloom, multiplied. Like a brave army, it moved steadily forward, occupying every crevice, cranny and hollow. These the hardy plants held, like forts, against all cold comers; yes, even resisting the avalanches that tried to crush these little strangers.

In a few hundred years, thousands of the Noble White plants dotted, or made beautiful, the bare rocks, or hung over the precipices. In vain did the icy breath of polar winds, or the blasts of the rude Frost Giants, or even the hurtling avalanches, drive the Edelweiss away. Nor was the hot south wind, the Föhn able to wither it.

Swiss maidens made this flower the emblem of their own purity, and also of the tenacity of faithful lovers. At the wrestling and shooting matches, the young men wore its flowers in their hats, or twisted them among the ropes, which marked off the boundaries of their games and wrestling bouts. To heroes, it was the symbol of perseverance, endurance and that quiet force which compels victory. Patriots so loved it because of its resisting power – the spirit of advance instead of retreat – that they would gladly make it the national flower. Switzerland – the Edelweiss among nations – has held its own for ages, maintaining her life and independence despite the alien power of invaders and tyrants, and the Swiss still sing their national hymn, "Stand fast, O Fatherland!"

So also Edelweiss, the Noble White, remains for ever as the Swiss emblem of their republic, and of its beauty and permanence. To destroy this flower, the Frost Giants make their continual assaults in vain. Just as mighty monarchs have tried again and again to overwhelm, as with avalanche of invasion, the freedom of the Swiss, and have always failed, so the Edelweiss never yields. Its white banner hangs for ever on the heights. To every boy and girl, it is as a living motto, bearing, amid snow and ice, the message of Excelsior – Higher yet and ever onward!

The Frost Giants and the Sunbeam Fairies

MANY PEOPLE THINK SWITZERLAND the most beautiful country on earth. It is certainly the world's playground. Every year, many hundreds of thousands of persons from various countries go there to spend either the winter or the summer. They come to enjoy the good sleep that comes from the bracing air, to climb the high peaks, to see the flowers, to hear the echoes of the Alpine horn, to ride over the mountain roads, or to be whisked up, on electric railways, to summits among the clouds. With most of the tourists, the effect of the sharp atmosphere is to whet their appetites, even more than their wits; but perhaps this is what they seek.

The sick and the well alike get vast benefit. They think it great fun to find so much ice and snow, and also so much sunshine, as if winter and summer liked to play together. In February, hardy and strong people enjoy sledding and sliding, besides skis and skittles, and many other merry sports. Children go out on sleds, with almost nothing on them, to enjoy the air baths.

Yet Switzerland was not always a flowery playground, rich in splendid hotels, where the boarders' bills catch the spirit of the place and become mountain climbers. For ages, it was a sort of North Pole, set in the middle of Europe, frozen in, tight and fast, and with mountains of snow and rivers of ice, where no animals could live. In this age, everything was white. Then there were no animals, men, women, children or babies; no flowers, no birds, no fish; no farms, no vineyards, but only dreadful cold, all the year round, and for millions of years.

Then the Frost Giants ruled a land for ever white with snow, that never melted, and their king sat on the top of a solid mountain of ice. These Frost Giants would not allow anything alive to come near them. They made it the law that, whatever had eyes or nose, feet or hands, or paws or wings, should be instantly frozen to death, and their solid carcasses packed away in a refrigerator, a million years old.

The queen of the fairies, that lived down in the warm meadows, felt sorry that so fine a place should have nothing in it that was alive, or had any colour, red, pink, blue, or yellow, violet or green. She believed that the land could be conquered from the Frost Giants and made a country in which boys and girls could play and pick flowers.

It might, indeed, take several millions of years to melt the ice and cover the ground with flowery meadows. But what was that? Because fairies never care anything about days, months or years. They never grow old and do not use almanacs, because not dwelling in bodies like ours, and never having lived like us mortals, they do not get sick or have any funerals or cemeteries. They are saved all expenses of being buried, for they do not have any graves. There are no doctors, or undertakers, in fairy land, even though the immortelle flowers bloom everywhere. It seems to be that because some are wiser than others that they may be called old, or mothers, aunts or grandmothers.

To carry out her purpose, the fairy queen made a friend of the sun and asked his help. This, Old Sol, as the fairies called him, was very glad to give; because he had rescued other parts of the world from the ice-kings and made many lands bright and beautiful. He thought that the monarch of the frost world and his white giants had reigned long enough in Switzerland. Besides, Old Sol wanted to show that he had not yet done his best work. It is true that he had made other lands look lovely, changing them from barren rocks and sand to fruitful fields, groves and gardens, rich in wheat and corn, fruit trees and berry bushes, besides peaches and apples and pears, roses and lilies.

Old Sol declared that, with the aid of the fairies, he would make Switzerland the most beautiful of all countries, so that many people from foreign lands would come to see it. He would scoop out lakes, channel out rivers, smooth the face of the country, and make it lovely with pastures, rich in cows and goats, and spangled with flowers of many hues. Yes, if the fairies would promise to put enough clothes on their favourites, and wrap them up in downy undergarments, with lots of fur and wool for overcoats, he would help the prettiest flowers to climb up to the high mountains. Then he would promise to furnish heat enough, so that they could keep warm and live there. He would make it so pleasant for them, that they would never get homesick, or want to go back to their mothers in the valley below. In spite of the Frost Giants, the storms and winds, the tempests, and the icy breath of the giants, these flowers would bloom, and nod, and laugh at and defy all enemies.

What was even more wonderful, Old Sol promised that every flower, as it climbed higher, should have a richer colour on its cheeks, so that all the world would wonder. Then, the plants, in the warmer regions lower down, should envy the brilliant faces of their sisters so high up. In fact, it was to be a beauty contest. "Nothing venture nothing have," should be the rule. They might not grow to be so tall. Their feet might be larger, for they would need strong toes, to hold on tight to the ground, when old Boreas, the wind giant, tried his best to blow them away; but to win out, they were sure to do, in the end, and beat Jack Frost and all his army.

When the fairies were called together, and told by their queen that the sun would be their friend and help them every day, and never tire of his good work, you ought to have seen how happy they were. They all clapped their hands, and everyone, big and little, wanted to be brave and go out to fight the Frost Giants. Each volunteer said, "I am not afraid. The Frost Giants can't freeze me."

It was wonderful how the pretty fairies were perfectly willing to be changed into humble-looking plants, that never could grow very tall, but lie quite flat on the ground, and have deep roots in the crannies. They would have to live without much society, or excitement, and spend their lives in clefts and hollows. What was hardest to bear, was, that most of them would have to live like nuns; for in the case of many of them, their beauty would never be appreciated or even seen.

Some were glad even to become plain meadow grasses. When one plump fairy was told she would become an Alpine Poa, and must carry her babies on her back, she gladly consented saying, "I am willing."

The enthusiasm for the war became an epidemic. Some of the big fairies asked to be changed into trees – oak, maple, spruce, pine or birch. This was hard, for those who had been regular chatterboxes would now be able only to sough in the breeze, or whisper in the winds, and they could roar only in a gale or tempest. Some even begged to be allowed to take on the form of the old-fashioned arolla, the most ancient of all the Swiss trees.

It was astonishing to note how ready these pretty fairies were to put off their lovely gossamer-like robes, lay aside their wings, and wear such plain clothes, as some of them must, who volunteered to be meadow and rock plants. But then, the idea of fighting the Frost Giants, and rescuing the land from ice and snow, had filled them all with enthusiasm. It was like patriotism among mortals. But then, they loved the children and wanted them to have a pretty playground made ready for them, so that, when babies and cradles came into the land, the flowers would be in bloom, for the little folks to pick and string around their necks.

So the queen of the fairies and her wise counsellors enrolled and equipped an army of her fairies, who had agreed to be turned into plants, for the long war against the Frost Giants. Of all these, Old Sol was to be the general. Heaps of fur and flannel, wool and velvet, and hair and down, were stored up, to make thick underclothes and stout overcoats to keep warm, and all sorts of wiry stuff, for toes to grip tight and keep hold of the rocks. Then, with plenty of rich paints and dyes to colour their cheeks, the Fairy Queen summoned the volunteers to come forth.

As each name was called, and a fairy stepped out, the queen waved her wand. First, she pointed it upward, to where the stars were playing hide and seek among the snowy peaks. Then, touching each kneeling fairy, she tapped with her star-tipped wand upon the neck of each.

Presto! What change! Eyes, nose, ears, lovely yellow, or raven black, or shining auburn hair, limbs, hands and feet and wings disppeared in a golden mist.

When one looked again, there was, where each fairy had kneeled down, a flower. Never was the like seen before, in all the wonderful floral world, either as to the kind, or blossom, or the shape of the stalk, leaves or petals of the plants. Some hardly looked like flowers at all, while others were recognized at once, as cousins or sisters of old friends; but so dressed up, as if for an arctic journey as scarcely to be recognized. One had a family of little folks on its back – "As hairy and furry as an Esquimaux baby," whispered one fairy to the other.

Here was one creature, dazzlingly splendid in colours, while, alongside of her, was a little lady robed entirely in white, as if she were to be the bride of Jack Frost, and marry him in a country where the tint of ermine and ptarmigan bird was the only one in fashion.

The lowliness of some of these newborn flowers was perhaps the most astonishing thing about them. Even when in bloom they were not over an inch in height, while their neighbours, down in the valley, were all nearly as tall as yardsticks. One group became only plain meadow grass, while their relatives seemed dressed for Fifth Avenue, or the main street of Zurich or Berne.

Although, when the fairies were turned into trees and were, at first, hardly higher than a needle, and not one of them had a body as thick as a thimble, they at once began whispering, for it was hard to give up the old habit of talking every minute.

Of one pretty creature, shaped like a bluebell, with scalloped edges, it was noticed that she shut up her mouth and did not say a word. At this, one wise old fairy looked up at the sky and said, "It is certainly going to rain." Thereupon, since flowers were so cheap, this one they called "the poor man's weather glass." Another, that had a curiously shaped blossom, they named Lady's Slipper. To still another, very reddish, tufty, and strong, they gave the title of Prince's Feather; while an unusually pert and active one, that had a very expressive face, they christened Johnny-jump-up. This fairy had whimpered a little at the idea of being named after a boy; but, when told she would have clothes of many colours, she was instantly happy, and welcomed her change into a flower with a face that would never need rouge, or lily-white powder.

While these, thus far mentioned, were mostly valley or pasture flowers, and not expected to live very far up the mountain slopes, several others volunteered to lead what some called 'the forlorn hope,' but they were too full of 'pep' for that and took the name of the advance guard. These were especially equipped for fighting the cold. These were the edelweiss, the Alpine rose, and the octopetalla. They were made so frostproof, by fur and thick clothes, that they could laugh in the very faces of the Frost Giants, and dare them to do their worst in trying their best to freeze them out.

Of the one that seemed done up entirely in white flannel, and that kept its blooms in a bunch, like a rosette, everybody knows, for it was the edelweiss – proud of her name, the noble white.

Millions of fairies gathered together on the hill slopes, to see the procession start, and did not mind waiting a thousand years or so. They hung on bushes, sat on top of rocks and boulders and on the tree-branches, or stood or hovered, wherever they could get either a peep or a good view of the fairy flower army that was to march up to the heights and wrestle with the giants.

Some wondered how the battle would go, and if the war would ever end. Could they possibly march up the mountainsides and hold their own amid the blasts of winter and amid the eternal snow and ice, and win the land now covered up? Not a sign of field, or pasture, or road, or any space clear of snow was then visible. There was nothing but ice, many miles thick and looming so far up in the air, as to seem, at night, to touch the stars. The jagged rocks, splintered by the lightning, and the mountainsides, clothed with glaciers, like armour, and which were billions of tons in weight, seemed very forbidding.

"Just give us a few millions of years, and we'll surely win," cried the fairy queen, who was proud of her beautiful army, and who, with them all, knew or cared nothing for what we call time.

Fairies never cry, but some felt as if they might weep, to see so many pretty flowers killed, as they feared they would be. Even the idea of the chills and shivers they would have to suffer made some of the timid ones feel creepy.

Even suppose they could survive ice and frost, and the cold breath of the strong winds that might uproot them, how could they resist the avalanches that might overwhelm and crush them? If whole forests of giant trees were often levelled, like eggshells, and flattened like flounders by these rolling terrors, or torn up by landslides, or ground to gravel by falling rocks, or carried away by landslides, how could tiny and tender flowers hope to escape?

But the fairy queen knew the power of her friend, the Sun, and the tenacity and perseverance of her flower children. So, laughing at such forebodings, she bade the lovely flowers and little trees begin their march. Their orders to advance were steadily "forward and upward." They were to hold the ground gained, inch by inch. They must even try, again and again, to split the rocks, and be willing to suffer cold, wet, wind, and not be out of sorts, or show bad temper, when it rained too much, or the clouds hid the sun. They must take advantage of every nook, crevice, crack and cranny.

"Don't be alarmed," said one wise fairy to her neighbour. "I'll warrant you they will pretty soon complain that it is too hot, and sometimes even ask the sun to veil his face with clouds. When the evil imps, that ride on the Föhn, or south wind, visit them, one or more will be eager to marry a Frost Giant to keep cool."

But the other fairy said, "That is only gossip," and she did not believe they would "ever be sorry and want to change back."

When, after their first victories, the cows and goats should come, and the birds make their nests, and men and women arrive, and the boys and girls play, these fairies, thus changed into flowers, were not to object to have their stalks eaten up by the cattle, or their seeds to be swallowed by the birds, or their blossoms to be plucked by the children. Even when they should come to their best bloom, and seem too pretty to be touched, they were to welcome the cows and goats.

To all these directions, the new plants, trees and flowers nodded their heads, and the war began. The older fairies went back to the vineyards, groves, forests, dales and meadows in the lower lands of sunshine of mild climate and of fair weather, and the battle was on.

Several millions of years slipped away, and some of the fairies in the warm countries had almost forgot their cousins in the high Alps. Then it happened that some thousands of them made up a party to go and visit what they had once left long ago, as a polar region, of thick ice where no land was visible.

What a change, and how lovely! When they reached Switzerland, and looked over the landscape, they could not, at first, believe their own eyes. True, it was midsummer when they arrived; but, as far as the eye could reach, they beheld valleys and meadows spangled with flowers, from which floated the sound, or echoes, of tinkling bells, where contented cows and goats were browsing. On the sweet perfumed air wafted the aromatic odours of the delicious herbage, freshly cropped by the cattle. Pretty houses, on the flat spaces, or perched on the hill slopes, told of happy homes. Children were playing games, or picking flowers. Church spires pointed towards Heaven. In one village, a great long parade of sleek cows, their well-groomed coats shining in the sun, and one with a milking stool between her horns, was moving up, where the grass was most luscious. Donkeys and horses, laden with cheese and garden produce, were moving in lengthened lines to the markets. Here and there, castles, chalets, bridges, church spires and thickly clustered houses told of villages, towns and cities; for man was now in possession, and all the world rejoiced. It was like an heiress receiving her fortune, for human beings thus to enter into the enjoyment of the lovely landscape and beautiful country, which the fairies had helped so grandly to create.

The Whimsical Avalanche

IT MAY HAPPEN in Switzerland that mighty masses of snow and ice, sometimes as big as the capitol at Washington and as high as Bunker Hill monument, will roll down the mountainsides without giving any notice. These crush whole forests, bury villages, tear rocks to pieces, knock off bits of the mountainsides and kill thousands of people, cows, goats and horses.

Though large enough to engulf an army or a battleship, they are very small when first born up in the very high Alps.

Starting as a snowball, they grow large, very quickly, every moment, and finally become immense. Then they roll along over many miles, carrying destruction in their path, until they tumble over precipices, or reach low land that is level. That is the reason why they are so named, for avalanche means 'to the valley'.

There are many causes of an avalanche and a little thing may start one of these terrors. The irregular melting by the morning sun of ice, in light or shade, the fall of an icicle, the tumbling of a stone or a sliver of rock, or even the firing of a gun, which shakes the overhanging or piled-up snow, will begin one of these revolving globes.

Now in old times, all Swiss folk used to think that an avalanche was alive, and was having a jolly time enjoying itself when sliding and rolling, leaping and dashing down the mountain slopes in its mad race from the sky to the plain. This was its way of enjoying itself, with a short life and a merry one. It grew faster than anything else known. For while a glacier might take a thousand years to develop, from snowflakes into miles of solid ice, like a frozen river, it required only a few minutes for an avalanche to spring from babyhood into full size, with a power exceeding that of a thousand giants.

Being, at its birth, only an inch or two in diameter, this infant son of the King of the Frost Giants, the avalanche soon became the child, which, as it grew up so terribly fast, took after its daddy. It liked to flatten out trees and houses, and smash things. It generally so frightened men, dogs, cats and the big animals that dared to come near the everlasting heights of ice and snow, where the Frost Giants lived, that, in old times, no one in winter went up to the high peaks.

As a rule, nobody knows, either in summer or winter, just when the avalanches will fall, or whether they will be made of light, powdery, dry snow, or of snow that is heavy, wet, and like what the boys call 'soakers'. Yet there are some old men in Switzerland who can foretell avalanches, as our wise men try to do with the weather.

Once upon a time, the Frost Giants' baby, of which we are going to tell, was born, and great things were expected of it, even when it was only as big as a snowflake. But when it grew up to be a real avalanche, it behaved very differently from all the others. It disappointed its daddy and its uncles awfully. The Frost Giants like to make all the mischief they can, while this one wanted to help men instead of hurting them, and made a new record in the history of colossal snowballs.

It was on a summer's day, when the Frost Giants all gathered together on a big mountain top, to celebrate the birthday of their king. On his part, he was to treat them to a sight of an unusually wonderful baby. It was to be in the form of a ball of snow that, when it became a mighty mass, would wipe out one great forest and two big villages with all the people and cattle in it, and would then roll into the valley. There it would destroy hundreds of acres of farms and vineyards, block up the roads, multiply funerals, and waste so many millions of men's dollars that years would pass before prosperity and good times would come again. The Frost King had a map of the route that the young avalanche was to travel, and he showed it around freely. This was what the Frost Giants loved to do, for they hated flowers and butterflies, and cows and men.

When the white Frost Giants had come together, and all had arrived, in their coats of hard snow and with long beards of icicles, the Frost King invited them to gather at the edge of a precipice, under a jagged peak that had many times been riven and splintered by lightning. Then he bade them look down over the landscape while he pointed out the track which he expected his hopeful offspring, the newborn avalanche, was to take, from the time it started until it had done its work in levelling forests, villages and vineyards. Then, using the big palm of his hand as a diagram, and his five fingers as pointers – just as a fortune-teller finds out and assures a girl what kind of a husband she will have – he told them just what he was sure would happen. On reaching the valley, the big ball would spread itself over a square mile or two, while covering up and ruining the grain fields.

After that, it would take the sunshine and warm south wind at least two or three years to melt the mass, while thousands of people would be in mourning for their dead children and kinsfolk. Or, reduced to beggary, they would bewail the loss of all they had in this world. To hear the old Frost King, as his tongue wagged, and the icicles of his beard flopped up and down, as the chief chin-chopper of the party, you would have thought that this baby avalanche that was to start today was the greatest and most famous ever known.

"Now watch," said the Frost King.

It was midday in midsummer, and the heat was great as he took up a mass of wet snow, hardly more than a dipper full, but already made soft by the sun's rays. He squeezed the mass hard, between the palms of his hands. To the Frost Giants, it seemed scarcely bigger than a pill.

Then, striking an attitude, like a baseball pitcher, or a man playing tenpins, and about to roll the ball along down the alley, the Frost King held up before them the dark grey, sticky ball. As he fondled and patted it, as his own child, the Frost King called out, "I name thee, my son, 'Soaker Smash-All,' and I expect thee to break all records. Make the widest swathe of ruin, my son, ever known among men. The sun is mine enemy, and, through thee, I shall spoil his work and give him plenty of labour to restore it. Go!"

Saying this, the toss was made and the ball set rolling.

At first, for several seconds, with Soaker Smash-All, it was more like ploughing than rolling its way through the drifts, for the slope was slight. Then, as the incline grew steeper, the tumbling became more rapid, until about half a mile from the starting point, the baby avalanche had by its leaps and bounds grown so fast as to be already as big as a barn. It was bouncing swiftly along when, instead of going straight ahead as its daddy, the Frost King, had planned and expected, it rolled against a rounded rock that curved up and backward like the dashboard of a sleigh or the roof of a pagoda.

At once, it swerved to the right and bounded high up in the air, as though some Frost Giant was playing football, and was trying to hit the goal.

Then all sorts of funny things began to happen.

The Frost Giants were terribly disappointed at seeing their pet mount up in the air like a pigskin ball from the foot of a first-class kicker, even before it was half grown. To behave so differently from what its daddy had felt sure of, and told the Frost Giants it would do, seemed like disobedience. For, was not this avalanche the Frost King's son? Instead of rolling straight down the valley, gathering force for its final plunge at every yard, it was apparently trying to climb up to the moon.

"That youngster is altogether too smart," whispered one old giant to another.

Just a second or two before this baby avalanche seemed to have lost both its head and its path to go aside and play in the deep valley below, there was a hunter on one side of the ravine who had climbed up the high rocks to get a shot at a herd of chamois that were feeding quietly on the other side.

Besides the buck or daddy chamois there were four mothers, each with a pretty little kid, hardly two months old, beside her. Now it was not the season for hunting, and it was against the law, which allowed the mother chamois a quiet interval, and the kids time to grow up; for a chamois kid needs to be educated just as a child does.

But this fellow, named Erni, was both cruel and lawless. He had brought his spyglass with him and, pulling it out, swept the distant faces of the great cliffs to find his game. Just as this promising family – a buck, with a harem of four does, and as many kids – hove in sight, his fancy was tickled. Law or no law, he would shoot. He laid down his glass, pointed the rifle and took cool aim, hoping to bring down two of the chamois at a shot. Then he pulled the trigger. With that gun, it was a case of 'a fire at one end and a fool at the other'.

Alas, for human hopes! There is many a slip between muzzle and game. In his case, a miss was as good as a mile, or even a league. In the cruel hunter's brain there had been already a fleeting vision of venison pot-pie and chamois steak. He even saw, in his daydream, two fine pairs of mounted horns adorning his parlour walls.

But the daddy of the chamois family had, a second before, thrown up his nose and caught a whiff of some human being near. Looking up in alarm, he saw the huge snowball in the air above him. Giving the usual sort of whistle, as chamois sentinels do, the whole family started to run, as if racing with the wind, to get under the shelter of an overhanging rock.

Already the bullet had sped, and, despite their speed, one or two chamois might have fallen, but the movement of an avalanche had so thickened and condensed the air that it was like firing a pellet of lead into molasses, making the ball go slowly. This was what is called 'the wind of the avalanche,' which sometimes kills men and beasts.

Instead of the heart of a chamois, the rifle bullet struck the monster snowball in the centre, but it hurt the avalanche no more than a flea bite on the end of an elephant's tail.

We cannot here tell what Erni, the enraged hunter, said.

Having lost the whole day in climbing and now, tired, hungry and vexed with disappointment, he trudged back. When he reached home, his wife kept quiet, his children had to keep away from him, and he did not say his prayers that night.

On the contrary, in the forest home of the chamois, there was much rejoicing, for they had heard the ring of the rifle and seen its flash. In fact, avalanches were very popular in chamois society, for even when one was seen coming, soon enough, the bucks and does could easily dodge them.

The Ice King and His Wonderful Grandchild

IN THE FAR-OFF AGES, all the lands of northern Europe were one, for the deep seas had not yet separated them. Then our forefathers thought that fairies were gods. They built temples in their honour, and prayed to them. Then, in the place where is now the little town of Ulrum in Friesland was the home of the spirit in the ice, Uller. That is what Ulrum means, the home of the good fairy Uller.

Uller was the patron of boys and girls. They liked him, because he invented skates and sleds and sleighs. He had charge of things in winter and enjoyed the cold. He delighted also in hunting. Dressed in thick furs, he loved to roam over the hills and through the forests, seeking out the wolf, the bear, the deer, and the aurochs. His bow and arrows were terrible, for they were very big and he was a sure shot. Being the patron of archery, hunters always sought his favour. The yew tree was sacred to Uller, because the best bows were made from its wood. No one could cut down a yew tree without angering Uller.

Nobody knew who Uller's father was, and if he knew himself, he did not care to tell anyone. He would not bestow many blessings upon mankind; yet thousands of people used to come to Ulrum every year to invoke his aid and ask him to send a heavy fall of snow to cover the ground. That meant good crops of food for the next year. The white snow, lying thick upon the ground, kept back the Frost Giants from biting the earth too hard. Because of deep winter snows, the ground was soft during the next summer. So the seed sprouted more easily and there was plenty to eat.

When Uller travelled over the winter snow, to go out on hunting trips, he strapped snow-shoes on his feet. Because these were shaped like a warrior's shield, Uller was often called the shield-god. His protection was especially invoked by men who fought duels with sword or spear, which were very common in early days; or by soldiers or hunters who wished to be very brave, or had engaged in perilous ventures.

Now when Uller wanted a wife to marry him, he made love to Skadi, because she was a huntress and liked the things which he liked. So they never had a quarrel. She was very strong, fond of sports and of chasing the wild animals. She wore a short skirt, which allowed freedom of motion to her limbs. Then she ranged over the hills and valleys with wonderful swiftness. So rapid were her movements that many people likened her to the cold mountain stream, that leaps down from the high peaks and over the rocks, foaming and dashing to the lowlands. They gave the same name to both this fairy woman and the water, because they were so much alike.

Indeed Skadi was very lovely to look at. It was no wonder that many of the gods, fairies and men fell in love with her. It is even said that she had had several husbands before marrying Uller. When you look at her pictures, you will see that she was as pretty as bright winter itself, when Jack Frost clothes the trees with white and makes the cheeks of the girls so rosy. She wore armour of shining steel, a silver helmet, short white skirts and white fur leggings. Her snow-shoes were of the hue of winter. Besides a glittering spear, she had a bow and sharp arrows. These were held in a silver quiver slung over her shoulders. Altogether, she looked like winter alive. She loved to live in the mountains, and hear the thunders of cataracts, the crash of avalanches, the moaning of the winds in the pine forests. Even the howling of wolves was music in her ears. She was afraid of nothing.

Now from such a father and mother one would expect wonderful children, yet very much like their parents. It turned out that the offspring of Uller and Skadi were all daughters. To them – one after another – were given the names meaning Glacier, Cold, Snow, Drift, Snow Whirl, and Snow Dust, the oldest being the biggest and hardiest. The others were in degree softer and more easily influenced by the sun and the wind. They all looked alike, so that some people called them the Six White Sisters.

Yet they were all so great and powerful that many considered them giantesses. It was not possible for men to tame them, for they did very much as they pleased. No one could stop their doings or drive them away, except Woden, who was the god of the sun. Yet in winter, even he left off ruling the world and went away. During that time, that is, during seven months, Uller took Woden's throne and governed the affairs of the world. When summer came, Uller went with his wife up to the North Pole; or they lived in a house, on the top of the Alps. There they could hunt and roam in their snow-shoes. To these cold places, which the whole family enjoyed, their daughters went also and all were very happy so far above the earth.

Things went on pleasantly in Uller's family so long as his daughters were young, for then the girls found enough to delight in at their daily play. But when grown up and their heads began to be filled with notions about the young giants, who paid visits to them, then the family troubles began.

There was one young giant fairy named Vuur, who came often to see all six of Uller's daughters, from the youngest to the oldest. Yet no one could tell which of them he was in love with, or could name the girl he liked best; no, not even the daughters themselves. His character and his qualities were not well known, for he put on many disguises and appeared in many places. It was believed, however, that he had already done a good deal of mischief and was likely to do more, for he loved destruction. Yet he often helped the kabouter dwarfs to do great things; so that showed he was of some use. In fact he was the fire fairy. He kept on courting all the six sisters, long after May Day came, and he lengthened his visits until the heat turned the entire half dozen of them into water. So they became one.

At this, Uller was so angry at Vuur's having delayed so long before popping the question, and at his daughters' losing their shapes, that he made Vuur marry them all and at once, they taking the name of Regen.

Now when the child of Vuur and Regen was born, it turned out to be, in body and in character, just what people expected from such a father and mother. It was named in Dutch, Stoom. It grew fast and soon showed that it was as powerful as its parents had been; yet it was much worse, when shut up, than when allowed to go free in the air. Stoom loved to do all sorts of tricks. In the kitchen, it would make the iron kettle lid flop up and down with a lively noise. If it were confined in a vessel, whether of iron or earthenware, when set over the fire, it would blow the pot or kettle all to pieces, in order to get out. Thinking itself a great singer, it would make rather a pleasant sound when its mother let it come out of a spout. Yet it never obeyed either of its parents. When they tried to shut up Stoom inside of anything, it always escaped with a terrible sound. In fact, nothing could long hold it in without an explosion.

Sometimes Stoom would go down into the bowels of the earth and turn on a stream of water so as to meet the deep fires which are ever burning far down below us. Then there would come an awful earthquake, because Stoom wanted to get out, and the earth crust would not let him, but tried to hold him down. Sometimes Stoom slipped down into a volcano's mouth. Then the mountain, in order to save itself from being choked, had to spit Stoom out, and this always made a terrible mess on the ground, and men called it lava. Or Stoom might stay down in the crater as a guest, and quietly come out, occasionally, in jets and puffs.

Even when Jack Frost was around and froze the pipes in the house, or turned the water of the pots, pans, kettles and bottles into solid ice, Stoom behaved very badly. If the frozen kettles or any other closed vessel were put over the stove, or near the fire, and the ice melted at the bottom too fast, Stoom would blow the whole thing up. In this way, he often put men's lives in danger and made them lose their property.

No one seemed to know how to handle this mischievous fairy. Not one man on earth could do anything with him. So they let him have his own way. Yet all the time, though he was enjoying his own tricks and lively fun, he was, with his own voice, calling on human beings to use him properly, and harness him to wheels; for he was willing to be useful to them, and was all ready to pull or drive, lift or lower, grind or pump, as the need might be.

As long as men did not treat him properly and give him the right to get out into the air after he had done his work, Stoom would explode, blow up and destroy everything. He could be made to sing, hiss, squeal, whistle and make all kinds of sounds, but unless the bands that held him in were strong enough, or if Vuur got too hot, or his mother would not give him drink enough, when the iron pipes were red with heat, he would lose his temper and explode. He had no respect for bad or neglected boilers, or for lazy or careless firemen and engineers.

Yet properly harnessed and treated well, and fed with the food such as his mother can give, and roused by his father's persuasion, Stoom is greater than any giant or fairy that ever was. He can drive a ship, a locomotive, a submarine or an aeroplane, as fast as Fro's boar, horse or ship. Everybody today is glad that Stoom is such a good servant and friend all over the world.

The Biter Bit

ONCE UPON A TIME there was an old man who, whenever he heard anyone complain how many sons he had to care for, always laughed and said, "I wish that it would please God to give me a hundred sons!"

This he said in jest; as time went on, however, he had, in reality, neither more nor fewer than a hundred sons.

He had trouble enough to find different trades for his sons, but when they were once all started in life they worked diligently and gained plenty of money. Now, however, came a fresh difficulty. One day the eldest son came in to his father and said, "My dear father, I think it is quite time that I should marry."

Hardly had he said these words before the second son came in, saying, "Dear father, I think it is already time that you were looking out for a wife for me."

A moment later came in the third son, asking, "Dear father, don't you think it is high time that you should find me a wife?" In like manner came the fourth and fifth, until the whole hundred had made a similar request. All of them wished to marry and desired their father to find wives for them as soon as he could.

The old man was not a little troubled at these requests; he said, however, to his sons, "Very well, my sons, I have nothing to say against your marrying; there is, however, I foresee, one great difficulty in the way. There are one hundred of you asking for wives, and I hardly think we can find one hundred marriageable girls in all the fifteen villages which are in our neighbourhood."

To this the sons, however, answered, "Don't be anxious about that, but mount your horse and take in your sack sufficient engagement cakes. You must take, also, a stick in your hand so that you can cut a notch in it for every girl you see. It does not signify whether she be handsome or ugly, or lame or blind, just cut a notch in your stick for everyone you meet with."

The old man said, "Very wisely spoken, my sons! I will do exactly as you tell me."

Accordingly he mounted his horse, took a sack full of cakes on his shoulder and a long stick in his hand, and started off at once to beat up the neighbourhood for girls to marry his sons.

The old man had travelled from village to village during a whole month, and whenever he had seen a girl he had cut a notch in his stick. But he was getting pretty well tired, and he began to count how many notches he had already made. When he had counted them carefully over and over again, to be certain that he had counted all, he could only make out seventy-four, so that still twenty-six were wanting to complete the number required. He was, however, so weary with his month's ride that he determined to return home. As he rode along, he saw a priest driving oxen yoked to a plough, and seemingly very deep in anxious thought about something. Now the old man wondered a little to see the priest ploughing his own cornfields without even a boy to help him; he therefore shouted to ask him why he drove his oxen himself. The priest, however, did not even turn his head to see who called him, so intent was he in urging on his oxen and in guiding his plough.

The old man thought he had not spoken loud enough, so he shouted out again as loud as he could, "Stop your oxen a little, and tell me why you are ploughing yourself without even a lad to help you, and this, too, on a holy day!"

Now the priest – who was in a perspiration with his hard work – answered testily, "I conjure you by your old age leave me in peace! I cannot tell you my ill-luck."

At this answer, however, the old man was only the more curious, and persisted all the more earnestly in asking questions to find out why the priest ploughed on a saint's day. At last the priest, tired with his importunity, sighed deeply and said, "Well, if you *will* know: I am the only man in my household and God has blessed me with a hundred daughters!"

The old man was overjoyed at hearing this, and exclaimed cheerfully, "That's very good! It is just what I want, for I have a hundred sons, and so, as you have a hundred daughters, we can be friends."

The moment the priest heard this he became pleasant and talkative, and invited the old man to pass the night in his house. Then, leaving his plough in the field, he drove the oxen back to the village. Just before reaching his house, however, he said to the old man, "Go yourself into the house whilst I tie up my oxen."

No sooner, however, had the old man entered the yard than the wife of the priest rushed at him with a big stick, crying out, "We have not bread enough for our hundred daughters, and we want neither beggars nor visitors," and with these words she drove him away.

Shortly afterwards the priest came out of the barn, and, finding the old man on the road before the gate, asked him why he had not gone into the house as he had told him to do. Whereupon the old man replied, "I went in, but your wife drove me away!"

Then the priest said, "Only wait here a moment till I come back to fetch you." He then went quickly into his house and scolded his wife right well, saying, "What have you done? What a fine chance you have spoiled! The man who came in was going to be our friend, for he has a hundred sons who would gladly have married our hundred daughters!"

When the wife heard this she changed her dress hastily, and arranged her hair and headdress in a different fashion. Then she smiled very sweetly, and welcomed with the greatest possible politeness the old man, when her husband led him into the house. In fact, she pretended that she knew nothing at all of anyone's having been driven away from their door. And as the old man wanted much to find wives for his sons, he also pretended that he did not know that the smiling house-mistress and the woman who drove him away with a stick were one and the self-same person.

So the old man passed the night in the house, and next morning asked the priest formally to give him his hundred daughters for wives for his hundred sons. Thereupon, the priest answered that he was quite willing, and had already spoken to his daughters about the matter, and that they, too, were all quite willing. Then the old man took his engagement cakes, and put them on the table beside him, and gave each of the girls a piece of money to *mark*. Then each of the engaged girls sent a small present by him to that one of his sons to whom she was thus betrothed. These gifts the old man put in the bag wherein he had carried the engagement cakes. He then mounted his horse, and rode off merrily homewards. There were great rejoicings in his household when he told how successful he had been in his search, and that he really had found a hundred girls ready and willing to be married; and these hundred, too, a priest's daughters.

The sons insisted that they should begin to make the wedding preparations without delay, and commenced at once to invite the guests who were to form part of the wedding procession to go to the priest's house and bring home the brides.

Here another difficulty occurred. The old father must find two hundred bride-leaders (two for each bride); one hundred kooms (witnesses); one hundred starisvats; one hundred chaious (running footmen to go before the procession); and three hundred voivodes (standard-bearers); and, besides these, a respectable number of other non-official guests. To find all these persons the father had to hunt throughout the neighbourhood for three years; at last, however, they were all found, and a day was appointed when they were to meet at his house, and go thence in procession to the house of the priest.

On the appointed day all the invited guests gathered at the old man's house. With great noise and confusion, after a fair amount of feasting, the wedding procession was formed properly, and set out for the house of the priest, where the hundred brides were already prepared for their departure for their new home.

So great was the confusion, indeed, that the old man quite forgot to take with him one of his hundred sons, and never missed him in the greeting and talking and drinking he was obliged, as father of the bridegrooms, to go through. Now the young man had worked so long and so hard in preparing for the wedding-day that he never woke up till long after the procession had started; and everyone had had, like his father, too much to do and too many things to think of to miss him.

The wedding procession arrived in good order at the priest's house where a feast was already spread out for them. Having done honour to the various good things, and having gone through all the ceremonies usual on such occasions, the hundred brides were given over to their 'leaders,' and the procession started on its return to the old man's house. But, as they did not set off until pretty late in the afternoon, it was decided that the night should be spent somewhere on the road. When they came, therefore, to a certain river named 'Luckless,' as it was already dark, some of the men proposed that the party should pass the night by the side of the water without crossing over. However, some others of the chief of the party so warmly advised the crossing of the river and encamping on the other bank, that this course was at length, after a very lively discussion, determined on; accordingly the procession began to move over the bridge.

Just, however, as the wedding-party were halfway across the bridge, its two sides began to draw nearer each other, and pressed the people so close together that they had hardly room to breathe – much less could they move forward or backward.

They were kept for some time in this position, some shouting and scolding, others quiet because frightened, until at length a black giant appeared, and shouted to them in a terribly loud voice, "Who are you all? Where do you come from? Where are you going?"

Some of the bolder among them answered, "We are going to our old friend's house, taking home the hundred brides for his hundred sons; but unluckily we ventured on this bridge after nightfall, and it has pressed us so tightly together that we cannot move one way or the other."

"And where is your old friend?" enquired the black giant.

Now all the wedding guests turned their eyes towards the old man. Thereupon he turned towards the giant, who instantly said to him, "Listen, old man! Will you give me what you have forgotten at home, if I let your friends pass over the bridge?"

The old man considered some time what it might be he had forgotten at home, but at last, not being able to recollect anything in particular that he had left, and hearing on all sides the groans and moans of his guests, he replied, "Well, I will give it to you, if you will only let the procession pass over."

Then the black giant said to the party, "You all hear what he has promised, and are all my witnesses to the bargain. In three days I shall come to fetch what I have bargained for."

Having said this, the black giant widened the bridge and the whole procession passed on to the other bank in safety. The people, however, no longer wished to spend the night on the way, so they moved on as fast as they could, and early in the morning reached the old man's house.

As everybody talked of the strange adventure they had met with, the eldest son, who had been left at home, soon began to understand how the matter stood, and went to his father saying, "O my father! you have sold *me* to the black giant!"

Then the old man was very sorry, and troubled; but his friends comforted him, saying, "Don't be frightened! Nothing will come of it."

The marriage ceremonies were celebrated with great rejoicings. Just, however, as the festivities were at their height, on the third day, the black giant appeared at the gate and shouted, "Now, give me at once what you have promised."

The old man, trembling all over, went forward and asked him, "What do you want?"

"Nothing but what you have promised me!" returned the black giant.

As he could not break his promise, the old man, very distressed, was then obliged to deliver up his eldest son to the giant, who thereupon said, "Now I shall take your son with me, but after three years have passed you can come to the River Luckless and take him away."

Having said this the black giant disappeared, taking with him the young man, whom he carried off to his workshop as an apprentice to the trade of witchcraft.

From that time the poor old man had not a single moment of happiness. He was always sad and anxious, and counted every year, and every month, and week, and even every day, until the dawn of the last day of the three years. Then he took a staff in his hand and hurried off to the bank of the River Luckless. As soon as he reached the river he was met by the black giant, who asked him, "Why are you come?" The old man answered that he came to take home his son according to his agreement.

Thereupon the giant brought out a tray on which stood a sparrow, a turtle-dove, and a quail, and said to the old man, "Now, if you can tell which of these is your son, you may take him away."

The poor old father looked intently at the three birds, one after the other, and over and over again, but at last he was forced to own that he could not tell which of them was his son. So he was obliged to go away by himself, and was far more miserable than before. He had hardly, however, got halfway home when he thought he would go back to the river and take one of the birds which he remembered had looked at him intently.

When he reached the River Luckless he was again met by the black giant, who brought out the tray again, and placed on it this time a partridge, a tit-mouse and a thrush, saying, "Now, my old man, find out which is your son!"

The anxious father again looked at one bird after the other, but he felt more uncertain than before, and so, crying bitterly, again went away.

Just as the old man was going through a forest, which was between the River Luckless and his house, an old woman met him and said, "Stop a moment! Where are you hurrying to? And why are you in such trouble?"

Now, the old man was so deeply musing over his great unhappiness that he did not at first attend to the old woman; but she followed him, calling after him, and repeating her questions with more earnestness. So he stopped at last, and told her what a terrible misfortune had fallen upon him. When the old woman had listened to the whole story, she said cheerfully, "Don't be cast down! Don't be afraid. Go back again to the river, and, when the giant brings out the three birds, look into their eyes sharply. When you see that one of the birds has a tear in one of its eyes, seize that bird and hold it fast, for it has a human soul."

The old man thanked her heartily for her advice, and turned back, for the third time, towards the River Luckless. Again the black giant appeared, and looked very merry whilst he brought out his tray and put upon it a sparrow, a dove, and a woodpecker, saying, "My old man! find out which is your son!" Then the father looked sharply into the eyes of the birds, and saw that from the right eye of the dove a tear dropped slowly down. In a moment he grasped the bird tightly, saying, "This is my son!" The next moment he found himself holding fast his eldest son by the shoulder, and so, singing and shouting in his great joy, took him quickly home, and gave him over to his eldest daughter-in-law, the wife of his son.

Now for some time they all lived together very happily. One day, however, the young man said to his father, "Whilst I was apprenticed in the workshop of the black giant, I learned a great many tricks of witchcraft. Now I intend to change myself into a fine horse, and you shall take me to market and sell me for a good sum of money. But be sure not to give up the halter."

The father did as the son had said. Next market day he went to the city with a fine horse which he offered for sale. Many buyers came round him, admiring the horse, and bidding for it, so that at last the old man was able to sell it for two thousand ducats. When he received the money he took good care not to let go the halter, and he returned home far richer than he ever dreamt of being.

A few days later, the man who had bought the horse sent his servant with it to the river to bathe, and, whilst in the water, the horse got loose from the servant and galloped off into the neighbouring forest. There he changed himself back into his real shape, and returned to his father's house.

After some time had passed, the young man said one day to his father, "Now I will change myself into an ox, and you can take me to market to sell me; but take care not to give up the rope with which you lead me."

So next market-day the old man went to the city leading a very fine ox, and soon found a buyer who offered ten times the usual price paid for an ox. The buyer asked also for the rope to lead the animal home, but the old man said, "What do you want with such an old thing? You had better buy a new one!" and he went off taking with him the rope.

That evening, whilst the servants of the buyer were driving the ox to the field, he ran away into a wood near, and having taken there his human shape, returned home to his father's house.

On the eve of the next market-day, the young man said to his father: "Now I will change myself into a cow with golden horns, and you can sell me as before, only take care not to give up the string."

Accordingly he changed himself next morning into a cow, and the old man took it to the market-place, and asked for it three hundred crowns.

But the black giant had learned that his former apprentice was making a great deal of money by practicing the trade he had taught him, and, being jealous at this, he determined to put an end to the young man's gains.

Therefore on the third day he came to the market himself as a buyer, and the moment he saw the beautiful cow with the golden horns he knew that it could be no other than his former apprentice. So he came up to the old man, and, having outbidden all the other would-be purchasers, paid at once the price he had agreed on. Having done this, he caught the string in his hand, and tried to wrench it from the terrified old man, who called out, "I have not sold you the string, but the cow!" and held the string as fast as he could with both hands.

"Oh, no!" said the buyer, "I have the law and custom on my side. Whoever buys a cow, buys also the string with which it is led!" Some of the amused and astonished lookers-on said that this was quite true, therefore the old man was obliged to give up the string.

The black giant, well satisfied with his purchase, took the cow with him to his castle, and, after having put iron chains on her legs, fastened her in a cellar. Every morning the giant gave the cow some water and hay, but he never unchained her.

One evening, however, the cow, with incessant struggles, managed to get free from the chains, and immediately opened the cellar-door with her horns and ran away.

Next morning the black giant went as usual into the cellar, carrying the hay and water for the cow; but seeing she had got free and run away, he threw the hay down, and started off at once to pursue her.

When he came within sight of her he turned himself into a wolf and ran at her with great fury; but his clever apprentice changed himself instantly from a cow into a bear, whereupon the giant turned himself from a wolf into a lion; the bear then turned into a tiger, and the lion changed into a crocodile, whereupon the tiger turned into a sparrow. Upon this the giant changed from the form of a crocodile into a hawk, and the apprentice immediately changed into a hare, on seeing which the hawk became a greyhound. Then the apprentice changed from a hare into a falcon, and the greyhound into an eagle; whereupon the apprentice changed into a fish. The giant then turned from an eagle into a mouse, and immediately the apprentice, as a cat, ran after him; then the giant turned himself into a heap of millet, and the apprentice transformed himself into a hen and chickens, which very greedily picked up all the millet, except one single seed, in which the master was, who changed himself into a squirrel; instantly, however, the apprentice became a hawk, and, pouncing on the squirrel, killed it.

In this way the apprentice beat his master, the black giant, and revenged himself for all the sufferings he had endured whilst learning the trade of witchcraft.

Having killed the squirrel, the hawk took his proper shape again, and the young man returned joyfully to his father, whom he made immensely rich.

The Giants and the Herd-Boy

THERE WAS ONCE UPON A TIME a poor boy who had neither father nor mother. In order to gain a living he looked after the sheep of a great lord. Day and night he spent out in the open fields, and only when it was very wet and stormy did he take refuge in a little hut on the edge of a big forest. Now one night, when he was sitting on the grass beside his flocks, he heard not very far from him the sound as of someone crying. He rose up and followed the direction of the noise. To his dismay and astonishment he found a giant lying at the entrance of the wood; he was about to run off as fast as his legs could carry him, when the giant called out: "Don't be afraid, I won't harm you. On the contrary, I will reward you handsomely if you will bind up my foot. I hurt it when I was trying to root up an oak-tree." The Herd-boy took off his shirt, and bound up the giant's wounded foot with it. Then the giant rose up and said, "Now come and I will reward you. We are going to celebrate a marriage today, and I promise you we shall have plenty of fun. Come and enjoy yourself, but in order that my brothers mayn't see you, put this band round your waist and then you'll be invisible." With these words he handed the Herd-boy a belt, and walking on in front he led him to a fountain where hundreds of giants and giantesses were assembled preparing to hold a wedding. They danced and played different games till midnight; then one of the giants tore up a plant by its roots, and all the giants and giantesses made themselves so thin that they disappeared into the earth through the hole made by the uprooting of the plant. The wounded giant remained behind to the last and called out, "Herd-boy, where are you?" "Here I am, close to you," was the reply. "Touch me," said the giant, "so that you too may come with us underground." The Herd-boy did as he was told, and before he could have believed it possible he found himself in a big hall, where even the walls were made of pure gold. Then to his astonishment he saw that the hall was furnished with the tables and chairs that belonged to his master. In a few minutes the company began to eat and drink. The banquet was a very gorgeous one, and the poor youth fell to and ate and drank lustily. When he had eaten and drunk as much as he could he thought to himself, "Why shouldn't I put a loaf of bread in my pocket? I shall be glad of it tomorrow." So he seized a loaf when no one was looking and stowed it away under his tunic. No sooner had he done so than the wounded giant limped up to him and whispered softly, "Herd-boy, where are you?" "Here I am," replied the youth. "Then hold on to me," said the giant, "so that I may lead you up above again." So the Herd-boy held on to the giant, and in a few moments he found himself on the earth once more, but the giant had vanished. The Herd-boy returned to his sheep, and took off the invisible belt which he hid carefully in his bag.

The next morning the lad felt hungry, and thought he would cut off a piece of the loaf he had carried away from the giants' wedding feast, and eat it. But although he tried with all his might, he couldn't cut off the smallest piece. Then in despair he bit the loaf, and what was his astonishment when a piece of gold fell out of his mouth and rolled at his feet. He bit the bread a second and third time, and each time a piece of gold fell out of his mouth; but the bread remained untouched. The Herd-boy was very much delighted over his stroke of good fortune, and, hiding the magic loaf in his bag, he hurried off to the nearest village to buy himself something to eat, and then returned to his sheep.

Now the Lord whose sheep the Herd-boy looked after had a very lovely daughter, who always smiled and nodded to the youth when she walked with her father in his fields. For a long time the Herd-boy had made up his mind to prepare a surprise for this beautiful creature on her birthday. So when the day approached he put on his invisible belt, took a sack of gold pieces with him, and slipping into her room in the middle of the night, he placed the bag of gold beside her bed and returned to his sheep. The girl's joy was great, and so was her parents' next day when they found the sack full of gold pieces. The Herd-boy was so pleased to think what pleasure he had given that the next night he placed another bag of gold beside the girl's bed. And this he continued to do for seven nights, and the girl and her parents made up their minds that it must be a good fairy who brought the gold every night. But one night they determined to watch, and see from their hiding-place who the bringer of the sack of gold really was.

On the eighth night a fearful storm of wind and rain came on while the Herd-boy was on his way to bring the beautiful girl another bag of gold. Then for the first time he noticed, just as he reached his master's house, that he had forgotten the belt which made him invisible. He didn't like the idea of going back to his hut in the wind and wet, so he just stepped as he was into the girl's room, laid the sack of gold beside her, and was turning to leave the room, when his master confronted him and said, "You young rogue, so you were going to steal the gold that a good fairy brings every night, were you?" The Herd-boy was so taken aback by his words, that he stood trembling before him, and did not dare to explain his presence. Then his master spoke. "As you have hitherto always behaved well in my service I will not send you to prison; but leave your place instantly and never let me see your face again." So the Herd-boy went back to his hut, and taking his loaf and belt with him, he went to the nearest town. There he bought himself some fine clothes, and a beautiful coach with four horses, hired two servants, and drove back to his master. You may imagine how astonished he was to see his Herd-boy returning to him in this manner! Then the youth told him of the piece of good luck that had befallen him, and asked him for the hand of his beautiful daughter. This was readily granted, and the two lived in peace and happiness to the end of their lives.

Reygoch

I

ONCE UPON A BEAUTIFUL SUMMER NIGHT the men were watching their horses in the meadow. And as they watched, they fell asleep. And as they slept, the fairies flew out of the clouds to have some sport with the horses, as is the fairies' way. Each fairy caught a horse, mounted it, and then whipped it with her golden hair, urging it round and round the dewy meadow.

Among the fairies there was one quite young and tiny, called Curlylocks, who had come down to earth from the clouds for the first time that night.

Curlylocks thought it lovely to ride through the night like a whirlwind. And it so happened that she had got hold of the most spirited horse of all – a Black – small, but fierce as fire. The Black galloped round and round with the other horses, but he was the swiftest of all. Soon he was all in a lather of foam.

But Curlylocks wanted to ride faster still. She bent down and pinched the Black's right ear. The horse started, reared, and then bolted straight ahead, leaving behind the rest of the horses, the meadow and all, as he flew away like the wind with Curlylocks into the wide, wide world.

Curlylocks thoroughly enjoyed her lightning ride. The Black went like the wind, by field and by river, by meadow and mountain, over dale and hill. "Good gracious! what a lot of things there are in the world!" thought Curlylocks, full of delight as she looked at all the pretty sights. But what pleased her best was when they came through a country where there were mountains all covered with glorious forests, and at the foot of the mountains two golden fields like two great gold kerchiefs, and in the midst of them two white villages, like two white doves, and a little further on a great sheet of water.

But the Black would not stop, neither there nor anywhere, but rushed on and on as if he were possessed.

So the Black carried Curlylocks far and far away till at last they came to a great plain, with a cold wind blowing over it. The Black galloped into the plain, and there was nothing there but yellow sand, neither trees nor grass, and the further they went into that great waste, the colder it grew. But how large that plain is, I cannot tell you, for the good reason that the man does not live who could cross it.

The Black ran on with Curlylocks for seven days and seven nights. The seventh day, just before sunrise, they reached the centre of the plain, and in the centre of the plain they found the ruinous walls of the terribly great city of Frosten, and there it is always bitterly cold.

As the Black raced up to the ancient gates of Frosten, Curlylocks threw her magic veil on the wall, and so caught hold of the wall. The Black galloped away from under her, and so continued his wild career up to his old age to and fro between the huge walls of Frosten, till at last he found the northern gate and galloped out again into the plain – God knows whither!

But Curlylocks came down from the wall and began to walk about the city, and it was cold as cold! Her magic veil, without which she could not fly among the clouds, she wound about her shoulders, for she took great care of it. And so Curlylocks walked and walked about the city of Frosten, and all the time she felt as if she must come upon something very wonderful in this city, which was so marvellous and so great. However, nothing did she see but only great crumbling walls, and nothing did she hear but now and again a stone cracking with the cold.

Suddenly, just as Curlylocks had turned the corner of the very biggest wall, she saw, fast asleep at the foot of the wall, a huge man, bigger than the biggest oak in the biggest forest. The man was dressed in a huge cloak of coarse linen, and the strap he wore for a belt was five fathoms long. His head was as big as the biggest barrel, and his beard was like a shock of corn. He was so big, that man, you might have thought there was a church tower fallen down beside the wall!

This giant was called Reygoch, and he lived at Frosten. All he did was to count the stones of the city of Frosten. He could never have finished counting them but for that huge head of his, as big as a barrel. But he counted and counted – he had counted for a thousand years, and had already counted thirty walls and five gates of the city.

When Curlylocks spied Reygoch, she clasped her hands and wondered. She never thought there could be such an immense creature in the world.

So Curlylocks sat down by Reygoch's ear (and Reygoch's ear was as big as the whole of Curlylocks), and called down his ear:

"Aren't you cold, daddy?"

Reygoch woke up, laughed, and looked at Curlylocks.

"Cold? I should think I was cold," answered Reygoch, and his voice was as deep as distant thunder. Reygoch's big nose was all red with the cold, and his hair and beard were all thick with hoar-frost.

"Dear me!" said Curlylocks, "you're such a big man, and you aren't going to build yourself a roof to keep out the cold?"

"Why should I?" said Reygoch, and laughed again. "The sun will be out presently."

Reygoch heaved himself up so as to sit. He sat up. He clapped his left shoulder with his right hand, and his right shoulder he clapped with the left hand, so as to beat out the hoar-frost; and the hoar-frost came off each shoulder as if it were snow slipping off a roof!

"Look out! look out, daddy! you'll smother me!" cried Curlylocks. But Reygoch could scarcely hear her, because it was a long way from Curlylocks to his ear, so big was he when he sat up.

So Reygoch lifted Curlylocks on to his shoulder, told her his name and his business, and she told him how she had come.

"And here comes the sun," said Reygoch, and pointed for Curlylocks to see.

Curlylocks looked, and there was the sun rising, but so pale and feeble, as if there were no one for him to warm.

"Well, you are a silly, Reygoch!" said Curlylocks – "you are really silly to live here and spend your life counting these tiresome stones of Frosten. Come along, Reygoch, and see how beautiful the world is, and find something more sensible to do."

Now it had never occurred to Reygoch to want a finer home for himself than Frosten city, nor had he ever thought that there might be better work than his in the world. Reygoch always thought, "I was meant to count the stones of Frosten," and had never asked for anything better.

Curlylocks, however, gave him no peace, but persuaded him to come out and see the world with her.

"I'll take you to a lovely country," said Curlylocks, "where there is an ancient forest, and beside the forest two golden fields."

Curlylocks talked for a long time. And old Reygoch had never had anybody to talk to, and so he couldn't resist persuasion.

"Well, let's go!" said he.

Curlylocks was mightily pleased with this.

But now they had to contrive something, so that Reygoch could carry Curlylocks, because Reygoch himself had nothing.

So Curlylocks drew out from her bosom a little bag of pearls. It was her mother who had given Curlylocks these pearls before allowing her to go down to earth, and told her: "If you ever should need anything, just throw down a pearl, and it will turn into whatever you want. Be very careful of those pearls, because there are so many things in the world that you will want more and more as you go on."

Curlylocks took out a tiny seed-pearl, threw it down, and lo, before their eyes there grew a little basket, just as big as Curlylocks, and the basket had a loop attached, just big enough to fit Reygoch's ear.

Curlylocks jumped into the basket; and Reygoch picked up the basket and hung it on his ear like an ear-ring!

Whenever Reygoch laughed, whenever he sneezed or shook his head, Curlylocks rocked as if she were in a swing; and she thought it a capital way of travelling.

So Reygoch started to walk, and had already taken a ten-yard stride, when Curlylocks stopped him, and begged:

"Couldn't we go underground, perhaps, Reygoch dear, so that I might see what there is under the earth?"

"Why not?" answered Reygoch; for he could break into the earth as easy as fun, only it had never entered his head to look what might be underground.

But Curlylocks wanted to know everything about everything, and so they agreed to travel underground until they should arrive under the forest by the golden fields, and there they would come up.

When they had settled that, Reygoch began to break up the earth. He lifted up his great feet and stamped for the first time, and at that the whole of the great city of Frosten shook and a great many walls tumbled down. Reygoch raised his feet a second time and stamped again, and the whole plain quaked. Reygoch raised his feet a third time and stamped, and lo, half the world trembled, the solid earth gaped under Reygoch, and Reygoch and Curlylocks fell into the hole and down under the earth.

When they got there, they found the earth all honeycombed with pillars and passages on every side, and heaven alone knew where they all led to. And they could hear waters rushing and the moaning of the winds.

They followed one of the passages, and for a while they had light from the hole through which they had fallen. But as they went on it grew darker and darker – black darkness, such as there is nowhere save in the bowels of the earth.

Reygoch tramped calmly on in the dark. With his great hands he felt his way from pillar to pillar.

But Curlylocks was frightened by the great darkness.

She clung to Reygoch's ear and cried: "It's dark, Reygoch dear!"

"Well, and why not?" returned Reygoch. "The dark didn't come to us. It's we have come to it."

Then Curlylocks got cross, because Reygoch never minded anything and she had expected great things from so huge a man.

"I should be in a nice fix with you but for my pearls," said Curlylocks quite angrily.

Then she threw down another pearl, and a tiny lantern grew in her hand, bright as if it were lit with gold. The darkness crept back deeper into the earth, and the light shone far through the underground passages.

Curlylocks was delighted with her lantern, because it showed up all the marvels which had been swallowed by the earth in days of old. In one place she saw lordly castles, with doors and windows all fretted with gold and framed in red marble. In another place were warriors' weapons, slender-barrelled muskets and heavy scimitars studded with gems and precious stones. In a third place she saw long-buried treasures, golden dishes and silver goblets full of gold ducats, and the Emperor's very crown of gold three times refined. All these treasures had been swallowed up by God's will, and it is God's secret why so much treasure should lie there undisturbed.

But Curlylocks was quite dazzled with all these marvels; and instead of going straight ahead by the way they had settled upon, she begged Reygoch to put her down so that she might play about a little and admire all the strange things and gaze upon the wonders of God's secret.

So Reygoch set Curlylocks down, and Curlylocks took her little lantern and ran to the castles, and to the weapons, and to the treasure-hoards. And lest she might lose her little bag of pearls while she was playing, she laid it down beside a pillar.

As for Reygoch, he sat down to rest not far off.

Curlylocks began to play with the treasures; she looked at the beautiful things and rummaged among them. With her tiny hands she scattered the golden ducats, examined the goblets chased in silver, and put upon her head the crown of gold three times refined. She played about, looked round and admired, and at last caught sight of a very slender little ivory staff propped up against a mighty pillar.

But it was just that slender staff that kept the mighty pillar from collapsing, because the pillar was already completely hollowed out by the water. And therefore God had caused that little staff to fall down there, and the staff held up the pillar under the earth.

But Curlylocks wondered:

"Why is that little staff just there?" And she went and picked up the staff to look at it.

But no sooner had Curlylocks taken the staff and moved it than the subterranean passages re-echoed with a terrible rumbling noise. The great pillar trembled, swayed and crashed down amid a whole mountain of falling earth, closing and blocking up the path between Reygoch and Curlylocks. They could neither see nor hear one another, nor could they reach one another....

There was the poor little fairy Curlylocks caught in the bowels of the earth! She was buried alive in that vast grave, and perhaps would never again see those golden fields for which she had set out, and all because she would not go straight on by the way they had intended, but would loiter and turn aside to the right and to the left to pry into God's secrets!

Curlylocks wept and cried, and tried to get to Reygoch. But she found that there was no way through, and that her plight was hopeless; and as for the bag of pearls, which might have helped her, it was buried under the landslide.

When Curlylocks realized this she stopped crying, for she was proud, and she thought: "There is no help for it, and I must die. Reygoch won't come to my rescue, because his wits are too slow even to help himself, let alone to make him remember to help me. So there is nothing for it, and I must die."

So Curlylocks prepared for death. But in case folk should ever find her in her grave she wanted them to know that she came of royal blood. So she set the crown of gold three times refined upon her head, took the ivory staff in her hand, and lay down to die. There was no one beside Curlylocks except her little lantern, burning as if it were lit with gold; and as Curlylocks began to grow cold and stiff, so the lantern burned low and dim.

Reygoch was really an old stupid. When the pillar crashed down and there was the big landslide between him and Curlylocks he never moved, but sat still in the dark.

Thus he sat for quite a long time, before it occurred to him to go and find out what had happened.

He felt his way in the dark to the spot where Curlylocks had been, groped about, and realized that the earth had subsided there and that the passage was indeed blocked.

"Eh, but that way is choked up now," considered Reygoch. And nothing else could he think of, but turned round, left the mound of fallen earth and Curlylocks beyond it, and went back by the road they had travelled from Frosten city.

* * *

Thus old Reygoch went his way, pillar by pillar. He had already gone a goodish bit; but there was all the time something worrying him. Reygoch himself couldn't imagine what it was that worried him.

He arranged the strap around his waist – perhaps it had been too tight; and then he stretched his arm – perhaps his arm had gone to sleep. Yet it was neither the one nor the other, but something else that worried. Reygoch wondered what in the world it could be. He wondered, and as he wondered he shook his head.

And as Reygoch shook his head, the little basket swung at his ear. And when Reygoch felt how light the basket was, and that there was no Curlylocks inside, a bitter pang shot through his heart and breast, and – simpleton though he was – he knew well enough that he was grieved because he missed Curlylocks, and he realized also that he ought to save her.

It had taken Reygoch a lot of trouble to think out all that; but once he had thought it out, he turned like the wind and flew back to the place where the landslide was, to find Curlylocks behind the heap of earth. He flew, and arrived just in time. Reygoch burrowed away with both hands, and in a little while he had burrowed a big hole, so that he could see Curlylocks lying there, the crown of fine gold on her head. She was already growing cold and rigid, with her little lantern beside her, and the flame of it as feeble as the tiniest little glow-worm.

If Reygoch had cried out in his grief the earth would have rocked, and the little lantern would have gone out altogether – even the little glow-worm light by the side of Curlylocks would have died away.

But Reygoch's throat was all tight with pain, so that he could not cry out. He put out his great big hand and gently picked up poor Curlylocks, who was already quite cold, and warmed her between the hollowed palms of his huge hands as you would warm a starved dicky-bird in winter. And lo! in a little while Curlylocks moved her little head, and at once the lantern burned a little brighter; and then Curlylocks moved her arm, and the lantern burned brighter still. At last Curlylocks opened her eyes, and the lantern burned as brightly as if its flame were pure gold!

Then Curlylocks jumped to her feet, caught hold of Reygoch's beard, and they both of them cried for pure joy. Reygoch's tears were as big as pears and Curlylocks' as tiny as millet-seed, but except for size they were both the same sort; and from that moment these two were mightily fond of one another.

When they had finished their cry, Curlylocks found her pearls, and then they went on. But they touched no more of the things they saw underground, neither the sunken ships with their hoards of treasure, which had worked their way down from the bottom of the sea, nor the red coral, nor the yellow amber which twined round the underground pillars. They touched nothing, but went straight along by the way that would take them to the golden fields.

When they had gone on thus for a long time, Curlylocks asked Reygoch to hold her up; and when he did so, Curlylocks took a handful of earth from above her head.

She took the earth, looked at her hand, and there, among the soil, she found leaves and fibres.

"Here we are, daddy, under the forest beside the golden fields," said Curlylocks. "Let's hurry up and get out."

So Reygoch stretched himself and began to break through the earth with his head.

II

And indeed they were under the forest, just underneath a wooded glen between the two villages and the two counties. No one ever came to this glen but the herd boys and girls from both villages and both counties.

Now there was bitter strife between the two villages – strife over the threshing-floors, and the pastures, and the mills, and the timber-felling, and most of all over the staff of headmanship, which one of the villages had long claimed as belonging to it by rights, and the other would not give up. And so these two villages were at enmity with one another.

But the herd boys and girls of both villages were just simple young folk, who understood nothing about the rights of their elders, and cared less, but met every day on the boundary between the two villages and the two counties. Their flocks mingled and fed together, while the boys played games, and over their games would often be late in bringing the sheep home of an evening.

For this the poor boys and girls would be soundly rated and scolded in both villages. But in one of the villages there was a great-grandfather and a great-grandmother who could remember all that had ever happened in either village, and they said: "Leave the children alone. A better harvest will spring from their childish games than ever from your wheat in the fields."

So the shepherds kept on coming, as before, with their sheep to the glen, and in time the parents stopped bothering about what the children did.

And so it was on the day when Reygoch broke through the earth at that very spot. The boys and girls happened to be all gathered together under the biggest oak, getting ready to go home. One was tying up his shoes, another fixing a thong to a stick, and the girls were collecting the sheep. All of a sudden they heard a dreadful thumping in the earth right underneath their feet! There was a thud, then a second, and at the third thud the earth gaped, and up there came, right in the midst of the shepherds, a fearsome large head as big as a barrel, with a beard like a shock of corn, and the beard still bristling with hoar-frost from Frosten city!

The boys and girls all screamed with fright and fell down in a dead faint – not so much because of the head as big as a barrel, but because of the beard, that looked for all the world like a shock of corn!

So the shepherds fainted away – all but young Lilio, who was the handsomest and cleverest among the lads of both villages and both counties.

Lilio kept his feet, and went close up to see what sort of monster it might be.

"Don't be afraid, children," said Lilio to the shepherds. "The Lord never created that monstrous giant for evil, else he would have killed half the world by now."

So Lilio walked boldly up to Reygoch, and Reygoch lifted the basket with Curlylocks down from his ear and set it on the ground.

"Come – oh come quickly, boys!" cried Lilio. "There is a little girl with him, little and lovely as a star!"

The herd boys and girls got up and began to peep from behind each other at Curlylocks; and those who had at first been the most frightened were now the foremost in coming up to Curlylocks, because, you see, they were always quickest in everything.

No sooner had the herd boys and girls seen dear little Curlylocks than they loved her. They helped her out of her basket, led her to where the turf was softest, and fell to admiring her lovely robes, which were light as gossamer and blue as the sky, and her hair, which was shining and soft as the morning light; but most of all they admired her fairy veil, for she would wave it just for a moment, and then rise from the grass and float in the air.

The herd boys and girls and Curlylocks danced in a ring together, and played all kinds of games. Curlylocks' little feet twinkled for pure joy, her eyes laughed, and so did her lips, because she had found companions who liked the same things as she did.

Then Curlylocks brought out her little bag of pearls to give presents and pleasure to her new friends. She threw down a pearl, and a little tree grew up in their midst, all decked with coloured ribbons, silk kerchiefs and red necklaces for the girls. She threw down a second pearl, and from all parts of the forest came forth haughty peacocks; they stalked and strutted, they flew up and away, shedding their glorious feathers all over the turf, so that the grass fairly sparkled with them. And the herd boys stuck the feathers in their caps and doublets. Yet another pearl did Curlylocks throw out, and from a lofty branch there dropped a golden swing with silken ropes; and when the boys and girls got on the swing, it swooped and stooped as light as a swallow, and as gently as the grand barge of the Duke of Venice.

The children shouted for joy, and Curlylocks threw out all the pearls in her bag one after another, never thinking that she ought to save them; because Curlylocks liked nothing in the world better than lovely games and pretty songs. And so she spent her pearls down to the last little seed pearl, though heaven alone knew how badly she would need them soon, both she and her new friends.

"I shall never leave you any more," cried Curlylocks merrily. And the herd boys and girls clapped their hands and threw up their caps for joy over her words.

Only Lilio had not joined in their games, because he was rather sad and worried that day. He stayed near Reygoch, and from there he watched Curlylocks in all her loveliness, and all the pretty magic she made there in the forest.

Meantime Reygoch had come out of his hole. Out he came and stood up among the trees of the forest, and as he stood there his head rose above the hundred-year-old forest, so terribly big was Reygoch.

Over the forest looked Reygoch, and out into the plain.

The sun had already set, and the sky was all crimson. In the plain you could see the two golden fields spread out like two gold kerchiefs, and in the midst of the fields two villages like two white doves. A little way beyond the two villages flowed the mighty River Banewater, and all along the river rose great grass-grown dykes; and on the dykes you could see herds and their keepers moving.

"Well, well!" said Reygoch, "and to think that I have spent a thousand years in Frosten city, in that desert, when there is so much beauty in the world!" And Reygoch was so delighted with looking into the plain that he just stood there with his great head as big as a barrel turning from right to left, like a huge scarecrow nodding above the treetops.

Presently Lilio called to him:

"Sit down, daddy, for fear the elders of the villages should see you."

Reygoch sat down, and the two started talking, and Lilio told Reygoch why he was so sad that day.

"A very wicked thing is going to happen today," said Lilio. "I overheard the elders of our village talking last night, and this is what they said: 'Let us pierce the dyke along the River Banewater. The river will widen the hole, the dyke will fall, and the water will flood the enemy village; it will drown men and women, flood the graveyard and the fields, till the water will be level above them, and nothing but a lake to show where the enemy village has been. But our fields are higher, and our village lies on a height, and so no harm will come to us.' And then they really went out with a great ram to pierce the dyke secretly and at dead of night. But, daddy," continued Lilio, "I know that our fields are not so high, and I know that the water will overflow them too, and before the night is over there will be a lake where our two villages used to be. And that is why I am so sad."

They were still talking when a terrible noise and clamour arose from the plain.

"There!" cried Lilio, "the dreadful thing has happened!"

Reygoch drew himself up, picked up Lilio, and the two looked out over the plain. It was a sad sight to see! The dyke was crumbling, and the mighty Black Banewater rolling in two arms across the beautiful fields. One arm rolled towards the one village, and the second arm towards the other village. Animals were drowning, the golden fields disappeared below the flood. Above the graves the crosses were afloat, and both villages rang with cries and shouting. For in both villages the elders had gone out to the threshing-floors with cymbals, drums and fifes, and there they were drumming and piping away each to spite the other village, so crazed were they with malice, while over and above that din the village dogs howled dismally, and the women and children wept and wailed.

"Daddy," cried Lilio, "why have I not your hands to stop the water?"

Terrified and bewildered by the dreadful clamour in the plain, the herd boys and girls crowded round Reygoch and Lilio.

When Curlylocks heard what was the matter she called out quick and sprightly, as befits a little fairy:

"Come on, Reygoch – come on and stop the water!"

"Yes, yes, let's go!" cried the herd boys of both villages and both counties, as they wept and sobbed without stopping. "Come on, Reygoch, and take us along too!"

Reygoch stooped, gathered up Lilio and Curlylocks (who was still carrying her lantern) in his right hand, and all the rest of the herd boys and girls in his left, and then Reygoch raced with ten-fathom strides through the forest clearing and down into the plain. Behind him ran the sheep, bleating with terror. And so they reached the plain.

Through fog and twilight ran Reygoch with the children in his arms and the terrified flocks at his heels in frantic flight – all running towards the dyke. And out to meet them flowed the Black Banewater, killing and drowning as it flowed. It is terribly strong, is that water. Stronger than Reygoch? Who knows? Will it sweep away Reygoch, too? Will it drown those poor herd boys and girls also, and must the dear little Fairy Curlylocks die – and she as lovely as a star?

So Reygoch ran on across the meadow, which was still dry, and came all breathless to the dyke, where there was a great breach, through which the river was pouring with frightful force.

"Stop it up, Reygoch – stop it up!" wailed the boys and girls.

Not far from the dyke there was a little mound in the plain.

"Put us on that mound," cried Curlylocks briskly.

Reygoch set down Lilio and Curlylocks and the herd boys and girls on the hillock, and the sheep and lambs crowded round them. Already the hillock was just an island in the middle of the water.

But Reygoch took one mighty stride into the water and then lay down facing the dyke, stopping up the breach with his enormous chest. For a little while the water ceased to flow; but it was so terribly strong that nothing on earth could stop it. The water pressed forward; it eddied round Reygoch's shoulders; it broke through under him, over him, about him – everywhere – and rolled on again over the plain. Reygoch stretched out both arms and piled up the earth in great handfuls; but as fast as he piled it up, the water carried it away.

And in the plain the water kept on rising higher and higher; fields, villages, cattle, threshing-floors, not one of them could be seen any more. Of both villages, the roofs and church steeples were all that showed above the flood.

Even around the hillock where the herd boys and girls were standing with Lilio and Curlylocks the flood was rising higher and higher. The poor young things were weeping and crying, some for their mothers, others for their brothers and sisters, and some for their homes and gardens; because they saw that both villages had perished, and not a soul saved – and the water rising about them, too!

So they crowded up higher and higher upon the hillock; they huddled together around Lilio and Curlylocks, who were standing side by side in the midst of their friends.

Lilio stood still and white as marble; but Curlylocks' eyes shone, and she held up her lantern towards Reygoch to give him light for his work. Curlylocks' veil rose and fluttered in the night wind and hovered above the water, as though the little fairy were about to fly away and vanish from among all these terrors.

"Curlylocks! Curlylocks! don't go! Don't leave us!" wailed the herd boys, to whom it seemed as if there were an angel with them while they could look upon Curlylocks.

"I'm not going – I'm not going away!" cried Curlylocks. But her veil fluttered, as if it would carry her away of its own accord, over the water and up into the clouds.

Suddenly they heard a scream. The water had risen and caught one of the girls by the hem of her skirt and was washing her away. Lilio stooped just in time, seized the girl, and pulled her back on to the hillock.

"We must tie ourselves together," cried the herd boys; "we must be tied each to the other, or we shall perish."

"Here, children – here!" cried Curlylocks, who had a kind and pitiful heart.

Quickly she stripped her magic veil off her shoulders and gave it to the herd girls. They tore the veil into strips, knotted the strips into long ropes, and bound themselves together, each to other, round Lilio and Curlylocks. And round the shepherds bleated the poor sheep in terror of being drowned.

But Curlylocks was now among these poor castaways, no better off than the rest of them. Her pearls she had wasted on toys, and her magic veil she had given away and torn up out of the goodness of her heart, and now she could no longer fly, nor save herself out of this misery.

But Lilio loved Curlylocks better than anything else in the world, and when the water was already up to his feet he called:

"Don't be afraid, Curlylocks! I will save you and hold you up!" And he held up Curlylocks in his arms.

With one hand Curlylocks clung round Lilio's neck, and with the other she held up her little lantern aloft towards Reygoch.

And Reygoch, lying on his chest in the water, was all the time steadily fighting the flood. Right and left of Reygoch rose the ruins of the dyke like two great horns. Reygoch's beard was touzled, his shoulders were bleeding. Yet he could not stop the Banewater, and the flood round the hillock was rising and rising to drown the poor remnant there. And now it was night – yea, midnight.

All of a sudden a thought flashed through Curlylocks, and through all the sobbing and crying she laughed aloud as she called to Reygoch:

"Reygoch, you old simpleton! why don't you *sit* between these two horns of the dyke? Why don't you dam the flood with your shoulders?"

The herd boys and girls stopped wailing at once. So dumbfounded were they at the idea that not one of them had thought of that before!

"Uhuhu!" was all you could hear, and that was Reygoch laughing. And when Reygoch laughs, mind you, it's no joke! All the water round him boiled and bubbled as he shook with laughter over his own stupidity!

Then Reygoch stood up, faced about, and – in a twinkling – he sat down between those two horns!

And then happened the most wonderful thing of all! For the Black Banewater stood as though you had rolled a wall into the breach! It stood, and could not rise above Reygoch's shoulders, but followed its usual course, as before, the whole current behind Reygoch's back. And surely that was a most marvellous rescue!

The boys and girls were saved from the worst of the danger; and Reygoch, sitting comfortably, took up earth in handfuls and all slow-and-surely rebuilt the dyke under himself and on either hand. He began in the middle of the night, and when the dawn broke, the job was finished. And just as the sun rose, Reygoch got up from the dyke with his work done, and started combing his beard, which was all caked with mud, twigs, and little fishes.

But the poor boys and girls were not yet done with their troubles; for where were they to go, and how were they to get there? There they stood on the top of the hillock. All around them was a waste of water. Nothing was to be seen of the two villages but just a few roofs – and not a soul alive in either. To be sure, the villagers might have saved themselves if they had taken refuge in their attics. But in both villages everybody had gone to the threshing-floor with cymbals and fifes to make merry, so that each could watch the destruction of the other. And when the water was up to their waists, they were still clanging their cymbals; and when it was up to their necks, they still blew their fifes for gratified spite. And so they were drowned, one and all, with their fifes and cymbals – and serve them right for their malice and uncharitableness!

So the poor children were left without a soul to cherish or protect them, all houseless and homeless.

"We're not sparrows, to live on the housetops," said the boys sadly, as they saw only the roofs sticking out of the water, "and we're not foxes, to live in burrows in the hills. If someone could clear our villages of the water, we might make shift to get along somehow, but as it is, we might as well jump into the water with our flocks and be drowned like the rest, for we have nowhere and no one to turn to."

That was a sad plight indeed, and Reygoch himself was dreadfully sorry for them. But here was an evil he could in no wise remedy. He looked out over the water and said: "There's too much water here for me to bale out or to drink up so as to clear your villages. Eh, children, what shall I do for you?"

But then up and spoke Lilio, that was the wisest lad in these parts:

"Reygoch, daddy, if *you* cannot drink so much water, *the Earth can*. Break a hole in the ground, daddy, and drain off the water into the earth."

Dearie me! and wasn't that great wisdom in a lad no bigger than Reygoch's finger?

Forthwith Reygoch stamped on the ground and broke a hole; and the Earth, like a thirsty dragon, began to drink and to drink, and swallow, and suck down into herself all that mighty water from off the whole plain. Before long the Earth had gulped down all the water; villages, fields, and meadows reappeared, ravaged and mud-covered, to be sure, but with everything in its right place.

The young castaways cheered up at the sight, but none was so glad as Curlylocks. She clapped her hands and cried:

"Oh, won't it be lovely when the fields all grow golden again and the meadows green!"

But hereupon the herd boys and girls were all downcast once more, and Lilio said:

"Who will show us how to till the ground now that not one of our parents is left alive?"

And indeed, far and wide, there was not a soul alive older than that company of helpless young things in the midst of the ravaged plain, and none with them but Reygoch, who was so big and clumsy and simple that he could not turn his head inside one of their houses, nor did he know anything about ploughing or husbandry.

So they were all in the dumps once more, and most of all Reygoch, who was so fond of pretty Curlylocks, and now he could do nothing for her nor her friends!

And, worst of all, Reygoch was getting horribly homesick for his desolate city of Frosten. This night he had swallowed mud enough to last him a thousand years, and seen more than enough of trouble. And so he was just dying to be back in his vast, empty city, where he had counted the stones in peace for so many hundred years.

So the herd boys were very crestfallen, and Lilio was crestfallen, and Reygoch the most crestfallen of all. And really it was sad to look upon all these poor boys and girls, doomed to perish without their parents and wither like a flower cut off from its root.

Only Curlylocks looked gaily about her, right and left, for nothing could damp her good spirits.

Suddenly Curlylocks cried out:

"Look – oh look! What are those people? Oh dear, but they must have seen sights and wonders!"

All looked towards the village, and there, at one of the windows, appeared the heads of an aged couple – an old man and an old woman. They waved their kerchiefs, they called the young people by name, and laughed till their wrinkled faces all shone with joy. They were great-grandfather and great-grandmother, who had been the only sensible people in the two villages, and had saved themselves by taking refuge in the attic!

Oh dear! If the children had seen the sun at his rising and the morning star at that attic window, they would not have shouted so for joy. The very heavens rang again as they called out:

"Granny! Grandad!"

They raced to the village like young whippets, Curlylocks in front, with her golden hair streaming in the wind, and after them the ewes and lambs. They never stopped till they reached the village, and there grandfather and grandmother were waiting for them at the gate. They welcomed them, hugged them, and none of them could find words to thank God enough for His mercy in giving grandad and grandma so much wisdom as to make them take refuge in the attic! And that was really a very good thing, because these were only quite simple villages, where there were no books nor written records; and who would have reminded the herd boys and girls of the consequences of wickedness if grandad and grandma had not been spared?

When they had done hugging each other, they remembered Reygoch. They looked round the plain, but there was no Reygoch. He was gone – gone all of a sudden, the dear huge thing – gone like a mouse down its hole.

And Reygoch had indeed gone like a mouse down its hole. For when grandpa and grandma appeared at the attic window, Reygoch got a fright such as he had never yet had in his life. He was terrified at the sight of their furrowed, wrinkled, withered old faces.

"Oh dear! oh dear! what a lot of trouble these old people must have been through in these parts to have come to look like that!" thought Reygoch; and in his terror he that very instant jumped down into the hole through which the Black Banewater had sunk down, and so ran away back to his desolate Frosten city.

* * *

All went well in the village. Grandad and Grandma taught the young folk, and the young folk ploughed and sowed. Upon the grandparents' advice they built just one village, one threshing-floor, one church, and one graveyard, so that there should be no more jealousy nor trouble.

All went well; but the best of all was that in the heart of the village stood a beautiful tower of mountain marble, and on the top of it they had made a garden, where blossomed oranges and wild olive. There lived Curlylocks, the lovely fairy, and looked down upon the land that had been so dear to her from the moment when she first came to earth.

And of an evening, when the field work was done, Lilio would lead the herd boys and girls to the tower, and they would sing songs and dance in a ring in the garden with Curlylocks, always lovely, gentle, and joyous.

But under the earth Reygoch once more fell in with the Black Banewater as it roared and burbled underneath, while he wrestled with it till he forced it deeper and deeper into the earth, and right down to the bottom of the Pit, so that it might never again serve the spite and envy of man. And then Reygoch went on to Frosten city. There he is sitting to this very day, counting the stones and praying the Lord never again to tempt him away from that vast and desolate spot, which is the very place for one so big and so simple.

The Peach's Son

ONE DAY, WHILE AN OLD WOMAN stood by a stream washing her clothes, she chanced to see an enormous peach floating on the water. It was quite the largest she had ever seen, and as this old woman and her husband were extremely poor she immediately thought what an excellent meal this extraordinary peach would make. As she could find no stick with which to draw the fruit to the bank, she suddenly remembered the following verse:

Distant water is bitter,
The near water is sweet;
Pass by the distant water
And come into the sweet.

This little song had the desired effect. The peach came nearer and nearer till it stopped at the old woman's feet. She stooped down and picked it up. So delighted was she with her discovery that she could not stay to do any more washing, but hurried home as quickly as possible.

When her husband arrived in the evening, with a bundle of grass upon his back, the old woman excitedly took the peach out of a cupboard and showed it to him.

The old man, who was tired and hungry, was equally delighted at the thought of so delicious a meal. He speedily brought a knife and was about to cut the fruit open, when it suddenly opened of its own accord, and the prettiest child imaginable tumbled out with a merry laugh.

"Don't be afraid," said the little fellow. "The gods have heard how much you desired a child, and have sent me to be a solace and a comfort in your old age."

The old couple were so overcome with joy that they scarcely knew what to do with themselves. Each in turn nursed the child, caressed him, and murmured many sweet and affectionate words. They called him Momotaro, or 'Son of a Peach.'

When Momotaro was fifteen years old, he was a lad far taller and stronger than boys of his own age. The making of a great hero stirred in his veins, and it was a knightly heroism that desired to right the wrongs.

One day Momotaro came to his foster-father and asked him if he would allow him to take a long journey to a certain island in the Northeastern Sea where dwelt a number of ogres who had captured a great company of innocent people, many of whom they ate. Their wickedness was beyond description, and Momotaro desired to kill them, rescue the unfortunate captives, and bring back the plunder of the island that he might share it with his foster-parents.

The old man was not a little surprised to hear this daring scheme. He knew that Momotaro was no common child. He had been sent from heaven, and he believed that all the ogres and demons could not harm him. So at length the old man gave his consent, saying: "Go, Momotaro, slay the ogres and bring peace to the land."

When the old woman had given Momotaro a number of rice-cakes the youth bade his foster-parents farewell, and started out upon his journey.

While Momotaro was resting under a hedge eating one of the rice-cakes, a great dog came up to him, growled, and showed his teeth. The dog, moreover, could speak, and threateningly begged that Momotaro would give him a cake. "Either you give me a cake," said he, "or I will kill you!"

When, however, the dog heard that the famous Momotaro stood before him, his tail dropped between his legs, and he bowed with head to the ground, requesting that he might follow 'Son of a Peach,' and render to him all the service that lay in his power.

Momotaro readily accepted this offer, and after throwing the dog half a cake they proceeded on their way.

They had not gone far when they encountered a monkey, who also begged to be admitted to Momotaro's service. This was granted, but it was some time before the dog and the monkey ceased snapping at each other and became good friends.

Proceeding upon their journey, they came across a pheasant. Now the innate jealousy of the dog was again awakened, and he ran forward and tried to kill the bright-plumed creature. Momotaro separated the combatants, and in the end the pheasant was also admitted to the little band, walking decorously in the rear.

At length Momotaro and his followers reached the shore of the Northeastern Sea. Here our hero discovered a boat, and after a good deal of timidity on the part of the dog, monkey and pheasant, they all got aboard, and soon the little vessel was spinning away over the blue sea.

After many days upon the ocean they sighted an island. Momotaro bade the bird fly off, a winged herald to announce his coming, and bid the ogres surrender.

The pheasant flew over the sea and alighted on the roof of a great castle and shouted his stirring message, adding that the ogres, as a sign of submission, should break their horns.

The ogres only laughed and shook their horns and shaggy red hair. Then they brought forth iron bars and hurled them furiously at the bird. The pheasant cleverly evaded the missiles, and flew at the heads of many ogres.

In the meantime Momotaro had landed with his two companions. He had no sooner done so than he saw two beautiful damsels weeping by a stream, as they wrung out blood-soaked garments.

"Oh!" said they pitifully, "we are daughters of *daimyos*, and are now the captives of the Demon King of this dreadful island. Soon he will kill us, and alas! there is no one to come to our aid." Having made these plaints the women wept anew.

"Ladies," said Momotaro, "I have come for the purpose of slaying your wicked enemies. Show me a way into yonder castle."

So Momotaro, the dog and the monkey entered through a small door in the castle. Once inside this fortification, they fought tenaciously. Many of the ogres were so frightened that they fell off the parapets and were dashed to pieces, while others were speedily killed by Momotaro and his companions. All were destroyed except the King, and he resolved to surrender, and begged that his life might be spared.

"No," said Momotaro fiercely. "I will not spare your wicked life. You have tortured many innocent people and robbed the country for many years."

Having said these words he gave the Demon King into the monkey's keeping, and then proceeded through all the rooms of the castle, and set free the numerous prisoners he found there. He also gathered together much treasure.

The return journey was a very joyous affair indeed. The dog and the pheasant carried the treasure between them, while Momotaro led the Demon King.

Momotaro restored the two daughters of *daimyos* to their homes, and many others who had been captives on the island. The whole country rejoiced in his victory, but no one more than Momotaro's foster-parents, who ended their days in peace and plenty, thanks to the great treasure of the ogres which Momotaro bestowed upon them.

He of the Little Shell

ONCE UPON A TIME, all the people of a certain country had died, excepting two helpless children, a baby boy and a little girl.

When their parents died, these children were asleep. The little girl, who was the elder, was the first to awake. She looked around her, but seeing nobody beside her little brother, who lay smiling in his dreams, she quietly resumed her bed.

At the end of ten days her brother moved, without opening his eyes.

At the end of ten days more he changed his position, lying on the other side, and in this way he kept on sleeping for a long time; and pleasant, too, must have been his dreams, for his little sister never looked at him that he was not quite a little heaven of smiles and flashing lights, which beamed about his head and filled the lodge with a strange splendour.

The girl soon grew to be a woman, but the boy increased in stature very slowly. It was a long time before he could even creep, and he was well advanced in years before he could stand alone. When he was able to walk, his sister made him a little bow and arrows, and hung around his neck a small shell, saying:

"You shall be called Dais Imid, or He of the Little Shell."

Every day he would go out with his little bow, shooting at the small birds. The first bird he killed was a tom-tit. His sister was highly pleased when he took it to her. She carefully prepared and stuffed it, and put it away for him.

The next day he killed a red squirrel. His sister preserved this, too. The third day he killed a partridge, and this they had for their evening meal.

After this he acquired more courage, and would venture some distance from home. His skill and success as a hunter daily increased, and he killed the deer, bear, moose and other large animals inhabiting the forest.

At last, although so very small of stature, he became a great hunter, and all that he shot he brought home and shared with his sister; and whenever he entered the lodge, a light beamed about his head and filled the place with a strange splendour.

He had now arrived at the years of manhood, but he still remained a perfect infant in size.

One day, walking about in quest of game, he came to a small lake.

It was in the winter season, and upon the ice of the lake he saw a man of giant height, employed killing beavers.

Comparing himself with this great man, he felt that he was no bigger than an insect. He seated himself on the shore and watched his movements.

When the large man had killed many beavers, he put them on a hand-sled which he had, and pursued his way home. When he saw him retire, the dwarf hunter followed, and, wielding his magic shell, he cut off the tail of one of the beavers and ran home with the prize.

The giant, on reaching his lodge with his sled-load of beavers, was surprised to find one of them shorn of its tail.

The next day the little hero of the shell went to the same lake. The giant, who had been busy there for some time, had already loaded his sled and commenced his return; but running nimbly forward and overtaking him, he succeeded in securing another of the beaver-tails.

"I wonder," said the giant, on reaching his lodge and overlooking his beavers, "what dog it is that has thus cheated me. Could I meet him, I would make his flesh quiver at the point of my javelin."

The giant forgot that he had taken these very beavers out of a beaver-dam, which belonged to the little shell-man and his sister, without permission.

The next day he pursued his hunting at the beaver-dam near the lake, and he was again followed by the little man with the shell.

This time the giant was so nimble in his movements that he had nearly reached home before the shell, make the best speed he could, could overtake him; but he was just in time to clip another beaver's tail before the sled slipped into the lodge.

The giant would have been a patient giant, indeed, if his anger had not been violent at these constant tricks played upon him. What vexed him most was that he could not get a sight of his enemy. Sharp eyes he would have needed to do so, inasmuch as he of the little shell had the gift of making himself invisible whenever he chose.

The giant, giving vent to his feelings with many loud rumbling words, looked sharply around to see whether he could discover any tracks. He could find none. The unknown had stepped too lightly to leave the slightest mark behind.

The next day the giant resolved to disappoint his mysterious follower by going to the beaver-dam very early; and accordingly, when the little shell man came to the place he found the fresh traces of his work, but the giant had already gone away. He followed hard upon his tracks, but he failed to overtake him. When he of the little shell came in sight of the lodge, the stranger was in front of it, employed in skinning his beavers.

As Dais-Imid stood looking at him – for he had been all this time invisible – he thought:

"I will let him have a view of me."

Presently the man, who proved to be no less a personage than the celebrated giant, Manabozho, looked up and saw him.

After regarding him with attention, "Who are you, little man?" said Manabozho. "I have a mind to kill you."

The little hero of the shell replied:

"If you were to try to kill me you could not do it."

With this speech of the little man, Manabozho grabbed at him; but when he thought to have had him in his hand, he was gone.

"Where are you now, little man?" cried Manabozho.

"Here, under your girdle," answered the shell-dwarf; at which giant Manabozho, thinking to crush him, slapped down his great hand with all his might; but on unloosing his girdle he was disappointed at finding no dwarf there.

"Where are you now, little man?" he cried again, in a greater rage than ever.

"In your right nostril!" the dwarf replied; whereupon the giant Manabozho seized himself by the finger and thumb at the place, and gave it a violent tweak; but as he immediately heard the voice of the dwarf at a distance upon the ground, he was satisfied that he had only pulled his own nose to no purpose.

"Goodbye, Manabozho," said the voice of the invisible dwarf. "Count your beaver-tails, and you will find that I have taken another for my sister;" for he of the little shell never, in his wanderings or pastimes, forgot his sister and her wishes. "Goodbye, beaver-man!"

And as he went away he made himself visible once more, and a light beamed about his head and lit the air around him with a strange splendour; a circumstance which Manabozho, who was at times quite thick-headed and dull of apprehension, could no way understand.

When Dais-Imid returned home, he told his sister that the time drew nigh when they must separate.

"I must go away," said Dais-Imid, "it is my fate. You, too," he added, "must go away soon. Tell me where you would wish to dwell."

She said, "I would like to go to the place of the breaking of daylight. I have always loved the east. The earliest glimpses of light are from that quarter, and it is to my mind the most beautiful part of the heavens. After I get there, my brother, whenever you see the clouds in that direction, of various colours, you may think that your sister is painting her face."

"And I," said he, "I, my sister, shall live on the mountains and rocks. There I can see you at the earliest hour; there are the streams of water clear; the air is pure, and the golden lights will shine ever around my head, and I shall ever be called 'Puck-Ininee, or the Little Wild Man of the Mountains.' But," he resumed, "before we part for ever, I must go and try to find what manitous rule the earth, and see which of them will be friendly to us."

He left his sister and travelled over the surface of the globe, and then went far down into the earth.

He had been treated well wherever he went. At last he came to a giant manitou, who had a large kettle which was for ever boiling. The giant, who was a first cousin to Manabozho, and had already heard of the tricks which Dais-Imid had played upon his kinsman, regarded him with a stern look and, catching him up in his hand, he threw him unceremoniously into the kettle.

It was evidently the giant's intention to drown Dais-Imid, in which he was mistaken, for by means of his magic shell, little Dais, in less than a second's time, bailed the water to the bottom, leaped from the kettle, and ran away unharmed.

He returned to his sister and related his rovings and adventures. He finished his story by addressing her thus:

"My sister, there is a manitou at each of the four corners of the earth. There is also one above them, far in the sky, a Great Being who assigns to you, and to me, and to all of us, where we must go. And last," he continued, "there is another and wicked one who lives deep down in the earth. It will be our lot to escape out of his reach. We must now separate. When the winds blow from the four corners of the earth, you must then go. They will carry you to the place you wish. I go to the rocks and mountains, where my kindred will ever delight to dwell."

Dais-Imid then took his ball-stick and commenced running up a high mountain, and a bright light shone about his head all the way, and he kept singing as he went:

Blow, winds, blow! My sister lingers
For her dwelling in the sky,
Where the morn, with rosy fingers,
Shall her cheeks with vermil dye.
There my earliest views directed,
Shall from her their colour take,
And her smiles, through clouds reflected,
Guide me on by wood or lake.
While I range the highest mountains,
Sport in valleys green and low,
Or beside our Indian fountains,
Raise my tiny hip-hallo.

Presently the winds blew and, as Dais-Imid had predicted, his sister was borne by them to the eastern sky, where she has ever since lived, and her name is now the Morning Star.

White Feather and the Six Giants

THERE WAS ONCE AN OLD MAN living in the depths of the great forest with his young grandson whom he had taken charge of when the boy was still an infant. The child had never encountered any other human being apart from his grandfather. He had no parents, brothers or sisters, no friends or relatives, and although he frequently questioned the old man on the subject of his family, he could not get even the smallest scrap of information from him.

His guardian insisted upon this silence for the boy's own protection, for he felt certain that he would attempt to avenge the death of his brothers and sisters before long. They had perished at the hands of six great giants after the villagers had challenged the giants to a race they believed they would win, casually offering their children as the forfeit. All were slain by the victorious giants except for the old man's grandson who, by some miracle, managed to escape through the trees to the safety of the isolated lodge.

Here the boy, who was named Chacopee, grew up relatively content. He learned to fish and he learned to hunt, beginning with smaller animals such as rabbits, until he became so highly accomplished with his bow and arrow that he could bring down deer and larger game almost with his eyes closed. Of course, as he developed into a more expert hunter, he longed to roam even further and his curiosity to know what lay beyond the tiny lodge increased with every passing day.

One day he wandered to the edge of the prairie where he happened upon several mounds of ashes, encircled by lodge-poles left standing in the earth. Returning home, he described to his grandfather what he had seen and asked him to explain the presence of these things. But the old man grew agitated and responded that the boy had surely lost his senses, for nothing of the kind existed except in his imagination.

Another day, however, Chacopee had followed a different path through the forest when suddenly he heard a voice calling to him: "You do not wear the white feather yet, but the hour is not far off when you will prove yourself worthy of it. Go home now and sleep. Soon you will dream of a pipe, a smoking-sack, and a large white feather. When you awake you will find these items by your side."

Chacopee turned in the direction of the voice and came face to face with a man, an encounter in itself quite shocking for a boy who had only ever seen his grandfather, but made even worse by the man's very peculiar body which was carved of wood from the breast downwards. "Put the white feather on your head," the stranger continued, "and you will become a great hunter, a great warrior and a great leader. If you need proof of my words, smoke the pipe and soon you will see the smoke turn into pigeons."

After this, the stranger informed Chacopee of his real identity and told him the story of how his family had perished at the hands of the giants, urging him to avenge the wrongs of his kindred.

"Take this enchanted vine," he told him, "you will need it when your enemy challenges you to a race. No giant can see it for it is invisible. You must throw it over your opponent's head while he runs. It will entangle him and bring him crashing to the ground."

Chacopee listened keenly to all of this advice and then returned homeward, extremely bewildered by the meeting. Everything happened just as the Man of Wood had predicted, however. As soon as he lay down the boy fell into a deep sleep and when he awoke he was surrounded by the promised gifts. The old grandfather was greatly surprised to see a flock of pigeons emerge from his own lodge, followed by his grandson wearing on his head a white feather, but then he remembered the old tribal prophecy, and knowing that the day would soon come when he would be forced to relinquish control of Chacopee, he sat down and began to weep inconsolably.

Next morning the young boy set off in search of his enemies. The giants, he had learned, lived in a very tall lodge at the centre of the woods, but this lodge was surrounded by little spirits who carried news to the giants of Chacopee's arrival. The monstrous creatures hastened out of doors and spotted the young boy approaching in the distance.

"Here comes the little man we are supposed to call White Feather," they mocked among themselves. "Haven't we been warned that he is destined to achieve great things. Let us welcome him as a great hero and encourage him to attempt some foolhardy trial of strength."

But Chacopee paid no heed to the giants' fine speeches, and without awaiting an invitation, marched fearlessly into their lodge where he challenged every one of them to a race. It was eventually agreed that the youngest among the giants would be the first to run against him and without wasting any more time, they set off across the fields in search of an appropriate starting-point.

They had soon mapped out a course which extended from an old, rugged tree as far as the edge of the horizon and back again. A war-club of iron was placed at the foot of the tree, to be used by the winner on his defeated opponent. As soon as they had taken their places, a gong was sounded and each of the runners shot off with as much speed as he could muster. Chacopee knew that his little legs would not carry him to victory over such a great distance and so he waited for the giant to overtake him and cast his vine out in front of him, tugging on it sharply as it wrapped itself around the giant's ankles. The hideous creature fell to the ground and when he attempted to rise again, Chacopee lifted the war-club high in the air, bringing it down on the giant's great skull over and over again until he was certain that the giant lay dead.

The next morning, Chacopee ran against a second giant and killed him in exactly the same manner. For five mornings he managed to conquer his foes in this way, but then, on the sixth morning, as he set off confidently to meet the last of the giants, he was met by his old counsellor, the Man of Wood, who informed him that his last opponent was far more cunning than any of the others.

"He is out to deceive you, White Feather," he told the boy. "Before you even reach his lodge you will encounter a very beautiful young woman. Do not pay her any attention, for she is there for your destruction. As soon as you catch her eye, you must transform yourself into an elk. Lower your head and feed on the grass and do not look at the maiden again."

White Feather thanked his kind adviser and walked on towards the lodge, mindful of the advice he had received. Before long, as had been foretold, he met the most beautiful woman. Quickly he transformed himself into an elk and began rooting in the earth, his eyes lowered as he had been instructed. But the woman only moved closer to him and began weeping softly.

"I have travelled a very long way to meet you," she sobbed. "Your great achievements have made you famous throughout the land, and I wanted, more than anything, to offer myself as your bride."

Filled with compassion and remorse, White Feather raised his eyes towards the woman and wished aloud that he might resume his natural shape. At once, he became a man again and sat down under a tree with the beautiful maiden, wrapping her in his arms to comfort her. Soon her tears and sighs had abated and he lay his head in her lap and fell into a peaceful slumber.

After she had listened a while to his deep breathing and had satisfied herself that White Feather was not likely to wake up, the beautiful woman transformed herself into the sixth giant and, taking up an axe, struck the young man on his back, changing him into a dog. The white plume immediately fell from his hair unto the earth, but as soon as he noticed it, the giant stooped and picked it up, putting it in his own hair. Now stripped of his powers, Chacopee gave a pitiful whimper, and followed wretchedly in the path of the giant towards the neighbouring village.

There were living in this particular village two sisters, the daughters of a chief, who had been bitter rivals for many years. Having heard the prophecy concerning the wearer of the white feather, each had made up her mind to have him for her husband and each was constantly on the look-out from her lodge door, hoping that White Feather would soon appear. When the day finally arrived and the sisters spotted a stranger wearing a white plume heading towards their home, they were filled with excitement. The eldest sister, who was the more ambitious of the two, dressed herself up in all her finery and ran ahead to meet the giant, inviting him into her lodge. The youngest, who did not possess any flamboyant clothes, remained dressed in her simple shawl and moccasins and invited the poor dog into her home where she prepared for him a good supper and a neat bed. The giant, pleased with the attention lavished upon him by the eldest sister, soon agreed to marry her and together they mocked the younger sister for having landed herself a dishevelled old dog as a life-long companion.

It was not long, however, before the villagers began to demand a demonstration of the skill and courage they had come to associate with the famous name of White Feather. The giant, who readily supposed that whoever wore the white plume would possess all of its virtues, boasted of the fact that he could bring back enough food in one day to supply the entire village and set off with the dog across the plains towards the forest.

Immediately, he began shouting and waving his great hands in the air, calling to the animals to come and be killed. But they fled in terror at the sight of him and he failed to catch a single one of them. The dog, on the other hand, stepped into a nearby river and drew out a stone which instantly changed into a fine, fat beaver. The giant stood staring in amazement, but as soon as he had recovered himself, he waded into the water and successfully performed the same feat. He was delighted with himself and having tied the animal to his belt, he called for the dog to accompany him back home.

When he had been seated a short time, savouring in advance the impact of his great achievement on the villagers, he called to his wife to come and examine his hunting girdle. Obediently, she knelt on the floor, but when she lifted his shirt to reveal his belt, she discovered only a massive stone secured to it. The giant stood up furiously and ordered his wife to keep her silence until he had gone out again and returned with the food he had promised.

Next morning, he took the dog along with him as before and watched its every movement closely. This time, the dog plucked a charred branch from a burned-out tree and threw it to the ground where it instantly transformed itself into a bear. The giant did exactly as the dog had done, and managed to produce a bear in precisely the same fashion. He carried the creature homewards to his wife, but again, as soon as he had called for her to inspect it, the bear disappeared and all the woman found was a black stick tied to her husband's belt.

And so it continued on. Everything the giant attempted failed miserably, while everything the dog undertook was a great success. Every day the youngest sister had more and more reason to be proud of the poor dog she had adopted, while every day the eldest sister received yet another reminder that the man she had married did not possess any of the virtues associated with the white feather. But in spite of this, the eldest sister insisted on keeping up appearances and departed the following morning for her father's lodge to inform him what a skilful hunter her new husband was.

As soon as she had set off, the dog began making signs to the younger sister that he wished to be sweated in the traditional manner of the Indians. Accordingly, his mistress built a little lodge just large enough for him to creep into and placed within it a number of heated stones on which she poured water until a thick vapour rose up into the air. When she imagined the dog had been completely sweated, she stooped down to unblock the entrance and was astonished to find, in place of the dog, a handsome young warrior lying on the earth. But she could not get a word out of him and realizing that he was quite dumb, she decided to lead him to the village where she hoped one of the medicine-people might be able to help restore his voice.

As soon as the chief heard his youngest daughter's story, he assembled all the old and wise heads of the tribe for a general meeting. He was now convinced, he told them, that there was some kind of magic at work and was keener than ever to discover the truth about the giant and the young man. And so he called for a pipe to be brought forward and began passing it among the circle. One after another, the elders puffed on the pipe, handing it around until eventually it was the young man's turn. But the handsome warrior signalled politely that it should be given to the giant first. The giant took the pipe and began smoking, swelling his chest and shaking the white feather on his head. But nothing came of this exhibition except a great cloud of smoke. Then the handsome young warrior took hold of the pipe and made a sign to them to put the white feather upon his head. As he drew the smoke deep into his lungs, his voice suddenly returned, and as he breathed out, the smoke became a flock of white and blue pigeons.

From that moment, the villagers turned on the giant and after the young man had recounted his strange adventures, indignation rose to a fever pitch. The chief then ordered that the giant should be transformed into a dog and stoned to death by the people. The villagers were more than delighted to carry out this instruction and danced in a circle around the dead body, greatly relieved that the six giants would trouble them no longer.

The handsome young warrior now gave them all the proof they needed of his right to wear the white feather. Calling for a buffalo robe to be brought to him, he cut it into thin strips and scattered them on the prairie in every direction. Next day he summoned the braves of the tribe to accompany him on a hunt. When they arrived at the edge of the prairie they found it covered with a great herd of buffalo. The people hunted as many of these buffalo as they pleased and afterwards a great feast was held to celebrate White Feather's triumph over the giant.

The Adventures of a Fisherman's Son

LONG AGO THERE WAS A MAN AND WOMAN who lived in a little mud hut under the palm trees on the riverbank. They had so many children they did not know what to do. The little hut was altogether too crowded. The man had to work early and late to find food enough to feed so many. One day the seventh son said to his father, "O, father, I found a little puppy yesterday when I was playing on the bank of the river. Please let me bring it home to keep. I have always wanted one."

The father consented sadly. He did not know how to find food for the children, and an extra puppy to feed seemed an added burden. He went to the riverbank to fish that day with a heavy heart. He cast his net in vain. He did not catch a single fish. He cast his net from the other side with no better luck. He did not catch even one little *piabinha*.

Suddenly he heard a voice which seemed to come from the riverbed itself, it was so deep. This is what it said: "If you will give me whatever new you find in your house when you go home I will give you fisherman's luck. You will catch all the fish you wish."

The man remembered the request which his seventh son had made that morning. "The new thing I'll find in my house when I get home will be that puppy," said the man to himself. "This will be a splendid way to get rid of the puppy which I did not want to keep anyway."

Accordingly the man consented to the request which came from the strange voice in the depths of the river. "You must seal this covenant with your blood," said the voice.

The man cut his finger a tiny bit with his sharp knife and squeezed a few drops of blood from the wound into the river. "If you break this vow the curse of the river giant will be upon you and your children for ever and ever," said the deep voice solemnly.

The fisherman cast his net where the river giant commanded, and immediately it was so full of fish that the man could hardly draw it out of the water. Three times he drew out his net, so full that it was in danger of breaking. "Truly this was a fortunate bit of business," said the man. "Here I have fish enough to feed my family and all I can sell in addition."

As the fisherman approached his house with his enormous catch of fish one of the children came running to meet him. "O father, guess what we have at our house which we did not have when you went away," said the child.

"A new puppy," replied her father.

"O no, Father," replied the child. "You have not guessed right at all. It is a new baby brother."

The poor fisherman burst into tears. "What shall I do! What shall I do!" he sobbed. "I dare not break my vow to the river giant."

The fisherman's wife was heartbroken when she heard about the business which her husband had transacted with the river giant. However she could think of no way to escape from keeping the contract which he had made. She kissed the tiny babe goodbye and gave it her blessing. Then the fisherman took it down to the riverbank and threw it into the river at the exact spot from which the deep voice had come.

There in the depths of the river the river giant was waiting to receive the newborn babe. He took the little one into his palace of gold and silver and mother-of-pearl with ornaments of diamonds, and there the baby received excellent care.

Time passed and the little boy grew into a big boy. At last he was fifteen years old and a handsome lad indeed, tall and straight, with eyes which were dark and deep like the river itself, and hair as dark as the shades in the depths of the river. All his life he had been surrounded with every luxury, but he had never seen a single person. He had never seen even the river giant. All he knew of him was his deep voice which gave orders in the palace.

One day the voice of the river giant said, "I have to go away on a long journey. I will leave with you all the keys to all the doors in the palace, but do not meddle with anything. If you do you must forfeit your life."

Many days passed and the lad did not hear the voice of the river giant. He missed its sound in the palace. It was very still and very lonely. At last at the end of fifteen days he took one of the keys which the river giant had left and opened the door which it fitted. The door led into a room in the palace where the boy had never been. Inside the room was a huge lion. The lion was fat and well nourished, but there was nothing for it to eat except hay. The boy did not meddle with anything and shut the door.

Another fifteen days passed by, and again the lad took one of the keys. He opened another door in the palace which he had never entered. Inside the room he found three horses, one black, one white and one chestnut. There was nothing in the room for the horses to eat except meat, but in spite of it they were fat and well nourished. The boy did not touch anything and when he went out he shut the door.

At the end of another fifteen days all alone without even the voice of the river giant for company, the lad tried another key in another door. This room opened into a room full of armour. There were daggers and knives and swords and muskets and all sorts of armour which the boy had never seen and did not know anything about. He was very much interested in what he saw, but he did not meddle with anything.

The next day he opened the room again where the horses were kept. This time one of the horses – the black one – spoke to him and said, "We like hay to eat very much better than this meat which was left to us by mistake. The lion must have our hay. Please give this meat to the lion and bring us back our hay. If you will do this as I ask I'll serve you for ever and ever."

The boy took the meat to the lion. The lion was very much pleased to exchange the hay for it. The lad then took the hay to the horses. All at once he remembered how he had been told not to meddle with anything. This had been meddling. The boy burst into tears. "I shall lose my life as the punishment for this deed," he sobbed.

The horses listened in amazement. "I got you into this trouble," said the black horse. "Now I'll get you out. Just trust me to find a way out."

The black horse advised the boy to take some extra clothes and a sword and musket and mount upon his back. "I have lived here in the depths of the river so long that my speed is greater than that of the river itself," said the horse. "If there was any doubt of it before, now that I have had some hay once more I am sure I can run faster than any river in the world."

It was true. When the river giant came back home and found that the boy had meddled he ran as fast as he could in pursuit of the lad. The black horse safely and surely carried the lad beyond his reach.

The black horse and his rider travelled on and on until finally they came to a kingdom which was ruled over by a king who had three beautiful daughters. The lad at once applied for a position in the service of this king. "I do not know what you can do," said the king. "You have such soft white hands. Perhaps you may serve to carry bouquets of flowers from my garden every morning to my three daughters."

The lad had eyes which were dark and deep like the depths of the river, and when he carried bouquets of flowers from the garden to the king's daughters the youngest princess fell in love with him at once. Her two sisters laughed at her. "I don't care what you say," said the youngest princess. "He is far handsomer than any of the princes who have ever sung of love beneath our balcony."

That very night two princes from neighbouring kingdoms came to sing in the palace garden beneath the balcony of the three princesses. The two oldest daughters of the king were proud and haughty, but the youngest princess had love in her heart and love in her eyes. For this reason she was one whom all the princes admired most.

The lad from the river listened to their songs. "I wish I looked like these two princes and knew songs like theirs," said he. Just then he caught sight of his own reflection in the fountain in the garden. He saw that he looked quite as well as they. "I too will sing a song before the balcony of the princesses," he decided.

He did not know that he could sing, but in truth his voice had in it all the music of the rushing of the river. When he sang even the two rival musicians stopped to listen to his song. The two older princesses did not know who was singing, but the youngest princess recognized him at once.

The next day a great tournament took place. The lad from the river had never seen a tournament, but after he had watched it for a moment he decided to enter. He went to get the black horse which had carried him out of the depths of the river and the arms he had brought with him from the palace of the river giant. With such a horse and such arms he carried off all the honours of the tournament. Everyone at the tournament wondered who the strange *cavalheiro* could be. No one recognized him except the youngest princess. She knew who it was the moment she saw him and gave him her ribbon to wear.

The next day all the *cavalheiros* who had taken part in the tournament set out to slay the wild beast which often came out of the jungle to attack the city. It was the lad from the river who killed the beast, as all the *cavalheiros* knew. When they returned to the palace with the news that the beast had been slain, the king said, "Tomorrow night we will hold the greatest *festa* which this palace has ever witnessed. Tomorrow let all the *cavalheiros* who are here assembled go forth to hunt for birds to grace our table."

The next day the *cavalheiros* went out to hunt the birds, and it was the lad from the river who succeeded in slaying the birds. None of the other *cavalheiros* were at all successful. The two neighbouring princes who were suitors for the hand of the youngest princess made a contract. "We cannot let this stranger carry off all the honours," said one to the other. "You say that you killed the beast, and I will say that it was I who killed the birds."

That night at the *festa* one prince stood up before the king and told his story of slaying the beast, and the other prince stood up and told how he had killed the birds. The other *cavalheiros* knew that it was false, but when they looked around for the *cavalheiro* who had done the valiant deeds they could not find him. The lad from the river had on his old clothes which he wore as a servant in the garden and stood at the lower part of the banquet hall among the servants.

When the king had heard the stories of the two princes he was greatly pleased with what they had done. "The one who killed the beast shall have a princess for a bride," said he, "and the one who killed the birds he too shall have a princess for his bride."

The youngest princess saw the lad from the river standing among the servants and smiled into his eyes. The lad came and threw himself before the king. "O my king," said he, "these stories to which you have listened are false, as all these assembled *cavalheiros* will prove. It is I who killed the beast and all the birds. I claim a princess as my bride."

All the assembled *cavalheiros* recognized the lad in spite of his changed appearance in his gardening clothes. "*Viva*!" they shouted. "He speaks the truth. He is the valiant one of us who killed the beast and the birds. To him belongs the reward."

The youngest princess had a heart filled with joy. The wedding feast was celebrated the very next day. The river giant found out about it and sent a necklace of pearls and diamonds as a wedding gift to the bride of the lad whom he had brought up in his palace. The fisherman and his wife, however, never knew the great good fortune which had come to their son.

The Princess of the Springs

ONCE, LONG AGO, the Moon Giant wooed the beautiful giantess who dwells in the Great River and won her love. He built for her a wonderful palace where the Great River runs into the sea. It was made of mother-of-pearl with rich carvings, and gold and silver and precious stones were used to adorn it. Never before in all the world had a giant or giantess possessed such a magnificent home.

When the baby daughter of the Moon Giant and the Giantess of the Great River was born it was decreed among the giants that she should be the Princess of all the Springs and should rule over all the rivers and lakes. The light of her eyes was like the moonbeams, and her smile was like moonlight on still waters. Her strength was as the strength of the Great River, and the fleetness of her foot was as the swiftness of the Great River.

As the beautiful Spring Princess grew older many suitors came to sing her praises beneath the palace windows, but she favoured none of them. She was so happy living in her own lovely palace with her own dear mother that she did not care at all for any suitor. No other daughter ever loved her mother as the Spring Princess loved the Giantess of the Great River.

At last the Sun Giant came to woo the Spring Princess. The strength of the Sun Giant was as the strength of ten of the other suitors of the fair princess. He was so powerful that he won her heart.

When he asked her to marry him, however, and go with him to his own palace, the Spring Princess shook her lovely head. "O Sun Giant, you are so wonderful and so powerful that I love you as I never before have loved a suitor who sang beneath my palace window," said she, "but I love my mother, too. I cannot go away with you and leave my own dear mother. It would break my heart."

The Sun Giant told the Spring Princess again and again of his great love for her, of his magnificent palace which would be her new home, of the happy life which awaited her as queen of the palace. At length she listened to his pleadings and decided that she could leave home and live with him for nine months of the year. For three months of every year, however, she would have to return to the wonderful palace of mother-of-pearl where the Great River runs into the sea and spend the time with her mother, the Giantess of the Great River.

The Sun Giant at last sorrowfully consented to this arrangement and the wedding feast was held. It lasted for seven days and seven nights. Then the Spring Princess went away with the Sun Giant to his own home.

Every year the Spring Princess went to visit her mother for three months according to the agreement. For three months of every year she lived in the palace of mother-of-pearl where the Great River runs into the sea. For three months of every year the rivers sang once more as they rushed along their way. For three months the lakes sparkled in the bright sunlight as their hearts once more were brimful of joy.

When at last the little son of the Spring Princess was born she wanted to take him with her when she went to visit her mother. The Sun Giant, however, did not approve of such a plan. He firmly refused to allow the child to leave home. After much pleading, all in vain, the Spring Princess set out upon her journey alone, with sorrow in her heart. She left her baby son with the best nurses she could procure.

Now it happened that the Giantess of the Great River had not expected that her daughter would be able to visit her that year. She had thought that all the rivers and lakes, the palace of mother-of-pearl, and her own mother heart would have to get along as best they could without a visit from the Spring Princess. The Giantess of the Great River had gone away to water the earth. One of the land giants had taken her prisoner and would not let her escape.

When the Spring Princess arrived at the beautiful palace of mother-of-pearl and gold and silver and precious stones, where the Great River runs into the sea, there was no one at home. She ran from room to room in the palace calling out, "O dear Mother, Giantess of the Great River, dear, dear Mother! Where are you? Where have you hidden yourself?"

There was no answer. Her own voice echoed back to her through the beautiful halls of mother-of-pearl with their rich carvings. The palace was entirely deserted.

She ran outside the palace and called to the fishes of the river, "O fishes of the river, have you seen my own dear mother?"

She called to the sands of the sea, "O sands of the sea, have you seen my darling mother?"

She called to the shells of the shore, "O shells of the shore, have you seen my precious mother?"

There was no answer. No one knew what had become of the Giantess of the Great River.

The Spring Princess was so worried that she thought her heart would break in its anguish. In her distress she ran over all the earth.

Then she went to the house of the Great Wind. The Giant of the Great Wind was away, but his old father was at home. He was very sorry for the Spring Princess when he heard her sad story. "I am sure my son can help you find your mother," he said as he comforted her. "He will soon get home from his day's work."

When the Giant of the Great Wind reached home he was in a terrible temper. He stormed and raged and gave harsh blows to everything he met. His father had hid the Spring Princess in a closet out of the way, and it was fortunate indeed for her that he had done so.

After the Great Wind Giant had taken his bath and eaten his dinner he was better natured. Then his father said to him, "O my son, if a wandering princess had come this way on purpose to ask you a question, what would you do to her?"

"Why, I'd answer her question as best I could, of course," responded the Giant of the Great Wind.

His father straightway opened the closet door and the Spring Princess stepped out. In spite of her long wanderings and great anguish of mind she was still very lovely as she knelt before the Giant of the Great Wind in her soft silvery green garments embroidered with pearls and diamonds. The big heart of the Giant of the Great Wind was touched at her beauty and at her grief.

"O Giant of the Great Wind," said the Spring Princess, as he gently raised her from her knees before him, "I am the daughter of the Giantess of the Great River. I have lost my mother. I have searched for her through all the earth and now I have come to you for help. Can you tell me anything about where she is and how I can find her?"

The Giant of the Great Wind put on his thinking cap. He thought hard. "Your mother is in the power of a land giant who has imprisoned her," he said. "I happen to know all about the affair. I passed that way only yesterday. I'll gladly go with you and help you get her home. We'll start at once."

The Giant of the Great Wind took the Spring Princess back to earth on his swift horses. Then he stormed the castle of the land giant who had imprisoned the Giantess of the Great River. The Spring Princess dug quietly beneath the castle walls to the dungeon where her mother was confined. You may be sure that her mother was overjoyed to see her.

When the Spring Princess had led her mother safely outside the castle walls she thanked the Giant of the Great Wind for all he had done to help her. Then the Giantess of the Great River and the Spring Princess hastened back to the wonderful palace of mother-of-pearl set with gold and silver and precious stones, where the Great River runs into the Sea. As soon as she had safely reached there once more the Spring Princess suddenly remembered that she had stayed away from her home in the palace of the Sun Giant longer than the three months she was supposed to stay according to the agreement. She at once said goodbye to her mother and hastened to the home of the Sun Giant, her husband, and to her baby son.

Now the Sun Giant had been very much worried at first when the three months had passed and the Spring Princess had not come back to him and her little son. Then he became angry. He became so angry that he married another princess. The new wife discharged the nurses who were taking care of the tiny son of the Spring Princess and put him in the kitchen.

When the Spring Princess arrived at the palace of the Sun Giant the very first person she saw was her own little son, so dirty and neglected that she hardly recognized him. Then she found out all that had happened in her absence.

The Spring Princess quickly seized her child and clasped him tight in her arms. Then she fled to the depths of the sea, and wept, and wept, and wept. The waters of the sea rose so high that they reached even to the palace of the Sun Giant. They covered the palace, and the Sun Giant, his new wife, and all the court entirely disappeared from view. For forty days the face of the Sun Giant was not seen upon the earth.

The little son of the Spring Princess grew up to be the Giant of the Rain. In the rainy season and the season of thunder showers he rules upon the earth. He sends upon the earth such tears as the Spring Princess shed in the depths of the seas.

Fables & Morality Tales

Introduction

THE BIGGER THEY ARE, the harder they fall. A giant is a cautionary tale in waiting. We can go further: the more arrogant they are, the more satisfying their discomfiture. Traditionally told by Mexico's Aztecs, 'The Giant Pyramid-Builder' describes a Mesoamerican Tower of Babel. The giants who once ruled Mexico's Central Valley tried to build a pyramid that would reach to the heavens themselves. Their angry gods hurled down a huge mass of flaming rock and laid it low. Too sure of himself in his enormous powers, the genie in the Middle-Eastern tale 'The Story of the Fisherman' finds himself deftly outwitted by the humblest man.

Not that it's always the giant who comes a cropper. In the French tale 'The Girl Fish', the giant is the punishment for the girl who selfishly kills and eats the fish: she has to win a crown back from an evil giant before she can resume her human form. A reminder that size as well as beauty can be in the eye of the beholder comes in the story of 'A Japanese Gulliver', who travels to a land of tiny people and finds himself a giant.

The Giant of the Flood

JUST BEFORE THE WORLD WAS DROWNED all the animals gathered in front of the Ark and Father Noah carefully inspected them.

"All ye that lie down shall enter and be saved from the deluge that is about to destroy the world," he said. "Ye that stand cannot enter."

Then the various creatures began to march forward into the Ark. Father Noah watched them closely. He seemed troubled.

"I wonder," he said to himself, "how I shall obtain a unicorn, and how I shall get it into the Ark."

"I can bring thee a unicorn, Father Noah," he heard in a voice of thunder, and turning round he saw the giant, Og. "But thou must agree to save me, too, from the flood."

"Begone," cried Noah. "Thou art a demon, not a human being. I can have no dealings with thee."

"Pity me," whined the giant. "See how my figure is shrinking. Once I was so tall that I could drink water from the clouds and toast fish at the sun. I fear not that I shall be drowned, but that all the food will be destroyed and that I shall perish of hunger."

Noah, however, only smiled; but he grew serious again when Og brought a unicorn. It was as big as a mountain, although the giant said it was the smallest he could find. It lay down in front of the Ark and Noah saw by that action that he must save it. For some time he was puzzled what to do, but at last a bright idea struck him. He attached the huge beast to the Ark by a rope fastened to its horn so that it could swim alongside and be fed.

Og seated himself on a mountain near at hand and watched the rain pouring down. Faster and faster it fell in torrents until the rivers overflowed and the waters began to rise rapidly on the land and sweep all things away. Father Noah stood gloomily before the door of the Ark until the water reached his neck. Then it swept him inside. The door closed with a bang, and the Ark rose gallantly on the flood and began to move along. The unicorn swam alongside, and as it passed Og, the giant jumped on to its back.

"See, Father Noah," he cried, with a huge chuckle, "you will have to save me after all. I will snatch all the food you put through the window for the unicorn."

Noah saw that it was useless to argue with Og, who might, indeed, sink the Ark with his tremendous strength.

"I will make a bargain with thee," he shouted from a window. "I will feed thee, but thou must promise to be a servant to my descendants."

Og was very hungry, so he accepted the conditions and devoured his first breakfast.

The rain continued to fall in great big sheets that shut out the light of day. Inside the Ark, however, all was bright and cheerful, for Noah had collected the most precious of the stones of the earth and had used them for the windows. Their radiance illumined the whole of the three storeys in the Ark. Some of the animals were troublesome and Noah got no sleep at all. The lion had a bad attack of fever. In a corner a bird slept the whole of the time. This was the phoenix.

"Wake up," said Noah, one day. "It is feeding time."

"Thank you," returned the bird. "I saw thou wert busy, Father Noah, so I would not trouble thee."

Thou art a good bird," said Noah, much touched, "therefore thou shalt never die."

One day the rain ceased, the clouds rolled away and the sun shone brilliantly again. How strange the world looked! It was like a vast ocean. Nothing but water could be seen anywhere, and only one or two of the highest mountain tops peeped above the flood. All the world was drowned, and Noah gazed on the desolate scene from one of the windows with tears in his eyes. Og, riding gaily on the unicorn behind the Ark, was quite happy.

"Ha, ha!" he laughed gleefully. "I shall be able to eat and drink just as much as I like now and shall never be troubled by those tiny little creatures, the mortals."

"Be not so sure," said Noah. "Those tiny mortals shall be thy masters and shall outlive thee and the whole race of giants and demons."

The giant did not relish this prospect. He knew that whatever Noah prophesied would come true, and he was so sad that he ate no food for two days and began to grow smaller and thinner. He became more and more unhappy as day by day the water subsided and the mountains began to appear. At last the Ark rested on Mount Ararat, and Og's long ride came to an end.

"I will soon leave thee, Father Noah," he said. "I shall wander round the world to see what is left of it."

"Thou canst not go until I permit thee," said Noah. "Hast thou forgotten our compact so soon? Thou must be my servant. I have work for thee."

Giants are not fond of work, and Og, who was the father of all the giants, was particularly lazy. He cared only to eat and sleep, but he knew he was in Noah's power, and he shed bitter tears when he saw the land appear again.

"Stop," commanded Noah. "Dost thou wish to drown the world once more with thy big tears ?"

So Og sat on a mountain and rocked from side to side, weeping silently to himself. He watched the animals leave the Ark and had to do all the hard work when Noah's children built houses. Daily he complained that he was shrinking to the size of the mortals, for Noah said there was not too much food.

One day Noah said to him, "Come with me, Og. I am going around the world. I am commanded to plant fruit and flowers to make the earth beautiful. I need thy help."

For many days they wandered all over the earth, and Og was compelled to carry the heavy bag of seeds. The last thing Noah planted was the grape vine.

"What is this – food, or drink?" asked Og.

"Both," replied Noah. "It can be eaten, or its juice made into wine," and as he planted it, he blessed the grape. "Be thou," he said, "a plant pleasing to the eye, bear fruit that will be food for the hungry and a health-giving drink to the thirsty and sick."

Og grunted.

"I will offer up sacrifice to this wonderful fruit," he said. "May I not do so now that our labours are over?"

Noah agreed, and the giant brought a sheep, a lion, a pig and a monkey. First, he slaughtered the sheep, then the lion.

"When a man shall taste but a few drops of the wine," he said, "he shall be as harmless as a sheep. When he takes a little more he shall be as strong as a lion."

Then Og began to dance around the plant, and he killed the pig and the monkey. Noah was very much surprised.

"I am giving thy descendants two extra blessings," said Og, chuckling.

He rolled over and over on the ground in great glee and then said:

"When a man shall drink too much of the juice of the wine, then shall he become a beast like the pig, and if then he still continues to drink, he shall behave foolishly like a monkey."

And that is why, unto this day, too much wine makes a man silly.

Og himself often drank too much, and many years afterward, when he was a servant to the patriarch Abraham, the latter scolded him until he became so frightened that he dropped a tooth. Abraham made an ivory chair for himself from this tooth. Afterwards Og became King of Bashan, but he forgot his compact with Noah and instead of helping the Israelites to obtain Canaan he opposed them.

"I will kill them all with one blow," he declared.

Exerting all his enormous strength he uprooted a mountain, and raising it high above his head he prepared to drop it on the camp of the Israelites and crush it.

But a wonderful thing happened. The mountain was full of grasshoppers and ants who had bored millions of tiny holes in it. When King Og raised the great mass it crumbled in his hands and fell over his head and round his neck like a collar. He tried to pull it off, but his teeth became entangled in the mass. As he danced about in rage and pain, Moses, the leader of the Israelites, approached him.

Moses was a tiny man compared with Og. He was only ten ells high, and he carried with him a sword of the same length. With a mighty effort he jumped ten ells into the air, and raising the sword, he managed to strike the giant on the ankle and wound him mortally.

Thus, after many years, did the terrible giant of the flood perish for breaking his word to Father Noah.

The Story of the Fisherman

SIRE, THERE WAS ONCE UPON A TIME A FISHERMAN so old and so poor that he could scarcely manage to support his wife and three children. He went every day to fish very early, and each day he made a rule not to throw his nets more than four times. He started out one morning by moonlight and came to the seashore. He undressed and threw his nets, and as he was drawing them towards the bank he felt a great weight. He though he had caught a large fish, and he felt very pleased. But a moment afterwards, seeing that instead of a fish he only had in his nets the carcase of an ass, he was much disappointed.

Vexed with having such a bad haul, when he had mended his nets, which the carcase of the ass had broken in several places, he threw them a second time. In drawing them in he again felt a great weight, so that he thought they were full of fish. But he only found a large basket full of rubbish. He was much annoyed.

"O Fortune," he cried, "do not trifle thus with me, a poor fisherman, who can hardly support his family!"

So saying, he threw away the rubbish, and after having washed his nets clean of the dirt, he threw them for the third time. But he only drew in stones, shells, and mud. He was almost in despair.

Then he threw his nets for the fourth time. When he thought he had a fish he drew them in with a great deal of trouble. There was no fish however, but he found a yellow pot, which by its weight seemed full of something, and he noticed that it was fastened and sealed with lead, with the impression of a seal. He was delighted. "I will sell it to the founder," he said, "with the money I shall get for it I shall buy a measure of wheat."

He examined the jar on all sides; he shook it to see if it would rattle. But he heard nothing, and so, judging from the impression of the seal and the lid, he thought there must be something precious inside. To find out, he took his knife, and with a little trouble he opened it. He turned it upside down, but nothing came out, which surprised him very much. He set it in front of him, and whilst he was looking at it attentively, such a thick smoke came out that he had to step back a pace or two. This smoke rose up to the clouds, and stretching over the sea and the shore, formed a thick mist, which caused the fisherman much astonishment. When all the smoke was out of the jar it gathered itself together, and became a thick mass in which appeared a genius, twice as large as the largest giant. When he saw such a terrible-looking monster, the fisherman would like to have run away, but he trembled so with fright that he could not move a step.

"Great king of the genii," cried the monster, "I will never again disobey you!"

At these words the fisherman took courage.

"What is this you are saying, great genius? Tell me your history and how you came to be shut up in that vase."

At this, the genius looked at the fisherman haughtily. "Speak to me more civilly," he said, "before I kill you."

"Alas! why should you kill me?" cried the fisherman. "I have just freed you; have you already forgotten that?"

"No," answered the genius; "but that will not prevent me from killing you; and I am only going to grant you one favour, and that is to choose the manner of your death."

"But what have I done to you?" asked the fisherman.

"I cannot treat you in any other way," said the genius, "and if you would know why, listen to my story.

"I rebelled against the king of the genii. To punish me, he shut me up in this vase of copper, and he put on the leaden cover his seal, which is enchantment enough to prevent my coming out. Then he had the vase thrown into the sea. During the first period of my captivity I vowed that if anyone should free me before a hundred years were passed, I would make him rich even after his death. But that century passed, and no one freed me. In the second century I vowed that I would give all the treasures in the world to my deliverer; but he never came.

"In the third, I promised to make him a king, to be always near him, and to grant him three wishes every day; but that century passed away as the other two had done, and I remained in the same plight. At last I grew angry at being captive for so long, and I vowed that if anyone would release me I would kill him at once, and would only allow him to choose in what manner he should die. So you see, as you have freed me today, choose in what way you will die."

The fisherman was very unhappy. "What an unlucky man I am to have freed you! I implore you to spare my life."

"I have told you," said the genius, "that it is impossible. Choose quickly; you are wasting time."

The fisherman began to devise a plot.

"Since I must die," he said, "before I choose the manner of my death, I conjure you on your honour to tell me if you really were in that vase?"

"Yes, I was," answered the genius.

"I really cannot believe it," said the fisherman. "That vase could not contain one of your feet even, and how could your whole body go in? I cannot believe it unless I see you do the thing."

Then the genius began to change himself into smoke, which, as before, spread over the sea and the shore, and which, then collecting itself together, began to go back into the vase slowly and evenly till there was nothing left outside. Then a voice came from the vase which said to the fisherman, "Well, unbelieving fisherman, here I am in the vase; do you believe me now?"

The fisherman instead of answering took the lid of lead and shut it down quickly on the vase.

"Now, O genius," he cried, "ask pardon of me, and choose by what death you will die! But no, it will be better if I throw you into the sea whence I drew you out, and I will build a house on the shore to warn fishermen who come to cast their nets here, against fishing up such a wicked genius as you are, who vows to kill the man who frees you."

At these words the genius did all he could to get out, but he could not, because of the enchantment of the lid.

Then he tried to get out by cunning.

"If you will take off the cover," he said, "I will repay you."

"No," answered the fisherman wisely.

A Story About a Giant, and the Cause of Thunder

THIS STORY IS ABOUT a forest giant, about him and a man called A-Man-among-Men.

A story, a story. Let it go, let it come.

There was a certain man by name, A-Man-among-Men, always when he came from the bush he used to lift up a tree and come, and throw it down, and say, "I am A-Man-among-Men." His wife said, "Come now, leave off saying you are a-man-among-men; if you saw a-man-among-men you would run." But he said, "It is a lie."

Now it was always so, if he has brought in wood, then he would throw it down with force, and say, "I am A-Man-among-Men." The wife said, "Come now, leave off saying so; if you have seen a man-among-men, you would run." But he said, "It is a lie."

Now one day his wife went to the stream. She came to a certain well; the well bucket, ten men were necessary to draw it up. She came, but had to do without the water, so she turned back. She was going home, when she met another woman who said, "Where are you going with a calabash, with no water?" She said, "I have come and seen a bucket there. I could not draw it; that is what caused me to turn back home." And this second woman, who had this a son, said, "Let us return that you may find water." She said, "All right."

So they returned together to the well. This woman, who had the son, told the boy to lift the bucket and draw water. Now the boy was small, not past the age when he was carried on his mother's back. Then he lifted the bucket then and there, and put it in the well, and drew up the water. They filled their large water-pots, they bathed, they washed their clothes, they lifted up the water to go home. This one was astonished.

Then she saw that one who had the boy has turned off the path and was entering the bush. Then the wife of him called A-Man-among-Men said, "Where are you going?" She said to her, "I am going home, where else?" She said, "Is that the way to your home?" She said, "Yes." She said, "Whose home is it?" She said, "The home of A-Man-among-Men."

Then she was silent; she did not say anything till she got home. She told her husband. He said that tomorrow she must take him there. She replied, "May Allah give us a tomorrow." Next morning he was the first to get up from sleep. He took the weapons of the chase and slung them over his shoulder. He put his axe on his shoulder and wakened her his wife from sleep. He said, "Get up, let us go. Take me that I may see, that I may see the one called A-Man-among-Men."

She got up, lifted her large water-pot, and passed on in front. He was following her until they got to the edge of the well. Now they found what they sought indeed. As they were coming, the wife of A-Man-among-Men came up, both she and her son. They greeted her, and the wife of this one showed him the bucket and said, "Lift it and draw water for me."

So he went and lifted the bucket in a rage and let it down the well; but the bucket pulled him, and he would have fallen into the well, when the little boy seized him, both him and the bucket, and drew out and threw them on one side. Then the boy lifted up the bucket, put it in the well, drew water, and filled their water-pots.

His wife said, "You have said you are going to see him called A-Man-among-Men. You have seen this is his wife and son. If you still want to go you can go together. As for me, I am not going." The boy's mother said, "Oh, what is the matter? You had better not come." But he said he would come; and she said, "Let us be off." They set out.

When they arrived at the house then she showed him a place for storing meat, and he got inside. Now he, the master of the house, was not at home; he has gone to the bush. She his wife said, "You have seen he has gone to the bush; but you must not stir if he has come." He sat inside till evening came.

The master of the house came. He keeps saying, "I smell the smell of a man." His wife said, "Is there another person here? It is not is not I." Thus, if he said he smelled the smell of a man, then she would say, "Is there another person here. Is it not I? If you want to eat me up, well and good, for there is no one else but I."

Now he was a huge man, his words like a tornado; ten elephants he would eat. When dawn came, he made his morning meal of one; then he went to the bush, and if he should see a person there he would kill him.

Now he A Man-among-Men was in the store-house, hidden. The man's wife told him, saying, "You must not move till he is asleep. If you have seen the place dark, he is not asleep; if you have seen the place light, that is a sign he is asleep; come out and fly." Shortly after he saw the place has become light like day, so he came out.

He was running, he was running, until dawn, he was running, till the sun rose he was running, he did not stand. Then that man woke up from sleep and he said, "I smell the smell of a man, I smell the smell of a man." He rose up, he followed where the man had gone. He was running. He also, the other one, was running till he met some people who were clearing the ground for a farm, and they asked what had happened. And he said, "Someone chased is chasing me." They said, "Stand here till he comes."

A short time passed, and the wind caused by him came; it lifted them and cast them down. And he said, "Yes, that is it, the wind he makes running; he himself has not yet come. If you are able to withstand him tell me. If you are not able, say so." And they said, "Pass on."

So he ran off, and came and met some people hoeing. They said, "What chased is chasing you?" He replied, "Someone pursued is pursuing me." They said, "What kind of a man chased is chasing one such as you." He said, "Someone who says he is A-Man-among-Men." They said, "Not a man-among-men, a man-among-women. Stand till he comes."

He stood. Here he was when the wind of him came, it was pushing about the men who were hoeing. So he said, "You have seen, that is the wind he makes; he has not yet come himself If you are a match for him tell me; if not say so." And they said, "Pass on"; and off he ran. He was running. He came across some people sowing; they said, "What are you running for?" He said, "Someone chased is chasing me." And they said, "What kind of a man is it who chased is chasing the like of you?" He said, "His name is A-Man-among-Men." They said, "Sit here till he comes." He sat down.

In a short time the wind he made came and it lifted them and cast them down. And they said, "What kind of wind is that?" He, the man who was being pursued, said, "It is his wind." And they said, "Pass on." They threw away the sowing implements, and went into the bush and hid, but that one was running on.

He came and met a certain huge man; he was sitting alone at the foot of a baobab tree. He had killed elephants and was roasting them, as for him, twenty elephants he could eat; in the morning he broke his fast with five. His name was 'The Giant of the Forest.'

Then he questioned him and said, "Where are you going in all this haste?" And he said, "A-Man-among-Men chased is chasing me." And the Giant of the Forest said, "Come here, sit down till he comes." He sat down. They waited a little while. Then a wind made by A-Man-among-Men came, and lifted him, and was about to carry him off, when the Giant of the Forest shouted to him to come back. And he said, "It is not I myself who am going off, the wind caused by the man is taking me away." At that the Giant of the Forest got in a rage, he got up and caught his hand, and placed it under his thigh.

He was sitting until A-Man-among-Men came up and said, "You sitting there, are you of the living, or of the dead?" And the Giant of the Forest said, "You are interfering." And A-Man-among-Men said, "If you want to find health give up to me what you are keeping there." And the Giant of the Forest said, "Come and take him." And at that he flew into a rage and sprang and seized him. They were struggling together.

When they had twisted their legs round one another they leaped up into the heavens. Till this day they are wrestling there; when they are tired out they sit down and rest; and if they rise up to struggle that is the thunder you are wont to hear in the sky; it is they struggling.

He also, that other one, found himself escaped, and went home, and told the tale. And his wife said, "That is why I was always telling you whatever you do, make little of it. Whether it be you excel in strength, or in power, or riches, or poverty, and are puffed up with pride, it is all the same; someone is better than you. You said, it was a lie. Behold, your own eyes have seen."

The Story of the Wonderful Goat

ONCE UPON A TIME there was a man called Kato who had a large herd of goats, and he noticed that one goat was larger than all the others. It grew and grew, and at last it was so enormous that people came from all parts of the Province to see it, and they said, "This goat is a fit present for the King, no one has ever seen its equal." Kato determined to go to the Capital and give his wonderful goat to the King.

Now, in the mountains near his village there lived a band of robbers, who used to plunder passersby and take their goods and sometimes kill them. So Kato was afraid to make the journey to the Capital alone, and his brother agreed to go with him, but first he went to the witchdoctor to have his fortune told, which was a very silly thing to do, as you will see.

The robbers had seen the enormous goat and wondered how they could steal it, and, unfortunately, while the chief robber was returning from the village market, he saw Kato going towards the witchdoctor's hut for he lived alone on a hilltop. The robber knew of a shortcut, and he hurried round and arrived first at the hut, and promised the witchdoctor a large reward if he gave certain advice to Kato.

When Kato arrived the witchdoctor said, "You are going on a journey, but you must go alone, and until you reach your destination you must eat no salt and drink no banana beer, if you do either of these things misfortune will overtake you."

When Kato returned home he told his brother, and he also told his wife to use no salt in the kitchen until he had started for the Capital. Then he made his preparations, and one morning at dawn he started out, driving his goat before him, with a gourd of water tied round his waist by a thong, and a parcel of food in a bag slung over his shoulder and carrying in his hand a spear wrapped round with plantain fibre for no traveller may carry a naked spear.

By midday he had reached the mountains, where the road passed between great boulders of rock, on which the turquoise-blue lizards played all day. He was hot and tired, so he sat down in the shade to rest and eat his dinner. He was so hungry that at first he ate without thinking, but as he felt rested he realized that the dinner was very good, and suddenly he remembered the witchdoctor's warning, and he wondered if there was salt in it. The more he thought over it the more convinced he was that he had eaten salt.

He started off again on his journey much agitated, and he had not gone very far when one of the robbers met him, and after giving him a friendly greeting, said, "Why are you driving a pig? That is a very unusual thing to do!"

Kato looked at the robber in amazement. "A pig!" he cried. "I have no pigs! This is my wonderful goat I am taking to the Capital to give to the King."

"Oh, really!" said the robber; and he said goodbye very quickly and hurried away. Kato was still thinking that the man must have been at a drinking feast to say such an extraordinary thing, when another of the robbers met him. "That is a fine pig!" said the robber. "Where did you get it?"

"It is a goat," said Kato; "my wonderful goat that I am taking to the Capital to give to the King."

The robber looked very much surprised and went on his way. Three more men of the robber band met Kato on the mountain path, and each one stopped in surprise and made some remark about his pig. Suddenly the witchdoctor's warning flashed across his mind: "If you eat salt or drink banana beer misfortune will overtake you." "I have eaten salt, and my goat has been bewitched and become a pig," he cried; and he was so frightened that he left the goat and ran all the way back to the village and his home. When he arrived he told his wife and his brother,

"I have been bewitched, I shall surely die."

The hot journey in the sun, the fright he had had, and the exhausting run home brought on a fever, and he died.

And the robbers took the goat and made a great feast and sent a large joint to the witch doctor with the present they had promised him; but Kato's family not only lost him and the wonderful goat, but they were more firmly convinced than ever before that the witchdoctor was a marvellous man.

The Story of the Three Billy Goats Gruff

THERE WERE ONCE THREE BILLY GOATS who lived in a meadow at the foot of a mountain, and their last name was Gruff. There was the Big Billy Goat Gruff, and the Middle-sized Billy Goat Gruff, and the Little Billy Goat Gruff. They all three jumped about among the rocks in the meadow and ate what grass they could find, but it wasn't very much.

One day the Littlest Billy Goat Gruff looked up at the high mountain overhead, and he thought to himself, "It looks as though there were a great deal of fine grass up on the mountain. I believe I'll just run up there all by myself, without telling anyone, and eat so much grass and eat so much grass that I'll grow to be as big as anybody."

So off the Little Billy Goat Gruff started without telling his brothers a word about it. He ran along, tip-tap, tip-tap, tip-tap, until at last he came to a wide river, with a bridge over it.

Now the Little Billy Goat did not know it, but this bridge belonged to a great, terrible Troll, and the little goat had not gone more than halfway across when he heard the Troll shouting from under the bridge.

"Who's that going across my bridge?" shouted the Troll in his great loud voice.

"It's me, the Littlest Billy Goat Gruff!" answered the Little Billy Goat in his little bit of voice.

"Oh! it's the Littlest Billy Goat Gruff, is it? Well, you won't go much farther, for I'm the Troll that owns this bridge, and now I'm coming to eat you up." And with that the Troll looked up over the edge of the bridge.

When the Little Billy Goat Gruff saw him, he was very much frightened. "Oh, dear, good Mr Troll, please don't eat me up," he cried. "I'm such a very little goat that I would scarcely be a mouthful for you. I have a brother who is a great deal bigger than I am; wait till he comes, for he'd make a much better meal for you than I would."

"But if he's much bigger than you are he may be tough."

"Oh, no, he's just as tender as I am."

"And a great deal bigger?"

"Oh, yes, a great deal bigger."

"Very well then, I'll wait for him. Run along!"

So the little goat ran on, tip-tap! tip-tap! tip-tap! across the bridge, and on up the mountain to where he was safe. And glad enough he was to be out of that scrape, I can tell you.

Now it was not very long after this that the Middle-sized Billy Goat Gruff began to think he'd like to go up on the mountain too. He did not say anything about it to the Great Big Billy Goat Gruff, but off he set, all by himself – trap-trap! trap-trap! trap-trap! After a while he came to the bridge, where the Troll lived, and he stepped out upon it, trap-trap! trap-trap! trap-trap!

He'd barely reached the middle of it when the Troll began shouting at him in his great, terrible voice:

"Who's that going across my bridge?"

"It's me, the Middle-sized Billy Goat Gruff," answered the Middle-sized Billy Goat in his middle-sized voice.

"Oh, it is, is it? Then you're the very one I've been waiting for. I'm the Troll that owns this bridge, and now I'm coming to eat you up."

At that the Middle-sized Billy Goat Gruff was in a great fright. "Oh, dear Mr Troll, good Mr Troll, please don't eat me up! I have a brother that's a great deal bigger than I am. Just wait till he comes along, for he'd make a much better meal for you than I would."

"A great deal bigger?"

"Yes, a great deal bigger."

"Very well then, run along and I'll wait till he comes. Only the biggest goat there is is fit to make a meal for me."

The Middle-sized Billy Goat was not slow to run along as the Troll bade him. He hurried across the river and up the mountain as fast as he could go, trappity-trap! trappity-trap! trappity-trap! And just weren't he and his little brother glad to see each other again, and to be safely over the Troll's bridge, and up where the good grass was!

And now it was the turn of the Big Billy Goat Gruff to begin to think he'd like to go up on the mountain too. "I believe that's where the Little Billy Goat Gruff and the Middle-sized Billy Goat Gruff have gone," said he to himself. "If I don't look out they'll be growing so fat up there that they'll be as big as I am. I think I'd better go and eat the long green mountain grass too." So the next morning off he set in the pleasant sunshine. Klumph-klumph! klumph-klumph! He was so big you could hear his hoofs pounding on the stones while he was still a mile away.

After a while he came to the bridge where the Troll lived, and out he stepped on it, klumph-klumph! klumph-klumph! and the bridge shook and bent under his weight as he walked. Then the Troll that lived under it was in a fearful rage. "Who's that going across my bridge?" he bellowed, and his voice was so terrible that all the little fish in the river swam away and hid under the rocks at the sound of it.

But the Big Billy Goat was not one bit frightened.

"It's me, the Biggest Billy Goat Gruff," he answered, in a voice as big as the Troll's own.

"Oh, it is, is it? Then just stop a bit – for you're the one I've been waiting for. I'm the Troll that owns this bridge, and now I'm coming to eat you up!" and with that the great grey Troll poked his head up over the bridge, and his eyes looked like two great mill-wheels, and they were going round and round in his head with rage. But still the Big Billy Goat was not one bit frightened.

"So you're a Troll, are you! And you own this bridge, do you? And now you're going to eat me up? We'll just see about that:

"I have a forehead as hard as stone,
And I'll mash you all up, body and bone!"

When the Troll heard the Big Billy Goat talk to him that way he bellowed so that the Middle-sized Billy Goat and the Little Billy Goat heard him all the way up on the mountain where they were. He jumped up on the bridge and put down his big, bushy head and ran at the Billy Goat, and the Big Billy Goat put down his head and ran at the Troll, and they met in the middle of the bridge. But the Billy Goat's head was harder than the Troll's, so he knocked him down and thumped him about, and then he took him up on his horns and threw him over the edge of the bridge into the river below, and the Troll sank like a piece of lead and never was seen or heard of again.

But the Big Billy Goat went on up the mountain; and you may believe that his two brothers were glad to see him again, and to hear that the great wicked Troll was gone from under the bridge.

And after that they all stayed up on the mountain together, and the smaller goats ate so much grass and grew so fat and big that after a while no one could have told one Billy Goat from the other.

Litill, Tritill, the Birds, and the Peasant Lad

THERE ONCE REIGNED A KING AND A QUEEN, and in the same country there also lived a poor old man and his wife. The king had an only daughter, called Enid, who was greatly beloved by both her father and mother. They spared no expense, and she had the best masters and governesses, and a number of servants to wait upon her; but notwithstanding that she was so carefully watched and looked after, she suddenly disappeared. The head governess said she had left her in her room only for a few minutes practicing her harp, with two of her maidens in attendance, and when she came back she found both the girls fast asleep, and the princess gone. Enquiries were made of everyone, but nothing could be heard of the princess. No one had seen her; she had vanished in the most mysterious manner. The king, in despair, sent out messengers in all directions, and spent a great part of his treasure searching for her; but all in vain. Then, at last, he vowed that he would give the princess in marriage to whoever should be fortunate enough to find her, and also give him the half of his kingdom. But though many of the knights and nobles about the court, eager to secure so great a prize, went off in search of her, they one and all returned empty-handed.

Now, the poor old man who lived outside the palace grounds had three sons. Their names were Osmond, Tostig and Harald. The two eldest boys were greatly beloved by their parents; but Harald, the youngest and handsomest, was disliked by his father and mother, and both his elder brothers ill-treated him and made him do all the work, while they went out shooting and fishing.

When the boys were grown up, Osmond came to his parents, and said he would like to start off and see the world, and try to win fame and riches for himself.

His father and mother were quite willing he should do so, and providing him with a new pair of boots and a large bag of food, he started off on his journey.

After he had gone a long, long way, he arrived at a little hillock. Here he sat down to rest, and unpacked his bag of provisions.

Just as he was beginning to eat, a tiny little man dressed in grey came up to him, begging for a morsel of food. Osmond angrily ordered him away, threatening to beat him if he did not go quickly.

After he had rested, Osmond went on again a long, long way, till he came to another hillock. Here he again sat down to rest, and began to eat. But he had hardly commenced than a still smaller and shabbier little man, dressed in green, came up to him and asked him for a morsel of food. Osmond spoke angrily to him, and sent him away with a volley of abuse.

He then went on again a long, long way, till he reached a large open glade in the wood. Here he sat down on the soft, mossy grass at the foot of a big beech tree, and thought he would eat another morsel. But no sooner had he opened his bag and taken out the food than a whole flock of birds flew down beside him; but he angrily chased them away, and then, having rested himself, went on his way, till he came to a big cave. Looking in and seeing no one, only a lot of cattle, he thought he would go in and wait till the dawn arrived.

Just as the sun was setting, an enormously big giantess walked in. Osmond was greatly startled, but, taking courage, he went up to her and asked whether he might stay the night there.

The giantess said yes, on condition that in the morning he would do the work she would require of him. This he promised he would do; so she allowed him to remain the night, she herself retiring into an inner cave.

The next morning the giantess told him that he must clean out the cave, and put down fresh bedding for the cattle, and that he must have it all finished before the evening, else she would take his life. With these words she went away.

Osmond took up a prong he saw standing in a corner, but no sooner did he begin to turn up the straw than the prong stuck fast in the bedding. In vain he pushed and pulled and tried to drag it out, the prong remained firmly fixed; and when in the evening the giantess came home and found that the cave had not been cleaned out, she took hold of Osmond and hung him up to a nail in the cave.

Meanwhile Tostig, the second son, thought he, too, would like to go out into the world to seek his fortune, for he felt sure his brother by this time must be quite a rich man. So he told his parents that he did not care to remain at home now his elder brother was away, and with only that stupid Harald at home; so having gained their consent, he, too, started off, provided with a pair of new boots and a big bag of provisions.

But he was not more fortunate than Osmond had been. He flouted the little men while he rested on the hillocks, he chased and killed some of the birds who came flocking round him for crumbs; and when he reached the cave, he also received leave from the giantess to remain the night, on condition that he cleaned out the cave next morning. When he went and took up the prong to throw out the old bedding, it stuck fast in the straw, and no efforts of his could move it. So the giantess coming home, and finding that he had failed to accomplish his task, took him and hanged him beside his brother.

So now there was only the youngest son, Harald, left. But though he was the only one at home, his parents did not love him any better, and the poor lad often felt that his presence reminded them of their lost sons, and that they regretted not having sent him away in their place. So he also decided to go away.

"I do not suppose I shall win riches and fame. All I hope is that I may be able to earn enough to support myself, and be no longer a burden to you."

Then his parents told him he might go; but instead of nice strong new boots, they only gave him an old pair of his brother's, and his sack contained nothing but some hard, dry crusts.

But Harald started off with a light heart, and as it chanced he, too, took the same road his brothers had done, and presently he came to the first hillock. "I think my brothers must have rested here, if they felt as tired as I do," he said, "so I will do the same." And seating himself on the hillock, he began to eat one of his dry crusts, when, looking up, he saw a little old man in grey standing beside him.

"Will you share your crust with me? I am very hungry, and have had no food today," he said.

Harald pitied the old man, who looked so feeble and tired. He begged him to sit down beside him and share his meal. When they had done, the old man got up, and, after thanking him, said, "My name is Tritill. Although I am old and feeble, if ever you are in need of help, call me, and I will come to you." So saying, he went round the back of the hillock and disappeared.

Harald then continued his journey till he came to the second hillock.

"I feel sure my brothers must have rested here," he said. "It is a long way from the last hillock. I, too, will rest here a while." And he sat down, and opening his bag, took out another crust. Hardly had he done so when a tiny, shabby, little old man, dressed in green, came up to him and asked for a morsel of food. Harald very good-naturedly asked him to sit down beside him, and shared his crust with him. When they had finished eating, the little green man got up, and, after thanking Harald, said –

"Call me, if ever you think I can do you a service. My name is Litill." And he, too, went away, and was soon out of sight.

Harald then continued his journey until he came to the large open glade in the wood.

"I am sure my brothers must have rested here," he thought. "I will do the same." And he sat down and took out another crust. No sooner had he done so than a great flock of birds came down. They circled round and round him, and seemed so hungry and fought so eagerly over every crumb he threw them, that Harald's heart was filled with pity. "Poor little things!" he said, "they need it more than I do." And he broke up the remaining crusts and threw the crumbs among them.

When they had eaten up every crumb, the biggest bird alighted gently on Harald's shoulder and whistled softly –

"If ever you think we can do you a service, call us. We shall hear you wherever we are, for we are your birds." And ere he had recovered from his astonishment, they had all flown away and were out of sight.

Harald then continued his journey, until he, too, came to the big cave. Looking in, he saw it was full of cattle, and hanging from a beam in one corner he saw the bodies of his two brothers.

Startled at the sight, Harald's first impulse was to go away; but he thought he must first bury his brothers. So he took down the bodies, and seeing a spade near the entrance, he speedily dug a grave and buried them in the sand outside the cave. Just as he had finished, the giantess arrived.

Harald, who was very tired, asked her if he might stay the night there.

"You may do so, if you will promise to do what I tell you in the morning," answered the giantess.

This Harald agreed to, and he slept that night in the cave.

Next morning, the giantess, who had slept in an inner cave, told him that he would have to clean out the cave, and put down clean bedding for the oxen.

"But remember, if your work is not finished when I come home, I shall hang you the same as I did your brothers;" and so saying she went away.

Harald took up the prong standing in the corner and began his work. But no sooner had he pushed the prong into the bedding and tried to lift it than it stuck fast to the ground. In vain he used all his strength, the prong remained firmly fixed. In his despair he called out: "Oh, dear Tritill, come and help me!"

No sooner had the words passed his lips than he saw Tritill standing beside him, who asked what he could do for him. Harald showed him the difficulty he was in.

Then Tritill called out: "Prick prong and shovel spade!" and immediately the prong pricked up the bedding and the spade shovelled it away, till in a very short time the cave was all cleaned out and fresh straw put down. Harald thanked him warmly for his help, and Tritill went away.

When the giantess came home in the evening and saw that the work was done, she said to Harald –

"Oh, man, man! you have not done this by yourself! But I will let it pass!" and she retired into the inner cave.

The next morning the giantess told Harald that she had some fresh work for him to do. He was to carry her bedding outside the cave, take out all the feathers, spread them out in the sun to air, and then put them back again.

"But remember, if when I come back in the evening there is a single feather missing, I shall hang you as I did your brothers!" And with these words she went away.

Harald carried out the great feather bed and the big pillows; and as the sun was shining warm and bright, and there was not a breath of wind, he ripped open the seams and spread out the feathers in the sun.

No sooner had he done so than a strong wind arose, and in one moment all the feathers were whirled away, not a single one remaining.

In despair Harald called out: "Dear Tritill, dear Litill and all my dear birds – oh, come and help me if you can!" And almost before the words had passed his lips, Tritill, Litill and the whole flight of birds came bringing the feathers with them; and while Tritill and Litill helped Harald to fill the bed and the pillows, and sew them up again, the birds flew round picking up all the stray feathers, so that none were missing. But out of each pillow they took one feather, and, tying them together, told Harald that when the giantess missed them and threatened to kill him, he was to tickle her nose with the feathers.

Thereupon Tritill, Litill and the birds all disappeared.

When the giantess came home in the evening, she went up to her bed, and threw herself down on it so heavily that the whole cave shook. Then she began carefully feeling all over the bed, and when she came to the pillows she cried out –

"Aha, man! I have caught you – there is a feather missing in each pillow! Now I shall hang you like your brothers!"

But as she took hold of him, Harold quickly pulled the two feathers out of his pocket and tickled her nose with them.

In an instant the giantess fell back on her bed looking terribly white and frightened; but Harald laughingly gave her back her feathers, telling her he did not want to keep them.

"Ah, man, man!" said the giantess, "I know you did not do this alone; but I will let it pass this time!"

So this third night Harald also passed in the cave, and in the morning the giantess said to him –

"I have some fresh work for you today. You must kill one of my oxen. Then you must scrape and clean the skin to make a leather bag; cut up the animal in joints ready for cooking; clean all the entrails, and make spoons out of its horns. All must be finished ere I return this evening. I have fifty oxen, as you see, and it is one of these I want killed. I shall not, however, tell you which one I have fixed upon; that you must find out for yourself. If all is done as I wish when I return, you can depart in the morning and go wherever you like; and in addition, as a reward, you may choose three things from among such of my treasures as I value most. If, however, everything is not finished, or if you kill the wrong animal, then it will cost you your life, and I shall hang you the same as I did your brothers." And so saying the giantess departed.

Harald was sorely puzzled. How could he possibly decide which of the animals the giantess wished killed? Then he remembered his friends.

"Dear Tritill, dear Litill, come once again to my aid," he cried.

Hardly had the words passed his lips than he saw them both coming towards him, leading a huge ox between them. They at once set to work and killed him, and while Harald cleaned the entrails and cut up the joints, Tritill scraped the skin and prepared it for making the bag, and Litill began fashioning the spoons out of the horns.

So the work sped along quickly and merrily, and all was ready ere the sun sank to rest.

Harald now told his friends what the giantess had promised him if he should have finished his task ere she returned.

"Can you advise me what to ask for?" he said.

Then they told him he should first ask for that which was over her bed, then for the chest which stood beside her bed, and lastly for that which was behind the wall of her bed.

Harald thanked them warmly for all they had done for him, and said he would do as they had told him, whereupon the little men disappeared.

When the giantess came home in the evening and found that Harald had finished all the tasks she had set him, she exclaimed –

"Ah, man, man! you never did all this alone; but you have conquered, so I must let it pass." And so saying she retired to rest.

The next morning, the giantess called Harald into the inner cave and told him he might choose the reward she had promised him, and that then he might go where he liked.

"Then," said Harald, "if I may have whatever I like, I choose, first, that which is above your bed; then the chest which is beside your bed; and, lastly, that which is behind the wall of your bed."

"Ah, man, man!" cried the giantess. "You have not chosen these things by yourself; but I cannot refuse you; you are too strong for me, and you have conquered, and I must give you the reward you claim."

So saying, she mounted some steps above her bed cut into the rock, and, opening a secret door, she led forth a beautiful maiden. This was none other than the fair Princess Enid, who had disappeared so mysteriously some time ago.

"Take her back to her father, and he will reward you as you deserve," said the giantess as she placed the princess's hand in that of Harald.

She then opened the lid of the chest beside her bed. This was filled with gold, pearls and precious stones; and then moving aside the bed, she touched a secret spring, and the wall sliding back, they saw the blue sea, and anchored close to the cave lay a beautiful ship completely fitted out, her sails all set, and her pennant flying, and possessing the power of sailing wherever its owner wished, without aid of either captain or crew.

When the giantess had handed him over these gifts, she told Harald that he would henceforth be one of the happiest and luckiest of men.

Harald then carried the chest containing the gold and precious stones on board ship, and then having arranged some soft cushions for the Princess Enid, in the stern of the vessel, they quickly departed, and reached her father's country.

The delight of the king and queen on recovering their long-lost daughter can be more easily imagined than described. They never tired hearing of the wonderful adventures through which Harald had gone, and the king ordered a great feast in honour of the rescuer of his child, which ended with the wedding of Enid and Harald.

The king then made Harald his prime minister; and so well and so wisely did he rule the country, that on the king's death he was chosen to succeed him, and he and Queen Enid lived long and happily together, seeing their children and grandchildren growing up around them.

Old Hopgiant

ONCE UPON A TIME, there were two neighbours: one of them rich and the other poor. They owned a great meadow in common, which they were supposed to mow together and then divide the hay.

But the rich neighbour wanted the meadow for himself alone, and told the poor one that he would drive him out of house and home if he did not come to an agreement with him that whichever one of them mowed the largest stretch of the meadowland in a single day should receive the entire meadow.

Now the rich neighbour got together as many mowers as ever he could; but the poor one could not hire a single man. At last he despaired altogether and wept, because he did not know how he could manage to get so much as a bit of hay for the cow.

Then it was that a large man stepped up to him and said: "Do not grieve so. I can tell you what you ought to do. When the mowing begins, just call out 'Old Hopgiant!' three times in succession, and you'll not be at a loss, as you shall see for yourself." And with that he disappeared.

Then the poor man's heart grew less heavy, and he gave over worrying. So one fine day his rich neighbour came along with no fewer than twenty farmhands, and they mowed down one swath after another. But the poor neighbour did not even take the trouble to begin when he saw how the others took hold, and that he himself would not be able to do anything alone.

Then the big man occurred to him, and he called out: "Old Hopgiant!" But no one came, and the mowers all laughed at him and mocked him, thinking he had gone out of his mind. Then he called again: "Old Hopgiant!" And, just as before, there was no hopgiant to be seen. And the mowers could scarcely swing their scythes, for they were laughing fit to split.

And then he cried for the third time: "Old Hopgiant!" And there appeared a fellow of truly horrible size, with a scythe as large as a ship's mast.

And now the merriment of the rich peasant's mowers came to an end. For when the giant began to mow and fling about his scythe, they were frightened at the strength he put into his work. And before they knew it he had mown half the meadow.

Then the rich neighbour fell into a rage, rushed up and gave the giant a good kick. But that did not help him, for his foot stuck to the giant, while the latter no more felt the kick than if it had been a flea-bite, and kept right on working.

Then the rich neighbour thought of a scheme to get free, and gave the giant a kick with his other foot; but this foot also stuck fast, and there he hung like a tick. Old Hopgiant mowed the whole meadow, and then flew up into the air, and the rich man had to go along hanging to him like a hawser. And thus the poor neighbour was left sole master of the place.

The Girl-Fish

ONCE UPON A TIME THERE LIVED, on the bank of a stream, a man and a woman who had a daughter. As she was an only child, and very pretty besides, they never could make up their minds to punish her for her faults or to teach her nice manners; and as for work – she laughed in her mother's face if she asked her to help cook the dinner or to wash the plates. All the girl would do was to spend her days in dancing and playing with her friends; and for any use she was to her parents they might as well have no daughter at all.

However, one morning her mother looked so tired that even the selfish girl could not help seeing it, and asked if there was anything she was able to do, so that her mother might rest a little.

The good woman looked so surprised and grateful for this offer that the girl felt rather ashamed, and at that moment would have scrubbed down the house if she had been requested; but her mother only begged her to take the fishing-net out to the bank of the river and mend some holes in it, as her father intended to go fishing that night.

The girl took the net and worked so hard that soon there was not a hole to be found. She felt quite pleased with herself, though she had had plenty to amuse her, as everybody who passed by had stopped and had a chat with her. But by this time the sun was high overhead, and she was just folding her net to carry it home again, when she heard a splash behind her, and looking round she saw a big fish jump into the air. Seizing the net with both hands, she flung it into the water where the circles were spreading one behind the other, and, more by luck than skill, drew out the fish.

"Well, you are a beauty!" she cried to herself; but the fish looked up to her and said:

"You had better not kill me, for, if you do, I will turn you into a fish yourself!"

The girl laughed contemptuously, and ran straight in to her mother.

"Look what I have caught," she said gaily; "but it is almost a pity to eat it, for it can talk, and it declares that, if I kill it, it will turn me into a fish too."

"Oh, put it back, put it back!" implored the mother. "Perhaps it is skilled in magic. And I should die, and so would your father, if anything should happen to you."

"Oh, nonsense, mother; what power could a creature like that have over me? Besides, I am hungry, and if I don't have my dinner soon, I shall be cross." And off she went to gather some flowers to stick in her hair.

About an hour later the blowing of a horn told her that dinner was ready.

"Didn't I say that fish would be delicious?" she cried; and plunging her spoon into the dish the girl helped herself to a large piece. But the instant it touched her mouth a cold shiver ran through her. Her head seemed to flatten, and her eyes to look oddly round the corners; her legs and her arms were stuck to her sides and she gasped wildly for breath. With a mighty bound she sprang through the window and fell into the river, where she soon felt better, and was able to swim to the sea, which was close by.

No sooner had she arrived there than the sight of her sad face attracted the notice of some of the other fishes, and they pressed round her, begging her to tell them her story.

"I am not a fish at all," said the newcomer, swallowing a great deal of salt water as she spoke; for you cannot learn how to be a proper fish all in a moment. "I am not a fish at all, but a girl; at least I was a girl a few minutes ago, only—" And she ducked her head under the waves so that they should not see her crying.

"Only you did not believe that the fish you caught had power to carry out its threat," said an old tunny. "Well, never mind, that has happened to all of us, and it really is not a bad life. Cheer up and come with us and see our queen, who lives in a palace that is much more beautiful than any of your queens can boast of."

The new fish felt a little afraid of taking such a journey; but as she was still more afraid of being left alone, she waved her tail in token of consent, and off they all set, hundreds of them together. The people on the rocks and in the ships that saw them pass said to each other:

"Look what a splendid shoal!" and had no idea that they were hastening to the queen's palace; but then, dwellers on land have so little notion of what goes on in the bottom of the sea! Certainly the little new fish had none. She had watched jellyfish and nautilus swimming a little way below the surface, and beautiful coloured seaweeds floating about; but that was all. Now, when she plunged deeper her eyes fell upon strange things.

Wedges of gold, great anchors, heaps of pearl, inestimable stones, unvalued jewels – all scattered in the bottom of the sea! Dead men's bones were there also, and long white creatures who had never seen the light, for they mostly dwelt in the clefts of rocks where the sun's rays could not come. At first our little fish felt as if she were blind also, but by-and-by she began to make out one object after another in the green dimness, and by the time she had swum for a few hours all became clear.

"Here we are at last," cried a big fish, going down into a deep valley, for the sea has its mountains and valleys just as much as the land. "That is the palace of the queen of the fishes, and I think you must confess that the emperor himself has nothing so fine."

"It is beautiful indeed," gasped the little fish, who was very tired with trying to swim as fast as the rest, and beautiful beyond words the palace was. The walls were made of pale pink coral, worn smooth by the waters, and round the windows were rows of pearls; the great doors were standing open, and the whole shoal floated into the chamber of audience, where the queen, who was half a woman after all, was seated on a throne made of a green and blue shell.

"Who are you, and where do you come from?" said she to the little fish, whom the others had pushed in front. And in a low, trembling voice, the visitor told her story.

"I was once a girl too," answered the queen, when the fish had ended; "and my father was the king of a great country. A husband was found for me, and on my wedding-day my mother placed her crown on my head and told me that as long as I wore it I should likewise be queen. For many months I was as happy as a girl could be, especially when I had a little son to play with. But one morning, when I was walking in my gardens, there came a giant and snatched the crown from my head. Holding me fast, he told me that he intended to give the crown to his daughter, and to enchant my husband the prince, so that he should not know the difference between us. Since then she has filled my place and been queen in my stead. As for me, I was so miserable that I threw myself into the sea, and my ladies, who loved me, declared that they would die too; but, instead of dying, some wizard, who pitied my fate, turned us all into fishes, though he allowed me to keep the face and body of a woman. And fished we must remain till someone brings me back my crown again!"

"I will bring it back if you tell me what to do!" cried the little fish, who would have promised anything that was likely to carry her up to earth again. And the queen answered:

"Yes, I will tell you what to do."

She sat silent for a moment, and then went on:

"There is no danger if you will only follow my counsel; and first you must return to earth, and go up to the top of a high mountain, where the giant has built his castle. You will find him sitting on the steps weeping for his daughter, who has just died while the prince was away hunting. At the last she sent her father my crown by a faithful servant. But I warn you to be careful, for if he sees you he may kill you. Therefore I will give you the power to change yourself into any creature that may help you best. You have only to strike your forehead, and call out its name."

This time the journey to land seemed much shorter than before, and when once the fish reached the shore she struck her forehead sharply with her tail, and cried:

"Deer, come to me!"

In a moment the small, slimy body disappeared, and in its place stood a beautiful beast with branching horns and slender legs, quivering with longing to be gone. Throwing back her head and snuffing the air, she broke into a run, leaping easily over the rivers and walls that stood in her way.

It happened that the king's son had been hunting since daybreak, but had killed nothing, and when the deer crossed his path as he was resting under a tree he determined to have her. He flung himself on his horse, which went like the wind, and as the prince had often hunted the forest before, and knew all the shortcuts, he at last came up with the panting beast.

"By your favour let me go, and do not kill me," said the deer, turning to the prince with tears in her eyes, "for I have far to run and much to do." And as the prince, struck dumb with surprise, only looked at her, the deer cleared the next wall and was soon out of sight.

"That can't really be a deer," thought the prince to himself, reining in his horse and not attempting to follow her. "No deer ever had eyes like that. It must be an enchanted maiden, and I will marry her and no other." So, turning his horse's head, he rode slowly back to his palace.

The deer reached the giant's castle quite out of breath, and her heart sank as she gazed at the tall, smooth walls which surrounded it. Then she plucked up courage and cried:

"Ant, come to me!" And in a moment the branching horns and beautiful shape had vanished, and a tiny brown ant, invisible to all who did not look closely, was climbing up the walls.

It was wonderful how fast she went, that little creature! The wall must have appeared miles high in comparison with her own body; yet, in less time than would have seemed possible, she was over the top and down in the courtyard on the other side. Here she paused to consider what had best be done next, and looking about her she saw that one of the walls had a tall tree growing by it, and in the corner was a window very nearly on a level with the highest branches of the tree.

"Monkey, come to me!" cried the ant; and before you could turn round a monkey was swinging herself from the topmost branches into the room where the giant lay snoring.

"Perhaps he will be so frightened at the sight of me that he may die of fear, and I shall never get the crown," thought the monkey. "I had better become something else." And she called softly: "Parrot, come to me!"

Then a pink and grey parrot hopped up to the giant, who by this time was stretching himself and giving yawns which shook the castle. The parrot waited a little, until he was really awake, and then she said boldly that she had been sent to take away the crown, which was not his any longer, now his daughter the queen was dead.

On hearing these words the giant leapt out of bed with an angry roar, and sprang at the parrot in order to wring her neck with his great hands. But the bird was too quick for him, and, flying behind his back, begged the giant to have patience, as her death would be of no use to him.

"That is true," answered the giant; "but I am not so foolish as to give you that crown for nothing. Let me think what I will have in exchange!" And he scratched his huge head for several minutes, for giants' minds always move slowly.

"Ah, yes, that will do!" exclaimed the giant at last, his face brightening. "You shall have the crown if you will bring me a collar of blue stones from the Arch of St. Martin, in the Great City."

Now when the parrot had been a girl she had often heard of this wonderful arch and the precious stones and marbles that had been let into it. It sounded as if it would be a very hard thing to get them away from the building of which they formed a part, but all had gone well with her so far, and at any rate she could but try. So she bowed to the giant, and made her way back to the window where the giant could not see her. Then she called quickly:

"Eagle, come to me!"

Before she had even reached the tree she felt herself borne up on strong wings ready to carry her to the clouds if she wished to go there, and seeming a mere speck in the sky, she was swept along till she beheld the Arch of St. Martin far below, with the rays of the sun shining on it. Then she swooped down, and, hiding herself behind a buttress so that she could not be detected from below, she set herself to dig out the nearest blue stones with her beak. It was even harder work than she had expected; but at last it was done, and hope arose in her heart. She next drew out a piece of string that she had found hanging from a tree, and sitting down to rest strung the stones together. When the necklace was finished she hung it round her neck, and called: "Parrot, come to me!" And a little later the pink and grey parrot stood before the giant.

"Here is the necklace you asked for," said the parrot. And the eyes of the giant glistened as he took the heap of blue stones in his hand. But for all that he was not minded to give up the crown.

"They are hardly as blue as I expected," he grumbled, though the parrot knew as well as he did that he was not speaking the truth; "so you must bring me something else in exchange for the crown you covet so much. If you fail it will cost you not only the crown but you life also."

"What is it you want now?" asked the parrot; and the giant answered:

"If I give you my crown I must have another still more beautiful; and this time you shall bring me a crown of stars."

The parrot turned away, and as soon as she was outside she murmured:

"Toad, come to me!" And sure enough a toad she was, and off she set in search of the starry crown.

She had not gone far before she came to a clear pool, in which the stars were reflected so brightly that they looked quite real to touch and handle. Stooping down she filled a bag she was carrying with the shining water and, returning to the castle, wove a crown out of the reflected stars. Then she cried as before:

"Parrot, come to me!" And in the shape of a parrot she entered the presence of the giant.

"Here is the crown you asked for," she said, and this time the giant could not help crying out with admiration. He knew he was beaten, and still holding the chaplet of stars, he turned to the girl.

"Your power is greater than mine: take the crown; you have won it fairly!"

The parrot did not need to be told twice. Seizing the crown, she sprang on to the window, crying: "Monkey, come to me!" And to a monkey, the climb down the tree into the courtyard did not take half a minute. When she had reached the ground she said again: "Ant, come to me!" And a little ant at once began to crawl over the high wall. How glad the ant was to be out of the giant's castle, holding fast the crown which had shrunk into almost nothing, as she herself had done, but grew quite big again when the ant exclaimed:

"Deer, come to me!"

Surely no deer ever ran so swiftly as that one! On and on she went, bounding over rivers and crashing through tangles till she reached the sea. Here she cried for the last time:

"Fish, come to me!" And, plunging in, she swam along the bottom as far as the palace, where the queen and all the fishes gathered together awaiting her.

The hours since she had left had gone very slowly – as they always do to people who are waiting – and many of them had quite given up hope.

"I am tired of staying here," grumbled a beautiful little creature, whose colours changed with every movement of her body, "I want to see what is going on in the upper world. It must be months since that fish went away."

"It was a very difficult task, and the giant must certainly have killed her or she would have been back long ago," remarked another.

"The young flies will be coming out now," murmured a third, "and they will all be eaten up by the river fish! It is really too bad!" When, suddenly, a voice was heard from behind: "Look! look! what is that bright thing that is moving so swiftly towards us?" And the queen started up, and stood on her tail, so excited was she.

A silence fell on all the crowd, and even the grumblers held their peace and gazed like the rest. On and on came the fish, holding the crown tightly in her mouth, and the others moved back to let her pass. On she went right up to the queen, who bent and, taking the crown, placed it on her own head. Then a wonderful thing happened. Her tail dropped away or, rather, it divided and grew into two legs and a pair of the prettiest feet in the world, while her maidens, who were grouped around her, shed their scales and became girls again. They all turned and looked at each other first, and next at the little fish who had regained her own shape and was more beautiful than any of them.

"It is you who have given us back our life; you, you!" they cried; and fell to weeping from very joy.

So they all went back to earth and the queen's palace, and quite forgot the one that lay under the sea. But they had been so long away that they found many changes. The prince, the queen's husband, had died some years since, and in his place was her son, who had grown up and was king! Even in his joy at seeing his mother again an air of sadness clung to him, and at last the queen could bear it no longer, and begged him to walk with her in the garden. Seated together in a bower of jessamine – where she had passed long hours as a bride – she took her son's hand and entreated him to tell her the cause of his sorrow. "For," said she, "if I can give you happiness you shall have it."

"It is no use," answered the prince; "nobody can help me. I must bear it alone."

"But at least let me share your grief," urged the queen.

"No one can do that," said he. "I have fallen in love with what I can never marry, and I must get on as best I can."

"It may not be as impossible as you think," answered the queen. "At any rate, tell me."

There was silence between them for a moment, then, turning away his head, the prince answered gently:

"I have fallen in love with a beautiful deer!"

"Ah, if that is all," exclaimed the queen joyfully. And she told him in broken words that, as he had guessed, it was no deer but an enchanted maiden who had won back the crown and brought her home to her own people.

"She is here, in my palace," added the queen. "I will take you to her."

But when the prince stood before the girl, who was so much more beautiful than anything he had ever dreamed of, he lost all his courage, and stood with bent head before her.

Then the maiden drew near, and her eyes, as she looked at him, were the eyes of the deer that day in the forest. She whispered softly:

"By your favour let me go, and do not kill me."

And the prince remembered her words, and his heart was filled with happiness. And the queen, his mother, watched them and smiled.

The Mountain Giants

LONG AGES AGO, when the round earth was being shaped, and the ice was melting to give way to the green fields and flowers, huge monsters, bears, wolves and other wild animals were the only living creatures in Switzerland. Then the giants arrived on the world.

When, by and by, human beings came into the land, they told their children that the mountains were what were left of the earth's crust after it had shrunk into peaks and ridges, humps and hollows, like an apple when baked in the oven, making crusts, points and wrinkles. The valleys had been sunk by the giants walking about on the earth while it was yet soft. The rivers were formed by the weeping of the giants' wives and daughters, when they were badly treated; for these rough fellows, husbands and brothers, did not know how to be kind to their female kin. The only way the giants were able to make their women obey them when they were bad tempered, or naughty, or scolded too much was to use shovels, pokers, clubs and straps on them. This clumsy and cruel way of keeping the family in order was because the giants had not yet learned to love, but were like brutes and knew only about force.

These giants, though so big, were very stupid as compared with men. Their brains were more like those of babies, and they were not half as smart as boys and girls are today. They did not know enough even to plough the ground, and raise wheat, and rye and oats, and to make porridge, to say nothing of bread and cakes, and pies and doughnuts. They could not melt lead, or work iron, or make tools, but depended on their muscles, because these were huge and tough, so that they bulged out; for the giants had terrific strength, like bulls and elephants. Though their brains were so small, their limbs were like pillars, much thicker than piano legs, and their arms were like iron. They could only make hammers or chisels, knives and scrapers of stone, and clubs of wood, for they knew no better and never went to school or college.

When men finally arrived on the earth and began to plough the ground and to raise wheat for bread, and brought cows for milk, the giants, and especially the giantesses, were mightily interested. Their curiosity was great to see how the things were done and how houses were built, and cradles were made for babies to sleep in.

The giants told their sons and daughters not to meddle with the human folks, but rather to help them; for the giants, dull as their wits were, were afraid of any creature, that, though smaller than they were, had more brains. They wondered how human beings got such big heads, and they often pounded on each other's skulls to see if they were hollow inside, like a coconut.

Now the biggest of all these big fellows was their king, named Gargantua, but men learned to call him 'Old Gargy'. He had only one daughter, Bertha, who was his pet. She was a pretty good giantess, but she always wanted to have her own way, and this often made trouble in the family. Daddy and Mamma could not always agree about her. Bertha knew how to get on Old Gargy's soft side, and sweeten his temper.

Too often, her indulgent father either let her have her own way or gave what she begged of him, or else he winked at, and overlooked, some of her foolish pranks.

One day, when her daddy and mamma were asleep, she sneaked out from the cave on her tiptoes, and slipped down a glacier. When on solid ground, she ran like a deer up into the valley, where she saw a farmer with two horses making furrows in the field.

Amused at this, she stood and watched while perched on a boulder, looking on with wonder. Then the young giantess burst out laughing.

"How funny, to make stripes and little gutters all along the ground," she said to herself. Then she walked up to where the man was and lifting him, his plough, and both his horses in one of her big hands, she held out her apron, open wide, and dropped the whole lot, man, team and tools, into it. These she took home to play with on the cave floor. Her mother looked on and enjoyed the fun, as her daughter pulled the horses' tails, and made them kick. She forced the man to dance on her thumbnail, and used the iron end of the plough to clean her fingernails. The man talked and whined and wanted to go home to his wife and babies, but the giantess Bertha could not understand a word he said. So she spoke to her mother thus:

"This must be his way of frowning, like a wolf cub. Or maybe he is chattering, like a monkey. Or is he crying, do you suppose?"

At this, the shadow of Old Gargy darkened the cave door. He saw what was being done, and instantly ordered the release of the man and his horses. Then he lifted his club, as a sign of securing obedience.

The jolly giantess Bertha, having had her fun, took back the man and his team into the valley. The farmer's wife was so grateful that she wanted to make her visitor a nice present. So she took from the corner of the room something brown. It was four feet long and stood there on the end with others like it. They looked like clubs, but seemed very light. These were loaves of Swiss rye bread that were kept standing on their ends in the spring house and were called the staff of life. A thick round cheese, a pot of honey and a full pail of milk were also given Bertha for a present. The giantess ate heartily. She drank a bucket full of the milk, chewed up a cheese and a yard of bread, and then asked for more to take home, which was willingly given.

When back in the cave, the giant family had a jolly feast; at least, each one had a mouth full. They all smacked their lips, and murmured, "Um, um, um," in their delight.

Down in the valley, the farmer's wife, although the sky was blue and the sun shining, thought it was thundering, or that an avalanche had fallen down the mountain; but it was only the giant family showing how happy they were at eating the food of human beings.

"So you see, daughter Bertha," said Old Gargy, her daddy, "what these human creatures can do for us. So, do you let them alone; and, in the future, harm them not, even in play. Then they will give us more bread and cheese and milk."

The good daughter placed one of the big cheeses, still uneaten, upon her thumbnail, as a sign of truth. Then she declared she never would disturb anything, man or beast, in the valley.

Now there was another giant, named Hotap, who, in disposition, was very different from his neighbour, and often played bad tricks on the farmers. He loved to start avalanches, by making a wet snowball called a soaker and then flinging it over the snow and down into the valley upon the villages. In this way, he ruined many houses, barns and stables, killing men, goats, sheep, donkeys, chickens and cattle.

Besides this, Hotap used to lie in wait for nice little boys, especially those that were rosy and plump, and to catch them and eat them up. He sometimes came back to his cave home with his pocket full of small boys. He thus ruined so many families, and made so many mothers cry, that they sometimes called him Old Schoppe, which means something like Boy-Eater, or, more exactly, our John Barleycorn.

But Schoppe was a giant who destroyed many more small boys than any other giant or ogre, and in a different way. By and by, Hotap and Schoppe, who at first were rivals, became partners. Instead of living in caves, they went into business and set up shops all over Switzerland. They lured young men into these shops, and set them to drinking poisonous stuff that the giants made, so that the roads, and streets, and gutters at nights, and early in the morning, were often full of fellows lying asleep on the ground, or like pigs in the mud.

Then, further, the two giants made it the general fashion of putting Schoppe's drink even into things cooked for children.

Hotap found that, as partner to Schoppe, he could catch and destroy more boys in this new business than in the old way. So he laid aside his club and stopped trying to destroy villages by rolling avalanches on them. He put on fine clothes and made his shops very attractive by looking-glasses, and pretty pitchers and tumblers. But finally, he himself got so fond of the drink which Schoppe made out of barley and rye and other grain that he drank himself to death and was buried in a cemetery. Over his grave a monument was carved, in the shape of a barrel, with a bung and spout and tap, as if he were continuing business in the next world.

But Schoppe kept on in the business. He ground up grain, and wasted so much, that he made the price of bread very high, so that poor people often had to go hungry. Out of the good barley and rye, he made the stuff that poisoned the brains of the young men and turned them into flapjacks, so that they lay as stupid as stones in the ground. He filled up the men until they were hardly better than swill barrels. In this way, many boys were ground up into poverty or stupidity, and the graveyards were filled so fast by old Schoppe that people called his saloon the Mill. At last, the big fat fellow, with a red nose, died also.

So at Berne, one sees the monument of Schoppe or the Boy-Eater. He stands in bronze over a fountain. He has boys in his pocket, samples of boys in his hands and mouth, some more at his feet, and a good supply at hand to chew up and swallow.

Everyone goes to see the statue of the Boy-Eater. Yet many others still follow his business and eat up the boys.

The Wonderful Alpine Horn

WHEN THE LITTLE BOYS AND GIRLS, who read these Swiss fairy tales, grow up to be big and travel in Switzerland, they will enjoy the Alpine horn.

Nearly every shepherd lad in the mountains knows how to blow it. It is made of wood, and is about half as long as an ordinary broom. Its butt, or heavy end, rests on the ground. When a man blows a long blast, the sound, at first, when one is too near, does not seem to be very pleasing; for distance lends enchantment to the sound. But wait a moment, and listen! Far off across the valley, the strains are caught up, and sent back from the tops of the high mountains. Then it sounds as if a great choir of angels had come down from Heaven to sing glory to God, and to bring greetings to all good souls. Nowhere in all the world is there such sweet music made by echoes.

Sometimes there is a double set of echoes, like one rainbow inside of another. Then, it makes one think of a choir of little angels, that sing a second time, after the first heavenly chorus has ceased.

How the Swiss people first received the Alpine horn, as a gift from the fairies, is told in the story of a faithful shepherd's boy, named Perrod. He had to work hard all day in tending the cows that grazed on the high mountain pastures, which the natives call the Alps. But when foreign people speak of 'the Alps,' they mean the ranges of mountains themselves.

In winter, these level stretches of ground are covered with snow and ice, but by the month of June, it is warm enough for the grass and flowers to grow. Then the cowboys and cheese makers go up with their cattle. At night, Perrod, having milked the cows, skimmed the cream off the milk, hung the great cauldron over the fire, and made the cheese.

By this time, that is, well into the late hours, Perrod was almost tired to death. After calling 'good night' to Luquette, his sweetheart, who lived across the valley, and hearing her greeting in answer, he climbed up the ladder into the loft, and lay down on his bed. This was only a pile of straw, but he was asleep almost the very moment he touched it, for he was a healthy lad and the mountain air was better than medicine. It was especially good for sound sleep, and he knew he must get up early, at sunrise, to lead the cows and goats out to pasture. Then the all-day concert of tinkling bells began.

But this night, instead of slumber, without once waking until day dawn, Perrod had closed his eyes for only about three hours when he heard a crackling sound that woke him up. He thought at first the wind was blowing hard enough to rip off some of the bark strips from the roof of the chalet, and was tumbling down some of the heavy stones laid on to keep them in place. But when he saw the reflection on the walls and ceiling of a bright fire, he crawled quietly out of bed. Then he peeped down and through the cracks in the board floor, to see what was going on.

Three men were around the fire. One, the biggest fellow of the three, was hanging up the cauldron on the hooks. The second piled on more wood, while the others warmed their hands in the bright blaze.

The three men were all different in appearance, the one from the other, and an odd-looking lot they were. The tremendously tall man seemed to be a giant, in weight and size. His sleeves were rolled up, showing that his arms were sunburnt until they were very dark. When he lifted up the cauldron, to hang it up or take it down, his muscles stood out like whipcords.

But the man sitting on a milking stool, at the right-hand side of the fireplace, was entirely different, being smaller, and with white skin and golden hair. He had a long horn, which rested on the floor beside him.

The man on the left-hand side of the fireplace appeared to be a woodman or hunter. At least, he seemed to be used to the forest. Though it was pitch-dark night, he knew where the wood lay, piled up under the eaves of the chalet; for, when the fire burned low, he went outdoors and returned with an armload of fagots. Then he piled up the wood, and the fire blazed, and crackled, and roared, until the boy in the loft thought the hut would be burned up, too. Yet, though he trembled at the strange sight, he was brave. He resolved not to be quiet if the big men tried to steal his cheese, which was to be food for the family during the winter.

Just as he was wondering whether his sisters and old daddy would have enough to eat during the long cold winter of eight months that was soon coming, when snow and ice covered the fields, he saw a curious thing happen. Sweet music began, such as had never met his ears since he was in his cradle and his mother sang to him.

It was the man with the golden hair, who seemed to be the real gentleman of the party. He it was who made the music. He first handed something to the giant, who dropped it into the cauldron. Then, with his horn, he disappeared through the door. When outside, he lifted the instrument to his lips and blew a blast.

Perrod was so interested in watching the giant that he paid little attention to the man outside, or to the sound he had made, for he saw the hunter take a bottle out of his pocket and hand it over to the biggest fellow, who stood at the cauldron over the fire. This one poured the liquid, which seemed to be blood red, into the big iron pot. Then, with a ladle as big as a shovel and long as a gun, he stirred vigorously. Then, three beakers, or cups, were set upon the table.

By this time, the golden-haired man outside had finished his blast of music, which seemed to float across the valleys down into the defiles, over the pastures, and through the wood. It grew sweeter and sweeter as it swelled on the gentle night breeze, until all the mountains seemed to have awakened, turned into living angels and lifted up their voices. The sweet strain ended with a prolonged sad note, as if melancholy had fallen on the musicians, and then it ceased.

A strange thing happened. All the cows and goats woke up from their sleep, and one, from all directions, could hear the tinkling of their neck bells, all over the pastures, far and near. The poor creatures thought it was time to get up and be milked, but they were puzzled to find it was yet dark. In fact, they were all still quite sleepy and very slow to move.

Something even far more wonderful happened next. Perrod, after first hearing the horn blow, thought the music had ceased: when, suddenly, it all seemed to come back in vastly greater volume. The sounds were multiplied, as if a thousand echoes had blended into one and all heaven had joined in the melody. Perrod was entranced. He even closed his eyes lest he might, by looking down at the strange men, lose some of what seemed to him a choir of angels singing.

When the last strain had ceased, Perrod opened his eyes. The golden-haired musician had re-entered the chalet and resumed his seat, sitting down again on the milkstool at the right of the fire; while the hunter rearranged three glass goblets, on the rough wooden table from which Perrod ate his meals.

All three of the strangers then solemnly watched the cauldron as the liquid boiled, just as the cream does when cheese is to be made; the big man stirring up with his huge ladle. At a particular moment, the giant lifted the cauldron and emptied out the contents into the three glass vessels. To the amazement of Perrod, there issued, from the same vessel, three very different colours.

In the first glass, filled to the brim, the draught was as red as blood, and it foamed at the top. The drops, flying out on the board, left crimson stains.

Giving a tap on the cauldron, with the big ladle, the tall man let flow, into the second glass, what seemed to be the same liquid; but this time, it was as green as grass, but hissing hot, and bubbling.

Another loud ladle tap on the cauldron, and out flowed a stream as cold as snow water, and as white as the edelweiss flower. The liquid rested in the goblet as quiet as milk, but seemed to be frosty on the top.

Now the giant-like fellow, shaking his huge ladle in his right hand, and putting his left at the side of his mouth, shouted with a voice of thunder:

"Come down, you boy, and make your choice of one of these three. Each has a glorious gift to him who drinks. Come quick, for it will soon be daylight."

Perrod knew he was discovered, but he was a brave boy. If his legs trembled, his heart was big. Moreover, the golden-haired man gave him a nod, and winked his eye, to encourage the lad.

So Perrod at once climbed down and stood before the table, on which were the three chalices.

"Drink, young friend," said the giant, "from any one of these, but know that in the red liquid is a gift to the Swiss men. Drain this cup, and then you will have strength, like me." At that, he bent his arm to show his mighty muscles. "You will be able to conquer the strongest man or fiercest beast. Besides, I shall give you a hundred fat cows, each of which will yield much milk, rich in butter. Drain this cup, and, according to my promise, you will see the kine tomorrow."

Then the hunter spoke: "Better drink from my goblet. After this green draught, you will have all the gold you want, and heaps of coins; and then you can marry, and still easily support your old father and mother." So saying, he tossed handfuls of gold pieces on the floor, piling them up until they reached the lad's knees. Perrod opened his eyes wide in astonishment, for here was not a promise in words, but the actual thing, that he could see for himself.

He was just about to stretch both his hands and drink the green liquid when the golden-haired man, speaking gently to Perrod, said:

"I cannot promise you either cows or coins, but if you drink the liquid in the white goblet, you will be able to use this horn, make music in the mountains and call your cows, as I have done. Thus your flocks and herds also will share with you my gift."

Not a minute did Perrod wait to decide. "I care more for music than for money or strength," he said, and, lifting the glass, he put it to his lips and drained the cup dry.

"What was it, and how did it taste?" do you ask? It was what the cows gave him every day – pure fresh milk, but cold as glacier water.

"Good," cried the man with the golden hair. "Any other choice would have meant death. Here is the horn. Blow it tomorrow, and see what will happen."

As if lifted up on wings to his straw bed, but holding on to his horn, Perrod heard the door shut and bang as the three men went out, two of them scowling. Then the fire cooled to ashes. He fell asleep and dreamed of the time when, in the church, he should lead his bride to the altar, his lovely sweetheart, Luquette, to be married, and the two should have a chateau and home of their own.

Awakening at the first moment when the rosy light of the rising sun made the face of the mountains blush, even while the valleys below were still in darkness, and long before his sisters in the village far away had awakened, he rushed out to the edge of the pasture. Then he drew in a man's breath, filled his lungs and, putting his lips to the mouthpiece of the horn, blew a long blast. He listened eagerly for the far-off echoes. A pleasant double surprise awaited him.

All over the pastures, in the chalets of the high plateau and along the mountain slopes, even down to the valleys, there was heard, at once, the tinkling of goat bells, cow bells, and the sound even of what hung in the metal collars of donkeys and horses, until the chorus of bell music was wonderful.

"Very fine, but is that all?" thought Perrod.

But another surprise! From across the great ravine, or chasm, out rushed his beloved Luquette. Hastily throwing a wrap around her shoulders, she stood in bare feet, threw a kiss to Perrod, and shouted to him her joy.

Now came the crowning wonder. From the high peaks, miles distant, and now rosy red in the dayspring, came back the music, in multiplied echoes, as if all the snow ranges of the Alps were singing. Pure, sweet, prolonged, the boy thought of what he had heard read in the church, that at creation, 'the morning stars sang together.' So it seemed now to him.

Through many centuries, and to this day, to call the cows together, to make the goats look up and turn homeward to seek shelter of the night, for men's evening prayer and chant of thanksgiving, for the signals of defence against enemies, for beginning the festal dance, or, to sound the wedding joy, the Alpine horn is the delight of the Swiss. It is like the carillons of the Belgic folk, the chimes of Normandy, the tower music of Holland, or the bagpipes of the Highlander. In a foreign land, in dreams, in its memories it tells of 'home, sweet home.'

A Japanese Gulliver

SHIKAIYA WASOBIOYE WAS A MAN OF NAGASAKI, and possessed considerable learning, but disliked visitors. On the eighth day of the eighth month, in order to escape the admirers of the full moon, he set off in his boat, and had proceeded some distance, when the sky looked threatening, and he attempted to return, but the wind tore his sail and broke his mast. The poor man was tossed for three months on the waves, until at last he came to the Sea of Mud, where he nearly died of hunger, for there were no fishes to be caught.

At length he reached a mountainous island, where the air was sweet with the fragrance of many flowers, and in this island he found a spring, the waters of which revived him. At length Wasobioye met Jofuku, who led him through the streets of the main city, where all the inhabitants were spending their time in pursuit of pleasure. There was no death or disease on this island; but the fact that here life was eternal was regarded by many as a burden, which they tried to shake off by studying the magic art of death and the power of poisonous food, such as globe-fish sprinkled with soot and the flesh of mermaids.

When twenty years had passed by Wasobioye grew weary of the island, and as he had failed in his attempts to take his life, he started upon a journey to the Three Thousand Worlds mentioned in Buddhist Scriptures. He then visited the Land of Endless Plenty, the Land of Shams, the Land of the Followers of the Antique, the Land of Paradoxes, and, finally, the Land of Giants.

After Wasobioye had spent five months riding on the back of a stork through total darkness, he at length reached a country where the sun shone again, where trees were hundreds of feet in girth, where weeds were as large as bamboos, and men sixty feet in height. In this strange land a giant picked up Wasobioye, took him to his house, and fed him from a single grain of monster rice, with chopsticks the size of a small tree. For a few weeks Wasobioye attempted to catechise his host in regard to the doctrines of the old world whence he came, but the giant laughed at him and told him that such a small man could not be expected to understand the ways of big people, for their intelligences were in like proportion to their size.

The Stone Giantess

IN BYGONE TIMES it was customary for a hunter's wife to accompany her husband when he sought the chase. A dutiful wife on these occasions would carry home the game killed by the hunter and dress and cook it for him.

There was once a chief among the Iroquois who was a very skilful hunter. In all his expeditions his wife was his companion and helper. On one excursion he found such large quantities of game that he built a wigwam at the place, and settled there for a time with his wife and child. One day he struck out on a new track, while his wife followed the path they had taken on the previous day, in order to gather the game killed then. As the woman turned her steps homeward after a hard day's work she heard the sound of another woman's voice inside the hut. Filled with surprise, she entered, but found to her consternation that her visitor was no other than a Stone Giantess. To add to her alarm, she saw that the creature had in her arms the chief's baby. While the mother stood in the doorway, wondering how she could rescue her child from the clutches of the giantess, the latter said in a gentle and soothing voice: "Do not be afraid: come inside."

The hunter's wife hesitated no longer, but boldly entered the wigwam. Once inside, her fear changed to pity, for the giantess was evidently much worn with trouble and fatigue. She told the hunter's wife, who was kindly and sympathetic, how she had travelled from the land of the Stone Giants, fleeing from her cruel husband, who had sought to kill her, and how she had finally taken shelter in the solitary wigwam. She besought the young woman to let her remain for a while, promising to assist her in her daily tasks. She also said she was very hungry, but warned her hostess that she must be exceedingly careful about the food she gave her. It must not be raw or at all underdone, for if once she tasted blood she might wish to kill the hunter and his wife and child.

So the wife prepared some food for her, taking care that it was thoroughly cooked, and the two sat down to dine together. The Stone Giantess knew that the woman was in the habit of carrying home the game, and she now declared that she would do it in her stead. Moreover, she said she already knew where it was to be found, and insisted on setting out for it at once. She very shortly returned, bearing in one hand a load of game which four men could scarcely have carried, and the woman recognized in her a very valuable assistant.

The time of the hunter's return drew near, and the Stone Giantess bade the wife go out and meet her husband and tell him of her visitor. The man was very well pleased to learn how the newcomer had helped his wife, and he gave her a hearty welcome. In the morning he went out hunting as usual. When he had disappeared from sight in the forest the giantess turned quickly to the woman and said:

"I have a secret to tell you. My cruel husband is after me, and in three days he will arrive here. On the third day your husband must remain at home and help me to slay him."

When the third day came round the hunter remained at home, obedient to the instructions of his guest.

"Now," said the giantess at last, "I hear him coming. You must both help me to hold him. Strike him where I bid you, and we shall certainly kill him."

The hunter and his wife were seized with terror when a great commotion outside announced the arrival of the Stone Giant, but the firmness and courage of the giantess reassured them, and with something like calmness they awaited the monster's approach. Directly he came in sight the giantess rushed forward, grappled with him and threw him to the ground.

"Strike him on the arms!" she cried to the others. "Now on the nape of the neck!"

The trembling couple obeyed, and very shortly they had succeeded in killing the huge creature.

"I will go and bury him," said the giantess. And that was the end of the Stone Giant.

The strange guest stayed on in the wigwam till the time came for the hunter and his family to go back to the settlement, when she announced her intention of returning to her own people.

"My husband is dead," said she; "I have no longer anything to fear." Thus, having bade them farewell, she departed.

The Fatal Pride of Vukub

THE SUBMERGING WATERS had returned to their appointed places on, above, and below the earth; but the face of both sun and moon were still veiled, and shone not with their wonted splendour.

In this twilight period there lived a gigantic being named Vukub-Cakix, for his countenance shone with seven times the brilliance of flame.

His eyeballs gleamed like silver set with precious stones; the enamel of his teeth was so brilliant that to look at them was like gazing at some gleaming emerald, or the light-filled face of the sky. There was nothing in all the world that gave forth light like the eyes and teeth of Vukub.

Great as was his radiant beauty, his pride was greater still. Orgulous was he and puffed-up. And he said:

"Of a truth, only those have been saved from the flood who were above their fellow men. And of all those left alive there is not one like unto me. I am their sun, their dawn, and their moon. It is my splendour by which men come and go. I can see to the limits of creation, and it is so."

Thus he spoke in his arrogance. Nor was his pride lessened when he looked upon his two giant sons: Zipacna, who ruled the cloud-piercing peaks, and Cabrakan, at whose word the mountains belched forth fire, and the earth trembled in sudden convulsions. Moreover, there was none who dared deny that only when he advanced from his throne did the world come to life.

But the gods on high were not deaf to this boasting. They heard and smiled when Vukub said: "I am the Sun"; they smiled when Zipacna said: "I heaped-up and rule the mountains"; and again they smiled when Cabrakan said: "I shake the sky and earth."

Nevertheless, when they perceived that all on earth bowed in assent before these vain boasters, they stirred up against them the hearts of the marvellous twin brothers Hun-Apu and Xbalanque. Miraculously born of an earthly princess, these brethren had become heroes of many surprising adventures; none might compete with them at tlachtli, that universal form of hockey by which a man's prowess was measured; deadly were the long blowpipes they carried over their shoulders; and withal they were very crafty.

"It is not good that this should be," said the brethren, when they heard the vaunts of Vukub. "Let us put an end to the jewels by reason of which he is so puffed-up."

Now, next to his light-giving features, the thing dearest to Vukub was a huge nanze tree, a tapal, loaded with its round, yellow, aromatic fruit; and each morning he was wont to breakfast on this delicious fare.

Coming one day as usual, he climbed up to the summit of the lofty tree that he might take his choice of the most luscious fruit. Very wrathful was he this morning, when he perceived that the spreading branches were almost completely stripped of the bountiful supply which had hung there the day before.

He glared about to see who had dared to do this thing, and his anger grew ten times greater when he perceived the twins, almost hidden in the thick foliage.

Before he could attack them, Hun-Apu raised the blowpipe to his mouth and sped a dart which buried itself in the giant's cheek. With a frightful screech he fell from the treetop to the ground.

Quickly the brothers descended, and ran to seize the groaning giant; but he grasped the arm of Hun-Apu with so fell a grip that he tore it completely away from the shoulder; whereupon they fled from him in haste.

Still holding his enemy's arm, and pressing his hand against the wounded jaw, Vukub made his way home, groaning aloud.

"What has happened to my lord?" asked his wife.

"Those wicked ones have shot a dart into my cheek which tortures me beyond endurance. But I have torn off the arm of one of them; and I shall revenge myself by roasting it over the fire till the pain drives that demon to come for it."

So he suspended the arm before the fire, bidding his wife never cease turning it over the blaze, and lay down groaning more than ever: for the teeth of which he was so proud now caused him an anguish he could not bear. Moreover, the pain had extended even to his shining eyeballs.

Meanwhile the brothers, in order to combat this magic torture, had consulted a pair of mighty sorcerers. Man and wife were this ancient couple; their hair was white as the snows upon the mountain peaks, and the woman was bent double when she sat or stood or walked. Between them they fashioned a subtle plan.

Vukub lay before his golden throne, moaning and howling with the pain that affected him, so that his cries could be heard afar off without the palace.

There came one who told him that two doctors were at the door, enquiring who it might be that suffered so greatly. He ordered that they should be admitted.

In hobbled a very ancient white-haired man and woman. Even in his agony the heart of Vukub was pleased to notice that the woman bowed almost double as she came before him.

"Who are you, and what do you wish?" said the giant king.

"We are doctors, mighty Lord. Hearing one cry out we stopped to enquire the trouble: for we make our living by curing ailments."

"Who are those behind you – your sons?" demanded Vukub suspiciously, noticing two slim figures, dressed in skins, in the rear.

"Not so, Lord. These are our grandchildren. Their father and mother are both dead, and they follow us everywhere as we go about to heal, since only thus can we get food for us all."

"What can you heal? Can you ease this pain which devours me?"

"Doubtless we can, for we are wise in all arts – though our special knowledge is that of removing aching teeth."

"Teeth!" exclaimed the king, groaning afresh, and scarcely able to speak. "That is what is killing me – they and my eyes."

"Let me see," said the old man. He bent forward and examined the wounded cheek. "Ah, you have a bad wound there. No wonder you suffer."

"It was those demons who shot me with a blowpipe," said Vukub thickly. "Cure me if you can, and you shall not complain of your reward."

"It will be necessary to remove those teeth," said the sorcerer. "Also I think the eyeball is diseased already."

"What! Remove my teeth which give light to all the world! Impossible."

"Are they not loose in the jaw anyhow?"

"Yes, yes, they move in their sockets – and when they do so, deadly pains run throughout my body."

"You see they must come out. But have no fear: such is our skill that we will replace them with others more beautiful by far. More, we will remove them all, so that the new set will be alike. Even the eyeballs we will match as before."

"If you are sure—" began Vukub. Then, as the pain gripped him – "Quick! Do as you say. I cannot eat; not once have I slept since those evil ones shot me; surely I shall die if I be not healed speedily. But use all your arts: for it is because of the beauty of my teeth and my eyes that I am king."

"Rest assured. Pure and strong and polished will be the new teeth that we shall put in their place."

"Hurry," said Vukub.

Then the two cunning sorcerers, aided by the disguised twins, removed the shining teeth, while the giant howled and wept. And in place of them they inserted only grains of white maize.

Immediately his splendour fell. He knew within himself that he was no longer the dawn and the moon. Nor was he able to resist when they proceeded to remove the gleaming eyeballs which still gave lustre to his countenance.

But when these also were gone, Vukub-Cakix ceased to be. For without his colossal pride he was not.

All this time his wife had been busily turning the severed arm over the fire, to increase the torments of its absent owner. Hun-Apu now snatched the arm, and with the aid of powerful incantations by the sorcerers, replaced it firmly in its socket. Whereupon the brothers went away, well content in that they had humbled the pride of Vukub.

The Giant Pyramid-Builder

IF YOU TRAVEL THROUGH that beautiful land of lakes and mountains north of the City of Mexico, you will hardly fail to visit the ancient sacred city of Cholula. Nor can you fail to marvel at the remains of that incredible Pyramid, four times as large as the famous Pyramid of Cheops in Egypt.

Cortés and his followers wondered at the fifty-acre structure nearly four centuries back. Humboldt measured it, studied it and speculated about it a hundred years ago. The general belief was that it had always been devoted to the worship of Quetzal, that Fair God of old Mexico. But there were once wise ancients among the Acolhuan Indians who remembered the truth passed down by tradition from times immemorial.

This is the tale of the Pyramid-builder.

As everyone knows, for 4800 years after the creation of the world the land of Anahuac was inhabited by a race of vast giants. Have not their mighty bones, dwarfing those of modern men, been dug up time and again through the centuries?

These monsters were enemies both of gods and men. Fierce were the wars waged against them by the people of Tlascala, and many a giant was overcome by their multitudes, or driven forth into the wilderness to perish of starvation.

Always, however, there were enough of the dreadful race left to keep the land in an uproar; and particularly one Xelhua and his six brothers defied all attempts against them, holding themselves above laws, and doing only that which pleased their own ruthless cruelty. Very crafty as well as very strong they were, and the land of Anahuac groaned beneath their devastating tread. Finding there was none alive who might resist them, they waxed arrogant past belief, and scorned the very gods above, confident that there was no power on earth or in heaven which could resist their will.

But at last the heavenly rulers grew wearied of this senseless tumult below. They determined to put an end to it all, and poured forth an overwhelming deluge on the earth. The clouds burst wide and precipitated their inexhaustible reservoirs; the irresistible ocean itself was loosed from its bounds; the underground rivers shot up from beneath the earth upon men and giants alike, and those who were not drowned were transformed into fishes.

All except crafty Xelhua and his six brothers: as the flood from above met the rising sea, they fled northward, climbed the lofty slopes of Mt. Tlaloc and hid themselves in seven caverns within its sides, rolling huge boulders in front of the openings to shut out the waters should they rise so high. Here they lay secure while the deluge raged unchecked throughout the universe.

When the appointed time came, the destroying waters withdrew to their stations above the clouds, beneath the earth, and in the ocean. Xelhua and his brothers came forth from their caves of refuge, the only living creatures, and by their arts peopled the earth with a new race, who were to be their servants.

They were now more arrogant than before – for had they not succeeded in evading the utmost wrath of the gods? So Xelhua, who was skilled in building, determined to erect a structure such as the world had not yet seen – to serve not only as a perpetual memorial of his triumph, but also as an easier means of escape from any future attempt made against him by the lords of the winds and waters.

On the plain of Cholula this edifice was staked out, four sided, in girth like some great hill, in height planned to pierce the very clouds aloft.

In far-away Tlamanalco, at the foot of the Sierra, a multitude of men were set to work at digging clay, shaping it in moulds and burning it into bricks. Instead of having these heavy loads carried across the hills, Xelhua stationed a line of workmen all the way from the brickyard to Cholula: these passed the bricks from hand to hand continually, so that the builders never lacked a supply. Bitumen too was similarly brought from a great distance to plaster the bricks firmly in place.

Under the hands of these myriads of workers the foundation of the incredible Pyramid grew as if it were a living thing. Day by day it mounted upwards, and the heart of Xelhua waxed high with pride when even he had to climb laboriously to reach the dizzy level where the swarming ant-like labourers still built themselves aloft bodily. Looking upwards, he regretted that he had not planned an even larger base: for surely that was the only thing which in any way limited this monument to his power and guarantee of future security. There was one consolation: when this reached the apex of its sloping sides, he could build another, infinitely larger and loftier. Meanwhile, a future deluge must be worse than the former one to reach him upon the summit of this almost completed structure.

But the gods do not sleep, though they be long silent.

With rising wrath they beheld the growth of this presumptuous edifice and the increasing audacity of its builder. Still they bided their time, and the pyramid of Xelhua crept upwards till the low-hanging clouds often lay far beneath its upper courses.

The day came when a man might easily count the space of time still needed to complete the structure. Xelhua urged on his host of workers.

Then suddenly the heavens opened. A huge mass of flaming rock fell with irresistible force upon the proud pyramid and those who built it. The upper portion crashed down in ruins, carrying to destruction thousands of the labourers and the master-builder Xelhua himself.

Wherefore men doubted no longer that there were eternal powers on high. The fragment of the building which remained was dedicated thenceforth to the Fair God, Quetzal. And down to the time of that worthy Dominican, Pedro de los Ríos, the priests showed to unbelievers a portion of the very thunderbolt, a stone shaped like a toad, which had confounded the mad presumption of Xelhua; while the dancing celebrants sang in their festival hymn the tale of these happenings, that reverence might no more perish among men.

Moreover, since that day the tribes have no longer spoken the same tongue, but each has a language of its own, unintelligible to the others.

Biographies & Text Sources

The stories in this book derive from a multitude of original sources, often from the nineteenth century and often based on the writer's first-hand accounts of tales narrated to them by natives, while others are their own retellings of traditional tales. Authors, works and contributors to this book include:

Debbie Felton
Foreword
Debbie Felton is Professor of Classics at the University of Massachusetts Amherst. Her specialty is folklore in classical literature. She is the author of *Haunted Greece and Rome: Ghost Stories from Classical Antiquity* (1999), *Monsters and Monarchs: Serial Killers in Classical Myth and History* (2021), and many articles about the supernatural in the ancient world. She is also the editor of *A Cultural History of Fairy Tales in Antiquity* (2021), *The Oxford Handbook of Monsters in Classical Myth* (2024) and *A Cultural History of Monsters in Antiquity* (forthcoming, 2025).

Emilie Kip Baker
The Eleventh Labour of Hercules
Emilie Kip Baker (1873–1951) was an American author, and a significant figure in the realm of education and literature of her time. Taking a scholarly approach to her retellings of ancient myths and stories, her work gained popularity among both academics and ordinary readers alike. She is the author of the popular collection *Stories of Old Greece and Rome* (1913), as well as *Stories from Northern Myths* (1914).

Rosetta Baskerville
The Story of the Wonderful Goat
Rosetta Baskerville (1880–1966) was a British author. She often published her work under the penname "Mrs. George Baskerville". Her work includes the collections *The Flame Tree and Other Folk-Lore Stories from Uganda* (1900).

Jean de Boschère
Sponsken and the Giant
Jean de Boschère (1878–1953) was a Belgian painter and writer. Born in Uccle, Boschère attended the École d'Horticulture in Ghent in 1893, after which he attended the Royal Academy of Fine Arts between 1896 and 1900. He wrote articles for the magazine *L'Occident and L'Art Flamand et Hollandais*, and his first published book was his poetry collection *Béâle-Gryne* (1909). During World War I he fled to London, where he came into contact with several significant fellow writers including Ezra Pound. His works of prose include the story collection *Folk Tales of Beasts and Men* (1918) and the novel *The Closed Door* (1917).

Ivana Brlić-Mažuranić
Reygoch
Ivana Brlić-Mažuranić (1874–1938) was a Croatian author. She was born in Ogulin, to a well-known family of writers and politicians. Writing initially in French, she kept diaries and composed poetry and essays. By the early twentieth century, her work was being published

frequently by journals and magazines. Her most popular work today remains her short story collection entitled *Croatian Tales of Long Ago* (1916), translated by F.S. Copeland.

Abbie Farwell Brown
How Odin Lost His Eye; The Giant Builder
American author Abbie Farwell Brown (1871–1927) was born in Boston and attended the Girls' Latin School. While attending school she set up a school newspaper and also contributed articles to other magazines. Brown's books were most often retellings of old tales for children such as in *The Book of Saints* and *Friendly Beasts*. She also published a collection of tales from Norse mythology, *In the Days of Giants*, which became a common text held by many libraries for several generations.

Samuel Butler
The Odyssey: Book X (Extract)
Samuel Butler (1835–1902) was born in Nottinghamshire, England. He was a novelist, essayist and critic. His most famous works include *The Way of All Flesh*, an autobiographical novel largely considered his magnum opus; and *Erewhon*, a utopian satire of the mentality and lifestyles embraced by Victorian England. The chapters of *Erewhon* which comprise 'The Book of the Machines' were adapted from articles he submitted to *The Press*, which posited that machines might undergo evolution in a similar way to humans.

J.F. Campbell
Conall Cra Bhuidhe; The King of Lochlin's Three Daughters
J.F. Campbell (1821–1885) was a Scottish author, folktale collector, and scholar of Celtic studies. Campbell, also known as Iain Òg Ìle, or Young John of Islay, was born on the island of Islay, in the Inner Hebrides. Throughout his life he travelled widely throughout Scotland recording traditional tales, anecdotes, and songs. He became known as an authority on the subjects of Celtic folklore and the Gaelic peoples. His best-known collection, *Popular Tales of the West Highlands*, was published in four volumes in 1890. He also published a collection of ballads entitled *Leabhar na Feinne*, which he self-published in 1872.

F.S. Copeland
Reygoch
Fanny Susan Copeland (1872–1970) was an Irish translator, journalist, linguist and mountaineer. Born in Birr, in County Offaly, Ireland, Copeland spent her childhood in numerous cities across Europe, and spent much of her adult life in Slovenia. She published numerous articles in various journals, and worked at the University of the Kingdom of Serbs, Croats and Slovenes in Ljubljana, in the Faculty of Arts' English department. She was the translator for Ivana Brlić-Mažuranić's story collection *Croatian Tales of Long Ago* (1916).

Jeremiah Curtin
The Son of the King of Erin and the Giant of Loch Léin; The Weaver's Son and the Giant of the White Hill
Jeremiah Curtin (1835–1906) was a Detroit-born ethnographer and folklorist. While much of his work focused on collecting myths and folktales from around the world, Curtin was also renowned for his translations of works by Polish author Henryk Sienkiewicz. Between 1883 and 1891 Curtin's interests would focus closer to home, when he worked as a field

researcher recording the myths and customs of Native American people, which would later result in the publication of the book *Creation Myths of Primitive America* (1898).

F. Hadland Davis

A Japanese Gulliver

Frederick Hadland Davis (1882–1956) was a writer and historian. His works include *The Land of the Yellow Spring and Other Japanese Stories* (1910) and *The Persian Mystics* (1908 and 1920). His books describe these cultures to the western world and tell stories of ghosts, creation, mystical creatures and more. He is best known for his book *Myths and Legends of Japan* (1912).

Elsie Spicer Eells

The Adventures of a Fisherman's Son; The Forest Lad and the Wicked Giant; The Princess of the Springs

Elsie Spicer Eells (1880–1963) was an American author and researcher of folklore. She travelled widely throughout her life, leading to her publication of several short story collections which were based on oral traditions from Brazil, the Azores, and other regions. She lived in Brazil for three years, and visited numerous other countries as a researcher for The Hispanic Society of America. Her works include *Fairy Tales from Brazil* (1917), *Tales of Giants from Brazil* (1918), and *The Islands of Magic: Legends, Folk and Fairy Tales from the Azores* (1922).

Elizabeth W. Grierson

Assipattle and the Mester Stoorworm; Peerifool

Elizabeth Grierson (1869–1943) was born on a farm near Hawick, in the Scottish Borders. Throughout the course of her life she published more than thirty books, many of which covered Scottish fairy tales and folklore. In addition to these, she also published travel guides to the cities of Edinburgh, Scotland, and Florence, Italy. Her best-known works are her collections *The Scottish Fairy Book* (1910) and *Children's Tales from Scottish Ballads* (1906).

William Elliot Griffis

Brabo and the Giant; The Fairy of the Edelweiss; The Frost Giants and the Sunbeam Fairies; The Great Stone Fire Eater; The Ice King and His Wonderful Grandchild; The Mountain Giants; The Tailor and the Giant; The Whimsical Avalanche; The Wonderful Alpine Horn

Born in Philadelphia in 1843, William Elliot Griffis served as a corporal in the American Civil War, and later graduated from Rutgers University in 1869. In 1870, Griffis went to Japan and became Superintendent of Education in the province of Echizen. Throughout the 1870s, Griffis taught at several subsequent institutions and wrote for numerous newspapers and magazines. His works include the collections *Japanese Fairy Tales, Korean Fairy Tales, Belgian Fairy Tales*, and *Swiss Fairy Tales*. He died in Florida in 1928.

Hélène Adeline Guerber

The Titans

Hélène Adeline Guerber (1859–1929) was a British historian who published a large number of works, largely focused on myths and legends. Guerber's most famous publication is *Myths of the Norsemen: From the Eddas and Sagas*. She also published retellings of legends from the classical world in her collection *Myths of Greece and Rome*. Her other works include *The Story of the Greeks* and *Legends of the Middle Ages*.

Mrs. A.W. Hall

Litill, Tritill, the Birds, and the Peasant Lad; The Five Brothers; The Giantess and the Granite Boat

Mrs. A.W. Hall was a translator and editor. She is best known for her editorship and translation of the collection *Icelandic Fairy Tales*, published in 1897. The collection preserved many traditional pieces of Icelandic folklore that might otherwise have been lost. She also published under the penname of Angus W. Hall. Her other works include the short story collection entitled *The Giantess in the Granite Boat* (1897).

Hesiod

The Theogony of Hesiod

Thought to have been active between 750 and 650 BCE, Hesiod was an Ancient Greek poet who lived around the same time as Homer. Though little is known of his life, scholars have inferred from references in his writings that he was born in Aeolis. He is credited along with Homer for helping to establish Ancient Greek religious customs, and academics look to his writings for insights into Greek mythology, archaic astronomy and time-keeping, and economic thought of the time, among other aspects of the ancient world.

Homer

The Odyssey: Book X (Extract)

Little is known for certain about the life of Homer, the Greek poet credited as the author of the great epics *The Iliad* and *The Odyssey*, although he is believed to have been born sometime between the twelfth and eighth centuries BCE. *The Odyssey* describes the trials of the hero Odysseus on his journey home to Ithaca following the Trojan War. It has had a huge influence on Western literature, inspiring extensive translations, poems, plays and novels.

Joseph Jacobs

Jack the Giant-Killer; Nix Nought Nothing; The Golden Ball

Joseph Jacobs (1854–1916) was born in Australia and settled in New York. He is most famous for his collections of English folklore and fairy tales, including 'Jack and the Beanstalk' and 'The Three Little Pigs'. He also published Celtic, Jewish and Indian fairy tales during his career. Jacobs was an editor for books and journals centred on folklore, and he was a member of The Folklore Society in England.

Gertrude Landa

The Giant of the Flood

Gertrude Landa (1881–1941) was a journalist and writer often referred to simply by her pseudonym Aunt Naomi. Landa wrote a number of plays and novels with her husband, the writer Myer Jack Landa, and published a collection of classic tales and folkloric stories in the book *Jewish Fairy Tales and Legends* (1919).

Andrew Lang

The Story of the Fisherman; The Story of the Hero Makóma; The Third Voyage of Sinbad the Sailor; Bedik and the Invulnerable Giant; How Ian Direach Got the Blue Falcon; Mirza; The Brave Little Tailor; The Frog and the Lion Fairy; The Giants and the Herd-Boy; The Girl-Fish; The Horse Gullfaxi and the Sword Gunnfoder; The Master-Maid; The Strong Prince; The Three Treasures of the Giants

Poet, novelist and anthropologist Andrew Lang (1844–1912) was born in Selkirk, Scotland. He is now best known for his collections of fairy stories and publications on folklore, mythology and religion. Inspired by the traditional folklore tales of his home on the English-Scottish border, Lang compiled twelve fairy books of different colours which collected 798 stories from French, Danish, Russian and Romanian sources, amongst others. This series was hugely popular and had a wide influence on increasing the popularity of fairy tales in children's literature. His fairy tale collections include *The Red Fairy Book* (1890), *The Lilac Fairy Book* (1910), and *The Book of Dreams and Ghosts* (1897).

Henry Wysham Lanier

A Son of Anak; Amadis Among the Giants; Gogmagog; How Zeus Fought with Titans and Giants; The Biter Bit; The Fatal Pride of Vukub; The Giant Behind the Waterfall; The Giant of St. Michael's Mount; The Giant Pyramid-Builder; The Giant Who Shines in the Sky; The Man Who Lost His Legs; The Outwitting of Polyphemus; The Peach's Son; The Turke and Gawain; When Thor Went to Jotunheim

Henry Wysham Lanier (1873–1958) was an American author and professor. The son of the musician, author and poet Sidney Lanier, he followed in his father's footsteps to pursue a creative career in the arts. His best-known work, *A Book of Giants* (1922), collects tales from around the world concerning the omnipresent figure of the giant found in numerous mythologies. His other works include *The Book of Bravery* (1918).

Frederick H. Martens

Anent the Giant Who Did Not Have His Heart About Him; Trouble and Care

Frederick H. Martens (1874–1932) was an American translator and music journalist. His translation work mainly consisted of books for children, and he worked several times with the author Clara Stroebe to translate her collections of stories and fairy tales into English. Martens was the translator of Stroebe's *The Norwegian Fairy Book* (1922) and *The Swedish Fairy Book* (1921). He also translated Elsie Spicer Eells' *The Brazilian Fairy Book* (1926) and R. Wilhelm's *The Chinese Fairy Book* (1921). His original works include *Violin Mastery* (1919) and a number of newspaper and magazine articles.

Cornelius Mathews

He of the Little Shell; White Feather and the Six Giants

Cornelius Mathews (1817–99) was an American author. After attending Columbia College, Mathews went on to study at New York University, where he graduated in 1834, and then proceeded on to law school. Mathews rebelled against the literary status quo of the time, which had viewed American literature as inferior to British literature. He pursued the development of a new, distinctly American literary style. He is best known for helping to form the literary group Young America in the 1830s. He wrote for and co-edited the Young American's journal, *Arcturus*, from 1840 to 1842. Throughout the 1840s and 50s, Mathews was involved in a number of American journals and magazines, either as a contributor or editor, including the *New-Yorker*, the *Comic World* and the *New York Dramatic Mirror*.

Elodie L. Mijatovich

Sir Peppercorn

Elodie L. Mijatovich (1825–1908) was a British author. During the 1850s she lived in Boston, Massachusetts, where she advocated for the abolitionist movement. Following her marriage to a Serbian politician, she moved to Belgrade, and then to London. She was the translator of several Serbian literary works, including *Serbian Folk-Lore* (1874), *Serbian Fairy Tales* (published posthumously in 1918) and *The History of Modern Serbia* (1872). She also translated numerous Serbian national songs of the Kosovo cycle into English.

Anthony R. Montalba

The Dragon-Giant and His Stone Steed; The Feast of the Dwarfs

Anthony R. Montalba (1812–84) was an author and painter. Swedish-born, Montalba married Englishwoman Emeline Davies in 1839 and lived in London. He came to raise a family of renowned painters who would base themselves in Venice during the latter half of the nineteenth century. Montalba is best known for his collection of stories entitled *Fairy Tales from All Nations* (1849).

Mara L. Pratt

The Apples of Life: Part I; The Apples of Life: Part II; The Finding of the Hammer; The Stolen Wine: Part I; The Stolen Wine: Part II; The Theft of the Hammer

Mara L. Pratt (1857–1921) was an American author, educator and physician. She studied at the Boston University School of Medicine. Her literary output mainly consisted of educational books for children. Her best-known work is *Legends of Norseland* (1894), which collects a number of traditional Norse and Scandinavian tales. Her other published works include *American History Stories, Volumes I and II.*

Katharine Pyle

The Blue Belt; The Giant's Cliff; The Story of the Three Billy Goat Gruffs

Katharine Pyle (1863–1938) was an American author and illustrator. She primarily wrote books for young adults, as well as works on the colonial history of her home state of Delaware. She became interested in writing and art as a child, and later attended the Philadelphia School of Design for Women. Pyle initially published poems in *St. Nicholas Magazine* and *Harper's Bazaar*, and she co-wrote the book *The Wonder Clock* (1887) with her brother Howard Pyle. She contributed to America's Golden Age of Illustration and collaborated with fellow creatives on many books as both a writer and an illustrator.

R. Sutherland Rattray

A Story About a Giant, and the Cause of Thunder

R. Sutherland Rattray (1881–1938) was a Scottish translator and barrister. Born in India to Scottish parents, he later worked for the Gold Coast Customs Service, and eventually became the head of the Anthropological Department of Asante in 1921. He learned the local languages, and came to translate several works into English. Rattray is the translator of Maalam Shaihua's *Hausa Folk-Lore* (1913).

Maalam Shaihua

A Story About a Giant, and the Cause of Thunder

Hailing from the Hausa people of West and Central Africa, Maalam Shaihua collected and transcribed scores of traditional Hausa folktales between 1907 and 1911. Published in his collection *Hausa Folk-Lore* (1913), his work preserves the culture and mythology of the Hausa people. Working closely with Africanist, anthropologist and translator Robert Sutherland Rattray, Shaihua produced a pronunciation guide and some information on

Hausa customs in addition to the stories. The significance of his work is due in part to the fact that it was first written in Hausa and then carefully translated, resulting in English versions that accurately reflect the originals.

Lewis Spence

The Stone Giantess

James Lewis Thomas Chalmers Spence (1874–1955) was a scholar of Scottish, Mexican and Central American folklore, as well as that of Brittany, Spain and the Rhine. He was also a poet, journalist, author, editor and nationalist who founded the party that would become the Scottish National Party. He was a Fellow of the Royal Anthropological Institute of Great Britain and Ireland, and Vice-President of the Scottish Anthropological and Folklore Society.

Clara Stroebe

Old Hopgiant; The Mount of the Golden Queen; The Three Dogs; Anent the Giant Who Did Not Have His Heart About Him; Trouble and Care

Clara Stroebe (1887–1932) was a German author, born in Freiburg im Breisgau. She attended Heidelberg University in 1907, followed by Ludwig Maximillian University of Munich from 1909 to 1910. Stroebe gathered and edited a number of fairy tale collections, including *The Swedish Fairy Book* (1921) and *The Norwegian Fairy Book* (1922), among several others. These books were published as part of the *Fairy Book* series produced by the Frederick A. Stokes Company. She is also often credited as Klara Stroebe.

W.D. Westervelt

A Giant's Rock-Throwing

W.D. Westervelt (1849–1939) was an American author and pastor. He settled in Hawaii in 1899 and served as the Corresponding Secretary for the Hawaiian Historical Society beginning in 1908. His enormous interest in Hawaiian mythology and culture led him to publish numerous articles and books on the subject. His best-known works include *Legends of Gods and Ghosts (Hawaiian Mythology)* (1915), *Legends of Old Honolulu* (1915), and *Hawaiian Legends of Volcanoes* (1916). He is considered one of the foremost authorities on Hawaiian folklore in English.